Excerpts from Editorial :
Secrets of Ravenshire:

Award-winning author Inge-Lise Goss:
"Dialogue, settings and protocols for the era are exceptional."

Excerpt from Readers' Favorite Review by Ray Simmons
"The dialogue in this story is excellent. The nuances of society are displayed in every conversation and this is a strong point of Noëlle de Beaufort's writing. Read this novel. It steps outside the boundaries of the usual historical fiction tale."

Excerpt from Readers' Favorite Review by Christian Sia
"The characters are fleshed out, each with a solid background. The writing is awesome and it leaps off the pages with unusual grace and lyricism....This is a very engaging story, fast-paced and beautifully plotted. I couldn't stop reading, thanks to the drama and the emotional depth of the story."

Excerpt from Readers' Favorite Review by Francine Zane
"Secrets of Ravenshire: Romance and Revenge by Noëlle de Beaufort is a work of art that truly reflects the best of what historical fiction is all about. The author is a brilliant wordsmith who has interwoven the complexities of beautifully crafted characters with the subtle yet intriguing historical references that transport a reader back in time....The romantic component of the story is complex and smart without being overly erotic, which makes it the perfect story to share with family and friends. While the text is long, is does not drag....I was equally intrigued with the full cast of secondary characters who provide Gabriella with the support, and sometimes conflict, necessary to make the story feel real."

Customer review by LJF:
"If you like historical fiction then buy this book. A great, character-driven piece that has obviously been well-researched. The people and plot are backed by a fascinating look into London in the Regency era. It kept me up well into the wee hours for several nights. I'm hoping the next installment comes out soon."

BY NOËLLE DE BEAUFORT

Secrets of Ravenshire, an epic historical series

The Gabriella Trilogy

Secrets of Ravenshire: Romance and Revenge
Book One (1811)

Secrets of Ravenshire: Temptation and Treachery
Book Two (1811-1812)

Coming Soon
Secrets of Ravenshire: Venom and Valor
Book Three (1812-1813)

Prequels and Sequels in process
Publication updates and character lists available on
www.noelledebeaufort.com

Short Stories

"The Search for the Snow Tribe"
"The Flight of the Eagle Feather"
"The Promise of the White Buffalo"

A series of short stories centering on Jean-Louis Chevalier in North
America, available for Kindle at www.amazon.com

Other short stories on secondary characters will be published from
time to time

Secrets of Ravenshire
Temptation and Treachery

Noëlle de Beaufort

Musée de Merbeau Press

Musée de Merbeau Press

ISBN: 1-7328827-1-1
ISBN-13: 978-1-7328827-1-3

DEDICATION

To my family and friends

ACKNOWLEDGMENTS

Originally conceived as a single novel, the story and characters in *Secrets of Ravenshire* demanded a trilogy as the first segment in a planned epic series spanning centuries.

A special thanks to the members of my critique group: Jo Anne Plog, Inge-Lise Goss, Ernie Walwyn, and Debbie Prince, who continue to challenge and inspire me every week.

Beta readers Bobbi Eve, Vicki Buford, Lin Hellman, Linda Flanagan, Susan Rybos, LeeAnne Tait, and Sandy Allendorph provided invaluable insights and feedback to improve this book.

Any remaining mistakes are, of course, my own.

Secrets of Ravenshire: Temptation and Treachery
Quick Reference for Main Characters

Character names are varied partly for proper address by others, and partly to avoid constant repetition. A "Lady" is a title designated by birth, not marriage. Lady Gabriella is of noble birth. Someone who is a lady by marriage, like Aelwyn, who married Henry's brother Rychard, was known as Lady Rychard Wyndward, not as Lady Aelwyn.

M., Mlle., and Mme. are abbreviations for French forms of address meaning Monsieur, Mademoiselle and Madame, respectively. Sig. is an Italian form of address for Signor.

Gabriella is known as Bri to family and close friends, Lady Gabriella to others, and more formally as Lady Gabriella Wyndward. Servants occasionally call her "milady." She secretly acts as her father's "man-of-affairs."

Henry Wyndward is the 11th Earl of Ravenshire and Bri's father. Friends call him Ravenshire. He is formally addressed as Lord Ravenshire. Servants call him "milord." In the narrative, he is referred to variously as the earl, Lord Ravenshire or Henry. Teasing names by old friends include Young Viscount (before he became earl), and His Excellency. He founded Wyndward Trading as a young man.

Gwyneth Wyndward Craigfell de Merbeau is Henry's sister and Gabriella's aunt. She is Lady Gwyneth, or the Comtesse de Merbeau, and referred to by some as Madame la Comtesse or the comtesse or her childhood nickname, Wynnie. Servants occasionally call her "milady." Her first husband, Jamie Craigfell, died in a riding accident. Her second husband, Luc de Merbeau, died in a mysterious carriage mishap.

Rychard Wyndward, brother of Henry and Gwyneth, is the late husband of Aelwyn and father of Ian. He was found dead, thrown from a horse, before Ian's birth.

Aelwyn, was the wife of the late Rychard Windward and is the mother of Ian Wyndward. She was found as a stowaway by Henry and taken in as a ward by the 10th Earl of Ravenshire.

Duff MacNeill **Blackburn** is the illegitimate brother of Henry, Gwyneth and Rychard. For twenty years, he worked with Henry at Wyndward Trading as his right-hand man. Bri nicknamed him Blackie as a child. His alternate identity is The Pharaoh and other identities as assumed for subterfuge or survival.

Edward James is banker to the Ravenshire family and the fiancé of Bri. He is called Mr. James, the banker, or the fiancé.

Vanessa Craigfell, the Duchess of Pytchley, is Bri's grandmother, mother of the Oliver as well as the late Lady Jane, Henry's wife and Bri's mother, and the late Vincent. Most address her as Duchess or Your Grace.

Oliver Craigfell is the sole surviving child of Vanessa and Bentley, the Duke and Duchess of Pytchley. His wife is Lady Abigail.

Charlotte Winters, Baroness Glasspool, is a widow. She was Henry's paramour and partner for fifteen years after the death of Lady Jane. She is often called the baroness. She is not of noble birth. As a widow, she may be addressed as Lady Winters, but most call her Baroness.

Taita is the love Henry found when shipwrecked on a South Pacific island twenty-five years earlier. Unbeknownst to Henry, she was rescued by Sultan Sarduba of Madagascar and reappeared in Henry's life in Book One.

Jean-Louis Chevalier met Henry in Canada in 1790 and returned with him to England in 1792. He is called The Frenchman, the fur trapper, the former trapper, the tracker or the driver.

Nashmir met Henry in Tibet many years earlier, and is known as the Tibetan, the herbalist, and serves as Henry's valet.

Nate Parker is a university friend of Henry's, who became a ward of the 10th Earl of Ravenshire after being stranded in England during the American Revolution. He is often called The American, the philosopher, or the professor.

Laurence (rarely used first name Philip) tutored Henry, Gwyneth, Rychard, Nate, Aelwyn and Bri.

Gio da Garfagnini is a dwarf and renowned artist who taught Gwyneth as a child and is a close family friend. Also called the dwarf, the artist, or Lord Ostwold, he is a confidant of many *grandes dames* in London Society, known as the *ton*. His son is Maximilian and his grandson is Charles.

Aneira, Blackburn's grandmother, originally born Galda, changed her name as circumstances and survival demanded. Galda became Sorcha, then Catherine, and now Aneira.

Mirela is Aneira's Gypsy companion. She is a mistress of poisons, the Tarot, and the occult.

CHAPTER ONE

Sunday, April 14, 1811 – Aboard *Nut's Night Sky*, The London Docks
Blackburn

A drunken crewman wandered into the storage closet and mumbled, "Who the hell are you?"

Despite being exhausted from his injuries and lack of sleep, Blackburn's adrenaline spiked. He grabbed a discarded section of steel pipe leaning against the wall and hit the intruder first in the left shoulder, and then on the back of the head.

Once the drunk had been rendered unconscious, Blackburn pulled off the man's rancid clothing, followed by his own. He stabbed his prey in the left shoulder to mirror his wound from the fight earlier that night at the Wyndward Trading offices, and then took out his pistol to shoot the crewman's right hand to match his other injury inflicted during the skirmish. Blackburn pulled a flour sack over the dead man's hand, and then used his left index finger on the trigger. The sound echoed more like the thud of a falling crate than a pistol shot. Tossing the sack aside, he examined his work. He twisted his lips into a crooked smile as he inspected the lifeless body covered in flour. *Perfect. Rocks and water will do the rest.*

He struggled to dress the unresponsive body in the dead Bow Street Runner's clothing and felt hat he had donned earlier in the evening to disguise himself. *Damn! Dead weight is hard to maneuver.*

Snorting in disgust at the foul odor, Blackburn put on the dead man's garb.

The storage closet was on the other side of the ship from where Blackburn intended to dump the body, so he threw the inanimate crewman over his good shoulder, opened the door, edged out and kept his back to the wall as he slipped around the corner and made his way to his chosen spot. *Darkness and the small crew of a cargo ship has its advantages—they can't man all decks. Luck is with me.* Blackburn heaved the hulk over the side, where he calculated it would be dashed on the rocks below. It quickly sank beneath the surface, and was carried away by unseen, fast-moving currents.

Staggering back to the obscure storeroom, his energy waned. He collapsed on the remaining pile of flour sacks.

***

Tuesday, April 16, 1811

Blackburn blinked into consciousness after sleeping for more than a day. Enveloped in darkness, sharp pains pierced through his left shoulder and right hand. He closed his eyes again, inhaled deeply a few times, and then smiled as a rough tongue licked his cheek. "How long have I been sleeping, Midnight?"

She meowed.

Raising himself on one elbow, Blackburn waited for his eyes to adjust to the dusky light coming from under the door frame. He scanned his surroundings. Small bones and furred skin were scattered in one corner of the dark room. He grinned as he petted his black cat. "I see you found some food."

Hunger gnawed at his gut. Slowly, Blackburn rose to his feet. He peeled off the shirt he'd purloined from the intruder, gritting his teeth as the fabric that had stuck to the wound ripped off the nascent scab to which it had become attached. The gash in his shoulder bled anew.

He spotted a stack of clean linens on a shelf, and a bottle of whiskey, no doubt secreted there by the inebriated sailor. *He's now met his death, interpreted by those watching as my final fall from grace to ignominy.*

Dousing one of the linens with whiskey, he cleaned the area punctured by the knife thrown by Count von Dusterberg. Blackburn grimaced, swallowing cries of pain as he cleaned the shoulder. *That damnable Prussian throws with precision.* Using his left hand to clean his left shoulder required twisting his arm into an awkward position, but his right hand was too damaged to function. The knife wound on his shoulder looked clean, but his right hand was red and swollen. *I didn't expect James could aim so true. I'm lucky I got a clear shot at the Frenchman.*

The impact of the embedded flecks from the small musket ball and residual black powder had torn his hand when the bullet ripped through his skin. From his boot, he removed a small knife with his left hand and dug out lead flecks and black powder residue. Luckily, the round ball had pierced and passed through the fleshy area between his thumb and index finger, but foul-smelling yellow pus dripped out as he worked on clearing out any remaining debris from the shot.

He poured the remaining whiskey on the open wound to stanch the infection and his facial features twisted and recoiled from the intense, searing pain. Fashioning more clean linens into makeshift bandages, Blackburn ripped strips to create ties to hold them in place. *Once the wounds look clean and the pus is gone, I can stitch them.*

From his travails in jungle, desert and mountainous terrain, Blackburn was uniquely advantaged in self-medicating and cleaning wounds or he would have been dead many times on many continents. He kept a medical kit in the travel bag he had grabbed as he left London. With breathing holes and netting specially designed for Midnight, the travel bag also held a variety of passports, currencies, letters of credit. A first aid kit and a change of shirt and breeches lay beneath a false bottom. In addition, the bag secreted small weapons slipped into hidden pockets.

"Preparation cheats death, Midnight. Let's find some food."

***

Wednesday, April 17, 1811 – Alexandria, Egypt
Alia

Alia worked by candlelight later into the night to complete documents required to advance The Pharaoh's interests in Alexandria. *My interests.* With The Pharaoh abroad and his date of return unknown, she attended to her tasks in the diligent manner that had attracted her master's attention years earlier. Tired, Alia yawned.

"More tea?" Sefu, her bodyguard whose name meant "sword" in Swahili, never missed a nuance of her behavior. He had saved Alia's life more times than she could count.

"Not tonight." She stretched her arms to the ceiling. "I need a few hours of sleep. The coming weeks will be very busy." She donned her half-*niqab* that conveniently shielded her identity.

The bodyguard extinguished the candles, saving two to guide their exit. After the door was bolted, they made their way through the winding near-empty streets of Alexandria. Looking around to be sure they were alone, the bodyguard swept away dirt and sand that camouflaged the door to a cellar under a restaurant. Alia crawled down the ladder, taking one candle with her. The bodyguard followed with the other candle, closing the door as he descended, enveloping them in near-darkness until Alia lit their tapers from the flickering flames of the never-extinguished wall torch. The dust of Alexandria would cover the wood-plank entry door within the hour and it would be invisible except to those who knew its exact location.

Moving through the cellar to a dead end, Sefu pushed a tall cabinet aside, revealing an arched doorway. They ducked under the low arch. After Sefu pulled the cabinet back into place, they passed by a pile of blankets to one side, and then entered the catacombs, carved out centuries earlier. After ushering Alia to her quarters, the bodyguard asked, "What time tomorrow?"

"Dawn."

Sefu nodded and walked back the way they had come, disappearing into the blackness.

Alia watched Sefu's candle flicker out. Her protector would sleep on that pile of blankets, guarding their secret entrance. She smiled. *We truly are the underworld. The devil's disciples.*

***

Saturday, April 20, 1811 – Aboard *Nut's Night Sky*
Blackburn

As his energy returned, Blackburn prowled the ship's passageways at night, finding the kitchens and stealing food, water, whiskey and salt to survive. The markings on the posted ship's calendar told him the date.

The storeroom had attracted no visitors so far. He attributed his lucky solitude to the nature of a cargo ship. Carrying a spare crew, using dockworkers at each port to load and unload, the ship allowed room to hide. Still, he could not count on being undetected for long. A few more days of invisibility remained, he guessed, before he would be discovered. *I must regain my strength soon.* If not, the crew, often recruited from an assortment of disreputable thugs along the docks, would sense his vulnerability and strike. He arranged a mattress of sorts from sacks of rice and flour. A stash of blankets in the storeroom served to mitigate the cold nights. *'Tis a far cry from the relative luxury of the Wyndward fleet. But I'm alive. Alive to fight another day. I will not be defeated until I am free of the Wyndward curse.*

He finished a meal of dried beef and a hunk of bread, holding back a torn section of meat for his cat. "Midnight, my only friend," he whispered. "My father abandoned *me*, but I shall never abandon *you.*"

She rubbed her head against his chin.

Blackburn reclined on the sacks and closed his eyes. The cat climbed onto his chest, stretched out, and purred herself and her master to sleep.

***

Saturday, April 20, 1811 – Dumfries, Scotland
Arthur

Arthur, an estate agent from Glasgow, arrived in Dumfries with an urgent message for Aneira.

Forty years earlier, Arthur's nervous fidgeting on another mail coach had annoyed a fellow traveler. Galda, as she was then known, delved into Arthur's past during that coach ride, eliciting a confession that he had narrowly evaded capture fleeing London. He clutched a bag holding a cache of currency he'd embezzled from his former employer. Since that day, their lives had been entwined. Arthur forged whatever documents Galda needed, transferred money, disguised himself to participate in her schemes, and owed his success to her patronage.

Tonight, after fourteen hours of traveling in a cramped stagecoach in need of new springs, Arthur, tense and sore, alighted an hour before midnight at the way station in Dumfries. He stretched, but the stiffness in his limbs did not subside. He rented a horse from the station stables and rode to the inn where Galda, now known as Aneira, and her Gypsy companion were staying.

The day before, Arthur had received two letters from Aneira's grandson, Duff Blackburn. One was addressed to him and the other to Catherine, a prior identity assumed by Galda. Unbeknownst to Blackburn, Catherine's name had been changed in his absence to Aneira Rhys-Jones.

Arthur's talent for forgery had created flawless identity documents for each of his benefactor's various name changes over the years, allowing her to avoid detection. In the letter addressed to him, Blackburn instructed Arthur to sell Blackburn's London townhouse and give the proceeds to his grandmother. The forger had not opened Aneira's letter, but the burden of other news that he must impart weighed on him. *I dread delivering this message.*

Aneira's driving motivation in life was to protect the life of her grandson and mold him into her instrument of revenge against the Wyndward family. The 10th Earl of Ravenshire had seduced her daughter, Brigid, and then banished the girl from his life. Brigid died shortly after giving birth to Duff.

Arriving at the inn where Aneira and the Gypsy crone were staying, Arthur rang the outside bell, rousing the proprietor from his bed. "It's nearly midnight. Can't you read the sign? We close at ten."

"I need a room for one night. It's urgent that I speak with my friends who are your guests. I've traveled a great distance to get here."

Grumbling, the elderly innkeeper shuffled to a desk, and retrieved a key. "Go down the hall and up the stairs to Room 206. Who are your friends?"

"Mrs. Rhys-Jones and her companion."

The proprietor spat into a spittoon. "She paid in advance or I wouldn't have let that Gypsy across my threshold."

For the first time, Arthur felt a pang of pity for Mirela. *It must be degrading to be treated with such disrespect wherever one goes. No wonder she's so distrustful.*

"They're in Room 202 the other end of the hall. Breakfast is at seven sharp. Sign here. *You* can pay when you check out."

"I'll pay now. Keeps it simple." *I wouldn't trust me.* Arthur tossed the money on the desk and then climbed up the stairs to the second level. He dropped his bag in Room Six, walked down the hall, and knocked on the door to Room 202.

***

Aneira

Incessant knocking awakened Aneira. *What does that proprietor want at this hour?* She gathered her strength, got out of bed, wrapped a shawl around her shoulders, and opened the door a crack. "Arthur! What's wrong?"

Arthur entered and sat at the small table. He extended his hand with the letter. "From Blackburn. In one to me, he instructed that I am to sell his townhouse and give the proceeds to you. It appears he had to leave London in haste."

Aneira grabbed the letter and ripped it open. Her lips pursed as she read it. Crumpling the missive, she rose to her feet, and trudged over to the fireplace. After throwing some twigs and a log onto the waning flames, she stirred the kindling with a poker to fan the blaze before tossing the letter into the now-crackling bark. Silent, she watched the letter touch the burning embers and curl, wafting in tiny pieces to rise in the airflow up the chimney.

By now, Mirela had stirred and sat up in bed. A sign of her vanity was a wide white streak on one side that contrasted with the unnatural blackness of the rest of her hair.

Turning to the Gypsy, Aneira ran her fingers through her gray hair. "He asks me to wait one year. Another delay while the Wyndwards prosper. Who knows if I will live to see the passing of another year? All Wyndwards must die."

Mirela shook her head. "You will living long. I seeing it in the cards—"

"—and 'the cards do not lie.' " Aneira finished Mirela's familiar refrain.. She walked back to the table where Arthur waited and lowered herself into a chair. "How much do you think the townhouse is worth?"

Arthur offered an estimate that caused Aneira to raise her eyebrows. "A tidy sum." She stared into the fire for a few moments.

"I have a new idea." Directing her gaze to Arthur, she said, "I will require another name change."

Arthur rolled his eyes. "Again? No one knows you under this name."

"The innkeeper does. I will keep Aneira. I like it. My last name will be 'd'Aix.' " She glanced over to the bed. "Mirela, we are going to open an omelet parlor and tea café in London—*Omelettes de Mme. d'Aix.* The proceeds from the sale of the townhouse should permit us to get a lease, outfit the business, and I can bake again. There we shall await my grandson's return."

Clearing his throat, Arthur said, "There's more." He took a page ripped out of the *Glasgow Gazette* and passed it to her. A glance at the article's headline tore at her heart.

Blackburn of Wyndward Trading Feared Dead

London, April 20, 1811 – Mr. Duff Blackburn, the long time associate of Lord Ravenshire at Wyndward Trading Company, is feared lost in a boating accident that occurred early in the morning of April 14, 1811. His body has not yet been found. No further information is available at this time.

Private funeral arrangements have been made.

As she read it, Aneira betrayed no sign of emotion. "Mirela, get out your cards."

***

Sunday, April 21, 1811 –Aristotle Drummond's Townhouse
Drummond

In his study, Drummond reviewed his slate of candidates for Parliament. No elections would occur until Parliament was dissolved, at the call of the Prime Minister, but he kept a list of candidates he could control. Someone always died, or suffered from some scandal, leading to unexpected openings from time to time. Yet few of those openings were unexpected to Drummond. If necessary, he could persuade a Member of Parliament to resign, blackmail being his stock-and-trade, or merely threaten opposition. *I wasn't wrong about Charlotte. With the right set of circumstances, I could make her Prime Minister.*

While he would never permit himself the luxury of trusting a woman, the usefulness of a well-connected wife was not lost on him, but he had to admit that Charlotte Winters, Baroness Glasspool, was too strong-willed, independent and rich to bend to his will. Marrying Charlotte would have been an excellent piece of treachery, but she knew him too well. He couldn't stop thinking about her because she was truly a match for his wit and skillful at making her way in a man's world. He admired her immensely. But, to his chagrin, she remained besotted with Henry Wyndward, the man who knew his darkest secret. Ravenshire had never revealed it. Drummond scoffed at the irony. *Too honorable.*

Always swirling around in his head were schemes to hurt the earl financially. Known as "Tottie" to old friends, a term he used loosely, Drummond knew that the elegant Lord Ravenshire referred to him as 'The Nemesis.' Early on, after their rift at Merton College, Oxford, Drummond had tainted the earl in some circles as a man enamored of commerce, not befitting a gentleman. Unfortunately for Drummond, that impression was short-lived, as the earl's success had negated the whisper campaign conducted against him.

Next, Drummond organized a consortium to back a trade competitor of the earl's, but that venture had failed spectacularly when all ships were lost at sea. The master political manipulator had successfully smeared other partners instead of himself with that failure, but it still rankled him. Lloyd's had covered only a small portion of their losses. Drummond, however, as the agent, claimed a commission off the top before the sailing.

Despite his considerable skills, Drummond couldn't put anyone in the House of Lords who wasn't already a lord of the realm. He could, however, place their deputies, the staff members who accomplished the real work that he could influence. In the House of Commons, he ran campaigns, controlling who won and who lost. Grateful members rewarded him financially and by voting as he instructed.

Drumming his fingers on the desk, the man devoted to the downfall of Henry Wyndward analyzed his opponent. *How can I make the earl's life intolerable?* Rumors of a liaison with the exotic island woman, a slave of an Eastern potentate, had diminished the earl's standing in the eyes of Society. *To a man as wealthy as Ravenshire, tawdry details splashed over the pages of the gossip rags matter not a whit.*

A scheme to bring down the earl had not yet struck Drummond, but he knew there must be an unexploited vulnerability in the earl's life that he had missed. *I'll find it. And whenever it happens, he won't know it was I who ruined him. I'll play him as a card sharp plays his victims.*

His butler knocked on the study door.

Drummond looked up and raised his eyebrows.

"A most disreputable sort is outside the stables demanding to see you, sir. In broad daylight."

"It's barely past dawn. Take him some tea and biscuits, keep him isolated and tell him I'll be down soon." *It must be that footpad. Damnation! How did the man know where I live?*

After stacking papers on his desk, Drummond went out to the stables across the back alley and found the man. *As I guessed, it's that malodorous brigand.* "I thought I made it clear that you were to pass a message to me through the barkeep at The Errant Hound."

"Just so, guv'nor, but this is too hot to trust to anyone but you." He guffawed, emitting breath that could fell a horse.

Drummond coughed. "For a man who follows people for a living, your stench precedes you, eliminating stealth as a tactic."

The footpad shrugged. "In my world, were I not to have this foul stink, I would get no information. No perfumed Molly or fop could go where I go. Tactics be damned! I have information you said you'd pay for."

"I'll be the judge of that. Tell me."

His informant grinned, revealing a near-toothless mouth. "That Earl of Ravenshire you wanted me to listen about, there's rumors down at the docks. A man fell from a ship onto the rocks. A bloke named Blackburn. The official word is the dead man had a boating accident. But one of my contacts saw him fall from the ship, and overheard the Bow Street Runners talk about him. They were looking for him. No one knew what he had done, but there was something about a woman."

There was no public information released about a fall. Blackburn was the earl's most trusted associate. *Why would Ravenshire invent a false story about his death?* Reaching into his pocket, Drummond pulled out enough to keep the informant in spirits for a month. "This is good information. Spread it. Tell all the other footpads. Make it common knowledge. Embellish if you wish. Rumors take on a life of their own." Drummond turned to go, but looked back and said, "Never come here again. Follow the protocol we established. You will not get another warning."

The footpad saluted. "Got it, guv'nor." He started to count the money, but glanced at Drummond, stopped, and quickly pocketed the money. "Good day to you, sir."

Drummond exited the stables. *Ravenshire is no killer, but Blackburn is no midnight sailor, either. There is more to this story.* A crooked smile formed on his mouth. *The simple law of momentum—a little push and human curiosity propels a rumor forward. Truth matters not.*

He ate breakfast, and then summoned his carriage. *Always politic to be seen in church with the faithful at St. George's.*

***

Tuesday, April 23, 1811 – Aboard *Nut's Night Sky*
Blackburn

The first nights onboard the ship has been dreamless, but one night Blackburn awoke abruptly.

The cat dug her claws into his chest as she jumped, startled by his unexpected movement.

Visions tortured his mind. Unable to discern their meaning, the images faded only when Blackburn descended into the deepest level of sleep.

Figures in his dreams shouted silent messages, assaulting his consciousness.

His grandmother's irises stared at him—the same blue with specs of turquoise as his. Her mouth moved. *What is she saying?* Her facial movements, distorted by screams of rage, left her message undecipherable. Finally he made out the word formed by her lips: "Revenge!"

Bri's laughing face at age three came into focus. The redheaded child hugged him and said, "Blackie, you're my best friend." That image faded, replaced by Bri's face twisted in horror as he'd pulled her from James's carriage, a look that haunted his dreams. On that fateful night he had been stabbed, shot and presumed dead from the fall he'd staged after his lucky encounter with the intruder. But his task remained unfinished. *They don't know. They don't know the truth.* Blackburn tossed and turned.

Other faces loomed in the translucence before him, floating from side to side across his field of vision. Henry, the 11th Earl of Ravenshire, his mentor and half-brother, and Gwyneth, the Comtesse de Merbeau, his half-sister, shrank from him. His other half-brother, the now-dead Rychard, and Gwyneth's dead husband, Luc, reached out toward him. *Do they hate me? Don't they understand? Surely, in death, they must understand.*

***

Thursday, April 25, 1811

Blackburn's shoulder appeared to be healing, and his infected hand, stitched and clear of residual infection, was almost back to normal. As his strength returned, he became more daring while he explored the ship.

After shadowing the captain for several days, Blackburn seized a moment of opportunity late one night, sticking a pistol in the captain's back as he opened the door to his quarters. Blackburn pushed him inside and locked the door.

The captain turned his head without moving his body and squinted at Blackburn. In Arabic-accented English, he said, "You are not one of my crew. You are…the man the constable sought." His lips narrowed into a line. "A member of my crew is missing."

Blackburn shrugged. "He was a drunkard."

"As are many sailors. What do you want?"

"Better accommodations. I can pay and pay well. No doubt you are aware of the reach of The Pharaoh."

"All who sail the waters off North Africa have heard stories about The Pharaoh. Do you mean to suggest you know him?"

"I am his closest and most trusted associate. When we get to Alexandria, you will be well compensated."

The captain scoffed. "Future promises are worthless."

"Not from The Pharaoh." Blackburn removed the pistol from the captain's back. "Turn around slowly."

Fixing his gaze on Blackburn, the captain shrugged. "That *is* the rumor. They say The Pharaoh always keeps his word. But you are not The Pharaoh. You are a blackguard, a murderer and a scoundrel usurping the name of The Pharaoh to threaten me."

"Perhaps. You can die now or live to see another day. It's your choice."

"Are you so clever that you can captain a sailing ship?"

A confident smile curled Blackburn's lips. "I have sailed the world in many capacities, Captain. There is nothing I cannot do."

"Hubris has been the death of many men. But perhaps you will be history's exception." The captain stood his ground without averting his eyes from Blackburn. "The cabin next to mine is free. We stop at Oran tomorrow morning. I will say you boarded there as my new first officer, Lieutenant—?"

"Roland."

"Lt. Roland, we'll soon know if your boast of ships' knowledge is fact or folly." He stared at Blackburn. "My crew has learned not to question my decisions."

Blackburn bowed his head while holding the captain's gaze. "I am in your debt." He put the pistol back in his pocket.

"You reek. There is a bath next to your cabin. Avail yourself of it. Cold water is better than nothing. My former first officer met with a sad fate in London, killed trying to stop a pub brawl on the docks. I had no time to replace him before sailing. You'll find clothes in his cupboard. Stay out of sight until I summon you, immediately before we leave Oran. In the meantime," the captain swept his hand toward the sideboard, "take some fruit, bread and cheese for today. Starting with dinner tonight, you will dine with me in my cabin."

"Thank you for your hospitality, Captain—?"

"Alif. Abdul Alif."

"One more thing. Do you have a ship's cat?"

"Not at the moment. I intended to get one in Oran."

"Then you'll have two. My Midnight is not a polydactyl, but she's sailed many seas and is an effective mouser nonetheless."

***

Thursday, April 25, 1811 – A Newsagent's Stall in London
Lady Patricia

Newsagents's stalls dotted many corners on busy London streets. These merchants displayed multiple gossip rags which came out every Tuesday morning. Political treatises as well as bawdy drawings of sexual escapades printed on a single page vied for the attention of passers-by.

Lady Patricia purchased *Scandal & Shame* because it was of particular interest to her, specializing in often-lurid details about the romantic liaisons in the *ton*. She quickly darted into an adjacent stationer's store, out of sight, to scan the latest items. A prominent entry caught her attention:

> One hears that the Heiress of the Season, now engaged, is a devotee of the notorious Mlle. Bellerobe, rumored to have had an affair with Napoleon.

> Lady X, a respectable dowager countess, was overheard saying, "Is this heiress setting the proper example for other young ladies by frequenting such a disreputable atelier? I am thoroughly shocked."

Lady Patricia's heart beat so loudly that she glanced around to make sure others didn't hear it. *Perhaps Bri will find this item amusing. I simply can't continue to provide snippets for this gossip rag. Eventually I will be exposed. How can I protect myself and my friends too?*

***

Friday, April 26, 1811 – Aboard *Nut's Night Sky*
Blackburn as Lt. Roland

Captain Alif performed as promised. He introduced Lt. Roland as the new first officer when the crew lined up for final inspection before the ship left Oran.

No longer exhibiting weakness, with gloves covering the stitches in his wounded hand, Blackburn exploited his purported role of aide to The Pharaoh on the ship. The captain met his every need. Blackburn admired the man's practical compliance, executed without a trace of obsequiousness. A bargain with the devil, Blackburn assumed, met the captain's code of personal enrichment, but the bargainer would not kiss the pitchfork.

Blackburn had created the legend of The Pharaoh over a decade—a master criminal who demanded unwavering loyalty but rewarded those who proved themselves. His reputation had spread throughout North Africa and beyond. Though absent from Alexandria for more than a year, The Pharaoh harbored no doubt that his underlings were carrying out his instructions, collecting protection money, and managing various enterprises to his specifications. *The legend is stronger than the man. Followers are believers. It is almost as if they worship me.*

Some did. He had rescued young girls—and young boys—from sexual exploitation in Asia and Northern Africa, and shrewdly picked local Egyptians who were ambitious. But for every choice as a watcher, there was another he tapped to watch the first. He had assembled a network, a spider web of spies, spun from interlocking strands of greed, vengeance, and fealty. Those few who dared to cross him never escaped The Pharaoh's web. They were eliminated, as the spider eats the fly.

He trusted men far less than women, though he truly trusted no one. Women were grateful for power. Men demanded it. And some day, he knew, some man's ambition would spur an attempt to depose The Pharaoh. To forestall such a possibility, he set spies upon spies upon spies.

Only two in his entourage were taken into his full confidence. Xie Xie Li, whom he had rescued from sexual exploitation in China, had a fine mind for commerce and the sophistication to match—an international sophistication he had educated her to assert. Her training in the Asian fighting arts equipped her to use guile and skill to counter the physical strength of an opponent, should she ever be in a dangerous fight for her life. Now she was ready for her final test. The other, Alia, an Egyptian and one-time belly dancer, happened to be a whiz with numbers as well as a master forger who brooked no malfeasance among her agents. Reflecting on Alia's strengths, Blackburn smiled. *She's far more deadly than I.*

CHAPTER TWO

Friday, May 3, 1811 – The Old Tower at Ravenshire
Edward

While they lay side-by-side on the mosaic floor of the old tower, Edward tucked a stray wisp of Bri's auburn hair behind her ear. "It may be a bit obvious what's just gone on."

"Nonsense. The wind blew my hair from our ride. 'Tis nothing out of the ordinary." She reached over to pull him to her when the dinner gong sounded one reverberation. "An hour to dinner. We'd better get back to change our clothes."

"A gong?"

"A bit too Mongol for you, Mr. James? Father brought it back with some story that it once belonged to Genghis Khan. I thought he embellished the tale for his own amusement, but one can never be certain."

"As we are now engaged, can we dispense with 'Mr. James' and 'Lady Gabriella'?"

"Some married couples never address each other in any other manner."

She is baiting me. Edward rose and extended his hand to Bri to stand up. As they brushed off the dust and dirt from the floor, he directed his gaze at her green eyes. *Don't make it sound like a command.* "I wish to call you 'Bri' and that you call me 'Edward.' "

"Until you annoy me, Edward." Her eyes sparkled with amusement. "And then, Mr. James, you will know it."

They exited the last standing tower remnant of the original Ravenshire Castle, gathered their horses' reins, and walked their steeds to the stables.

***

The Earl's Library at Ravenshire
Henry

Opposite the earl, Jean-Louis leaned back in his chair. "All is arranged for our sailing."

Henry glanced up at the ceiling. "Excellent, if they don't all set upon me with knives at dinner."

"It was my doing. You were unaware."

"Your instincts were correct. If Blackie had known that Rychard had fathered a child, the child and Aelwyn would most likely be dead. You have insured their safety. But next time—"

"Next time, circumstances will determine actions, as always. The grandmother and her Gypsy friend evaded my men, but they will be found."

"Until they are found, Bri, Aelwyn and Ian will need extra security.". The earl picked up a paperweight and rolled it in his hand. "Will you ever...want to return to France? Or Canada?"

"Not to France while Napoleon rules, save for the odd smuggling mission. It's almost child's play to evade the inept French navy, but it buoys my spirits." His eyes moved to focus on the view of Ravenshire Castle outside the window of the earl's study. "Canada...or America...someday. But not yet."

Despite their over twenty-year association, the Frenchman's past remained mysterious and the earl respected the privacy of the former fur trapper. Rising to his feet, Henry said, "I insist that you join us for dinner. Some of the abuse that awaits me should fall on you as well."

A smile turned up the edges of the Frenchman's lips. "Why not?"

***

Bri

Jane Anne extended a hand to Bri to help her out of the bath, and then wrapped her in a thick robe.

"You won't be a Lady's maid much longer, Jane Anne. After your sister, Dana, arrives, you'll have a few weeks to train her before your hairstyling salon is ready. Viscount Vaux told me that he has completed the drawings for the salon's interior for us to review when we meet him next week."

Bri slipped out of the robe and into her silk chemise.

Evaluating the options Jane Anne had selected for her, Bri pointed to a lavender linen dress with puffed sleeves in the empire style, trimmed in lace.

"My stomach jumps when I think about running my own hair salon, milady. What if no clients come? After all, most ladies have their hair done at home."

"I will come and set the pattern for others I know. And there is no reason you could not go to a lady's home…you could just charge more for your time. And you'll have to add one or two other workers."

"Do you mean I should train *other* women to fix hair?"

Bri nodded. "You have an excellent idea." She tilted her head. "It would be like an academy. I think I know where we might find some candidates." *The salon would provide a respectable profession for some of Charlotte's charges after their confinement.*

Once dressed, Bri sat at her vanity and watched in the mirror while Jane Anne styled her hair. "How about something different for tonight?" She used her hands to lift her tresses. "Up on one side with loose curls extending to my shoulder on the other. What do you think?"

"A lovely change. It won't take long."

The gong rang twice. "Ten minutes to dinner."

When Jane Anne was finished arranging her hair, Bri went downstairs to the parlor where Thompson, the head butler who'd accompanied them from London, stood pouring sherry. His son, the under butler, addressed as 'Young' to distinguish him from his father, passed out the glasses.

Bri walked over and took Edward's arm.

Her fiancé smiled. "Not a moment to spare."

Gio, a renowned artist, dubbed "Dwarf Extraordinaire" by the gossip rags, leaned back in his chair. The diminutive Lord Ostwold, a viscount whose right to the title had been restored late in life, possessed a droll wit. "Ravenshire thrives on punctuality, James."

Edward nodded. "Correct, as always, Gio."

Lady Gwyneth held up her glass of sherry and glanced toward her niece. "The terrors of the last months are over and we all are safe from Blackburn's treachery. Forever. Here's to a new beginning for us all."

Young handed Bri a glass, and she raised it to accept the toast.

"To a new beginning," echoed the other guests.

Thompson opened the double doors to the massive dining room and announced, "Dinner is served."

Gio raised an eyebrow. "Jean-Louis, you normally prefer to dispense with the formalities of a structured dinner."

The Frenchman revealed the hint of a smile. "*Normally.*"

"Come, now." The dwarf artist's persistence was legendary. "To what do we owe your presence?"

Jean-Louis shrugged in silence, his reaction of preference.

The footmen served a clear chicken broth and a basket of freshly baked bread.

"A light soup. To ease our digestion, Lord Ravenshire?" Decades spent painting portraits of the aristocracy had honed Gio's mastery of reading facial expressions. "Are you about to make an announcement of consequence?"

The earl looked at his soup. "Perhaps, after dessert."

"No." Bri put down her soup spoon. "We've had too much death and too much playacting lately. What is going on?"

Henry looked at Jean-Louis, then at Gwyneth and Bri, and took a deep breath. "Aelwyn is alive."

"What!" Gwyneth blanched and her hand flew to her throat. "How? Where? Why would she hide from us?"

"Because I made her swear to it." Jean-Louis moved his eyes around the guests. "To protect her."

"All this time? More than three years have passed!" Bri's face flushed with anger. "How could you keep this secret?"

"Because I feared for her life and your father has charged me with protecting this family. I followed my instincts."

Henry cleared his throat. "We leave Monday for Wales and sail to Ireland on Tuesday to see her. She's been hidden at our castle there."

"No wonder you discouraged me from visiting that estate." Bri turned to Jean-Louis. "And is *that* where you've disappeared to from time to time without explanation?"

The Frenchman shrugged again.

Edward raised a glass. "This is good news, isn't it? A woman thought dead is actually alive! Let us toast her return to your lives."

No one stirred.

Gwyneth stared at Henry. "Why didn't you tell me? She was like a sister to both of us and the dearest of friends to Charlotte."

"I didn't know. I found out little more than a month ago."

"A *month!*" Bri leaned forward. "And you said *nothing?*"

Gio shook his head. "To speak might have given Blackburn another easy target. I must agree with your father and Jean-Louis. Aelwyn is alive due to the Frenchman's actions."

Bri fumed as the guests finished their soup in awkward silence. She glared at Jean-Louis.

The footmen brought in hearty slices of beef roast, with buttered potatoes. Each person's portion was cooked to his or her preference.

Gio clinked a spoon on his glass. "Cease being petulant, all. I shall paint a portrait of Aelwyn the Resurrected."

Gwyneth frowned. "Gio, don't be sacrilegious."

"Why not? It's all superstition to me. Heaven or hell, we make our own."

Slowly, conversation returned. Bri noticed looks passing between Jean-Louis and her father. As dessert was being served, a pecan pie with whipped cream, she couldn't control her curiosity. "Is there more? Why are you two stealing surreptitious glances at each other?"

Edward reached over and put his hand on Bri's arm. "Don't keep the scab open—" He stopped when she scowled at him.

Henry sighed. "Bri's correct. There is more and it concerns her future. When Rychard died, Aelwyn was with child. She birthed a son. The earldom of Ravenshire has a male heir."

Stunned, Bri's mouth dropped open. After a few moments, she began to laugh.

The others stared at her unexpected reaction.

"What a relief! The trading company and the estate are both huge responsibilities. I welcome the help."

Gio took a sip of wine before speaking. "For a woman who relishes control, you are relinquishing it more readily than I would have imagined."

"I'm surprising myself," Bri acknowledged. "A first cousin!"

"His name is Ian Rychard Neyl Wyndward," said Henry.

At a loss for words for a moment, Gwyneth grasped the meaning. "Ian is a form of John...*Jean.*"

"She was grateful for his help." Henry waited for Thompson to pour more tea. "Aelwyn and Ian can now return to England or stay in Ireland, if they prefer. The important point is that they no longer have to hide in the shadows. I've sent a bird to alert them that we'll be there Tuesday evening."

"I'm *free.*" Bri sat back. "I am no longer 'Heiress of the Season.' I am simply a daughter, a niece and a fiancée."

"Nonsense. You are still my heir. Only Ravenshire Forest is tied to the earldom. No need to be so melodramatic."

Gio raised his eyebrows. "I think she has a knack for it. Actually, it's rather charming."

Bri looked at Jean-Louis. "You've met Ian. Does he look like Uncle Rychard?"

"Red hair like Rychard's and yours but with Aelwyn's blue eyes instead of the green shade that you and Rychard shared. Ian's a clever boy. Reminds me of you at that age."

"I'll be more like an aunt than a cousin, with such an age difference." Turning toward her father, she asked, "Don't you think they should live here at Ravenshire?"

Henry shrugged. "It will be up to Aelwyn. If there's anything you, *and* Gwyneth, *and* Charlotte, *and* Taita have taught me, it's that I should not make decisions for women."

Gwyneth reached over to take Henry's hand. "Charlotte must accompany us to Ireland, Henry. She loves Aelwyn as we do."

Henry nodded. "I planned to ask her to join us, even though she will probably not speak to me."

The dwarf waved his glass of wine in the air. "Then *I* must come along on the voyage to keep the conversation light!" He looked around the table. "Is there any objection?"

The earl threw back his head and laughed. "Would you listen if there were? You're a member of the family, Gio. No need to ask."

Gio raised his glass in a mute toast to the earl. He turned to Jean-Louis. "Frenchman, tell us about Ian.

"He's precocious. He's demonstrated some skill at archery."

Gwyneth was aghast. "Archery! At the age of three? Are you mad?"

Jean-Louis swirled his wine glass, but set it down without taking a sip. "Not at all, Lady Gwyneth. One day Ian and I were walking through the woods. I was teaching him about the differences among the trees and how to read animal tracks. While he was looking up at the leaves, I put my hand on his arm to curb his stride. In front of us, a fox was killing a rabbit. In the six months since that day, he's refused to eat rabbit. He asked me to kill the fox with my bow and arrow, and we buried them both. Ian said a short prayer, ending with 'Maybe they will love each other in heaven.' He looked up at me and said, 'Teach me bow and arrow.'

"I told him a weapon was not a toy, and he said, 'Me protect rabbits.' I winnowed a small bow and made appropriately sized arrows for him. I set up practice targets and his aim was true. The boy has an unerring eye and a strong arm. Within less than a month, his proficiency exceeded that of boys ten years older. Aelwyn approved."

Gio smirked. "We shall be meeting a *petit* Jean-Louis. Does he wear the fox's fur as a fully outfitted trapper would?"

"As a matter of fact, he wears the tail on his hunting hat."

Edward tilted his head. "A hunting hat for a child?"

"Inclement weather plagues the British isles, Mr. James."

Edward smiled. "*Touché*, Jean-Louis. *Touché*."

***

Friday, May 3, 1811 – Madagascar
Ariapses

Holding the office of *kâtib* of the sultanate, Ariapses served as the official scribe or prime secretary of Sultan Sarduba. When the Sultan left Madagascar, the word of Ariapses was law. Third in hierarchy after the Sultan and his vizier, Xerxes, the official scribe held court, adjudicated disputes, and conducted trade negotiations on behalf of the Sultan. Even more important, in his mind, he kept the sultanas, the Sultan's many wives, as well as his sons and daughters under watch.

Ariapses, a shrewd judge of character, kept his impressions to himself. In his opinion, the Sultan's eldest son, Szilard, exhibited a malicious streak and an undisguised ambition. His mother, Anja, the chief wife, was regal and kind, and the Sultan generally conducted himself with fairness, but their son's demeanor conveyed a sense of entitlement and an attitude of arrogance. His actions were too often deceptive, demanding, and cruel. A preening dandy on some days, he wielded the crossbow with deadly accuracy. His absence from the sultanate during the Sultan's foray in London had allowed Ariapses and the court a pleasant interlude. Walking through the Sultan's gardens on his way to his offices, Ariapses smiled. *How the palace life thrives without Szilard's pernicious influence.*

The scribe had derived the formula for the Sultan's success in maintaining power in his mountainous seaside territory. To keep the population at a manageable level, licenses were granted for marriages, and children limited to two per couple without special permission. Ariapses smiled. *Taita's herbal knowledge has ensured the Sultan's long dominance of his land by limiting births.* As a result of the policies, each tribe was prosperous with enough food and housing for all. His initiative directing that the Sultan marry one woman from each tribe conveyed honor on the family and ensured the Sultan's continuing control of his realm.

In truth, though many in the western world made assumptions in ignorance of the facts, Sultan Sarduba was not *the* Sultan of Madagascar, but one of many who ruled small sultanates. His particular land was rich in spices valued by Westerners, and Ariapses had exploited connections with traders to secure lucrative contracts. His deft administration of the land and resources filled the coffers of the royal household and allowed the Sultan freedom to travel the world at will. Fertile volcanic soil covered mountains that gently sloped to sea, and nourished gardens, flowers, staple crops, spices and other herbs. Animal herds grazed on fields bordering virgin forests while seaside lagoons nestled among the swaying palms. Courtesy of the natural mountainous barrier to invasion or conquest, the protected area seemed like a Garden of Eden to Ariapses.

The scribe sighed. *I don't miss the Sultan. But I am a poor substitute for Taita, the healer. I have used her healing lessons to keep the Sultan's young son,*

Rija, hovering between life and death after a severe seizure. I must keep him alive until Taita returns.

***

Friday, May 3, 1811 – Aboard *Nut's Night Sky*
Captain Alif

Blackburn took an unmarked red leather-bound volume from the ship's library to peruse its content one evening, and his brow wrinkled in surprise. "The pages are blank."

Captain Alif tilted his head toward the shelves of books. "There are several blank volumes my predecessor stockpiled to be used as adjuncts to the ship's logs. I have no such need. Take it with my compliments."

"A gracious gesture, Captain. I am partial to recording my thoughts. Perhaps Nut, the goddess of the night sky, is looking upon me with favor."

"May she inspire you." *This man has the air of a dangerous predator. If a blank book buys goodwill, 'tis a small price to pay.*

***

Friday, May 3, 1811 – A Townhouse in London
Lord Merrick

Lord Merrick awaited the arrival of his secret lover, Lady Patricia, in the townhouse of an old friend who rarely came to London. By prearrangement, each lover entered separately.

Lady Patricia's ample bosom never failed to attract male attention. Her wickedly satirical view of life amused her older paramour. *She's besotted with me. I'll have no trouble keeping her on the hook despite my decision.*

Often over the last eighteen months, he had promised her that as soon as his sickly wife died, they could marry. Lady Patricia stood to inherit a respectable fortune, and were it not for the untimely death of the extremely wealthy Lord Exton, he would have made good on his promise. However, newly widowed Countess of Exton, ten years Lord Merrick's senior, had always had an eye for him, and days earlier they had secretly agreed to marry after a suitable mourning period for each. *Now all I have to do is wait out my wife's demise.*

***

Lady Patricia

On her way to meet Lord Merrick, Lady Patricia imagined their life together. *Lady Margaret is near death, so it won't be long now. Clarissa is married. Bri and Penelope are engaged, and soon I will be too. This Marriage Season has been intolerable, rife with immature boys at balls that make me yawn.*

Evan, Lord Merrick, was thirty years older than Lady Patricia. She didn't have to worry about conceiving a child because it was a rare evening when Evan could perform. That was just as well. Lady Patricia had no interest in seeing her supple body stretched and misshapen by carrying a child in her belly. In truth, the thought repulsed her. She'd heard women complain of childbirth pains, and pain terrified her. Worse, many women died, like Bri's mother. Lady Patricia shivered in revulsion. *Not the path for me. Lord Merrick has a son and grandson from his marriage. His line of succession is secured.* She craved the social status that Lord Merrick enjoyed. And he wrote her such naughty love letters, more fantasy than reality, given his impotence. Hidden behind a painting in her bedroom, the *notes d'amour* thrilled her. *Someday I must take a lover to find out what it's like to lie with a virile man.*

When her Hackney arrived at their rendezvous, she almost danced her way into the townhouse.

"Darling!" Evan took her into his arms, smothering her face with kisses. "My love, my wife's condition is worsening. I may not be able to see you for a while. I must play my part during her last weeks. I know that you understand."

Crestfallen, Lady Patricia nodded. "Of course."

"I will send you more letters, my sweet. Fear not, we will be together soon."

"I'll miss our clandestine meetings. It's exhilarating to keep our secret."

"Our illicit liaisons are exciting. Passion, my pet, is an elixir one cannot easily relinquish." He pulled away from her. "I will write you as in the past, but we must be careful. Now more than ever there cannot be a whiff of scandal."

"Soon, our love will be out in the open. No skulking around like thieves in the night. Patience, my dearest. It won't be long now."

***

Friday, May 3, 1811 – *Chez Michel*
Vaux

The wealthy scion of a family with real estate holdings throughout the *ton*, Viscount Vaux had become known for designing cutting-edge interiors. Among the elite, his name drew potential clients to see the latest interiors carved from his imagination. Beyond that, his facility for clever banter made him a sought-after dinner party companion.

With Lady Gabriella and James, two of his favorite dinner companions, away at Ravenshire for the weekend, he gathered a small group together at the last minute for dinner. In addition to his maiden aunt, Lady Elena Vaux, other attendees included Banfield and Rogers, who had been classmates at Merton with Vaux and James. Sir Reginald of the Foreign Office, his niece Lady Patricia, Lady Melanie, and Lady Marianna rounded out the crowd.

Lady Elena indulged her nephew. She appreciated fine wine and good company. The added benefit of Sir Reggie, a companion her own age, joining her to act as *de facto* chaperones for the unmarried young people in the last throes of the Marriage Season, delighted her.

"Tell me," asked Lady Elena, "do any of you young ladies frequent Mlle. Bellerobe's atelier? *Scandal & Shame* called her 'notorious.' "

"Be frank. Auntie loves gossip." The dark-haired urbane viscount winked at his henna-coiffed aunt.

Lady Melanie leaned in. "I wonder who told the gossip rag of Lady Gabriella's patronage?"

"Well, Lady Melanie, you should go as soon as you can. That little tidbit in *Scandal & Shame* has doubled Mlle. Bellerobe's trade. You may not be able to get a gown for the rest of this Marriage Season."

Lady Patricia quickly raised her glass to her lips, hoping the color in her cheeks would be attributed to a flush from the wine.

CHAPTER THREE

Saturday, May 4, 1811 - Ravenshire
Henry

Early that morning, a carriage left for London to gather whatever extra clothing or other items the travelers needed for the voyage to Ireland. Henry wrote out a message for Jean-Louis to send to Aelwyn via one of his birds.

In addition, he dispatched a messenger to invite Oliver, Lord Darlemont to accompany them because he, Rychard and Aelwyn had been exceptionally close despite Oliver's differences with Henry. Their enmity centered on Oliver's belief that Henry's frequent abandonment of Lady Jane, Bri's mother, had deepened her melancholy and hastened her death. In truth, many women, wealthy and poor, died in childbirth as had Lady Jane. For the sake of Bri, whom Oliver adored, he maintained a cordial but distant relationship with his one-time brother-in-law.

The earl summoned the housekeeper. "Configure a suite of rooms for Aelwyn and Ian, whether for visits or permanent residence."

Mrs. Connor could not hide her tears. " 'Tis a miracle, milord."

"Tell Jane Anne that she will accompany us to Ireland to serve the ladies. Jean-Louis has arranged for her sister, Dana, to meet us at Castle Glaslough to accompany us back to Ravenshire. In addition, ask Nashmir to send that new under valet he's training, Wilson, to see to the gentlemen."

"Yes, milord."

***

Later that morning, Henry suggested a tour of the castle project. Bri, Edward, Gwyneth, and Gio accompanied him. They walked past the old crumbling tower to the foundation and outer walls of the first level of the main central hall of Ravenshire Castle.

Bri pointed to a cherub over the entrance. "The design and layout are based on the engraving that hangs behind Father's desk."

"That cherub bears a striking resemblance to someone I know." Gwyneth kept a straight face.

Gio shrugged. "Immortalized as a cherub? It could be worse. My countenance might grace a gargoyle."

"Cherub or gargoyle, the figure is distinctive." Bri squinted at the sculpture and shielded the sun from her eyes. Gesturing to the wide expanse before them, Bri continued, "Arches and Laurence have been searching for the original plans at the Bodleian Library at Oxford, but used the etching to design the construction. They solved most of the conundrums that baffled them."

Henry nodded. "Edward, you may not know that the restoration was designed by your father's and my old schoolmate, AJ Smithton, an architect now based in Italy, and Arches, a former servant who accompanied me to Merton when I was a student there. Arches is better known by his true name, Peter Groom."

Edward's mouth dropped open. "The renowned architect was once a servant here?"

Henry nodded. "From a family of grooms, hence the surname. Arches is a nickname based on his hero, Archimedes. He became a student under my father's sponsorship after he passed a series of mathematical and spacial tests. Smithton and Arches are working together to make my long-held dream come true—the restoration of Ravenshire Castle to its former glory."

Bri waved her hand toward the construction. "Imagine the history! This castle, built centuries ago for war and defense, will now house part of our family's extensive art collection and serve as a venue for balls, weddings and unique events. The crumbling Old Tower, the only remnant of the original castle, will remain as a testament to the relentless power of time and nature."

Henry pointed to future areas of construction as he spoke. "The main reception and ballroom areas will be completed in the center, flanked by rooms on either side. When completed, it will accommodate up to 500 guests in the main area with over 100 bedrooms and a staff of nearly 200 for special events, although a core staff of about fifty will be permanent."

"Boosting the local economy, no doubt." Gio was uncharacteristically impressed. "Fit for a king, Henry. Are you planning a usurpation?" Gio shook his head in wonder. "This is a massive undertaking. It could be decades before it is done."

"Perhaps, but the builders have promised that the center reception area will be done within the year."

Gwyneth's face betrayed her disbelief. She waved her hand toward the façade. "You can see the attention to detail. Look at Henry's framed etching of the castle when we go back to the main house. It's been faithfully replicated."

"Can we go inside?" Gio gingerly stepped toward the door.

Henry put out his arm to stop the dwarf. "Too much construction material. Perhaps in a few months. I don't want to lose anyone to falling debris."

"I shan't lose myself to such an ignominious end. Wait I must."

***

Gwyneth

Gio and Gwyneth split off from the others, walking around the perimeter of the castle.

The dwarf squinted into the sun as he imagined the final tableau. "I'd like to paint Ravenshire Castle when it's completed, if I live long enough."

"Why not paint it as it is being built?" Gwyneth pointed to the beginnings of the central hall. "Envision is as a series of scenes of construction progress."

Gio nodded. "An excellent suggestion…for an old man."

"Better to paint a portion of the castle's story than leave nothing but an intention."

"It annoys me to admit that you're right, as usual. What about *your* legacy? When am I going to see Musée de Merbeau Press publish the faerie stories and alphabet book? Don't dawdle, Gwyneth. You're not getting any younger, either."

Playfully, Gwyneth pretended to punch him. "Never remind a lady of her age."

"Never hit a dwarf. It's beneath you."

"Ha! You are incorrigible."

"I hope so. I wouldn't want to soften in my old age."

"And who will write the autobiography that you envision to be published by my press? A memoir that I know must take precedence over faeries and alphabets?"

Gio shrugged. "You are the writer. I can regale you with resonant tidbits and anecdotes to weave into a laudatory tome."

"Vainglorious and eccentric as always."

"That can be in the title, if you like."

"Don't tempt me. If I write it, it will be a biography, and from *my* point of view. *You* must write about your life. I can, however, act as your editor."

"And rip heart-wrenching scenes of despair or triumph from the manuscript of my life? Lady Gwyneth, you wound me."

"Then write it yourself and present it as a *fait accompli*. Don't wait too long. *Tempus fugit*."

***

Saturday, May 4, 1811 – Interior of Lady Clarissa's Carriage
Clarissa

Dr. Nicholas St. Cloud helped his wife, Lady Clarissa, climb into their carriage after the evening's performance of *The Princess*. In wigs and costumes, disguising their true identities, she had performed the title role and he the role of The Wizard.

Clarissa collapsed onto the leather carriage bench, letting her head fall back. "I'm exhausted. I don't know why I'm so tired. Four nights a week didn't seem like too much of a commitment, but now I wonder. How can I keep this up another five-and-a-half months? Or longer, if the run is extended?"

"I too am finding it difficult to give my full attention to my practice during the day. My clerk has tapped me on the shoulder more than once to wake me up."

"I hesitate to admit that my father and Mr. James may have been correct."

"I know your father was skeptical of your participation, but what did James say?"

"He told Bri that you would not be able to build your veterinary enterprise *and* appear onstage so frequently. She dismissed his concern, expressing her opinion that appearing onstage was no more demanding than attending a Society dinner party."

Nick sighed and shrugged. "I was of the same opinion before I tried it."

"What do we do now? The operetta is a hit, Wyndward Investments has funded it based on our performances, and the theatre is leased for a long run. We are trapped by our own success."

"We have understudies. Perhaps we should have them take over two nights a week and then move to four before the demands on us get worse."

Clarissa raised her eyebrows. "Worse? What do you mean?"

"I overheard Herr Kramer talking about extending performances of *The Princess* to include one more evening as well as adding a matinee."

Paling at the thought, Clarissa reached for Nick's arm. "Tell the driver to pull over. I feel that I am about to be sick."

Nick signaled the driver to pull over, leapt from the carriage, and helped Clarissa step down.

Retching bile onto the street, Clarissa's expectorations alternated with dry heaves. When she finally caught her breath, tears were running down her cheeks. "I feel terrible. I don't know what I ate that could have made me so sick."

Steadying her with his arm, he asked, "Are you ready to get back in the carriage?"

She nodded mutely.

Nick embraced her as they rode through the streets. "Our next performance is two nights from now. Perhaps you will have recovered by then. Even so, I will speak to Herr Kramer about the understudies. All theatrical companies have performers who substitute for the main players from time to time."

"Or for *all* time. The career of Violetta Vinci may be a short one."

"And that of Drew Wood as well."

"The operetta is a critical and financial triumph. The music is wonderful and we were part of its creation." She shook her head. "But others must take over our performing obligations soon. I will remain on the governing board for investment purposes and you can concentrate on what you love—the health of pets. I hope Bri doesn't see it as a failure on our parts. I don't want to disappoint her."

"Lady Gabriella is a practical woman. She will not cast blame. She wanted to prove to James that the operetta would win over the *ton*. It has earned universal acclaim and our stage names have allowed us to maintain anonymity."

Clarissa closed her eyes and yawned. "The last few months have passed like a whirlwind. Maybe once the understudies have proven themselves, we could go away on a honeymoon. With some rest, I should regain my usual energy."

Nick kissed Clarissa's forehead. "Whatever you wish, my darling."

By the time they reached their home, the Hanforth Mansion, Clarissa had fallen asleep. Nick picked her up and carried her inside.

***

Saturday, May 4, 1811 – Dumfries, Scotland
Mirela

Mirela trudged along the cobblestones after a visit to a bookseller who specialized in unusual volumes, many on the occult. With her hand around a paper-wrapped book of incantations and spells, the back of her neck tingled. *Someone watching me.*

Out of the corner of her eye, she saw a figure dart behind a building. *The hat. The same hat as in Inverness. A watcher.*

Knocking the prescribed code on the door, Mirela waited for Aneira to open it. "We having watchers."

"Do you think they tracked us from Inverness?"

The Gypsy shrugged. "Same hat."

"We've been here too long. I thought the fire would throw them off our trail, but this is a small town. Strangers bring unwanted attention. We'll need more subterfuge this time"

"London hiding us better."

Aneira looked out the window. "I have an idea." She returned to the small table and opened a bag to retrieve a quill, an inkwell and paper. "Arthur must be informed of our plans."

***

Sunday, May 5, 1811 – Castle Glaslough in Ireland
Gilles

Gilles O'Malley, the son of a French mother fleeing Napoleon and an Irish soldier who helped her escape, eyed the dawn's horizon through his spyglass and spotted a bird heading for the dovecote. From his perch above the castle, he could see for miles. The locals were known to him by gait, favored hat, hair color, horse, and wagon. Anyone out of the ordinary was flagged to be tracked by one of his underlings. Trained by Jean-Louis, he'd vowed to protect Aelwyn and Ian as long as he breathed.

A stocky but fast-moving adversary, Gilles could wrestle a larger man to the ground in seconds. He'd snapped more than a few necks in ambush, employing battle tactics taught him by his uncle, a French army captain who'd deserted Napoleon and emigrated to Ireland to be with his sister.

During his uncle's military service in Southeast Asia, he'd learned lethal fighting methods that struck old-line European fighters as ungentlemanly. "You can be a dead gentleman or a live soldier," his uncle would say. "It's up to you."

Gilles laughed as he remembered the words.

A bird alighted on the sill, and cooed to his old friend. "Let's get the message, Bertie." Gilles named all the birds. No one else could tell them apart, but he noticed a misshapen eye, a discolored feather, a malformed foot, or the tone of its song. Bertie regularly flew from Ravenshire to Glaslough and back. As Gilles read the message from the earl, his eyes widened. "At last!" He bounded down the curved stone steps in the lookout tower and ran to the kitchen entrance.

The cook, Mrs. Kerry, looked up from her luncheon preparations, her ruddy complexion even redder from the soup's rising steam. "Catch your breath, Gilles. What's wrong?"

"Nothing. Everything's right. Where is Lady Sheffield?" Lady Sheffield, the surname of Rychard's mother's family, was a subterfuge to shield Aelwyn's identity while in residence.

"In the parlor. Master Ian is with her."

Gilles went to find the butler, Bidey, and whispered in his ear. After Bidey had lured Ian away from his mother with a challenge to play a game of hide-and-seek out of earshot, Gilles walked into the parlor and handed her the message.

Tears misted over Aelwyn's blue eyes. "We're safe? We're free to go home?"

Her protector nodded.

Aelwyn stood and walked to the window and ran her fingers through her ebony tresses, revealing the first few emergent strands of white. "Castle Glaslough feels like home now, but—" She stared out the window for a few moments. "—Ian may be earl someday, so he should grow up at Ravenshire."

"I hope you will visit us from time to time, milady."

Whirling around to face Gilles, Aelwyn looked stricken. "Aren't you coming *with* us? I feel safe only when you are nearby."

"I serve *you*, milady. I am gratified that you value my service."

"Always, Gilles. And Ian would miss you terribly. It's settled then. You will come to Ravenshire with us."

***

Sunday, May 5, 1811 – Baroness Glasspool's Mansion
Charlotte

Charlotte walked into her dining room for breakfast.

Morgan, the butler, signaled to the footman, who disappeared into the kitchen and returned shortly with a platter. "Mrs. Holdart has prepared your favorite, Baroness."

"*Payn perdu?* You know how to cheer me, Morgan."

Day-old bread dipped in beaten eggs and cream, *payn perdu* was fried in butter, sprinkled with sugar and doused in maple syrup from America. *A gift from Henry, but its flavor is irresistible.*

The doorbell rang, distracting Charlotte. *Who would be calling early on a Sunday morning?* She stiffened when she heard Morgan's greeting.

"Lord Ravenshire, we weren't expecting you."

"May I see the baroness?"

Charlotte called out, "Come join me for breakfast, Henry. I'll have Mrs. Holdart fry up some bacon to accompany the *payn perdu.*"

Henry walked into the pale green silk-walled dining room and took a seat on the chintz floral upholstered chair opposite Charlotte. "I've missed your cook's *payn perdu.* Jean-Louis told Mrs. Jones never

34

to make it. She ignores him, but the dish is still a rare treat at Ravenshire."

Charlotte directed her hazel eyes at her former lover. "Is *payn perdu* the reason for your visit?"

"No. I've come to invite you to Ireland—"

"Stop! Haven't I—"

Henry held up both hands. "Please listen to the reason." He paused, took a deep breath, and sighed. "I found out barely a month ago that Aelwyn is still alive."

Dropping her fork, Charlotte's face blanched as she stared at him.

Henry picked up a spoon and twirled it between his fingers as he spoke. "Jean-Louis believed her life was in danger and spirited her away to my estate in Ireland, where she has been ever since. Now that we know Blackie is dead, we are sailing to Ireland to see her. You love her as do we all, so I am inviting you to join us."

Wordlessly, Charlotte nodded.

The footman came in with Henry's platters of *payn perdu* and bacon.

Charlotte leaned forward. "Aelwyn and I were like sisters, Henry. I've mourned her these last three years." Her brow furrowed into a scowl. "Why did you not tell me as soon as you knew?"

"Bri and Gwyneth are also furious with me, but Jean-Louis only told me a month ago. Until we knew Bri was safe from Blackie, I feared revealing Aelwyn's secret. And there's more."

After hearing the rest of the story, the baroness reached over to Henry's plate and took a piece of bacon for herself. "When do we sail?"

***

Monday, May 6, 1811 – Dumfries, Scotland

Colvert

While Voutain watched the front of the inn from the shadows, Colvert was relegated to the delivery entrance.

Over the time they had been watching the two old women, Colvert had become familiar with the delivery patterns of the local tradesmen and farmers who supplied the small kitchen of the inn.

Their wagons rolled up on a predictable schedule. Deliveries began at dawn with the dairyman

Colvert had arranged with him to trade him a small tin of milk every morning for a touch of snuff.

The dairyman uncovered the tarp over this large tins of milk and handed them to the cook. After that, he walked over to Colvert and completed their daily transaction.

***

The Dairyman

Returning to his wagon, the dairyman pulled the tarp back over his cargo, covering the shoes of his unseen passengers from the prying eyes of Colvert.

He climbed up to the driver's bench, took the reins, and edged the carriage in the direction of his next stop.

CHAPTER FOUR

Tuesday, May 7, 1811 – Aboard *Airmid's Wynd*
Jean-Louis

S wansea lay a day's coach ride from Ravenshire. After a night at the Swansea Waterview Inn, the earl's traveling party boarded *Airmid's Wynd* just after dawn. The earl had a penchant for naming his sailing ships after goddesses—Celtic, Greek or whatever culture struck his fancy.

Gio frowned and rubbed his chin. "My proficiency in Celtic mythology has faded."

Gwyneth scoffed. "You *never* had any proficiency in Celtic mythology."

Henry smiled. "Airmid is the Celtic goddess of medicinal plants and keeper of the spring. Her spirit regenerates, bringing the dead to life again."

Edward squinted. "*Is?* You speak as if she exists."

"How do we know she does not?" Henry didn't wait for an answer, leading the group to the captain's dining room, a compact teak-paneled area set at the back of the ship. It featured multi-colored diamond-shaped window panes of leaded glass, a trademark of the Wyndward fleet. Henry, Bri, Edward, Gwyneth, Oliver, Gio and Charlotte took their seats at the captain's table. After a conducting a final security check of the vessel, Jean-Louis arrived.

Gio yawned. "When will we depart?"

At that precise moment, the boat lurched from its moorings.

Stretching, Gio gazed at the multi-colored hues beaming through the window that spanned the width of the captain's quarters. "I should get up this early more often. The light dancing on the clouds is amazing."

Charlotte smiled. "Gio, you are an artist *and* a poet."

The earl offered a breakfast toast, holding up a goblet of water. "To a good sailing!"

A staccato of echoes reverberated around the cabin.

***

Bri

Edward and Bri strolled arm in arm on deck after breakfast.

Losing balance, Edward stumbled, unfamiliar with the movements of a ship.

Bri steadied him. "You'll get used to it."

Gulping, Edward's face paled and he ran to the side of the ship. He retched, spewing his breakfast into the sea. He retrieved a handkerchief from inside his waistcoat and wiped his mouth. "Will I? You Wyndwards have it in your blood. I'd forgotten how much I hated the sea."

"Nonsense. Comfort with the roll of a ship is acquired over time. Ginger tea will help. Let's find the chief steward."

Silently, Edward nodded and clung to Bri's arm, weaving from side to side as the ship lurched.

"Duck!" Bri pulled Edward's head down as the sail flew low overhead as it was repositioned.

He meekly let her lead him below decks.

***

Edward

After taking a sip of ginger tea in the ship's library, Edward appeared on the verge of gagging again. "How much longer must I endure the Irish Sea?"

Bri tilted her head. "With favorable winds, the voyage is about ten hours to the Irish coast and about another hour by carriage to reach to the castle. We'll be there for dinner."

Putting up his hands, as if to stop her from speaking, Edward closed his eyes. "Do not mention food until we are on dry land."

"How ever did you travel to Asia? Is sailing something you abhor? It *is* my family's habit to travel frequently by ship. We own a fleet, Edward. This is not a particularly bad passage."

"Am I the only one who is out of sorts? These seas pitch and roll more than I remember."

The captain walked in and put his hand on Edward's shoulder. "You lean in the same direction with your body, so it's not as disorienting. Fight it and it will win. Watch Lady Gabriella. She unconsciously rolls with the ship to maintain her equilibrium. Come, stand."

Edward struggled to his feet.

"Don't take a rigid stance. Bend your knees and rock with the waves. If you go against it, you will reel with vertigo. Go with it, and you maintain your balance."

Bri stood and said. "Keep your eyes on mine. Forget your body."

The captain stood in back of Edward to catch him if he lost his footing.

Summoning all his strength, Edward fixed his gaze on Bri's eyes. "I imagine my face is as green as your eyes." He rolled, mirroring her movements. After a minute or two, he turned to the captain. "It's working. I think I have it."

Gio walked in and hopped onto a chair. "Practicing the rock and roll stance, I see." Gio looked to the captain. "Any wine around here?"

"It's not yet noon, Gio."

"It's noon somewhere, Bri."

Bri rolled her eyes as she and Edward left the captain's quarters.

Back on deck, Edward maintained his balancie.

"It takes time to get your 'sea legs,' but soon it will be second nature."

Edward grimaced. "As long as I don't fall overboard. I can't swim."

"What?"

Edward immediately regretted revealing his weakness. He withered under the scrutiny from his fiancée's eyes

"That is unacceptable, Edward. You must set an example. Every passenger on a boat should know how to swim. Oceans and storms are unpredictable." She looked out over the deck where Ireland's verdant hills loomed on the horizon. "There's a pond at Glaslough. I'll teach you how to swim tomorrow."

"It is a practical solution, but I can't say I look forward to it." Her scolding had interrupted his focus. Vertigo overwhelmed him and he vomited over the side of the ship.

***

Tuesday, May 7, 1811 – Castle Glaslough
Gilles

A bird flew overhead, directly into the dovecote.

Gilles dashed up the circular steps to the high perch of the birds' homing station. "Here, Sallie girl, You're home, darling." He carefully removed the message, then gave the bird a treat and placed her in a cage to be returned to Ravenshire with Jean-Louis.

After reading the message, he descended and walked to the kitchen entrance. "Is Lady Sheffield about?" The cook nodded. "She's in the drawing room with the housekeeper."

Gilles strode down the long hallway and found Aelwyn and the housekeeper reviewing the tasks to be completed before the Ravenshire party arrived.:

"Milady, their arrival on the coast is estimated about five o'clock today. "Would you like to meet them on the beach?"

Aelwyn brushed a white-tinged ebony strand from her face. "Yes! It's been too long to wait any longer than necessary."

"We'll leave around half-past three." Gilles waited to be dismissed.

"Perhaps some wine, bread and cheese for the ride home would be welcome."

The housekeeper stood. "I'll see to it that the cook prepares several baskets."

Nodding, Aelwyn added, "I'll wake Ian from his nap in a couple of hours. He'll enjoy the adventure of the ride."

Gilles tilted his head toward the woman known as Lady Sheffield. "He'll want to ride up with me."

"Have you tested the straps to protect him from being thrown? He's up so high in the driver's perch, it unnerves me to think of it."

"Yes, the system Jean-Louis designed has functioned well. And he loves the perspective."

"Gilles, I'm afraid that you and Jean-Louis have turned Ian into a daredevil."

"He was born that way, milady. Fearless."

"Fearless can be foolish. I'm relying on you and Jean-Louis to temper any tendencies of my son to act without thinking."

"With all due respect, milady, we would not encourage rash, impulsive behavior. We do, however, respond instinctively to danger. He may try to imitate us, and I am mindful of your concerns."

"Confronting danger is second nature to you and Jean-Louis. At his age, Ian sees what you two do as an exciting game. He does not grasp the consequences."

Gilles nodded. "I will temper his will." He left to prepare the carriage.

***

Tuesday, May 7, 1811 – Aboard *Airmid's Wynd*
Charlotte

Charlotte and Gwyneth stood on the deck.

Gwyneth pointed to the dock. "I see a carriage!"

"Aelwyn must have been lonely these last three years, fearing that her child might be in danger if the truth ever came out." Charlotte sighed. "At least Blackburn is dead. I am so thankful that she is alive and that Ian is safe. I can no longer be angry with Jean-Louis or Henry."

The comtesse laughed. "Don't let on this soon that you've forgiven them."

"Don't worry."

Gwyneth shook her head. "I thought I knew Blackie. I am still stunned at his duplicity and hatred."

Henry and Gio sauntered up behind them.

Gio hoisted himself up on a barrel lashed to the inner deck so he could look over the edge of the ship. "Sunset over the Emerald Isle. Quite a sight." He pulled out a spyglass and peered through it. "I'll be damned."

"Undoubtedly," said the earl.

"A lame riposte, Henry." The dwarf did not lower the spyglass as he spoke. "That redheaded boy could be a double for Rychard. Perhaps there is a God, or gods, or something in the universe."

Stealing a glance at Henry, Charlotte saw his eyes mist over. Silently, she put her hand in his, looking straight ahead while he regained his composure. *Tottie is right. I still love him.*

***

Jean-Louis

The former trapper had served in the French army as an act of rebellion against his extended family of naval officers. Miraculously, not one had lost his head during the Terror. An uncle who still served as an admiral had told Jean-Louis, "Being on the high seas has its advantages during a revolution where one marks the passage of time by avoiding the fall of a blade." Knowing his actions before deserting the army had eliminated any chance to see his remaining family, the forays that Jean-Louis made into France on behalf of the earl were fraught, even before the ascendance of Napoleon. He let others overstate the danger he faced. *I am protected by the incompetence and insouciance of the local gendarmerie.*

Jean-Louis had learned one important lesson from that uncle. One or more of what the English called jolly boats, used to row to shore from anchor in deeper water or to traverse the distance between boats in a fleet, were roped to the stern of a French naval vessel. His uncle called them "officer exits" because none were provided for the general crew. In a moment of crisis, shipboard discipline vanished. The officers were "exited" over the decks and it was every man for himself to secure a place on the jolly boats. The sad truth was, in the middle of a battle at sea, or a storm, or a mutiny, being in a small boat in the middle of an ocean rolling with massive waves guaranteed escape for neither officer nor crewman. Only in rare circumstances did anyone survive.

Former officers from various world navies commanded most of the earl's vessels. The Wyndward fleet consisted of cargo vessels with minimal crew. Loading and unloading required extensive coordination, but labor was contracted dockside at ports of call.

Prior to their first voyage together, Jean-Louis had brought the jolly boat issue to Henry's attention. Impressed, the then-viscount had mandated that an adequate number of jolly boats be attached to each ship in his fleet to accommodate all crew and officers. Passengers were unusual on most of the earl's ships. Only a few cabins were available, primarily kept for family, friends and well-heeled travelers who gladly paid the extra expense for the relative luxury the Wyndward fleet offered. Extra jolly boats were attached for passengers when cabins were full.

Over the previous thirty years, despite the odds, over five hundred men in the Wyndward fleet had survived calamities at sea, while twice that many had perished. The oceans were treacherous to all shippers at one time or another, but no other shipping company could document a survival record even close to that of Wyndward Trading. On the occasion of any survival, the earl always credited Jean-Louis with the foresight to suggest an adequate supply of jolly boats.

***

The Irish Coast
Aelwyn

Seeing the jolly boat being lowered with the landing party, Aelwyn's heart leapt. Signaling to Gilles to open the carriage door, Aelwyn waited for the footman to help her alight from the carriage.

Gilles placed one foot on the lift-step to the driver's perch, unfastened the leather straps keeping Ian safely in place, and lowered him into Aelwyn's arms.

The sight of him in his floppy hat with a fox tail hanging down for half his height made her smile. "You're about to meet your Uncle Henry, Aunt Gwyneth, Cousin Oliver and Cousin Bri. Baroness Glasspool, Mr. James and Lord Ostwold are in the boat with Jean-Louis, too."

"The dwarf Jean-Louis told me about? Will he draw me?"

"Perhaps. He is prolific."

"Prorific? What is that?"

"*Prolific*. It means he paints many paintings."

As the boat neared the shore, Aelwyn's breaths became shallower.

In Aelwyn's arms, Ian felt his mother's anxiety. "It's all right, Mother. Gilles and Jean-Louis will protect us."

When the boat rowed ashore, Aelwyn's tears flowed.

Henry bounded out of the boat to embrace Aelwyn. "Until a month ago, I thought you were dead." Taking Ian's chin in his hand, he added, "And I didn't know you existed, Nephew."

"But I knew all about you, Uncle Henry. Jean-Louis told me about your castles and your horses and your ships." He pointed at Gwyneth. "You are the blonde Aunt Gwyneth!" Looking at Charlotte, he smiled. "And you are the black-haired baroness."

"What a clever boy you are." The baroness smiled. "Coached by a certain Frenchman, I'd wager."

Henry lifted Ian into his arms. "Who do you think the rest of these people are?"

"The red-haired lady is Cousin Bri. The blond man is Cousin Oliver. And the dwarf is the famous artist, Lord Ostywild."

"Ostwold," said the artist, "but you may call me Gio."

"Gio, will you paint me?"

"Absolutely, my boy."

"But you—" Ian stared at Edward with a frown. "Who are you?"

"I am Edward James. I am engaged to be married to your cousin, Bri."

"Are you a duke or a prince?"

"No."

"An earl or a viscount?"

"No."

Ian's face fell. "A baron?"

Edward shook his head.

The boy. "A knight?"

"No, but my father is a knight."

"So you're not important?"

"Edward is important to me, Ian," said Bri.

The boy bit his lip, not knowing what to say.

Henry handed Ian to Jean-Louis. He nestled his head in the Frenchman's neck.

Aelwyn embraced Oliver, Charlotte, Gwyneth and Bri.

Even Oliver fought back tears.

Bri composed herself. "We have two carriages. I think one should be for the women and one for the men."

Gilles helped the women enter their carriage, while Jean-Louis opened the door for the men and Ian.

"I want to ride with you, Jean-Louis."

"Not this time. Your face is ruddy from the ride over. You'll ride inside with your uncle."

The boy didn't argue as the Frenchman handed him into Henry's arms.

When Henry, Edward, Gio, Oliver and Ian were seated inside, Jean-Louis took two large and two small baskets of bread, cheese and pastries from the back of one of the carriages. The large ones were provided to each coach's passengers, and the smaller ones were given to the drivers and footmen. A footman was assigned to act as driver for the men's carriage .

A third carriage transported Jane Anne and Wilson, the valet-in-training.

Jean-Louis ascended to the driver's perch of the women's carriage next to Gilles and they began their trek over rutted roads to the Castle Glaslough, the Irish seat of an extinct branch of the Wyndward clan.

***

On the way to Castle Glaslough

Gilles

Gilles brought Jean-Louis up to date on events on the estate. "Lady Sheffield—I guess I can now call her Lady Wyndward— has requested that I accompany her to England."

"*Bien.* You are the right man to protect her."

"I thought the danger was over."

"Blackburn had a grandmother who still lives and may be hell bent on revenge. We'll keep that fact to ourselves for the time being."

Gilled nodded.

"Is that Gypsy boy still—"

"*Oui.* He is a horse groomer."

"Do you trust him?"

"I have no reason not to trust him, but I have not tested him."

"Then let us speak to him. We can bring him to England where he could be an informer for us to smoke out any confederates of the Gypsy companion of Blackburn's grandmother."

***

Aelwyn

Inside the coach, the women brought Aelwyn up to date on the events of the prior three years.

Aelwyn's brow wrinkled as she stared at the baroness. "But Charlotte, how could Henry throw you over for a woman he hadn't seen for five-and-twenty years? It's inconceivable."

"Taita is an extraordinary woman, we all agree." Bri leaned back in the tufted leather bench seat. "But I'm not convinced that she sees herself in Father's world. The protocols of Society are unimportant to her."

Gwyneth shrugged. "Henry has little patience for arbitrary rules."

"But he plays his role when needed." Bri shook her head. "I think she is wary of our ways."

Charlotte held up her hands. "Stop. Whatever happens with Henry, my life goes on. I have the foundling hospital to oversee and a future to build for myself. I am free."

Aelwyn leaned forward and squeezed her friend's hand. "Then why do you sound so sad?"

"Because I know that my time with you will be limited. Henry invited me for your sake, Aelwyn. But now your life is changing. You will be at Ravenshire. I will be in London. Our visits will be rare."

"No! Do not say so."

"It is the way of it, Aelwyn."

No one missed the sadness in Charlotte's eyes.

To divert attention, Aelwyn sat back and smiled at Bri. "Now tell me all about the dashing Mr. James."

Bri blushed and regaled Aelwyn with stories of the balls, her intellectual duels with Edward, the terror inflicted by Blackburn, a man she'd once admired and called a friend, and the horror of watching that man fall to his death.

CHAPTER FIVE

Tuesday, May 7, 1811 – Aboard *Zainab's Dream*
Taita

The months' long voyage back to Madagascar from London on Sultan Sarduba's magnificent sailing ship, named after his eldest and favorite daughter, included stops at various ports to take on supplies and explore the coastal cities.

Taita, healer to the Sultan, stood on the deck and looked into orange clouds tinged with flashes of purple as the sun set over the Mediterranean. The shock of learning that Henry, Lord Ravenshire, had not died in the typhoon five-and-twenty years earlier still clutched at her heart. *A part of me believed he still lived, but I thought it naught but a wishful fantasy.*

No longer a slave after the Sultan freed her as a gesture of gratitude for her long service to him, the events in London haunted Taita. Henry had asked her to stay in London, but she needed more time. Much had happened since that typhoon had separated them. *Henry does not understand why I did not remain behind. How will he react when he learns the truth?*

***

Tuesday, May 7, 1811 – Castle Glaslough Dining Room
Gio

A huge fireplace dominated the two-story stone dining room. Gio's vision swept over the display of medieval swords and weapons of war that decorated the mortared stone walls. "I hope arguments at the

47

table don't reach a fever pitch. Any one of these implements could be wielded to inflict a swift stroke of death."

Gwyneth scoffed. "A charming thought, Gio. Those swords weigh more than you do. I doubt you could pick one up."

"Proving my point. I am at a significant disadvantage."

Henry glanced around the table and then back at Gio. "Which one of us do you expect to smite you?"

"One must always be aware of one's surroundings. Perhaps I need a bodyguard. Does Nambotha have a brother?"

Gwyneth shook her head. "His entire family died in a village fire when he led us on a safari. That is why he left and vowed never to return to East Africa. To me, it is Earth's most magical spot, but to him, despite its beauty, it looms as a place of death and despair."

Gio's sense of being watched caused goose bumps to erupt on his neck. Out of the corner of his eye, he detected Ian peering around the wall, staring at him. "What is it, Ian? Have you never seen a dwarf sit at a table?"

Wordlessly, the boy shook his head.

Aelwyn tilted her head. "Why are you not in bed?"

"I want to be here with everybody else."

Henry smiled. "Come, Ian, sit on my lap."

As the boy climbed onto Henry's legs, the butler and footmen brought the soup.

Aelwyn caught the butler's shock at seeing Ian in the earl's lap. "Shannon, ask a footman to fetch the special chair for Master Ian."

"Of course, milady."

Aelwyn turned back to her guests. "Gilles built a chair for Ian so he could sit at the big table with me."

A footman entered, carrying a chair with a high seat. Hewn of oak, it had a leather strap to fasten the child in securely.

Gio hopped to the floor and examined Gilles's creation closely. "An ingenious contraption. Better than all the pillows I sit on."

"Me too. I used to fall off at least once an evening," remembered Bri.

Edward laughed. "A fall from grace? Now that would have been a sight to see."

"Indeed, Mr. James—" She corrected herself. "Indeed, Edward, do you think it funny for a child to fall on the floor?"

"Of course not." His tone was not convincing.

"She got right back on, like riding a horse." Henry laughed. "She instructed Jean-Louis to strap the pillows more tightly to the chair."

"And he said to sit still. It was a bit of a game." Bri inclined her head toward her fiancé, started to say something, but then appeared to have thought better of it.

Shannon placed the high chair between the earl and Aelwyn, and lifted Ian into it. The boy now sat at the right position to reach the table.

"Soup for me, Shannon."

Smothering a smile, the butler nodded. "Yes, Master Ian."

Momentarily dumbfounded, Gio feigned umbrage. "Why has no one constructed such a chair for me?"

"This is the first I've seen anything like it." Henry leaned forward. "If you want one, I will have an assortment made for all of our homes and yours as well."

Ian shook his head. "You're not supposed to ask for presents, Gio. Mother says asking for a gift is impertinent and impudent."

"Clever boy." Oliver smiled. "Do you know what those words mean?"

"Of course I do. Impertinent means disrespectful and impudent means rude." He slurped a spoonful of soup, spilling it on his nightshirt.

"Well, young Ian, your vocabulary may be extraordinary," acknowledged Gio, "but in Society, one does not slurp one's soup. One sips, silently."

Ian watched Gio demonstrate, and then performed his sipping flawlessly.

As the conversation returned to London, politics, and rumors of war, Ian became bored. His head fell to one side and he fell asleep.

After the maid took Ian upstairs, Henry clinked his knife on his glass to silence conversation. "Blackburn's grandmother is alive and escaped the surveillance team Jean-Louis set upon her."

No one spoke.

"Aelwyn, you have the choice to remain her in secret or to return with us. You, Ian and Bri are at most at risk from the grandmother's vengeance, although we all must be vigilant. It is your decision."

Glancing around the table, Aelwyn said, "Danger is ever-present. I do not wish to cower in the shadows. We will return with you to Ravenshire. We are stronger together than separated."

Henry smiled. "That was the answer I'd hoped for."
Aelwyn raised her glass. " We sail into the wind."
All echoed the Wyndward motto in response.

***

Wednesday, May 8, 1811 – Grounds of Castle Glaslough
Gilles

Before breakfast, Jean-Louis and Gilles rode their horses around the grounds of the castle at a slow enough pace that they could talk about their voyage back to England. Gilles had long been fascinated by the descriptions Jean-Louis had given of Ravenshire and the various Wyndward homes in London. "I often imagined the earl, Lady Gabriella, the comtesse, and the baroness. Your descriptions were, as always, uncannily accurate. I am looking forward to a new focus, and Lady Sheffield, I mean Lady Wyndward, is relieved to no longer live in fear for herself or Master Ian. But—"

Pulling up on his horse's reins, Jean-Louis stopped.

Gilles did likewise, knowing his mentor was waiting for his unuttered thoughts. "Though the others appear convinced of their safety after Blackburn's death, I detect a lingering wariness in your eyes. Do you doubt that devil's demise?"

The former trapper sighed deeply. "I saw a body, badly damaged and unrecognizable. The location of the wounds matched the injuries we inflicted upon him. That, of course—"

"—is what you would have done if you wanted to make others think you were dead." Gilles nodded. "I grasp your perspective. Our vigilance must not cease."

Jean-Louis rubbed his chin. "Is there a Gypsy encampment nearby?

"No. There used to be a caravan that came through this area annually, but we haven't seen a caravan for a few years."

"Where did you find the groomer?"

"On a provisioning trip, I observed a young Gypsy boy picking pockets in the market. His moves were predictable, but expertly executed. The bump-distract-lift routine. I watched for a few days, followed, and then confronted him. I thought he might be a useful informant.

"Manfri was unhappy in the caravan. 'Twas a familiar tale. A raging, drunken father beat his sons and the mother cowered before her husband, failing to protect her children from his wrath." Gilles's facial muscles tensed and then released in revulsion. "One day the caravan left without him and it never returned.

"When I next saw Manfri, he told me the story. The hollow look in his eyes convinced me his pain was real. I brought him to work in the castle stables. He has a way with horses and all animals. He took a new name after leaving—Orion Majić. He loves that constellation and is fascinated by the concept of magic. He works closely with the young local animal doctor."

Jean-Louis raised an eyebrow and directed his gaze at Gilles. "And Orion never heard from his family again?"

"No. But they left of their own volition. No unmarked graves have been dug on my watch."

***

Glaslough Pond
Edward

Edward splashed in the water, gasping for breath.

Bri pushed him under again.

He stood up in the shoulder deep water. "Stop pushing me under!"

"A wave would engulf you in seconds. You must develop breathing reflexes." She lay back and breathed steadily. "Float to conserve your energy. Like this."

Edward leaned back and sank beneath the water.

Bri pulled him up. "You have to try. Shall I have Jean-Louis throw you off the ship to force you to swim?"

Blanching, Edward shook his head. He laid back again and breathed. "It's working."

After he remained afloat, she said, "Tread water like this." She demonstrated. "You might have to do it for hours if you can't find a piece of wood to cling to."

"What? Hours! It's hopeless, then. No one can survive out in the ocean."

"Develop the skills and be prepared. That gives you a fighting chance. Do nothing and you will surely die."

Edward began to tread water. "I see. Establish a rhythm."

"There are cork vests in the rooms. Didn't you wonder what they were?"

"No."

"There are cork life buoys fastened by ropes to the deck rail every ten feet or so. Did you notice those?"

"No."

Bri sighed. "It seems to me, Mr. James, that your powers of observation need to be honed."

"And it seems to me, Lady Gabriella, that your pedantic skills need to be tempered with a touch of humility."

"Is that so? See if you can catch me." Bri began to swim away from Edward into deeper water.

"Come back here. I can't go out that far."

"Yes, you can. Try."

As Edward dug his feet into the dirt bottom of the pond, a splashing noise caused him to turn his head.

Ian was swimming out to join Bri, followed by Aelwyn. The boy called out, "Come on, Mr. James. Follow me."

Damnation! If Ian can do this, I must or I'll never hear the end of it. Holding his head up, Edward gamely tried to match Ian's strokes and finally reached Bri. They all treaded water for a few minutes while Edward caught his breath.

"It will be second nature to you before you know it," said Aelwyn.

Edward's expression conveyed doubt. "I feel like a frog."

Bri smiled. "Let's swim back to shore. Race you!"

Ian turned and sped through the water with his mother within reach. Edward trailed all three, but managed to reach the neck-high depth and gratefully stood and walked to the shore, where he fell on a blanket spread on the grass and wrapped himself in it.

Ian sat next to him. "Swimming is fun!"

"For you, Ian. It's a bit of a chore for me."

"I'll teach you."

The boy's earnestness touched Edward. "I'd appreciate that. Your cousin is a very tough taskmistress."

"She said she'd teach me to breathe so I can put my head down in the water to move faster."

All the blood drained from Edward's face. He turned to Bri. "Must I?"

Bri nodded, wordlessly.

***

Wednesday, May 8, 1811 – Aboard *Zainab's Dream*
Anja

Anja, the Sultan's head wife, saw Taita deep in thought and walked up next to her. "I knew I'd find you lost in the sunset. The cycles of nature are reassuring—they precede us and outlast us."

"Yes, it is comforting. I miss Vaitea. Months of travel remain ahead of us."

"I'm afraid it will be longer than that before you see Vaitea again."

Taita's face paled.

Seeing her reaction, Anja gripped her arm. "Nothing is wrong with Vaitea. I'm sorry to have frightened you." She sighed. "The Sultan just informed me that we are turning back and will disembark in Portugal. Word is that naval battles are raging around Madagascar. The Sultan has decided that some of us will remain there for a few months until his palace in London is restored, and then return to London. It may be more than a year before we set foot again on Madagascar. Szilard will sail home on another ship with many of the courtiers in hopes that the battles will be over by the time they arrive."

Taita's pinched face told Anja all she needed to know, although she tried to keep up the conversation.

The healer said, "I'm sure Ariapses will be gratified to have Szilard back in the sultanate."

Anja shrugged. "Perhaps, perhaps not. Ariapses is a wise steward, but Szilard believes his instincts are more important than the facts that Ariapses likes to recite. The scribe's penchant for analysis doesn't fit with Szilard's view of governing the sultanate by fiat." Anja felt Taita's sadness. "Do you want to see the earl again?"

"Not until I have had enough time to consider the implications. The earl is my past. Vaitea is my life."

***

Wednesday, May 8, 1811 – Castle Glaslough

Aelwyn

After breakfast, Henry and Aelwyn wandered around the perimeter of Castle Glaslough.

"Henry, you and Jean-Louis have each saved my life. If you hadn't found me as a stowaway on that ship—"

"I choose to believe another would have rescued you or you would have survived in spite of the odds against you. The life of indentured servitude you escaped is a stain on our way of life."

"But it was you who rescued me, who persuaded your father to take me in as a ward, just as he later sheltered Nate at your request." Nathaniel Parker, an American friend of Henry's, had become stranded at Oxford during the American Revolution and remained at Ravenshire until the war ended. "And Jean-Louis intervened again to protect me."

"If I had only known—"

Aelwyn shook her head. "No, painful though it was for all of us, the thought of Blackie effecting revenge through hurting Ian chills my soul. Jean-Louis kept our secret. He kept us safe. Now we move forward together."

Henry embraced her as both shed tears of relief.

***

Castle Glaslough Stables
Jean-Louis

When Jean-Louis and Gilles returned to the stables, someone else's carriage was parked nearby.

"One of our mares is near to foaling." Gilles nodded toward the rig. "Perhaps there is some difficulty that has brought the animal doctor here."

They dismounted and led their horses into the stables. One of the grooms saw them and went to take the reins. "Nosey is in labor. The doctor says the foal is breech."

Jean-Louis frowned. "But it's daylight. Mares only give birth at night."

"We blocked all the light this morning because she was acting strangely. The doctor feared Nosey would delay labor, causing the foal or her to die."

"Like Goddess." Gilles looked pained. "Before I came here, I was unaware that horses could delay labor by force of will."

Jean-Louis nodded, remembering that Goddess had been a favorite of the stables.

Gilles signaled to Jean-Louis to follow him to the birthing stall.

On the fluid-soaked straw, a young man knelt at the mare's head, stroking and calming her with soft tones while another man, who appeared only slightly older, struggled to move the foal into birthing position by massaging the mare's abdomen.

Jean-Louis moved to help, but Gilles restrained him, shaking his head. He whispered, "Do not alarm her. She knows those two well."

Most mares foaled without incident, but Jean-Louis had seen the deaths of mares and foals over the years. Their suffering affected him deeply.

Nosey groaned and threw back her head.

"Almost, Nosey. Almost." The man Jean-Louis assumed to be the doctor gave the mare a final nudge. Movement within the mare was abrupt and fluids spilled out. "Now!" The doctor moved back. "The foal is coming."

One leg appeared, then another, then the head. The foal struggled and wiggled and exited with a muffled neigh as he took his first breath.

Nosey rubbed her nose against the younger man's cheek while he stroked her head.

"Good work, Nosey."

Jean-Louis nodded to him. He'd seen Orion around the stables in prior visits, but had done little more than acknowledge a greeting in passing. *Will he fit my requirements? Can any Gypsy be trusted?*

***

Wednesday, May 8, 1811 – Viscount Wexington's Townhouse
Lady Patricia

None of her Society friends knew that Lady Patricia Roswell, daughter of Viscount Wexington, had been a source for *Scandal &*

Shame during the Marriage Season. Everyone wondered how items of minutiae ranging from the unflattering color or fit of a dress or waistcoat, or tidbits from overheard conversations could show up in a published gossip sheet soon after an event, sometimes even with ribald depictions to underscore rumors of infidelity. Such illustrations, often colored with inks, included images such as the drawings of a man climbing out of a woman's window, pursued by her husband, or a woman flirtatiously raising her skirt, or a couple clearly *in flagrante delicto*.

As the summer loomed, balls waned. As a result, Lady Patricia faced enormous pressure from the publisher to deliver more salacious details from private conversations. He recently had demanded in-person meetings instead of her previous letters listing the little details he printed. She stared at herself in the mirror in her boudoir. *I could be unmasked by such private particulars. It's one thing to be at a ball full of other people. But private meetings are too risky. I cannot continue along this path.*

∗∗∗

Thursday, May 9, 1811 – Dining Room at Castle Glaslough
Bri

Bri nudged Edward as they filled their plates at the breakfast buffet. "Ready to practice breathing whilst swimming?"

Edward sighed. "It's not how I expected to spend my birthday."

Bri blanched. *I didn't know today was his birthday.* She gamely forged on. "If you want to celebrate another one, then you must learn how to swim properly. Ian will join us."

Gio piped in. "You risk being shown up by a three-year-old, James."

Bri didn't look up as she scooped eggs onto her plate. "Drowning would be worse."

"I cannot argue with your logic." Edward glanced at Gio. "Do *you* swim?"

"Like a dolphin at dawn."

"What does 'dawn' have to do with dolphins' swimming habits?"

"They swim fastest when the sharks are prowling."

Bri smiled. "Don't worry, Edward. There are no sharks in Glaslough Pond."

***

Thursday, May 9, 1811 – Castle Glaslough
Orion

Orion dipped his hands in the water bowl in his room over the stables and smoothed back his jet-black hair. *Jean-Louis wants to talk to me. The man is a legend. He killed a polar bear with his bare hands. What can he want of me?*

As a stable hand, Orion had spent little time in the main castle. This summoning would mark his first glimpse of the innermost castle beyond the kitchen. When he had once tried to peek at the main entry and library, Gilles had pulled him back by the collar.

"No place for a stable boy. You stink of manure."

Remembering that moment, Orion lifted his shirt, detecting no odor. He'd washed up after the birth, and changed into his other set of clothes, but the sensitive noses of Lady Sheffield and the others might still be offended by his scent.

The stable hand took a deep breath and traipsed toward the kitchen entry.

Gilles was there, bantering with the cook and "testing" her fare for the evening. Seeing Orion, he waved him in and put one arm around the Gypsy's shoulder. "Ready?"

Orion shrugged. "Am I in trouble?"

The security man threw back his head and laughed. "Just the opposite, boy. You'll see."

Knots in Orion's stomach churned and he was grateful he had not eaten anything. *What could be worse than vomiting on Jean-Louis?*

CHAPTER SIX

Thursday, May 9, 1811 – Glaslough Pond
Edward

Gamely, Edward mastered the art of breathing while moving through the water, as did Ian.

Drying off with a blanket on the shore of the pond, Ian pulled Edward on the grass and whispered in his ear. "Cousin Bri is planning a surprise for your birthday with a big chocolate cake. Don't tell her I told you."

Edward whispered back, "It will be our secret."

Bri brought over a picnic basket. "You've earned a hearty lunch. After we eat, Ian will take a nap and you and I shall ride around the estate."

"I am as a jinn in the *Thousand and One Nights*, forced to obey your every command."

"I assume you know my wish, Mr. James."

Edward winked at her.

Ian looked confused. "What is a jinn?"

Edward explained. "It is described in a story as a magic lamp that has captured a jinn, or genie. When you rub the lamp, the jinn appears and grants a wish."

The boy's eyes widened.

"But it's just a story, Ian. Like a game," said Bri.

"Can I play the game with you and Edward?"

Bri choked on her baguette.

Edward threw his head back and laughed. "Pretend you found a magic lamp, Ian. What would you wish for?"

Thinking for a moment, Ian beamed. "A pony!"

***

Thursday, May 9, 1811– Castle Glaslough
Orion

Gilles guided Orion to the small suite of rooms off the kitchen with a separate entrance that served as the security station for the castle.

Jean-Louis rose from behind Gilles's desk and shook Orion's hand. He motioned to the boy to sit down.

No man has offered to shake my hand before. A man who is a legend is treating me with respect. Orion lowered himself in the designated chair.

Gilles pulled over an adjacent stool and placed it next to Jean-Louis.

They're staring at me. He cleared his throat. "The foal is thriving, and Nosey seems to be recovering well."

"You have a way with animals, Orion. They sense the soul of a man. You've passed the second test."

"What was the first, sir?"

Jean-Louis laughed. "I am no 'sir,' Orion. Reserve your flattery for those who crave it."

Orion glanced from Jean-Louis to Gilles and back to the former trapper. "What was the first test?"

"Gilles vouched for you. He has recommended that you accompany us back to Ravenshire to train to care for the animals there."

Leaning forward, slightly lifting out of his chair, Orion's face lit up. "Really? Thank you!"

Gilles put up a hand. "Wait. There is one more test."

Orion's face betrayed his disappointment as he fell back into the chair.

Jean-Louis shook his head. "Actually, that is not accurate. Not one. There will be many more tests. We are all tested by life, Orion. I have more plans for you than minding horses. I need eyes and ears in the Gypsy world. There are Gypsy connections to the man who killed Lady Wyndward's husband and the Comte de Merbeau, the late husband of Lady Gwyneth. The killer also kidnapped Lady Gabriella, and then shot Mr. James and me. His grandmother poisoned the 10th Earl of Ravenshire."

Orion felt the blood draining from his face. *Am I expected to die for this family?*

Noticing Orion's discomfort, the French former trapper leaned forward. "I don't expect you to risk your life, Orion, but I cannot promise there will be no peril. We know the grandmother was in Scotland, but she has evaded our surveillance. We believe she may be on her way to London. As long as the grandmother breathes, she will try to kill all Wyndwards. She doesn't know about Ian. When she learns that Ravenshire has an heir, he will be in mortal danger."

"Then why not keep Lady Sheffield—I mean Lady Wyndward—and Ian here, unknown to this evil woman?"

Gilles grimaced. "Because no one can hide forever. We are safer together. We left the decision in Lady Wyndward's hands and she prefers to live as a free woman."

Orion looked down and rubbed his sweaty palms on his breeches. "I left the Gypsy world. If I see my father, I will kill him." He directed his gaze at Jean-Louis. "You should know this."

Jean-Louis did not blink. "If you find him, I will back up your actions. You need only ask. Some men need to die."

The trapper is everything I imagined and more. Orion cleared his throat again, but before he could summon words, Jean-Louis spoke.

"Orion, a man must learn not to signal his actions. Clearing your throat indicates hesitation. Speak or do not speak. Learn to mask your feelings. You are about to become a spy."

The stable boy sat back in his chair. "I have a suggestion."

"We're listening." Jean-Louis tapped his fingers on the desk.

"The animal doctor who saved Nosey and her foal today wants to live abroad. You saw how skilled he is. Would there be a place for him at Ravenshire?"

Jean-Louis looked at Gilles, his lips curving into a wry smile.

"You were right. This young man has bold instincts under a controlled exterior. Precisely the kind of infiltrator we need." Turning back to Orion, the Frenchman smiled. "Welcome to the staff of the Earl of Ravenshire. Bring the farm doctor to see me tomorrow morning. We sail in on Friday." He stood. "I'll let Gilles fill in the rest of the details. And remember, shield your reactions of fear or shock—it comes with practice. Gilles and I will train you." Jean-Louis reached the door, and then turned around. "If it would please you, when Nosey and the foal are strong enough, we can bring them to Ravenshire."

Orion beamed. "Thank you, Jean-Louis."

"Call me J-L. You're one of us now."

***

Thursday, May 9, 1811 – Dining Room at Castle Glaslough
Edward

The cake was a pièce de resistance: a three-tier chocolate cake with blueberry flavored butter cream icing.

"Was it a good surprise, Edward?"

"Yes, Ian. I want you to have the first section to be cut."

Bri cut the cake and gave the second piece to Edward. "For the birthday celebrant—twenty-nine years old."

"Thank you for my gift." He kissed her.

Ian stretched his neck. "What is the gift? I want to see it."

"We all do," said Gio.

Bri blushed, but Edward came to her rescue.

"Your cousin taught me to swim. Maybe she saved my life today. Who could receive a better gift than that?"

***

Friday, May 10, 1811 – Aboard *Airmid's Wynd*
Gilles

The return trip benefited the travelers with swift winds on calmer seas.

Gilles had arranged for Dana Kelly, Jane Anne's sister, to return with them. He shepherded Orion Majić and Dr. Elton Derry around the deck and introduced them to the Wyndward party.

Oliver, Lord Darlemont, nodded to Orion. "Perhaps Jean-Louis will take you to Tattersalls sometime. It's a market for horses. I shouldn't suggest it because you might select a winner for Lord

Ravenshire, to the detriment of my racing stables. I sense that your assessment would be valuable."

Bri had listened with intensity to Gilles's explanation of Orion's and Dr. Derry's backgrounds. Gilles, trained to detect minute changes in facial muscles, deduced that her interest in the new retainers was more than perfunctory.

The earl's daughter smiled. "Orion, perhaps you could come to London occasionally. We have a stable man there, Ali, who has fashioned some unique riding and tack accessories. Perhaps you and he could devise other useful gadgets."

Edward shook his head and laughed. "Orion, Lady Gabriella is always envisioning new roles for us all. Welcome to her world."

Bri ignored her fiancé. She turned to Dr. Derry. "Do you treat primarily horses and large farm animals, Doctor?"

"That has been my focus to date, although the occasional small farm animals like dogs and cats have required attention."

"Hmmm."

"There she goes, Doctor. You're next." Edward appeared to be enjoying himself.

"Mr. James, your ability to annoy me has grown in equal measure to your seaworthiness. I'm simply mulling over the possibility that Dr. St. Cloud and Dr. Derry might have common interests."

"Well, my darling, let that be a topic for another day." He pulled out his pocket watch. "The captain asked us to meet him in a few minutes."

Orion blurted out his first thought. "Is the captain going to marry you on shipboard?"

Oliver threw back his head and laughed. "Most people don't speak the unfiltered truth, Orion."

Visibly drawing back, Bri's face blushed as she addressed Orion's inquiry. "Of course not. We shall not marry for months, perhaps a year."

Edward bid adieu to the three men, took Bri's arm and steered her toward their appointment.

Oliver took a stroll around the deck in another direction. Amused, he twisted his neck to see Gilles box Orion's ears.

Gilles widened his stance and put his hands on his hips. "Impudence will not be tolerated, Orion."

"But she is so beautiful! Mr. James should marry her before she changes her mind. If he dallies, she may fly away," he fluttered his fingers up in the air, "like a butterfly."

Gilles scoffed. "Since when are you an expert on love and marriage?"

The Gypsy shrugged and smiled, stealing a side glance to Dr. Derry. "Since never."

As Gilles nudged them to walk to the front of the ship, he heard Orion whisper to the animal doctor, "But I think I am not wrong."

***

Dana

Waiting for Lady Gabriella to return from the mid-day meal, Dana pulled the letter from Jane Anne out of her pocket and read it again while Jane Anne moved between the rooms of the other ladies to meet their needs. *I must not fail Lady Gabriella.* Absorbed in its lessons, she didn't hear the door open.

"Dana?"

The Irish girl of sixteen, startled, turned around to see Lady Gabriella. "L-Lady Gabriella. M-milady, I would like to know what you expect of me."

Bri walked over to Dana, and extended her hand. "Welcome. When we get to Ravenshire, Jane Anne can help you understand our routine. Let's just sit down and you can tell me more about yourself."

***

Charlotte

Charlotte stood on the deck, hands firmly on the railing to steady herself, staring out at the horizon. *My life was once linked with these companions, this family. I imagined it would last forever. I've had Aelwyn back in my life for these last few days, but as she eases back into her life at Ravenshire, will I be eased out of hers?*

"Lost in thought or do you see something out there?"

The sound of Henry's voice startled her. Her heart wrenched as her pulse accelerated. *Calm down.* She turned her head toward his and smiled. "The former. Thank you, Henry, for letting me share these days with Aelwyn and your family."

Henry moved next to her and leaned slightly over the edge of the rail. He twisted his neck to the side to catch her eye. "It meant a lot to me to have you with us on this trip. It was almost as if—"

"—No, Henry. Please don't pretend it can be the same as it was. It never can be."

He hung his head and looked over the softly rolling seas. "I have been an utter fool. Taita is sailing back to Madagascar, you are building a new life, and I am feeling the toll of my folly, my arrogance. I never should have taken you for granted, Charlotte. Forgive me."

"Had we been married when Taita appeared, our lives would still have been up-ended. I know you thought her long-dead, but if I'd known the truth of your past, the present might be less painful. But probably not. I suppose it is natural to wonder 'what if.' I, however, have no such long lost loves."

"But now you have a current love. You know what a manipulative cad the man is. Pulling strings for the ambitious, molding them to his dark purposes."

"I told you he said he could make me Prime Minister if only I weren't a woman. Then he spun a tale of how he might actually achieve making a woman Prime Minister."

Henry furrowed his brow.

"I know who Tottie is. He is not my love, Henry. He is a convenient companion. Nothing more. He is using me to annoy you, and I am using him to re-enter Society. A devil's bargain, perhaps, but my eyes are open."

"Could we—"

"—be together again? Until Taita returns?" Charlotte moved away from the deck rail. "I think not, Henry. Not as it was. But as friends, on occasions such as this, perhaps we can find our way to be cordial to each other."

"Cordial is more than I deserve."

"Quite true." Charlotte kissed him on the cheek, turned on her heel, and walked away, swaying in perfect synchronicity with the ship's movements.

***

Friday, May 10, 1811 – Theatre Royal Hayrmarket
Herr Kramer

From his seat in the theatre's orchestra, Herr Kramer listened to the auditions for the replacement cast for his operetta, *The Princess*. *I knew this day would come, but I expected a few more months to find replacements.* Violetta Vinci and Drew Wood, the stage names of his main players, wanted to abandon their roles as soon as practically possible.

He couldn't fault them. The runaway success of the operetta had strained all the players, stagehands and orchestra. Additional performances had been scheduled during the week and the probability of a long run, perhaps up to a year, thrilled as well as challenged him as the director of the production.

Today's voices were passable, even fine, but so far, no singer had matched the lyrical trills of Violetta nor had any magician demonstrated the proficiency of Drew. The originators of the roles had set a high standard for others to follow, but Herr Kramer remained convinced that the appeal of the operetta would prove lasting.

His mind wandered to the magician auditions as the current singer executed the notes without any color or dynamism. Silence brought him back to the present. "Thank you. Next up is Miss Giuliana Mergetti." He settled back, resigned to disappointment.

The Italian soprano, a dark-haired beauty who, save for her zaftig physique, might have been mistaken for Violetta in her black wig, began to sing the audition aria.

Within moments, Herr Kramer sat forward in his chair and smiled. *I have found my new Violetta.*

***

Saturday, May 11, 1811 – Aboard *Nut's Night Sky*
Blackburn as Lt. Roland

In the early hours of the new day, Lt. Roland opened the diary given to him by Captain Alif.

Midnight lay sleeping next to his feet.

The candle flickered, casting its intermittent light over the pages as he rested his wrist on the table. He dipped the quill into the India ink and recorded his thoughts, always with a care to conceal the full meaning of his words. No one who found it could discern the truths that lay within. *Subterfuge has served me well. I am still alive.*

The ancient Egyptians lived
according to rituals that
foretold entry into the
afterworld.

Their paths were carved in stone.
Mine is unknown.
Scratches on parchment mean little.

The Wyndward curse is ever in my
thoughts.
There is no escape.
There is only one end.
I must wield the final blow or
breathe my last.

There is still time for treachery.
Temptation will weaken my foe.

CHAPTER SEVEN

Saturday, May 11, 1811 – Swansea, Wales
Aelwyn

After landing in Wales, the arrivals again spent the night at the Swansea Waterview Inn.

The next morning, the travelers divided into smaller groups to board the caravan of carriages for the return trek to Ravenshire.

Aelwyn turned to Jean-Louis. "Thank you for protecting us." She bent down and lifted Ian into her arms. "Going home to Ravenshire has been my dream for so long. It's difficult to believe I stand again on Welsh ground, the land of my birth."

Jean-Louis tipped his black felt hat in acknowledgment of her gratitude. "We'll keep you safe."

"I would never doubt you, Jean-Louis." She placed Ian in the first carriage, then climbed in, joined by Gwyneth, Oliver and Gio.

***

Gilles

Henry, Charlotte, Bri and Edward climbed into the second carriage.

Gilles led Dr. Derry and Orion to two horses, while Dana and Jane Anne rode in the baggage carriage along with Wilson, the valet.

This voyage had been a test for him, devised by Nashmir, to attend to the gentlemen on this unexpected journey.

Orion looked puzzled. "How did you get a message to have more horses? Our plans were not settled until yesterday."

His Irish-French mentor smirked. "Maybe we exchange messages through the ether."

The Gypsy frowned. "If that is a reference to Gypsy fortune telling, those charlatans use Tarot cards, not wordless messages from the beyond."

Seeing Gilles raise an eyebrow, Orion smiled. "I am not ignorant. Uneducated, perhaps, but not ignorant."

"Can you read?"

"My mother taught me the basics."

"Then we'll see to your further education."

Once they were mounted, Gilles handed them sandwiches wrapped in paper.

The carriages were stocked with Swansea delicacies as well as bread, cheese, dried meats and wine for the several hours they would be riding over roads that ranged from areas of level hard-pack to stretches with uneven rutted tracks.

Gilles noted that Hans Steiner, second in command to Jean-Louis at Ravenshire, had driven over from Ravenshire to meet the group at Swansea and supervised the departure. He'd brought additional guards from Ravenshire to ride along and provide protection from attacks by highwaymen. His close-cropped blond hair and stern demeanor had earned him the nickname "Sterner."

The line of carriages, horses and baggage wagons pulled onto the road as the sun rose in the sky.

***

Dana

Dana, Jane Anne and Wilson were crammed into the carriage loaded with excess baggage.

While Jane Anne slept, it took all of Dana's patience to tolerate Wilson's complaints.

"I hate traveling, whether by coach or by ship. I just want to stay at the main house. The earl isn't in residence much and I can do as I please."

"And what would that be, Mr. Wilson?"

He leaned across the bench and smiled. "Nothing. I like the leisurely life of a gentleman. I take a walk around the grounds and imagine the land is mine."

"But you are not a gentleman, Mr. Wilson, you are in service. What if the earl found out that you do nothing?"

Wilson scoffed. "He pays no attention."

Dana frowned. "I fear you may mistake restraint for disinterest."

"I should be paid more for this last week. Acting as valet for the earl, Lord Darlemont, Lord Ostwold and Mr. James. It's too much. And what's worst of all, I am subject to the direction of a Chinaman!"

"I thought Mr. Nashmir came from Tibet."

"Tibetan, Chinaman, Mongol—all those slanty-eyed dogs look alike to me."

Repelled by Wilson's prejudice and indiscreet comments, Dana tried to ignore him. Even when she didn't respond, he continued his tirades. After Wilson railed for more than an hour with incessant complaints about the earl, his family, and the staff, Dana could tolerate his whining no longer. "Mr. Wilson, I'd like to nap a bit."

"No wonder, you lazy Irish never do a full day's work. Join your sister in slumber. I don't care." He sniffed in disdain. "Think you'll be able to sleep on the job with that uppity Lady Gabriella? She'll put you through your paces."

Dana held back any retort. *I'll ask Jane Anne how to respond. I don't want to appear shrewish in my first days with this family, but Wilson is a most detestable man.*

***

Orion

Riding at the rear of the carriage train, Orion's awe at his incredible luck washed over him. *I am embarking on a new life in a new land. I face the future with a friend, a challenging set of tasks, and soon I will be reunited with Nosey and Sunny.*

After several hours on the road, a sixth sense interrupted Orion's thoughts. The back of his neck tingled. He turned to his left. Shadows moved closer. He squinted. *Men on horseback.* He spurred his

69

horse and sped to reach Gilles. He shouted up to the drivers. "Highwaymen approaching!"

Steiner signaled to the guards escorting the caravan to fan out.

They quickly surrounded the three highwaymen, outnumbering them two to one.

Steiner made demands. "Sheath your weapons. Identify yourselves."

Two of the three highwaymen looked to their leader.

The leader smiled. "We're just out for a hunt."

He spoke with an accent that Orion could not identify.

Steiner scoffed. "In daylight? With pistols drawn? I doubt it. I repeat, sheath your weapons and identify yourselves."

One of the highwaymen spat. "We can take 'em." His finger moved on the trigger.

Before he got off a shot, Steiner put a bullet in the thief's head. Toppling off his horse, the would-be robber hung by one stirrup, dead.

Steiner didn't flinch, his gaze still leveled at the others. "You have a choice. Toss your guns, dismount, and surrender."

"And if we do not?"

"You'll join your friend in hell."

"He was a fool. I am not." The leader tossed his gun and signaled to the other man to do the same. They dismounted.

Two of Steiner's men jumped down and checked the thieves for other weapons, and found knives secreted in their boots. Steiner tossed rope to his guards, and they tied the men's hands, and led them to one of the wagons. They were pushed to climb in. When their dead companion was disentangled from his horse, he was carried to the wagon and dumped next to the others as a warning.

The leader wrinkled his nose. "He stinks."

Steiner scoffed. "No one ever said death is fragrant. You'll find out when you are hanged."

The horses were tied to the wagon, and Steiner signaled to Jean-Louis that all was secure. He rode over to Orion and patted him on the back. "Good eye, Orion."

He remembered my name. His chest bursting with pride, the Gypsy sat up straighter on his horse, and rode back to take his place behind the last wagon. Dr. Derry rode back to join him. "Were you scared?"

"Yes. The first thing I'm going to do when I get to Ravenshire is ask Gilles to teach me to shoot. I want to be ready if this ever happens again."

The animal doctor tilted his head toward Orion. "We were all transfixed. You are a hero. The hunters chose the wrong prey."

***

Dana

Steiner jumped off his horse, and threw open the door to the carriage where Jane Anne, Dana and Wilson were traveling.

Terrified, Dana sighed with relief to see Steiner. Color began to come back to her cheeks. "Is everyone safe?"

Steiner nodded. "Yes, Miss Kelly. And you?"

Jane Anne answered with a roll of her eyes toward Wilson. "*We're fine*."

Wilson sputtered, "What about me? I'm not fine! Why did you risk our lives on this road? You don't give a whit for us. Only for the quality."

Steiner glared at the valet.

Whining, Wilson cowered on the floor, huddled in a corner. He had soiled himself.

Steiner shook his head in disgust and closed the door.

***

Bri

Once the volley of shots ended, no one in the carriage moved.

Out of the corner of her eye, Bri saw Jean-Louis open the door to the carriage.

At the sound of the gunshot, Henry had pulled Charlotte under him and ducked away from the window.

Similarly, Edward had thrown his body over Bri's and pushed her to the floor.

Taking in the scene of splayed arms and legs, Jean-Louis laughed. "I see everything is in order here." He reached out to pull Henry back to a seated position.

The earl helped Charlotte sit up.

Bri couldn't move under Edward's weight.

Edward rolled to the side and lifted himself back onto the carriage's leather bench and leaned over to help Bri.

Glancing at Jean-Louis, Bri raised her eyebrows. "Well? Aren't you going to tell us what just happened?"

"Orion spotted three highwaymen. One is dead, the others are tied up in one of the wagons to be delivered to the sheriff."

Bri leaned over and kissed Edward on the cheek. "Edward, darling. What a gallant fiancé you are."

Her fiancé shook his head. "The Gypsy stable hand is the hero. But my mind went to Blackburn opening the door to the carriage—"

The earl grimaced. "He is out of our lives forever and Bri is safe."

Squeezing Edward's hand, Bri sighed. "That moment flashed before me as well. We escaped Blackie's vengeance, but tonight is a reminder that danger is ever present. I refuse to quake at the unknown."

Henry smiled. "Ah, that's my Bri. Wyndwards sail into the wind, unafraid."

***

Aelwyn

With the sound of the first pistol shot, Oliver threw himself over Aelwyn and Ian, while Gwyneth and Gio hunkered down below the window.

Gilles threw open the door. "All is clear. Is anyone hurt?"

"No."

Oliver frowned. "Highwaymen?"

"Yes. Cocky opportunists who won't see the sky for a long time when the sheriff takes over. We were more than a match for them. We take no chances, right Ian?"

"You protect us, Gilles."

"It was Orion who suspected we were being tracked. His warning prevented disaster."

"Orion is a hero!" Ian beamed.

"Indeed he is, Master Ian."

"Remind me to ask Jean-Louis for a bodyguard. I don't fear death, but I don't want it to be a violent one." Gio wiped his forehead with a handkerchief.

"Fast is best," said Gilles.

"For you, perhaps. For me, a pleasant sleep, awakening in the Elysian Fields, is more appealing."

Gwyneth shrugged. "Are you so sure your awakening won't be on the shores of the River Styx?"

Ian frowned and looked up at his mother for a translation.

"Never mind, darling. The only thing that matters is that we're safe."

CHAPTER EIGHT

Saturday, May 11, 1811 – Ravenshire
Jean-Louis

Ever alert for the balance of their journey, the French former trapper was relieved to see the torches lighting the entry to Ravenshire shining in the distance. The attack by the highwaymen had delayed their arrival. *Safe. For now.*

Jean-Louis supervised the unloading of the carriages, and then showed Orion and Dr. Derry to their rooms alongside the stables. "Doctor, we can build a clinic for you to work on sick animals and attach a suite of rooms in the back. For now, I hope this will suffice."

The veterinarian looked around the room. "You've offered me a new life. I am not one to complain."

***

Bri

As the normal Ravenshire dinner hour had passed, Bri alerted the kitchen staff to prepare a light supper.

The staff gathered around Lady Wyndward, some in tears, to welcome her back. Lilyanne, one of the maids, took Ian from her arms. "I'll put him to bed straightaway, milady. We've set up a nursery next to your room."

Tired from their bumpy and interrupted journey, Henry, Charlotte, Gwyneth, Gio, Oliver and Edward filed into the parlor.

Young poured small glasses of sherry.

Bri came in and took a glass.

The earl waited and then raised his glass. "Welcome home, Aelwyn."

"Here, here!" echoed her companions.

A tear appeared in Aelwyn's eye. "It is good to be at Ravenshire again."

***

Jane Anne

Dana shadowed Jane Anne as she helped Bri prepare for bed.

"Over the next few weeks, you'll learn." Bri touched Dana gently on the arm. "It's all new right now, but soon it will be second nature to you."

"I hope so, milady." Dana's shyness showed in her soft voice.

After they left, Jane Anne showed Dana to the room they would share. Haltingly, Dana told her about Wilson's comments while Jane Anne had been sleeping. "How should I handle such a situation?"

Jane Anne narrowed her eyes and shook her head. "You shouldn't have to. Come with me. We're going to find Jean-Louis. He's the one to take care of something like this."

Pulling her terrified sister by the hand, Jane Anne led her toward the stables, where they saw Jean-Louis completing his nightly walk of the perimeter. "May we speak with you, Jean-Louis?"

Grim-faced as he listened to Dana's experience, the Frenchman directed his gaze at the frightened girl. "He's been warned twice before. Fear not, Dana. Wilson will be gone by morning."

***

Aelwyn

After dinner, Aelwyn settled back in the room she had shared with Rychard before her flight after his death. The adjacent sitting room had been turned into a nursery. Ian's favorite toys and décor had been brought in from one of the wagons so that he would feel at home. *Home.* She reached down to Ian's head on the pillow and ran her hand along his cheek.

Aelwyn had asked for privacy this first night, so Heather, who had been her Lady's maid before she'd left, set out her nightclothes on the bed and drew her bath.

"Good night, milady. We are ever so grateful that you are back. And with a *bairn* for us to spoil."

"I won't have him spoiled, Heather." Seeing the maid's face fall, she added, "At least not too much."

Breaking into a smile, the maid nodded and closed the door.

Looking around the room, Aelwyn remembered the night her life had ended. Now it had begun again. She opened the armoire, and marveled that the clothes she had left behind were still folded, just as she'd left them. *There is a marker with my name over an empty grave, yet nothing here has been disturbed.*

Disrobing, Aelwyn walked into the bath, stepped into the tub, and slipped beneath the water, cleansing herself of travel dust and dirt. Rising up to breathe again, she laid her head on the back of the tub, closed her eyes, and let the heat of the water ease her muscles, sore from the jarring ride over uneven roadways that had returned her to her home.

***

Charlotte

Back in the guest room she'd inhabited for years, a contrivance to maintain the appearance of propriety despite her long romance with the earl, Charlotte thought back to the happy years she had spent at Ravenshire. Though she comported herself with dignity in public, private pain stabbed deeply into her heart.

After Lucy, the Lady's maid who had tended to her until her break with Henry, had taken her clothes to be cleaned, the baroness bathed. When Lucy returned, she helped Charlotte don her nightclothes before bidding her goodnight.

"I'm glad to see you again, Baroness."

" 'Tis only for tonight, Lucy. Perhaps I shall visit Lady Wyndward occasionally and see you again."

"Yes, Baroness." The maid closed the door as she left.

Charlotte ran her hands over the blue silk nightgown. *I'd forgotten that I'd left clothing here.*

After climbing into the bed, Charlotte stared into the fire's flames, shooting sparks of amber, orange and scarlet up the chimney.

Memories flooded her mind. Her calm façade broke as tears flowed down her cheeks. She wept with such despair that she didn't hear the door open.

Startled to feel Henry's arms around her, she turned her tear-streaked face toward his.

"I stood outside your door, debating whether or not to bid you goodnight, and heard your sobs. Please don't cry, Charlotte. I hope you can forgive me someday." He kissed her forehead.

She tucked her head between his chin and shoulder and wept. "Oh, Henry, I still love you."

The earl kicked off his slippers and eased her over on the bed, lying next to her. "Let me hold you."

Silently, she agreed and they fell asleep in each other's arms.

***

Sunday, May 12, 1811 – Ravenshire Village
Wilson

Steiner pulled up on the reins of the wagon he drove to the Coach Inn on the edge of Ravenshire village. "The morning coach to London leaves in five hours, at seven o'clock. Be on it."

Wilson radiated hatred. "You can't do this. You can't throw me out in the middle of the night with no references."

"We can and we have. You're lucky to have one month's wages. You weren't here long. You're not suited for service. Find another vocation. Never mention you worked for the earl."

Standing in the street watching the wagon head back to Ravenshire, Wilson burned with outrage. He walked over to a bench and sat down outside the inn. *I don't want to spend money on a room for a few hours. I'll just wait here. I won't be treated like this. They'll be sorry.*

***

Sunday, May 12, 1811 – Ravenshire
Charlotte

Charlotte woke up at dawn and nudged Henry. "You'd better return to your room before the servants begin their day."

The earl didn't open his eyes, but smiled. "Just like old times." He turned toward her, rubbing his eyes and then fixing his gaze on her. "I slept better than I have for months."

The baroness sighed. "So did I. Go now, and I'll see you at breakfast."

"Ride back to London with me."

"Maybe." Charlotte sat up and put her hand on his shoulder. "Much has come between us."

"I want you in my life Charlotte. On your terms, not mine. You set all conditions and I will comply."

"Maybe."

"That's better than 'Never.' "

He rose in his wrinkled clothing, picked up his boots, and peeked out the door. With a quick turn of the head back to his once-paramour, he nodded adieu and left, closing the door softly behind him.

Charlotte fell back on the pillows and frowned. *I can't lose myself in him again.*

Half an hour later, Lucy knocked on the door to help Charlotte begin the day.

***

Gio

Gio awoke with the first rays of the sun. *These people are early risers. Dawn is not my usual time to rise, but I do like the first pure beams of daylight.* He splashed water on his face and dressed himself, having told Young he could dispense with a valet. *That Wilson is a prig.* Gio had never become accustomed to a valet, although once his title had been restored, others expected it of him. Over the years, Gio had become self-sufficient out of necessity and relished his privacy. His butler Hawkins also served as his valet and could read Gio's moods.

The dwarf left his room and walked down the hall. *I'll sketch the castle in the early light, before the others wake.* Coming around the corner, he ducked back. *Henry coming out of Charlotte's room? Has she lost her mind? We have not seen the last of the island woman.*

The rift between Henry and Bri has not yet completely healed. She must not hear of this.

Bri's fury to discover that her father's dalliance—a "joining" in island terms—had occurred while still married to her mother simmered beneath her veneer of control. She had fumed to Gio about her father's betrayal, oblivious to the dwarf's arguments that her father thought himself lost to civilization forever and the will to live outweighed societal conventions.

I must speak with Charlotte after we return to the city.

Peering around the corner to confirm that Henry had disappeared, Gio went downstairs and went into the kitchen. "Good morning, Mrs. Sawyer."

The cook, Sallie Sawyer, was the niece of Nellie Jones, the earl's cook in London. She jumped when she heard the artist's voice. "Lord Ostwold! You're not usually the first to appear. But despair not." She sported a mischievous grin. "I have all the ingredients for your favorite omelet right here."

"Fresh eggs from the henhouse, mushrooms and spinach fresh from the greenhouse?"

She nodded as she bustled around the kitchen.

"And I smell the bread baking. You are a sorceress with food, Sallie." Gio had first met Sallie's mother, Pollie, when she was a small child learning at the side of Sallie's grandmother, Rosie. "Rosie and Pollie made sure you and Nellie were always at home in a kitchen."

Sallie looked around the large kitchen. "This was our home. But Aunt Nellie and I have no children to pass on our secrets to."

"Come now, just because the convention is to call you Mrs. Sawyer doesn't mean the menfolk don't fancy you. Never fear. Cupid's arrow will fly."

"Ha! You just want a larger omelet than usual. Do you want to wait for the others?"

"No, I'm starving, breaking my fast, as it were. I'll eat twice to accelerate my growth spurt."

"Out not up, I'd wager. Now let me work."

"A wily one you are, Sallie."

Gio left and returned with the sketchbook he'd left in the parlor after they'd returned the night before. Taking out charcoal, he sat on a stepstool and sketched the trim woman of six-and-twenty as she cracked eggs, added some cream, whipped them into a froth, and then spooned the mixture into a pan sizzling with butter. Next she added thinly sliced mushrooms and chopped spinach, scattered dashes of herbs and timed its finish expertly.

Gio ripped off his quick sketch, signed it, and said, "For you."

Sallie's eyes widened as her mouth fell open. "For me?" She looked at her hands covered in flour and herbs. Her face flushed as she fidgeted. "Thank you."

"I'll set it aside until later." Gio walked into the dining room, nearly bumping into Bri.

Moving to see the sketch, Bri smiled. "You've captured Sallie at work. A snippet of time." She bent over to kiss him on the forehead. "You are a master, Gio."

"You promised to pose for me."

"Soon."

"What's soon?" Edward took his seat.

"A portrait of your fiancée. I want to capture that wild, fiery red hair while she's in her prime."

Edward smiled. "And that steely determination in her eyes."

"I shall always be in my prime, thank you very much." Bri pouted in *faux* umbrage as she sank into her chair.

Ian came running in and hugged Bri. He climbed onto her lap and looked around the table.

Aelwyn entered, followed by Gwyneth and Henry. Charlotte was the last to appear.

Gio looked at Bri. "Practicing?"

Edward blanched.

"That's a long way off." Bri balanced Ian on her knee.

Gio scoffed. "Everyone says that...and then, voila!" The dwarf lifted his arms to the ceiling, palms upward. "It happens."

Aelwyn lifted Ian out of Bri's arms and into the high chair fashioned by Gilles that had come in one of the wagons.

Gio peered at the contraption more closely. "I have made my decision. I will simply commission a furniture maker to fashion a chair made higher so that I can reach the table more comfortably."

Gwyneth walked in and frowned at Gio's empty plate. "You ate without us?"

"Only my first serving. I've missed Sallie's cooking. I'm looking forward to the next few days at Ravenshire."

The footmen brought pans to the sideboard filled with breakfast selections for the guests to serve themselves.

Bri looked up. "You're not coming back to London with us?"

Gio shrugged. "You don't need a chaperone now that you are engaged. And Henry and Charlotte don't need my banter, charming though it may be. No, I'm staying here with Aelwyn and Gwyneth, doing sketches for a portrait of Aelwyn and Ian, and whatever else pleases my fancy. Gwyneth wants me to record the raising of the castle in stages…just in case I die before it's done."

"You're immortal, Gio. At least that's what you've always told us." Bri glanced at the dwarf.

"Immortal in the sense of my work, not in the sense of my physical body."

Henry helped Charlotte from her chair. "Ladies first." The other women stood to serve themselves from the buffet.

The earl, Oliver and Edward followed, filling their plates.

Gio selected pastries and fruit. "Sweets are a privilege of the old and infirm."

Back in his seat, Henry buttered a piece of toast.

"You're in your mid-sixties, Gio." Gwyneth took a bite of her omelet, filled with bits of bacon and chives. "Please don't start with that drivel about facing death for at least another fifteen years."

"Will the castle be done by then?"

"Probably." Henry shrugged and smiled. "Maybe."

"Proving my thesis." Gio speared a mushroom with his fork.

***

Tuesday, May 14, 1811 – Ravenshire
Jean-Louis

After a lazy day at Ravenshire, while Bri and Aelwyn talked about the changes at the estates, some of the group prepared to return to London.

Oliver borrowed a horse to ride to Pytchley Manor.

Jean-Louis watched as Edward's driver, François, whom he had personally trained and assigned to Edward, helped Bri into their new carriage, an engagement gift from Henry. Shepherding a network of informants in his native country, through companies secretly owned by Wyndward Trading, Jean-Louis kept an eye out for talent. The Corsican, as he derisively referred to Napoleon, might rule, but *gendarmes* were no match for the intrepid former trapper. François, recommended by associates in France, became the Frenchman's most recent protégé.

François could pierce wild prey with an arrow, stop a cut-purse with a well-thrown knife, shoot a quail with a fowling piece at a distance unmatched by anyone Jean-Louis had ever seen, and wrestle a larger man to the ground in seconds. After Bri's brush with near-death at Blackburn's hands, Jean-Louis was taking no chances. Edward might be expert in the Asian fighting arts, but he had been stopped by one of Blackburn's bullets. Two protectors were better than one.

After Bri, Edward and Spotty were in the carriage, François leapt up to the driver's perch.

Jean-Louis walked back to the earl's carriage and helped the baroness climb in, followed by the earl, Hector at his heels. The Frenchman lifted up the stairs, fastened them to the door, and closed it.

Standing next to his mother, Ian waved goodbye. "See you Friday!"

After taking his position, Chérie jumped up next to him, and Jean-Louis pulled on the team's reins. Followed by François and his charges as they left Ravenshire, Jean-Louis caught a glimpse of Gio carrying his easel and painting bag toward the rising Ravenshire Castle.

***

Interior of Edward's Carriage
Edward

"Alone at last." He pulled Bri to him in a long, lingering kiss.

Bri smiled, but didn't resist. "Edward, it's not even noon yet."

"Does it matter?" The carriage lurched a bit over a rut, nearly tossing Edward to the floor. He recovered his footing and sat back on the leather-tufted bench. "That's François following instructions, no doubt."

"When we get back to the city, we need to meet with Vaux to finalize decisions for our new home. He has an excellent eye for architecture and interior design."

"You don't need me for that."

"Edward, I at least need to know your preferences for your study."

"Not 'our' study?"

"Hmm. I was thinking we could each have our own space. Do you disagree?"

Edward shrugged. "I have some Asian décor that I had shipped back. It's in storage at the Wyndward warehouse. There is a magnificent desk and matching display cases. It's a long story, but they were a gift from a friend before he died." Edward looked off into the distance. *I can't tell her more than that. Not yet.*

"I'll go with Vaux to take a look and measure the pieces you have there. I'd like to schedule a meeting once a quarter to review the progress of Wyndward Investments. But first, let's go over our criteria for evaluating their performance."

Edward nodded. *I thought we'd have more private time once we were engaged. The sooner the house is renovated, the sooner we can gain that privacy, although we'll still have to meet in secret.* He sat back and began to cite his preferred criteria.

∗∗∗

Interior of Lord Ravenshire's Carriage
Henry

Inside his carriage, Henry reached for Charlotte's hand. "I can make no promises as to the future, Charlotte, but I want you to be part of my life. Bri, Aelwyn and Gwyneth will never waiver in their love for you. Let me see you occasionally. I meant what I said—you set the terms."

Charlotte gently released her hand from his. "Oh, Henry." She sighed and shook her head. "Another time. Another place. Another life." She stared away from him, watching leaves in the high branched oaks of the Ravenshire Forest blow in the soft late-spring breeze.

"I've been thinking a lot, Charlotte. Examining my life. And you're right. I see it now. I have been selfish. Telling myself I was looking out for everyone else was untrue. It was selfish of me to sail away so often." He took a deep breath. "On my first voyage, Gwyneth stood on the shore, waving until my ship was over the horizon. She felt abandoned."

"I know. She's often talked of it. As if her life were bookended between episodes of waving goodbye to you."

Henry's face clouded. "It pains me to know I caused her such anguish. She must have been so lonely while I was off on my adventures. And Jane...Jane harbored a deep distaste for the sea, terrified that she would be swept overboard. She remained in our cabin, rarely venturing on deck." He hung his head, but then slowly smiled. "Bri insisted on accompanying me after I returned from a long trip when she was barely three. It was the first day she met Jean-Louis. She captured his heart in that moment."

"Bri is an adventurer too, Henry, but of a different sort. She is so much like you. My focus is the foundling hospital, and now I have agreed to be a trustee for the Seminary for Women's Work. Did Bri tell you Blackburn founded it?"

The earl nodded. "I suppose it shows no one is all good or all bad. Still, I cannot truly believe that I could have been fooled for so long—"

"All of us were fooled, but he was your most trusted associate. To be betrayed at such a level. And to find out he was your brother—"

Henry ran his hand through his hair. "I'll never get over his treachery. But we have to move on. I want you to know something about Bri. She has been acting as my 'man-of-affairs' for the last couple of years."

Charlotte sat back on the bench and stared at him. Then she tossed her head back and laughed. "No wonder she and Edward bicker! She is, in effect, in a position to give him orders. The man is more impressive than I realized. He clearly adores her, but she challenges him at every turn."

"That's what appeals to him. Our Bri is unique."

" 'Our?' "

"You are the closest to a mother she's ever known. She needs you. You, Aelwyn and Gwyneth are like her faerie godmothers."

"If only I had a magic wand that would work on you, Henry."

"Or Tottie? Must you socialize with that devil? A man who plays at politics and discards associates as others play at Whist?"

"In a country that has been at war for over a decade with Napoleon, with a king who's gone mad, and a prince who'd rather go clubbing with Beau Brummell than see to his duty, politics is a game of the petty and the powerful." Charlotte raised an eyebrow. "Remember, Tottie told me he could make me Prime Minister."

"I remember, but you never told me how."

"Not in a straight line, of course, but by a circuitous, deceptive, manipulative route."

"That's the only route he knows." His brow furrowed. "How deceptive?"

"First, by getting me elected as a Member of Parliament from an obscure district. A woman, an anomaly, that he would propel to power by any means necessary."

"In other words, a well-timed death would be no problem?"

"That is the implication he conveyed. It was meant to impress me. Instead, it repulsed me." She closed her eyes and shivered. Turning her gaze to Henry, she frowned. "What was the source of your rift? You two were at Merton together."

Henry nodded with a frown. "We were never close. He resented my birthright. I cannot tell you the cause of the final fissure. 'Tis not that I mean to keep another secret from you, but that secret is not mine to tell." He took her hand. "I promise that I will tell you someday, but only with the permission of the ones I am protecting."

"Take care, Henry. Tottie is capable of anything, as are most men who seek power. He resents you and sees you as an enemy."

"He is correct."

CHAPTER NINE

Wednesday, May 15, 1811 – JAK, Jane Anne's Hair Salon
Bri

B ri and Jane Anne reached the location for her hair salon where they were scheduled to meet Vaux.

The viscount greeted them. "We have a few decisions to make. If all goes well, I think we can anticipate an opening in about two months." Directing them around the space, he pointed to specific areas, and then showed them renderings of how the salon would look.

"The colors I've chosen were influenced by a treatise I just read, *Theory of Colors*, by Goethe."

"Really? The poet and writer from Frankfurt?" Bri leaned forward.

"The same. His theory posits the emotional impact of color. The 'scientific' community scoffs, but, to me, the intuition of a poet is not to be dismissed. In the salon, you want to create an atmosphere, a feeling of warmth, a welcoming space. I propose that walls be a pale yellow. The Carrara marble floor will go with any color scheme you might use in the future. But my recommendation is that we do the unexpected. I propose a sea-green and yellow patterned upholstery on the chairs, with a white-lacquered chair frame and matching individual vanity tables and mirror frames."

The watercolor renderings had a softness, an ethereal quality that took Bri's breath away. "Did you paint these?"

"Perhaps I had a bit of instruction from a certain dwarf."

Jane Anne choked up. "It's more beautiful than I imagined."

Vaux smiled. "Then you approve?"

Nodding, Jane Anne looked toward Bri.

"It's your salon. I defer to your preferences. The space is perfect. Now, we need to build your clientele."

"A year from now, I predict that not even you, Lady Gabriella, will be able to secure an appointment." Vaux turned to another rendering. "I thought perhaps a little tea area where clients might wait for service would be useful."

Bri and Jane Anne agreed.

Vaux pulled a copy of *Scandal & Shame* out from under his drawings. "Have you seen this?"

Scoffing, Bri said, "I try to avoid it."

"A few weeks ago, there was a reference to the 'notorious Mlle. Bellerobe.' Instead of being scandalous and frightening ladies of the *ton* away, it had the opposite effect. She's been inundated with clients ever since."

"That item alluded to the 'Heiress of the Season,' " Bri grimaced. "but I think I see where your mind is headed. Word-of-mouth is valuable, but publicity may be the way to attract new clients."

"Control your own destiny. Plant the seed and watch it grow."

***

Wednesday, May 15, 1811 – *Scandal & Shame* Offices
Rollins

Rollins removed the cigar from his tar-stained mouth and spoke through fleshy oversized lips. "And so, Mr. Wilson, as a result of what you consider to be unfair treatment, you wish me to publish a story about your dispute with Lord Ravenshire?"

"Haven't you been listening to me? He employs thugs who run rampant. His recklessness nearly cost me my life!"

"The earl is a powerful man, not a reckless one." *And the Frenchman is a force unto himself.*

"I possess negative information that could sell more copies of your gossip rag. I can always take my information elsewhere. Perhaps you mean to discard me as callously as the earl did."

Rollins leaned forward in his chair and chomped on his cigar. "Mr. Wilson, my readers are not interested in a valet who was tossed out for bigotry. Bigots thrive in darkness. Publicity brings you into the light. I have no interest in promoting your version of hatred. Your story makes the earl into the hero and makes you out to be the villain. Perhaps you have never read my sheet. It satirizes hypocrisy. You have given me nothing of the kind."

Wilson stood and glared at Rollins. "You'll be sorry."

"As I recall your story, those were your parting words to Herr Steiner. He could break your neck faster than you could blink. You're fighting a losing battle."

"Am I? Wait and see."

"Is that a threat?"

"No. A promise." Wilson stomped out of the offices of *Sandal & Shame,* seething with rage.

Rollins watched Wilson depart with nary a glance to the rows of artists and printers preparing the following week's issue. *If he were of any importance, I'd skewer him with his own insolence.*

***

Wednesday, May 15, 1811 – The Hanforth Mansion
Clarissa

Before taking Jane Anne back to Lord Ravenshire's townhouse, Jean-Louis dropped Bri at Clarissa's home for lunch.

Wolfberger, the butler, showed her to the parlor where Clarissa was waiting.

Clarissa looked pale.

"Are you unwell?"

She nodded. "I've not been able to perform lately, but Herr Kramer has found a marvelous Milanese soprano to replace me. Her reviews have been wonderful. And he is deciding between two potential wizards. Bri...I feel we have disappointed you. The strain of appearing onstage so often, with the additional performances now scheduled, and Nick's practice, it's too much. The operetta is a success and will not suffer for our absence."

"I agree *The Princess* will endure. What concerns me now is your health."

"It will pass. The spells come and go."

"You must see a doctor. It could be a deadly affliction—"

Clarissa smiled. "No, Bri. It is nature taking charge."

"Taking charge of what? Don't sound like a Fatalist."

"I am with child."

Bri sat back, speechless. Recovering, she rose to hug Clarissa. "A baby! What a wonderful surprise!"

"Sooner than we'd like. We'd planned a honeymoon after the play, so we may go in two or three weeks. The doctor says the spells of nausea will end soon. And once there's a baby, it will be hard to get away. Will you and Edward still join us?"

"To Africa?"

"No, that is too far now that we know of the baby. I've been considering the Azores. About a week's sailing time, then a week or so visiting the various isles and basking in the sun. What do you think?"

"If we can get Viscount Vaux to complete the design for the changes to Edward's new house, perhaps the renovations will be underway by the time we return." Bri furrowed her brow. "Let me talk to Edward and Father. But we must have a chaperone...I daren't risk my reputation on such a voyage. Maybe Aunt Gwyneth and Gio could accompany us. Would you mind?"

"Not at all. I intend to rest and may not be very good company."

The butler knocked and entered. "Luncheon is served, milady."

***

Thursday, May 16, 1811 – Lord Ravenshire's Townhouse
Bri

As she walked downstairs for breakfast in a gray-and-white striped dress, Bri braced herself for Edward's disapproval at their morning meeting. *He warned me about the commitment of Clarissa and Dr. St. Cloud to the operetta, that it would be too much for them.*

She plopped down at the dining room table across from her father.

The footman placed her breakfast plate in front of her.

Bri sighed and ate listlessly.

Henry put down the morning paper. "What's wrong?"

"Edward was right and I was wrong. He's going to gloat."

"Would you?"

"Yes."

"Maybe he's a tad more mature than you are."

Bri bristled at the criticism.

"Stop squirming."

Putting down her fork, Bri sat back and crossed her arms.

"Now you are being petulant. Not everything is always going to go your way. Learning that now will save you a lot of heartache later."

"That is *such* a cliché, Father."

"Clichés express truths about human behavior." He picked up his paper. "Eat."

Bri pushed her plate away.

"Isn't Edward coming for breakfast? I thought that was your normal plan." He turned the page of the newspaper.

"Normally, true. But he met Vaux for breakfast to go over the plans for the house so we could talk about that today."

"You and Vaux have been working on that house a lot the last couple of weeks."

"I am hoping renovations can begin before we leave for the Azores. We've set September as a target for Edward to move in."

"Leave for the Azores?"

Bri's face fell. "I forgot to mention it to you. Yesterday, I met with Clarissa and she suggested that Edward and I accompany her and Dr. St. Cloud on their honeymoon." Noticing her father's surprise, she added, "Don't worry, Aunt Gwyneth and Gio will chaperone."

"Did you forget to tell them too?"

"I intend to ask them soon."

"Then perhaps you shouldn't present a trip to the Azores as a *fait accompli*."

"Perhaps you have a point." Bri relented, took a piece of toast, doused it in raspberry jam, and took a bite.

Henry lowered the newspaper to look directly at his daughter. "How do you think the *ton* will react when people learn that you and Edward are taking a honeymoon before you've even set a wedding date?"

"Since when have you cared what the gossip rags say?"

"Since your name began to appear there. And mine. And Blackie's."

"Maybe we'll marry next June, after Lady Penelope's wedding to Baron Beauchamp in April."

"I never would have guessed my old Merton classmate would marry a contemporary of yours." Henry sighed. "I have no objection to your travel. I'll arrange one of our ships. And Jean-Louis will accompany you. For protection."

"For surveillance, you mean." Bri stood, tossed her red locks in frustration. She headed to her father's study to prepare for her meeting.

Spotty scampered to keep up with her.

*****

Henry

Henry looked down at the Dalmatian lying at his feet. "Hector, run next to me while I ride."

The dog jumped up on his master and then raced down the back stairs to the stables.

He glanced at Monkey, stretched out under the table on the lush Persian carpet. *If only solitude cane so easily to me. Uncertainty haunts.*

*****

Bri

When Edward was announced, Bri looked up from the designs for his new home, which were spread out in front of her on the earl's desk in his study. She rose and walked around the desk to kiss her fiancé on the cheek. "Good morning. Did you have a good breakfast with Vaux?"

Edward kissed her forehead. "Yes. Rogers staggered in. Drunken fool. He crashed another carriage last night. It rolled over. Only his drunkenness saved him from injury." Edward sat across from the desk.

Bri moved back to her chair and lowered herself while asking, "How would drunkenness save him?"

Edward leaned back. "When the body is gripped in fear, muscles tense and the rigidity can lead to injury. When inebriated, the muscles relax and injuries are less severe. Rogers has bruises and a few lacerations, that's all. I saw holy men in Asia fall when totally relaxed, as if in a trance. Injuries that would have killed had no impact. Rogers has a taste for the oblivion alcohol brings. This time, it saved him." Edward shook his head. "Someday he may not be so lucky."

"And Vaux?"

"He told me about your sojourn in the warehouse cataloguing the furniture I brought back from the Orient. He says he has a place for everything. He described the changes to the building's structure. His engineer says it is stable. So we can move forward."

"Excellent! I have his room designs here, but first, there's something I need to tell you. I want to get it out of the way." Bri stood and paced behind the desk.

Edward sat in silence, waiting for her to speak.

"The operetta is sold out for months in advance, and Herr Kramer scheduled additional performances. Some new players have relieved Clarissa and Dr. St. Cloud of the constant pressure of performing over the last couple of weeks." Bri took a deep breath. *How will he react?* "In fact, the new players will be taking over their roles effective immediately." She stopped pacing. "You were right, Edward. The performance demands were too much for Clarissa and Dr. St. Cloud. In fact, she is with child and unable to continue."

Tenting his fingers, resting his elbows on the chair arms, Edward nodded. "You were right that the operetta would be a financial success. And a baby is not unexpected."

"And you were right that the commitment would be too much for non-professionals. I was wrong to compare the rigors of performing to attending a dinner party." *He is not angry.*

"It will not be the first time an investment succeeds in one respect and fails in another."

Bri sat down and leaned back in the chair, musing aloud. "Someday Napoleon will be gone. We could expand the operetta into other European capitals with local performing companies. Perhaps we could even set up a season in America."

"That makes sense. The bank is establishing a branch there, so we will have ready access to capital."

Bri straightened herself in the chair. "We could publish the music and commission translations of the lyrics. In fact, Aunt Gwyneth's publishing company has been preparing Uncle Luc's compositions for publication. Herr Kramer can work with Musée de Merbeau Press. There are multiple income streams."

Edward nodded. "We have both learned from this experience."

"I promise to listen to your point of view in the future without judgment."

Edward acknowledged her offer with a nod. "And I, yours." He stood, and walked around to stand beside Bri to look more closely at the plans. "Now let's talk about my house—our house."

Bri smiled and began to explain how the home would look when the renovations were complete.

"Am I to understand that my only input is for my study? All other decisions have been made by you and Vaux?"

Startled at his tone, Bri was taken aback. "I thought you said that was the only area you cared about. You waved your hand dismissively regarding décor."

Edward smirked. "That's correct, I was just testing your memory."

"By the way, Clarissa has invited us to accompany them on their honeymoon to the Azores with Gwyneth and Gio as chaperones."

"Since when do others 'accompany' a couple on their honeymoon? Must I anticipate a crowd on *our* honeymoon?"

Taking a deep breath, Bri said, " 'Sometimes' to the first question and 'No' to the second. Would you be able to get away for three weeks?"

Leaning forward, Edward gazed directly at his fiancée. "Bri, we are taking on more and more obligations at Wyndward Investments, let alone Ravenshire and Wyndward Trading that you oversee. We can't go gallivanting around the world without risking the loss of control over those operations. Such dalliances are neither prudent nor responsible."

"Nonsense. I've thought of a proper structure for decision-making in light of my misjudgment on *The Princess*. Aelwyn is back and will resume running Ravenshire. Father is restructuring Wyndward Trading to provide more depth in directorships while he is traveling. He relied on Blackie more than he realized to handle interpersonal spats among directors. I meet with the directors only once a quarter. And I have drawn up a proposed board of trustees for Wyndward Investments, with Eli and Charlotte as the first two trustees. And what you refer to as dalliances, others would refer to as living a full life."

"That's the outline of a way forward. But the Azores...another sailing?"

"We're Wyndwards. We sail everywhere. Adapt or—"

"—die? Now you sound like the Bri I know and love. You've been so polite this morning that I thought you might have taken ill."

***

Thursday, May 16, 1811 – *Scandal & Shame* Offices
Lady Patricia

After delivering mild but embarrassing anecdotes in the last few weeks, Lady Patricia agonized over her predicament for days. *I will refuse to meet the demands of Rollins.* The dilemma was never far from her mind. One morning, as she examined her image in the mirror, she was gripped by panic. *What if I never attract a husband? What if I age in an unbecoming manner, with graying hair and sagging skin?* That was the moment the solution came to her in a flash.

Lady Patricia spent a few days testing her hand at adapting the secrets of those who appear on the stage. She couldn't risk being recognized entering *Scandal & Shame,* so she sent her Lady's maid to shop at the Blue Bazaar, located in the part of London that catered to immigrants.

The maid returned with a choice of three different wigs, several items of used clothing and working class shoes. Lady Patricia changed her appearance each week before she entered the offices of *Scandal & Shame* by the back entrance.

For the last two meetings, she had invented anecdotes about vaguely described denizens of the *ton.* Today, she resolved to end the charade. *This will be my last visit. I will not return.*

A clerk escorted Lady Patricia into the publisher's office. The walls were decorated with framed caricatures and cartoons of scandalous scoops. Tan elderly man, with mere wisps of hair on his mole-speckled bald head, hunched over a layout of the next week's sheet. Ruthless, driven by greed and suspicion, the publisher looked up at his visitor and then sat back in his chair. "An excellent disguise. What tidbits do you have for me today?"

"Nothing, Mr. Rollins. I can no longer do this. It's tearing me apart."

"It's not that easy, Lady Patricia. You cannot walk away."

"People are suspicious of me. They stop talking when I approach."

"Then you'll have to be better at your playacting. Have you forgotten that I have intercepted several of the lurid love letters Lord Merrick wrote to you? I *will* publish them." He puffed on his cigar.

"You can't!"

"I can and I will."

"I will not defame anyone else."

"You're not defaming them if you are reporting their behavior and comments accurately. If you cease to deliver information to me, you will be ruined. It's your choice. And no more of those oft-whispered non-secret secrets. I want more tantalizing parlor gossip." He clasped his fingers together. "As we say around here, lewd is good."

Lady Patricia hung her head in surrender. "The Season is ending soon. People are preparing to leave London for the summer. Few parties are scheduled during the summer months."

"Very well. Take a week off. But in two weeks, I'd better have something. If not, you will not be able to show your face in public again."

Leaving the office, Lady Patricia felt trapped. *What can I do? I have no choice at this point. There is only one person who can help me.*

***

Thursday, May 16, 1811 – Wyndward Trading Offices
Henry

Avery Sheldon, George Gonzales, Hiram Fong and retired Royal Navy Commodore Christopher Darnell, head of the Wyndward fleet, sat around the Wyndward Trading teak meeting table as Henry revealed all the details of Blackie's deception.

Gonzales shook his head. "I never heard anything but praise for him in South and Central America. I can't believe I worked with him so closely for so long and never saw it."

Fong nodded. "He was respected throughout Asia. I am shocked."

Sheldon sat back. "I had doubts only recently with losses of shipments in Egypt and an intransigence in him, a refusal to share responsibility. Still, he fooled us for so long."

"He fooled me most of all. To think Blackburn was my half-brother!" Henry shook his head. "Trade is built on trust. The story for the outside world must remain a boating accident, which has an element of truth. Say nothing more than that. None but you know he was a Wyndward bastard.

"Moving forward, Sheldon will assume Blackie's duties, consulting with Gonzales and Fong in my absence. No one man will have as much concentrated power as Blackburn did. We will consider a new head for Africa once Sheldon has evaluated his people. In fact, we should have succession plans in place for all of our key positions. An event like Blackburn's death should have been anticipated."

Pausing for a moment, Henry exhaled. "In the event of *my* death, Lady Gabriella will administer my affairs with advice from our bankers and solicitors." Henry saw the looks of surprise on the faces of his associates. "She is clever and adept with numbers. It is unorthodox, but I believe she will prove worthy to the task. In preparation, she will be attending our quarterly meetings as an observer."

Sheldon tilted his head as the hint of a smile crossed his lips.

Henry noted Sheldon's reaction and shrugged. "She may have a suggestion or two, but she learns quickly. You will not be disappointed. Comments?"

Gonzales tapped his fingers on the table, and then laid his palm down against his papers. "Triumvirates have a negative connotation."

Fong nodded. "Someone is always odd man out."

"This is not ancient Rome. No one here is Lepidus, and it won't be a triumvirate. Sheldon and his to-be-designated head of Africa will make four. Lady Gabriella will have the deciding vote when I travel. Now, the Commodore and I have other news. Commodore?"

Commodore Darnell cleared his throat. "Rumors persist of war with America over the impressment of sailors. As you know, we have planned alternate routes for our fleet, which may affect delivery times, but we expect that most cargo will get to the intended destination port. However, contracts should mandate alternatives in the event of war. Not an unusual stipulation in the Age of Napoleon. We stand ready to divert most trade with America to the southern hemisphere, to the extent possible."

Henry added, "Unfortunately, the markets of the southern hemisphere are more sources of imports to European markets than destinations for our exports. Those markets are not as developed as the United States, and Canada is not large enough to absorb all cargo originally destined for America. We'll deliver perishables to the closest port, and hope that non-perishables will find other markets. We can use ships registered in other countries and transfer cargo to avoid obvious origin. It can be done."

Leaning forward, the commodore observed, "We've been active in smuggling to avoid the Continental Blockade as well as avoiding the patrols enforcing the American trade embargo, but out luck can't last indefinitely. We must pay attention to cargo markings and provide instructions to crews as to re-marking cargo for alternate delivery. We can do the same on the seas of the American coastline."

"Let's move to the competition." Henry looked at each of his directors in turn. "We are vulnerable. How will our competitors and trading partners react to another war with America?"

CHAPTER TEN

Friday, May 17, 1811 – The Foreign Office
Lady Patricia

Lady Patricia sat in the anteroom of the dark-paneled reception area outside the office of Sir Reginald of the Foreign Office. Her mother's brother, called Sir Reggie by everyone who knew him well, handled delicate matters of diplomacy for the Empire as well as his family. He was the only one she could think of who could help her. *He is, after all, a diplomat. How did I ever let myself get into this position?*

A clerk appeared. "Sir Reginald will see you now."

Lady Patricia rose and followed the clerk into Sir Reginald's office. He walked over to greet her with a hug as the clerk closed the door.

"To what do I owe—"

Lady Patricia's tears fell as she gasped, "Oh, Uncle Reggie—"

He held her until she stopped sobbing. "Tell me."

"I'm so ashamed."

"Sit down and tell me." He led her to the divan and sat next to her, holding her hand.

Her tear-streaked face looked up at his. "I've been having an affair with Lord Merrick for over a year."

Sir Reggie's practiced diplomacy betrayed no shock. "Go on."

"He said we couldn't announce our engagement until after his wife died. But she died ten days ago. And now he won't return my messages. The publisher of *Scandal & Shame* is blackmailing me,

98

forcing me to feed him private information on other Society people to keep from printing the truth about Lord Merrick and me. Somehow, months ago, the publisher intercepted some of Lord Merrick's love letters to me. Were they to be published, I would be ruined, and I am in turmoil every day. First I submitted gossip about ill-fitting gowns, then I documented minor *faux pas*, then he demanded evidence of more serious breaches of etiquette. Now he is demanding salacious gossip. I can no longer maintain a façade with my friends while feeding their secrets to him."

Sir Reggie sat back. "It's worse than that, my dear. It's been whispered that Lord Merrick will marry the Countess of Exton."

All the blood drained from Lady Patricia's face. "But she is old!"

"And wealthy. Wealth trumps beauty for men such as Lord Merrick. He is land-rich but illiquid as are so many large landowners. He is twenty years your senior, a greedy man who takes advantage of young women." He squeezed his niece's hand. "You are not the first, nor, I fear, will you be the last.

"Patricia, *Scandal & Shame* is fed with tidbits by many sources. It might surprise you to know that some prominent people deliver private information about themselves. They are partial to the notion that seeing their name in print, no matter what the story, enhances their reputation." He tilted his head. "Notoriety, to be more precise."

"What shall I do?"

"Go on with your life. Forget about Lord Merrick and find yourself a suitable young man. Leave *Scandal & Shame* to me. You did the right thing by coming here. Tell no one else."

Lady Patricia nodded, kissed her uncle on the cheek and left.

***

Sir Reggie

The middle-aged diplomat ran his hand through his partially dyed hair, leaving a bit of gray at the temples, symptomatic of a man fighting the march of time. He sighed. *Telling a young girl to forget a man she believes herself to love is a waste of breath.*

Sir Reggie dipped his quill into the India ink, penned a note, blew on it to dry, folded it, dripped sealing wax on the edge, and rang for his clerk.

The clerk entered with a note for Sir Reggie. Exchanging that note for Sir Reggie's missive, the clerk left.

The Foreign Officer unsealed the note, read it, and shook his head. *Another diplomat needs to be sent home, but this one requires a more firm approach. No gentle suggestion will do. There's only one man for the job.* He composed another missive, but this one would have to be delivered by another means. *It's not prudent for the Foreign Office to know about this conduit.*

***

Friday, May 17, 1811 – Lord Ravenshire's Townhouse
Vanessa

The last to arrive at the family party for Aelwyn and Ian were the Duke and Duchess of Pytchley. They joined Oliver and Lady Abigail, Gwyneth, Gio, Edward and Bri. Charlotte had declined the invitation, opting instead to meet Aelwyn for lunch the following day.

Sweeping into the parlor, followed by the duke, the duchess smiled. Embracing Aelwyn, she whispered, "Oh, my darling, I am so glad you are still with us."

The duke walked slowly with a cane.

Turning to Ian, Vanessa knelt so that her eyes were level with his. "You look like your father, Rychard. He was a fine man." Rising to her feet, she directed her gaze at the earl. "Well, Henry? What is the plan to announce Aelwyn's resurrection before it leaks to *Scandal & Shame*?" She sat down on the divan next to Gwyneth.

"I hadn't thought of it—"

"Well, luckily for you, I have." She waved at Thompson to bring her and the duke a glass of sherry. "We will take the initiative. Alert the *Times* that we are prepared to sit for an exclusive interview to celebrate the young possible-earl-to-be. At the same time, someone," she glanced at Jean-Louis, "will sell an item to *Scandal & Shame* along the lines of, 'Which heiress has been displaced by a heretofore unknown heir?' *Scandal & Shame* will be trumped by the *Times*, and we will have controlled the release of the information."

Bri laughed. "Blast the truth all over the front page and beat *Scandal & Shame* at its own game."

**

Bri

Bri caught a glimpse of Vanessa winking at Jean-Louis. *Grandmother is full of surprises, from sponges to spies.*

Thompson appeared. "Dinner is served."

Henry stood. "Before we move into the dining room, I have a toast for Aelwyn and Ian."

The rest of the guests stood. Henry offered his arm to steady the duke.

"Whatever forces there are for good in the universe, be they set in motion by God or Zeus or Odin or Epona, the return of Aelwyn and discovery of Ian are gifts beyond measure. Welcome home!"

All raised their glasses of sherry. "To Aelwyn and Ian!"

Gio nudged Bri, and whispered, "Who is Epona?"

"I thought you knew everything."

"I will after you tell me."

Bri leaned in closer to the dwarf. "Epona is the Celtic horse goddess. Jean-Louis has an old coin showing her image that he found in France. It's his lucky piece."

Twisting to see the Frenchman leaning against the entry to the parlor, Gio raised his eyebrows. "Found? I never envisioned you digging in architectural ruins."

Jean-Louis pulled the coin out of his pocket and held it up. "There are ways."

Gio walked over to examine the ancient coin, turning it in his fingers. "So you are superstitious?"

"Only fools are *not* superstitious."

**

Vanessa

The duchess pulled Bri aside as they walked into the dining room. "Let's have lunch out somewhere, a little excursion, soon. I'll find the *au courant* place. We need to talk about your Engagement Ball."

"Engagement Ball? Didn't the Masquerade Ball serve as that announcement?"

"Certainly not. That announcement was unplanned, unintentional and unsatisfactory."

Bri surrendered. "I'll be happy to join you on whatever date you select, Grandmother."

"Of course you will. I'll send a note when it's set up. I'll pick you up in my carriage."

Thompson appeared. "Dinner is served."

***

Aelwyn

After all the toasts to Aelwyn's return, the footman brought the first course. It was Aelwyn's favorite soup, an onion cream soup with chives.

Ian tried some and wrinkled his nose. "I don't like this."

The duchess looked at him. "Of course you don't. What is your favorite food, Ian?"

"Lasagna." He grinned.

Aelwyn laughed. "Our cook in Ireland married a Greek, who claimed the origin of lasagna was Greece, not Italy."

Vanessa craned her neck to see the butler. "Thompson!"

Glancing at Henry, Aelwyn remained silent. *The duchess may be in Lord Ravenshire's house, but she outranks him, so no one can be surprised that she is usurping his role.*

Thompson appeared at her side. "Yes, Your Grace."

"Instruct the cook to prepare potatoes au gratin for Ian. It's the closest thing to lasagna she probably has on hand."

Thompson looked to the earl for approval.

"The duchess makes an excellent suggestion." He nodded to Thompson to fulfill the duchess's command. Turning to Ian, he said, "I think you'll like potatoes with cheese. For tomorrow night, we'll have the cook make fresh lasagna."

"Thank you, Uncle Henry."

Everyone laughed at the boy's serious tone.

Oliver tilted his head closer to whisper to Aelwyn. "He reminds me so much of both of you. Rychard's red hair, your blue eyes."

"I know. It brings me heartache and joy in the same moment."

After Ian devoured his potatoes au gratin, the footman brought dessert, a chocolate cake followed by a bowl of whipped cream. After he dropped a dollop of whipped cream on each serving of cake.

When Ian's last bite of cake ended up on the floor, Aelwyn signaled Thompson. "Please ask Lilyanne to come take Ian to bed. He's nodding off."

"Yes, Lady Wyndward."

Ian didn't resist, and fell into the maid's arms, immediately asleep.

Aelwyn finished her dessert. "I remember this delicacy from Summerfest. Have you continued that tradition?"

"Yes." Bri beamed. "But this year, it should be a big celebration to welcome you back and introduce Ian to our litany of games and diversions."

Henry spooned a bite of dessert into his mouth. "What about mid-July?"

Bri frowned. "We might still be in the Azores."

***

Bri

Vanessa put down her spoon. "Azores?"

"Yes. Edward, Aunt Gwyneth, Gio and I are accompanying Clarissa and Dr. St. Cloud on their honeymoon to the Azores."

"Is traveling while engaged appropriate?" The duchess looked to the earl as if expecting him to make a pronouncement.

"Gwyneth will be acting as chaperone, and Gio will adapt to being in a cabin with Edward. Just be certain," the earl looked sternly at his daughter, "that it is *their* honeymoon, not yours."

Bri pulled back from the table. "Father, Edward and I would never do anything inappropriate." Silently, she knew her grandmother would understand. *We'll take care not to get caught, thanks to your introduction to the sponge-and-vinegar regimen, Grandmother, if we steal a few private moments, there will be no consequences.*

"Of course not, my dear. We all know that." The duchess took a sip of wine. "Edward wouldn't want to be torn limb by limb by Jean-Louis. Just ask that polar bear."

"That is quite true." Edward took a sip of wine.

Aelwyn tilted her head, appearing puzzled. "Duchess, how do you know about that myth?"

"Myth? I never doubted it." Oliver smirked.

Vanessa raised an eyebrow. "It is my place to know everything about my family. And dismissing all tales as myths is foolish. Myths contain truths."

Whirling her wine around the glass, Bri returned to the matter at hand. "How about scheduling Summerfest for the middle of August?"

The duchess nodded her approval. As everyone rose to depart, she directed her gaze to the earl. "Henry, I must speak with you in private."

***

Friday, May 17, 1811 – Aboard *Nut's Night Sky*
Blackburn as Lt. Roland

The test of Blackburn's skills as Lt. Roland came in a swift and sudden manner. A couple of weeks after leaving Oran, Lt. Roland noticed that tall vertical clouds rested overhead. He spoke to the captain in a low voice so as not to alarm the crew. He raised his eyes but not his head.

The captain's gaze followed the eyes of his new first officer. Nodding, he said, "Dense vertical clouds often appear before a gale."

Lt. Roland glanced around the deck as he felt it roll. The once-calm sea churned as a squall enveloped the ship. Pelted by torrents of rain and tossed by gusts of wind, the craft pitched wildly. Never losing his focus, Lt. Roland shouted, "Clear loose gear from the deck, stow it and secure the hatches!"

The captain grabbed the wheel, signaling with a tilt of the head to the crew that the first officer's orders should be followed.

As the crew scrambled to clear any unsecured items, Lt. Roland continued to yell over the shrieks of the wind as he and a ship's hand worked to shorten the mainsail to avoid capsizing. "When the hatches are shut, rope yourselves to the rail! I want no one overboard!" Blackburn knew the danger of crew being flung across reeling decks as ships were abruptly heaved from side to side by the fierce energies of water and wind.

"Roll the jib," shouted the captain.

Lt. Roland fought the wind to get to the jib. After he rolled it, he spotted something off the bow. "Waterspouts starboard! Pilot 90 degrees from that direction!"

Maintaining a course to avoid the watery volcano-like waterspouts, whirlwinds that could lift a ship off the sea and hurl it through the air, required all the captain's skills.

The intense fury subsided about twenty minutes after the squall blew them off course. Whitecaps stirred up by blasts from the storm disappeared as the sea reverted to a normal pattern of rolling waves.

No crew member was lost, although one was thrown overboard. He remained tethered to the deck rail, but was injured by repeated ramming against the ship. It took three men to pull the man onto the deck by the rope he'd fastened to the deck rail under Lt. Roland's order. They carried him below decks to be examined by the medic.

The captain saluted Lt. Roland. "You expertly handled the sails and crew, anticipating my orders. I've never sailed with a more skilled officer."

Lt. Roland saluted in return. "Nor I with a man of such controlled temperament in face of danger. We both know that languid seas occasionally precede a squall." He tilted his head toward the sails. "Let's assess the damage and plot our new course."

***

Friday, May 17, 1811 – Lord Ravenshire's Townhouse
Vanessa

Preceding Henry into his study, the duchess took a seat while he sank into the chair behind his desk.

Vanessa sighed. "The duke is ailing. He has moments where he appears confused and doesn't know who or where he is. For the time being, I've hidden it from Oliver, but that harridan he married, Lady Abigail, is drooling over becoming duchess. She'd like nothing better than dispatching me to the dower house near Pytchley Manor."

Henry leaned forward and frowned. "It always seemed to me that Lady Abigail preferred the pace of London Society over the pastoral life at Pytchley."

"True, but that craven, greedy woman chafes at the thought of my continued existence."

"The duke appears quite well tonight. A bit tired, perhaps, but nothing too far out of the ordinary."

"The moments of confusion are not frequent, but in public, frankly, I ply him with wine to make any *faux pas* attributable to overindulgence."

"I'll help you however I can when the time comes."

"I'm counting on you. We're not there yet, but Oliver needs an heir. Otherwise—"

Henry sat back with a look of shock on his face. "It never occurred to me until now. Bri's son would be Duke of Pytchley."

"If Bri has no son, the duke's sister's son, Adam, will inherit the title. He has three daughters. The Craigfell line will die out unless Oliver divorces Lady Abigail, marries again, and fathers a child."

"Divorce is a difficult proposition, but if anyone could engineer it, you could. Does Oliver want a divorce?"

"He's accustomed to her nastiness. Why do you think he disappears most days, buying more horse stock for his racing stables or playing cards with that awful Drummond? If Oliver ever knew—"

"—we agreed he never would be told. He might take revenge."

"I don't need to lose another son."

"Whatever I can do to help you, Vanessa, I will. Your wiliness in disguising any weakness in the duke with wine is clever."

"It won't work forever, but maybe a couple of more years will rid me of the objectionable Lady Abigail."

"Be careful. Henry II made a similar statement about a Becket and some took him literally."

"She longs to be called 'Duchess' and tires of waiting. Ambition is always dangerous. But don't worry. I won't mention it to Jean-Louis."

The earl sat up and leaned forward. "Jean-Louis doesn't kill for sport or grudge. His code is one of justifiable self-defense."

"Forgive me, Henry. I said that in jest."

Henry smiled. "And you know what Will said."

Vanessa rose to leave. "The next time you're at Ravenshire, invite the duke and me. I'd like to see the beginnings of the new Ravenshire Castle."

Smiling, Henry rose to escort her out. "The south wing might suit you."

"I'll be the judge of that."

CHAPTER ELEVEN

Saturday, May 18, 1811 – Interior of Lady Wyndward's Carriage
Aelwyn

Passing by soot-covered buildings and melancholy faces of people on the teeming streets saddened Aelwyn. She preferred the verdant countryside of Ravenshire to the clogged, foggy, smoky city of London. But she knew Ian would someday need to feel at home in both places, and she loved the company of her friends, lost to her the last three years, so she reconciled herself to adjust to a future of regular visits to London that the earl expected.

Gilles slowed the horses as the carriage neared Winters Foundling Hospital.

Aelwyn noted that the new building was not covered by the black dust of the older structures that surrounded it. She exited the carriage and walked under the canopy into the reception area.

***

Saturday, May 18, 1811 – Winters Foundling Hospital
Charlotte

Although Charlotte wanted to attend the dinner for Aelwyn the night before, she had declined the invitation. *I can't pretend things are the same. Taita hovers over Henry and me like a storm cloud. I never know when it will burst.* In order to see her friend away from the rest of the family, Charlotte had invited Aelwyn to visit the foundling hospital.

At the time Aelwyn disappeared, the foundling hospital had occupied a dilapidated building in another part of town. Partly to assuage her grief at the loss of Rychard and Aelwyn, Charlotte had spent the last few years expanding operations, taking over an abandoned hospital and refurbishing it as well as hiring and training a professional staff. Her goals were to improve basic hygiene, provide maternal counseling, childbirth and specialized treatment of women's ailments. As her vision expanded, she established a school of midwifery, engaged tutors to apply scientific principles to the study of childhood development, and nurtured an association with the Seminary for Women's Work that Blackburn had endowed. *How can I hate him and be grateful to him at the same time?*

Charlotte fervently hoped that Aelwyn would be drawn to the foundling hospital's mission. And, selfishly, she wanted to see Aelwyn on her terms, not through a series of sympathetic invitations to Ravenshire or London dinner parties, gestures made by Henry, for which she would have to wait and express gratitude.

When Aelwyn arrived, Charlotte was already in the reception area, and walked over to embrace her. "I'm excited to show you all that's changed since you left."

Aelwyn's eyes swept around the large foyer with hallways spoking out from the center like a half-wheel. "It's an amazing transformation from the old location. I admire your tenacity and vision...to have created all this—"

Dr. Northcliffe approached Aelwyn and Charlotte, his mouth agape. "Lady Wyndward, w-we thought you were dead."

"Forgive me, Dr. Northcliffe. Everything happened so fast the day Rychard died. Jean-Louis spirited me away to Ireland for protection."

Charlotte placed her hand on the doctor's arm. "I learned it less than a week ago. Not even Henry knew until recently. Once Blackburn was dead, Jean-Louis and Henry believed Aelwyn would be safe. She has truly come back from the dead."

"Only Rychard knew I was with child when he died, Doctor. In Ireland, I gave birth to his son, Ian."

Dr. Northcliffe grasped Aelwyn's hands. "Finally, a piece of good news after so much death and despair." Releasing his grip, he added,

"I have set up a practice in Ravenshire village and come into London periodically to assist here and look into establishing a general clinic for the indigent. After you were presumed dead, I left with my family to do missionary work in the Cape Colony. I returned earlier this year, after my wife's death."

Aelwyn's face wrinkled in pain. "Not Claudia! I am so sorry to hear that."

He nodded in acknowledgment of her sympathy. "I have my children, our two daughters and one we adopted when her parents died."

"Please bring them to Ravenshire to meet Ian. I worry that he will be isolated and know only servants and relatives. He deserves a childhood. I'm hoping Summerfest will introduce him to more children."

Charlotte took Aelwyn's arm. "Come, before we eat, let me show you what our mission is." As they headed down the hallway, a scream diverted their attention to the main door.

A woman, covered in blood, staggered in.

***

Saturday, May 18, 1881 – Aboard *Nut's Night Sky*
Blackburn as Lt. Roland

Midnight and the pterodactyl tomcat that Captain Alif picked up in Oran a month earlier prowled the decks mousing at will. In fact, the captain named the tom Mouser.

His role as Lt. Roland has worked out well. The captain had taken note of his comfort at the helm and the crew respected his vast knowledge of the intricacies of a sailing ship.

After dinner with the captain, his nightly ritual was to re-read and make notations in the new diary the captain had given him. It served as a map to plot his new strategy to achieve his goal. *There is only one outcome that will serve my interests, but there are many routes to my goal.*

Blackburn looked over the recent entries in his diary. *Xie Xie must find James's weakness. All men have secrets. There is still time.*

His mind turned to Alia. *Things should be functioning well. Alia always has firm control over her men. And the occasional woman. There were few like*

109

Alia. He laughed silently. *She has a lot in common with Bri. I wonder if they would like each other?*

Before he extinguished the candle and retired for the night, Blackburn glanced at the cats. Wound up in a ball, head to tail, the two slept. *Midnight will miss Mouser when we arrive in Alexandria.*

***

Saturday, May 18, 1811 – Winters Foundling Hospital
Charlotte

Late in the afternoon, Dr. Northcliffe came out of a birthing room, spotted Charlotte and Aelwyn, waiting for news of the bleeding woman who had collapsed in front of them. He shook his head. "It was too late to save the mother. We won't know for a few days if the baby will survive the trauma. A girl."

Charlotte grimaced and her lips narrowed into a thin line. "Too many women die in childbirth."

"The mother fell unconscious before we could learn anything of her plight. Not even her name. Her clothing was torn. Infection was evident throughout her womb." Dr. Northcliffe sighed in surrender. "I will notify the coroner."

Aelwyn's eyes flashed in anger. "Poverty is a scourge. Charlotte, I want to help you change things so that fewer women and babies die."

***

Saturday, May 18, 1811 – Drummond's Gentlemen's Club
Drummond

Drummond regularly held court at a table in his club's card room. He was flanked by two members of Parliament who owed their careers to him and his unmatched political acumen, one fat and florid, the other wiry and twitching. Sitting directly across from him, Oliver, Lord Darlemont, blond and patrician in demeanor, moved his cards around in his hands.

A tap on Drummond's shoulder caused him to turn his head. *Who needs a favor?* Wherever he went, someone always needed a favor. "Sir Reggie?"

Sir Reggie twirled a finger around his dyed mustache. "May I pull you away for a private word?"

Drummond placed his cards face down on the table. "Give me a moment, gentlemen." He followed Sir Reggie to a quiet corner out of earshot. "I received your message. What is the urgent matter?"

"Tottie, I need your help again with *Scandal & Shame.*"

Nodding, Drummond waited. *Sir Reggie is building up quite a debt of favors I can call in at my pleasure.*

"My niece, Lady Patricia, is being forced to do the bidding of Rollins, that brigand of print. He has some private letters that should not be made public."

"He is a devil, that one." *My devil.* "How can I help?"

"Rollins is in possession of purloined love letters to my niece from a certain married, or then-married, now recently widowed, lord of the realm." Sir Reggie stopped, looked around to be certain no one was listening, and whispered the name, "Merrick." He took a deep breath and continued, "The publisher is forcing her to deliver gossip on others in the *ton* by threatening to publish the letters for all to read. She hasn't seen the missives, but, given the nature of the ones she previously received from her paramour, they might contain obscene and indecent descriptions of lewd and vulgar acts he would like to perform on my niece."

Drummond struggled not to raise an eyebrow in surprise. *Lady Patricia must be quite a delightful bed partner. And Rollins is a clever thief, intercepting private mail.* "I understand your need to protect your niece. A lovely young woman, as I recall."

Sir Reggie inclined his head in recognition of the compliment. "I know I can rely on your utmost discretion, given our past confidences. My niece is of marriageable age and must not be ruined in Society."

Putting his hand on Sir Reggie's shoulder, Drummond made a commitment. "I will retrieve the letters for her to destroy. I can crush Rollins and he knows it. Give me a week."

Visibly relieved, Sir Reggie pulled out his handkerchief to blot his puffy, sweat-splotched face. "I am once again in your debt, Tottie. Any time—"

With a smile that only raised one side of his lip, Drummond bowed. "I know." Taking Sir Reggie's arm to steer him back to the card table, the political mastermind asked, "Will you stay for a hand?"

"Not tonight. Some urgent diplomatic issues have emerged. I stole away for but a moment to seek you out. Thank you."

Drummond patted Sir Reggie on the back and waved good night. Retaking his seat, he picked up his cards.

The pudgy Member of Parliament stared at Drummond, adjusting the curl of his hair around one ear, the newest fashion. "What did Sir Reggie want?"

"You should know better than to ask me that, Wilkins. Would you be so eager for me to reveal your secrets?" *Trying to look young and in fashion for a man of Wilkins's age is ridiculous.*

Wilkins sputtered as his face turned a grayish tone. "Of course not...not that I have any, you understand."

"No one is questioning *your* honor, Wilkins." Darlemont's tone mocked the flushed, paunchy player.

The wiry man sat rigidly upright in his chair, staring at his cards.

"And as for you, Pemberly, stop acting so guilty." Drummond enjoyed these opportunities to demonstrate his power. "No one suspected you of anything, before you revealed yourself. Learn to be inscrutable or give up cards. Your hand is written on your face."

As they played their hands, Darlemont glanced at Drummond. "Are you and the Baroness Glasspool still an item?"

"Unclear. Charlotte is besotted with your damnable former brother-in-law and, most likely, will be until the end of her days."

"Then why do you see her?" The fidgeting player's hands shook.

"To irritate Ravenshire, of course. And because I genuinely like the baroness. She has a fine mind."

Darlemont raised an eyebrow. "She is a lovely woman. Ravenshire treated her shabbily, as is his way. Thrown over for some pagan island woman. His behavior is unconscionable."

"You'll get no argument from me." *The earl's honor has compelled him to keep my secret all these years. Darlemont is a crack shot. Should he ever learn the truth, I might be spitting up blood.* Never one to dwell on his own shortcomings, Drummond's mind went to the issue of Lady Patricia as he discarded. *Young, attractive, wealthy and a woman of experience...perhaps it is time for me to meet Sir Reggie's niece.*

The heavyset man played a card and picked up another. "Did you see the brief notice in the *Times* that Ravenshire's man, Blackburn, died? Seems to be a bit of a mystery. Some kind of a boating accident on the Thames in the middle of the night."

Darlemont frowned. "Blackburn was highly competent. What the devil would he be doing out on the river in the middle of the night?'

Shrugging, Drummond picked up a card and discarded. "Maybe working with Ravenshire drove him mad." *'Tis indeed a mystery to be unraveled. And one that might tarnish the vaunted earl. I can set my dog, Rollins, to dig up that bone.*

***

Saturday, May 18, 1811 – Mlle. Sabine's Brothel
Sir Reggie

After midnight, Sir Reggie sat on the bed in a small room decorated in late 18th century opulence with red silk moiré lining the walls and gilded furniture outfitting the room. *Reminds me of what Marie Antoinette's bedroom must have looked like on the last night before she was dragged to the Bastille.*

A double knock on the door startled him.

"I'm glad you came. I am in need of your services again. The payment will be the same." He held out a leather pouch.

The black-clad man accepted the pouch, feeling its weight to determine the amount."What is the situation?"

Sir Reggie explained.

"It will be handled."

"But how?"

"There are ways." He tipped his black felt hat to Sir Reggie and left.

A few minutes later, a single knock came. The door opened.

"Angelique." He smiled and lay back on the bed. "It's been a difficult day."

CHAPTER TWELVE

Monday, May 20, 1811 – *Scandal & Shame* Offices
Drummond

Drummond sat across from the publisher of *Scandal & Shame*. "Rollins, you're stuck in a rut, like a wheel in mud. Forget the petty *faux pas* and naughty proclivities of the swells and debutantes. You're onto something real, but squandering its proper use."

Rollins inhaled the smoke from his pungent cigar and exhaled it into Drummond's face. "And you propose to enlighten me, no doubt."

"Information is power. It may be false, but if it is perceived to be true, and spread broadly enough, often enough, it gathers its own momentum."

"My coffers are full, Tottie. Why should I change what works?"

"Because the law of the jungle rules men—there is always a bigger predator stalking you. Adapt or die."

"Surely you aren't suggesting that I should replace my gossip features about the goings-on in the *ton* with drivel about the somnambulant politicians you hold on a leash?"

Drummond shook his head as an amused grin animated his face. "Politicians are not sleepwalkers. They toil in shadows affecting all areas of our lives unbeknownst to most until laws are enacted that limit our freedom. Wouldn't you like to have an impact in directing their activities?"

Leaning forward, Rollins removed the ever-present cigar from his mouth. "You mean to say there's money in it?"

"More than your customary blackmail of an unsuspecting young woman whose virtue is suspect or of Miss Mollies fearing discovery of their foul preferences."

Adjusting his position in his chair, Rollins shook his head. "Why do I sense that you want me to abandon a self-replenishing fountain of income for an unproven one?"

"Not all, just one. Lady Patricia. I want all the letters you intercepted from Lord Merrick."

"And in return?"

"I will pay you a monthly fee that will far exceed the pin money of any young lady and most molly-boys, and feed you stories to print that will increase your paper's circulation beyond the *ton*." Drummond pulled out a wad of currency and placed it on the desk. "To be sure, there's always a market for the Prince Regent's or Lord Byron's or Beau Brummell's latest escapade, forbidden love or scandal. But don't ruin the lives of young people who could be of much more use to us later."

"I've always prided myself on verifying what I print or suggest between the lines. My sources have always been good. That's how I stay on top."

"And so you will remain. Don't get tangled up in your feet preaching 'truth' to me. The world, as we know, is constantly changing. War, pestilence and infamy will ever be with us. You and I are not only in the business of peddling information for profit. We are in the business of molding public perception. You publish it, people talk about it. You publish it again, people begin to believe it. Words in print become taken as accepted facts. True or not, the printed word takes on a life of its own." Drummond paused, and leaned forward, hand extended. "Give me the letters."

Rollins reached out and picked up the money. "We are in agreement." Pulling a key from his waistcoat pocket, he unlocked a drawer. Lifting out a packet of broken-seal letters tied with twine, he handed them to Drummond.

The political manipulator, in turn, handed him a note for publication.

After reading it, Rollins curled the edges of his lips. "I used to laugh when people called you the devil incarnate. I now am a believer, a convert to the dark, shadowy world of Aristotle Drummond."

"My involvement is not to be revealed, or else...." Drummond rose to his feet.

Standing with his outreached hand to shake on the deal, Rollins nodded. "Understood. The devil will have his due."

***

Tuesday, May 21, 1811 – Riding along Rotten Row
Oliver

In accordance with family custom, Gwyneth rode back a bit to let Bri and her uncle speak in private. Often their conversations revolved around Oliver's memories of his sister Jane. Those remembrances kept Bri's late mother alive in both their minds.

"What do you think about Edward and me accompanying Clarissa and Dr. St. Cloud on their honeymoon?"

Oliver sat back in his saddle and laughed. "I hated my honeymoon. Lady Abigail and I went to Portugal and were set upon by brigands one evening. The food was too spicy, the wine too strong, and the weather too hot. So all in all, having friends around would have made it at least somewhat enjoyable. There appears to be some romantic notion going around in this age of Lord Byron that the ecstasies of love can smooth over rough edges. Don't believe it. Moonlight and roses do not make up for a lack of mutual interests. You and Edward are well matched in that regard. Of course, it's almost as if you two are taking your honeymoon *before* you are wed. That may set the *ton* atwitter."

"When is Society *not* atwitter about someone or something?"

Darlemont shrugged. "True enough. The Azores are lovely. I sailed there once with Henry and Jane, back when things were good among us all. I remember it as an idyllic and unspoiled string of islands to explore. Some say that it is all that remains of Atlantis."

"And you pretend you never read Plato."

"I didn't. But I listened to the philosophy don drone on about it. The Atlantis story was more interesting than drivel about shadows on a wall and all that pointless musing."

"Is philosophy 'pointless musing' to you?"

"Isn't it to everyone? Except that American friend of Henry's. Race you to that post?" He spurred his horse to get a head start.

Bri smiled, leaned forward on her horse, and her lesser weight allowed her horse to make up the delay. They sped neck-to-neck until Oliver inched a bit ahead at the end.

Darlemont leaned over to pet his horse and glanced at Bri. "Couldn't let you win. It might go to your head."

Gwyneth caught up with them. "It looked like a tie to me."

"No. Uncle Oliver had the edge."

"Don't pout," Gwyneth scolded. "You know what your grandmother would say—. "

"—'It's unattractive, unnecessary and unladylike.' "

Laughing, Oliver warned, "I hope she never hears you mimic her so perfectly."

Bri tossed her pony tail back over her shoulder. "I would be iced over like a statue."

"And the thaw would be a long time in coming. Court my mother's wrath at your peril."

***

Lord Ravenshire's Townhouse
Bri

Reaching the stables, Bri dismounted, handed off the reins to the groom and bounded up the back stairs, famished.

Startled to see Edward talking with her father and Jean-Louis, she stopped abruptly. "Edward, you've arrived early."

Henry took a sip of tea and leaned back in his chair. "Are you committed to the Azores?"

Bri shrugged as she took her seat. "We talked about going to Africa with Lord Hanforth to help establish his Conservancy, but that endeavor would have taken over eight months. Now that Clarissa is with child, such a lengthy and demanding trip is out of the question. Sailing to the Azores would take about three weeks from our schedules during the summer, which is *not* the busiest time of year."

Henry picked up a piece of bacon and bit into it. "The trading company is active somewhere in the world no matter what the season."

"I'm sure you can spare me for a mere three weeks, Father. Your voyages take you away for months at least once a year."

The earl grimaced. "Must you always have facts at your disposal?"

"I was tutored by a master." Bri smirked.

Looking up at the ceiling, Henry mused, "Let's see if I remember Laurence's exact words—'Facts trump assumptions.' "

Edward laughed. "Remind me not to argue a point with both of you at once. I would be at a distinct disadvantage."

The footman served Bri and Edward.

Jean-Louis nodded when offered more tea, and used tongs to add two slices of lemon followed by inserting a rock-shaped wedge of brown sugar into his cup. Once enough sugar to meet his preference had melted, he used the tongs to remove the sugar chunk and place it on a silver dish to dry out. "The vessel will be secure."

Bri scoffed. "*All* Wyndward vessels are secure."

"You can shoot passably, for a woman—"

Bri flared at the barb. "I am a crack shot and you know it. You taught me all you know about shooting."

"Not *all* I know." The French former trapper stirred his tea. "To enjoy your voyage, you need not be concerned with such matters. Your safety is my responsibility."

Bri threw up her hands, knowing it was folly to argue with Jean-Louis. "Very well."

She used her fork to put a small layer of eggs on top of a piece of toast.

Edward followed her eyes to the lumpy mound of sugar. "What is that devious mind of yours conjuring about a slab of sugar?"

"The block of sugar is too large for the teacup. Perhaps a chisel could carve it into bite-sized pieces."

Henry scoffed. "I hardly think Mrs. Jones would agree. And I don't see you in the kitchen applying a chisel to an unformed hunk of sugar."

Bri glanced around the table. "The scullery maid could do it, or a footman."

"To how many new tasks do you intend to set the staff?" Henry took another slice of bacon. "If you can convince them, I have no objection."

"And if you did object, Lord Ravenshire, do you think that would matter to our Bri?" Edward spread raspberry jam on his toast.

The earl shrugged. "Not for the last two-and-twenty years, but I am by nature an optimist."

***

Edward

The earl and Jean-Louis pushed back from the table. When he got to his feet, Henry turned to his daughter.

"I'll be at the trading company all day. We need to restructure the directors' functions now that Blackburn is gone. Who would you recommend to be my main advisor?"

Without hesitation, Bri replied, "Sheldon."

"Good. He's my preference also."

"Father," Bri frowned, "I think we might consider dividing responsibilities into smaller territories. Given wars and the far flung reach of our trading territories, three directors plus Sheldon may not be enough. Who do you envision replacing Sheldon as director of African trading operations?"

"I intended to leave it to him. He knows his staff better than I."

Bri nodded her agreement.

"Tonight at dinner we can discuss new geographical options." Turning to Edward, the earl added, "Feel free to join us, Edward."

"Seven?"

"Excellent." Henry and Jean-Louis went toward the back stairs to the stables. "Come, Hector."

The dog followed his master and looked back at Jean-Louis.

The Frenchman smiled. "I'm coming, Hector. Chérie is waiting for you."

As their bootsteps echoed down the stairway, Edward glanced at Bri. "Those Dalmatians raised both their spirits. Clever of you, as usual."

Bri smiled. "Chérie loves to ride on the carriage perch next to Jean-Louis."

The affianced couple walked into the earl's study, where Bri took her place at her father's desk.

Sinking into his chair, Edward leaned back. "What parameters do you propose for Wyndward Investments to allow for issues such as Clarissa's condition?"

"I've been thinking about that. I am used to the large, sprawling trading company as a challenge, with experienced directors who can handle most any problem. Father and I simply review their recommendations and approve or reject them.

"However, these early stage new ventures require more hands-on direction. It is more than you and I can deal with on our own. As I mentioned last week, that's why I think adding Eli and Charlotte as a board of trustees or some similar structure to advise the companies on an oversight basis is prudent. As a case in point, our trip to the Azores will remove us from an advisory role. What if there is a crisis?"

"Precisely my thinking. My brother-in-law Eli has an excellent mind for very small businesses, dealing with Jewish shopkeepers, diamond dealers and cutters, and family-owned businesses. His particular area of expertise is the analysis of the financial and development needs of the very small businesses at the early stages of development you're interested in."

"I agree. He would be ideal. And frankly, I think he would champion the drive and ingenuity of people who might be disdained by Society's unfounded prejudices."

"You're thinking of Jane Anne being Irish. I regret doubting that she would be accepted by women in the *ton*. You were correct that her skills would win over any skeptics—that's been demonstrated." Edward took a sip of tea and a chunk of sugar. "Clever to think of a chisel to make smaller wedges of sugar. It *would* be easier to sweeten tea."

"I'll talk to Mrs. Jones and solicit her views." Bri leaned forward. "Dr. St. Cloud needs to formally designate people to take over in his absence. Maybe Dr. Derry or Dr. St. Cloud's assistant could fill in as a vet, but the pet food formulations require a different set of skills. Furthermore, we're looking at acquiring or building a warehouse, offsite from his shop and clinic, to meet growing demand. What shall we call this need? Succession planning?"

"That's a good phrase. A small business just beginning to grow doesn't have the depth of directors that the trading company has. Those individuals are used to autonomy in your father's long absences. You review things at the level of broad oversight, while they execute hands-on decision-making. We need to set clear parameters for succession and direction of small enterprises that thrive under the vision and effort of one person. Driving the enterprise forward requires a second-in-command at a minimum. The initial investments of Wyndward Investments in Jane Anne, Dr. St. Cloud, and Nashmir are all based on a singular leader."

"I've been thinking about what you said about funding charity projects versus businesses with real profit potential. I think the five-year experiment Father set in motion could accommodate a wide range of investments. All of our charity efforts have been anonymous to date. But perhaps some of these investments that prove to be valuable but not viable as self-funding enterprises could be migrated into an entity we could call Wyndward Charities." Bri dipped a quill into the inkwell. "Let's make a list of what ideas we come up with and see if there is really a significant market for them."

"Your quill-in-hand has jarred a memory. Eli says that in family-owned businesses, the whole family works together. Often the women keep the accounts while the men do the hard or skilled labor. I wonder if that academy Blackburn started could train women to be clerks to employ in the Wyndward Investments portfolio."

Tilting her head, a smile crept over Bri's face. "Seeing me with a quill spawned this concept?"

Edward shrugged. "Your twists of inspiration are contagious."

CHAPTER THIRTEEN

Wednesday, May 22, 1811 – Ravenshire
Orion

Orion tended the horses in the earl's stables at Ravenshire, acclimating to his new surroundings. He groomed the steeds, talked softly to the workhorses, and learned about their natures. There were horses for riding, horses for carriages, and horses kept for breeding purposes. *Nosey will like it here.*

Gilles spent most mornings with Steiner riding the property, evaluating points to mount defenses if necessary. Late in the evening, he would seek out Orion and they'd talk.

To Orion's surprise, Gilles came to see him one morning while the Gypsy exercised one of the riding horses.

"Saddle up two horses. We're going on a quest."

Barely containing his excitement, Orion prepared the horses. They maintained a brisk pace but one that allowed them to talk about their impressions of Ravenshire. "It's even bigger than I imagined." Orion shook his head in amazement. "I thought the Castle Glaslough and its grounds were beautiful, but Ravenshire is a wonder."

Gilles smiled. "It is one of the largest estates in England. Only Ravenshire Forest is by grant of the monarch to the earls of Ravenshire. All the rest is owned outright by the Wyndward family. That is very different than most estates."

"What does it matter?"

"If an earl or another noble were to fall out of favor with the king, his title could be made forfeit and lands could be seized, but only the lands granted by the monarch. The Wyndwards are almost as rich as the king's family."

"We are lucky, then." Orion hesitated before speaking again. "I've been wondering...what is expected of me now?"

"We'll generally go to London on the weekends, and there will be time to look for Gypsy enclaves. Once we identify them, we'll come up with a plan for you to infiltrate the band."

"My condition hasn't changed." *If I see my father, I will kill him with my bare hands.*

"Understood. Just be sure that nothing leads back to the earl. Agreed?"

"Agreed."

Gilles pulled up on the reins. "Here we are. One of the earl's tenants raises ponies. We're here to select one for Ian as a surprise gift from Jean-Louis. The pony will be Ian's responsibility. You'll be his riding instructor."

Orion's chest puffed with pride. He dismounted, and tied the horses to the tenant's fence. Ponies were grazing in the adjacent field. "I count a dozen. They look hardy."

"Shetlands are excellent working ponies, and are used to carrying weight on their backs. More are in the stables. We'll start there."

Inside the stables were ponies of all colors. From black to chestnut to dappled versions, Orion placed his hands on each. After reviewing them all, he turned to Gilles. "Let's look at the ones outside."

Gilles tilted his head toward the door and they walked around the fence enclosing the grazing field.

As Orion's eyes scanned the ponies, one raised its head. The pony gazed directly at him, threw his head back, neighed and stepped toward the Gypsy. Picking up the pace, the dapple gray pony, sporting a white mane and tail, approached Orion.

Gilles glanced back and forth between Orion and the pony. "You've made a connection."

The pony reached the fence and raised its head to nuzzle Orion.

The Gypsy put his hand on the pony's head and stroked it.

"I guess we have our choice." Gilles pushed his hat back on his forehead and put his hand on Orion's shoulder. "You are a master with these beasts."

"They are not beasts. They are magnificent creatures." Orion placed his head on the pony's mane and closed his eyes. "Yes, my friend, I know." He rose and pulled back the horse's lips. "Looks to be about three. Good age, like Ian."

As they walked back to the front of the field, the dapple gray followed them.

The tenant farmer came out. They met his price, and he left to get a harness and saddle.

Orion tested the equipment, made sure the horse was comfortable, and then led him to their horses. "These ponies are built for endurance, not speed, so we'll have to limit our pace."

When they arrived back at Ravenshire, they spotted Jean-Louis and Ian playing with Chérie, throwing a stick for the dog to fetch. Seeing the two horsemen approaching, Ian squinted to peer more closely. "Is that a baby horse?"

"Let's go see." Jean-Louis hoisted the boy on his shoulders, walked over to greet Gilles and Orion, and then lowered him to the ground as the two riders dismounted.

Ian's expectant eyes looked up at the men, and then directly at the pony.

Orion smiled. "You can pet him."

The boy reached out and the pony buried his head in the boy's neck. Ian giggled and hugged the pony.

Jean-Louis tipped his hat to the boy. "He's yours, Ian. To make you feel at home at Ravenshire. Give him a name."

Ian looked into the pony's eyes. "Gio."

The former trapper shrugged. "Lord Ostwold might not appreciate a pony being named after him."

"Why not? A pony is like a dwarf. And I'll let Gio ride pony Gio."

Orion lifted Ian onto pony Gio's back, and led him to the stables.

Gio sat nearby, sketching the old tower.

"Look Gio! Look! I have a pony!"

Gio turned his head, rose from his stool, put down his sketchpad, and walked over to examine the Shetland. He nodded approvingly. "A steed fit for a dwarf. You'll grow too big for the pony, but he'll always be the right size for me when I visit Ravenshire." He rubbed the pony's face.

Ian turned to Jean-Louis. "See? I knew he'd understand." Glancing at Gio, he beamed. "I named him after you."

Momentarily speechless, Gio laughed so hard he fell down in the grass.

***

Friday, May 24, 1811 – Musée de Merbeau
Gio

Back in London, Gio arrived for a planned mid-day meal with Gwyneth.

The reception clerk hurried out around the desk. "Lord Ostwold, let me escort you to the office of the comtesse."

Gio found Gwyneth sorting paintings on a long table.

She glanced at him and smiled. "Any suggestions?"

He reviewed the artwork piece by piece. "True, a special exhibition of your original watercolors would be wonderful. But to bring these to a broader public, in book form, is a different matter. Woodcuts are generally not as detailed in reproduction. Copper plates can produce details close to a watercolor, but, like woodcuts, would have to be individually hand-colored on paper. It is not impossible, but there must be a more efficient way." He looked down at his feet, and then out the window. He tilted his head and walked over to the chintz draperies. "This is the answer!"

"Draperies? Are you mad as a hatter?"

"A book of cotton prints—samples—stitched into a binding in the same way a book is produced. We can use copper plates, maybe even the rollers since we don't need a large fabric sample. They can reproduce eight colors. That's it! We could even have quilts produced from the artwork, or frame the fabric as paintings. Maybe someday they'll develop a way to reproduce paintings by lithography more easily than today. I've talked to some of them, but the size of my portraits are daunting. Yours might be more suitable. In the meantime, we might achieve vibrant color prints on fabric."

Gwyneth raised an eyebrow. "That may be the most ludicrous idea you have ever proffered."

Throwing his hands up toward the ceiling, Gio shrugged. "Sometimes my cleverness exceeds prudence."

Scoffing, Gwyneth picked up a painting of a zebra. "I've hand-written text describing the characteristics of each animal. I think engravings that are hand-colored offer the best possibility."

"That's what we must investigate."

"We?"

"You?"

Together they both came to the same conclusion in the same breath. "Bri!"

"She is most definitely adventurous." Gio sorted through the paintings. "There are only twenty-four paintings. What letters are you missing?"

" 'X' is troubling, and 'Q' has been difficult."

"Quail?"

"My goal is not to include birds. I prefer wild animals, and will consider birds for another volume."

"A Latin name, perhaps?"

Gwyneth scoffed. "This book is meant for children. It is not a scientific or medical treatise."

"*Ergo*, you—I mean Bri—needs to find a specialist in rare animals. Surely on some continent there are creatures whose names begin with those letters. Henry must know someone at the British Museum."

"*Verum.*"

"*Touché*, Madame la Comtesse. Now what delicacy have you planned for our mid-day repast?"

"Poached chicken under a cream sauce of spinach and bacon. And some kind of chocolate creation for dessert. I'm testing the chef's recommendations for our next gala."

"Test away."

***

Saturday, May 25, 1811 – Lord Merrick's Gentlemen's Club
Lord Merrick

Lord Merrick recognized the man approaching him. *Damn. His step is confident. What nefarious scheme is this Machiavellian up to?* He put down his newspaper. "Drummond."

"May I congratulate you on your engagement?"

"You may." *I must be wary.*

Without invitation, Drummond sat down next to Lord Merrick. *This man's impudence never ceases to amaze me.*

Drummond leaned closer and whispered, "Some of your letters to Lady Patricia were intercepted."

Blanching, Lord Merrick looked around to be sure they couldn't be overheard. "Good God, man! How do you know this?"

"That is not your concern. I am simply here to inform you that *Scandal & Shame* will *not* be publishing them, as was their intent."

"Publish? No...I'd be a laughing stock. And my engagement would be broken off by my intended."

"The letters will not be published. I've seen to that. But I've read them, Merrick. You are overly fond of purple prose. The letters will be delivered to Lady Patricia." He paused for his words to take effect. "Threw her over for a richer heiress, did you?"

Sputtering, Lord Merrick emitted no coherent sound.

"Luck is with you, for Lady Patricia has vowed to burn your love notes. But I know of them, as does the owner of *Scandal & Shame.* We may call on you from time to time for a favor."

Damnable menace! "I'll do what I can to be of service."

"I know you will. And I'm sure the future countess will be gratified by your compliance."

"You wouldn't—"

Inscrutable as ever, Drummond smiled. "I wouldn't *want* to, unless...." He shrugged, rose to his feet, and made a *faux* salute to the impoverished earl, turned on his heel and left.

Lord Merrick picked up the paper to hide his flushed face. *I should have responded to Lady Patricia's entreaties. Now I am compromised. Forever. Tottie Drummond never releases his trapped animals.*

***

Saturday, May 25, 1811 – The Blue Bazaar
Orion

Orion wandered the Blue Bazaar with Jean-Louis. "Why do they call it the Blue Bazaar?"

"You alerted us to the highwaymen because you were aware of potential danger. Hone your powers of observation when you are not at risk. If you do, then noticing something out of the ordinary will become second nature." The Frenchman stopped and pointed to the tall poles surrounding the boundaries of the bazaar. Blue triangle-shaped flags flew in the breeze.

Orion grimaced. *I feel like a fool. I will pay more attention.*

Jean-Louis led Orion on a stroll around the perimeter of the market stalls, Chérie at his heels. He pointed out which stall keepers were honest, which sold fake souvenirs, and which could be trusted. He took the young Gypsy on a circuitous route through the rabbit warren of interior stalls, and then he put his hand on Orion's arm to signal that they had arrived.

Orion stared at the colorfully painted canopy. The stall overflowed with an assortment of East Indian wares.

The Frenchman rang the bell.

A bald, clean-shaven man appeared from behind a curtain. He clapped his hands and bowed his head. "J-L, J-L! Welcome!"

"Tej, this is Orion. If he needs help, he will come to you. Say nothing to anyone else. Do as he asks."

"For you, J-L, always. I am the soul of discretion. You know this."

Jean-Louis smiled. "For a price."

Tej shrugged. "I am a mere merchant." He turned to Orion. "Perhaps you would like a small gift from my stall." He picked up a light blue shawl. "For your love?"

Orion felt the soft fabric. "Not for a girl, but for my horse."

Jean-Louis elbowed him in the ribs. "I'm sure Tej doesn't mean for this lovely shawl to go to a horse."

The Gypsy stammered. "It's...it's for a baby horse, coming soon from Ireland. I was there at the moment of his birth."

Tilting his head, Tej smiled. "Then the horse is your love. I can see it. Take the shawl for the baby horse. What is his name?"

"I call him Sunny." Accepting the gift, Orion marveled at his luck. *The wild colors and scents of this bazaar are intoxicating.*

Jean-Louis leaned in and whispered to Tej. "Where is the Gypsy stall?"

Following Tej's directions, Jean-Louis pulled Orion back into the shadows as they approached their target. "We'll watch for a while, perhaps for several weeks, while I am still here, then you can go back to Ravenshire until we return from the Azores. Do not approach the Gypsies under any circumstances until I return."

"Won't they recognize us?"

"Why do you think we are in the shadows? Don't disappoint me, Orion. Use your head. Think of them as prey, as untamed animals who might strike out if surprised. You will infiltrate the band, gain their trust, and listen. I have a theory, but I don't want to reveal it too soon."

After a few moments of silence, Orion asked, "Is it true you killed a polar bear with your bare hands?" He spoke while keeping his eyes on the Gypsy stall.

Jean-Louis laughed. "No. With a knife. Still, an animal over one thousand pounds is quite an adversary. Ten times as big as a cougar, but not as swift or cunning."

"What's a cougar?"

"A lion that roams the mountains and plains of the Americas."

"Did you kill those too?"

The Frenchman pushed back his black felt hat. "Yes. And ate them on the trail. Similar to pork in taste."

Orion was enthralled with Jean-Louis but shocked to hear he'd eaten a lion. "I couldn't eat a beautiful animal."

The former trapper shrugged. "Survival instincts kick in. You'd be surprised what you might do. You eat beef, don't you?"

The Gypsy nodded.

"What about those lovely sweet cows in the pastures of Ravenshire? Could you slaughter one of them for food?"

Appalled, Orion turned to glance at Jean-Louis, and shook his head.

"Then you are overly civilized. You live on a farming estate but ignore the ongoing butchering of animals for your dinner."

"That's different."

"How?"

"I don't have to do it."

"Precisely." Jean-Louis nudged him and indicated that he should direct his gaze to the activity in the Gypsy stall. "Keep your eyes on the target. Distraction can get you killed."

Orion paled.

"How many do you count?"

"Five. Three in front and two on the side."

The Frenchman nodded. "Good. You're learning. This task I've set you to may be dangerous. You shy away from killing a cow, but you might have to kill a man in self-defense."

"That's not a problem. I've often thought of how I'd kill my father."

Jean-Louis scoffed. "Revenge can make you careless. I'll test your skills later. For the time being, you will merely observe. What is your weapon of choice?"

Orion's silence and stiffened stance betrayed the truth.

"I see. We'll start your training tomorrow."

CHAPTER FOURTEEN

Saturday, May 25, 1811 – Lord Ravenshire's Townhouse
Jean-Louis

Jean-Louis took the steps up two at a time from the courtyard to the kitchen, Chérie at his heels. He grabbed an apple from the cook's pile before walking through to the dining room. He eased into the chair opposite the earl. Chérie and the earl's dog, Hector, snuggled together on the floor, a spray of Dalmatian spots in the Persian rug under the table. "Gilles will be your driver for a few days next week."

Henry looked over his spectacles and put down the newspaper and waited for the Frenchman to explain.

"Orion is untrained in weaponry. He's bold but untested. I mean to take the measure of his strengths and weaknesses around Ravenshire. When I'm in the Azores, Gilles will continue his training."

"Trial by fire for the boy, eh? Are you sure he's not better off in the stables?"

"Uncertain, as yet. He may fall short of my expectations, but I think not." The former trapper reached for the teapot, poured a cup and took a wedge of sugar to melt in it. "I see the chunks are smaller."

Henry lowered his voice. "Mrs. Jones swore quite colorfully as she spiked that hard rock of sugar, but she was determined to try Bri's idea. The cook adores her."

Jean-Louis shrugged. "As do we all. Where is our lady fair?"

"In the study reviewing accounts."

"Ha! James has an interesting life ahead." The Frenchman smiled as he stirred his tea. He took another sip, nodding approval. "The sugar melts faster." He glanced at the earl. "What did you have for breakfast?"

"*Payn perdu.*"

Shaking his head, Jean-Louis raised an eyebrow. "Amazing how the wealthy adopt the 'delicacies' of the poor. As for me, I had far too many servings of that stale bread to ever want another. We had no butter, no sugar, and no maple syrup imported from America."

"What do you propose to eat in its stead?"

"A meal fit for a gout-plagued glutton. It's half a day's ride to Ravenshire."

As if on cue, the footman brought a platter of eggs, bacon and fried potatoes.

"How do you remain so trim?" Henry patted his near-flat belly and exaggerated. "My girth is expanding."

Between bites, the Frenchman answered. "I avoid *payn perdu.*"

"And you ride half a day to Ravenshire twice a week as routine." Henry sighed. "You've shamed me. As soon as I finish the paper, I'll take Hector out to accompany me on a jaunt around town on Hermès."

"The dog and the horse have a friendly rivalry."

"One named for a Greek, the other for a Trojan. Both like to win. As do we."

***

Lord Ravenshire's Gentlemen's Club
Henry

Later that afternoon, Henry went to his club. He'd received a note from his confidant inside the Foreign Office requesting a meeting. He arrived, took a seat, and in keeping with their standard arrangement, placed his newspaper on the table.

The man from the Foreign Office arrived and placed his newspaper on top of Henry's.

The earl never greeted him by name, as the bureaucrat preferred anonymity in public. He looked like any other graying functionary. He was, however, anything but ordinary. Van Malcolm had spent years as a diplomat on secret missions serving the king and Prince Regent. He and the earl had saved each other's lives on more than one occasion on multiple continents. Their bond of trust was unbreakable.

Henry waved over a server, and each took a small goblet of sherry. Cut-crystal facets sparkled in the rare ray of afternoon sun filtering through the leaded glass windows.

"Not used to seeing your name in *Scandal & Shame,* Ravenshire." The guest took a sip of sherry.

Grimacing, Henry shrugged. "Neither am I."

"You thought you would die on that island. It's understandable. The baroness is an unfortunate casualty of the unexpected resurrection of your lost love. The Sultan left in a bit of a huff."

"I still have his spice contract. For now."

"The Prince Regent hopes that continues. The king may be mad, but he still craves his spices."

Henry held his goblet in both hands, leaning forward, eyes downcast. His voice, barely audible, took on a hushed tone. "Any optimism on the Atlantic issues?"

Malcolm shook his head. "Tension is building, but nothing appears imminent."

"It's bad enough already. I've recast my fleet under the flag of Portugal to maintain shipping routes, but it adds time to each voyage to travel via Porto. Still, to be unable to ship to America at all for fear of encountering warships will require more adjustments. Another six months would be helpful."

"That should be satisfactory. But not much longer than that. The powder keg is dry and ready to blow."

Nodding, the earl sat back up and drained his glass and a server's tray appeared to remove it from his hand. *Ears are never far away. I must be on guard.* Running his hand through his still-thick dark-brown hair, now streaked with a few white strands, Henry leaned closer. "I suppose you've heard Blackie's dead."

"I saw the notice, but I sensed there was more."

"Kidnapper. Killer. Thief. I trusted him more than anyone for twenty years." Henry scoffed. "And I always prided myself on being a shrewd judge of character."

Malcolm squinted. "His age is about right. Don't tell me he's—"

"Correct. By God, I suppose diplomats must cultivate a devious turn of mind. Blackie was my half-brother. Said he didn't kill me because he liked me."

The Foreign Officer raised his glass to Henry. "At least there's that." He sipped his sherry and smiled. "My sources may not be as good as I thought. Next time I'll try your Frenchman first. It will no doubt be more efficient." Malcolm stood to leave.

Henry rose to his feet and retrieved the top newspaper. "Maybe I should have brought *Scandal & Shame.*"

Picking up the bottom newspaper, the Foreign Officer shrugged. "You'd be surprised what we find out that way."

***

Monday, May 27, 1811 – Wyndward Trading Offices
Henry

Inside the intricately restored trading company near the docks, a monumental building more than a century old, Henry sat in the office of the director of African operations. "Sheldon, I'd like you to spearhead an analysis of all areas of the company to increase the depth of our directorial teams. If war comes, we'll need experienced hands in locations beyond frequent communication.

"You know the whole of Africa, where Blackburn had many longstanding contacts. Can you reconstruct his activities?"

"Maybe. This Pharaoh character he referenced is one I will investigate. Maybe our people there know something. Even with birds, though, information travels slowly."

"Agreed. If you think Africa is too big, split it. Ask Fong and Gonzales for the same recommendations—in fact, you should brief them with me to establish your authority. We need to be more nimble in the future. The world is changing and we must adapt."

"It may be counterintuitive after Blackburn's actions, but I think we have been correct in delegating authority to the local directors. Our training indoctrinates them with our systems, expectations and values. There will be mistakes, but time and distance from headquarters requires timely decisions."

"Make a list of who you think is ready for more responsibility." Henry looked down at his hands and then back at Sheldon. "Napoleon will not reign forever, and expansion will spur growth now and position us for the future. A larger fleet will require more oversight."

***

Monday, May 27, 1811 – Ravenshire Forest
Orion

Jean-Louis and Orion rode west from London for several hours until they were deep into Ravenshire Forest. The Frenchman led the Gypsy to a clearing. Straw targets stood in a semi-circle.

"Could you find your way back to the main road?"

Orion looked around. "I noted markers as we came. I think so."

"We'll find out. Dismount, tie up the horses and wait here."

Doing as he was told, the pit of the Gypsy's stomach churned. He steeled himself for the tests to come.

Jean-Louis came back carrying a leather bag. He threw it on the ground, opened the flap, and exposed an assortment of bows, arrows, pistols, shotguns, and knives. "We even have tomahawks—"

Orion looked perplexed. "What are tomahawks?"

"Like a small axe, wielded with an adept flick of the wrist by Indian warriors of the North American plains. Next, we have poison darts."

"I have never seen such things." He picked one up and turned it in his hand. "How do they work?"

"South American natives sail along in canoes to attack those on the banks, or hide in foliage along the shore to ambush strangers. They blow pointed poison-pellets through these cane leaf-wrapped cylinders to pierce the neck or skin of their enemies, be they local or white would-be conquerors. The poison is deadly. And if their target were to survive, falling into the river to feign death, man-eating fish strip the flesh from their bones. No escape."

"Your wild tales—"

"Wild but true. We'll test your skills until twilight. Then we'll see if you can guide us out of this wooded maze."

Orion's arrows went far askew of the series of targets. His pistol shots hit half their intended bulls-eyes. Recoil from the blast of a fowling piece, a long-barreled shooting implement designed to bring down birds, knocked him off his feet. With knives, however, he excelled. Mark after mark, he hit inside the painted red circle with precision. He could even throw the tomahawk with passable skill.

"Arrow, no. Pistol, fair. Fowling piece—," Jean-Louis turned to Orion, "which you should learn to use, should you ever need to eat, no."

The Frenchman's acerbic delivery unnerved Orion. *I have failed.*

"But with knives, you have an unerring eye and agile handwork. The blades flew on the wind like invisible birds in flight. You have found your *métier.* You need little refinement. The tomahawks are heavier and will require a different thrust, but I see promise there." Pride surged in Orion. *I have not failed at all tasks.*

"Can I try the poison dart blower?"

"Not with real poison and not in my direction." Jean-Louis put a berry in the blower. "If it hits the target, it will splatter and we can see how accurate you are."

Orion squinted, took a deep breath with the cylinder in his mouth. He began to choke and spat out the berry.

Jean-Louis shook his head. "Think, boy! Breathe *before* you place your mouth on the blower. You would have killed yourself." He placed another berry in the leaf-wrapped implement and handed it to Orion.

The Gypsy took a deep breath, placed the cylinder in his mouth and blew. The berry flew like an arrow and splotched as a tiny mass in the center of the target's bulls-eye.

Jean-Louis cocked his head. "If you can remember to breathe first, you may carve out a name for yourself. If not, you'll at least have a fast death." He looked off into the distance, then back at Orion. "I could call you Blower."

Orion hung his head. "I've disappointed you with other weapons."

"No. You disappoint *yourself.* I can shoot my dinner with a fowling piece." He pushed his black felt hat back on his head, put his hand on Orion's shoulder and smiled. "You're a master with a knife, decent with a tomahawk and not bad with a pistol."

"But I missed half the targets with a pistol."

"Most trained men miss more."

***

Wednesday, May 29, 1811 – Darlemont's Gentlemen's Club
Oliver

At their club, Oliver, called "Darlemont" by his friends, Sir Reggie and Duncan Mitchell-Dawson, Member of Parliament, waited for Drummond to arrive.

Oliver shuffled the cards absentmindedly, over and over. "It's not like Tottie to be late." *What intricate political schemes are afoot? The man prides himself on punctuality.*

A copy of *Scandal & Shame* flew onto the table. Drummond sank into the empty chair.

"Your reading tastes have devolved, Tottie," said Mitchell-Dawson, known as M-D to this group.

Sir Reggie's forehead glistened with perspiration. He reached into his pocket for a handkerchief.

"Gossip drives the *ton*. And you would be wise to pay attention, M-D. There's a snippet about you on page one."

Nonplussed, M-D reached for the paper, but Oliver beat him to it.

"Ah, here it is. 'What Member of Parliament from a far northeastern city has been tapped for Tory leadership? Fond of claret and beefsteak, with a gouty foot to prove it, this man-on-the-move holds court at a certain gentlemen's club. He keeps track of who's voting for Tory principles and who must be disciplined. Cross him at your peril.' "

Oliver raised an eyebrow. "This makes you sound fearsome, M-D. I hope you play politics better than you play cards."

Sir Reggie nearly ripped the paper out of Oliver's hands and scanned its contents. Visibly relieved, he took a deep breath, but then looked more closely at a small entry at the bottom of the page. "I say, Darlemont. Your brother-in-law is referenced here."

"Ravenshire? More on that island woman? I hate the way he degrades my family. My niece should not be tainted nor my late sister's memory tarnished by his philandering."

"No. It's speculation about the nature of Blackburn's death."

Oliver took the paper from Sir Reggie. "Where?" He found it and read the copy aloud. " 'What was Mr. Blackburn, deputy to Lord Ravenshire at Wyndward Trading, doing in the early hours of April 14th of this year when he went missing? Boating to his death? His battered body washed up on the rocks two weeks later. Was it a natural death or is a crime being covered up?' "

Gasps came from his Whist partners.

Oliver's face clouded."I am no acolyte of Ravenshire's, but the suggestion of murder seems far-fetched." He stared at Drummond. "Are you responsible for this?" *Denial is Tottie's first lesson of manipulation.*

"Ravenshire and I have a known animosity. He calls me his 'Nemesis.' I wouldn't tweak his nose in public." He took a sip of wine. "It's too easy to do in private."

"I need to get to the bottom of this. This taints the Wyndward name. My niece should not be mired in scandalous rumors of murder." Oliver pushed back his chair, bid the others *adieu*, and stormed off into the night, *Scandal & Shame* in his hand.

***

Wednesday, May 29, 1811 – Lord Ravenshire's Townhouse
Henry

Thompson knocked on the door of the earl's study.

The earl looked up from his reading and removed his spectacles. "Yes?"

"Lord Darlemont has arrived unannounced. He seems a bit agitated."

"This late? It's after eleven. Show him in and bring some tea."

Henry stood as Oliver entered. They nodded to each other in a perfunctory manner.

Oliver tossed *Scandal & Shame* on Henry's desk. "Drummond denies he planted it, but I don't believe him. He controls the owner. I don't want this scurrilous speculation to affect Bri." He pulled up a chair and leaned toward the earl, watching him intently for a reaction.

The earl read the item. "We issued a simple statement that *Scandal & Shame* embellished. We can't dispute the fact that Blackburn's body was found bashed on the rocks at the water's edge. I generally lean toward ignoring rather than inflaming such comments."

"You've told us that Blackburn fooled you for twenty years, embezzling funds and falsifying contracts. How did you discover your half-brother's treachery?"

"Bri uncovered it—"

"How would Bri have any idea of your company's operations?"

Henry leaned back. "You know how clever she is. She is secretly acting as my 'man-of-affairs'."

Oliver raised his eyebrows. "She is a clever girl. But to hide Aelwyn and her child from us? Rychard was my closest friend, Henry. I shall never forgive you for keeping Aelwyn's survival from me."

One more thing to never be forgiven for. "I knew nothing of her whereabouts until a month ago. We all thought she'd been killed or had taken her own life."

"Blackburn's body—"

"—was smashed on the rocks and eaten by fish until it was beyond recognition."

"Doubt is in your voice. Do you suspect he lives?"

"We do not know." Henry shrugged. "He is comfortable in many parts of the world."

"Illicit funds at his disposal on several continents, no doubt."

"Jean-Louis believes the traitor's grandmother is intent on finishing his plan of revenge."

Oliver leaned back in his chair, keeping his gaze on Henry. "The mother of the nanny?"

Henry nodded.

"I remember the nanny, you know, from that summer I spent with your family at Ravenshire. Rychard and I were around four."

"When the duke and duchess took Vincent and Jane to Europe? I'd forgotten that Brigid was with us then."

"I love my mother, of course, but she was not particularly attentive to children, nor was our nanny. Brigid was warm and kind. I've never forgotten how she made me feel loved."

The sad, wistful tone of Oliver's voice deeply affected Henry. *He has never revealed himself to me on this level.* "We all loved Brigid. To lose her so soon after my mother died was difficult." He averted his eyes to regain his composure. "Jean-Louis has confirmed that the grandmother is alive. He has people searching for her. Bri is not aware of this fact and I prefer that you maintain secrecy. No need to upset her unnecessarily.

"Since you ride with Bri every week, I ask you to be on alert for strange characters. Did you notice anything unusual in the park yesterday?"

Oliver looked off as if summoning an image to the front of his mind. "Not that I recall. It was an ordinary ride. We were absorbed in conversation about Jane's love of horses." Oliver smiled. "I told her how Jane always wanted a unicorn. Nothing could convince her they were naught but creatures of fantasy."

"And Bri couldn't understand that, I'd wager."

"She requires scientific proof for all unicorn sightings."

Henry laughed. *When was the last time Oliver and I had a pleasant conversation?* Henry sighed. "I don't know how to protect the ones I love from an unknown danger. Bri and Aelwyn are adamant that they won't cower in the shadows." Henry leveled his gaze at Oliver. "Let us decrease the tension between us for the sake of Bri, Aelwyn and Ian. You and Rychard were friends. We should be able to socialize without rancor."

Oliver nodded. "Their safety is paramount and requires secrecy. Perhaps I've misjudged your Frenchman. Aelwyn is no doubt alive because of his action. Mother holds him in high regard."

He stood to leave and extended his hand to Henry. "I'll let you know if I hear anything more from Drummond. His denial of involvement in fueling gossip strikes me as probable confirmation."

Henry rose to his feet and took Oliver's hand. "Thanks. And keep Blackburn's grandmother in mind. We believe she is somewhere in Scotland, but she could be in London as we speak. We've lost her trail. Be on alert for any odd elderly women."

Hector stretched on the floor to the side of Henry's desk, and then rose to his feet. The Dalmatian walked over to Oliver, and rubbed against his leg.

Oliver bent down to pet the dog.

Hector jumped up, put his paws on Oliver's shoulders and licked his face.

Laughing, Henry said, "Now there is no doubt, Oliver. You are always welcome here."

CHAPTER FIFTEEN

Wednesday, May 29, 1811 – Ravenshire
Jean-Louis

When Jean-Louis and Orion arrived back at Ravenshire after their third day of training, the moon hung low over the horizon as the last violet-tinged clouds faded into a dull gray. After reaching the stables, they left their mounts to the groomers.

Orion headed out of the stables.

Jean-Louis called out to him. "Wait. I have something to show you."

The Gypsy boy turned and followed his idol. As he turned the corner, he heard a familiar neigh. "Nosey! You're here!" He ran to her and stroked her head. She nuzzled him, joined by the foal. Sunny rested his head against Orion's chest. Turning to Jean-Louis, he asked, "How did you know they'd arrived? We've been in the forest all day."

"Tomorrow, I'll show you. Tonight, let's eat a hearty meal and let the cook spoil us."

"I'll be back later with a surprise," Orion whispered to the horses.

They walked through the kitchen door and Jean-Louis grabbed Sallie from behind and hugged her. The cook, in her mid-twenties, cooed at the attention. "We have something special for you, J-L, and," she pinched Orion's cheek, "this pretty boy. Go wash up."

They did as they were told, and then took their places at the servants' table next to the kitchen. Jean-Louis and the doctor would normally eat separately from the staff, but when the earl was not in residence at Ravenshire, meals were less formal. The permanent staff, standing, waited until Young sat at the head of the table before pulling out their chairs.

Orion smiled at Dr. Derry. "Nosey and Sunny must have been happy to see you."

The veterinarian smiled. "Not as happy as they were to see you, I'd wager."

Knowing Jean-Louis was partial to lamb, Sallie had instructed the butcher to prepare one. He fashioned several cuts, but the chops were reserved for Jean-Louis. Mint jelly, roasted potatoes with rosemary, and fresh bread rounded out the evening's fare.

The Frenchman regaled the diners with stories of Orion's artistry with knives as well as his artlessness with the bow and fowling piece. He never forgot to charm the cook. "Best chops I've ever had, Sallie. You spoil me."

"Of course I do." Sallie, her face flushed from the heat of cooking, beamed.

After dinner, Orion took a few chunks of sugar in his pocket, and he squinted. "These are smaller."

Jean-Louis laughed. "Lady Gabriella's idea. Was it an annoying task, Sallie?"

"Not at all. I had the butcher chop it up."

After dinner, Jean-Louis accompanied Orion back to the stables. "Do you smoke?"

Orion shook his head.

"Good. Surveillance requires attention to smells as well as sights. Wash your body and clothes often. Nothing traverses the wind faster than stink."

***

Orion

Interesting J-L didn't talk about my skill with the pistol or the blower. He never reveals everything. After feeding the sugar wedges to the horses, Orion told them about his day, as had been his habit in Ireland. His listeners appeared rapt. These one-way conversations helped the Gypsy boy adjust to the facets of his new life.

When Orion finally opened the door to his new quarters, he found it completely outfitted. New clothes were folded inside an armoire and polished boots stood next to it. A leather jacket hung on the back of the door. And the light blue shawl for Sunny was set on the table. *I'll present the shawl to Sunny, so he can sniff it and recognize it in the future when it is placed under a saddle.*

Astounded by his good fortune, Orion stood immobile until a soft knock rapped on the door. He opened it.

"Shh! We must be careful." His visitor closed the door.

Their embrace quickly turned hungry with passion.

***

Thursday, May 30, 1811 – Ravenshire Dovecote
Orion

Early in the morning, before they headed back to London with Aelwyn and Ian, Jean-Louis took Orion to a wall in the back of the stables. The Frenchman pushed on it and it moved.

Orion's eyes widened in anticipation. *A false wall?*

A staircase appeared that led to an upper level above the stables.

Peering up, Orion said, "I thought nothing was up there but an attic."

"That's the idea."

"Only a few know of this, and you must keep it a secret. Speak of it to no one but Gilles, Steiner, or me."

"I won't."

"Including Dr. Derry."

Orion nodded. "No one but Gilles, Steiner or you." *I hear odd noises. Bats?* The Gypsy shivered at the repellent thought.

After unlocking the door at the top of the stairs, Jean-Louis motioned for Orion to walk in.

A large number of cages were placed around the attic. Most contained a single bird.

Two workers Orion didn't recognize moved from cage to cage, feeding the birds.

"Are they what are called 'homing pigeons'?"

"Yes. We have them at Ravenshire, Glaslough, the trading offices, and on our ships. That's how I knew when Nosey would arrive. That's how Aelwyn knew when to meet us on the shore. It's a competitive advantage in a dangerous world."

"Why show me? I'm not important."

"Not yet. But if something were to happen to Gilles or Steiner, I like to have insurance. You are that insurance. If there's ever an emergency that threatens Aelwyn or Ian while you are here, send a bird with a note attached in one of these carriers." He showed him how to insert a note in one of the leather carriers and strap it to a bird's leg. "Use a bird in one of the cages marked 'Trading.' The earl or I will get the message immediately. "

"I understand."

Jean-Louis put his hand on Orion's shoulder. "Good. I'm counting on you."

Orion's chest swelled.

***

Friday, May 31, 1811 – The Blue Bazaar
Orion

Back in London after his training, Orion continued his surveillance of the Gypsy stall at the Blue Bazaar in the late afternoon. By now, he recognized the regulars. Repeat visitors seemed to have a pattern of certain shopping days. He listened to them haggle over prices. *Each haggler believes he surpasses the other in cunning.*

An elderly Gypsy woman shuffled to the stall, a bit unsteady on her feet. She picked up items of Bohemian glass, crystal balls and decks of Tarot cards, examined them closely, and then replaced each one on the table. Orion had never believed in fortune tellers or superstition. Though he had heard there were a few who truly had the gift of prescience, he guessed that any prediction that came true had been vague, revealing nothing more than mere coincidence.

Orion noticed her stance first. The woman's back was slightly hunched and the back of her hands were veined with age, but her face appeared unlined. *How?* Her eyes were a dark shade of brown that bordered on black. *A pure Roma.*

She spoke with a loud voice, so Orion did not have to edge closer to the Gypsy stall to overhear her. "Perhaps I reading cards here one day a week, Vano. I having time. Charge what you please." She waved her arm dismissively. "I having no need for money."

The swarthy, mustachioed stall keeper scoffed. "Everyone wants money. I trust no one who says otherwise." The heavily muscled man towered over her.

The Gypsy crone shrugged. "Some things being more valuable than money."

His face lit up with understanding. "You seek secrets."

A sly smile crept over her face.

He's hooked.

"Come back tomorrow."

CHAPTER SIXTEEN

Monday, June 3, 1811 – Interior of The Duchess's Carriage
Bri

Rain pelted Vanessa's carriage as it moved through the slippery streets. Claude, the Pytchley driver, trained by Jean-Louis, guided the rig expertly through the uneven and partially flooded roadways.

Bri looked out the window. "It's a good thing we wore boots today. Our skirts will be soaked."

Vanessa tilted her head and turned it toward her granddaughter. "Bri, this is London. It rains. You sound uninformed, unprepared and uneducated. You can hike up your skirts a bit and step gingerly. We're going to *La Pâtisserie entre les fleurs.*"

Bri's eyes widened. "But we'll have to trek over an uncovered path through the park."

Her grandmother's stare silenced her. *I can always buy new clothing.*

"Has your father discussed the Marriage Settlement with you yet?"

"No. Everything happened rather quickly. I've not had much time to think about legalities."

"Well, you'd better start thinking about legalities and you'd better start now. A married woman's property becomes the sole property of her husband upon marriage."

"But surely the trading company—"

"—is property."

"But Edward would never restrict me—"

"You think not, but many things can change with time."

"What do you recommend? I know Father would want me to be protected. His legacy is the trading company."

"I want you to meet with Lord Judge Todd-Hatton. He has very enlightened views on the equality of women. He may still wear a powdered wig and prance around in robes in court, but he is in possession of a keen mind. Henry has the advantage of holdings in many countries with different laws and customs. The law of corporations could be used to your benefit. I don't mean to suggest Edward is untrustworthy. Far from it. And a private trust held by his bank under another's private administration could be a form of protection for you.

"But I have learned that different courts have different approaches to jurisprudence, even within the *ton*. The world may change and the position of women may improve in your lifetime, though doubtful in mine." Vanessa sighed and shook her head. "Oliver can't be bothered with such details. He dreams only of his title, racing horses, and playing a grand role in the Society. You have ingenuity, drive and ambition. I will not permit you to fritter away your gifts on a fleeting romance."

Bri's annoyance flared. "What I have with Edward is not a fleeting romance. I will not fritter away anything, Grandmother."

The carriage pulled to a stop. To Bri's surprise, a canopy had been erected over the pathway to the *pâtisserie*, driven into the wet ground with stakes. Boards had been laid in a cross-wise pattern to avoid sinking into the mud. "This canopy and walkway are rather clever." She glanced at her grandmother. "You knew."

"Of course."

Claude opened the door, lowered the steps, and assisted the women as they exited the carriage.

Continuing their conversation as they approached the *pâtisserie*, Bri stepped gingerly to avoid twisting an ankle as she traversed the boards. "When can I meet with the Lord Judge?"

"He's joining us for lunch. Tonight, speak to Henry about his intentions regarding your Marriage Settlement."

"Did you receive any such advice before your marriage?"

"More than fifty years ago? No. That is why I want you to be prepared. If your son were to marry a wicked, nasty piece of work like Lady Abigail, your life would be intolerable. That shrew is not even as competent as the meaning of her name."

"It is a bit odd to name a child 'Abigail' and risk the ridicule of her being taunted as an 'abigail,' a Lady's maid."

The duchess sniffed. "Her parents possessed rather limited intellect. She inherited the worst attributes of each—the dullness of her father and the arrogance of her mother combined to create a sorry spectacle."

They reached the *pâtisserie* to find a few intrepid patrons, but only one man, seated at a corner table, sans powdered wig.

***

Monday, June 3, 1811 – Kensington Press
Corning

Roger Corning adjusted his spectacles as he read a manuscript. Piles of them covered his desk. Each was stamped in red ink—*Accepted*, *Rejected*, or *Tabled*. A knock on the doorjamb alerted him to a delivery. He nodded to the clerk to enter.

The clerk brought in a manuscript wrapped in paper and tied with twine and put it on Corning's desk. *The usual method of delivery from Penelope Peabody or Drusilla Dorset.* In accordance with procedure, the clerk left and closed the door behind him.

Corning marked the page he had been reading, put down the manuscript and sat back in his chair. *My best-selling author never disappoints. She delivers like clockwork.*

He cut the twine with scissors and unwrapped the volume. The title page made him smile—*The Calculating Countess and the Doddering Dotard* by Drusilla Dorset. Corning scoffed at his previous disbelief. *I was wrong. Readers want to know the plot from the title.*

He settled back in his chair to read. Before he'd reached the end of the first page, a smile came over his face. *She's done it again.*

***

Monday, June 3, 1811 – *La Pâtisserie entre les fleurs*
Bri

Bri assumed the distinguished looking man smoking a pipe must be Lord Judge Todd-Hatton. She took note of his stylish gray jacket and steely blue breeches. *Impeccably polished boots. His valet must be a former military man.* The man rose and removed his pipe to speak. "Your Grace." He bowed, and then kissed the duchess's outstretched gray-gloved hand. Directing his gaze to Bri, he smiled. "And you must be the indomitable Lady Gabriella. May I extend my best wishes upon your engagement?"

"Thank you, Lord Judge." He gallantly kissed her glove as well. "Shall we make our selections? I'm not used to such an informal method, but I appreciate evaluating an array of choices."

Vanessa led the way to the display cases, her light pink dress with pale gray stripes swooshing around the tables. "We must adapt to the ways of modernity, mustn't we?" She scanned the choices. "French onion soup and a plate of greens, nuts and *chèvre.*"

Bri and the Lord Judge glanced at each other. He nodded to Bri to make her selection next.

"I'll have the same," she said.

"As will I," the judge intoned. "And a bottle of dry white wine for the table."

He reached into his pocket, but Vanessa swept him away from the counter. "I invited you here. The bill has been paid."

"As long as you have no cases pending before me, ethics permit me to say, 'Thank you.' "

They retook their seats. The server appeared almost immediately, carrying three plates. Each held a small freshly baked baguette, butter and preserves.

The Lord Judge tore off a morsel of bread, buttered it, and dropped a spot of strawberry preserves onto it. "Now, what advice do you seek?"

Bri listened to the duchess explain the purpose of their meeting, exhibiting uncharacteristic deference. She examined the jurist's face as he absorbed the details. *No trace of reaction. He has the practiced gaze of an impartial arbiter.*

The judge ate while the duchess explained her concern for Bri's future.

Putting down his fork, the judge cleared his throat. "Marriage Settlements are delicate things. Laws vary among jurisdictions, and the laws of corporations differ from the laws governing land and estates. A woman's property is subject to the control of her husband, and later, her eldest son. From what you've told me, however, you have a number of distinct advantages. Mainly, your family's property in Scotland."

Turning to Bri, he continued, "If you married in Scotland, and set that as your primary domicile, it might be possible to maintain separate property." He absentmindedly rubbed his ear as he spoke. "I will have to do some research."

Bri leaned forward. "Is there a solicitor adept at fashioning agreements for women in my situation?"

"In a word, no, although..."

The duchess had no patience. "Although what?"

"I have heard that one woman has continued to operate a law stationer's office after her husband's death. Clerks copy legal documents for property transactions, wills, settlements, mortgages and perhaps some marriage settlements. The word is that they sometimes create these documents, which are later reviewed by a member of the bar for a fee. These are rumors, mind you. But I can make discreet inquiries."

"Do you foresee changes in property laws, Lord Judge?" Bri tried to hide her disappointment, but she was not as practiced as the jurist. She brushed a stray strand of hair from her eyes, and adjusted her position in the cushioned chair. Its light blue plaid blended with her ombré blue linen dress, navy at the top, shading to the palest of blue at the hem.

"I see your discomfort, my dear. The law moves slowly. It is, by its very nature, conservative. Maybe if England has a queen again, such a monarch would spur change."

Vanessa scoffed. "The king has seven surviving sons and five surviving daughters! The prospect of a queen in Bri's lifetime is ludicrous."

Ever practical, Bri pressed her point. "What about Parliament? Rights of women are discussed more often in the press. Could not change be effected without a queen? Monarchs are figureheads. The power is in the law."

"Idealism is admirable, Lady Gabriella, but men make laws, not women." The judge picked up his pipe.

"What if my Marriage Settlement put forth an agreement between Mr. James and me that varies from the law? If he did not object, what would happen?"

The judge puffed on his pipe before answering. "Your persistence is laudable, but the Marriage Settlement must be filed in court. While I seem to recall that some courts have recognized private trusts between parties in Marriage Settlements, it is unlikely that a document diverging from governing law would be accepted."

"Unlikely or impossible?"

"Nothing is impossible, Lady Gabriella, but let me complete my research and we can discuss what is possible to achieve within the law. Taking a course that diverges from prevailing law is not prudent."

Bri sighed. "Forgive me if I appear combative. I simply want to explore all my options."

"If women could practice law, you would be a formidable opponent." The judge emptied his pipe into the ashtray. "Let's meet again in about a month or two and I will give you a summary of what I have learned on your behalf."

After the judge departed, the ladies pulled on their gloves, rose and walked along the path to their waiting carriage. The duchess put her arm around Bri. "Someday women will practice law—perhaps not in my lifetime, but in yours." She climbed into her carriage.

Bri followed. "I trust Edward, but one never knows what will happen in the future."

The duchess held firm. "We'll exploit every legal angle available to protect you."

"I love you, Grandmother. Thank you for looking out for me."

"Although I didn't turn a blind eye to my daughter's melancholy, I felt constrained by Society and did not follow my instincts to intervene." Her jaw set in defiance. "After her suffering and death, I vowed to never again curb my tongue where my family is concerned. That would be uncaring, uncourageous, and unconscionable."

Grandmother doesn't want me to face the same future she does.

***

Monday, June 3, 1811 – Lord Ravenshire's Townhouse
Henry

Bri's voice echoed around the marble-framed foyer, so Henry knew she was home. In moments, she appeared at the earl's door and sat down in the chair across from him. "As a Lord, can you introduce legislation in Parliament to change the property laws governed by marriage?"

Removing his spectacles, Henry leaned back in his chair. "Were you daydreaming when Laurence instructed you on the processes of Parliament?"

"I didn't think I'd need to master the minutiae of legislation."

"And now you do?"

"I will if I must, but I thought you would know."

"Most legislation is introduced by the government, meaning the Prime Minister. A private member's bill can be introduced in either House, but, as you know, I attend only when absolutely required, so I have neither a deep sense of the place nor relationships with people who do. Not to mention the fact that changing the laws of property governed by marriage would be a major undertaking requiring massive public support. It's not realistic."

"Maybe your Nemesis could do it. You said he manipulates politicians."

"You're not listening to me. Such legislation is not remotely possible. Even if it were, I would never deal with Drummond. The man is a cur, a scandalous threat to the rule of law, and utterly devoid of decency. Merely asking for his help would compromise your future."

Bri tilted her head and stared at her father. "Your distaste for the man you call 'The Nemesis' predates his interest in Charlotte. Why won't you tell me what it is?"

"Perhaps I will someday, but it is best that you do not know. And to temper your curiosity, he has no compromising information on me. Just the opposite. But I withhold that secret to protect others."

"What has prompted this interest in the law? Your Marriage Settlement?" He watched her nod. "I suppose I should have thought of it long ago from your perspective. Jane had wealth, I had wealth—it didn't seem relevant to us. And now, with Ian as the presumptive earl, I should consider all the potential legal and inheritance issues."

"Grandmother and I had lunch with Lord Judge Todd-Hatton. He is researching whether I should be domiciled at our Scottish estate and if Edward and I should marry in Scotland."

Henry shrugged. "We could still have a reception at the new center hall at Ravenshire Castle. I defer to your choice, but I tend to believe your maneuverability will be limited."

"I will evaluate all the potential paths."

"I know you will. Do what you always do—analyze your options and make an informed decision."

***

Wednesday, June 5, 1811 – Ravenshire Castle
Gio

Gio sketched different views of the castle, with an eye toward the architectural details. "That cherub *does* look like me."

"I advised the sculptor." Gwyneth dipped her brush in water, then dabbed at the watercolor tiles, laying down light sketches on studies to use for her final painting.

Gio finished a sketch, stood and stretched. "Let's move over to the old tower."

The footman standing behind them picked up the chairs, easels and satchels.

"When I was young, I had to do all that myself," Gio observed. "I *do* appreciate a life of privilege."

"You've earned it."

The dwarf stopped in his tracks and stared at his former art student. "I don't have a retort for that."

Gwyneth rubbed her hand on his cheek. "You are irascible and imperious, but you almost always speak the truth. As do I." She glanced toward the old tower. "Let me show you the mosaic floor again."

Walking inside the circular structure, Gwyneth swept away dirt and dust to reveal the ancient Roman-style tiled floor.

Gio knelt down. "The colors are still vibrant. Incredible."

"The sun beams in only from the arrow slits between the stones."

"Show me where you found the treasure."

***

Wednesday, June 5, 1811 – Pytchley Manor
Oliver

Oliver finished up a meeting with the estate manager, a function he had handled for his father for several years.

As heir to the dukedom, the Pytchley estates consumed at least one day a week of his time. His family title, Earl of Darlemont, conferred by a long-ago marriage of one of the Craigfell clan. That small, seaside estate was in the far south of England. As a young boy, Oliver had loved it. His older brother, Vincent, was slated to be duke under the laws of primogeniture, so Pytchley would have been Vincent's domain and Darlemont Oliver's. Views of the sea, small flat fields of wheat, hilly pastures for grazing sheep, and a lovely, if not grand, home at its center beckoned, but he rarely visited. *I must plan a fortnight's sojourn soon.*

In the midst of his preparations to return to London, Oliver realized he had nothing of import awaiting his attention there. *I could go to Ravenshire for the day.* He notified his driver to drive his loaded carriage to Ravenshire for the trip back to London. "I'll ride over. Tell the stable master to saddle up the new Arabian, Scheherazade. I'll take her back to London with me."

***

Ian

Ian awoke from his nap, and saw that Lilyanne was asleep too. He quietly got out of bed, grabbed a satchel that looked like a saddle bag, and tiptoed out of the room. After silently closing the door behind him, he went downstairs and through the kitchen.

Sallie was sitting at her desk in the hours between mid-day meal and tea, making lists for the grocer and butcher. "Awake, are we, Master Ian?"

The boy nodded. "Where's Gio?"

"The artist or the pony?"

Ian giggled. "The artist."

"He's out by the castle with your Aunt Gwyneth." She stood, walked over to the back kitchen door, and opened it for him. "See? They're over by the Old Tower."

"I see them!"

"Tell your aunt that I'm sending over some lemonade and biscuits."

Nodding, Ian rushed over to the Old Tower.

Ian stopped by the entrance to catch his breath and overheard Gio say, "Show me where you found the treasure."

"What treasure?"

Gwyneth and Gio turned to see Ian.

"That's a long story. Your aunt found something here when she was a little older than you are now." Gio looked at Ian's saddle bag. "You brought the paints?"

The boy put it on the exposed mosaic floor. "You promised to teach me art."

"So I did. Now, Gwyneth, where was the treasure?"

"Pirate treasure?" Ian's eyes sparkled.

"Not exactly." Gwyneth felt along the stones near the spiraling tower staircase to the upper level. "I used to go up to the top to read and imagine I was a princess in a tower." A stone moved, and she pulled it out. "Here is where I found it."

Ian edged closer and stood on his tiptoes to peer inside. "Nothing's there."

"Inside this empty space, I found a rolled piece of parchment, like a diary, and a leather pouch with a knotted string of rare pearls and a cache of sapphires. Runes and other strange writings on that parchment were deciphered by a don at Merton College, Oxford."

With a wrinkled brow, Ian squinted in puzzlement.

"Pearls and sapphires are jewels, and the rest is just a story about the people who used to live in this castle." Gwyneth saw the boy's disappointment. "Your father found a dagger with a jeweled hilt hidden behind another stone. And a little faerie told me there might be more hidden here. Perhaps you'll find more hidden treasure if you look."

"But not now. I see lemonade is coming!" Gio walked over to the footman and gave each a glass. "To Ian's search for treasure!"

"What treasure are we seeking?"

They turned to see Oliver under the arched entrance. He took the extra glass of lemonade and held it up to the others, clinking each in turn.

They all echoed, "To Ian's search for treasure!"

CHAPTER SEVENTEEN

Wednesday, June 12, 1811 – Dr. St. Cloud's Veterinary Care Clinic
Bri

D r. St. Cloud waved Bri into the clinic and led her to his office. He collapsed into his chair. "To what do I owe your visit?"

"I've just come from lunch with Grandmother, and thought I'd stop by. Edward and I were talking this morning about establishing a board of trustees to watch over Wyndward Investments in our absence, and I had a couple of ideas I wanted to discuss with you."

"I think Carolyn can handle routine treatment in my absence, but an emergency surgery, which happened today, is beyond her current skill level. Brian is merely a stocking clerk and occasional groomer. I don't see how I can leave for three weeks, longer if the winds are weak."

"I may have a solution for you. We have a new vet at Ravenshire, who cares for large and small farm animals. He came back with us from Ireland. I'd like you to meet him. Perhaps he could be a resource for Carolyn while you are gone."

The vet leaned forward. "I've thought about developing some kind of cooperative venture, but there are few vets in the city."

"Have you thought of training assistants who might learn basic animal care methods, as apprentices?"

"You mean as a formal endeavor?"

Bri nodded.

"Not really, but it strikes me as a practical approach if we grow as you envision."

"If we plan to expand your food preparation to a warehouse and free up more clinic space, we have to consider growth and additional staff to operate efficiently."

"That sounds—"

A high-pitched barking interrupted their conversation.

Carolyn came out of the animal care area to find Dr. St. Cloud. "I can't calm down the Yorkshire Terrier who was dropped off this morning. The note said his owner died. He's probably missing his normal environment."

Dr. St. Cloud rose to his feet. "Let me go check."

Bri waited a few minutes, until the vet came back, holding the dog, now docile. "How did you manage to quiet him?"

"He wanted to be held. Dogs become attached to their owners. I must find a new home for him soon. He's healthy, probably about two years old."

"May I hold him?"

"Of course. Let's see how he reacts."

After a whimper, the dog settled into Bri's arms. "I know just the person to adopt this social creature, but I'd like it to be a surprise for him."

"Edward?"

Bri shook her head. "Gio."

"I'll have Carolyn prepare our standard adoption kit—a bed, a leash, water and food dishes, and an assortment of food."

"Perfect." Looking into the dog's eyes, she said, "You'll have a home soon." Glancing back at the doctor, she asked, "How is Clarissa feeling?"

"The sickness is subsiding. She's looking forward to our trip. We're sorry that we'll miss seeing Africa with her cousin Hanforth, but that long a journey will have to be another time."

"I'm disappointed too. I so wanted to see Nambotha's homeland. The stories he's told me of the animals and their habitats sound ethereal."

"A far off look is on your face. What are you thinking?"

"When my father and aunt were children, a menagerie existed at Ravenshire. Aunt Gwyneth painted a series of watercolors of the wild animals. She kept them in a portfolio, in the form of an alphabet book, and I'd always ask her to read it to me when I stayed over at her house.

"In any case, the duke once visited for a hunt with my grandfather and became enthralled by the animals. I am told that Lady Jane, my mother, especially loved the birds. After years of discussion, my grandfather offered the entire menagerie to the duke after Aunt Gwyneth left for boarding school in England, and it was installed at Pytchley."

"The Pytchley Menagerie was once the holding of your family? I've heard it's an astonishing collection of wildlife on a savannah-like plain. It's almost as if they are roaming free, although there are barriers and fences."

"Yes. The duke is one of few who have the vast area needed for the wide variety of animals in the menagerie and the fortune to maintain it. We generally visit once a season. Many of the animals came originally from Africa and have reproduced and thrived here. I'm certain you'd enjoy it." Bri smiled. "It would be an ideal location for Viscount Hanforth's farewell dinner!"

"That's an inspired idea."

"We could tour the menagerie and have the dinner in the greenhouse near the reflecting pool."

The veterinarian agreed. "Observing wild animals roaming free would be gratifying, but I could learn more by examining them up close."

"Just not too close." Bri laughed. "Let's make sure you keep your head."

***

Wednesday, June 12, 1811 – Atelier Maximilian
Bri

Bri guessed she'd find Gio in his back studio painting in the late afternoon light. Because the dog was so small, she was able to cover him in a basket with a blanket.

The staff knew Bri and greeted her warmly. She made her way through the hallway. Classrooms flanked each side, and then opened into a broad back area where several studios were available for students as well as established artists.

Gio's space was the largest with the best view. Bri caught him in mid-brushstroke, and didn't want to startle him.

Without turning, he said, "You have a distinctive footfall, Bri." He dabbed another bit of paint on the canvas, and then turned to see her. "To what do I owe this visit?" He raised his brow. "Is that a basket of wine?"

"Not exactly." She lifted the blanket to reveal the Yorkie. "I thought you might like a companion."

Gio tilted his head and the dog tilted its head as if mirroring the dwarf's move. He walked over and petted the dog.

The dog licked him and Gio laughed.

Bri sighed with relief. "He was left on Dr. St. Cloud's doorstep last night. Apparently, he cried all night because he doesn't like cages."

"Who does?" Gio lifted the dog up to look him directly in the eyes. "You will never see a cage again, Dog."

" 'Dog?' That's the best you can do?"

"He will show me who he is. The choosing of a name is a process, like a painting."

***

Monday, June 24, 1811 – Aboard *Nut's Night Sky*
Blackburn as Lt. Roland

Blackburn dined with the captain each night and skillfully questioned him, gaining useful intelligence to employ when he retook the helm of his operations.

One evening, as the flickering candlelight reflected off the diamond-paned, multi-colored leaded glass at the back of the ship where the captain's quarters were located, the captain made an apparently offhand remark. "Your eyes are an unusual color of blue, nearly the turquoise of the Caribbean Sea." The captain took a sip of wine. "Unforgettable in a brown-eyed land."

Nothing is offhand with this man. Ambition drives his every move. "And your point is?"

"The eye color gives you instant recognition as The Pharaoh's man."

So he asked around Oran and learned something about The Pharaoh's 'man' but has not revealed it until now. Clever and calculating.

"But—"

Blackburn interrupted the captain. "It gives me instant recognition as The Pharaoh's man." He emptied his glass of the remaining wine. "Shall I gouge them out?"

The captain flinched. "Of course not. But there is an apothecary in Alexandria I've heard of, a woman from Southeast Asia, who has unusual potions. Your unusual eyes, her unusual potions…this juxtaposition of the unusual has brought me a moment of insight."

Blackburn leaned back and swirled the wine in his glass without taking his eyes off the captain. "Go on."

"It is said…that she has potions and poisons for all purposes. A crewman once told me she gave him a potion to change his eye color from green to brown. With time, on a long voyage, I saw his eyes change from brown back to green. He needed the potion only for a short time to evade those who wanted him dead. He became just another man with brown eyes, not the one they were looking for."

"How much for her location?"

"*Gratis.* Just a good word about me to The Pharaoh. Perhaps I could carry some of his cargo from time to time."

"I can suggest that."

"Then we have an understanding?"

Blackburn nodded.

The captain pulled out some writing paper, dipped his quill in the inkwell, wrote down an address, blew on it to dry the ink, folded the paper, and handed it to the man who sat before him, not knowing he was speaking to The Pharaoh himself. "With my compliments to your master."

***

Tuesday, June 25, 1811 - Riding along Rotten Row
Bri

Bri raced her uncle Oliver's latest acquisition from Tattersalls, Scheherazade, a blue-black filly who seemed to fly with stride-lengths Bri had never seen before. Gazelle struggled to keep up, but her lineage was no match for the bloodline of the racer.

When Bri caught up to Oliver, she was out of breath. "Impressive runner you've acquired. What black magic have you worked on her?"

Oliver leaned over to pat the horse's neck. "She is a natural. I was lucky—Jean-Louis and Orion were otherwise engaged during the last auction."

"So you had an unfair advantage."

"I paid a very high price and no other bidders dared test my resolve."

"I've been thinking about your advice over the last month on the nature of men, Marriage Settlements and the stream of life. I'll have more time to think while we are sailing in the Azores. I look forward to continuing our discussions when I return. It's easier to talk with you about these subjects than Father or Edward."

"That's the nice thing about uncles. We have a more removed perspective on things. More rational, less emotional." Oliver smiled. "Game for another race?"

***

Tuesday, June 25, 1811 – James & Co., Bankers
Edward

As the date neared for their voyage to the Azores, Edward met with bank associates to inform them of the needs of clients they might have to service in his absence. He knocked on Eli's door.

His brother-in-law looked up from his work. "Edward, come in." He pushed aside his papers and took out some clean sheets of parchment. "Do you have any particular requests of me while you are on your journey?"

Edward closed the door. "Father knows what I am about to tell you, but no one else." Edward took a seat opposite his brother-in-law. "Bri has been acting as Lord Ravenshire's man-of-affairs for over two years."

Eli sat back in his chair, a wry grin animating his face. "I'm not surprised. During the time you were in the Far East, her knack for identifying the key point of any analysis—on any subject—struck me as unusually insightful. No banal dinner conversation from Lady Gabriella. In fact, she eviscerated several would-be Society beaux."

He shook his head in amusement. "The two of you must have some spirited disagreements."

Edward leaned back in his chair. "Too true. Sometimes that woman is so exasperating—"

"That is the nature of marriage. Annabelle and I erupted in spurts of anger in the early years. No subject was too insignificant to spark an argument."

"I remember. When I returned, you both seemed different, more accepting of each other's points of view."

Eli scoffed. He leaned forward and raised his eyebrows. "My dear brother-in-law, you will find all men in happy marriages will give you the same advice: Agree with your wife."

Taken aback, Edward's face clouded. "You mean I should dissemble for comity's sake?"

"Indeed. For good measure, remind her that she once suggested your current point of contention—whether she did or not—in an earlier 'discussion.' Without guile, ask her why she's changed her mind. That often brings concession." Eli sat back. "You'll get the hang of it."

"I doubt it. We argue, but Bri and I come to agreement in time."

"How much time?"

Edward shrugged. "I am no actor. She knows how I think. She'd be onto my deception. No." He shook his head. "With Bri, pretending to agree with her when I did not would backfire as fast as an improperly loaded cannon."

"Ha! You would be obliterated." Eli picked up his quill and twirled it in his fingers. "Be more subtle, Edward. Say that you understand her point of view, but if she could shift it a bit, perhaps she could see yours. Just as you guide a recalcitrant client to the appropriate conclusion, you mold the client's perception."

"Perhaps you should attempt to mold Bri's perception. You can relay the result to me from an infirmary."

Eli threw up his hands. "I surrender! No more advice from me."

"Actually, that is exactly what I need from you." Edward explained the principles of Wyndward Investments. He handed a file to Eli, which detailed the principals of each venture, the parameters of each investment, and instructions as to how to fund any needs that arose during his absence.

"This is intriguing. I might have some clients who could provide support, quarters or products. While you're gone, I'll prepare proposals for you and Bri to consider."

"I'll watch you mold her perception."

"Maybe I won't have to. Maybe she'll agree with me."

Edward smiled. "That should be interesting to watch." He rose to his feet. "I have to pick up some final items for the sailing. We depart on July 2nd."

Eli stood and extended his hand. "Have a good trip. Accompanying another couple on their honeymoon is a novel escapade."

"Gwyneth and Gio will be chaperones."

"Chaperones can be evaded."

"I will be sharing a cabin with Gio. He misses nothing. And Jean-Louis is sailing with us."

"Ah." Eli raised his eyebrows. "The Frenchman will brook no untoward behavior. Dally at your peril."

***

Thursday, June 27, 1811 – Drea & Co. Tailors, Ravenshire Village
Miss Drea

Valerie Drea, scion of a long line of tailors, stood to address a group of ten seamstresses sitting at worktables in the tailoring shop known as Drea's. A woman of five-and-thirty, Valerie had more than an eye for style and a deft hand at fashioning garments. She understood her customers, both the Wyndward family and the local townsfolk. For decades, her family's shop had made the livery for the Wyndward staff at Ravenshire as well as for their other estates. When Bri was a child, Valerie had made her clothes, as her mother had done for Lady Jane and Lady Gwyneth.

Every year, Bri made it a point to order several items from Valerie and to wear them to local functions. Valerie knew that Lady Gabriella had ball gowns and other clothing made in London, but her ladyship made it a point to support local businesses in Ravenshire village. Now that Lady Wyndward had returned from the dead, as it were, she would be a consistent client again.

The sandy-haired owner waited for silence, and then began her introduction. "Lady Gabriella and Lady Wyndward will be here shortly, delivering the materials for the smock prizes in the women's footraces at the Ravenshire Summerfest, including the linen for the drawers all the runners *must* wear to participate. We have the patterns here—" She turned her head, hearing horses outside.

The doorbell rang and Lady Gabriella entered, followed by Lady Wyndward and footmen carrying bundles.

"Good afternoon, Miss Drea." Bri waited while the footmen placed the bundles on the table and left the shop. "I'm sure you and your staff will be as delighted as I am to see Lady Wyndward again after her harrowing escape. None of us in the family knew her fate until her recent return. Jean-Louis spirited her away to Ireland for her protection from the itinerant brigands who killed my Uncle Rychard. She will explain the smocks for this year."

Aelwyn smiled. "It's wonderful to see you all again."

Bri unwrapped the bundles while Aelwyn spoke.

"We have white linen and a multicolor assortment of silk ribbons along with silk thread for embroidery, silk scarves and linen handkerchiefs with edges rolled, ready for embellishment. The races will have a winner's smock for runners in four age ranges: under ten, ten to fifteen, sixteen to twenty, and one for widows of any age. In addition, this year, in celebration of my return, we are including extra yardage so that each of you may fashion a separate smock for yourself and decorate it to your own preferences."

Gasps and murmurs came from the group. Their eyes lit up and one "Thank you" after another echoed around the room.

"For each age-limited race, the first prize will be the smock, second prize the scarf, and third prize the handkerchief, so four of each will be needed."

Bri moved forward. "And, as I mandated several years ago, all runners must wear drawers. Based on past races, and the addition of a castle tour this year, we are estimating twice as many entrants as last year. So forty sets of drawers will be needed. As with the smocks, there is extra fabric for your own use."

A woman who had recently moved to Ravenshire from the far north appeared confused. "How can the foot-racers carry sets of wood drawers?"

The others laughed.

Valerie raised her hand to signal that they stop. "Evelyn is new to our village. Her question is not unusual outside of Ravenshire." She turned to their new neighbor. "Drawers are a form of women's undergarment."

Evelyn blushed.

Bri tilted her head and shrugged. "This is a new idea, Evelyn. The garments are called drawers because the wearer draws them up to her waist one leg at a time, and then ties the two leg coverings together in front and back."

Evelyn grasped the point. "So if a foot-racer falls, the men won't see her private parts."

"Precisely," said Bri. "No point in encouraging bawdy behavior."

"There's enough of that without encouragement," agreed another seamstress.

"My hope is that more women will want drawers and this demand will increase your shop's offerings. When the castle is finished, Ravenshire will grow and so will opportunities for all the villagers." Bri looked at Aelwyn, but she had nothing to add. "At Summerfest, Lady Wyndward and I will both be wearing dresses designed by Miss Drea. We hope to see you all there!"

Bri and Aelwyn went around the room and shook hands with each seamstress before leaving.

In the carriage on way back to Ravenshire, Aelwyn glanced at Bri. "Do you think all women will be wearing drawers someday? The ties can be constricting. I must confess that I find them uncomfortable."

"I agree," Bri said, "The ties can be too tight or loosen over the course of the day. You've given me an idea. I'm going to ask the French dressmaker I told you about, Mlle. Bellerobe, what improvements to drawers she might recommend."

"When you get back from the Azores, we'll have about three weeks until Summerfest. We should go over the prizes for the various contests now so that we have time to make adjustments after you return in case something is not ready."

Bri nodded. "Months ago, I commissioned the rifles, the throwing knives, the bows and arrows, carved chess sets, and so on. I have some ideas for the other races and contests to discuss when we get home." She sat back in the carriage. "With the expected increase in attendance, I hope our preparations are adequate. Do you think we should require tickets next year? The main part of the castle will be completed and should draw a larger crowd."

"I see no other way to be certain we have enough food and drink, seating, shelter and contests."

"Perhaps I should have thought of it for this year, recognizing that with the construction taking shape, the rising castle would inspire curiosity." Bri sighed. "I'm so glad you're back, Aelwyn. I don't know how I thought I could do so much by myself."

"Our responsibilities here will increase as the castle draws crowds."

Nodding, Bri continued, "We must change to meet new challenges. While we have performed all tasks of running Ravenshire up to now, perhaps specialization by some assistants to particular functions would make the direction of the estate more efficient."

"Exactly what I was thinking. The castle expansion will change everything. Guests, tours, and special events." Her voice was tinged with regret. "Ravenshire will no longer be simply a home."

CHAPTER EIGHTEEN

Saturday, June 29, 1811 – The Hanforth Mansion
Edward

After greeting the guests, Count von Dusterberg bid a pleasant evening to the young people his daughter had invited to dinner. As he took his leave, he kissed Lady Clarissa goodbye. "Enjoy your meal. I am dining with Gio, Charlotte and Lady Gwyneth tonight."

The dinner party, hosted by Clarissa and Dr. St. Cloud, took place before their scheduled departure on a delayed honeymoon. The guests included Hanforth and Lady Clemmie, Bri and Edward, Baron Beauchamp and Lady Penelope, Vaux, Banfield, Lord Lt. Thornton, Lady Melanie, Lady Patricia and Lady Marianna.

During soup and the main courses, the diners talked to the guests seated next to them. It wasn't until the dinner plates were cleared that the entire table engaged in conversation as a group.

Clarissa sighed. "Violetta Vinci will sing no more. The new singers are triumphant in the roles we debuted. Our runs as The Princess and The Wizard will be forgotten."

"Never among the cognoscenti." Edward raised his glass of Riesling. "To the eternal memory of Violetta Vinci and Drew Wood!"

"Here! Here!" The guests drank their toasts.

Turning to Hanforth, Clarissa said, "Cousin, I'm sorry we won't be able to travel with you to East Africa. I was so looking forward to it."

"So was I, but Africa is a wild, tempestuous and unconquered world. In your condition, it would be too difficult to traverse the terrain." Hanforth glanced at Clemmie. "Maybe in a few years we will have established a suitable camp."

"We?" Edward leaned forward. "Are *you* still going, Lady Clemmie?"

She nodded. "My parents are accompanying us, so there will be no impropriety."

Edward shook his head. "Impropriety is not my concern. Your safety is."

Hanforth sat back in his chair, with an approving sideways glance at Lady Clemmie. "It may interest you to know that Lady Clemmie is a crack shot with a fowling piece."

"Forgive me," Banfield interrupted, "but of what use is a fowling piece against a charging elephant or pouncing tiger?"

Vaux nodded. "I must echo my friend. Danger lurks in every direction."

"Tigers roam Asia, not Africa, but I get your meaning. We will have Maasai guides, who throw spears like Jean-Louis is rumored to flick a knife. And we'll have Lord Lt. Thornton with us. We'll survive."

Lady Clemmie agreed. "We'll more than survive. We'll thrive."

Lord Lt. Thornton swirled the wine in his glass as he spoke. "I'm more concerned about my sister being left alone to manage the ways of the *ton* as well as our estates in my absence. James, I hope I can rely on you to provide her with advice and counsel."

"I will be honored to be at your service." Edward glanced at Lady Melanie. *I wonder how Lady Melanie likes being dismissed as incapable in front of her friends.* He caught himself. *I never would have given his comment a second thought before I met Bri.*

The servants brought dessert. A bowl of iced cream churned with vanilla bean, courtesy of Wyndward Trading's spice trade, was placed in front of each guest. Wolfberger returned with a crystal pitcher filled with syrup and poured it over each mound of ice cream. " 'Tis a concoction of sugar, cream and cocoa simmered over a low flame," he explained. A dollop of whipped cream was spooned on top of the dripping syrup after each plate was served.

Vaux closed his eyes as he savored the delicacy. "Isn't chocolate from Africa?"

Bri shook her head. "Vanilla beans, yes. Chocolate, no. We import it from South America. The cacao beans grow on trees. 'Food of the gods,' they call it."

Lady Patricia changed the subject. "Tell me, Dr. St. Cloud, what is the origin of your name? There are no saints with that name, as I recall, and it doesn't sound particularly French."

" 'Tis a fanciful story, perhaps, but I am told there are papers somewhere in France documenting it. The only remaining male relative besides my father lost his head on the guillotine during the French Revolution, and I will never go back, so it matters little to me. In terms of history, the gardens of Louis XIV's brother, Philippe, Duc d'Orleans, were called Saint-Cloud, and a hamlet nearby carries the same name.

"There was a Saint Clodoald, son of a King of Orleans in the 500s, who gave his name to the area, which became corrupted in usage to Cloud from Clodoald over time. The Anglican Church does not recognize Clodoald's sainthood. At some point in the last thousand-plus years, some ancient ancestor of mine revived the gardens and was named comte of the area."

Vaux tilted his head toward the doctor. "I'd feel a bit intimidated to carry the name of a saint."

"The Pope would have reclaimed it from you, if he had any clout in England." Banfield raised his glass. "To the non-Saint Vaux. May he inspire us all to lives of piety."

"Unlikely." Edward raised his glass and led the others in the toast. "To non-Saint Vaux!"

Lady Patricia joined the others in the toast, and then continued her questioning of Dr. St. Cloud. "What kind of dog do *you* have, Doctor?"

"None. We have a cat, at present. The count's hunting dog died a couple of years ago. We may consider a dog. I hesitate to breed animals when people are abandoning pets so frequently."

Clarissa leaned forward. "Every morning, there is at least one animal on the doorstep of the shop. He finds them shivering, often soaked from rain, near-starving. It would break your heart to see them."

Bri nodded. "Dr. St. Cloud provides nurture and nourishment for abandoned pets, and finds suitable homes for adoptions."

Lady Marianna's face contorted. "'Suitable'? Like baby adoptions? Do you actually investigate people?"

"Not usually. It's instinct. If I sense a problem, I don't permit the animal to leave my care."

Lady Patricia took a spoonful of ice cream. "I think I would like a cat or small dog. I need some company. I'll come by your shop when you return from the Azores."

***

Bri

I never thought of Lady Patricia as interested in animals. She must be lonely. Bri assumed Lady Patricia's suspected secret lover had disappeared because she flattered the count after their initial introduction and seemed disappointed that he wasn't staying for dinner. For his part, the count had fixed his attention on Lady Patricia's ample cleavage. The thought of Lady Patricia as Clarissa's stepmother might not be improbable. *Would Clarissa accept Lady Patricia as her stepmother? At least she doesn't have to worry about losing her home like Grandmother.*

When Clarissa and Lord Hanforth's grandfather decided to build a new house, where Hanforth's parents now lived, he'd given the mansion they were in tonight to his daughter, to be passed on to the eldest daughter through an unusual legal trust. Bri made a mental note to discuss with Clarissa any similar provisions she might incorporate in her Marriage Settlement.

Banfield took another sip of wine. "I too would like a dog or cat. I'll come by after your honeymoon too."

Bri finished her dessert and sat back in her chair. "That was delicious. Let's talk about our sailing to the Azores."

Lady Penelope sat forward. "We've been talking about where to go next spring for our honeymoon. We'll be interested in hearing about your trip."

Baron Beauchamp reached over and squeezed his fiancée's hand. "Or maybe we'll go visit Hanforth and Lady Clemmie." He glanced at Hanforth. "Build us a lodge of twigs and mud and we'll live as barefoot natives."

The look of shock and horror on Lady Penelope's face sparked laughter around the table.

"By the time you arrive, a year or more from now, perhaps Hanforth will have proper accommodations for you. But if not, the experience will still be incomparable." Bri raised her glass. "To the wild savannah of East Africa!"

The group clinked glasses and echoed her toast.

The future baroness shrugged her shoulders. "Adventure awaits in all directions."

"Don't worry, darling." The baron smiled at his fiancée. "We'll go wherever *you* want to go." Turning toward Clarissa, he said, "Now tell us about the Azores. I've heard the weather is sunny and pleasant most of the time."

Clarissa smiled. "Gio thinks the Azores are the remnants of Atlantis. He's enamored of the legend."

"Is there evidence?" Lord Lt. Thornton leaned forward. "I'm skeptical of legend."

"We'll see what we find." Edward took a sip of wine.

"I say, James. You're going on a honeymoon to celebrate your engagement. How did you talk the earl into that?" Vaux twirled his wine glass as he spoke.

"Gio and Lady Gwyneth are accompanying us as chaperones. And Jean-Louis."

Hanforth tilted his head. "Watch out, James. Speaking of legend, there are many around Jean-Louis. Rumor is the Frenchman killed a polar bear with his bare hands. He'd make quick work of you."

Bri shook her head. "Jean-Louis had a knife, but the kill is legendary in Canada. The animal weighed over a thousand pounds. Edward will be sharing a cabin under the watchful eye of Gio."

"Gio?" Vaux laughed. "Will James return as a slave to wine, an artist, or a raconteur of tall tales?"

Edward shrugged. "Who knows? Adventure awaits."

***

Tuesday, July 2, 1811 – Aboard *Nut's Night Sky*
Blackburn as Lt. Roland

More than two months of sailing allowed Blackburn to rest and heal. In the final two weeks on the ship, he disguised himself as a crewman during the day, worked the decks and sails to rebuild his strength, and reverted to his role as Lt. Roland in the evening. *Weakness makes men vulnerable. I must exude vigor when I return.*

"You look hale and hearty." The captain had provided Blackburn with appropriate clothing for his disembarkation.

"My robust state of health is thanks to your cuisine, medicinal stores, and discretion. Use the code name Seagull when you contact me at this address." Blackburn handed the captain a piece of paper with instructions. "The Pharaoh's men will deliver the cargo we discussed before you sail on Wednesday. Do not identify yourself as Seagull to them—use it only on written communications to The Pharaoh or me. To them, you are simply a ship's captain with a contract to deliver cargo. They will present the normal bills of lading for you to sign. When you land in Marseille, you will be paid and more cargo will be delivered. Your contact there will be listed on the bill of lading."

"You are a man of honor."

Blackburn pulled an envelope from his jacket. "Payment for my accommodations, as promised."

The captain opened the envelope and thumbed through the currency. "This is more than I expected."

"Good. I like to surprise people who help me. I can be generous or vengeful—it's up to you."

"Understood. I am at your service."

"As my brother would say, "Excellent." Blackburn smiled at the irony of his reply. *My brother hasn't heard the last of me yet. My task is not finished.*

***

Tuesday, July 2, 1811 – Aboard *Taygete's Wynd*
Jean-Louis

Under the direction of Jean-Louis, crewmen pushed wagons carrying the final load of provisions onto the ship. He and Captain Treadway went over the final checklists. "Dana Kelley will serve as Lady's maid to the ladies and Quincy Shore will serve as valet to the gentlemen."

The captain shook his head. "This is primarily a cargo ship with a few cabins. The ship's quarters are at capacity. We have hung a curtain in the cabin that the maid and the valet must share, but I cannot promise that she will emerge with her virtue intact."

The Frenchman didn't take his eyes off his list as he spoke. "*I* can. The valet has been made aware of the consequences should he violate her."

"I wouldn't want to cross *you*, Jean-Louis."

Jean-Louis raised his eyes to meet the captain's. "Prudent." He walked to the edge of the deck and scanned the docks. "Our passengers are here."

The captain nodded. "I'll see to the final preparations for departure. My first officer, Lt. Gibson, will direct the travelers to their cabins."

The first night onboard ship, Captain Treadway and Lt. Gibson welcomed the passengers to dinner in the captain's quarters. It was crowded, but wine flowed freely. Chérie, Hector, Spotty and Gio's "Dog," lay under the table, hoping to catch scraps. The ship's cats, Stem and Stern, curled on the bookshelves above, too high for the dogs to reach them.

Gio took a swig of his wine. "My recollection of the Greek goddesses has faded. Bri, who was Taygete?"

"If Father were here, he would tell you that she is one of the seven sisters, known as The Pleiades. Taygete is a mountain nymph."

" 'Is'?" Gio raised one bushy eyebrow.

Gwyneth smiled. "You know Henry. His theory is that the Greek gods and goddesses really are immortal and invisibly walk among us."

The dwarf shrugged. "One has to be very, very rich to advance such a theory and not be committed to Bedlam."

***

Tuesday, July 2, 1811 – Baroness Glasspool's Mansion
Henry

After sending Bri, Jean-Louis and the rest of the travelers off to the Azores in the morning, Henry rode Hermès through the streets of London's Mayfair section later that afternoon. He guided the horse through a back alley to the stables across from Charlotte's home. Hector ran next to them. After Henry dismounted, Charlotte's stable master took the horse's reins.

Climbing the steps up to the servants' entry, the earl and his dog found the butler holding the door. "Good evening, Lord Ravenshire." *Morgan can't hide his disdain for me. But Charlotte deserves his loyalty.*

Morgan led the earl into the parlor. "Please wait here for the baroness." He glanced at the dog. "Will your dog require food?"

Charlotte's voice answered from a distance. "Morgan, Dominique set aside a juicy bone for Hector." At the sound of the word 'bone,' Hector jumped up and paced in a circle. Charlotte came down the curved stairwell.

Henry reached for Charlotte's hands, raised them to her lips, and kissed them. "You look beautiful tonight. Your hair is different. It's stunning."

"I went to Jane Anne's salon today and she suggested a softer, longer look with curls. I must admit, I didn't think you'd notice."

"A year ago, I might not have. I'm learning to observe more details. It's partly Bri's influence, partly Blackie's betrayal, and partly my late-in-life realization that assumptions are not facts." Hector rubbed his nose on Henry's leg. The earl petted the dog. "Lie down."

The dog obeyed.

Charlotte and Henry moved to the settee and sank down onto the cushioned bench while the butler prepared their drinks.

Henry jumped when the cork popped on a bottle of Champagne. He looked stricken. "Have I forgotten an important occasion?"

"No. I thought it fitting to celebrate a new beginning. As friends."

Uncharacteristically, Henry's eyes misted. It took him a moment to compose himself. "I don't deserve it."

The butler could not suppress his scoff.

"You're right to hold me in disdain, Morgan. I have behaved in a selfish and insensitive manner."

"Morgan, despite the earl's remark, kindly refrain from grunting in disagreement with my guests."

"Forgive me, Baroness."

"Forgiven and forgotten."

After pouring the Champagne, the butler handed the glasses to them and exited without a sound, followed by Hector.

Charlotte raised her glass. "To our new beginning."

"Uncharted territory for both of us."

They clinked their glasses and drank to their unknown future.

CHAPTER NINETEEN

Wednesday, July 3, 1811 – Alexandria
Blackburn as The Pharaoh

Before Blackburn returned to his cohorts in the persona of The Pharaoh, he pursued one critical task. After settling into the inn that he'd purchased in secret years earlier, he ventured out to reacquaint himself with Alexandria.

Intrigued about the particular powers of potions described by the ship's captain, Blackburn walked through dusty alleys in the Asian sector in his disguise as a ship's mate. Reaching a red door with an arched entry in a nondescript building on a side alley near the harbor, he knocked in a pre-arranged pattern, as Captain Alif had described in his note.

A slave boy opened the door, causing the overhead bell to ring. The urchin scampered out of sight. Listening to the boy speak a language he only partially understood, the sound of a slap startled Blackburn. A high-pitched voice cursed the slave. Curse words were the first ones Blackburn learned in any language. A rough translation meant "An easy mark is here." *They are fooled by my western dress.* Blackburn smiled. *They do not know they are dealing with The Pharaoh.*

A petite Asian woman emerged from behind a curtain of colorful beads. Her hair was black, shiny as an English bulldog's nose.

Dyed with one of her potions, no doubt. She is of a certain age.

The apothecary spoke English with a French accent. "I am Mme. Anh. How may I be of service to you?"

177

A native of Indochina? "I come in search of a potion to change eye color from light to dark. Informers have told me of your offerings."

She eyed him warily.

He reached into his pocket and tossed a purse of silver on the counter. "This should more than suffice. My terms are non-negotiable. I require complete discretion. I work for The Pharaoh. You have no doubt heard of him."

"All in Alexandria have heard the legend of The Pharaoh."

"He is no legend. He rewards those who serve him. Generously. And he punishes those who thwart him. Mercilessly."

She bowed. "I am your servant."

"Your dialect has a familiar cadence. From the mountains of Viet Nam, I presume?"

Her eyes widened. "You are well traveled, sir."

"There is no continent I have not seen."

"What potions do you seek?"

"My eye color is too distinctive. I need brown eyes. I am told you have vials with a liquid that causes such a shift."

"A rare and unusual potion, to be sure. The change will manifest in about one week's time, but...."

"But what?"

"This potion must be formulated with extra potency for eyes of your coloration. It is not meant to force a permanent change."

"Tell me the risks."

"I, personally, have not seen what happens. I know only the warning I received I acquired the secrets of creating the formula from a now-dead practitioner. She had trained under an alchemist who possessed an ancient book of spells. Her warning to me was that the dye, if used for too long a period, might migrate from the eyes into the brain and affect judgment, perhaps leading to death."

Blackburn shrugged. "I might need it for a few months, but less than a year."

"My warning said no more than six months to be safe, but the usual portion would not be as strong as what I must give you."

"Understood." Blackburn then peppered her with questions about how much should be taken a day and how often, how long one vial would last, and how long it would take to reverse the process.

Satisfied with her answers, he asked the price. "I'll take a supply to last two years."

Mme. Anh stared at him and shook her head. "Did you not hear my words, sir? No more than six months, and less for your eye color."

"Tales of old women do not frighten me. But I don't intend to take it longer than a few months. I may need it again sometime in the future. As life is uncertain for all of us, I'd prefer to secure my supply now rather than coming back in a year only to learn that you had met an untimely end and your secrets had died with you."

She is intimidated Good.

"Your silver is adequate for a two year supply."

"From this day forward, you will sell this potion to no one else. The Pharaoh commands it."

"It shall be done." The apothecary left to prepare the vials.

While he waited for her to return, Blackburn examined the shop's other wares. In addition to the assortment of herbs, powders, plant specimens, and items one would expect in an apothecary shop, large jars displayed on one wall held dead rats floating in liquid. Various desert lizards darted around in cages, and a variety of snakes curled up in baskets. He sniffed. An odd fragrance diffused the space, partially disguising the putrid odors of rotting roots and other plant detritus. He ran his finger along a shelf. *No dust. She is meticulous.*

Mme. Anh returned with a tray holding two dozen clear vials. "As I explained, for the two weeks, three drops a day under your tongue. By the end of the first week, your eyes should be light brown, by the end of the second week, a medium brown. After that, take the drops every other day for the next month, until your eyes reach the shade of dark brown you desire. Twice a week thereafter should be sufficient. There are rarely any ill effects with short term use, but please return if you feel any lightheadedness. I have a counter-potion for that."

"Give it to me now. I want to be prepared for any such reaction in advance."

"A man who thinks ahead is wise."

"Cease the useless flattery and fetch the counter-potion."

The apothecary bowed, left and returned with a violet glass vial. "A mere drop should eliminate any vertigo."

Blackburn threw another purse of coins on the counter.

She bent over to look inside and raised her eyes to him without moving her head. "Gold?"

He nodded. "I have another request. The Pharaoh is often the subject of assassination plots, although he never sleeps in the same place two nights in succession." *It is best for all to assume it is so.* "Standard weapons offer little threat to him, but poison is an insidious arrow, piercing with invisible entry. I require an assortment of poisons with a listing of their visible effects and a supply of antidotes."

"Sir, there are an innumerable array of natural substances that can render one dead by a massive dose. I assume what you seek are rare, undetectable, droplets of *toxicums* and venom that bring instant death, or—," she leaned in to whisper, "—that *appear* to bring instant death."

Immediately grasping the usefulness of such a drug, to incapacitate another or create a *faux* impression of his own death, Blackburn smiled. "You do not disappoint."

"Would you care for some Turkish coffee while you wait? I have some freshly brewed in the back."

"Yes." *Does she think me a fool? Dare I drink it?*

Mme. Anh turned to the urchin. "Bring the pot of coffee, two cups and sugar."

Glancing at Blackburn, she raised her eyebrows. "I will drink from the same pot. I can see the doubt in your eyes." She shrugged. "Brown eyes hide doubt better than those of your azure hue."

She donned a pair of gloves of supple patterned leather. "The leather allows for dexterity, but these are of snakeskin, impervious to stray drops of poison." With a tilt of her head to the snake baskets, she added, "I skin them myself to fashion the gloves. I have a large pair I will give you. They were intended for my husband, who *thought* he had hidden a young mistress from me." She scoffed. "He disappeared and will never be found."

"The Pharaoh will be impressed with your ingenuity." *You will live only as long as it serves me to permit it.*

She left and returned with three vials in various shades of colored glass and an envelope. Anticipating his query, she said, "Easier to avoid a deadly choice." Holding up a yellow vial, she continued, "Three drops of this potion will render your prey unconscious for approximately two hours—more for a small woman, less for a large man. The heart and breathing will slow to the point that the victim will appear dead. Sometimes they awake in their coffins." She shrugged, replaced the yellow vial, and picked up a blue one. "This potion will paralyze limbs and prevent speech, but the victim will remain conscious."

Blackburn reached for the red vial.

"Stop!"

Eyes narrowing in anger, Blackburn's gaze bored into the petite apothecary. "I am the client. Do not presume to give me orders."

The herbalist rose to her full, although diminutive, height. "A warning is not an order. I presume nothing, Monsieur. This vial is deadly and should not be touched by a human hand. I have taken all precautions, but a mere drop of this on the skin means instant death. This vial is constructed to release only a drop at a time. You must wear gloves or use a rag to hold it."

"My apologies, dear Madame. You have prepared precisely what I requested. "And the green vial?"

"An antidote for the yellow and blue vials. But be warned—there is no antidote for the red vial. Death is certain."

"And the envelope?"

" It contains a harmless sleeping powder that will work for six to eight hours, depending on the size of the person. No lasting impact. A dash in a cup of tea or wine is all that is needed."

Each vial was sealed with a cork stopper. She placed the vials in a cushioned velvet-lined box, the red vial in its own compartment, and locked the box with a key, which dangled from a chain that she handed to Blackburn.

He put the chain around his neck and tucked it underneath his shirt. "You've given me an idea. Do you have tiny vials that could be worn on a chain like the key?"

The hint of a smile crossed the apothecary's lips. "You are a clever man. Such vials can be procured, but it will take me a week to have them blown. Only one glassblower can do such delicate work. When you return, I can examine your eyes to measure the effect of the color change." Mme. Anh knelt down and brought out a large leather bag, untied the flap, and filled it with the assortment of vials for eye color change, first wrapping them in cloth to prevent breakage. The box was similarly prepared. She handed him the bag and put the purses of silver and gold in her pockets. "I will be honored to serve you and The Pharaoh."

"One more thing. I require a dark hair dye, preferably one I can easily concoct while traveling. I am forced to shave daily because my beard has too much white in it. I prefer to look younger than I am."

Mme. Anh nodded. "Plants are safest." She assembled an assortment of twigs, roots, barks, leaves, flowers, berries and shells from baskets under her work table. "Boil a variation of two or three of these at a time in vinegar and black tea until the liquid boils away and the blend reaches the consistency of clotted cream. Apply the mixture to your beard at night for seven days. It will turn your beard the color you seek. Then you can apply it once a week. You can replace these ingredients with almost any plant material that is available. It is the combination of vinegar and tea that sets the dye."

"Give me enough for a year."

The apothecary raised her eyebrows. She left to assemble a canvas bag with a larger supply than she had initially provided. "Test a little at a time. Waste is your enemy." She reached under the counter. "The gloves are essential for your protection."

Blackburn tried on the gloves. As she promised, they were supple yet appeared impervious to penetration. He removed them and placed them in the leather bag.

"Never touch them if a drop remains. Dry them in the sun and the poison will evaporate."

"I rely on your discretion."

"You were never here."

"The urchin?"

"He knows nothing."

Blackburn gave the apothecary a slight nod of his head in farewell. "Until next week." He swept through the door quickly and vanished into the crowded, dusty streets of Alexandria, becoming invisible, surrounded by the cacophony of voices in the growing, vibrant city.

She knows my secret but is useful to me. For now.

***

Wednesday, July 3, 1811 – Deck of *Taygete's Wynd*
Edward

On their second day at sea, Edward roamed the deck, having mastered the roll of the ship, and spotted Gio sketching, Dog at his side. He peered over the dwarf's shoulder, examining the artist's rendition of the ship's elaborately entangled rigging.

Gio peppered the crew with questions about types of knots.

Edward listened, looked up at the rigging, and then back at Gio's sketch. "The intricacy of the rigging is as intriguing as it is complicated. So are the processes of adjusting the masts and sails. I should put my time to good use on this voyage, as you are."

"I am determined to accomplish something during my days at sea. *Tempus fugit*, James. Would you like to join me? I have more paper and charcoal. Do you intend to sketch?"

"Ha! I have no artistic ability. No, Gio, but thank you for the offer. I intend to learn how to climb the rigging and work the sails." Edward walked over to a crewman, who led him to the sail master.

After listening to the banker's request, the sail master shrugged. "Not in those clothes." He called over one of the crew. "Find Mr. James suitable attire to climb the rigging and bring it back here." As the sail master pointed and explained how they determined the proper angle to set the sails according to the direction of the wind and the course they had set, Edward became completely absorbed in his lesson.

***

Bri

During the days onboard, Bri walked the deck in the early mornings after breakfast, and then spent most of the day in the cabin she shared with Gwyneth, jotting down notes about ideas for Wyndward Investments, Wyndward Trading, and Ravenshire.

Her aunt left the cabin each morning, making her way to a table in the captain's library, where she opened a box with ink and quill, pulled paper from her portfolio, and wrote.

Taking periodic breaks from her work, Bri meandered around the deck to clear her head in the sea air. She mulled over ways to expand the enterprises funded by Wyndward Investments. On one of the early days at sea, she realized that her focus had shifted away from the trading company, and that she needed to allocate her time to handle both, as well as Ravenshire. But now that Aelwyn had returned, she could turn the estate duties over to her. *How could I have handled all my responsibilities plus marriage and children?* Even with Aelwyn at Ravenshire, and Charlotte and Eli forming the board of Wyndward Investments, when the earl left on another voyage, she would have to focus on the activities of Wyndward Trading until Sheldon fully took over what Blackie had directed. *I may have miscalculated the limits of my energy.*

"You're going around in circles, making me dizzy." Gio's voice brought her back to her surroundings.

"Gio, do you ever worry that you've set yourself too many tasks?"

"Of course! That's how you keep your mind fresh. Shifting focus, changing direction. Don't get set into patterns."

"As my grandmother would say, 'Becoming set in your ways is'—"

"Wait! Let me guess. 'Unimaginative, uninteresting, and uninformed.'"

"Good choices. However, I believe I have been unwise to take on so much."

"Not at all, my dear. What you are learning is that you need other people. You cannot do it all yourself. I myself was reluctant to release the atelier and school to Maximilian, but both are thriving. Now that I am not breathing down his neck, we get on better. I can play with paint, and he keeps the candles lit."

"What about Charles?"

"Charles is part artist, part musician. He has one foot in each world." Gio waved his hand in dismissal. "He must chart his own life, as do we all."

"You are a philosopher hiding in the guise of an artist."

"Aren't we all? We each live our own philosophy."

***

Dr. St. Cloud

Clarissa told her husband that she planned to search for books in the captain's library that sparked her interest.

While she was occupied, Dr. St. Cloud ambled along the deck and stopped to see Gio at work. "That rigging is so detailed on your drawing, and the sail appears to fully encompass the wind." He looked up to see if Gio was accurately sketching the rigging, and squinted to peer more closely. "Is that someone in the lookout up there? What is that called?"

"It's called the Main Top Castle." Gio looked up. "If I'm not mistaken, that's James."

"What? It can't be!" The vet looked up, and put his hand on his forehead to block the sun's glare from obstructing his vision.

"Oh, it is. He changed into a crewman's clothes and climbed up."

"Isn't that dangerous for an untrained man?"

Gio shrugged. "We'll soon find out."

***

Wednesday, July 3, 1811 – An Inn in Alexandria
Blackburn as The Pharaoh

Waiting for the eye-color potion to take effect, Blackburn tended to other tasks, continuing a trick he'd learned from crews onboard ship. He rubbed butter on his skin to attract the sun. He dared spend no more than two hours a day exposed to the sun to avoid a burn. Lying naked on the roof of the small hotel on a cushioned chaise covered by Turkish towels, the thick cotton absorbed the fat, but the towels became rancid after a couple of days and were discarded. Despite his fair coloring, Blackburn's skin bronzed a deeper shade each day from the base coloring he'd acquired while working on the ship's decks as he'd rebuilt his strength. As he sunned, he plotted. *My plan requires me to transform from European to Arab.*

Each day his scheme took on more detail. A master of disguise, he'd discovered on the ship that his natural beard would betray him. It was an auburn color, like Rychard and Bri's heads. With his dark hair, he'd not expected a red beard. He'd remained clean-shaven once he realized it, and lied to the apothecary about it being white, but now that he had the coloring concoction, he let his beard grow. The dye also left a residual stain on his skin. *So much the better. It will appear darker faster.*

Blackburn settled on two *faux* personas for Europe to augment his Arab feint. He sketched out his facial looks. In one, his hair was longer and brushed forward in the current British fashion but with a tightly cropped beard in the style of a foppish Croatian count. The second transformation would require a wig to show a fully grayed

185

head along with a false beard, trimmed to about two inches, in the costume of an Italian merchant. In case he needed more, a blond wig in the style of a foppish Dandy and his normal appearance, but with brown eyes, would provide additional options.

Detesting the current styling of men's hair, Blackburn preferred the close-cropped trim of a Roman soldier that had always defined his appearance. He knew from past visits to the main bazaar that a master wigmaker had a stall and others specialized in used European clothing. *Probably stolen from tourists' hotel rooms.* Dressing a season or two out of fashion would suit his purposes, presenting himself as a man not given to the latest fashion. Appearing a step or two behind the times would fool his victims into thinking he was a bit of a bumpkin.

The Pharaoh's enemies used many words to describe him. "Bumpkin" was not one of them.

***

Wednesday, July 3, 1811 – The Captain's Library
Clarissa

While reading a short treatise on the history of the Azores, Clarissa couldn't help but notice the comtesse writing what appeared to be a manuscript. Feeling awkward about interrupting her, Clarissa waited until the comtesse put down her quill and stretched her arms. The pile of papers next to her measured at least half an inch high.

"Do you write poetry?"

"Sometimes. I decided to set up a press at the museum. I am reviewing some children's books I wrote years ago, some faerie stories and a fanciful alphabet book. Gio convinced me I should publish my work—I've talked about doing it for years. Of course, he wants the museum to publish his autobiography."

Clarissa tilted her head. "Is it written?"

"He wants *me* to write it."

"But it's an autobiography, not a biography."

"Precisely. He expects to dictate it to me, as Cicero dictated to Tiro. No doubt Gio feels his works will have the same lasting power."

"Will his autobiography be written in Latin?"

Gwyneth laughed. "You have a wry sense of humor, my dear. I can see why you and Bri get along so well." She picked up her papers and put them in a portfolio. Leaving it on the table, she rose to her feet. "Let's get some fresh air."

They climbed a ladder to the sun and walked along the deck.

Gwyneth squinted. "What is Dr. St. Cloud looking at?"

Clarissa and the comtesse followed the doctor's gaze. "Someone is standing in that basket-like well. A lookout?"

Bri came along. "What is everyone looking at?"

Gio waved them over. "It's James. He wanted a high vantage point. I'm going up next."

Gwyneth stared at him. "You most certainly are *not*."

Evaluating the situation, anger flashed in Bri's eyes.

"Curb your tongue, Bri," advised Gio. "Don't embarrass a man in front of a crowd."

"I don't have to. He may accomplish that feat without intervention on my part. Climbing up is easier than climbing down. Ask any cat."

The ship's mouser looked up from his nap, followed the others' gaze, rolled over and went back to sleep.

***

Edward

The mate tilted his head at Edward. "I warned you that I must remain in the Main Top Castle until my watch ends and that climbing up is easier than climbing down."

Edward nodded. He had discounted the mate's advice as cautionary but obvious. Now, contemplating how to get a foothold without plummeting to the deck, he realized he'd dismissed the warning too casually. Looking down, Edward saw people pointing at him. *Caught.*

Grasping the rope firmly, weaving his hand between knots, as the crewman had demonstrated, he placed his other hand on the rim of the basket, and extended one leg over the side. He secured his foot, and then lifted out his other leg.

"Good." The mate wrapped a length of rope around Edward's chest and tied a complex knot in seconds. "I've got you. Move one leg, then your hand. Easy does it."

Tentatively, Edward moved one foot, but lost his toehold, which left him hanging by one arm.

The crewman held him fast. "Breathe. Try again."

This time Edward's foot connected and he could grasp the rope with his hand. Slowly he made his way down. About halfway to the deck, he miscalculated his grip and slipped again, hanging by one arm.

He heard Bri cry out, "Edward!"

Damn. Everyone believes me inept. He grasped the rope and righted himself. *Breathe.* Each move was deliberate. The mate loosened his grip on the rope from above as Edward descended. All went well until the final ten feet. He slipped again and dangled, held only by the crewman's grip on the rope wrapped around his chest. The angle of the rigging kept him too far away to reach the rope. *If I swing out so that I can ride the momentum back to the rigging, the mate might lose his hold on the rope.* He extricated himself by bending his legs to soften his landing and raised his arms to slip out of the mate's rope.

Dr. St. Cloud and Jean-Louis caught him before he hit the deck.

Bri embraced Edward and sighed. "You're safe." She took a deep breath, then turned on her heel and continued her walk.

Sheepishly, Edward looked up at his travel companions. "I have new respect for climbers."

***

Thursday, July 4, 1811 – The Bazaar in Alexandria
Blackburn as The Pharaoh

Blackburn ambled around the multi-colored tents of the crowded bazaar, his ship's mate cap pulled low over his forehead. He searched for the stall selling foreign clothing, touted as coming from unclaimed trunks or valises of departed visitors, though no one really believed that fiction. A full selection of servant-to-gentlemen's wear covered the tables. Blackburn particularly liked a red cape. *A foreign dandy's choice. Perfect.* He picked up boots, breeches, gloves, jackets, shirts, cravats and hats from the displays. *All in all, an excellent selection.*

He negotiated, paid and also bought a large Turkish carpetbag to transport his purchases.

Next on his stop was the knife stall. Jeweled daggers and other deadly blades beckoned collectors and killers alike. A brass-handled sapphire-studded slender poniard appealed to Blackburn. *I like the French name. A weapon for the fist. This promises a deep thrust to the heart or throat. Not weighted for throwing—honed for a close kill.* Pleased to find a Scottish dirk, a reminder of his childhood, he added that to his cache, along with hilts designed for throwing.

With that purchase accomplished, Blackburn moved through the market's winding pathways, picking up the odd accoutrement. A rare book stall caught his eye. *Reading material on the long trip back to London would be welcome.* As he scanned the volumes offered, his hand touched frayed green leather bindings on a set of six volumes of Shakespeare's works. "How much?"

The stall keeper quoted a high price, and after a period of haggling, he and Blackburn settled on an amount that both considered fair. The proprietor wrapped the books in a rough undyed cotton fabric and tied them with twine.

With one hand on the twine and the other on the carpetbag strap, Blackburn wandered through the merchants hawking their stock, musicians playing for coins, and purveyors offering food and drink until he reached his final stop.

The wigmaker's stall was tucked in the back row, out of the main area. *Perhaps I am not the only client of the wigmaker who craves anonymity.* One of the tables before him held a wide selection of formal powdered courtly wigs.

Raising his eyes to the stall keeper, Blackburn said, "Those are rarely worn now. The nineteenth century *is* upon us." Brushing the dust off one of the tightly curled examples, he added, "More apt for a costumed affect by an actor," when a burst of inspiration hit him, "such as I."

"You don't talk like a shipman, so you are not an effective impostor." The wigmaker narrowed his eyes, tilting his head to peer more closely at his customer.

Blackburn shrugged. "I see Europeans on shipboard. They tell me of the latest styles in their capitals."

"Your Arabic is nearly flawless, but your nose looks more European."

Nearly? "Perhaps you should mind your own business." *And I must pay more attention to my pronunciation.*

"That *is* my business." His gaze was direct. "To appear as one you are not requires attention to detail."

Blackburn shrugged. "I am also a member of a troupe of actors when I'm not sailing. For my upcoming performances, I must acquire wigs and beards to appear as an older man of Croatian descent and one of Italian background. Perhaps you'll attend."

"Perhaps I shall. Here are some options for you to consider. We even have wigs for women, if that is something you require."

Picking up a woman's red-dyed wig, Blackburn smiled. *This with my natural red beard might give me the look of a pirate.* He chose several false beards and wigs to accommodate his needs. As a last gesture, he tossed the woman's wig onto the pile. *Why not?*

"You will need some paste to attach the beards, and hairpins to hold the wigs in place." The stall keeper went behind his curtain to gather them.

While he waited for the man to reappear, Blackburn saw a spread of other items he'd hoped to find—spectacles and monocles. He opted for two sets of spectacles and one monocle.

The proprietor brought the necessary items and added up the total purchases. They bargained back and forth again until both agreed.

Accepting payment, the wigmaker smiled. "I am pleased to serve you again. The eye color had me confused for a time, but the timbre of your voice revealed your true identity. It's a bit of a game for me, you see, as a purveyor of disguises."

How unfortunate. "I expect silence from all with whom I deal."

"Of course. Discretion is my most pronounced trait." The wigmaker's crooked smile, punctuated by spaces left by missing teeth, gave lie to his assertion.

***

Later than night, as the wigmaker left his stall for the evening, a poniard slit his throat from behind.

Now your silence is assured.

***

Thursday, July 4, 1811 – Aboard *Taygete's Wynd*
Bri

Bri and Edward promenaded along the deck, Spotty trailing behind. Bri took a deep breath of sea air.

Edward sighed. "You've said nothing about my climbing the rigging. I'm ready. Berate me."

"I have no intention of berating you." She raised her eyebrows as she directed her gaze to him. "Learn how to do it properly. Then you can teach *me*. I want to see the view from the Main Top Castle."

Her fiancé's mouth dropped open. "Are you mad? Your skirts will get tangled up in the rigging. It would be dangerous."

"I will wear a pair of your breeches and a shirt. 'Twill be no more dangerous for me than it is for you."

Edward smiled. "You will scandalize your aunt and the captain." He paused. "Well, perhaps only the captain."

Bri squeezed his hand as they walked. "I feel relaxed. For the first time since Blackie's death, I feel free. He can't reach out from the grave to harm us." Her voice became wistful. "As a child, I called him my best friend. Can you imagine?"

"No. The man betrayed your trust and nearly—"

Bri put her hand on his arm. "Don't utter the words. His treachery is behind us."

***

Thursday, July 4, 1811 – An Inn in Alexandria
Blackburn as The Pharaoh

Unable to sleep after his interlude with the wigmaker, Blackburn lay on his bed by the window in his room, petting Midnight, bathed in the diffused light of the desert moon. *The wigmaker knew me as Blackburn, not The Pharaoh. None but my top people know me by appearance. The legend of The Pharaoh is made more powerful by fear stoked by human imagination.* He spoke aloud as he petted his cat, the only companion he trusted. "I must take care to change my voice, my mannerisms and my phrasings, so as not to betray my real identity when I return to England. The wigmaker taught me a valuable lesson."

CHAPTER TWENTY

Thursday, July 4, 1811 – Ravenshire
Gilles

While Bri and Gwyneth were away, Aelwyn and Ian settled in to a routine, spending four days a week at Ravenshire and three days in London at Gwyneth's townhouse.

Gilles trained Ian to ride his pony, teaching him verbal commands and physical cues. As they finished their ride on Thursday afternoon, Gilles said, "Say goodbye to pony Gio. We'll be off to London early tomorrow morning."

"Why can't pony Gio come with us?"

The trainer tilted his head, bent down to look Ian in the eye and pointed. "Look at the length of his legs. How would he keep up with the horses, whose legs are much longer and more powerful?"

Ian's face brightened. "He could ride inside the coach with me."

"Come with me." Gilles tugged on the pony's reins and headed to the stables at a brisk pace, forcing Ian to run to keep up with him.

The boy stopped abruptly. "My legs are like pony Gio's. Slow down!"

The man who served as horse trainer, bodyguard, driver and protégé of Jean-Louis stopped, turned and smiled at Ian. "You're learning." He slowed down and they ambled toward the stables. When they reached the pony's stall, Gilles handed the reins to the groomsman to rub down the pony.

Gilles crooked his finger, signaling Ian to follow him to one of the earl's carriages. Opening the door, he asked, "Would pony Gio fit in here?"

Ian shook his head.

"Sometimes it is better for us to leave those we love where they are safe and happy, for their sake."

The boy nodded. "Like you and Jean-Louis protected us in Ireland."

***

Friday, July 5, 1811 – Alia's Offices
Alia

Within the warren of rooms behind a false wall in a non-descript warehouse in Alexandria, Alia plied her trade. Reviewing the completed travel documents she had forged for Xie Xie, Alia sighed with satisfaction. The Pharaoh's international protégé would soon leave for London under private orders.

Some people thought the two women were jealous of each other, but each turned such shallow, erroneous assumptions to her advantage. Xie Xie spoke Mandarin as well as Cantonese, English, French and Arabic, directing The Pharaoh's import-export activities, disseminating spices and drugs, and traveling off the African continent while Alia held the local criminal enterprises together, the day-to-day operations that oiled the graft machine. The Pharaoh insisted that operations be self-sustaining financially to continue in the event of his death.

Greedy bureaucrats, petty criminals, and spies took their orders and received their payoffs from Alia. If her agents came close to being apprehended, she had new papers ready for them. On a worst case basis, they could disappear and become mercenaries. On a best case basis, they could catch a fast ship to a new country and slip into a new life with a respectable nest egg.

Alia knew only the broad outlines of Xie Xie's task for the foreseeable future—setting up a new company in London to steal commerce from The Pharaoh's enemy, an English earl. Before Xie Xie left for London, Alia expected that someone else would be selected by Xie Xie to assume her duties. But that person would not have parity with Alia. She would assume command of all operations.

Alia had no idea what The Pharaoh's master plan was. She gave him total loyalty, fulfilling every task he assigned to her without question.

Both women had bested more than one ill-fated male rival. The Pharaoh trusted women over men, and, again, contrary to male assumptions, he did not exploit either woman for his personal pleasure. Alia admired The Pharaoh for rescuing abused children of all nationalities, educating them and integrating them into his network of eyes and ears, invisible butterflies transferring information to him. An eye for talent and a magnet for orphans, he became their father. None had ever abandoned him.

When a young boy named Mobi brought Alia a folded note, she set it aside while she focused on her minute scribing, magnifying glasses on her forehead to augment her vision. "No, you must read it now. He said so."

Alia pushed the glasses up and glared at the dark-skinned boy, a mixed race outcast of indeterminate parentage. "You know better than to speak to me in such a manner."

Mobi leaned closer and whispered, "I think it is from the master."

The forger frowned. "That would be most unusual." *It means something is terribly wrong if the master is back in Alexandria.* "Where did you encounter this man?"

"In the tourist bazaar, where you sent me to steal and listen. I attempted to pick the pocket of a ship's crewman, but he gripped my wrist. He said, in English, 'I knew one of you would find me. Take this note to Alia and use this phrase: 'The raven flies through fog.'"

Alia's copper skin turned gray. *We are all at risk.*

***

Friday, July 5, 1811 – Vaux's Gentlemen's Club
Vaux

Banfield, Rogers, and Vaux finished playing cards with Durwood.

Rogers enjoyed teasing Durwood, who valued propriety above all else. "Time to go home to Lady Rose, Durwood. Must be a dutiful husband and all that."

Durwood sighed. "Someday you will all know the vicissitudes of marital bliss. At times I feel—"

"Trapped?" Rogers drained his wine glass. "Men are women's prey."

"Not trapped, but limited. I miss the feeling of charting my own course on my own terms. Now, everything is negotiated."

"You're getting to be a bore, Durwood." Vaux stood to move to the open dining room. "Take up some new hobby."

"I don't know," said Banfield. "The thought of dinner waiting for me and a life companion isn't an unpleasant thought. No offense meant to you," he waved his hand among his friends, "but a woman offers something you don't."

Vaux's face betrayed no sign of the churning in his stomach. *I cannot stifle my fear—would my friends hate me if they knew the truth?*

Shrugging off his malaise, Durwood bid the others goodnight and left.

The three friends opted for the *menu du jour*.

Vaux waited for the server to pour the wine before speaking. "Perhaps we delude ourselves that independence isn't lonely."

"You just called Durwood a bore, Vaux. Don't pull a black fog down over our dinner." Rogers tore off a baguette and smothered it in butter. "Banfield, cheer us up. How goes the opera?"

"Lady Gabriella challenged me to find subjects for several operas, rather than be locked into one that sparks little or no interest. I have the story for *The Nymphs* in my head, but she set me on a broader path. She and James think they can find a theatre and arrange funding. I want a story with high dramatic impact." Banfield glanced back and forth at each of his friends as he spoke. "I've decided the subject must be Shakespearean. His stories build to unequaled moments of high drama, perfect for the power of an operatic aria."

"*Romeo and Juliet.*" Vaux shrugged. "It's a natural."

"Not exactly a happy ending," scoffed Rogers.

Banfield rolled his eyes. "Have you ever *seen* an opera, Rogers? The final aria is almost always sung immediately before the last gasps of death."

Rogers grinned and shrugged. "I'll see *yours*, Banfield."

"For my first effort, I want to make a major impact. A tragedy is the only choice. *Hamlet* is too daunting. I think *MacBeth* would be ideal."

Vaux nodded. "Witches, ghosts, murder, war. I'd love to design Birnam Wood coming across the stage. What a great martial tune you could compose for that!"

The composer leaned forward. "Exactly! I am inspired by the possibilities."

The designer moved his hand in a wave. "I can see the castles, the battlefields, the blood, and the witches. Costumes! I wonder—"

Even Rogers was entranced. "Wonder what?"

"I know an upholsterer and draper who stores bolts of leftover fabric that could be fashioned into costumes, certainly, and they would be sturdy. Good for the stage. I've never designed clothing, but why not?"

"Because you've never designed clothing, Vaux." Banfield shook his head. "Lady Gabriella has a designer or two she knows. Perhaps combining their expertise with your upholsterer—"

"And draper."

"—and draper. And you could give direction, as would I."

"If Gio came up with overall murals and backdrops, I could build the sets and execute our joint inspiration for costumes, colors, and so on." He paused for effect. "Damnation!"

"Damnation of what?" Rogers drained his glass mug of its remaining ale.

"Of my commitments. I'm going to be busy all the time."

"Now that is a tragedy worthy of an opera." Rogers smirked. "I can see the headlines in *Scandal & Shame:* 'Viscount Vaux too busy to dine out!' or "The diva swooned after singing her final aria, entitled: 'My designer didn't finish my wallpaper.' Tragic, indeed."

"Although you expect Vaux to fold like a used napkin beneath your contempt, kindly remember I still have to *compose* the opera. That will take months, if not more. It will be at least a year before it is performed."

"No contempt, Banfield. A bit of jealousy, to be truthful. You two will get all the glory. What about me?" Rogers pouted but then his face broke into a smile. "I can become the impresario!"

Banfield nodded. "You do have a flair for promotion. Everyone in the *ton* is talking about the Phaeton Meet."

Vaux agreed. "They're calling it, 'The Trot of the *Ton.*' "

"Catchy, eh?" Rogers sat back. "An impresario. With a big cigar. It might be a pleasant gentlemanly pursuit. God knows I need more to do. I can't sit around my estate like my father, or stroll around to pester the gardeners and tenants. I can barely tell a sheep from a pig."

"One is white and one is pink." Banfield shook his head.

Raising his eyebrows, Rogers grimaced. "My father calls me the black sheep."

"I've always said you were a rare and unique creature." Vaux signaled a server to bring more wine and ale. "How much do you think such a production would cost?"

Banfield shrugged. "I was going to speak to James about how much it cost to stage *The Princess*." He tossed out a number as a guess.

Rogers recoiled. "I may be out of the impresario business before I smoke my first cigar."

Vaux mused aloud. "I'll talk to James. Your promotional skills are valuable. Let's see what James and I can concoct."

Banfield inclined his head toward Rogers. "If you're going to concoct, don't forget the best concoctor."

"You're right. Lady Gabriella's insight is the most valuable."

Banfield lifted his glass. "To *MacBeth, The Opera*! Score by Banfield. Libretto Adapted from Will Shakespeare. Conceptual Design by Gio. Sets by Vaux. Costumes by the Upholsterer and Draper. Presented by Impresario Rogers. Financed by James & Co. With Concoctions by Lady Gabriella Wyndward."

They clinked their refilled glasses.

Just as the other two took a sip, Vaux asked, "Can't I come before the Bard in the credits?"

Rogers and Banfield spat out their drinks.

***

Friday, July 5, 1811 – Interior of a Hackney
Durwood

Why didn't I tell them that Lady Rose is with child? Durwood's family owned large tracts of farmland south of London. Tenant income was sufficient to support his lifestyle without concern. But his days were long and uneventful. And now, with Lady Rose in a delicate condition, he couldn't imagine the next phase of his life.

As the only son and youngest in a family of three children, Durwood did as was expected of him, without fanfare. Now, approaching thirty, he feared his chance to be his own man diminishing each day. Children annoyed him, bored him, and frightened him.

Rogers, Banfield, and Vaux led carefree lives. No wives, no demands, no children to worry about. He scoffed. *Get a hobby, say my friends.*

He rapped on the side of the carriage, alerting the driver to pull to the side of the street so that Durwood could give him another destination in the industrial part of town.

As the carriage pulled back into traffic, Durwood sat back on the leather tufted bench seat and smiled. *Why not?*

CHAPTER TWENTY-ONE

Friday, July 5, 1811 – A Turkish Coffee House, Alexandria
Alia

The Pharaoh's forger made her way through the teeming streets of Alexandria, followed by Sefu. *This was not The Pharaoh's plan. Something has gone terribly wrong.*
Their prearranged code led Alia on a circuitous route that would end near the docks in an alley that housed a Turkish coffee house. It had survived the battles of Napoleon, who was ultimately defeated by a coalition of British and Ottoman forces in 1801. The city had been nearly destroyed. The few wealthy who had not previously escaped left for Cairo where the new government was forming.

Alia thought about her years with The Pharaoh as she traversed narrow alleyways, often dodging rubble. Her master's experience in China had influenced his view of time. He often told her, "To the Chinese, a hundred years is but one night's sleep." To her knowledge, The Pharaoh had few heroes. None exceeded Alexander the Great in his admiration. "This city boasts a natural harbor. Alexander chose this spot for his capital because easy access to sea transport promised military and economic superiority." The Pharaoh's experience in trade around the world convinced him that Alexandria would be the best locus for his modern-day empire.

When a city was destroyed, opportunities abounded. Alia remembered The Pharaoh telling her, "I know I could never dominate Cairo. But Alexandria," its population decimated in 1800 to less than 10,000 from its once-great stature, "will rebound." He was correct. The Pharaoh became the underworld king of Alexandria, persuading, bribing and corrupting his way to power anonymously through a web of confederates. Away from the scrutiny of Cairo and government oversight, the territory was his to control.

The formula for domination began with his network, developed years before Alexandria became embroiled in war. Dealing with unsavory characters instilled a survival instinct in him and his few trusted associates, of whom Alia was one.

Through their connections, The Pharaoh learned about hidden catacombs beneath the city. Immediately grasping the advantage of such protected sanctuaries, with rivers of tunnels and secret exits under most of the city, he set up areas to house his people. They could emerge to gather food, by coin or by force, and keep abreast of above-ground turmoil, and retreat to their safe havens at will.

Slowly, over more than a decade, small but elegantly appointed apartments for The Pharaoh and his chosen favorites were created below the city. Word spread that if you worked with The Pharaoh, your family would be safe. His legend grew beyond the borders of the city.

In tales embellished by sailors, The Pharaoh's mythical exploits inspired fear and awe at the mention of his name. He was known in all countries where the coastline touched the Mediterranean. In Cairo, they dismissed him as a provincial annoyance, but those who crossed him never lived to tell the tale.

When she arrived at the coffee house, Alia took a seat in the back corner where the curved booth bench seat allowed a view of all who entered. She signaled to the proprietor to bring two coffees as well as some dates and cakes.

A man dressed as a member of a sailing crew, his hat pulled low to obscure his face, sauntered in and took a seat on the bench next to her. She kept her head facing forward, but shifted her eyes to the side. "A knife is pointed at your liver. Leave now or die."

The man smiled and leaned back. "I've always admired your audacity."

"Master!" she whispered. "You look different. Thinner, sinewy, bearded and bronzed."

"I recently survived bullets, knife wounds, and more. Recovery took weeks, but I am nearly ready to return. In ten days, I'll appear in the catacombs."

"What happened in London?"

"My initial plan was thwarted." He shrugged. "My enemies think me dead, therefore I have the advantage. We will accelerate Xie Xie's departure for London. Tell her to be ready to travel immediately after I meet with her. Set up a meeting in my catacomb apartments the day I return, when I will give her the final instructions. She should designate her replacement to act as intermediary with our Asian connections. Are there any pressing matters that require my attention?"

"No. All of our operations here are proceeding as planned. Recruits are growing and the coffers are full. We have only had to terminate one of our own since you left."

"Who?"

"The Serbian."

"I'm not surprised. A good collector, but a thug." He took a sip of coffee. "I missed this brew. Any trouble with the authorities about The Serbian's demise?"

"The death appeared so natural, no bribe was necessary. He choked on a chicken bone in a restaurant." Alia leaned forward and smiled conspiratorially. "A poisoned fig helped."

The Pharaoh popped a date into his mouth and glanced around the café to be certain no ears were listening. "I will be leaving for London a month or two after Xie Xie." He handed Alia a folded piece of paper. "I will require the items on this list when I next see you." He slowly twirled the coffee cup in his hand, staring into its swirling contents. "After I leave the next time, I may or may not return to Alexandria. Prepare to consolidate your power in my absence. Be ruthless. Many men will not accede to a woman's superior position. Eliminate them. Be wary. Keep my legend alive for your own protection. And select your replacement with care."

"You have given me all that I have, Master. I am your servant, always."

After drinking the remaining coffee, The Pharaoh continued, "Alia, some years ago, I advised you to always be ready for a rapid departure. Are you prepared?"

Alia nodded. "At all times, Master." She hesitated. "Master, what is happening to your eyes? They appear clouded. Do you have cataracts?"

"No. I am taking a potion to turn them brown. Tell no one. I need to disguise my appearance thoroughly for my return to London." He leaned forward. "With luck, you will never have to disappear, but should it become necessary, write 'on raven's wings' on the catacomb wall. If I ever return, I'll know from the code that your disappearance was at your volition. In these next weeks, I'll instruct you in whatever I can to complete your accession to become The Pharaoh and face the future without me."

A whisper escaped Alia's lips. "Understood."

The Pharaoh nodded toward the door. "You leave first. I'll wait a bit longer."

"Until we meet again, Master." Alia exited the café as casually as she had entered.

***

Friday, July 5, 1811 – Aboard *Taygete's Wynd*
Gio

After the dinner plates were cleared away each night, the steward appeared with a basket of tangerines, limes or lemons. Each guest took one.

Gio raised his glass. "I propose that we toast the most memorable act, whether outrageous or altruistic, of the person sitting directly to our left."

Gwyneth shook her head. "A sinister and cynical proposition. You have done so many outrageous things, Gio, how can I pick just one?"

"My behavior just makes the task easy for you, as you are seated to my right. To my left is seated the lovely Lady Clarissa. *Ergo,* I toast her bravery in donning the inspired disguise of Violetta Vinci, thus creating the unforgettable lead role in *The Princess.*"

All murmured, "Here! Here!" and sipped in agreement.

To Clarissa's left sat her husband. "I toast the moment I met Dr. St. Cloud—the light in his eyes projected kindness. He healed Spotty and gave me a kitten. At that moment, I fell in love."

Dr. St. Cloud kissed her on the cheek and clinked his glass to hers as his wife's toast was echoed.

"To *my* left sits the inimitable Lady Gabriella. Perhaps I would have met Clarissa in the audition for the operetta, but it was Lady Gabriella's concern for an injured dog that originally brought Lady Clarissa to my attention, and that is a moment I shall never forget."

After acknowledging the toast to her, Bri glanced at Edward, who was seated to her left.

Edward moved his eyes around the table. "Does anyone have a spare shield?"

The guests laughed.

Bri sat back. "So you *expect* a barb?"

"Don't we all?" asked Gio.

"Come back to me later."

"No, it's my game and you must play your turn." The dwarf leaned forward.

Bri started to say something, but stopped herself.

"Am I so unmemorable?"

His fiancée raised her glass and directed her gaze to him. "I think we all witnessed you climbing to the top of the Main Top Castle. Brave, but outrageous and reckless."

"So outrageous that you followed my lead that very afternoon."

"But *I* didn't fall."

"That *is* a barb and James *will* need a shield, like a Roman legionnaire." Gio shrugged.

"But I said he was brave first." Bri leaned over and kissed him.

Uncharacteristically, Edward's faced flushed and the guests repeated, "James the Brave!"

Gio smirked. "She got you, James! The compliment cancels the barb."

"Alternatively, the barb cancels the compliment, but I surrender," said Edward.

Gio waved his empty glass at the steward. "More wine!"

Edward cleared his throat. "Lt. Gibson, I am at a loss in this game, as I have no anecdote about you to relate."

Gio waved his hand. "James, you are excused. I'm sure the lieutenant has a story about Captain Treadway."

"Indeed I do. We were in the Royal Navy years ago, serving under a cruel, drunken commander who enjoyed flogging men over minor infractions." He glanced at the captain out of the corner of his eye. "On one occasion, the captain, who held the rank of lieutenant at that point, grabbed the whip from the commander's hand and tossed it overboard. He said, 'You have refused my repeated demands that you cease such heinous punishment. I hereby relieve you from command under the laws of the Admiralty.'

"Over the commander's sputtering curses of protest, the lieutenant ordered the commander escorted into confinement."

Bri leaned forward. "What happened when you returned to port?"

"No charges were brought against the lieutenant. The commander was found guilty of unjust punishment inflicted on inferiors, stripped of his rank, and thrown out of the Royal Navy. However, the lieutenant was reprimanded because the tribunal stipulated that he should have filed a formal complaint when the ship returned from its mission instead of placing the commander under confinement.

"How many other men would have been scarred, defiled or killed under that policy? The lieutenant was offered permanent shore duty. He refused and resigned.

"The next day, I did the same and followed him into service with Lord Ravenshire's fleet."

After toasting Captain Treadway, Gio refused to let the more somber mood dominate. "Captain, what do you know of our French friend?"

"More than you can imagine."

Gio pulled his head back, feigning shock, slightly in his cups. "No one has more of an imagination than I do. Test me."

"On another ship several years ago, the earl and many of you here, were on a voyage to the Caribbean, we sailed close to the shore of the dense jungles of the Yucatan. Winds were sluggish, and it seemed as if we barely moved for hours. Late one night, or early one morning, whichever you prefer, a group of wild, naked natives swam out, climbed up the side of the ship like centipedes, and dumped poisonous snakes in a woven bag over the deck. Silently, the natives scurried down the ship's hull like spiders, disappearing into the waters below.

"This man," he pointed to Jean-Louis, "must have eyes in the back of his head. He alone noticed the saboteurs' actions. Leaping in arcs from one side of the boat to the other, Jean-Louis wrangled the snakes back into the bag and tossed it overboard. An hour or so later, when I lowered my head to take a drink from the cup attached to the water barrel, a knife flew by my ear with a whoosh and speared the head of an errant snake to the side of the boat. I heard the Frenchman's laconic voice.

" 'Missed one.' "

Lady Gwyneth paled. "I was on that trip, but I never heard that story."

The captain shrugged. "I was advised to keep it a secret."

"Until now," Gio observed.

After the group toasted Jean-Louis, it was his turn. "Alas, I know too many secrets. Lady Gwyneth, with a pencil and a sketchbook, turns a door you enter every day into a magical entrance, a window into a portal of other worldly visions, a flower into a faerie's abode. Her sketches and paintings bring the world to life. She reminds me of what I often forget: Beauty is found in the little details that we pass by every day but rarely notice."

After nodding in acceptance of the toast, Gwyneth lifted her glass. "Now, 'tis true, I have the easiest task of this evening's amusement. Years ago, my late husband Luc and I were on safari in Africa with Gio, Henry, Charlotte, Bri and Laurence, her tutor. And, as always, Jean-Louis." Gwyneth could not suppress a laugh.

Gio squirmed. "No—not that story!"

She put her hands up. "Stop. This is my toast. A female chimpanzee wandered into our camp. Luc reached for a gun, but Jean-Louis restrained him with a touch on his arm. 'No one should move,' said our intrepid Frenchman. 'She could tear off your face in a flash.' "

Gio pouted. "One would think this was another toast to the Frenchman. This is supposed to be about me."

Gwyneth glared at Gio. "Silence. In a wine-induced deep sleep, our artist friend, whose hair was near-black then with only a whisper of white, heard nothing. The beast scooped him up with one muscled arm, cradling our Gio next to her breast. She used her other arm to climb a nearby tree. Gio stretched, awakened by the movement, opened his eyes and assessed the situation. The chimpanzee stared at him. 'Mama!' he cried, and kissed the chimpanzee on the lips, distracting her. She let him go and he fell into a blanket held by Henry, Luc and Jean-Louis. To Gio!"

Edward leaned over to Bri. "Is that true?"

Bri nodded. "I was terrified for him. Jean-Louis advanced the theory that the chimpanzee had probably lost a child recently and wanted a replacement."

In a wistful tone, Gio added, "I probably could have ruled the Land of the Chimpanzees."

Jean-Louis shrugged. "Until the lions came."

***

Friday, July 5, 1811 – Alia's Offices

Alia

Alia dispatched her message boy to Xie Xie with a coded note instructing her to meet her in the back of the needle the next morning at noon. If anyone intercepted the message, they would assume it meant Cleopatra's Needle, a monument in Alexandria that had stood, in truth, for more than a thousand years before Cleopatra's birth. The actual location for the meeting was a nondescript tailor's shop on a street only partially rebuilt from the war with Napoleon, resulting in little foot traffic. Anyone's approach could be detected by Alia's bodyguard, Sefu, who would remain in the shadows.

The Pharaoh had taught them never to conduct business in the same place all the time. "Vary the location, the time, the day. Assume people follow and watch, and take precautions. Enter separately from different entrances, at different times. Communicate in code."

Dealing with the rough characters of the underworld required vigilance to insure Alia's personal safety.

Xie Xie was never seen with her because they moved in different circles, following The Pharaoh's directives..

***

Saturday, July 6, 1811 – Aboard *Taygete's Wynd*
Dana

After dinner, Dana laid out the nightclothes for Lady Gwyneth and Lady Gabriella in their cabin.

Leaving there, she returned with the valet and gave it a final glance. All was ready.

Dana and Shore, the valet assigned to the gentlemen on the trip, would be spending an hour or two on deck, where the crew was having an evening of fiddling and dancing.

As the only woman, Dana expected to dance to exhaustion.

***

Bri

With their servants were occupied with the other crewmembers, Bri and Edward separately entered their servants' room, taking care to avoid detection.

Once inside, Bri carefully removed the pouch with sponge and vinegar from where she had secreted them in a hidden pocket in her shawl.

He kissed her, and then tilted his head toward the door. "How long do we have?"

"Long enough. We must steal these moments when we can."

During a kiss where Edward's tongue explored her mouth, Bri gasped for breath. "Edward!"

"Shh! The walls demand silence," he whispered, and kissed her again.

Pulling back from him, Bri handed him the pouch. She lifted her dress over her head and stood in her silk chemise.

Smiling, he removed the sponge, poured vinegar over it from a small vial, knelt down and inserted the sponge.

Bri closed her eyes in pleasure.

Edward rose to his feet and pulled her toward him.

Entwined in each other, they fell to the small sleeping hammock, but their ardor caused it to swing, dislodging them.

Tossed to the floor, Edward grimaced. "So much for our attempt at subterfuge." Pausing to see if anyone knocked on the door, they relaxed. Bri wrapped her arms around Edward and they became entangled in each other's limbs.

CHAPTER TWENTY-TWO

Saturday, July 6, 1811 – Alexandria
Xie Xie

As Xie Xie trekked through the alternately crowded and deserted streets to meet with Alia, she smiled. *I am close to my goal.*

The Pharaoh had founded a school in an old palace for girls and boys he rescued from servitude. One of the first to attend was Xie Xie. Located in a remote area outside Alexandria, the palace provided schoolrooms as well as living quarters for instructors and the children. Many of the instructors were eunuchs or women, as The Pharaoh distrusted the baser inclinations of men. He mandated that all students be taught English, the language of commerce, and French, the language of diplomacy, as well as receiving instruction in the manners of the European upper class.

When Xie Xie was young, eager for praise and thrilled to be singled out by her idol, she reveled in The Pharaoh's description of her as his 'masterpiece.' However, as she grew in confidence, knowledge and a sense of self, the term rankled. *I am no masterpiece crafted by another's hand. I learned from The Pharaoh, I absorbed the lessons, and I became my own person.* Tutored in hiding her emotions, Xie Xie never revealed her annoyance.

She readily acknowledged to herself that she owed The Pharaoh a great deal. He'd led the escape that released her from a life in sexual bondage in China. He'd provided her with an education in the

European model. He'd offered her an unmatched opportunity to visit Paris, Rome, Greece and ancient areas of Turkey. Such gifts could have come from no other.

Yet she yearned to break free. *I am a pawn in his and his grandmother's plan for revenge. I could be sacrificed at any time to achieve their checkmate. As soon as I can extricate myself, I will. I have learned secrets of disguise, duplicity and subterfuge from The Pharaoh and I intend to implement them for my own purposes.*

*** *

Saturday, July 6, 1811 – A Tailor's Shop, Alexandria
Alia

Alia sat in the tailor's back room. The proprietor had been dismissed for the duration of her meeting and knew better than to ask questions.

The Pharaoh's master forger watched over a pot of Turkish coffee and waited for Xie Xie. The Asian woman was no threat to Alia. *She may never return.* Her refinement would never mix with the rough-edged characters that inhabited Alia's world.

Xie Xie arrived through the back entrance.

"The time has come." Alia poured a cup of coffee for Xie Xie. "Our Master has returned. He says you must meet him on the fifteenth in the catacombs where he will provide you with final instructions. Be ready to leave immediately after the meeting. Passage has been booked for you and multiple passports created." Alia handed Xie Xie a book.

Opening it, Xie Xie nodded to Alia. The pages had been hollowed out. Several passports, cash and documents for her ship's passage were secreted within. She smiled. "You are efficient as always, Alia. I shall miss your counsel. Navigating my way through the hazardous maze of London will take all my skills."

"I have no doubt our Master has taught you well." She knew The Pharaoh had never seduced any of his workers. *The man is an ascetic when it comes to women.* "You have been trained for your part in his scheme for years."

"But our Master has returned to us unexpectedly early. Something must have gone wrong."

"My advice is that you wait for our Master to reveal his new plan to you. Do not confront him. Follow your instructions without fail."

"I always do. I am ready."

Alia sipped her coffee. *I watched this child grow into a woman. We have forged a relationship based on the divergence of our roles in The Pharaoh's plan.*

While they finished their coffee and sweets, Alia and Xie Xie reminisced about their years together.

Xie Xie sighed as she prepared to leave. "Neither of us knows what the future holds. I may or may not return. Farewell, Alia. I have valued your friendship."

"And I yours."Alia reached over and covered Xie Xie's hand with hers.

"*Au revoir.*" Carrying the hollowed out book, Xie Xie left.

Alia waited for half an hour, and then departed. On the way back to her offices, she reviewed the little she knew of Xie Xie's assigned tasks. *Her path now takes her to a new life. My Chinese friend thinks she knows British culture, but unknown obstacles await her.*

***

Sunday, July 7, 1811 – Aboard *Taygete's Wynd*
Bri

Within a few days, Bri, Edward and the doctor were climbing the ship's rigging expertly. Dr. St. Cloud urged them on from his perch on the Main Top Castle.

As Edward had predicted, Gwyneth objected. She called out as Bri ascended the rigging, "You two look like street urchins."

Edward turned toward Gwyneth and shouted loudly enough to be heard below. "My tailor would be offended."

Bri, who was lower on the rigging, between Edward above her and Jean-Louis below, brushed aside her aunt's admonition. "We are isolated on a ship with friends. No one cares about my choice of attire."

"Ahoy, there!" The lieutenant called out. "That's too many people on the rigging. Two at a time is regulation."

Jean-Louis yelled up to Bri. "We must try the Mizzen Top Castle. Come down. Now."

Bri nodded, and slowly descended.

Jean-Louis stayed close enough to intervene should Bri lose her footing.

When she reached the deck, Bri put her hand to her forehead to shade her eyes as she looked to the other mast. "The Mizzen isn't as high. We won't be able to see as far."

Jean-Louis scoffed. "We are on the open sea. The horizon is the horizon is the horizon. We won't be able to spot land for a few more days. Better to practice on a shorter mast."

Bri sighed in surrender, walked over to the other mast, and turned to look at the Frenchman. "Ready?"

Making a low bow with his hand extended to the side in a flamboyant flourish, Jean-Louis lowered his eyes. "As you command, my queen."

"Feigned obsequiousness is—"

In a mocking tone, the Frenchman echoed, " 'Feigned?' "

"—as Grandmother would say, 'uninspired, untrue, and unsuccessful.' "

Jean-Louis tipped his hat to his verbal sparring partner. "After you."

***

Sunday, July 7, 1811 – The Captain's Dining Room
Clarissa

At meals onboard, Clarissa related what she'd learned of the Azores from the travel diaries kept in the captain's library. At dinner one of those nights, she asked, "Does anyone know the origin of the name, Azores?"

"May I offer a guess?" Bri sat back in her chair. "In French, a variant on the word 'blue' is *azure*. In Italian, the term is *assurro*, and in Portuguese it's *azul*."

Clarissa nodded. "That is a possibility. It is said that the vegetation appears blue from a distance, and we will be able to see for ourselves soon enough if that is true. It is interesting that you mention Italian, because the first map where the Islands of the Azores appear is in the *Medici Atlas,* in 1351."

Jean-Louis suggested a blue bird might have led a ship there. "Birds always signal land, or ships, nearby."

Clarissa smiled. "There is a legend about birds nesting on the archipelago. Perhaps they had blue feathers."

The doctor asked, "Which is it?"

"No one knows. There is a town in Portugal named Açores that has a patron saint. Other islands in this archipelago have the names of saints, so there might be a connection. Many island names have changed over time. Perhaps they were known by other names in times before history was written."

Edward shrugged. "Perhaps. Maybe they're what Homer referred to as 'The Isles of the Blest' or 'The Fortunate Islands' in the west Atlantic. Who knows what early seafaring peoples might have stopped there and come back with tales of being blessed or fortunate to have found safe harbor there?"

Gwyneth leaned forward. "Islands in the far Atlantic are referenced in legends of the Irish and sagas of Viking explorers."

The captain smiled. "The Wyndwards' knowledge of ancient sea legends is steeped in the classical curriculum."

"The earl is passionate about understanding ancient myths and legends. He believes that legends hold truth disguised by hyperbole. He can speak for hours on the nature of the Greek gods of antiquity, Norse sagas, or ancient Celtic tales, and is determined to master Egyptian hieroglyphics now that the Rosetta Stone has revealed a basis for translation. He intends to study the monuments in Egypt in person to read the truths written in stone, undecipherable for millennia."

The captain took a sip of wine. "Napoleon's men discovered the Rosetta Stone. While he was defeated in Egypt, his ships continue to patrol the northern Mediterranean. We've evaded them many times, but one is not *always* lucky."

Jean-Louis lips took on a wry expression. "There are ways."

***

Monday, July 8, 1811 – Alia's Offices
Alia

Seven days remained until The Pharaoh's reappearance. In her office, Alia catalogued all that remained to be completed by that date.

People were accustomed to The Pharaoh as a concept, a man above day-to-day transactions. He appeared about once every two years to shore up his legend, absorb the energies and intangible measures of his empire. *It will be difficult to continue without him, but not impossible.* His unexpected visit would give her one year, perhaps as long as two, to consolidate her position. In truth, by then she might be ready to turn over the reins. She endured constant pressure to maintain power, tamp down revolts, control internal disputes and eliminate the occasional rogue henchman.

She ran an organization that relied on fundamentally unreliable blackguards to accomplish its objectives. Fear and intimidation were implied. She preferred to set rewards to achieve compliance with her goals. In retrospect, she realized that she had marginalized other women in her ascent. Perhaps it was as simple as female jealousy vying for The Pharaoh's approval. Perhaps she was more aware of feminine duplicity. Men were more predictable. Each gender was capable of lying with skill, but men were more susceptible to flattery.

There were three who might succeed her, one woman and two men. Xie Xie understood the finer points of The Pharaoh's traditional businesses, but she was no master of the underworld. Alia ran a latticework of pickpockets, forgers, blackmailers, informers, protection collectors and, occasionally, killers.

There was Layla, a feisty Ethiopian woman, whose name meant "dark beauty." She ran the blackmailers and informants, keeping the authorities at bay.

Jorgos, a half-Greek, half-Polish son of a deserter from the Greek army, ran the pickpockets and forgers, Alia's bread-and-butter operations.

The elimination of The Serbian had vaulted the Egyptian, Mert, whose name meant "lover of silence," into the head of protection collectors. He was too new to be raised to her position now, although in two years, he might be ready.

If assassins were required, she contracted for them separately through Sefu. He had told her many times that he preferred to remain in the background.

She let her mind wander to what she might do if she were forced to leave Egypt. She smiled. *Paris. I've always dreamed of Paris.*

***

Tuesday, July 9, 1811 – Ravenshire
Gilles

Gilles taught Orion patterns of surveillance, usage of weapons, and the ways of the *ton*.

The young Gypsy learned quickly to blend into the shadows. He tracked Gilles through Ravenshire Forest without a sound and jumped in front of his tutor.

Unsurprised, Gilles shrugged. "Not bad. You're learning. But the absence of sound is a signal too. There are diverse noises in the forest. Let the calls of birds, the steps of the wild ones, and songs of the wind teach you. Learn to sense the slightest change—such awareness could save your life. The woodland has a cadence of its own. Match it and no one will suspect you until it's too late."

With weapons, Orion improved steadily with the pistol, hitting targets eighty percent of the time. Taking up the bow again was not a success.

"Forget the bow. You're not a marauding Indian on the American plains or part of the Mongol horde conquering the world or one of the bowmen for Henry V."

Orion looked perplexed. "I have heard of the Indians, but what are Mongols?"

"Genghis Khan and his followers conquered most of the known world riding west from Mongolia, shooting arrows as they rode. Henry V won a war with France in good part due to the superior archers under his command."

"So you are saying that the bow is a weapon of the past?"

"The bow can release swift and fierce missiles of death. It is a formidable weapon, but has little use outside the greenwood. Wandering the streets of London with a longbow and quiver of arrows would attract attention. In the city, the knife and the pistol are concealable and practical. You hit most of the pistol targets in practice, but in a confrontation, accuracy will drop. But that is when reflexes take over. Practice trains the eye, the arm, and the fingers. Unpracticed hands are as useless as a crone's lips."

Gilles picked up a dagger. "Knives are different. A small dagger is ideal to wield in tight spaces, and are the weapon of choice for killers seeking deep personal revenge. 'Tis a rare man who can throw a knife like J-L. Like him, you have a natural flair for it."

Orion basked in the praise.

"Remember something about pistols. In real life, targets are moving. You have to estimate where to aim based on where the target will be, not where it was a moment earlier. Someone may be rushing toward you or away from you or toward someone you love or have a duty to protect. One way to simulate such a situation is to practice shooting a stationary target while moving on horseback. Mount your horse. Estimate their gait and direction and aim there."

Riding over a course laid out by Gilles, Orion had to twist to shoot at the straw targets, rush them and shoot, and ride away and turn back to shoot over his shoulder.

Gilles called out, "Stop!"

The Gypsy yanked the reins of his horse.

"I think you hit an animal." Gilles pointed. "I hear mewling in that direction." He ran toward the sound.

Following Gilles on his horse, Orion saw a wounded red fox. Its eyes expressed pain. He dismounted and turned to Gilles. "Can we save him?"

"A fox? They are not suitable for farm life. They'll prey on our chickens. No. the kindest thing to do is kill it to end its suffering. Go ahead. Shoot it."

"Maybe we could get the bullet out and let him go."

"Are you going to act this way when you have to kill to protect the Wyndwards? How will you kill your father if you can't kill a fox?"

Orion's face hardened. "That is different. This fox did not attack. I shot him by accident."

Gilles shook his head. "He's bleeding from the thigh. He will never walk or run normally again. You're sentencing him to a long and painful death by starvation."

"He's pretty fat. Maybe he can survive."

The reynard began to shiver and cry out.

"*Mon dieu*! It's a female ready to give birth! The trauma has forced her time."

"Where is her den?" Orion looked around for signs of a burrow. "There!" He ran over to inspect it. "Let us carry her over here for the birthing."

"Carry a squirming vixen with kits spilling out?"

"It's not far." Orion bent to pick her up and she lurched to bite him, but his reflexes retracted his hand in time to avoid injury. "We need a way to carry her." He took off his leather jacket and wrapped her head in it. "Come on!"

"*Foutre!* You are crazy!" Gilles picked up the lower body and they carried the birthing female to the burrow, settling her in. "Keep her head wrapped or she'll gnaw off your hand."

Orion struggled to control the vixen while Gilles examined the wound.

"It's a graze. She's bleeding, but should survive. The bullet is not inside her. She'll make it. Slowly pull your jacket off and back away."

Rolling the fox's head from his jacket, Orion released her. She snarled, but did not lunge forward.

"Satisfied?" Gilles shook his head and walked away. *This boy may be too soft for what J-L expects of him.*

Five kits were expelled from the vixen's body while Orion stood transfixed.

"Let's go before the skulk appears."

"Won't the rest of the skulk hide until we're gone?"

Gilles shrugged. "Probably, but we're done here." He mounted his horse.

Orion did the same, and then looked at Gilles out of the corner of his eye. "Thanks."

"You have a new leather jacket covered with fox blood. Explain that to J-L when he gets back."

"Maybe he won't notice."

Gilles turned away from his apprentice and laughed as they mounted. He spurred his horse to a gallop, leaving Orion sputtering from the dust kicked up by the lead horse's hooves.

CHAPTER TWENTY-THREE

Tuesday, July 9. 1811 – Turtin Upholsterers & Drapers
Vaux

Vaux walked through the door of the shop, activating the bell, alerting the proprietor of his arrival.

Hugh Turtin stood with his back to Vaux, examining bolts of fabric.

The viscount marveled at how trim the draper looked from the back. In profile, the girth of the draper's gut made him appear as a woman on the verge of giving birth. *How does he bend down and get up?*

"Lord Vaux. I'll get Rachel. She's expecting you." Turtin went through the curtain to the back part of the shop where well-muscled men labored on upholstering chairs, settees and divans, while seamstresses stitched the drapes and pillow coverings.

He returned with his daughter.

Rachel had a handsome look, a no-nonsense approach to her tasks, and a bit of an abrupt manner.

Vaux didn't care. She had the best eye in the *ton* for fabrics and their suitability for particular projects. With her light brown locks carelessly tossed into a pony tail, she appeared insouciant but was in fact obsessed with details, a quality that Vaux valued in his decorating and design work. "Did the blue-hued jacquard fabric arrive?"

"Yes, and the tanner sent over a sample for the light-hued leather chairs. I think you'll like it. I have more samples in my office. Come back with me and we'll review the color scheme for Mr. James."

Following her into the noisy work area, the sweat-tinged air offended his lungs. He coughed.

"I have the window open in my office for fresh air."

"Fresh air in London is a bit optimistic. I took you for a realist."

"I am. It's all we've got." She led him into her office and closed the door, reducing the din. Several long tables held books of fabric samples. Bolts of fabric leaned against the wall, and sketches of designs were splayed across her desk.

"His study is in these shades of gray, the jacquard for the draperies, and the leather for the chairs. The rug is a Moroccan design with gray and white, not as busy as a Persian rug. But the antique Asian black lacquer desk you found in his storage warehouse is magnificent and will stand out. I have a painter who can match the lacquer with a glossy paint finish for the bookcases and side tables.

"All we have to decide now is what accent color you'd like to use for accessories, drapery tassels, and so on. For the parlor, chintz with a yellow background features bursts of flowers on the divan. The wingback chairs are in a pale green leather. The draperies match. The rug is a pale green in the Greek key design that is subtle but rings texture and warmth. Lady Gabriella picked the combination."

Vaux nodded. "James has deferred to her on most decisions except his study."

"The dining room has the Greek key rug design on the draperies and cushions on the black lacquer chairs. Again, that black lacquer table is long and dramatic. It can seat twelve easily. Your carpenter matched the antique Chinese chairs with an unerring skill. The little touches on the underside are perfect."

The viscount designer smiled. "I love that you notice the details that I do. Most people say they like something, but they don't understand why it pleases the eye."

"And I appreciate that *you* notice the little touches that make a difference. That's why I wanted to take another look at the private spaces with you. You know these people and I don't. Mr. James requested a blue bedroom, but Lady Gabriella requested a pale yellow." She pointed to two sketches—one for each bedroom. "Each has a separate dressing room and bath, with a sitting room between the suites, so there is plenty of space."

After examining both designs, Vaux made a couple of suggestions and discussed furniture makers who could produce the bed frames, chairs, benches, desks, vanities and armoires they required. Finally, they covered the specifications for the servants' quarters, nursery and children's and guest rooms on the upper floors.

As the light faded, Vaux realized he had another appointment at his club. "I have to schedule the workers to properly time all the installations. I have rented a warehouse nearby where I will have all the furniture delivered.

"We can bring it here for you to upholster, and return it for storage at the warehouse until the house is ready. The inside construction has been completed, and the windows are ready for the final measurements.

"Assuming we can get the furniture delivered to you by the end of July, is that enough time for the upholsterers to complete their work by early September?"

Rachel shrugged. "That sounds reasonable, as long as I can get the yardage for the fabrics we've chosen. Now that our decisions are firm, I can place orders and I'll let you know if any availability problems arise."

She leaned over her work table, searching for something. She walked over to another table and pulled out a design portfolio. "Do you have just a moment?"

"Of course." Vaux looked over the sketches. "A French Provincial theme? A new restaurant?"

"An omelet parlor and *salon de thé*. Your source secured the bistro tables and chairs for me, but the proprietress would like to have a seating section that is like a parlor, to give an intimate feel. Could your furniture makers create an area with divans and chairs to accommodate ten to twelve people? I have some bolts of prints from France—I found them in the back cupboard from before Napoleon's ascension."

Vaux looked them over. "They're ideal! I can see how it would look. May I sketch my initial concept?"

"Of course!" Rachel cleared space for him. As Vaux sketched, she looked over his shoulder. "Perfect! Exactly as I'd imagined! I marvel at how fast your hand transfers what's in your head." She sighed. "My process is more pedestrian."

"Not pedestrian," Vaux replied without looking up from his work. "Deliberate and thoughtful." He put down the pencil and turned his gaze toward Rachel. "We make a great team, don't we?"

"For some reason, you're the only man I trust." She leaned back in her chair. "I worry about what will happen to the shop when my father dies. It will be mine as an unmarried woman, but if I had a husband, it would be his. I don't think I could tolerate that."

"I'd never really thought about the inequity of marriage until I got to know Lady Gabriella better. At the beginning, she'd argue with us at dinner parties over the limitations placed on women versus men."

"We'd roll our eyes, as if to say, 'There she goes again, running on about women's rights.' But over time, I've come to see things through her eyes. Society demands rigidity, setting arbitrary rules, when life requires flexibility, to my way of thinking."

Vaux sighed as if deflated and stared at the bolts of fabric. "I am being pressured to marry, to beget an heir."

"I thought the 'quality' married for else than love, disdaining the poetry and adventures of Lord Byron. Men of my class are rough, uncouth and dense of mind."

She touched his arm. "I sense the reason for your hesitation, Lord Vaux. Perhaps you could develop a friendship with a woman—a woman who appreciates you, a woman who understands your needs—a woman who has inclinations similar to your own...for her own."

Vaux shrugged. "Perhaps. And perhaps the sun will shine at night and the moon light the day."

"Our night is day on the other side of the world. Both exist at the same time." Rachel rose to her feet. "It's dark. You're quite late for your appointment."

The viscount stood. "So I am. We have accomplished a great deal today. I enjoy our time together." He walked to the door and turned toward Rachel. "What is the name of the *salon de thé*?"

"*Omelettes de Mme. d'Aix.*" Rachel smiled a wry grin. "Odd how we still look to the French for style and cuisine while in a state of war."

"We're always at war with France. Name a century without one."

"My sense of history is shallow. I don't know. Is there?"

"I don't know, either. It's a great line, though, isn't it?"

"Fit for a dinner party of swells. Use it tonight."

"Perhaps I shall, fair Miss Turtin. Perhaps I shall."

***

Wednesday, July 10, 1811 – An Apothecary Shop, Alexandria
Blackburn as The Pharaoh

The urchin held the red door open for the man wearing Arab robes and then darted out of sight.

Mme. Anh came out from the back area of the shop with a box and placed it on the counter. She opened it to reveal tiny blown glass vials on thin silk straps. "An assortment in different colors to coordinate with the potions I gave you."

Blackburn dropped a few gold coins on the counter.

Mme. Anh checked his eyes. "Blink rapidly."

Following her instructions, Blackburn waited.

"There are still light brown, almost gold areas. The natural hue of your eyes is so strong – use your judgment in dosing with the potion."

"One more suggestion."

Blackburn waited in silence.

"Let me remind you again: When filling those vials with the snakeskin gloves, should any drops get on the gloves, place salt on them and let them dry in the sun. But to protect yourself, never touch the outside of the gloves where any poison might remain."

"Understood." He bowed his head. "Until I return."

"As you say."

I may return someday. She is a useful tool.

The urchin peeked around the edge of the back area.

Blackburn gave him a withering look the slave would never forget.

The boy soiled himself and shrank away.

***

Wednesday, July 10, 1811 – Interior of a Hackney, London
Michelle

As she rode back to her rooms at Durrants, Michelle Matthews reviewed her moving schedule. The flat she just leased would be ready for occupancy in a few days. *Miss Jones is an efficient estate agent. The floor of the old palace is perfect, with servant's quarters in the back.* She glanced out the window, but the view was obscured by the driving rain. *I'll have to get used to this rain. It's incessant.*

Looking over the card Miss Jones had given her, she hoped she could find a cook and a Lady's maid from the Seminary for Women's Work. The flat came with a butler, housekeeper, scullery maid, and footman. *All in all, things are going well. I've been here less than a week, and I have a place to live, excellent contacts and—"*

Without warning, she was thrown to the side of the Hackney. Her head hit the door and the wobbling of the carriage caused her to fall to the floor where she rolled around with each jerk of the axle until the carriage came to a stop. Dazed, she couldn't focus when the door of the carriage opened. A man's hand extended toward her, but she felt faint.

The tall rescuer picked her up and carried her inside the adjacent hatter's shop, where he helped her sit on a bench and then knelt next to her.

The driver ran in after them with her reticule and package of papers that had been left in the carriage. "Are you all right, Ma'am? The wheel split in two after hitting a rut in the road."

Taking the papers from the driver, the tall man placed them on the bench next to the injured woman.

The hatter brought a wet cloth to wipe the blood off her forehead. "I think it's a minor laceration." He pressed the fabric against her skin until the bleeding stopped.

Slowly, the faces around her came into focus. "Th-thank you."

Her rescuer's face filled her eyes. "Ma'am, I can wave down another jervie to take you home."

"Not home. To my hotel. Durrants."

"I'll follow to make sure you arrive safely," said the tall man. "Protocol prevents us from riding in the same carriage." He turned to the hatter. "Briggs, box the hats for me." He looked at the woman. "Mrs.?"

"Miss. Miss Michelle Matthews." She picked up her reticule and papers, and stood. "That would be kind of you, sir."

"American?"

She nodded.

Durwood escorted her outside and waved down a Hackney. "Take her to Durrants."

Miss Matthews smiled. "Sir, I didn't catch your name to thank you properly."

The man smiled. "I didn't throw it. Durwood. Dennis Durwood."

"Thank you, Mr. Durwood."

He bowed his head slightly, closed the door to the Hackney and rapped on the side of the carriage, signaling the jervie to move into the traffic.

***

Durwood

Raising his hand, Durwood alerted his driver to pull up. He climbed into his carriage with the hatbox, sat back and wondered what this chance meeting might lead to. *She felt light in my arms. It's an exhilarating feeling to rescue someone. Perhaps she'll invite me for tea at the hotel, in clear view of the public. What could be improper about that?*

***

Wednesday, July 10, 1811 – Aboard *Taygete's Wynd*
Gio

On another evening, Gio leaned in after finishing his meal. "Lady Clarissa, what more should we know about our destination?"

"Settled in the early 1400s, the archipelago of the Azores, its clusters and individual islands have been called various things: the Goat Islands, the Islands of The Wind, the Island of Flowers, the Islands of the Dove, the Island of Sea Crows, the Island of Fire—"

"From volcanic eruptions?"

"Perhaps. There are nine volcanic islands, spread out in three groupings over the archipelago. The last major eruptions were in 1759-1760 extending from Christmas into the new year. There are two islands in the western cluster, five in the central area and two to the east as well as a reef. The captain has mapped out a course where we make our first landing on the farthest western island of Corvo. Whaling expeditions from New England provision there. We will pass Flores, named for its blue hydrangea flowers, which should be gloriously in bloom as we sail around the island."

Gwyneth leaned forward. "Why aren't we stopping there to see the flowers?"

The captain cleared his throat. "Both western isles are sparsely populated, Madame la Comtesse. Most of the population on Flores consists of slaves, mulattoes and badly treated servants who toil shoeless. I felt it might not be safe for a wealthy party such as yours."

The dwarf took a gulp of wine. "I fear you have depressed the festive mood, Captain. Talk of slavery and poverty are hardly lighthearted subjects of mirth."

Edward frowned. "The winds of change are upon us. Slavery cannot long prevail."

Bri shook her head. "Isn't poverty another form of slavery? Though people be not owned as chattel, they are exploited nonetheless. Human history is one of war, conquest and domination. We perpetuate the conceit that we are better than slavers, but are we?"

"We cannot rescue the population of Flores. Let us say a silent prayer for them." Clarissa bowed her head.

Gio started to retort, but Gwyneth poked him in the ribs, so he remained silent until Clarissa spoke again.

"Our planned itinerary after leaving Corvo and sailing by Flores, will head east to the central island grouping and first stop at Faial, also a haven for blue hydrangeas. Its name comes from the Faya tree, which appears blue from a distance. In fact, Faial was the only source for blue dye, called 'woad' from the plant of the same name, until the end of the 16th century when indigo began to be exported from the Far East. In the central grouping, we will also stop at Terceira, where lush vineyards spring from porous volcanic rock. Our final stop will be at San Miguel, with caldera lakes and the *Lagoa de Sete Ciudades*, which would be a long trek and a reason to return someday. Then we will sail past Santa Maria, where Columbus was blown in a storm returning from his first voyage to America in 1493."

"Come on, Clarissa, you know what Gio wants to hear. The oldest legend of all." Edward glanced at Gio. "Atlantis."

"There is a name linked to that myth on San Miguel, *Sete Cidades*—meaning seven cities—that might suggest the legend or merely be a later, fanciful name. We'll never know."

The captain demurred. "Perhaps, but knowledge is always expanding. Many who sail to the Caribbean also say those islands are the remains of Atlantis. One of my sailors stared at his reflection in the clear turquoise waters, like Narcissus.

"When he reached out to touch his face, the fool fell overboard. We thought him dead, but when he surfaced, we captured him in our fishing net and hauled him back onto the deck. He spoke of cobblestone streets and remnants of buildings on the ocean bed. He'd heard the legends and believed he had discovered the road to Atlantis."

"The city-continent of seven concentric circles, described by Plato as divided by canals, would have been massive to extend from the Azores to the Caribbean." Edward shook his head. "And to disappear in a day and a night? Impossible."

Bri disagreed. "Nothing is impossible. And who are we to say what is too massive? Our perspective is provincial. Remember what Hamlet said—"

" 'There are more things in heaven and Earth, Horatio, than are dreamt of in your philosophy.' " Gio smirked. "And I am one of them."

Gwyneth glared at him. "No. We are not dreaming that you exist, Gio. You are here. Must all conversation center around you?"

"Yes. But let's get back to the impossible destruction of the magnificent Atlantis. I imagine people in sun-filled villas, pursuing poetry, painting and the arts. Some clever one must have survived. Why else the legend? Perhaps Henry is correct."

"An earthquake or simultaneous volcanic eruptions could have induced a catastrophe." The captain narrowed his eyes as he spoke. "Tidal waves destroy all in their path. I saw the devastation one caused once from a distance. Only the grace of God prevented us from being swept away. We were exploring and were able to scramble to high ground.

"So, Lady Gabriella, I must agree with you. Nothing is impossible in the hands of Mother Nature."

Gio raised his glass. "A toast to Mother Nature!"

***

Wednesday, July 10, 1811 – Aboard *Taygete's Wynd*
Clarissa

Clarissa knocked on Bri's door. The latch wasn't fastened, and the door opened. "Bri?" Seeing no one, Clarissa thought she'd leave a note that she intended to take a nap. She noticed a stack of paper on the table, and sat down to write a note. She pulled what she thought was a blank piece, but then realized writing was on the other side. She glanced at it, and it captured her attention. Her mouth dropped open as she read. *This is a novel!* She turned over the bottom of the pile of papers to see the initial page—*The Scottish Laird and the Vicar's Widow* by Persephone Peabody. *What? The comtesse is Persephone Peabody? The writer of scandalous novels?* She quickly replaced the papers and left, fearing discovery.

CHAPTER TWENTY-FOUR

Thursday, July 11, 1811 – The Catacombs of Alexandria
Xie Xie

In her cave-like room in the catacombs, Xie Xie sat at a small desk and reviewed her checklist for her meeting on the fifteenth with The Pharaoh. Several large candles in tin holders illuminated the small space. Like The Pharaoh, she had procured traveling clothes from a stall at the bazaar, intending to acquire a fuller wardrobe when she reached London. Her arrival in the city would be about a month or two earlier than The Pharaoh.

She asked no questions about his travel plans. The Pharaoh had chosen her hotel and would contact her when he arrived.

Her most urgent task remained unfinished. She must learn James's secret weakness. All men had them.

As part of research into Edward James, Xie Xie extended her tentacles into old Chinese contacts on the trade routes. Through this incestuous and circuitous network, she had followed a link through a chain of informers that finally promised success. *Just in time. I can't disappoint The Pharaoh.*

An informer in the Far East claimed to have information on James. Money flowed freely through the chain on orders from The Pharaoh. A meeting with her original link was set for tomorrow in a restaurant in the Asian quarter.

London loomed in Xie Xie's imagination as the chance of a lifetime. The Pharaoh had told her that after she completed her part of this assignment, he would be successful, die or disappear. Then she would be free.

Not that she was a prisoner. In his true identity, which only she and Alia knew, The Pharaoh had saved her from an unspeakable life of sexual bondage and degradation. He had educated her, groomed her and encouraged her individuality, abnormal for the culture of her birth. He had promised to arrange for money to be left in her name in London, and told her that she could embark on whatever life she wanted after her assignment there was completed.

Xie Xie had never been involved in the criminal activities under Alia's direction, although, in Xie Xie's opinion, they were mostly petty crimes involving bribery, forgery, pickpocketing and other forms of minor theft—criminals preying on corrupt government officials, unsuspecting wealthy European tourists, or other criminals.

Occasionally, she'd heard rumors of a murder, but she didn't know whether such whispers were conjectures, embellishments, or facts. In rescuing her and other young girls from the brothel in China, the man who became The Pharaoh had not flinched at killing.

In Xie Xie's view of life and men, anything was possible.

***

Thursday, July 11, 1811 – Edward's Townhouse
Vaux

The viscount and the upholsterer walked through Edward's townhouse, marking off on a list the final items they needed to acquire, deliver, and install.

"You've done a fine job, Lord Vaux."

"We both have. And call me Vaux."

"Call me Turtin."

"Not Rachel?"

"No. Not unless you let me call you by your first name. I resent men being addressed with more formality than women."

"I never thought about that. No one ever calls me by my first name except my parents, and then it's usually with a tone of disdain." Vaux lowered his voice in an imitation of his father. " 'Rudy, stop dabbling. Collect the rents and inspect our properties.' "

He shrugged. "I devote one day a week to my holdings. That's enough."

"Rudy...Rudolph?" Rachel could not suppress a smirk. "That sounds Teutonic."

"It is. It means 'wolf of fame.' "

"You don't strike me as ferocious but you are famous in the *ton*."

"Ha! Being underestimated is my secret weapon. I leap for the kill when least expected."

***

Thursday, July, 11, 1811 – Winters Foundling Hospital
Eli

Eli Sterling exited his carriage for lunch with Charlotte. A short, intense bur affable Jew who'd married Annabelle James, Edward's sister, came from a family of Jewish bankers. Initial shock befell the *ton* when James & Co. absorbed their operations after the death of Eli's father and uncle in a robbery, but the surviving son won over most critics.

An expert in small, family-owned trades and service businesses, Eli looked forward to being a trustee of such a forward-thinking operation as the one Charlotte had created. He admired the drive and meticulous attention to detail the baroness had demonstrated in making the Winters Foundling Hospital a haven for working class women and abandoned children. And he knew his brother-in-law's future wife, Lady Gabriella, was not one to shirk a challenge.

A receptionist led him to a small room next to Charlotte's office. A round table had been set for their meal. "The baroness will join you shortly."

As he turned to thank the receptionist, he saw two women leaving Charlotte's office. He recognized one of them, but had practiced discretion long enough that he betrayed no indication of that recognition. He was certain she had not seen him. *I've never considered it, but Mlle. Sabine must have need of Charlotte's services for her workers from time to time.*

Charlotte entered and greeted Eli. "Mr. Sterling, I'm so glad you could meet today." Even though Charlotte knew Eli and his wife's family, protocol demanded that they address each other in a formal manner. "Wyndward Investments holds a great deal of promise." She gestured for Eli to sit down as she took her place behind her desk. "In addition, I have been working on a number of initiatives that I think you'll find equally compelling."

Eli sat back. "I look forward to hearing about them, Baroness. I've brought a summary of the current investments and what issues might come up with Bri and Edward away in the Azores."

***

Thursday, July 11, 1811 – Aboard *Taygete's Wynd*
Bri

"Land Ho!" called the lookout from the Main Top Castle.

The ship sailed past the Island of Flowers. The fields of blue shading to purple transfixed the travelers. It was late afternoon when they dropped the jolly boats to ferry them to shore to the port on the island of Corvo. Windy, but sunny, balmy weather beckoned them.

The travelers gathered behind them to board the jolly boat. The captain reached out to Gwyneth and helped her into the boat, then Clarissa and Bri. Edward, Dr. St. Cloud and Gio followed. The boat was lowered via ropes, rocking in the air as crewmen struggled to keep the ropes taut. Once it splashed gently into the water, the oarsmen rowed to shore.

The group took a leisurely walk, exploring the town, and opted for an early dinner in a small inn with a Portuguese chef who had a deft hand with fresh seafood.

At a nearby table, American ship captains from other docked whalers made bawdy toasts.

After dinner, Bri and Edward walked barefoot on the beach watching dophins at sunset.

Bri thought of how dolphins had saved her father after his shipwreck. As they playfully jumped in the air, she said, "I believe they have souls, as we do."

Edward tilted his head as he watched their antics. "That hypothesis can never be proven."

"I know. I choose to believe it."

"A sentimental choice, given your father's experience."

"Some things must be taken on faith, even by me."

***

Friday, July 12, 1811 – An Asian Restaurant in Alexandria
Xie Xie

Xie Xie sat at a booth in the back of a restaurant in the Asian quarter of Alexandria. Despite the noon hour, the interior was dark. Perfect for a clandestine meeting. Her secretive contact entered in traditional Bedouin robes, his skin nearly as dark as an Ethiopian from years of camel riding.

In truth, she wasn't sure Neri was Egyptian or Arab by birth. No one denied that his language skills were prodigious—he was known as The Translator, having mastered English, Persian, Greek, and Armenian as well as multiple Chinese and Indian dialects. Neri was much sought after in the caravanning trade, signing on whenever he craved adventure. He always more than earned his pay, translating the real cost of goods to the caravan leaders after eavesdropping on the purveyors' conversations. As for his real currency, it was information. Neri dealt in circles that spewed rumors, speculation, or gossip—deciphering the truth was a guess. But a guess from Neri was more reliable than testimony from a direct witness to a crime.

Neri took a sip of the black Turkish coffee Xie Xie had poured for him. She offered him sugar.

"No sugar. Bad for the teeth." He flashed a smile. "I intend to keep them as long as I can."

Xie Xie smiled and sipped tea. "I am anxious to hear what you have learned. The timing is perfect, for I will be leaving for Europe in a few days."

"England, no doubt. You always want to speak English. You do it so well."

The Chinese apprentice maintained an enigmatic face and passed him a purse filled with silver.

Neri leaned forward, taking a date from a dish and popping it in his mouth before speaking. He reached into a pocket in his robe, and brought out a book with a cover title written in Persian script. "A collection of Persian love poems." He opened it to reveal a dried flower pressed within its pages. "Here is your answer."

***

Friday, July 12, 1811 – *Omelettes de Mme. d'Aix*
Vaux

It was the end of a busy week for Rachel and Vaux.

The draper had introduced Vaux to Danforth, the estate agent who'd found the location for Mme. d'Aix's café. Danforth arranged a meeting for Vaux with the proprietress. At the appointed time, Viscount Vaux visited the shell of the abandoned space to develop an overall interior design based on Rachel's fabric choices that would appeal to the trendsetters of the *ton*.

The owner, Aneira d'Aix, welcomed him. "I look forward to hearing your concepts, Lord Vaux."

Vaux's eyes scanned the room. "Good light from the leaded windows. The name of the café says it all. I assume you want to recreate the ambiance of Provence."

Aneira nodded. "The colors of that countryside are unmatched."

"Agreed. Shades of lavender, yellows and whites are what I envision. We could *faux* paint the walls to look like the fortification walls built by the ancient Romans, then use bistro tables and divans for comfortable seating. Perhaps paintings depicting the lavender fields of Provence and Mt. Ste.-Victoire could be commissioned from expatriate artists who have fled Napoleon."

Clapping her hands together, Aneira smiled. "You have encapsulated my vision perfectly."

Moving his hand in an arc over the space, he added, "I see white-washed pine floors, with matching white-lacquered chairs and tables along with linens and upholstery from Miss Turtin displaying the paisleys and patterns of Provence that you have selected. She and I work well together."

"I defer to the experts." Aneira quoted a budget suggested by the estate agent, who had knowledge of similar project requirements. "Will that suffice?"

"I think so. My normal working process is to let you know when we have reached eighty percent of the budget, so we can review final choices, and add or cut as needed. I require forty percent in advance. Will that be satisfactory?"

"Yes. I can provide a draft from my bank tomorrow."

Vaux handed her his card. "It can be delivered here. Shall we meet in a week's time to review final sketches, samples of fabric, and so on? Miss Turtin will join me."

"Your efficiency impresses me, Lord Vaux. The same time a week from today."

As Vaux turned to leave, he caught a glimpse of an elderly woman with a distinctly foreign look heading up the stairs to what he assumed was a living area. Colorful clothing, necklaces and a bandana in her hair struck him as Gypsy attire. "Are living quarters upstairs?"

"Yes."

"Before you move in, I suggest that my engineer determine whether the construction is sound. Let me take a look now."

Aneira extended her hand, signaling him to take a look.

Vaux went up the stairs and examined the suite of rooms. He glanced at the Gypsy standing by the window. "I am Viscount Vaux, Madam—"

The Gypsy turned. "Mirela. I being simply Mirela."

Aneira reached the top of the stairs. "I see you've met."

The designer bowed his head in acknowledgement. "Madam Mirela, Mme. d'Aix, as long as we're outfitting a kitchen below, we can extend the venting up here as well, for a small kitchen for personal use, and an ice box.

"The floors can be the same as below, and if you'd like me to design and build the furniture, I'll be happy to do it for another ten to fifteen percent over the price for the lower area, depending on the finishes. I can provide you a proposal on this area when we meet next week."

"You are a most enterprising young lord."

"I have the luxury of indulging my interests, and a banker who instructs me on the financial minutiae that I find annoying."

Aneira glanced at Mirela and then directed her gaze back at Vaux. "We'll need a table, a divan and some comfortable chairs, and a large bed and two armoires for the bedroom."

Vaux nodded without betraying any surprise at the sharing of a bed her instructions implied. "Understood."

***

Mirela

After Vaux left, Mirela waited while Aneira locked the front door behind them. Aneira waved down a Hackney, and they climbed in.

As they pulled away, Mirela said, "When he shaking my hand, I knew. He understanding us because he being the same as us."

Aneira shrugged. "History was made by people like us."

***

Friday, July 12, 1811 – The Island of Horta
Gwyneth

The travelers admired the vista of the town of Horta from the bay. Classical bayside structures graced the circular walled road encircling the beach. Centuries-old churches and colorfully painted doors and shutters on stone buildings dotted the hillsides.

Gio pointed to a bench looking out over the bay. "Let's set up there. We can get the other shore, the boats, and the changing colors of the water." When they were situated, he reached into his bag and pulled out a tin about ten inches by six inches and handed it to Gwyneth.

She opened it and gasped. "A set of stamped Reeves watercolor cakes!" she stared at him. "These are perfect."

"The world doesn't *always* center around me—it sometimes includes other people." He handed her a canvas bag filled with bushes, and then pulled out two water dishes and a canteen, placing them on the bench between them. He poured a bit of water in each dish. "I was unable to fit two easels, but I have two boards and a supply of handmade cold-pressed paper."

"How did you get this from France? The embargo—"

"—as a certain Frenchman would say, 'There are ways.' "

"Why didn't he come with us?"

"He said he'd be along later."

Gio pointed to several interesting architectural structures. "Comtesse, let us sketch and paint *en plein air* while light permits."

***

Edward

"These islands have a near-tropical climate in the middle of the Atlantic. Such a difference from our foggy, cold home."

Bri closed her eyes and basked in the sun's warmth.

"You wouldn't want to live here all the time," Edward whispered as he kissed her neck. "It might make you indolent."

Her eyes opened and she smiled. "I was just thinking. These islands are mostly undeveloped, like a green refuge. We could begin with small hotels, trekking expeditions to the extinct volcanoes, tented camps as if on safari, but without six months of travel. Nature safaris, like Hanforth's wildlife viewing safaris."

"I continue to be impressed by your mind. Practical and visionary."

"Sounds a bit grand for a small travel business. Exaggeration is uncalled for." She turned her face toward his. "And indolence is not a fair description. Think of those who suffer from melancholy, like my mother. Perhaps a rest cure in a sunny place, a change of venue to a temperate climate, is another possibility. A way to escape one's burdens. Longer than a holiday. A way to heal one's mind."

"I often think I might need a rest cure from your constant inspirations." Thinking his retort a bit insensitive, Edward adopted a gentle tone, and placed his hand on her shoulder. "When the person returns to his or her home, wouldn't all the same concerns reappear?"

Bri's face fell. "You're probably right. Maybe a holiday is all we can offer."

"Come, let's explore."

They found several places for dinner, and then turned the corner and saw a restaurant on a small hill with tables out on a terrace. Bri pointed. "That's it!"

***

Gio

A dinner, Jean-Louis finally appeared.

Gio and Gwyneth showed their paintings, as course after course was brought to their table.

The travelers toasted each other and the island as the sun set over the mountains.

Reluctantly, as the moon rose in the sky, they made their way back to the jolly boat, turning around for a last look at Horta. Each held to the rim of the boat as it was raised back to the ship, clambered out onto the deck and staggered, exhausted, to their cabins and fell into their sleeping hammocks.

***

Monday, July 15, 1811 – An Inn in Alexandria
Blackburn as The Pharaoh

Assessing his appearance in a small mirror, The Pharaoh searched his eyes for any trace of turquoise. None remained. The transformation to subtle variations of brown was complete. The dye on his beard and the darkening of his natural brown hair to near-black made him almost unrecognizable as the man who had been known as Blackburn. A wry smile crossed his face. *The "Blackie" nickname Bri gave me still works.* His skin had bronzed to match the skin tone of a desert Arab and his robes made him seem as one ordinary man of many in a crowd.

He snapped his fingers, and Midnight jumped into the black leather bag. Camouflaged netting allowed her to breathe.

She meowed her approval.

"You will see our new home soon. You can wander through the catacombs at will again for the next month or two, mousing at your leisure."

With his leather bag in one hand, he gathered up the carpet bags with his purchases and descended the stairs to the reception area.

The manager, understanding The Pharaoh's requirements, had a carriage waiting for him. "Until your return."

The Pharaoh nodded. *I may never be back, but life holds many uncertainties.* As he rode through the town, he noted the steady improvements. *Alia is ready. Growth here means more opportunity for my people. My attention is no longer needed.*

The carriage delivered him to the edge of the bazaar, where he could easily disappear, descending below the streets, and vanish into one of many hidden conduits that led to the catacombs. When he reached one of the entry points, a guard he did not recognize stopped him.

"Identity code?"

Narrowing his eyes as he stared at the guard, The Pharaoh remained silent, fingering a silver ankh hanging from his neck on a silk cord. A black star sapphire, inset into the metalwork, sparkled in the torchlight of the dark cavern.

The man fell to his knees. "Master, I am your servant."

CHAPTER TWENTY-FIVE

Monday, July 15, 1811 – The Pharaoh's Catacomb Apartments
Xie Xie

At the appointed hour, Xie Xie appeared at the foyer leading to The Pharaoh's apartments. She had not seen him for more than a year, but their communications, delivered through coded letters and messengers carrying more sensitive information every six months, had prepared her for this moment.

She had established herself as the Egyptian representative of a wealthy Asian consortium, Silk Route Trading, seeking trade and natural resource partners.

Thanks to The Pharaoh, unlimited bribes had secured reliable contacts throughout Asia and Africa. Her cover story and viability could be verified. Particular attention to British banks operating in Alexandria, through personal and private dealings, ensured her credibility in London.

Raj, an Indian man of about twenty, had been assigned by Alia to guard The Pharaoh. He had an affectation for extravagance and color, sporting royal blue silk harem pantaloons, ankle bracelets, a yellow silk sash and a flowing white silk shirt with ruffled sleeves. No one knew his real name—the sobriquet for "rajah" played to his vanity. He was no prince.

Xie Xie recognized that the assignment of Raj to The Pharaoh's inner chamber was a test—a test where failure to please the Master would have fatal consequences.

"Miss Li, you arrive on time, as always." Raj spoke English well despite his heavy accent. "The Master awaits." He pushed aside a door that receded into the stone walls. Once she stepped inside, he closed it again.

Xie Xie stared at a man she did not recognize. Near-black hair and an Arab-like complexion stunned her. A black beard covered a thinner face than when she had last seen him. His eyes were completely different. She waited to hear his voice. *Is it really The Pharaoh?*

The Pharaoh smiled. "There was a time, Xie Xie, when I was not sure we would meet again, but I have survived." He lay stretched out on his side. The bed was piled high with soft pillows, a black cat slept draped over his hip, purring lightly. "I'd stand, but I don't want to disturb Midnight."

Xie Xie sat in an ornately carved chair opposite the bed. Rumored to have been looted from a true pharaoh's tomb, its gilded legs felt steady, even after the passage of millennia. "Master, I have missed Midnight. She and I would be lost without you."

"Nonsense." He absentmindedly petted his cat. "Felines are instinctive killers. She could forage for herself on a moment's notice. So could you." He gestured to the table. "Please pour some tea for us."

Dutifully, Xie Xie filled their cups and brought one to The Pharaoh.

He carefully nudged Midnight off his hip and sat up to sip his tea.

The cat rolled onto the down pillows, stretched, and reclined lazily in slumber.

While he sipped his tea, Xie Xie retook her seat. "Your eyes, Master, have changed. They no longer reflect shades of blue-green."

The Pharaoh shrugged. "A subterfuge to fool the British. I trust that Alia has informed you of your imminent departure?"

"I am booked for this evening's sailing. Silk Route Trading is established with the contacts you recommended." She handed him a portfolio of papers. "The details are contained here. Of all of our associates, I believe that Rao would be the best replacement for me to implement your objectives."

"Half-Egyptian and half-Chinese. Interesting." The Pharaoh frowned. "You trust him?"

"Yes, I have tested him. His loyalty has never wavered. He is aware that I am leaving tonight."

The Pharaoh picked up a hammer and rang a small brass gong.

The door opened, and Raj appeared. "Yes, Master?"

"Bring Rao to us. Keep him outside until Miss Li leaves."

Raj nodded and pushed the door back into place.

Xie Xie continued, "I have letters of introduction and Letters of Credit from British and Egyptian banks to establish banking in London for the Silk Route Trading offices in London. We will have full banking and capital support."

"Is the first shipment of silk on the same ship?"

"Yes, as well as bolts of fine Egyptian cotton. In addition, I am taking vases we will market as antiquities as well as counterfeit tomb relics. We will offer a selection of goods beyond silk, all with Asian provenance. The authentic will mask the inauthentic. You'd be impressed with the workmanship."

"Your cleverness has never been in doubt." He stood back and scanned her from head to toe. "By the way, you wear European clothing well. You will inhabit your role with typical panache.

"Have you any last questions for me?"

"No, master. I believe you have prepared me for whatever impediments I may encounter."

The Pharaoh's now-brown eyes scanned his apprentice. "You will be on your own, with only your wits at your disposal. In such situations, recall your training. Play for time if necessary. I will see you in London near the end of the year. Now, tell me how much of our scheme does Rao know?"

"Only what is necessary for him to function. Shipping details, import/export sources, and so on. Nothing of your broader purpose."

"Keep it that way. No last minute instructions. I will take over his grooming."

A knock on the door signaled that Rao had arrived.

The Pharaoh's eyes bored into her. "What have you learned about Mr. James?"

Xie Xie reached into her bag and brought out the Persian book she had been given by The Translator, and handed it to The Pharaoh.

He opened it and touched the delicate dried petals inside. Slamming the book shut, his lips betrayed the hint of a smile. "Now we know his secret."

***

Monday, July 15, 1811 – Aboard *Nekhbet's Wings*
Xie Xie

Standing onboard the ship, Xie Xie focused on Cleopatra's Needle as it receded from view. Stacked in the cargo were crates with bolts of Chinese silk, Egyptian cotton, Asian jade and pearls, and a mixture of real and fabricated ancient Egyptian artifacts.

The genuine ones would be donated to The British Museum, while the reproductions would be sold to unsuspecting collectors.

Alexandria had been Xie Xie's home since her rescue from China by Blackburn years earlier. During the months' long caravan journey along the Silk Road, Blackburn had formulated the concept of The Pharaoh.

Like her mentor, Xie Xie craved adventure and seeing new worlds. The Pharaoh had taken her on trips to Europe over the years, giving her limited first-hand experience of the western world.

As she gazed out over the lightly churning sea, her feet planted apart on the deck, she reflected on her balancing act. She bridged cultures just as she balanced her stance on the rolling deck. *I am not of my culture, nor am I a European.*

She had woven the contrasting strands of her experiences into the creation of her own persona. For years, she had suppressed her own wishes to learn and follow. She initiated action within narrow boundaries—so far, her instincts had been unerring. Now she stood on the cusp of directing her own life and her heart surged in anticipation. The Pharaoh's great promise was never far from her consciousness.

"After your task in England is completed, you can chart your own future." As the last vestiges of the ancient Alexandrian harbor vanished below the horizon, she breathed the salty air.

London awaits.

***

Monday, July 15, 1811 – The Island of Terceira
Gio

On Terceira, Gio, Edward, Jean-Louis and Bri took a bumpy wagon ride to see caves hollowed out of hillsides. "Natives say these hidden places were carved out of rock and pre-date any European settlements."

Gio looked into one of the caves and took a tentative step inside. "The mystery may never be solved. Who were they? Where did they go?"

Jean-Louis ducked to follow Gio inside. "Easter Island off the Pacific coast of South America has huge stone carvings of odd looking beings. Legends say the locals carved them, and they 'walked' to their positions. Over many years of accompanying the earl on his travels, I have seen monuments whose placement or construction defy explanation. We do not have ways to recreate them today."

"What does that tell you?" Edward held a torch up to see if any writing or cave drawings were on the walls.

"That we don't have answers to the mysteries of ancient cultures, let alone the stars." Bri sat on a boulder. "Perhaps an elder sat here to address her people."

Edward laughed. "A woman leader? Like the myth of the Amazons?"

The dwarf walked over to Bri and leaned against the rock. "Your fiancé no doubt prefers the myth of uncivilized club-wielding cave dwellers." Gio opened his arms as if enveloping the cave. "And here we are in his lair."

"The guide said these caves were used for burials." Edward felt the walls. "This rock feels carved rather than naturally formed."

Jean-Louis walked deeper into the cave, waving Edward forward. "People often label monuments they don't understand as tombs. Caves, pyramids and catacombs are unexplained. Man forces an explanation that fits his time."

Gio and Bri followed.

"There's nothing more back here." Edward's voice registered disappointment.

"Hold! I see something reflecting light." Gio dropped to his knees and brushed aside dirt. "A coin!" He retrieved it and turned to Edward. "No cavemen had coins."

The banker pushed back. "Caves no doubt had different inhabitants in different epochs. It was probably dropped by travelers like us."

The dwarf headed outside the cave to reach the sunlight. He spit on the coin to remove packed on dirt. He squinted to make out the writing. "Travelers, yes. Like us, perhaps. But from long before colonization in our era." He handed the coin to Jean-Louis.

The Frenchman looked carefully at both sides and a smile slowly came over him. "Perhaps the comtesse will accept this as a donation to the ancient artifact collection of the Museé de Merbeau."

Bri furrowed her brow. "The museum doesn't have an ancient artifact collection."

Jean-Louis shrugged. "It does now. This is an ancient Carthaginian coin."

CHAPTER TWENTY-SIX

Tuesday, July 16, 1811 – Aboard *Taygete's Wynd*
Dr. St. Cloud

B ri, Clarissa and Gwyneth reclined in deck chairs in the warmth of the early afternoon.

Gio stood on a stool looking out over the horizon. "I could watch the seas roll forever." He turned his head to see Chérie following Jean-Louis around the deck for his afternoon walk.

"You're dog's getting fat, Jean-Louis."

The Frenchman shrugged. "Maybe Sallie and Nellie give her too much food when I'm not looking."

Dr. St. Cloud knelt down and called Chérie over to him and palpated her abdomen. "Her weight is fine."

Gio scoffed. "Dr. St. Cloud, any fool can see she is not the lean runner she used to be."

"That's because she and Clarissa are in the same condition.

Jean-Louis was taken aback. "I thought she was too young."

The dwarf shrugged. "Apparently not."

Bri sat up. "How long until they're born?"

"Gestation is about two months."

"How many in a litter?"

The vet answered again, "Six to nine."

"Hmmm." Bri looked off into the distance.

Edward noticed. "There she goes, Jean-Louis. She's distributing the litter in her mind."

"Why not?" Bri sat up. "One for Ian, one for Oliver, one for Charlotte, one for Banfield, at a minimum. Lady Patricia expressed interest in a smaller dog, like Gio's Yorkie, but I'm sure we can place them all. Oh, and maybe you would like one, Dr. St. Cloud. And Edward."

Gio raised an eyebrow. "Nice of you to offer the entire *ton* the offspring of the Frenchman's dog."

Bri scoffed. "I doubt it was a virgin birth. Hector is no doubt responsible. And it is best for sibling dogs to be separated."

Dr. St. Cloud nodded. "If not separated, they never learn to socialize and cannot be separated after a few months together. And before you posit your theory, Gio, Hector and Chérie are *not* related."

***

Wednesday, July 17, 1811 – Aboard *Nekhbet's Wings*
Xie Xie

Dining at the captain's table the second night, Xie Xie concentrated on the attitudes of the other passengers. She picked up nuances of language, catalogued cultural references, and noted implicit and explicit prejudices. *What makes white people think they own the world? We Chinese were printing philosophical treatises when they were heathens grunting without a written language.*

In accordance with her teachings from The Pharaoh, she listened before speaking, to discern rather than reveal.

Alone in her cabin, she practiced her story looking in a small mirror until the words flowed freely from her lips. *I'm becoming the person I've invented.*

***

Wednesday, July 17, 1811 – Aboard *Taygete's Wynd*
Jean-Louis

The last stop in the Azores, the island of San Miguel, beckoned the travelers.

Gio's demand was insistent as they waited to climb into the jolly boat. "I want to see an extinct volcano."

The captain shrugged. "The trek is long. I'm not sure you could make it and get back in one day, but the weather is sunny, so it might work. You could hire horses." He looked at Bri. "They may not have side saddles, Lady Gabriella."

"Now you've done it," Edward sighed. "She refuses no challenge."

Bri acted nonchalant. "I wore a voluminous skirt today to accommodate that very possibility."

Gwyneth nodded. "She tested it by straddling the sleeping hammock. We both did."

Edward blanched and stared at Bri. "You mean to ride astride? In public?"

"You made that observation at Ravenshire. Again, I must point out that we will be on a private trek. It's not like I will be parading around the *ton* astride in Hyde Park. And Aunt Gwyneth is wearing the same type of skirt."

Jean-Louis smothered a laugh. "Mr. James, you appear to have been outmaneuvered."

The travelers climbed into the jolly boat and set off on their adventure.

***

Wednesday, July 17, 1811 – The Island of San Miguel
Bri

While the others relaxed with wine in a sidewalk café after abandoning the ride to the volcano, Bri excused herself. "I want to take a little walk and see what the local market stalls have to offer."

She stopped by one stall that had colorful shawls. "Locally woven from our own sheep, Miss." Thinking of gifts for Summerfest guests and Hanforth's farewell dinner, Bri scanned the rest of the stall's wares. "What do you have for men?"

"Ah, you are a discerning shopper, I can see that. We have an excellent selection of canes, carved from the local juniper trees. One particular artisan has a selection of wild animal heads and other toppings to gain a firm handhold, miniature top hats, initials, etc."

"How many do you have in your selections?"

"About fifty, give or take."

Bri bit her lip in concentration. "How much for all of your stock?"

Stammering, the stall keeper blurted out a number. Recognizing a bargain, Bri took out enough gold coins to cover the price. "Ship me another fifty on the next Wyndward ship when the artisan has made them." She gave him her card. "Ship them here."

"Lady Gabriella Wyndward? I'm honored to meet you. I've often admired your ships." He handed her his card.

She smiled. "Tell your artisan that I will take future shipments of fifty when he has them finished. Our agent here will contact you with the appropriate bills of lading and arrange future payments. And I'll take fifty of the shawls as well, in an assortment of colors. Give me your best price."

They haggled for a few moments, then settled on a sum.

"If I want more of them, I'll have our agent order from you."

"Crate these batches and I will send someone to collect it shortly."

Bri turned to leave, but Señor Pontes called her back. "I have something new, just arrived from Spain. Venetian glass, wire spectacles in many lens colors. I haven't even unpacked them yet."

"I'm intrigued. Let me see."

Jean-Louis ambled up to the stall and tipped his hat. "Need help?"

Brightening, Bri nodded. "Yes, Jean-Louis. Señor Pontes and I are discussing another transaction. Perhaps you can open this crate."

"Show me." Jean-Louis followed the stall keeper, and carried the crate out to the front. After opening it, he took out individual boxes of spectacles. The lenses were in shades of yellow, lavender, violet, blue, red, pink, green and gray. Bri put on a pair of lavender spectacles. "I love them! They shield my eyes from the sun."

"The sun in London *can* be blinding."

"You think you're so amusing," said Bri, not giving the Frenchman the satisfaction of a scowl. " I love these. How many do you have?"

"Two hundred pair."

"I'll take them all. Can you supply these on an ongoing basis?"

"I get them from a Basque village through a relative. I can work out a more direct shipping route to London."

"Good. Our agent here will take care of the details with you."

"Hold! What's this?" Jean-Louis held up a colored engraving of a man in Spanish dress wearing the spectacles. "A dandy's dream."

Lady Gabriella took it from Jean-Louis. "We could use that to advertise the merchandise. May I have this?"

"Of course, Lady Gabriella." He trilled the "r" in her name that gave it a lilting sound.

Jean-Louis filled three crates with merchandise and loaded them into the stall keeper's wagon.

Watching the wagon go by their table, Edward called out, "Is there anything left in that stall?"

Bri turned and waved. "Don't you wish you knew?"

***

Wednesday, July 17, 1811 – Aboard *Taygete's Wynd*
Gio

Returning to the ship, Gio was met by Dog. The small Yorkie's outsized bark announced his presence from a distance. Gio collapsed into a deckchair and the dog jumped into his lap. He held the dog's head in his hands as he spoke.

"Dog, the extinct volcano was too far away, so we will have to return another time. I would have liked to have seen the spectacular caverns and an underground lake, but I pushed my endurance to the limit and we had to turn back. Lucky for the horse that he didn't drop dead."

"Is he talking back yet?" Bri plopped down next to Gio and reached over to pet Dog.

"Not yet, but he's an excellent student. He understands my commands. If only you would."

"And what commands of yours have I ignored?"

Gio waved his hand in a flourish. "Convince your aunt to write my autobiography."

"She's mounting a major exhibition of your works at the Musée de Merbeau beginning on New Year's Day. And I believe that she has told you repeatedly that *you* are the only one who can write *your* autobiography."

"Dog, look at her. Bri has an agile mind, but she ignores her elders. Don't emulate her behavior."

Dog yipped several times.

"Good boy, Dog." Glancing at Bri, he said, "Dog agrees with me."

Bri smiled. "Then let Dog write your autobiography. Here comes Chérie."

Gio frowned. "Don't get any ideas, Dog. She's already made her choice."

Dog whined.

"Ah, yes, Dog. Life is a series of disappointments."

***

Wednesday, July 17, 1811 – Lord Wexington's Townhouse
Lady Patricia

Lady Patricia's initial relief from fear of exposure in *Scandal & Shame* morphed into rage at Lord Merrick. Infatuation twisted into hatred and a desire for revenge. *Lord Merrick's fiancée should know of his treachery.* But no matter what elaborate scheme Lady Patricia concocted in her head, it always ended with her role being exposed. *A Pyrrhic victory. I must let it go.*

Lady Patricia examined herself in a full-length mirror. In addition to being an heiress, she was a buxom, voluptuous beauty. *Uncle Reggie could introduce me to ambassadors. Maybe I could marry a titled foreigner.* She sighed, recognizing that Napoleon's conquests had reduced those prospects. *Lord Merrick picked a wealthier woman, but I am still desirable.*

Her mother, incapacitated by arthritis, required nursing care. Still sharp and lucid, she impressed upon her daughter the importance of a good marriage, by which she meant a well-established Society merger of wealth and status. Love was not a consideration. But Lady Patricia had become addicted to the thrill of a forbidden liaison.

Her father had gone mad, secretly locked up at Bedlam. The family developed a plausible story that he preferred tending to his gardens at the country estate over London. Never much for social occasions, the viscount was not missed.

With these thoughts swirling through her mind, Lady Patricia descended the stairs to enter the carriage to meet her Uncle Reggie for lunch.

***

Wednesday, July 17, 1811 – The Foreign Office
Lady Patricia

Lady Patricia's carriage arrived at the Foreign Office, she alighted, entered the imposing edifice, and was escorted to her Uncle Reggie's office.

Her mother's brother stood to greet her. "My dear, I was not expecting you today."

"Mother sent me with a request that you join us for dinner Sunday, and I fancied a jaunt around town. Are you free for lunch at Chez Michel?"

Sir Reggie closed the files on his desk, put his spectacles in his pocket and walked around his desk to embrace his niece. "Delightful suggestion."

Arriving at the café, Lady Patricia saw several friends. Vaux, Banfield and Rogers were there, so she waved and guided Uncle Reggie to their table.

The three men stood to greet Sir Reggie and Lady Patricia.

Banfield spoke first. "Sir Reginald." Turning to the Foreign Officer's niece, he added, "Lady Patricia."

"Mr. Banfield." She nodded. "Mr. Rogers."

Rogers, bleary-eyed, smiled. "Breakfast for me. Lunch for everyone else."

Banfield tilted his head toward his friend and added, "I ran into Rogers this morning stumbling into the club and prevailed upon him to join me for a bite. Why don't you sit with us? We've just arrived."

Lady Patricia glanced at Sir Reggie.

He nodded. "Why not?" After they sat down, Sir Reggie asked, "What is new in the world of young men of the *ton* now that the Marriage Season of balls and romance is over?"

"Rogers is racing this weekend." Banfield raised his eyebrows.

"What kind of racing? You don't strike me as a jockey." Sir Reggie laughed at his own observation.

Rogers appeared too robust to sit a horse in a race.

"More than mere *racing*, Sir Reggie. Rogers, here," Vaux put his arm around his bleary-eyed friend, "has organized a Phaeton Meet for this weekend. We're calling it 'The Trot of the *Ton.*' "

Rogers shrugged, evidently amused. "True. Carriage races. My friend Forester has built a racing track where we can test our Phaetons against other aficionados. I love the feel of speed, the rush of the wind against my face."

The idea intrigued Lady Patricia. "Do people come to watch?" *Rogers is a daring, dashing daredevil. Perhaps I have been wrong to fancy an older, more established man as a partner.*

"A few. Lady Gabriella and James are off in the Azores. I'm not sure who else from our crowd will be there." Rogers smiled. "Of course, you are both welcome. The festivities begin at two o'clock."

Banfield grinned. "Rogers rarely wakes before noon." He leaned back as a male server brought a basket of croissants, brioches and scones with butter, clotted cream and jam. They ordered a light lunch from the *menu du jour*.

A female server brought a painted ceramic pot of tea and placed it on a raised holder with a candle burning underneath. "Today's special is a rare white tea from the highlands of China." She poured a cup for each diner.

As they sipped the delicate flavor, another diner walked over.

"Sir Reginald." All recognized the tall, gray-haired legend of the halls of Parliament.

"Drummond." Sir Reggie moved to stand, but Drummond put up his hands to stop him. "Not necessary, old friend. We've all met before. Lady Patricia, you're looking as lovely as ever."

"You are too kind, Mr. Drummond."

The maker of politicians nodded in acknowledgement, then went to his next target. "Mr. Rogers, should you ever decide to enter politics like your father, let me know."

Rogers scoffed. "Never."

"Politics can be as thrill-seeking as racing, Mr. Rogers. Never say never. Opportunities must be taken as they arise." Turning to Banfield, he said, "I heard you play some of your compositions at one of Lady Genevieve's dinner parties, Mr. Banfield. You are very talented."

"Thank you."

Finally turning to Vaux, he said, "Lord Vaux, I understand that your interior designs are more sought after than ever."

Banfield laughed. "Vaux's complaining that he doesn't have the time to be a man of leisure anymore. But he's making time for the Phaeton Meet this weekend."

"The 'Trot of the *Ton*'? I'm impressed, Mr. Rogers."

Rogers shrugged. "Events require proper organization. If this weekend goes well, we might establish a regular Phaeton Season."

"Who's 'we'?" asked Drummond.

"Rogers is partial to the royal 'we,' Mr. Drummond." Banfield popped a bite of brioche in his mouth.

***

Wednesday, July 17, 1811 – *Chez Michel*
Sir Reggie

No one could miss Drummond's eyes focused on Lady Patricia's bosom peeking over the lace trim of her pale coral dress, least of all Sir Reggie. *I hate that I needed Tottie's help. He may think her an easy mark now.*

Rogers was staring at her too.

She'll play them both against each other. Rogers has the spark but Drummond has the power, unless Drummond can make Rogers a Member of Parliament. Sir Reggie sighed. *The perils of romance, the pull of lust versus status, consume my niece.*

Well known as an official in the Foreign Office, few were privy to Sir Reggie's additional role as a clandestine operator. He ran a network of secret informers around the world. *Rogers could be a good spy once Napoleon is toppled, if the young man keeps his drinking under control. With his racing reputation and connections, Rogers could infiltrate the upper levels of any foreign society. A brash bon vivant gains the confidence of the wary more than a polished, overly refined young man. Unguarded moments are the most productive in statecraft.*

"Then I'm even more impressed. Enjoy Michel's cuisine." Drummond left to join one of his clients.

"He's a rogue, that one." Vaux sighed. "But a powerful one, a puppet master." He raised his arms as if being manipulated by invisible strings. "I'll vote as you tell me, Tottie."

The viscount is an observant man. He could be of use to me as well as Rogers.

CHAPTER TWENTY-SEVEN

Wednesday, July 17, 1811 – Aboard *Taygete's Wynd*
Dr. St. Cloud

For their last night in the warmth of the Azores before heading back to London, the captain anchored the ship off the harbor at San Miguel and set a small table on deck with bottles of Champagne and plates of *hors d'oeuvres*. The night stars shone in the dark sky, sparkling above the deck. Candles flickered in tin holders on the table. The voyagers gathered for an *apéritif.*

The captain raised his glass to Lady Clarissa and Dr. St. Cloud. "I thought one last sight of the island as the moon rises and the stars reveal themselves might be a fitting end to your honeymoon adventure."

Dr. St. Cloud and Lady Clarissa raised their glasses in return. "A poetic farewell, Captain. Thank you. This has been a delightful sailing. To the captain and crew!"

"Here, Here! To the captain and crew," echoed the travelers.

"To the myth—or truth—of Atlantis." Gio lifted his glass. "To a magnificent civilization, even if it lives only in the imagination of humanity."

Bri smiled and clinked her glass with his.

"To Atlantis!"

"Yes, milady." Gio bowed. "I trust you noted that I did *not* say 'in the imagination of mankind.' We must change the language."

"One more small task." Edward's wry delivery elicited laughter as he raised an eyebrow.

Gwyneth tapped her glass on Gio's. "To the Carthaginians, for leaving a coin for our most ardent treasure hunter."

Gio beamed. "To the Carthaginians!"

The next toast fell to Edward. "To Poseidon, the builder of Atlantis. We know his name. Have we seen part of his empire? Was it real? All magic vanishes with time. Perhaps we have seen a glimpse of it."

"To Poseidon!"

It was Bri's turn. She held up her glass so that both starlight and candlelight reflected beams, and looked up to the heavens. "To the sun, moon and stars that have guided sailors since the dawn of time."

"To the sun, moon and stars!"

Jean-Louis was the last to toast. He gazed at each person in turn before elevating his flute of Champagne. "To love!"

"To love!"

***

Thursday, July 18, 1811 – Aboard *Taygete's Wynd*
Gio

Gio set up a special telescope known as a cometseeker, hoping that the black sky devoid of clouds would allow a glimpse of the comet.

Mumbling to himself as he peered through the eyepiece, making manual adjustments with multiple dials to focus the lenses, he cursed in frustration. "*Foutre!* How can it be termed The Great Comet of 1811 when 1811 is half over and I've not been able to see it with a telescope, let alone the naked eye?" Focused on his task, Gio didn't sense the presence of someone else on the deck.

"Appropriating my language to curse is a bit lazy, is it not?"

Gio jumped, causing the dials on the telescope to spin, obscuring the adjustments he'd painstakingly set. "Frenchman, you creep up on people. Lucky for you I don't have a pistol at the ready."

"*Very* lucky."

The Frenchman's laconic delivery elicited an icy stare from Gio.

"The scientists have warned us the Great Comet won't be visible until more than a month from now due to its low altitude and the diffusion of the light from the rising moon. Why do you think *you* will be able to see it?" Jean-Louis crossed his arms, awaiting an answer.

Directing his attention back to resetting the dials, Gio sighed. "Because we are out in the middle of the ocean, without clouds obstructing the stars above or gaslights obscuring the blackness of the sky. It's a reasonable assumption that one could have a clearer view here than in London." He peered through the comet seeker.

After a few minutes of silence, Jean-Louis tapped him on the shoulder. "Let me take a look."

Gio stood aside. "It's a magnificent instrument, but I couldn't discern any spray of light. The coma it leaves in its wake is supposed to be twice that of the sun."

Jean-Louis knelt down to avoid recalibrating the comet seeker. Putting his eye next to the eyepiece, he scanned the sky, moving the instrument from left to right and up and down. "No comet, but the brilliance of the starlight is stunning. I wonder—" He fell silent.

"Now you've piqued my curiosity. Wonder what?"

"What it would be like to ride a comet through the heavens."

Gio answered the man staring through the cometseeker. "A brief moment of ecstasy before you froze to the icy ball and became part of it for all eternity—to feel no more, to see no more, to be no more."

"You assume an ice crystal has no consciousness." Jean-Louis pulled back from the telescope and rose to his feet.

"*You* have spent too much time listening to Henry's musings on the nature of existence."

"And *you* have spent too little."

***

Saturday, July 20, 1811 – Interior of Vaux's Cabriolet
Banfield

Banfield rode with Vaux to The Phaeton Meet. "Not quite the buccaneer, are you, Vaux?"

"Rogers is the reckless daredevil, not I. Is this cabriolet too *quotidien* for your taste?"

"Pfft!" Banfield exhaled. "Quotidian is a word in English, too. An everyday carriage is a practical choice. Rogers has a stable full of racing carriages. I find it more convenient to take a Hackney than rent stable space or keep horses. I see no reason to spend my inheritance before I receive it."

"Why should you be different than the rest of us?"

"I don't have as much coming to me."

Vaux shrugged. "When your first opera is a hit, you will be famous and have more carriages than Rogers, no doubt."

"As the third son of a baron, I've already disappointed my family by not going into the military. The path to artistic success is an uneven one. I don't want more carriages than Rogers. I prefer to live to an old age."

Stealing a glance at his friend, Vaux shook his head. "Speed is a goddess, a dangerous siren. The lightweight construction of the Phaeton, and the High Flyer in particular they speak of coming soon, are more intoxicating than whiskey. But if you hit a bump—"

The blood drained from Banfield's face. "Hell's teeth! You don't think we'll witness something grim, do you?"

"Isn't that part of the allure?"

His face wrinkling in self-disgust, Banfield nodded, and then gazed at Vaux. "Are we animals?"

"Yes. Driven by instincts as base as those of the gladiators at the circuses of Rome."

"Base? They were fighting for their lives. Speed is not essential to life."

"Not for you, but it's an elixir for Rogers and his cohorts."

Vaux pulled up and parked his carriage with the footman. He and Banfield jumped down from their open cabriolet and walked toward Forester's Field.

***

Saturday, July 20, 1811 – The Phaeton Meet
Rogers

A track for timing horses being trained to race had been repurposed for the day's contest. The width of the mile-long course was not equal to that of Ascot's, so there would be intermediate races, and the two best times, as measured by the starter's stopwatch, would be matched for the final race.

The advertised prize was a prototype of a High Flyer Phaeton, donated by Hooper's, the manufacturer, to stir up demand for the new century's soon-to-be-produced chariots. The light-springed four-wheeled rigs sat one or two and could be pulled by one or two horses.

Young men about the *ton* drove themselves in curricules, a two-wheeled rig drawn by two horses, or a gig, a two-wheeled carriage drawn by a single horse. The Phaeton was light and fast and sexy.

Rogers had organized the meet, engaged an experienced starter, and convinced Hooper's to donate the prize. He had printed programs that delineated the five races that would precede the sixth final race, which would determine the winner. He held his hand up to shade his eyes to see the length of the course.

"You're lucky it's a sunny day. The grass looks good."

Rogers turned when he heard Banfield's voice. He playfully faux-punched his friends' shoulders. "Sure you two don't want to be added to the list to face off against each other?"

"Except for the facts—namely, that we don't have Phaetons and we think you're mad—why not?" Vaux looked around at the center line surrounded by rows of oak benches. "The benches look like pews in the Cathedral of Phaeton."

Rogers nearly lost his balance in laughter, grabbing hold of the back of a bench to steady himself. "A touch sacrilegious wouldn't you say?"

"Or instructive," Banfield countered. "Refresh my memory on Phaeton's myth."

Vaux shrugged. "You studied something useful—music. I studied something fanciful—the Greek and Roman classics.

"Here is my recollection from lo so many years ago. Phaeton's mother told him his absent father was, in truth, the sun god, Helios. She told her son to ask Helios directly for confirmation of his paternity. When Phaeton confronted Helios, the son asked for proof that would show that his father was really the sun god. 'I will grant you any wish,' the god replied. The son made his request: 'Let me drive the Chariot of the Sun.'" Warned that it was too dangerous, Phaeton insisted. When his day came, the son could not control the fire-breathing horses on the arc of their journey, and burned large parts of the earth as he fell from the sky, creating the Sahara Desert.

"Zeus, alarmed that his creation was being harmed, hurled a thunderbolt at the Chariot of the Sun, saving the Earth, but killing Phaeton."

Banfield grimaced. "I'm sorry I asked."

Vaux disagreed. "It's a universal myth. A son's desire to show up his father, overestimating his ability, miscalculating the price, and proving, as they say, that 'Pride goeth before a fall.' Or, as Ovid wrote, accepting the 'gift fatal.'"

"Stop spouting proverbs and quoting poets," said Rogers. "Today's theme is the thrill of speed and the rush of wind on your face. We are here to enjoy the races, not to send the onlookers into despair. It's only a mile on a set course. I've walked it. No stray rocks or ruts will trip a horse or jar a wheel. All will go well."

"Is anyone taking bets?"

They turned to see that Durwood had arrived.

Rogers shook his head. "I don't have a betting license, Durwood. Besides, you're in race number two. Don't even think about betting." He whispered in his friend's ear, "The local sheriff is nearby. The refreshment stand is taking bets. The code phrase is 'Fog is coming,' then you add the amount of your bet, so you say, 'Fog is coming in two days, Rogers.'. .That means two pounds on the race.

"And since when do *you* race, Durwood?" Vaux looked around as Durwood gestured toward his rig, a red-wheeled Phaeton in the distance. "Is that it? My God! Those back wheels are as high as the horses' ears. And the front ones nearly as high as their haunches."

"It's a new design, just out." Durwood grinned. "Make no mention of it to Lady Rose. She's not a devotée of carriage racing."

Banfield, put his arm around the racer. "You are an *impressive* impresario, Rogers. We should get seats before the benches are full. Good luck in," he looked at the printed order on the program, "Race Three."

Rogers waved them off as he attended to the last minute details, setting up the drivers in their heats, lining up the Phaetons in two-by-two formation. Durwood's rig wasn't the only one with red wheels. There were several in black, one in white, two in yellow, and one a deep shade of blue. A splash of color on the body of the carriages distinguished one from another. There were different varieties of Phaeton, but each had two horses and wheels of differing front and back heights.

"May I see your license, sir?"

The deep baritone voice of the local sheriff startled Rogers.

The impresario pulled the appropriate paperwork out of his pocket and handed it to the constable.

The sheriff looked it over, saw the approval signatures, and handed it back to Rogers. "We have a doctor and wagon in the event of an injury, as you requested."

***

Vaux

With about a half hour before the start of the races, a large wagon pulled by four horses drove up near the last row of benches. An awning was set up on poles, with the word, "Refreshments" lettered across the top. Barrels of water were displayed along the back end of the wagon, along with others marked "Lemonade" and "Wine."

Small metal cups hand-painted with "Trot of the *ton*" were set out for sale. Baskets of biscuits filled the table.

"Clever," Vaux observed. "You have to buy your own cup. A painted souvenir. Who thought of that?'

Banfield shrugged. "Probably Rogers."

"Lady Gabriella would be impressed. I never would have pegged Rogers as a promoter, but I am a convert." He put his arm around Banfield. "Maybe he *is* the right impresario for your operatic endeavors."

Looking over the list of racers, Banfield murmured, "We know most of these people. Viscount Armstrong, Lord Clyr—"

"That fat pile of jiggling lard will slow down the rig. Even I could probably out-drive him."

"Maybe he has powerful horses."

Vaux looked over Banfield's shoulder. "Portchallont? Is that the baron's sister's son?"

"Must be. I see Lord Lt. Thornton listed, and look—a couple of names I recognize from the club."

"This is a more popular sport than I imagined." Banfield scanned the gallery. "I see Lady Patricia and Sir Reggie. There is standing room only, like at the theatre."

"Or opera. This is a real production, isn't it?"

A trumpet sounded, startling the crowd into silence.

The starter announced, "The first race will begin when the flag is down." He held a blue-and-white striped flag above his head, looked to the first two racers, holding at the ready, and swiftly cast down the flag.

The first two teams of horses leapt forward pulling their Phaetons through the grass as if on a smooth field of ice, sailing by the assembled guests on their circular course.

TWENTY-EIGHT

Saturday, July 20, 1811 – Lady Gwyneth's Townhouse
Aelwyn

Aelwyn awoke in a guest room in Gwyneth's townhouse. Ian stirred next to her. *He should start sleeping alone soon.*
Nambotha and all the staff doted on Ian. Felicity and Dominique taught him a few French words to augment the ones Jean-Louis had taught him in Ireland..

Despite her relief at no longer needing to hide, Aelwyn felt as unsettled now as she had three years earlier when she was forced to disappear. Thrust back into her former life, she realized she had changed. In Ireland, the loss of Rychard wasn't as intense as it was now, finding herself surrounded by people from their years together. Memories flooded back, intruding on the present. She felt uncertain, out of sorts, and unfocused.

Ian finds both London and Ravenshire exciting. Will I ever adjust?

***

Saturday, July 20, 1811 – The Phaeton Meet
Banfield

Vaux and Banfield were stunned when the rotund Lord Clyr won the first heat.

"How can it be? Hell's teeth!" Vaux sputtered in disgust. "I bet on his opponent."

"I put all I could risk on Rogers, so that's the only race I care about. If I'd known Durwood planned to race, I would have split my bet, but I limit my gambling. I hope he knows what he's doing."

"I bet on him. Figured he was a long shot, so I got better odds. Durwood's red-rimmed wheels and black horse make him look somewhat dashing from a distance." Vaux raised his eyebrows and glanced at Banfield.

"I must admit, I always saw Durwood as a plodding, dependable sort without much imagination. What has overtaken him? Carriage racing has an edge of danger."

"He always sat a horse well, but this is different. He doesn't gamble. Could we know someone for so long and yet not know him?"

Banfield kept his eyes on the starter's flag. "Are you saying humans are immutable? You goaded him at our recent dinner. Why couldn't he develop a new hobby?"

"Hobby? This isn't whittling, Banfield."

The flag fell, signaling the beginning of the second heat.

It was neck and neck, and to the surprise of his friends, Durwood won his race.

Rogers caught their eyes and shrugged, as if to say, "Are you as shocked as I am?"

Banfield agreed. "Durwood? Who knew?"

Vaux elbowed Rogers. "Maybe she did."

A young woman, definitely not Lady Rose, had stepped forward to speak to Durwood. He leaned in to whisper to her, as if he knew her.

Banfield's mouth dropped open. "Here? In public? In front of us?"

Vaux shook his head. "She's simply congratulating him for all we know."

When Banfield turned to say something to Vaux, he recoiled as he watched the viscount walking toward Durwood. *What is Vaux going to say?* Banfield's brisk stride brought him to Vaux's side. He pulled on Vaux's arm and blocked his friend's view of Durwood. "Stop!"

"I just wanted to tell him I won several pounds on his race."

"You intended more than that and this is neither the time nor the place to confront him. Come back to our pew in the Cathedral of Phaeton, Vaux. Rogers is up next."

Vaux reluctantly complied. Back on their bench, Vaux and Banfield rose with the crowd as the third race came down to its final moments.

Rogers had soared ahead soon after the flag fell, but his opponent was gaining steadily.

"Can he maintain his lead?" Banfield strained to see over the heads of those in front of them.

"I hope so, or I stand to lose quite a bit."

"As do I." *Was I foolish to be seduced by the odds? Rogers' opponent has more experience.* Banfield hung his head. *I bet on the loser.*

Vaux shouted, "Rogers by a nose!" He slapped Banfield on the back. "You're a winner today, Banfield."

Banfield glanced around to locate the sheriff. "How do we collect our winnings right under the sheriff's nose?"

"Look on the bottom of your cup."

Banfield started to turn it over.

"Wait—don't spill it on your breeches."

Grimacing at his near *faux pas*, Banfield drained the cup before looking. A ticket was stuck on the bottom.

"How did you know?"

Vaux gave him a withering look.

"Of course." Banfield kicked the ground. "You're the risk taker who knows all the angles."

"You go back for more wine or punch for the ride home, hand over your payment, and your change includes your winnings tucked inside a folded flyer, a commemoration of 'The Trot of the Ton.'"

"And the sheriff is none the wiser."

Vaux shrugged. "Possibly, but in my experience a little extra payment for his trouble to come out and keep the peace eliminates excessive scrutiny."

"Who's your money on in the next race?"

"Viscount Armstrong. Apparently he has a way with horses."

"There he is. Yellow-rimmed wheels really catch the eye. That's a fine rig he's driving and the horse carries itself with pride."

"Nonsense, Banfield. You're reading too much into a horse's step."

Banfield squinted and stuck his head out beyond Vaux. "The green-rimmed wheels stand out on Armstrong's competitor's carriage. Hold! That driver looks familiar. There's something about him—"

Vaux nodded. "His face," he shielded his eyes from the sun, and then leaned in to get a better line of sight, "is obscured by the shadows and a wide-brimmed hat."

"The green gloves are a nice touch to match the wheels. A dandy?"

"A man of mystery. Let's see how well he guides his carriage. A side bet between us, Banfield?"

Banfield reached into his pocket, pulled out a one pound note and placed it on the bench between them. "Not a penny more. My money is on the dandy."

"Damnation! I didn't speak quickly enough." Exhaling in surrender, Vaux took out a matching amount and laid it on top of Banfield's wager. "I'm left with Armstrong."

As the flag went down, the green rig leapt ahead of Armstrong's yellow flash of color, but the viscount soon pulled even with the mysterious stranger. The stranger spared the whip but his steeds vaulted over the course with ease. At the very last stretch, he pulled ahead and Armstrong was hit in the face by a clump of dirt.

"Like a divot from a bad stroke," observed Vaux. "Looks like you made a lucky bet."

As the green-rimmed wheels crossed the finish line, Banfield smiled and picked up the two pounds. "Maybe I should reconsider the gambling trade."

"For you, two wins are unexpected, Banfield. Don't get cocky."

"Portchallont is in the last race. I see Lady Penelope, the baron and Lady Portchallont down in the front. The baron is a known connoisseur of horse flesh. Who's he up against?" Banfield unfolded the race list and whooped. "The man of mystery is Brien Kerry. No wonder!"

Vaux shrugged. "Should that name mean something to me?"

Banfield scoffed. "Vaux, I thought you were the arbiter of gossip. Perhaps you know him better under his official name, *Captain* Kerry, the Irish privateer, scandalous devil, and one who never shrinks from a battle. I read he's back in London for a few months to negotiate his next territory. Rumors are swirling that he wants to be named governor of some West Indies island as a reward for his plunder on behalf of the crown."

"Damn! I've been so busy renovating properties, I haven't indulged in my favorite pastime, reading *Scandal & Shame*. You've bested me at my own game, Banfield."

"We should root for Portchallont. I'm not familiar with his opponent, Ashfield."

"Khan knows him from his wife's family. He's from the coast, near Bath. He's come to town for the Season next year. A fine horseman, they say."

"You're not *that* disconnected if you know *those* details."

Vaux shrugged. "I know Portchallont's pedigree, so that's where my money went. But that approach may be sentimental rather than clear-headed. So far, I've won two and lost two." He caught Banfield's smirk. "Don't gloat over your lucky calls. Two of two—you played it safe."

Portchallont proved himself superior to his challenger, pulling ahead from the beginning and maintaining his lead throughout the race.

The trumpet blared, alerting the crowd to the announcement of the winners of the two best heats for the final race. The starter stepped forward and the crowd's murmurs lowered to a buzz. "The best times posted are from Mr. Durwood and Captain Kerry."

"What? Not Rogers? Now *this* will be a race! I'm betting on Durwood. Old school ties and all that." Vaux walked toward the refreshment stand, turned and raised his eyebrows at Banfield. "No support for our old friend?"

"Yes, but in spirit, not in currency. I bet on two races. Not a penny more." He picked up his 'Trot of the *Ton*' mug. "I'll come with you for more wine and to collect my winnings."

Vaux leaned over to speak with Banfield while they walked. "The red-rimmed wheels on Durwood's Phaeton contrast with the green-rimmed rig of Captain Kerry. It will be easy to follow who's ahead."

Banfield nodded. "Both teams of horses are strong and well-paired in color and size." After they reached the refreshment wagon, he handed his mug to the server, he said, "More wine and I'm done, Johnson." The code word 'Johnson' worked. Receiving his refilled mug back, Banfield noted the folded flyer pressed underneath.

Vaux paid for more wine with the code "Durwood" to place his bet.

He and Banfield walked back to their bench, and watched Rogers, who stood next to the starter. Vaux frowned. "I wonder if Rogers should be impresario and race in his own event. Wouldn't it have looked as though the race were fixed if Rogers had driven in the final heat?"

"The times were kept outside of his control."

"True, but the perception might taint his win."

Durwood shook the captain's hand, and they climbed up onto their Phaetons. Making a theatrical wave toward the Hooper's rig that stood nearby as the prize, Durwood bowed to the crowd.

"He's taking this with quite a flourish, eh?" Banfield grimaced. "Not the good old Durwood we know."

The captain waved to his smaller cheering section.

The rigs pulled into position, and the horses chomped at their bits. A light rain started to fall, and the ladies kept their parasols up, repurposed from covering their faces from the sun to protecting them from the rain. "We may be traipsing through mud at the end," said Vaux.

The flag went down, and the race began, with Durwood pulling ahead, but not for long. Captain Kerry gained on him until their horses were in lockstep. Both whipped their teams to go faster. The ground absorbed the rain, and the lightweight rigs bounced over unseen rivulets forming in the grassy course. The rain intensified, the course became treacherous, and the crowd's cheers grew louder. Thunder clapped, startling Durwood's horses, who came to a complete stop. The momentum of their previous stride propelled Durwood out of the carriage in head-over-heels somersaults beyond the horses landing in the mud on his left side, and then rolling to a stop.

While Rogers and the medics ran over to Durwood, Captain Kerry kept to the course and finished to win. He then drove back to where Durwood lay, and jumped down to help.

The sheriff kept the crowd at bay. "Stay back! Stay back!"

Vaux and Banfield ignored him and ran forward only to be blocked by the sheriff's men.

"The injured man is our friend," said Vaux.

"Wait here."

***

Vaux

Vaux searched the crowd for the woman who had spoken to Durwood earlier. She appeared stricken. He moved toward her, and said, "I am Durwood's friend."

Her plaintive eyes searched Vaux's. "I pray he is not badly injured."

An American accent. "As do we all. I am Rudolph Vaux."

"Forgive me, sir. I am Michelle Matthews from Virginia."

Unable to stop himself, Vaux asked, "Are you a friend of Lady Rose?"

"Who is Lady Rose?"

"Durwood's wife."

The distraught woman paled, glanced around the area, and gasped. "You have caught me unawares, Mr. Vaux. I shall take my leave of you." She reached into her reticule and pulled out a calling card. "Please get word to me about his condition. Privately."

"As you wish, Miss Matthews. And I am *Viscount* Vaux rather than Mr. Vaux. Here is my card."

"Viscount Vaux., I trust that because Mr. Durwood is your friend, I may rely on your discretion."

"You may. And just to be clear, as a foreigner, you may not be aware that the proper form of address is Lord Vaux, but I am simply Vaux to my friends, of which I shall now count you as one."

"Thank you, Vaux." She trudged through the mud to a waiting line of Hackney cabs, climbed in and disappeared into the rainy, fog-drenched twilight.

CHAPTER TWENTY-NINE

Monday, July 22, 1811 – Aboard *Taygete's Wynd*
Gio

Mere hours away from London on the last night of their voyage, after the usual toasting, Edward suggested a topic for their final dinner. "We have talked of Atlantis, of remembrances, of dreams for the future. Tonight, I propose we each offer up a myth or a fantastical tale we have been told or an experience beyond observable Nature that others might find improbable. No arguments, no criticism," he glanced at Bri. "Simply consider each story as a suggestion of possibilities we might not have considered. I have been told, more than once, by someone at this table, that my initial reactions can be thick-headed and biased. So I ask each of us to keep an open mind and listen, not lecture."

"I'll go last." Gio sat back. "It's your idea, James. You start."

Edward nodded. "Fair enough. I shall begin. As most of you know, I traveled in the Far East for over five years, searching." He paused and glanced around the faces at the table. "For what? Enlightenment, I suppose. On my journey of self-discovery, I engaged local guides to better understand the culture and learn a bit of the language of the areas I explored.

"One guide in particular exuded a peace I'd never seen or felt before. We trekked over vast expanses of desert, trudged through steep passes covered in snow, climbed up and down rock-faced mountains, and rested in meadows of brilliantly hued poppies. We foraged or hunted for food. We slept under the stars or stayed in huts with strangers. I told him of my life and world, and he told me tales of his ancestors—myths, I assumed—of hidden valleys and lamaseries with ancient holy men, hundreds of years old, who suffered from no disease or sign of aging.

" 'You don't believe it possible,' he observed, 'because your world doesn't believe it possible. You are a thoughtful man on a spiritual quest. Tomorrow I will show you that I speak the truth.' "

Edward leaned forward to his rapt audience. "We awoke at dawn, as was our habit. It was spring, cold at night but warm during the day. Snows melted in the sun, then froze again as darkness fell. Up, up into the high cliffs we scaled the heights until we reached a narrow pass into a high valley. Twilight was nigh. A lamasery rose in front of us. We reached it as the last beam of light vanished.

"A monk in saffron robes opened the door. 'We've been waiting for you. Please share our food.'

"How did they know we would arrive?" Edward shrugged. "It remains a mystery to me. We sat at rough-hewn tables and benches in front of a fire, and ate plates of vegetables and fruits that I had never seen, with a selection of dark breads, butters and goat cheeses, and a sweet wine. We ate in silence with five monks. I watched for a sign from my guide, but none came until we finished eating.

"My guide bade me goodnight and followed all except one monk out of the room. The remaining monk bowed to me and signaled that I should follow him down a long hallway. I thought I was being led to my room, but we ascended stone steps that spiraled to the top of a circular tower, where a lama sat, cross-legged, on a pillow. His eyes were closed, but as we approached, he opened them. 'Welcome,' he said, in English.

"Before I could ask how he knew my language, he explained that he had once lived in the outside world until he had been found near death, and brought to this lamasery. 'Like you, I was educated in England. I was posted to a nearby high-mountain kingdom as a diplomat, and found a new calling. One of healing, not war. Of listening, not preaching. Of patience, not demands.'

"He appeared to be slightly older than I, but he claimed his residency at the lamasery had lasted over one hundred years. 'Occasionally,' he said, 'we meet with those from the outside, to gauge its progress. Do men still solve disagreements with violence?'

"I nodded, confirming that war was still the way of men.

" 'It will not always be so,' he said. 'It may be hundreds of years, or a thousand, or more. We have solutions, meditations and practices, knowledge of healing powers of plants, and the secrets of rocks to give you. But these gifts are not for the greedy, the selfish or kings. These gifts remain to be claimed. The path is long and difficult, but humanity will reach its purpose.'

" 'And what purpose is that?' I asked.

" 'To learn to live in peace and respect all life. To ask the grass, "May I walk on you?" To ask the tree, "Would you like to become a table?" To ask the rock, "May I carve you into a new shape?" To ask the animal, "Would you like to nourish my body with yours?" To ask the plant, "May I consume you for my health?" And, in time, in a great deal of time, to reach the stars and live in harmony with the universe.' "

Edward stopped speaking.

The voyagers were transfixed.

Gio pointed to Bri. "You're next."

"How can I possibly speak now? My mind is swirling with questions."

The dwarf shook his head. "No comments. We are simply relating mind-opening experiences."

Bri took a deep breath as she glanced at Edward. "Once, on a trip to Brazil when I was seven, Blackie arranged for a small group—Father, Blackie, Jean-Louis and me—to stay with a tribe that had experienced no interaction with the outside world other than us. Wyndward Trading imported feathers, drums and artisan-crafted objects from them. The native women taught me basket-weaving, and we painted masks made of mud and dried them in the sun.

"Late one night, while the others were sleeping, I awakened to hooting sounds. I peeked under the tent to see what was happening. Men, covered in feathers, danced in a circle around a fire, surrounded by onlookers. I had started to wiggle under the tent flap when two hands pulled me back inside. Jean-Louis put his finger to his mouth, and carried me outside. The chief glanced up and waved us over to watch. He put me on a stool next to him. As you can imagine, my red hair was quite a novelty in Brazil. Jean-Louis sat native-style, cross-legged on the ground. The chief leaned over and whispered to me, 'The dancers summon the spirits of birds.'

"The birdmen chanted, breathing in the smoke of the fire, spiked by onlookers tossing what looked like grains of sand into its center, causing multi-colored flames to shoot up and make popping sounds. After several minutes, one dancing birdman fell to the ground. His body trembled as if seized by an unearthly power. He screeched, and then fell prone, unmoving. I feared he was dead.

"I turned to the chief, my eyes full of terror. The wise man allayed my concern. 'Fear not, child. Watch.' After what felt like a long time, but probably was only minutes, the feathers began to move, and the man rose to a kneeling position. He bowed his head to the chief, who translated for me. 'I saw two grand canoes in the big water. White wings on trees rose to the sky.'

" 'Our sailing ships...when did he see them?'

"The chief told me, 'His spirit flew as a bird to see your ships. He saw them in his mind.'

" 'But his mind never left his body.' I couldn't understand how he could have known what our ships looked like, because I had been told the tribe members had rarely ventured beyond their village and the stream that flowed to a river. No one had ever seen the ocean, the 'big water.' I turned to Jean-Louis. 'Did you tell them?' He shook his head.

"The chief put his hand on my shoulder, and I looked up into his ancient and endlessly deep near-black eyes.

" 'Child, few have the gift of spirit-flight. You are the only outsiders to have seen this ceremony. Remember this night, for it tells you the spirit world holds secrets. The earth is alive and can transmit truth to those who listen. Learn to listen.' "

Again, the silence was intense until Gio nodded to Dr. St. Cloud. "You are next."

"My tale is short, and also happened to me as a child, but it remains in my mind whenever I work with animals. When my parents were alive, and I was about twelve, we took a sojourn in Greece for the summer on the shores of the Ionian Sea. Dolphins jumped and played near the shore. In fact, sometimes I would wade out and they would come to me, encircling me, nudging me and making their squeaking sounds.

"One day when I was alone, an elderly, hunched woman was standing near me. 'Speak to them, boy. They will understand.'

"Startled by her appearance, I stared at her. 'How could dolphins understand human language?'

"She scoffed at me. 'Boy, dogs understand commands. Think you these creatures be less intelligent than dogs? I tell you, dolphins are more intelligent than humankind. They came to earth to help us.'

"I began to fear she was insane, escaped from some asylum. To avoid antagonizing a madwoman, I continued the conversation. 'To help us? In what way? And where did dolphins come from?'

"She smiled. 'Watch.' She spoke in Greek to the dolphins, something like 'Say six words.'

"Six very different sounds were emitted. I frowned. How could this be happening?

" 'Can I talk to them?'

" 'Of course,' she said. 'Extend your hand. Say "Peace to all beings," and wait.'

"I did as she instructed, and they came to me, one at a time, pressing a nose to my hand and squeaking out a greeting. I responded, 'Peace,' to each.

"I turned to the bent old woman, who smiled. 'All is not as it seems,' she said. 'Dolphins understand all languages. How will they help us? To remember we are all connected. You are destined to work with animals. They will trust you. They will teach you. Remember.'

"She began to swim away, escorted by the dolphins. I called after her, 'Where are you going?'

" 'My time among humans is ending. I am ready to transform.'

" 'But wait,' I called. 'You haven't told me where dolphins come from.'

"She turned around and swam back toward me. 'Boy, think you that earth is the only water planet in the universe? There is much you do not know. Open your mind. Let animals speak to you.'

"Rejoining the pod, she disappeared with the jumping, joyful creatures."

Awestruck, the guests said nothing.

Gio waited until the steward refilled his glass. "Lovely Lady Clarissa, we await your fable."

"Fable or truth? I often think of sacred trees in Teutonic, Germanic and Norse mythology. Like the Druids, who worshipped in groves among trees, pagan spiritual practitioners throughout

Europe gathered around trees. Not to worship them, as the Romans mistakenly assumed, but to draw on their wisdom. Legends were recited over millennia as melodious poems, with a musical cadence that enhanced their retention in memory.

"My governess came from the Norse tradition, and told me stories about the special powers of all the different types of trees. I don't remember them all, but I remember her telling me that if I have a question that is tormenting me, I simply need to walk into a forest, and stand before a tree. I must speak aloud, she told me, ask for guidance, and gently touch the tree and imagine a cloud of gratitude enveloping me and the tree. 'Trees hold the secrets of the living earth, from whence they spring,' she said.

"I hesitate to say this, but her words echoed in my head in the days after my mother died. I walked to the forest, while we still lived in Prussia, and knelt before a tree I'd always admired for its symmetry and majesty. I wept, thinking of my mother. Then I stood and followed the instructions, and imagined the cloud covering the tree and me when a vision inside the cloud appeared. My mother was with me. 'I am where I should be and you are where you should be. Each of us follows our own path. I will always love and watch over you. Whatever tree you select, I will be there with you.' "

Clarissa's voice broke as she held back tears. "Perhaps it was a dream of what I wanted to believe. My governess believed trees were conscious, just as we are. My heart wants to accept what my mind rejects as impossible." She took a few deep breaths and regained her composure. "All I can say is that the moment felt real."

A respectful silence enveloped the listeners.

"And now, Madame la Comtesse, we await your account." Gio titled his head in anticipation.

"The realm of the supernatural has always fascinated me. Like Lady Clarissa, I lost my mother at a young age. I spent a lot of time alone, playing in the old tower of Ravenshire Castle, topped with crenelated parapets, the last solid standing structure of the original battlement. Lost for hours in my imagination there, I conjured images of armored knights, ladies fair, swordfights, tournaments, all the typical fanfare that surround our myths of a glorious past. Occasionally, Henry and I fought mock battles with wooden swords.

"Roses thrive at Ravenshire, where varieties express a range of pinks, yellows, oranges and reds, pruned by our gardeners on a rotating basis with the seasons. Around the tower, there were a few ancient rose bushes in shades of pink. As a lonely little girl, I would say hello to them as I passed and sometimes pretended we had conversations. I gave them names—Twilight Pink, Blushing Pink and Petal Pink. One day I heard a high-pitched voice say, 'You can call me Petal.'

"At first, I thought Henry was hiding in the bushes pulling a trick on me, but I was alone. I sat down on the ground in front of the talking bush. 'Petal? May I see you?' I saw a flash of pink darting around the budding bush. Something was there, perhaps a bee. A tiny buzz scared me. I didn't want to be stung, so I scrambled away. I pushed past the broken wood-planked door through the arched entry to the tower. I sat down on the circular stone stairway and let my eyes become accustomed to the dark. The buzz followed. A blur hovered in front of me, and then flew to the stair step near my head. The buzzing stopped. Staring back at me was a spotted-winged creature garbed in pink petal-like clothing. Her skin glimmered with a pale green tint. Deep green eyes peered at me from a face framed in pink flowing hair.

"Over time, as we got to know each other, Petal told me of the faerie world, describing the lives of the faeries as well as those of the gnomes, the pixies, devas, the elders, the elementals, the evil ones, and more. She is over several thousand years old. Her stories are the ones in the two small volumes of faerie poems I wrote. I invented the fictional Foreword explaining my promise to publish the work of a friend who had died and left me manuscripts of her fantastical dreams. In tonight's conversation, we have all spoken of secrets hidden in Nature, awaiting discovery. I believe that faeries create a mysterious link bridging our world to the domain of magic."

Edward glanced at Bri, who appeared transfixed.

Looking at the Frenchman, Gio raised his glass. "We await your tale."

Jean-Louis smiled. "Before I speak, I would like to hear from the captain. Surely he has a story as well as each of us."

Gio sputtered. "Forgive me, Captain. Of course we would be interested in your narrative."

The captain sat back. "This may be the most unusual dinner conversation I've ever experienced. It's intriguing. The common line of inquiry strikes me as, 'Is there more to existence than what we perceive?'

"Think of this planet." He nodded at Dr. St. Cloud. "Recall the old woman's comment to the doctor. Earth is a water planet. Its surface is covered by seventy per cent water and thirty per cent land. We congratulate ourselves on 'discovering' land that clearly existed before we 'discovered' it. And there is ample evidence to travelers that many of these areas were visited by others before we 'discovered' them.

"There are monuments around the world that exceed our capabilities to build today. Are we really to believe that illiterate men in fur garments wielded tools to create precise right angles or stones of odd shapes fitting together perfectly? I think not. Do I know who left these monuments behind after their civilizations disappeared? I do not. Have I seen many things I cannot explain, just as you have described tonight? I have.

"I have seen bright orbs rise out of the seas and light up the night sky. Are these orbs truly fish emitting light? Fish who can hover in the air and circle a boat with incredible speed? I have seen octopi glow at night, illuminating the waters surrounding my ship, but octopi don't fly.

"I have seen circular boats emerging from deep waters on moonless nights, with odd flickering lights around their spherical shapes. These ships appear and disappear in a flash.

"I have seen the Northern Lights and would never confuse that phenomenon with what I have just described. Shift your belief patterns. The oceans are wide, deep and unexplored. What might exist there? Creatures who can breathe as easily in water as we breathe on land? Or might they do both? These mysteries puzzle many sailors, who hesitate to speak the truth of what they've observed. Secrets abound in the skies as well as in the depths of the oceans."

After a moment of peaceful reflection, Gio waved his hand toward Jean-Louis. "And now to our intrepid trapper."

The Frenchman leaned back in his chair. "As a young man, having left the French army to seek my fortune elsewhere, one summer I wandered around the plains of western Canada and met a shaman of the Snow Tribe of the Paiutes. We traveled together for a time, and after his death in the selfless act of saving my life, I completed his quest and returned his harvest of life-saving herbs to his people.

"I lived among the tribe for several months until winter ended. There were many caves in their sacred mountain lands. These caves were used as hunting, trekking, or vision quest shelters. One day during my last week in their lands, just as winter's frost lifted, I trekked on a private journey with the chief. That evening, I sat in the cave with the chief, talking of our different worlds. Into our small camp near the opening of the cave, a large, hairy giant emerged and sat with us.

"Although he, or she, did not speak, I heard words in my head as clearly as we are speaking to each other tonight: 'We are the original beings of this planet. We live in caves and navigate through tunnels deep beneath the earth that connect all continents. Over a time span you cannot comprehend, we welcomed many species from the stars to seed the Earth. The breadth of flora and fauna that populate this world make it a unique destination in the universe.'

"The word 'destination' struck me. I spoke, saying, 'Is Earth being visited, colonized by beings from other worlds?'

"The being answered, 'It has always been thus. Our task is to welcome all to Earth by creating a harmony of consciousness to support all life. In recent millennia, many species have been hunted to extinction. Others have left our sphere of their own volition. Earth's balance is delicate to maintain. War, fear and hate displace harmony.'

"I leaned closer to the flames of the fire, though I felt neither heat nor warmth that night. 'Task? From whence came your instructions?'

"In my head, came the answer: 'From the creative force of the universe.' He saw puzzlement in my eyes. 'My kind exists in a dimension beyond yours. We reveal ourselves to only a few. I bid you peace.' His form began to shimmer until it vanished."

Gio put down his glass and gazed at each person around the table in turn before he spoke. "It strikes me that none of us spoke of pre-destination, Fate, or an anthropomorphic God in the Biblical sense. Are we all given to pagan notions of Mother Earth or Mother Nature? Or is it that war, fear and hate separate us from our true nature?

"I spent years cursing God. Why was I born thus? Why was I cast out of my home? When I fell into a group of artists, I became lost in the creation of art. I touched the soul of the universe.

"One day, shortly after my wife died, I was bereft, holding a sleeping Maximilian in my arms. He opened his eyes and my heart wrenched in pain. How could I provide for him? A vision floated before me. My late wife, her image pale, ghostly and ethereal, spoke to me. Was it in my head or in my ear? I know not. But it was as real to me as is this evening's conversation. 'Gio, no one else can love our child as much as you. No one else can guide him as well as you. Love will show you the way.'

"After that moment, I no longer cursed God. I don't claim to understand the unexplainable. For me, the notion of the creative force of the universe, a consciousness of harmony, such as that hairy being described by Jean-Louis, is closer to my idea of God than any imposed dogma, forced catechism or doctrinal creed. Worship is an anthropomorphic projection of human desire onto an omnipotent being. Omnipotence does not require worship. The universe inspires awe. It does not demand obsequious kneeling. God is an allegory of love and peace expressed in the universe around us. The universe shows us secrets of stars and light, sun and shadow, moon and tides. Therefore, to me, the consciousness of the universe *is* God."

Gio raised his glass. "On this voyage, I didn't find Atlantis, but I found a deeper connection. To friendship!"

CHAPTER THIRTY

Tuesday, July 23, 1811 – The London Docks
Henry

Arriving in late afternoon, Steiner drove Henry to meet the ship returning from the Azores. Guy arrived to pick up Gwyneth and Gio, the count waited for Clarissa and Dr. St. Cloud, and Francois waited for Edward.

Amid the flurry of goodbyes, Edward kissed Bri on the cheek. "I'll see you on Thursday for breakfast. I'll need to spend all day tomorrow catching up at the bank."

Bri gave him a dazzling smile. "I enjoyed our pre-honeymoon."

"So did I." He kissed her again and helped her into the carriage.

Spotty scrambled onto her lap and licked her face.

Hector nuzzled her leg.

Jean-Louis lifted Chérie up to join Steiner, and then leapt to the step and reached the perch.

The earl's brow furrowed. "Why did Jean-Louis have to lift Chérie? Was she injured on your voyage?"

"She's going to have her first litter soon. You might need to have a stern talk with Hector."

Henry rubbed Hector's neck and laughed. "Dr. St. Cloud's adoption service will be busy."

"Probably not. I think I have homes for all of them."

"Why does that not surprise me?" He laughed. "Now, tell me about your trip."

"It was wonderful to be free of fear of Blackie. Edward and I are bickering less—the time away was a perfect interlude. Thank you."

"As if I could have stopped you."

"You had valid reasons for me to consider postponing the trip. And, after all, it *is* your fleet. I'm unlikely to commandeer a vessel."

" 'Unlikely' leaves a wide swath of possibilities."

"You taught me to always plot alternative scenarios."

"Well, here's an alternative scenario for you. We're going directly to Charlotte's for dinner."

***

Thursday, July 25, 1811 – The Blue Bazaar
Orion

After Jean-Louis returned from the Azores, Orion went to London to fulfill his promise to the Frenchman to help infiltrate the Gypsy band. *Will my father be there?*

Orion told Jean-Louis of events at Ravenshire during the Frenchman's absence. "Lord Darlemont came over once a week. He and Ian are quite taken with each other. Ian is determined to find treasure in the old tower.

"Nosey is good and Sunny is growing so fast. You wouldn't recognize him!"

Jean-Louis smiled at the Gypsy's enthusiasm. "You're hesitating. Is there something you're afraid to tell me?"

Orion looked at his feet. "I don't want to forget my place."

"Out with it."

"I think Lady Wyndward and Lord Darlemont might fall in love."

"Ha! You are a delusional romantic. Lord Darlemont is married to a harridan, but he would never besmirch the reputation of Lady Wyndward because he is an honorable man. *And he knows what I would do to him.* Find yourself a woman of your own. Then you'll stop imagining other people's love lives and have a basketful of new problems."

The Gypsy boy blushed.

Jean-Louis tilted his head. "So you already have?"

Nodding, Orion grinned.

"Don't tell anyone else until you know it's true between you. Initial lust can fade with time."

"Not this one. She is everything to me."

"Give it six months, then we'll talk."

Days revolved around observing the Gypsy stall in the bazaar but evenings allowed him time with the horses. The animals' companionship helped him sort through his conflicting emotions. Gypsies were his people, but they were no longer his family.

On one particular day in the shadows where he could observe the Gypsy stall, Orion felt the presence of Jean-Louis behind him. The Gypsy spoke in a hushed tone. "Something has changed since we were last here. I saw her approach Vano before you left on your sailing. An old Gypsy woman is reading Tarot cards, purporting to tell fortunes." He pointed to a makeshift piece of fabric that created privacy. Orion scoffed. "She's been seeing one gullible fool after another."

"You don't believe in fortune tellers?"

"No. Gypsies know it's a game to exploit weak minds."

"Stay here and don't let the old woman leave. Get your fortune read if you need to in order to keep her here. She is dangerous."

Jean-Louis disappeared into the crowd.

***

Felicity

Humming to herself as she shopped from the list Dominique, the comtesse's cook, had given her, Felicity was startled when a familiar voice called to her.

"Felicity."

"Jean-Louis—"

The Frenchman pulled her behind the tent of a nearby stall. "Would you agree to help me with a small matter?"

"*Oui.*"

"Do you believe in fortune tellers?"

Shaking her head, Felicity stared at Jean-Louis. "*Non.*" She made the sign of the cross.

"Would you pretend to do so for my sake?"

"*Bien sûr.* Of course."

"I just want your sense of the woman. Play along and give me your impressions." He dropped some coins in her hand. "This should cover it. Wander through the bazaar and act as if you're interested in the wares at the Gypsy stall. Inquire of the stall keeper as to the cost of the Tarot card reading and appear to waver. He's the tall muscled man. Be a bit of an actress. After all, men cannot resist you."

"Ha! But *you* can."

"I am the exception."

"Very well."

Jean-Louis pointed. "It's in that direction."

"See you soon. *À bientôt.*"

Following her instructions, Felicity strolled along a path lined by tents and stopped to look at the wares at the Gypsy stall. Seeing a woman exit the curtained fortune teller's section, she asked the tall man, with a feigned fascination, "Is that a real *fortune teller*?"

Vano nodded. "You could be next. Pay me whatever you think is fair. You are such a lovely lady. I love the accent of a Frenchwoman."

Felicity blinked her long lashes and took a couple of coins out of her purse. "Will this be enough?"

Without looking at the amount, Vano closed his hand into a fist. "For you, of course."

Mirela opened the curtain and saw Felicity. "Come in, my dear."

***

Jean-Louis

The Frenchman returned within ten minutes. "I saw one of the comtesse's servants shopping earlier. She's going to get her fortune told."

Orion nodded. "A light-brown-haired woman just went inside the curtained-off area. I overheard a French accent."

"That's her."

"*Bonjour.*" An unfamiliar voice behind Jean-Louis caused Orion to turn to see who it was.

Jean-Louis did not turn around. His voice dripped with disapproval. "Voutain."

"We got a tip and just found them. Colvert is watching the grandmother."

"You lost them for months! Don't lose them again. I can't do everybody's job."

"*Je comprends.*"

"No. You *don't* understand. The grandmother's companion is under our noses in the Gypsy stall." Jean-Louis still didn't turn around. He leaned toward Orion. "The grandmother is a killer. Bri and the earl are her targets. When she finds out about Ian—"

Orion paled. "Would she—could she—hurt a child?"

"Not hurt. Kill. She would not hesitate." Jean-Louis never released his steely-eyed gaze from the makeshift fortune telling privacy curtain. "Let this be a lesson to you, Orion. Voutain and Colvert were deceived by two old women. People die when men like us make misjudgments. We are players in a deadly game."

***

Felicity

About twenty minutes after she entered Mirela's lair, Felicity pulled aside the brightly patterned curtain and exited. She bought a trinket from the Gypsy tent, and ambled through the bazaar until she reached Tej's stall, where she had arranged to meet Jean-Louis.

He arrived a few moments later and pretended to look at the Indian's wares. "Well?"

Felicity shrugged. "At first, it seemed the ordinary drivel you would expect. 'An exotic man awaiting you,' in her odd way of speaking and so on. But then she turned over cards and I got a chill." Felicity reached for the Frenchman's arm. "She frightened me."

"In what way?"

"She said, 'One of your countrymen watching me. He knowing truth, which is dangerous for him.' I think she meant you. You must be careful, Jean-Louis."

Jean-Louis shrugged. "Could be Voutain. Or Colvert. What else did she say? You were in there for longer than I expected."

"Mostly she shuffled the cards and instructed me to cut them, over and over, asking me questions." Felicity's face looked pinched. "Just before I left, she touched my arm and said, 'A woman with a noble title having dead husband. His death being no accident. She should being careful crossing street too.'"

"*Foutre!* She's as much as admitted she knows of the manner of the comte's death and has threatened the comtesse. I never put much stock in Tarot cards. Perhaps she has not the gift of sight, but was complicit in the comte's death." His eyes narrowed into slits. "Anything else?"

Felicity shook her head.

Jean-Louis frowned. "The threat to the comtesse is real. Stay away from that Gypsy stall." He glanced around the immediate area. "Did Guy bring you here?"

"Yes. He's parked out near the front entry."

"I'll deliver you to him and alert him of the situation. Are you finished with your shopping?"

"Not quite."

"Let's get what you need. I don't want you to be alone in this bazaar. You may be a target." He took her arm and steered her away, turning back to cast a warning glare at Tej. "Say nothing of what you have heard."

Cowering under the former trapper's gaze, Tej nodded.

***

Thursday, July 25, 1811 – Dr. St. Cloud's Veterinary Care Clinic
Dr. St. Cloud

Back from the Azores, the pace of the veterinary clinic had not slowed to what was expected in the dog days of summer. Dr. St. Cloud came back to a silent war between his assistant Carolyn and Dr. Derry. He sensed a rift, but decided to speak to Carolyn before delving into Dr. Derry's viewpoint.

Dr. Derry had returned to Ravenshire the day before, but the plan was that he would relieve Dr. St. Cloud on the weekends starting in August.

When demands on him slowed down, Dr. St. Cloud called Carolyn into his office. "You seem unhappy. I'm sure you need some time off."

"Time off? I will need to work many *more* hours to repair the damage that man did while you were gone. He may be competent with horses, cattle and sheep diseases, but he sees small animals as nuisances. He is far too willing to euthanize them for the slightest complaint."

Dr. St. Cloud's face paled. "Dear God! You stopped him, I hope."

"Of course. He wanted to change established procedures, which I resisted, saying we must wait until you returned. The man is domineering and treated me with disdain on a daily basis. If he returns, I will quit."

"I need you, Carolyn. Tell me more."

She related several specific instances of incompetence.

"He came highly recommended. Lady Gabriella holds him in high regard."

"She has spent no time with him. From what I have learned, her opinion is based on what others observed in his work in Ireland with large farm animals. He has never worked with people and lacks the necessary skills. He is a dictator. And, for what it's worth, he does not hold *Lady Gabriella* in high regard."

Taken aback, Dr. St. Cloud sat forward in his chair. "He spoke ill of her?"

"Of all women. He thinks we are alive to serve men."

"Then he will have a short tenure at Ravenshire. I have faith that Lady Gabriella will exert her influence. I wonder how Lady Wyndward feels about him?"

"My guess is that no one pays attention unless an animal dies. It's probably the odd twist of Fate that permits him to *avoid* killing an animal."

"He seemed competent in my discussions with him, but the art of persuasion can mask incompetence. I'll tell him I've decided to train assistants myself, and that his time is too valuable at Ravenshire to abandon his post. Then I will somehow broach the subject of his incompetence with Lady Gabriella. Jean-Louis can advise me on how to present the facts.

"As for your position, I will increase your pay and train you in surgical techniques. Specializing in small pets is not a priority for veterinarians, so the fact that women cannot attend university will not be an impediment. We will find—and test—other candidates to work with us."

"So I can sleep tonight knowing that the Dr. Derry interlude will not be repeated?"

"Correct. He has spent his last day here."

***

Thursday, July 25, 1811 – Lord Ravenshire's Townhouse
Jean-Louis

Returning before the dinner hour from the Blue Bazaar, Jean-Louis found a sealed letter on his bed table, as well as a basket of cheese and sandwiches from Nellie. *She knows my habit of forgetting to eat.*

He broke the blue seal on the folded note from Dr. St. Cloud. After reading it, he grabbed a sandwich, and rode to the comtesse's townhouse to find Gilles. *I need to know if Gilles has seen similar problems with Dr. Derry and what Orion might know of his behavior.*

***

Thursday, July 25, 1811 – Lady Gwyneth's Townhouse
Gilles

As had become custom after Aelwyn's return, she and Ian stayed with Gwyneth in London on weekends and the family gathered for dinner.

Occasionally Vanessa and the duke came with Oliver and Lady Abigail, but this weekend, the group included only Bri, Edward, Aelwyn and Ian.

Once the family members were settled inside, Gilles and Jean-Louis met in the comtesse's stables. "The doctor is correct. Other than horses, Dr. Derry has little patience or concern for either farmyard animals or pets. He even made a comment about Chérie." Gilles grimaced.

"Out with it."

"He said, 'The bitch is having a litter. More disposable pests for the "quality." '"

"Dr. Derry's face hardened into a scowl. He could not hide his disdain, saying, 'The spoiled members of Society expect these large rat-like animals to be treated as if they were beloved children.'"

With an icy tone, Jean-Louis continued, "And your comment about farmyard animals?"

"He suggested one of the lambs born recently be killed because it had a lame leg. He refused to even look at the limb. He said, 'Nature's misfits die in the wild. So should they here.' "

"Orion recommended him."

"I believe their only interaction was in relation to horses. Orion is young and impressionable. His instincts are not honed by time and experience as ours have been."

Jean-Louis nodded. "He has a good heart. He will never be a security man. But he may be useful to me with the old Gypsy."

Gilles knew better than to question Jean-Louis when he set his jaw in such a manner.

"I'll ask the earl to terminate Dr. Derry and have a letter prepared for him to come to London mid-week for a meeting. Wait an hour after he leaves and send another coach with his belongings. I have an idea where our Dr. Derry can be put to good use, far away from us."

***

Monday, July 29, 1811 – The Blue Bazaar
Orion

Orion hid in the shadows where he kept an eye on the Gypsy stall. Voutain watched with him. "That old Gypsy witch made fools of Colvert and me."

"Who is she?"

Voutain shook his head. "That is for J-L to explain, not me. I'm in enough trouble as it is. I'm under instructions not to let her out of my sight. I want to follow those men, too, but I can't be in two places at once." Voutain shrugged. "Maybe J-L will send you to follow them."

Jean-Louis came up behind them. "Exactly what I planned. Closing time is near. Perhaps they will invite us to their camp."

"Is it nearby?"

The Frenchman inclined his head to the north. "In a rundown area near the river. They've set up their wagons and tents there." He looked at Voutain. "You can rejoin Colvert. I'll watch the old woman with Orion. I've engaged some footpads for more eyes."

As the stall keepers rolled down their flaps to protect their wares for the next day, a Gypsy began to play the fiddle and sing a catchy ditty:

Come, come along to our Gypsy camp,
To dance and sing and drink your fill,
Listen to the fiddler under the fiery lamp
You'll fall under our spell. You will, you will.
Follow us now, we'll lead the way
A perfect end to a perfect day.

Shoppers and proprietors fell in line, and soon a group was heading north. Mirela, cane in hand, moved slowly behind the fiddler's followers.

Jean-Louis and Orion kept her in sight, staying at the back of the crowd.

Voutain saluted adieu and faded into the twilight to resume his assignment.

The Frenchman scoffed at the trail of followers. "Like children under the spell of the Pied Piper's pipe, they follow."

Orion spoke softly. "Drunken men fall down, get bumped into, and don't realize their coin is gone until they regain their senses."

After following for about twenty minutes, the torches of the Gypsy camp came into view. Jean-Louis stayed on the far edge. "You go forward. See if you can get close enough to overhear any conversation."

The young Gypsy moved with a spring in his step as a fiddler played a tune for dancing.

Mirela stopped to listen and look around the camp.

Standing near her, Orion was startled when she turned and gazed directly at him. She took his arm. "Let me lean on you. I am a weak old woman and you are a fine young man."

Unsure of what to do, Orion smiled. "I am at your service, Madame."

"You being Roma, that much looking clear. And you having a way with horses." As his face clouded, wondering how she knew that, his heart clutched as a second fiddler played a familiar tune. He stepped out of the fiddler's line of sight.

"You no liking him, boy. You no wanting him to see you."

"I don't know him. That tune reminds me of someone I once knew."

"He *reminding* you of no one. He is the one. His memory living in a dark place in your heart. You meaning to kill him."

Orion blanched. "No! I would never—"

"Do not lie to me. It being pointless."

Stammering, Orion sputtered, "I w-will not l-let you read my cards."

"Foolish boy! Think you my secret lying in my cards or my crystal? No. It being my touch."

The Gypsy boy tried to pull away.

Mirela held fast to his arm. "I feeling your hate. I feeling your fear. This man being evil. You must taking him unawares. I help you. Let me thinking on it."

"But—"

"Meet me on Friday in Gypsy area of Blue Bazaar." She pointed up. "When sun being at zenith." She released his arm and hobbled away.

Moments later, Jean-Louis grabbed him by the arm. "I heard it all. Leave now. I will follow her."

***

Jean-Louis

A short time later, the former trapper arrived behind Voutain and Colvert. They watched Mirela go upstairs to a suite of rooms over a restaurant, *Omelettes de Mme d'Aix*. He signaled with his palm and two footpads appeared. "We'll just go by initials. 'V' and 'C', meet 'F' and 'T'. 'V' will assign shifts."

The grandmother and the Gypsy. Will she act alone, without Blackburn? Or wait for his return? Jean-Louis had always felt in his bones that Blackburn had survived. Too many loose ends were conveniently tied up. Now the Frenchman had an advantage. *I know where Blackburn will hide.*

CHAPTER THIRTY-ONE

Monday, July 29, 1811 – Dr. St. Cloud's Veterinary Care Clinic
Banfield

B anfield dropped by Dr. St. Cloud's clinic and ran into Lady
Patricia, who seemed enthralled by a fluffy white Pomeranian
in a cage.

Dr. St. Cloud came over to greet them. "Lady Patricia, this
Pomeranian was brought in by the daughter of a woman who died.
The dog is only about two years old, and appears to be well trained."

"I think he or she will be my choice, but I want to see all the
others before I decide."

"She."

While Lady Patricia looked at the other dogs, the doctor inclined
his head closer to Banfield. "If you'd be interested in a Dalmatian,
the Frenchman's dog is expecting a litter soon. Lady Gabriella put
your name on a list of those who might be interested. Edward is
getting one."

"They like to run, don't they?"

"Yes, and swim. Great companions, very loyal."

Banfield hesitated. "If there aren't enough in the litter..."

"Then we'll find another solution. I prefer to adopt out
abandoned pets, but Chérie and Hector seemed to have had other
ideas."

Lady Patricia rejoined them. "I love that Pomeranian. She and I
understand each other."

Banfield raised an eyebrow. *Why not? They're both showhorses.*

***

Tuesday, July 30, 1811 – Interior of a Hackney Cab
Orion

The day after seeing the Gypsy camp and talking with Mirela, Orion rode in a Hackney to the Blue Bazaar with Jean-Louis and waited for the Frenchman to speak.

"Touch, eh? That's her secret?"

Orion nodded.

"Meet her at noon on Friday as she requested. Stay in the shadows until then. I'll be close by." The Frenchman looked at Orion out of the corner of his eye. "Was the second fiddler your father?"

"I think so. That is his tune, but I was too far away to see his face. It's been many years."

"She'll probably offer you poison. Take it, but we won't use it."

"We?"

"You don't kill anyone on my watch without my approval unless it's for immediate self-defense. As I told you before, revenge killing is often fraught with regret. If you are determined to kill your father, it must be done without any link to you. The Gypsy crone must believe you had nothing to do with it. Then she will claim she made it happen to protect you. She is as dangerous as a jungle snake."

"Maybe I shouldn't kill him."

Jean-Louis sat back on the carriage bench. "Sons and fathers have many conflicts. Perhaps what you want is not his actual death, but the death of the past. You want him to change into the father you wanted him to be. That is a child's dream. Gratification from victory is fleeting."

"What should I do?" *Jean-Louis will know.*

"Only you can decide, but first, we could intercept him, and you could speak your piece. Then, if you want him to disappear, we can discuss that. But tell the Gypsy crone you do not want the fiddler dead. There is a risk that she might kill him to ingratiate herself with you."

Orion's horror contorted his expression. "She-she wouldn't—"

"She would. To people like her, you are a pawn to be used in a plan you do not understand. She may know that you work for the earl. Always assume your enemy knows more than you think. Plot two or three steps ahead before you move forward. Sometimes it is better to move to the side or retreat."

"I am not suited to this work. Stop the carriage."

Jean-Louis rapped a signal to the jervie to stop.

Before the carriage had fully halted, Orion pushed the door open and jumped out. He retched, emitting guttural sounds and spewing his breakfast onto the muddy ground.

***

Tuesday, July 30, 1811 – Palace of Westminster Offices
Drummond

Whether or not Parliament was in session, Drummond maintained a small suite of offices in the cavernous structure, technically a courtesy of the ruling party. In truth, the suite was provided no matter which party was in the majority. All recognized his power. The son of a former Member of Parliament, Drummond had a name well known to multiple generations of government representatives. His offices, located in a rarely used corridor, suited everyone. Fewer prying eyes wandered the halls to observe the comings and goings of politicians who sought campaign advice or support, funding for projects to enhance their constituent appeal, or the quashing of emerging crises that threatened their positions.

Burying scandal or creating a false impression of a rival's transgressions was Drummond's stock-in-trade. Over the years, he'd developed disdain for his clients. Their weaknesses, their secrets, were his to exploit. And when he needed a favor, he got it. He'd become wealthy due to the misdeeds of others—others who paid exorbitant fees to make their problems disappear.

Though the most recent session of Parliament had dissolved, clients continued to seek him out. He sat at this desk with his feet propped up as he leaned back, wondering what help he might seek from Sir Reggie in repayment for the favor he'd done for Lady Patricia, when a knock at the door disturbed his thoughts.

"Come in." Drummond lowered his legs and stood to receive his guest, a senior member of the party leadership. The man had come to him before. *Another one?*

The MP, Albert Pencheff, looked around furtively.

"I dismissed my staff for a month's holiday after the session's end." Drummond gestured to Pencheff to take a seat. "Calm yourself. We are alone."

Doing as instructed, the MP sat and pulled out a handkerchief to wipe his perspiration-beaded forehead. "I need your assistance, Tottie."

"For?"

"A shopgirl in my district is with child. She needs to disappear from the town before she shows. She must come to London until the child is born."

"Bertie, this is the third one in two years."

"Most of the time I'm careful. Three out of more than a hundred isn't bad." He guffawed and then began to spew phlegm into a handkerchief.

"No. It's not merely bad, it's stupid. You are reckless, Bertie. Liaisons with more than a hundred women in two years? That is many more than I can stop from speaking out, even if you could remember them all, and many more than even you can afford to silence. Maybe you need the Abelard treatment."

Pencheff paled. "Never!"

Drummond sighed. "If you recall the cautionary tale of Abelard and Héloïse, his castration was not voluntary. If you can't impose discipline on yourself, it may be imposed upon you from without. And that might end in your death. Do you want to die?"

"No one wants to die."

"Your behavior would suggest otherwise. A young girl's father, uncle, brother, or would-be lover might seek revenge. Why not avail yourself of high quality brothels in the *ton?*"

"I prefer fresh flesh, unsullied by the touch of another man."

Pencheff's crooked smile chilled Drummond. "Give me her name and town. I'll arrange for her to be cared for and the child to be adopted."

The MP gave him the information.

After Drummond made notes, he put down his quill. "I require something in addition to my usual fee this time."

"It's yours."

"You don't know what it is."

"Anything."

Drummond leaned forward in his chair. "Your resignation."

"But I'm in line to become Prime Minister in a few years!"

"No longer. This is the last mistake of yours that I will fix. You are not fit for office."

"No." Pencheff's face reddened. He reached to grasp Drummond's hand. "I'll change. You know I'll always do your bidding. What difference does another girl's ruined life mean to you?"

Drummond scoffed and withdrew his hand. "One thing I've learned in my lifetime of dealing with people like you is that people like you don't change. You're out. Now. I have several candidates who can move seamlessly into your position without dragging a trail of scandal behind them."

Pencheff sat back and slumped in his chair. "My life is over."

"Your government life is over. There are sinecures available to former Members of Parliament, so you can preserve an aura of power. Your life, what remains of it, gives you the opportunity to *prove* that you can change. I'll write out the press release of your resignation for health reasons right now for the *Times*. After six months, you can re-emerge, cured. Leave London today. Stay out of the limelight. Perhaps take the sun in Portugal."

The MP rose to leave. "I should thank you for your help in the past."

"You should, Bertie. And remember that you're leaving Parliament of your own volition. Cross me and you'll never be welcome in the *ton* again. I hold your ruin in my hands."

"Ruthless you are, Drummond. I'm done in by my own Faustian bargain with you. I see it, I know it, I admit it. But I won't pretend to be happy about it."

"Retirement won't be so bad. A lot of people our age are already dead."

As he walked out of the office, Pencheff called out over his shoulder, "Cold comfort, that."

***

Wednesday, July 31, 1811 – Winters Foundling Hospital
Charlotte

A clerk appeared at Charlotte's office door. "Baroness, Mr. Drummond is here to see you."

"Show him in." Charlotte sighed. *Another young girl no doubt.*

Drummond walked in and embraced Charlotte. "You look as lovely as ever, Charlotte. Please have dinner with me sometime soon."

"Dinner with old friends is always welcome, Tottie."

"Good. How about next week?"

"Done." Charlotte walked over to a seating area and gestured to Drummond to sit down. "Are you bringing me another guest?"

"Yes. I've arranged for her to be brought here tomorrow." He looked down at his hands and then directed his gaze back to Charlotte. "This will be the last one from that contemptible man. I have secured his resignation."

Charlotte leaned forward. "I'm surprised. I thought erasing the footprints of the errant politician was your main task."

"One of my tasks. But this man is indefensible. I know. I see the look in your eyes. Yes, even I set limits from time to time. Not often, but in a case as egregious as this, it was time."

"The usual arrangement?"

"Yes, I will provide funds for the young woman to establish a new life and I'm sure you can arrange a satisfactory adoption. As always, at the age of majority, the child will receive an annuity from an unknown benefactor. From these situations, Charlotte, I want to assure you that all fees paid by this client go to the woman and child. For pure political advice, I keep my exorbitant fees. But helping these women is, perhaps, penance for my many other less-than-honorable acts."

"Tottie, you've never told me what set you on this path, but your honesty with me is something I value."

"Sometimes..."

"What?"

"Nothing." *Sometimes I wish I'd taken a different path. And found a woman like you.*

CHAPTER THIRTY-TWO

Thursday, August 1, 1811 – Lord Ravenshire's Townhouse
Henry

Thompson ushered Dr. Derry into Henry's office. Jean-Louis sat to his right.

"Dr. Derry, I understand you have a hankering to travel. Through a friend of mine at the Foreign Office, I have arranged a posting for you to Portugal. The army needs horse doctors for the cavalry. We've packed up and transferred your belongings here so that you can take up your new post immediately. Jean-Louis will escort you to the regiment to be trained before you are sent to Portugal."

At first dumbstruck, Dr. Derry stammered. "B-but I don't want to join the army."

Jean-Louis stood. "Join the army or return to Ireland. Those are your choices."

The veterinarian paled. "I-I don't understand."

The earl stood. "I told you when you were hired that I require respect for people and animals from all I employ. You have failed that test. Where you go from here is up to you, but it will not be Ravenshire and it will not be London. I will see to it."

After a few moments of silence, he spoke. "I don't want to go back to Ireland, so it's the army, I guess." He slightly bowed his head and left the room.

Before Jean-Louis left the earl's study, he turned to Henry. "If he's as good with horses as we think, he'll survive. If not, they'll cashier him out. In any case, he won't be our problem anymore."

***

Friday, August 2, 1811 – Edward's Townhouse
Vaux

Showing Edward and Bri the progress that had been made over the month they had been gone, Vaux pointed to the roof before they entered.

Bri squinted and shielded her eyes with her hand as she looked up. "It's all new."

"Not just a new roof, newly reinforced attic, floors, stairs and landings. When the roofing contractors were tar sealing, we lost time when part of ceiling caved into one wing. Now that has been restructured, reinforced and inspected."

Edward frowned. "Were any workers hurt in the cave-in?"

Vaux shrugged. "Agility is helpful in the roofing trade."

"A rather dry observation, Vaux."

"One has to be flexible in construction projects. Miraculously, no one was injured. The older the structure, the more hidden problems are revealed when we update them."

Vaux took them on a tour and when they reached the bedrooms, he asked, "Do either of you know the purpose of canopies over beds?"

"I assumed it was for privacy," said Bri.

Edward nodded. "As did I."

Vaux shook his head. "It was to protect sleeping tenants from the fall of roofing detritus."

"Practical." Bri shrugged.

"Arches came by and gave me some suggestions. I've incorporated them all. The man is a genius."

"He continually implements maintenance projects on the Ravenshire manor house."

"Why do you call it a *house?* It's really a palace by any measure."

Bri smiled."My great grandfather didn't want to offend the then-duke, so he downplayed its size and grandeur. In those days, not so long ago, a personal affront to a duke could cost one his head as well as his title."

***

Friday, August 2, 1811 – Interior of a Hackney
Mirela

Mirela left the café to visit the Gypsy stall in the bazaar. When younger, she had traveled with the Gypsy wagons, from town to town and to the Continent and back before Napoleon made such travel so difficult.

After Duff left to pursue his long-planned revenge in London, she'd moved in with Aneira for companionship.

Their friendship had spanned Duff's lifetime. For the first twenty of those years, they had seen each other only for a short period each year when the caravan was nearby Aneira's home.

Mirela and Arthur had forged documents and covered Aneira's trail whenever she and Duff, under whatever names they were using at the time, moved.

Lately, seeing the Gypsy community again, Mirela felt pulled back to her roots. *These are my people.* She sighed in resignation. She loved her friend, but she would always long for the Roma and their ways.

Even the music from the other night kept playing in her head and she tapped her foot absentmindedly to the same rhythm as the carriage wheels click-clacked through the streets.

Walking through the market, she bought some fruit, and wandered until she came to the Gypsy stall.

Vano, the proprietor, smiled broadly. "We have people waiting for your readings. Come, come." He escorted her into the curtained space and helped her into her seat.

The fortune teller reached into her bag, retrieved her crystal ball and deck of Tarot cards, and placed them on the table. She encircled the crystal with her palms, closed her eyes and chanted in the language of the Roma.

When she opened her eyes, she nodded. "I am ready."

The first client came through the curtain.

***

Friday, August 2, 1811 – The Blue Bazaar
Orion

Colvert slid into the shadows of a stall behind Jean-Louis and Orion. "Voutain is watching the grandmother. I followed the old Gypsy here."

Jean-Louis motioned with his head. "I know the woman who just went in to get her fortune told. She's a friend of Lady Gabriella. I'll pull her aside when she leaves."

Colbert took a bit of snuff. "We have one of the workmen on the café reporting to us also. Ever heard of a Viscount Vaux?"

The Frenchman twisted around to glance at Colvert. "I know him." He looked at the snuff box. "Don't use snuff. It will cause sores in your mouth, rot your body, and shorten your life."

"Working for you has shortened my life. Of that I am certain. Must I give up one of life's pleasures?"

"Continue at your own peril."

"The viscount came with a woman in a wagon marked Turtin Upholsterers & Drapers."

"He has no idea that he's dealing with a killer."

Orion remained silent. *I thought I could kill my father, but when I saw him, the hatred left me. If J-L knew, he would think me weak.*

***

Friday, August 2, 1811 – The Fortune Teller's Tent
Lady Patricia

"Sit down, my dear. I being Mirela."

Taking a seat, Lady Patricia clasped and unclasped her fingers below the table level. "I've never had my fortune read before. How does it work?"

"Closing your eyes and relax. Focus on the questions you wanting to ask me. The cards do not lie."

Lady Patricia concentrated, and then opened her eyes. "What about the crystal ball?"

Mirela shrugged. "It adding to atmosphere. The cards tell all." She handed the cards to Lady Patricia, briefly touching her fingers. "Shuffle and cut the deck while thinking of your question."

Her client did as she was told.

The Gypsy picked up the cut deck and made a design on the table, murmuring as she did. She turned over the first card. "The lovers, upside down. Most young girls wanting to know this truth."

"If it's upside down, does that mean he does not love me?"

"Perhaps. More cards will telling us." She turned over the next card. "Death. Meaning change, not death of the body."

When Mirela revealed the third card, she sat back. "The Eight of Cups meaning betrayal, disappointment. You being now, or were, in love with a man now leaving you for another."

Blood drained from Lady Patricia's face. "It's true. It's all true." Tears welled up in her eyes. "He said he loved me, but he's asked someone else to marry him now that his wife has died."

"You turning over next card."

Lady Patricia picked up a card and turned it over. "The Five of Swords. What does that mean?"

"It meaning to cleaning up after conflict and studying what going wrong. Learning from mistakes."

"I'm trying. I feel so alone and unloved." Her body slumped.

"Stop crying. Man like that not deserving you."

Raising her head, Lady Patricia used her handkerchief to wipe her eyes. She reached out and turned over another card.

"The Queen of Swords. This being good sign. You must being independent, not pleasing man all the time."

Lady Patricia extended her hand to turn another card, but Mirela put her hand over the card to stop her.

"You having heard enough. Hold up your head. Other men will finding you. We being done."

Rising to her feet, Lady Patricia said, "Thank you. I shall consider your advice."

"Not advice. Truth." She pointed to Lady Patricia's heart. "You knowing this."

Pushing the curtain out of the way, Lady Patricia left.

She rushed through the bazaar, and hailed a Hackney. Before she could get in, Jean-Louis opened the door. "Lady Patricia, beware the old Gypsy. What did she tell you?"

"That my lover betrayed me and that I should learn from my mistake."

"Anyone could have told you that."

Lady Patricia rose to her full height, displaying indignation. "How dare you speak to me in such a way?"

"For your own protection. Get in the carriage." He closed the door. "And never visit that stall again. That Gypsy is evil incarnate."

***

Colvert

Colvert put his arm around Orion's shoulders. "What do you think of this work?"

"I'd prefer to be in the stables with the horses."

"Ha! An unambitious man is always welcome. No daggers in the back."

Orion's shoulders sagged.

Jean-Louis reappeared. "It's near closing time. When the piper starts, we'll follow. The footpads are nearby."

***

Vano

The Gypsy stall keeper had two more people waiting to see the fortune teller. The curtain parted and the client left, nearly dancing out into the bazaar. *What lies did she peddle to that one?*

The second to the last in line entered the Tarot card reader's lair.

Vano marveled at his luck. *The crone doesn't ask for money. I collect what I please from the Society fools who seek her out. Mostly women, and the occasional foppish dandy. Impressionable.*

He signaled to his workers that it was time to begin securing the tent for the evening. He always kept two men on guard. Unprotected property was too tempting, despite the Blue Bazaar's "security" watch guards. *They're as corrupt as any man who sees an easy mark.* He sniffed. *Not much better than a footpad.*

The fiddler and the piper began to close the tent flaps, tightening the ties and testing their fastness. Once that was done, they gathered their instruments, leaving one flap open to haggle over a few more sales before the bazaar closed. The tune was jaunty and late-afternoon shoppers walked in their direction to hear the music and see the players.

The curtain opened, and the client left in tears.

Vano distracted the last person in line with trinkets to avoid her seeing the teary woman and having to refund her advance payment. After the weeping one disappeared into the crowd, he escorted the last woman to the tent. He glared at Mirela as he closed the curtain. *She said she wouldn't give people bad news.*

***

Orion

The music from the Gypsy stall heralded day's end.

Orion's stomach churned at the thought of seeing his father again. *How can I be of use to Jean-Louis when all I can think about is my father? I must escape this task.*

Jean-Louis put his hand on Orion's shoulder and whispered in his ear. "I sense your hesitation. Now that we know where the Gypsy and the grandmother live, all I need to know is if she has recruited additional confederates. She may want you to perform a service for her. You should agree. I need to know how many men to gather around us to protect the family."

Involuntarily, Orion stiffened with fear.

"You don't have to join the band. Forget that. Just observe and report. I'll find a Gypsy footpad. The problem is, he could be working both sides. Double his blood money and betray both sides."

Orion twisted his neck to look back over his shoulder at Jean-Louis. "I don't want anything to happen to Ian, but I'm no hero."

"I'm not asking you to be a hero. Observe and report, as I said. Maybe a couple more evenings, that's it. Just enough to get a flavor of the conspiracies that the Gypsy witch is spinning."

The two footpads joined them.

"Either of you know a Gypsy footpad?" Jean-Louis studied their faces.

One spat. "Don't trust them. They'd as soon drink a mug of ale with you as slit your throat. They have no honor."

Orion couldn't stop himself from snapping at them. "And you do?"

The other footpad stepped forward with a menacing stare.

Jean-Louis held up his hands. "We deal in facts, not insults. Let's see how much we can glean from tonight's gathering. One night at a time. One detail or hunch to follow." He motioned to them. "Spread out in the crowd. We'll compare notes tomorrow at the same time. If anything urgent arises, you know how to find me."

***

Friday, August 2, 1811 – The Gypsy Camp
Django the Fiddler

Django the Fiddler liked London. People spent money freely and tossed coins or currency carelessly into the hat he placed at his feet. Even in the Gypsy camp, non-Gypsies followed the music. By the time the crowd dispersed at midnight, his hat overflowed.

No longer did he have to share his earnings with his wife. The once-compliant woman had ceaselessly hounded him after he forced her to abandon their younger son in Ireland. Django thought the soft boy unsuited to the life of a wandering fiddler. He regretted listening to his wife, who had prevailed on him to stay in Ireland for too long. *The Roma aren't meant to stay in one place.*

After leaving Ireland, they joined a tribe in Scotland and traversed the country. His other son, with a temperament more akin to his, had tweaked the nose of another man after too much drinking, inviting a knife fight that ended badly. Once his wife lost her second son, she turned into a screeching harridan, haranguing him from dawn to dark.

As a result, the other Gypsies forced them to set their camp out of earshot. One night he slapped his wife so hard that she fell back and hit her head on the rocks around the campfire. Her screeching stopped. Dead, accusing eyes stared back at him. Grateful for their isolation, he buried her in the forest, broke camp, and disappeared.

No one knew him in London and he liked it that way.

Django heard the other fiddler and the piper leading the bazaar crowd back to their camp. Over the years, he realized that his talent for composing rousing tunes was unique among fiddlers. He spent his days composing. Without the drag of a wife and children, his temper had lessened in sharpness. Left to his own devices, he reveled in his freedom. *I should have killed her years ago.*

***

Friday, August 2, 1811 – Heading Toward the Gypsy Camp
Mirela

Looking around the crowd moving toward the Gypsy camp by the river, Mirela spotted the boy. *So young and handsome he is. He could be useful.*

She reached him and slipped her arm through his. She felt him shiver. "It being only me." She smiled at Orion. "Besides horses, what inspiring you?"

"The stars."

"A dreamer." She nodded. "I have thinking your problem."

In a nervous tone, speaking very quickly, Orion said, "I don't want him to die."

"Don't you?"

Orion shook his head.

They walked a few steps in silence.

"I will touching him. I will learning his nature. You will knowing the truth of him."

"I already do."

***

Jean-Louis

A long-haired Gypsy man with a bandana around his forehead and one earring walked next to Jean-Louis. He smelled of tobacco.

"Want a smoke?" The man offered the Frenchman a puff.

"Never touch it."

The man shrugged. "I know who you are. I am Lash."

Jean-Louis steered Lash away from the crowd to a spot between two buildings where they could speak privately. "Are you a 'renowned warrior'?"

Lash nodded his head in recognition of the Frenchman's knowledge of the Roma language. "I've been told you know more than people might expect."

"There are ways."

"Boyd told me to seek you out. I have helped him in the past."

"I am wary by nature, Lash. Why approach me now? What do you want?"

"For the last week, I've been watching you watch the Gypsy stall."

The Frenchman pushed back his black felt hat. "I know." *My footpads were onto him after a day.*

"You won't believe me."

"Probably not. But try."

"I want to work for Boyd. A real job as a Bow Street Runner."

Jean-Louis looked off into the distance. "There are barriers built to keep out people like you, Lash. Barriers of class and education that may be beyond Boyd's ability to break down. Did he promise you a job?"

"No. He told me he couldn't promise me anything. But that if I worked for you, I might prove myself. A good word from you would make a difference."

"I'll talk to Boyd to verify your claims. In the meantime," he swept his arm toward the crowd moving toward the river, "tell me about this band of Roma."

"About a year ago, Vano, the stall proprietor, decided that setting up a stall in an international bazaar in one of the great cities of the world would be worth putting down roots. We Roma are wanderers, but the world is at war and we must be practical. I, like Vano, am tired of wandering. And I despise the slurs about my people. I want to show that we can be men of honor."

"How long have you been with this band?"

"Since birth."

"Does anyone in this band know of your ambitions?"

"No. They sense dissatisfaction but I've blamed my restlessness on a woman who spurned me. They've accepted that explanation because it's true."

"Good. The best deflection is the truth. Have any of the men in your band disappeared without a trace in the last few years?"

Lash glanced away for a moment and then returned his gaze to Jean-Louis. "Allowing for the occasional duel or revenge killing, there have been a few who have vanished. But in a band of Roma, that is not unusual."

"Do you have a good memory? A mind that recalls details, names and dates?"

"Others believe so."

"Meet me next Thursday at the Pelican's Beak at four." Jean-Louis inclined his head toward the river. "Go to the gathering. I'll follow on a different path."

"Until tomorrow." Lash ambled in a way that would look aimless to any observer.

Jean-Louis stared after him. An astute judge of character, the Frenchman detected no note of insincerity, but he couldn't be too careful. Not where the Wyndwards were concerned.

***

Friday, August 2, 1811 – The Gypsy Camp
Colvert

Colvert stationed himself away from Orion. From the sidelines, he watched Orion fixate on the camp fiddler.

Mirela, the Gypsy who had eluded Colvert and his partner for months, stood at Orion's side.

The fiddler who'd led the crowd moved into place next to the camp fiddler, deferring to the older man's pleasing baritone.

The camp fiddler's long, curled mustache struck Colvert as a ridiculous affectation. Trained to blend into the background, Colvert would never have adopted such a distinguishing trademark. *He's an entertainer. His appearance is part of a performer's desire to stand out.*

After the camp fiddler finished his song, the Gypsy fortune teller walked over to the fiddler, dropped some coins in his hat, and stumbled. The mustachioed singer caught her before she hit the ground.

Colvert noticed an odd look come over the Gypsy crone's face. *What the devil does that mean?*

***

Orion

The old woman hobbled with her cane back to where Orion stood. Walking past him, she whispered, "Follow me."

Orion waited a few moments and then followed her. He sensed Colvert strolling behind them.

When they were near a main road, Mirela stopped and waved down a Hackney. Before she entered, she turned to Orion. "That man is evil. There is blood on his hands. A woman with green eyes."

Pain creased Orion's face. "My mother?" His voice cracked.

"I fearing for you, boy. Staying away from that fiddler. I will seeing you at the bazaar tomorrow as the sun waning." She climbed into the carriage and drove away.

Colvert came up behind him.

Orion pointed to the carriage in the distance. "She is getting away!"

The watcher shook his head. "I know where she lives, and I know the driver." He waved down the next cab and opened the door for Orion. "Get in. Go home. Sleep. We'll see you tomorrow."

Dutifully, Orion nodded. As the carriage drove away, Colvert pretended not to see the boy's tears.

CHAPTER THIRTY-THREE

Saturday, August 3, 1811 – The Blue Bazaar
Orion

The next day, Orion dreaded his meeting the Gypsy crone. *How does she know secrets about my life?*

As the hours ticked away, Jean-Louis pulled Orion off their watch. "Let's get something to eat. Colvert will follow Mirela. You won't miss your meeting time and it's better to approach from an unexpected direction."

Orion took a deep breath. "I don't think I'm cut out for what you want me to do."

The Frenchman put his arm around the young man's shoulder. "You may not have to. I think I've found someone else who can bring me information. If so, you can go back to the horses tomorrow."

Relief shone on Orion's face. "Truly? I want nothing more than that."

They sat at the small café near the entrance to the bazaar and ordered the special of the day, which appeared almost immediately.

Orion took a bite. "This is good! We never ate in restaurants in Ireland. London is so different, so busy."

"Do you like it?"

The Gypsy shrugged. "I prefer Ravenshire. It's peaceful. And the pace suits me."

Jean-Louis sat back in his chair. "Your skill with a knife is impressive, but I know that you would only kill to protect yourself or another." He took a sip of tea. "Do you still want to kill your father?"

Orion's jaw hardened. "The fortune teller told me he killed my mother."

"Do you think that is possible?"

The young Gypsy nodded. "My father often beat my mother, my brother and me. My brother was more like him and sometimes fought back. My father liked that. He used to say that I was soft like my mother, and then spit in disgust."

"I ask again, do you still want to kill your father?"

The young man's eyes fixed on Jean-Louis. "I don't know. What would you do?"

"I am not you. What I do know is that a moment's hesitation could be deadly—for you. You must be ready to strike or not strike at all."

"Would you...would you kill him for me?"

"Never ask another man to kill for you. Do it by your own hand or banish it from your mind. But as I've warned you before—revenge is often less satisfying than you imagined."

Orion cast his eyes down. He clasped and unclasped his hands. "I never thought I'd have a conversation this casual about killing."

"Life is about death, a prelude to your final breath. The important thing is to know yourself. Most would kill to save another or himself. Many would kill out of anger or jealousy. Very few can kill with a calm mind."

***

Mirela

At five o'clock, Mirela left the curtained card-reading space.

She saw Orion approaching and smiled. *He being prompt.*

"Mme. Mirela, may I ask your advice?"

She nodded. "Come." Passing Vano, she said, "This being my friend. No charge."

Vano scowled but shrugged and made no argument.

Inside the curtained area, Orion scanned the space. His eyes fixed on the crystal ball. "Can you really see the future in that crystal?"

"Or the past, but only those having the 'sight'." *What he seeking?*

Orion plopped down on the client's chair, a rickety seat with uneven legs. He steadied himself.

Mirela sat in her larger, intricately carved chair, placed her hands on the crystal ball, closed her eyes and chanted ancient Roma words.

When she opened her eyes, Orion asked, "Will I be able to see anything in the crystal?"

The old Gypsy raised her palms in a gesture of uncertainty. "Look and you telling me."

Staring at the ball for a few minutes, Orion saw nothing. "It didn't work." He sat back and hung his head.

"What seeking you?"

Orion's eyes misted. "I wanted to see my mother once more."

"Remembering her from good times in life, not in death."

Orion nodded. "I cannot kill my father, even if he killed her. But I must stand up to him. I must show him I am strong."

"He being dangerous man."

"I know. After tonight, I will leave London. I wanted to say goodbye to you because you have been kind to me."

Mirela placed her hand over his. "I feeling your strength. You will having good life."

The young Gypsy turned his head. "I hear the piper. I'll walk with you to the camp."

They rose, left the stall and locked arms as they joined the crowd.

***

Jean-Louis

Jean-Louis followed Orion and the Gypsy crone from a distance.

After Orion's father, the camp fiddler, finished his first session, he walked away to have a smoke.

Orion kissed the old Gypsy on the cheek and followed his father, stopping a few feet from him.

His father opened a package of pipe tobacco. "Smoke?"

"No."

The camp fiddler shrugged. "I like a bit of it now and then. Prefer it to snuff." He packed some into a pipe, but just held it.

The French trapper hid behind a tree. *It's been years since the fiddler's seen his son. When will he recognize Orion?*

"I'm Django."

"I know."

Django squinted at the boy, and then scoffed. "Taller than I remember. Why London?"

"Did you kill my mother?"

The boy treads dangerously, revealing his purpose too quickly.

"Where did you hear that?"

"I demand the truth."

Django laughed. "*You* demand the truth? You are in no position to demand *anything*." He shrugged, retaining a smug grin.

"Your eyes betray you. And Timbo? Did you kill him too?"

The camp fiddler shook his head as he puffed on a cigarette. "No. Your brother's temper got him killed in a fight over a woman." He spat. "Fool."

Orion glared at his father. "You are dead to me. I have no father."

His father took a broad bow and then stared at him with malice. "Consider yourself an orphan."

"You have made me one." Orion turned and walked away.

Jean-Louis emerged from the shadows and approached the camp fiddler. "Be gone by dawn. This is your only warning."

"Or what?"

"Ask around. Ask if the French trapper means what he says."

Jean-Louis disappeared into the night.

***

Saturday, August 3, 1811 – JAK, Jane Anne's Salon
Charlotte

As the last guests left, confetti strewn on the floor and empty wine glasses littering the tables, Jane Anne, Dana, Bri, Aelwyn, Gwyneth and Charlotte nearly fell into chairs, exhausted.

Charlotte leaned toward Jane Anne. "It was a triumph! Young ladies of the *ton* as well as dowagers of a certain age, as the French say, mingled with each other and marveled at the demonstrations you and your assistants conducted."

Tears welled in Jane Anne's eyes. "I never could have imagined this without Lady Gabriella's vision and faith in me. Without the intervention of Jean-Louis and your father years ago, I might have died as an indentured servant to that wicked wigmaker."

Gwyneth offered Jane Anne her handkerchief to dab her tears. "You learned his secrets and turned that knowledge into this." Bri waved her arm around the salon. "We are the sum of all our experiences."

"And tonight's auction of a portrait by Gio will help fund the foundling hospital's operations. Commercial and charitable goals were met." Gwyneth smiled. "Lady Patricia surprised me by submitting the highest bid."

"No one's seen Viscount Wexington in years, but her father's coffers seem to be supporting Lady Patricia's wardrobe, jewels, carriages, and social escapades."

Dana squeezed her sister's hand. "I'm so glad I am here now to share this with you!"

Aelwyn looked around. "Mrs. Jones's staff has cleaned up the entire room while we've been talking. I'll just make sure the coaches are ready." She rose to speak to Young, who had directed the staff throughout the evening.

Edward and Jean-Louis appeared at the door.

"It looked like a success from the outside. Jean-Louis deputized me as a lookout to spot any dastardly characters. Perhaps you should consider doing more charitable events, and next time invite eligible men in the *ton*. This could become a matchmaking center."

"And frankly," Charlotte said, "some of the dandies might want their hair styled here too."

Bri recoiled. "I saw this more as a retreat for women to pamper themselves, a respite from the incessant demands on them to be on display as marriage fodder."

Gwyneth stood. "On that note, I think it's time to say, 'Goodnight.' One task at a time."

Edward frowned at Bri. "Surely you never thought of *yourself* as marriage fodder."

"Perhaps I exaggerate because I am tired." Bri kissed Edward on the cheek.

***

Jean-Louis

Young locked up after all the guests had departed. He, Jane Anne and Dana took a Hackney back to the earl's townhouse, arriving ahead of Jean-Louis and Bri.

When Jean-Louis pulled into the stables, he jumped down from his perch and opened the carriage door, and found Bri curled up on the bench, sound asleep.

***

Sunday, August 4, 1811 – Aboard *Nekhbet's Wings*
Xie Xie

Ever since she could remember, Xie Xie had taken morning moments to center herself in meditation. The Pharaoh had advised her to walk the ship's deck to maintain her strength. In addition, she began a practice of lifting books from the floor and extending them over her head in a series of repetitions. She practiced fencing moves, twisting, thrusting forward on bended knee, balancing on one leg, performing dance movements. While performing these actions, she cleared her mind, seeking inspiration.

After her exercises, her daily habits included a quick daily sponge bath. Once a week, on specific days assigned by the captain, each guest took a full bath, as the process to heat the water and fill the copper tub was time consuming for the crew. It took extra time to wash her long silky hair.

After dressing for breakfast, she headed to the captain's dining room. Xie Xie was acutely aware that without the aura of The Pharaoh around her, a woman traveling alone would not have been invited to dine with the other passengers. *Perhaps I should continue to use his reputation for my own protection even after I am out of his immediate entourage. The legend of The Pharaoh could be useful.*

The captain knew only that The Pharaoh had requested that Miss Li be extended all courtesies. That was all he needed to know. He had heard rumors of a man who had double-crossed The Pharaoh. The traitor's gruesome end was not one that the captain wished to contemplate for himself.

Xie Xie dined in the captain's quarters with a motley group of travelers from many backgrounds. None expected to see a woman traveling alone, as they all said to her whenever she ran into them on deck. Their voyage took the southern route due to Napoleon's control of shipping along the northern shores of the Mediterranean.

One night at dinner, the French-born wife of a Turkish official being posted from Cairo to London ate little and drank too much wine, releasing her from the normal constraints of polite conversation. Since all the guests spoke English, despite their languages of origin, it served as the established language at the captain's table.

An Arab professor on his way to Portugal glanced at Xie Xie. "Miss Li, how do you expect to conduct commerce as a woman and an Asian in London?"

Before she could answer, the Frenchwoman said, "Napoleon has blockaded England. We should be speaking French. *Nous devrions parler français.*"

The captain shook his head. "Not everyone speaks French, Madame."

"*We* control the world, not the *English.*" She nearly spat the last word.

Her husband spoke up. "Not the entire world, my dear." Turning toward the other guests, he continued, "You are well aware that my government, the Ottoman Empire, split from Napoleon after he invaded Egypt. After Egypt regained its sovereignty in 1801, we strengthened our ties to Britain. Hence, my upcoming position in London." The diplomat took a sip of wine. "During our thirty years of marriage, the life of a diplomat has become a great deal more complicated."

"Again, I say, *Nous devrions parler français.*"

"That, Madame, may be your *opinion*, but I am captain of this ship and I control the conversation at this table."

The Frenchwoman glared at him.

Xie Xie turned to the Arab professor. "To answer your question, Professor, my family has worldwide contacts and letters of introduction. I choose to believe that my ties to Chinese and other Asian products will overcome any prejudice in trade dealings."

The diplomat's wife scoffed and said under her breath, "*La pute fera des affaires comme tout de son genre.*"

Many at the table spoke French, reached for their wine, and averted their eyes from others. No one expected that Miss Li understood the insult: *"The whore will conduct business like all of her kind."*

The captain's voice took on an icy tone. "Madame, I do not tolerate such insults at my table. My steward can serve your meal in your cabin if you cannot maintain the decorum I demand. You must offer Miss Li an apology."

The Frenchwoman waved her hand dismissively. "Her sort could never master the French language."

Miss Li directed her gaze to the Frenchwoman and did not flinch. *"Vous vous trompez, Madame. Je parle couramment le mandarin et d'autres dialectes, l'arabe, l'anglais et le francais."*

"Madame, we await your apology." The captain drummed his fingers on the table, as if marking time.

Her husband nudged her.

"I apologize, Miss Li. Perhaps I have drunk too much of this fine vintage."

Miss Li bowed her head in acknowledgment. "I accept your apology, Madame. *J'accepte vos excuses.*"

Events like this remind me how lucky I am that The Pharaoh rescued me. He provided me an education as well as guidance, warning me about the ingrained prejudices of these so-called civilized people.

***

Monday, August 5, 1811 – Wyndward Trading Emporium
Bri

The space for the Wyndward Trading Emporium designed by Vaux from a quick sketch over dinner with Bri and Edward came together quickly. *The Emporium was Blackie's idea. A killer and a visionary—he was such an enigma.*

Bri smiled as she remembered giving Vaux a pair of spectacles with blue tinted lenses at that dinner. He had immediately donned the glasses and now rarely appeared in public without them. *"Must* you make them available to the *ton*? I like to stand out in a crowd," Vaux had complained.

Edward had scoffed at that. "Vaux, you will always stand out in a crowd."

Bri inspected the progress on the space. The aisles were being stocked before the opening in two weeks. The Emporium, initially envisioned as an experiment to sell unredeemed cargo from Wyndward ships and other overstock remainders, expanded its mission to offer whimsical items or new products from abroad that had not yet been widely introduced.

Gio had painted the image of a Wyndward Vessel on the wood sign over the door. "The *cognoscenti* of the *ton* will frequent this spot," Gio had promised. "The rich like bargains."

The footman brought in boxes of the spectacles that Bri had found in the Azores. *These will be very popular.*

She saw a supply of baskets on one aisle, and said, "*Voilà!*" Calling the footman over, she said, "Count these baskets and let me know if we have at least fifty. I want to make up Summerfest Favor Baskets for our weekend guests."

In addition to the merchandise she had acquired in the Azores—shawls for women and canes for men as well as a set of spectacles for each guest—Bri found samples of imported cosmetics, tooth powders, and other trinkets on the shelves. *We could print up gift vouchers for hair styling for Jane Anne's salon. The investment company can reimburse her for any usage. We can print Summerfest Favor on the vouchers and a number on each voucher so she can track them.*

The footman came toward her. "I found over eighty baskets, milady."

"Perfect. Load them all in the carriage, in case more guests show up at the last minute."

She had already arranged for bottles of the shampoo Jane Anne had concocted and jars of jam from Nellie's kitchen for the guest favors. *This will be the best Summerfest ever.*

CHAPTER THIRTY-FOUR

Tuesday, August 6, 1811 – Aboard *Nekhbet's Wings*
Xie Xie

Roused from a deep sleep, her consciousness still lodged in a dream of a lagoon on a beach sheltered by rocks, Xie Xie was thrown to the floor. She could feel the hull slamming into waves. Her body left the floor as the ship rose and fell, tossed about like a ball. She crawled into a corner between the bunk and the wall, gripping handholds to avoid being catapulted from one side of the cabin to another.

Hours of turmoil ensued. Her muscles tired, but she didn't loosen her grasp. "I'm not ready to die!" she cried aloud. *If I survive, I vow not to forget this moment. I have devoted myself to The Pharaoh's dreams and suppressed my own.* Then she realized that was not true. *I have not permitted myself to create my own dreams, except to dream of an abstract freedom. I need to create a specific plan for my life as The Pharaoh has done for his.* She invoked all the deities she could remember in a spoken vow: "Gods of China, gods and goddesses of Egypt, Greece and Rome, God of the western world, and gods unknown, guide me to my destiny."

A sense of serenity enveloped her. Certainty that she would not die in that moment grew. In time, the waves softened their assault, their turbulent punches subsided, and as the sea calmed, she calmed. The tempo of the ship slowed to a steady roll.

Exhausted from the terror of the past hours, Xie Xie fell asleep. An ethereal, transparent figure of a woman perched on the back of a

316

large white bird, with a wingspan larger than the ship, flew through Xie Xie's dream. "You called on me. I will protect you on the seas."

***

Thursday, August 8, 1811 – The Streets of London
Aneira

The hot afternoon caused Aneira to move more slowly than usual. Still, for a woman of eight-and-seventy, her step belied her years. She wanted to explore the immediate area where the café was located and try to develop connections with neighboring merchants. *If it were not for the Wyndwards, I might have had a happy life. Baking is my passion as well as my métier.*

The day before, she had received a letter from Arthur with another letter enclosed within. It was from Duff, posted from Alexandria. *Do nothing until I return to London in the new year. I have a new plan that cannot fail.*

Aneira sighed. *Waiting is against my nature, but I promised him I would wait until I knew of his Fate. He lives! The cards did not lie.* She stopped to catch her breath. *My legs ache. My back has been carrying this burden too long.* And then a gossip rag caught her eye.

Scandal & Shame featured a headline: "Summerfest at Ravenshire August 16-17-18." She paid for it and walked back to her hotel. *Duff wants me to wait. But I know Summerfest. I know Ravenshire. For years, I delivered goods for the baker's stall and watched the games. This opportunity will not come again. I cannot wait. This is the perfect time. All Wyndwards must die.*

***

Thursday, August 8, 1811 – Pelican's Beak Pub
Jean-Louis

Jean-Louis sat in the back booth where he had a full view of the pub. Paneled in dark wood, little light filtered into the candlelit pub. The walls featured a collection of framed bawdy prints, caricatures cut from the gossip rags or printed as flyers. Some depictions shocked even Jean-Louis.

Lash came in and sat across from him, a blue bandana identifying him as a Gypsy. He ignored the scoffs and taunts from patrons as he walked by.

Boyd, a hat pulled low over his forehead, joined them.

The Frenchman waved at the barkeep to bring ale. "We look like a thoroughly disreputable gang."

"We fit right in." Boyd laughed as the ale appeared.

Leaning forward, Jean-Louis raised his pewter mug. "To the gang!"

The Bow Street Runner and the Gypsy echoed his toast and clanked their mugs together. "To the gang!"

Inclining his head toward Boyd, Jean-Louis said, "We both need an informer inside your community. I think the fortune teller in Vano's stall will set men to follow me or others under my charge, and Boyd seeks knowledge of criminal activity that can be stopped in advance."

Nodding, Boyd directed his gaze at Lash. "Do you think you can pretend to be part of the watchers but report back to us? It's a role fraught with danger."

"Not all my people are thieves. I want to prove that to you and change the general perception of the Roma."

"Don't approach the crone directly. Make it known to Vano that you seek extra work."

"Vano will know what that means." Lash took a swig of ale. "He's used me for similar purposes before—to protect his interests from those who would steal from him."

Boyd swirled the ale in his mug, and then glanced at Lash. "I can't promise you can be a full member of the Bow Street Runners, but if you help protect the Frenchman's people, that will be an excellent recommendation." He narrowed his eyes. "That bandana is very distinctive and makes you instantly recognizable. Can you remove it?"

Lash pulled it off, revealing a diagonal scar from the top of his left temple to the base of his right eyebrow.

"You're lucky you didn't lose an eye." Jean-Louis sat back. "Recognizable either way. Maybe a hat with a deep front brim would be the best disguise."

"I have one." Lash shrugged. "I've used it before."

A smile crept over Boyd's lips. "Jean-Louis and I were right about you. You're clever and inventive."

"And reliable," added Jean-Louis. And we'll both

"One more thing." Lash drained his mug. "There's a notorious footpad that Vano uses for revenge killings. They call him The Jackal."

Jean-Louis nodded. "Jacques du Bois."

Boyd shook his head. "The Jackal hasn't been active for years."

"Not in your circles, but in ours, he is called in when all else fails. Your fancy constables don't investigate Gypsy deaths. We live outside your jurisdiction. The Jackal may be recruited by Vano if the fortune teller asks for a killer."

The Frenchman frowned. "I can handle him."

Lash leaned forward. "How? He's a ghost. Word is you never see him until he's slitting your throat."

"There are ways."

***

Monday, August 12, 1811 – The Gypsy Camp
Lash

Lash heard a soft step outside his tent. Always a light sleeper, a requirement in his line of work, he became instantly alert.

Vano lifted up the back flap. "Lash!" he whispered.

"Enter. I heard you." Lash sat up, resting against extra blankets.

Sitting cross-legged on the blanket-covered ground, Vano swore in Roma fashion. "That damned Mirela! *Scroafă! Gâscă!*"

"I agree that she is a bitch and a goose, but we know that. *Futu-i.* What has she done now?"

"She wants me to send men to her for a project at the end of this week that may last several days. She did not disclose the project, but of course she wants someone killed. She always wants someone killed. She never tells me who, but I read the newspapers. I can guess. It's been more than two years since the last one. My man drowned. Ha! He could swim like a fish. His throat was slashed down by the docks."

"It could have been anyone."

"True, but the dead man was a comte married to a Wyndward. Two years earlier, two other men I sent to Mirela never returned. A Wyndward died. Before either of those deaths, the 10th Earl of

Ravenshire, a Wyndward, died. The paper said it was natural causes. I doubted it then and I doubt it now. The Wyndwards are powerful people and I am nothing. I am no fool. If this gets traced back to me, my life is *over*."

Lash rubbed his chin.

"Let me hire footpads. How many men has she requested?"

"Four."

"Caló is desperate for money," Vano said.

Lash scoffed. "Caló's not even a good thief."

"Dangerous jobs attract the desperate or the foolish. Which are you?"

"Neither. You lead the band and I want to prove myself to you. I'm older now, not so impulsive." He pointed to his forehead. "Give me a chance."

"A chance to die, perhaps. The person who requested men is a harbinger of death. After I initially declined, the offer doubled." Vano whispered the amount to Lash. "I'm not risking *my* neck, but who am I to say *you* shouldn't?"

"That's a lot of men to corral, train and trust in a few days' time." Lash paused. "I'll meet with her. Caló' may be necessary for the task at hand. What about The Jackal?"

"He already refused. Mirela will be at the stall tomorrow at noon. You've proven yourself. Deal with her directly and charge her more than her first offer. I want none of it this time. You know you have to watch Caló. If you kill him after this venture, I won't object. But this is the last time I will provide men to her. I don't want her blood money."

Vano left.

Lash lay awake. *I must get word to Boyd and Jean-Louis.*

***

Wednesday, August 14, 1811 – Ravenshire
Aelwyn

Young sat across from Aelwyn in the earl's library, reviewing the final preparations for Summerfest.

"The family will arrive tomorrow, and the other guests the day after, in time for the Friday evening reception. We usually entertain around one hundred from the village on Saturday and Sunday, but with the castle as an attraction, the rumors coming to me suggest attendance may double."

Aelwyn looked up from her list. "The servants' wing of Ravenshire Castle must be completed by the winter, so that the staff can be housed for Lady Gabriella's wedding next summer. Our responsibilities will increase dramatically over the next few months, Young. We should start making lists of the skills we will be seeking and consider how to direct the hiring process."

The butler nodded. "We employ a large staff, but the massive castle structure vastly expands our operations. Perhaps we should engage staff with experience working in the royal household, in one of the lesser castles, or a large museum."

"We must impress upon the earl the urgency of the task. He is enamored with the architectural details, but the practical requirements loom larger in my mind." Aelwyn frowned. "And the village may need expansion planning for additional traffic, inns, etc. We should mention to the earl that we might need to build more housing and stables in and around the village itself for tradesmen, artisans, and new residents, as we did when the rebuilding of the castle began. We are but months away now."

Young agreed. "And days away from Summerfest. Next year, it will be much larger, attracting people for the games as well as to see the castle. We may have interlopers, peeping toms, and brigands in our midst."

Aelwyn crinkled her brow. "Jean-Louis has been augmenting the guard staff. I'm sure he's considered those risks."

A knock on the door startled them.

"Come in."

Hans Steiner walked into the room. The former Prussian soldier supervised security measures at Ravenshire when Jean-Louis was in London. "I wanted to alert you that we had a skirmish around the edge of Ravenshire Forest with some intruders."

"Young and I were talking about just such risks." Aelwyn glanced at the butler and then turned back to Steiner. "Do you think it is related to Summerfest? Thieves lying in wait for a gathering of the carriage trade? Or preparing to steal from villagers' homes when they attend the games?"

"I fear more than mere thievery is afoot. By chance, I was riding the perimeter with the Sheriff of Ravenshire, a monthly habit. We came upon a small encampment of a scurrilous crew, perhaps Gypsies. Before I knew it, a knife whizzed by my head. The invaders were on foot, and we chased them on horseback. I shot the one who tried to kill me, and we subdued the three who attempted to flee.

"It was the first time I'd tried the rope Jean-Louis taught me to use to capture an errant sheep or cow. He claimed he'd learned it from an Indian in the American west. I felled the runner, and he couldn't escape his ties. The third one cowered on his knees in front of me while the sheriff chased down the last one. We roped the three survivors together, and put them in the sheriff's wagon. I wanted to let you know I'm taking Orion with me to see if he recognizes any of them or if he can understand their gibberish. They spoke broken English with an accent and, as I said, looked like they might be Gypsies."

"Have you sent word to the earl?"

Steiner nodded. "Yes."

A bird must be flying as we speak.

***

The Sheriff of Ravenshire's Holding Cells
Orion

After being coached by Steiner, Orion sat in a cell across from the three prisoners. He scoffed, and said, *"Gadjos."* Hoping to get a reaction from calling their jailers non-Roma, he got no response from the other prisoners. *"Futu-i."*

The others spoke to each other in a language he didn't understand. He tried English. "I heard they killed one of your friends. They're rounding up all the people in the forest."

One of the men came over to the bars. "We heard rich people would be traveling the road from papers in London. Never got a penny before they captured us." He spat.

"Where are you from?"

"Persia."

Orion started shouting to the jailers. "Hey, you fools! Let me go! I've done nothing!"

On cue, the jailers came in and roughly grabbed him. "We're going to teach you a lesson now."

Yelling curses in Romani, Orion followed by screaming. "No! I did nothing wrong!" as the burly jailers dragged him from the holding area. He turned with pleading eyes toward the Persians.

The man to whom he'd spoken looked at him coldly and turned away.

Once they were out of sight, Orion told Steiner, "These are Persians, not Roma. They planned to rob people who were traveling to Summerfest."

***

Wednesday, August 14, 1811 – Ravenshire Forest
Sheriff of Ravenshire

Ned Gilchrist had been Sheriff of Ravenshire for ten years. He admired Jean-Louis and had worked in London for a time as a young man with Boyd of the Bow Street Runners.

Jean-Louis, and Lash had set up tents in the forest to serve as a staging area for the extra security patrols.

Gilchrist rode up with Orion.

The Gypsy boy dismounted and went to the horse corral.

Gilchrist took a folded piece of paper out of his pocket. "There's been publicity. These flyers are all around London. Turns out these brigands were just ordinary thieves out to rob the well-heeled gentry, not assassins sent by the grandmother."

***

Thursday, August 15, 1811 – Ravenshire
Young

Early in the morning that family and friends were due to arrive for Summerfest, which would take place on Friday and Saturday, the earl called Young into his library after breakfast.

As a man of one-and-thirty, Young ran Ravenshire while the earl was in residence in London. His father had served in the earl's household for over forty years, first as a footman, then rising to the position of butler, a position he had held for twenty years. Young wondered how duties would be divided over the next few days of Summerfest. He had played an integral part in the planning with both Lady Gabriella and, lately, Lady Wyndward after her return. He knocked.

The door opened and his father signaled Young to enter.

The earl nodded to him. "Young, you've proven yourself worthy of the challenges of running the Ravenshire manor house. Your father has some news. Thompson?"

"I've told the earl I would like to retire in the next year or so, to one of the tenant houses in Ravenshire village and tend to a flower garden. Of course, I will be available for the occasional event such as this or to train new staff."

Young's mouth dropped open. "Are you ill, Father?"

"Not at all. I am ready for a quieter, simpler life."

Henry smiled. "From now on, Young, you will serve as head butler at Ravenshire. Responsibilities here will increase as the castle center hall nears completion next year, so I will search for a new butler for my townhouse in London. Let me know if you have any suggestions. Tell me of the Summerfest plans."

Stunned, the newly designated butler-in-charge took a deep breath. "Thank you, milord. The family members, now including the James relatives, will be arriving around the noon hour, and the other guests in time for tea. I have a list of their assigned guest rooms and where their servants will be housed." He handed the lists to the earl and his father.

Charlotte knocked on the door. "Aelwyn, Bri and I are going to walk up to the castle and review the final layout. Young said he would accompany us. What about you, Henry?"

"Let's all go look at the tented area."

***

Thursday, August 15, 1811 – Ravenshire
Jean-Louis

Beginning shortly after noon, a steady caravan of carriages pulled into the wisteria-arced entry lane that led to the Ravenshire manor house, lasting long after twilight. Summerfest was timed to capture the bluish lavender flowering trees in full bloom.

Belying its grandeur, the elegant palace of Ravenshire had been termed a manor house specifically to downplay its massive size. The classic symmetrical architecture of the family home and its towering dominance over the surrounding pastures never failed to awe the first-time visitor. The rising walls of Ravenshire Castle, about half a mile's walk, would eventually dwarf the manor house, but both featured multi-colored stone quarried from British granite deposits.

Extra servants had been hired for Summerfest from the village.

A welcome dinner for family and friends would be staged in a tent across from the scaffold-clad Ravenshire Castle on Thursday evening before the villagers and visitors attended the opening fanfare on Friday morning.

Jean-Louis had a guest list and knew all of the invited weekend guests. His concern was the drivers, servants, or people who would pretend to be part of an entourage. *Have I imagined every scenario to protect them?*

***

Lash, Jean-Louis and Gilchrist rode the perimeter of the grounds, assigning watchers and setting up checkpoints.

"You can't be too careful," said the sheriff. "After the incursion into Ravenshire Forest by the Persians, we must consider the risk of other opportunists as well as run-of-the-mill highwaymen."

Lash leaned forward to pat his horse's head. "I have one man, Caló, from the Gypsy band and other 'footpads,' who are really your men in disguise. The grandmother's plan to be implemented by the Gypsies will be thwarted, but the other risks are up to you to stop." He looked up at the sun's position. "It's time for me to rejoin them. You know our position."

As he rode off, Jean-Louis sighed. "The worst risk is contained. The others we must imagine."

"We have the manpower. But next year, security has to be integral to your planning. With the castle going up, more lookers will come. The nature of our village may change. More people, more risk."

Jean-Louis tipped his hat to the sheriff. "Welcome to civilization."

CHAPTER THIRTY-FIVE

Thursday, August 15, 1811 – Ravenshire Village
Charlotte

Gio and Charlotte had arrived on Wednesday. On Thursday morning, they walked through the village to avoid being underfoot when the other guests were getting settled.

Charlotte sighed. "I've always loved this little town. Ancient and picturesque, it reminds me of a simpler time."

Gio shrugged. "Was it really simpler? You forget how much blood has been spilled on this countryside. Are we really more civilized now or is it just a veneer? After all, as Ravenshire Castle rises in the distance, it's a reminder that it served as a refuge in times of war, Viking raids and feudal disputes."

"Leave me with my imaginings of a pastoral life. Look around this lovely village. The church, its soothing bells, the unusual round shape of the Methodist meeting house, the fieldstone houses of local merchants whose shops are below their living spaces. One of the things I love are the colorful shutters and doors, the pets lying in the sun."

"August offers a rare respite from rain. Most of the time summer downpours drench these inhabitants, who scurry around with stringy and matted hair like drowning rats in a storm."

"You put a pall on a pleasant day. Stop being so negative. It's idyllic here. The little pubs, cafés, and—wait—there's the Ravenshire Bakery. Let's get some fresh-baked brioches and jam."

"Why not? We'll feast tonight. Perhaps a light lunch is best."

Small tables by the window allowed patrons to read the paper and have a bite.

"Dear God!" Charlotte shook her head.

Gio gave her a puzzled look.

The baroness pointed to the colorful sheets of paper. "That scurrilous *Scandal & Shame* gossip rag is strewn over the tables. Even here!"

"What's the topic?"

Charlotte picked one up. "Summerfest." She glanced at Gio. "We'd better tell Aelwyn. Attendance may be more than expected."

"Who'd travel four or six hours from London for a local fair?"

"People who love gossip and read *Scandal & Shame*."

"In other words, more than I can imagine."

***

Ravenshire

Aelwyn

Aelwyn oversaw welcoming the guests with assistance from Bri, Edward and the earl. Young directed the servants to escort the attendees to their rooms.

Family was housed in the main wing while guests fanned out into the visitors' wing. The manor house could accommodate more than fifty guests in well-appointed rooms and suites. It took several hours to get everyone situated.

***

Edward

In the tent erected for the Summerfest welcome banquet and other festivities across from the rising Ravenshire Castle, long tables were arranged around a central dance floor.

Edward, Bri, Vaux and Banfield chatted as the guests began to file up the path to the tent.

Bri took a sip of wine and glanced at Banfield. "Have you visited Durwood in the infirmary?"

"Yes," Banfield said. "Vaux, Rogers and I saw him a few days ago. He's still laid up with a leg broken in two places and a dislocated shoulder. He may be there several more weeks."

Banfield and Vaux exchanged glances before walking over to greet Rogers, who was talking to Lady Patricia.

Bri noticed. "Edward, is there something more to Durwood's injury? Is it worse than what we know?"

Hesitating, at first, Edward decided to reveal the truth. "It may mean nothing, but a young American woman came to watch Durwood's race. She was not aware that he was married. I only mention this to avoid hiding things from you."

"Has Durwood been unfaithful? Lady Rose is with child!"

"He says it was a mere infatuation. He helped the woman after seeing her carriage wheel break off. It was a freak accident."

"Infatuation? On his part as well?"

Edward shrugged. "I assume so."

Bri inhaled deeply. "Am I terribly naïve? Are all men susceptible to 'infatuation'?"

"Infatuation is not infidelity."

"Yet 'tis the first step, is it not?"

"Sometimes, but too many people know about it now. These liaisons thrive in secret, not in the open."

Bri's face flushed with color. "So the only thing stopping Durwood from engaging in an illicit love affair is that people know about his infatuation? If that infatuation were still secret, would he proceed?"

This conversation isn't going to end well. "Perhaps. No one truly knows the intentions of another."

"Promise me you will not humiliate me in such a way. Every time I see Lady Rose and Durwood, I will know something that I wish I did not. I'm sorry I asked you."

"So am I, but I want to be honest with you. And you have my promise. I will not humiliate you."

Bri took Edward's hand. "Let's continue to greet our guests."

***

Bri

As they walked toward the next group of guests, Bri maintained a calm exterior. Internally, she reeled. *Edward would never betray me, would he? Grandfather, Father, and other men have disappointed me. Can any man be trusted?*

***

Henry

The earl, dressed in shades of white and cream as he always did for Summerfest, stood next to Vanessa in front of a line of five cometseekers set up for guests. "The night is clear. The *Times* said the comet is streaking across Leo minor. We've trained the sights in that direction, but we have to wait until the light ebbs. Perhaps after dinner."

The duchess put her eye next to the lens and then pulled back. "You're right. It's too bright. There is not enough contrast." She brushed one hand to straighten her pale blue dress and fanned herself with the other. Inclining her head toward Charlotte, standing nearby, and then back at Henry, Vanessa raised her eyebrows and waited for a response.

"We are friends."

"For now. Remember my warnings."

Henry bowed his head in acknowledgment. "They are foremost in my thoughts."

"Diplomatic, though I'm not persuaded."

***

Gio

Tables for card games and chess were set up near the cometseekers.

Bri and Edward walked over to greet Gwyneth and Gio.

Gio smirked. "Ah, reminiscences of Summerfests past." Looking around, he glanced back at Bri. "Isn't this where you beat Edward at Whist so many years ago?"

"Must we constantly relive that moment?" Edward sighed as he took a sip of wine.

Gio demurred. " 'Tis hardly constant. Merely a reminiscence."

Gwyneth shook her head. "Edward, as long as you complain about it, Gio will keep needling you."

"James, while we were sailing the Azores, we missed the Phaeton Meet. I want to speak to Rogers about it." Gio looked around, but couldn't see over people's heads. "Where is he?"

Edward pointed in that direction.

After talking with Rogers, Gio wandered around the area, watching the stalls being set up to sell local products. Just as he popped a *petit fours* in his mouth, the duke and duchess came over. With a full mouth, he mumbled a greeting. "Your Graces."

Vanessa disapproved. "Your speech is unclear, unmannered, and unbecoming."

Gio bowed at the waist. "I apologize for my shortcomings."

The duke chortled. "Shortcomings. That's amusing, Gio. You are a droll dwarf."

"These stalls are but a small display of what will be offered at the main Ravenshire Market that is held around Samhain." Vanessa used an alternative Gaelic pronunciation that sounded like "Sow-een" instead of "Sow-in." "It almost immediately follows the Engagement Ball for Bri and Edward on October 26th."

"I hope we're not expected to costume ourselves for the Engagement Ball as if it were Halloween." The dwarf feigned insouciance when confronted by Vanessa's icy stare.

"The theme is the Great Comet of 1811 and costumes are *requested*, not required."

"Your Grace, costumes, costumes, costumes? Will it ever end?" He gestured with his arm in a wide arc and splashed wine on himself.

"In a word—no. I love costumes and fantasy. Grow up and abandon your adolescent whining."

Gio shrugged. "My apologies, Your Grace, but I *can't* grow up, can I?"

Vanessa glared at him.

The duke laughed. "Another dwarf joke." He patted Gio on the head. "You're a clever one."

***

After dinner, the toasts began.

Sir Reggie was the first to rise to his feet. "I've been told it's the enterprising Lady Gabriella we have to thank for the thoughtful and useful gift baskets in our rooms and Lady Wyndward for our accommodations." He waved his hand toward the scaffolding shielding Ravenshire Castle from view. "Next year, perhaps, we'll dine in the castle. Tonight, raise your glass to Lady Gabriella and Lady Wyndward!"

The toasts extended well into the night. Some guests retired, but most swarmed around the cometseekers to gaze at the sky.

Gio peered through the eyepiece now that the moon was overhead in the black sky. "I see it! Now I can finish my painting. What a marvelous sight is this comet!"

***

Friday, August 16, 1811 – Summerfest
Bri

Games and contests began at ten. Each event was scheduled on the hour, with trap shooting being the first bout of competition.

Shooting events were the most popular, always scheduled first at Summerfest. Traps were placed in a clearing in the forest about half a mile's walk from the tented area where stalls and refreshments were served. After a qualifying match, the earl announced the terms of the event. "The top fifteen contestants will shoot quail from multiple flights of twelve that will be released from one house trap. The fallen quail will be gathered, dressed, and prepared as our dinner entrée tonight." Baron Beauchamp won, hitting eight of twelve birds.

Stationary targets had been set up for the next match on another part of the broad clearing in Ravenshire Forest. Apples served as targets, placed on wood stakes at twenty paces. Pistols were unreliable, so skill was only part of a winner's success. Properly oiled and maintained weapons were critical. Twenty men and women competed. Bri placed third, after the local vicar. The winner was Sir Reggie, to everyone's surprise.

Bri overheard a disgruntled shooter say, "How can that old man be so adept with a pistol?" She leaned over to whisper to Lady Patricia. "How did your uncle became so proficient?"

"I think he was in the army when he was young."

Bri nodded, but was not convinced it was that simple. *There must be more to Sir Reggie than we know.*

The next meet was wrestling.

The earl leaned over to whisper to Aelwyn. "I decided against the Olympic practice of wrestling in the nude."

Aelwyn gave Henry a withering look. "Small mercy, that. Naked chests are shocking enough."

After several simultaneous matches, the two highest scoring wrestlers faced off in a final round. The local butcher bested a tenant shepherd, who had won that contest during the last three Summerfests. Shaking the butcher's hand, the loser said, "Guess I'm getting too old for this."

In the boxing event, few participants came forward. A local weaver easily beat a local carter. The carter appeared more muscular, but the weaver danced around him and distracted him with barbs until he delivered the winning blow.

Edward good naturedly entered the swimming contest. He'd been practicing on visits to Ravenshire, and had improved measurably. There was an island in the middle of the pond with a large oak tree and a tree house that Henry and Arches had built as a construction project using their mathematical and geometry skills as a test devised by Laurence years earlier. Today's course required the contestants to swim out to the island, run around the tree three times, then swim back to the grassy shore. Any stroke was permitted. While Edward was not last, a local girl of fourteen sped through the water like one of the Wyndward ships with a tailwind to best the other participants.

After lunch, there were sack races where entrants hopped fifty feet. Of more than forty hopefuls, Sallie Sawyer, the Ravenshire cook, beat all the others.

The last event of the day was an obstacle course of hurdles to jump, fences to slide under, ladders to climb, and a *faux* moat to jump. All the aspirants became filthy with dirt, sweat and grass stains and some, who miscalculated the final jump, arose doused in mud. The local arborist slithered through the mud to a win.

Gio shrugged. "Impressive, but the man *does* climb trees for a living."

The earl had provided clothing for all the day's events except shooting, and had set up two tents—one for men and one for women—to change their clothing and clean up after their competitions.

People milled around the stalls until the dinner bell rang, and locals dined with titled guests in a rare display of equality. The quail were roasted on outdoor spits, and the aroma heightened the guests' hunger pangs.

***

Steiner

While the events were underway, Steiner and the sheriff's men patrolled the perimeter of the Ravenshire manor house and event environs, staying out of sight of the guests. While many in the village were known to Steiner, there were many he didn't recognize. Trained security men acting as footmen were placed around the tents and events for safety.

Jean-Louis rode up to Steiner. "Anything unusual?"

"No, but it's not dark yet. That is when our defenses must be strongest."

"Lash has been silent. I trust he has Caló well in hand. One man can wreak havoc."

***

Orion

After dinner, Orion walked along the edge of the tent, where occasional outcroppings of trees punctuated the landscape, with wildflowers sprouting near the trunks in vivid colors. Away from the festivities, under the stars, he scanned the sky for the comet. *I'll have to look through one of the cometseekers. I can't make out much except*—he squinted—*could that streak be it?*

He heard voices and saw a couple walking toward the next grouping of trees. *It's the earl and the baroness.* He crouched behind one of the trees.

Henry and Charlotte embraced, silhouetted in the moonlight. He kissed her.

Orion spotted a man he recognized from the Gypsy stall, called a "ne'er-do-well" by Vano. *Caló!*

A beam of light flashed on a knife blade in Caló's hand.

A high-pitched voice cried out, "Pick up the rock."

Orion blinked and saw a pixie hovering in front of him.

"Pick up the rock and stop him."

Orion spied the rock, wrapped his fingers around it, and in one smooth motion, threw it like a knife.

The jagged rock hit Caló in the head. Grunting, he fell.

The earl, startled but agile, moved quickly and pinned the dazed assassin to the ground.

Orion ran over. "I got him!"

"Good job, Orion. Find Jean-Louis."

***

Jean-Louis

A birdcall Jean-Louis had taught Orion reached his ears. He turned his horse in that direction, signaling Gilchrist to follow.

Seeing Orion, Henry and Charlotte, Jean-Louis spurred his horse. When he reached them, he jumped off.

"Lord Ravenshire, I asked you not to leave the main area."

Henry nodded. "I erred."

"*Erred?* That is an understatement." The sheriff dismounted, questioned Orion and the earl to evaluate the situation, and then tied Caló's hands behind him. "Attempted murder. The penalty is hanging."

Caló spat. "I've had enough of this life."

"And we've had enough of you." The sheriff tied him to his horse and took him away from the tented area.

Charlotte grasped the situation. "Are we all in danger? I thought Blackburn was dead."

"His grandmother is alive, in London, and may be orchestrating mayhem through her Gypsy cohort."

The baroness paled. "There are many innocent people here. Are other killers about?"

Jean-Louis shook his head. "Only this man. We thought we had him under surveillance. Something has gone very wrong."

"Obviously." Charlotte's eyes bored into the Frenchman.

"Go back and look through the cometseekers. Act as though nothing has happened."

Henry nodded. "We'll talk after everyone else has retired."

CHAPTER THIRTY-SIX

Early Saturday, August 17, 1811 – Ravenshire Forest
Jean-Louis

Gilchrist and Jean-Louis took men and wagons to search for the missing deputies and Lash. They found a bloody trail and followed it to find a body of one of the deputies. Gilchrist dismounted. "He's alive, but he's lost a lot of blood."

Some of the other deputies lifted him into the wagon and a medic tended to him.

"Can he speak?"

"No."

Jean-Louis said. "See to his wounds. We'll keep searching."

They came upon the bodies of two deputies. Checking them for signs of life, Gilchrist said, "Their throats were slit."

This is worse than I could have imagined. An ambush? Did Caló have confederates waiting? The Frenchman heard something.

Faint voices floated on the wind.

The Ravenshire crew spurred their horses toward the sound. A deputy who survived the assault, despite a bloodied head, tended to Lash, applying pressure to his chest to stanch bleeding. "The knife thrust tore open his breast. This Lash is like a cat. He has so many scars that he should have died many times over, but he's still with us."

Gilchrist dismounted and knelt next to his deputy. "What happened?"

"Caló became suspicious and sensed a trap. He attacked a deputy who confronted him, then ambushed two of our men from behind. After slashing them, he took off through the woods. Lash and I chased him, and engaged him in a knife fight. Although wounding him slightly, he got the better of me. I hit my head as I fell and only recently regained consciousness. I heard Lash moaning. He was near death, but I think I've stopped the bleeding."

Jean-Louis turned his horse. "I'll bring the wagon and the medic."

Lash spoke in a feeble voice. "Did you get him?"

"Yes. Orion stopped him. Caló will hang."

***

Summerfest
Aelwyn

The program for Saturday attracted even more people than Friday's matches. The first and second contests were set up where the prior day's shooting events had taken place.

Archers mingled before their qualifying flights of arrows were loosed. Two shots in rapid succession would determine the order of shooting.

Aelwyn nudged Bri. "Isn't that a friend of yours?"

With a start, Bri nodded. "Lady Melanie? I had no idea she had mastered archery."

Gio ambled over. "Too bad no betting is permitted at Summerfest. I'd wager that the odds on Lady Melanie would win me a pretty penny."

"So you believe she will win?" Gwyneth raised her hand to shield her eyes from the sun to watch the contest.

The dwarf shrugged. "I always root for the underdog."

The final match was between Lady Melanie and a local tenant wheat farmer.

The farmer shot first and got both arrows in the bulls-eye.

Lady Melanie stepped into the shooter's box, aimed, and loosed her arrow. It landed in the center, touching one of the farmer's arrows.

The crowd applauded, then fell into silence as she readied her second arrow.

She released the missile. It flew with a whooshing sound and split the farmer's other arrow. The crowd cheered.

Gio pouted. "I knew she would win. What's up next?"

"Knife-throwing," said Aelwyn.

"I'd better get up there. Wish me luck."

"You? I thought those boasts about knife-throwing were mere jests." Gwyneth tilted her head in disbelief.

"Apparently, you don't know everything, Madame la Comtesse."

Bri, Aelwyn, Charlotte, Gwyneth and Henry followed Gio to the throwing mound, and stood transfixed as Gio threw his knives straight and true.

Edward ambled over. "Did I just see Gio throw?"

Henry shrugged. "Who knew?"

The final match was between Gio and Orion.

The young Gypsy was adept, but the dwarf won.

Bri's mouth fell open. "He wasn't kidding when he said he could have joined the circus." She pulled on Edward's arm. "Come on, we need to dress for our event."

The fastest horse and rider over the jumping course would be declared the winner.

Bri finished ahead of Edward, but behind a sixteen-year-old girl from the village. Dismounting, she approached the girl to congratulate her. "Fine riding, Miss—?"

"Jenna Vance, Lady Gabriella. I like to ride through the countryside." Sheepishly, she added, "I jump over your fences from time to time."

Bri laughed. "Good for you."

The next competition was racing horses on a flat course. At the end, Rogers was neck-and-neck with a young groom from the village stables. The young groom won.

Breaking for lunch, the group wandered back to the tented area.

Henry stopped short.

Charlotte glanced at him and followed his gaze. *Drummond? Here?*

Drummond walked over to them. "Ravenshire, a lovely day for your games."

"The public is welcome, Drummond."

Charlotte moved to lighten the tone. "Are you going to test your skills in any of the events?"

"Whist is my game."

"I thought politics was your game."

"*Touché*, Ravenshire."

While Banfield faced Drummond over Whist, chess pieces were set up at other tables.

The vicar and a boy of twelve were the last ones remaining in a chess match that attracted quite a crowd. The vicar was known to be an expert, but the boy seemed to have an unmatched focus.

Aelwyn whispered to Oliver. "They say he speaks little, and likes to do naught but play chess."

Oliver nodded. "He's a master. Single-minded focus is difficult to maintain."

The boy won.

At the same time, Drummond beat Banfield at Whist.

Banfield threw his cards on the table. "You were three steps ahead of me the entire game."

"Not really, only two. But you are an adept player. 'Twas a good match."

The final two events loomed. The men would run footraces, and the women would run the smock race.

Smock races were a tradition where unmarried women ran barefoot, competing to win the creations fashioned by Drea's workers: a smock dress with ribbons sewn in patterns for first place winners, a locally woven scarf as second prize, and an embroidered handkerchief as third prize. For Summerfest, there would be four age bands: under ten, ten to fifteen, sixteen to twenty, and widows of any age.

The men's footraces were run barefoot over the same course, laid out around the rising castle, and tent, ending in the front area where prizes would be given. The prizes for the men were sturdy boots, to be made to fit by the local cobbler, hats made by the local hatter, and gloves made by the local glover. Male runners were split into the same age bands as the women in the smock races, with widowers of any age making up the fourth group. Some believed that they would attract a wife by demonstrating their vigor.

Strips of linen dyed in different colors symbolizing age were tied around the entrants' arms.

First the men ran. Women lined the pathways and mocked them, much as the men would soon mock them. After a course of approximately one mile, the winners reached the finish line and were pulled aside so that their names could be recorded for the prizes.

Rogers, who had not run, came up to Bri. "Is it true that the female runners are wearing under drawers?"

"Correct." Bri had been horrified at men peeking at women's private parts when the runners had fallen in prior years. "You boys won't have as much fun this year."

"You *are* a killjoy. It's a wild thrill to see women barefoot and sweating as they run."

Bri rolled her eyes.

"Father vetoed naked men wrestling, as in Ancient Greece."

Rogers, Banfield and Vaux recoiled.

Edward scoffed. "Surely that wasn't a serious consideration."

"Why not? Women could examine your equipment as you ran by. All most of them have seen of men's anatomy is a Greek statue."

"Do not speak of such things!" Banfield blushed.

Lady Patricia piped up. "*You* can, but we can't? Someday things will be different."

Rogers shook his head. "Not in my lifetime, by God!"

Bri scoffed. "You race dangerous rigs, you gamble in the hells, and—don't deny it—you frequent brothels, you drink until you pass out, you gape at women's private parts when they fall in a race but the thought of a woman seeing naked men wrestle offends you?"

Lady Penelope agreed. "Oh, *quelle horreur*! A woman might compare men's attributes. You're really afraid of women, aren't you?"

Unable to resist, Bri nodded. "The Greeks have a word—misogyny—the hatred of women. You fear the power of the womb."

"Perhaps you suffer from misandry—the hatred of men." Vaux glanced at Bri. "No, I wasn't asleep in *all* my university lectures."

Rogers stared at a woman passing by.

Bri followed his gaze. "Why do you stare at women so? Are you imagining them naked?"

"Of course." Rogers shrugged. "You look at men the same way."

The women laughed.

Edward and the other men shifted their stance.

Lady Melanie shook her head. "No, we don't. We admire the handsome looks, the cut of their clothes, their manners, their smile."

The others nodded.

Lady Marianna added, "If we imagined all men we saw as if they were naked, we'd be laughing all the time."

Nonplussed, the men stole glances at each other.

Bri sighed. "Women must be practical until the world changes. Maybe someday women will run companies, countries, and have children under their own terms."

A village elder overheard the discussion as he walked by. "Hell will freeze over before that day comes. God put men in charge."

Bri leaned toward him. "*Men* put men in charge. And what a mess you've made of the world."

Charlotte pulled Bri away. "This is too contentious. You're influencing these women to spout off. You can get away with it, but they can't."

Gio intervened. "We are unlikely to solve this dilemma tonight. Men and women are different but need to come together to perpetuate the human race. If each side digs in, we shall become extinct."

Bri noticed that the female runners were gathering and left to organize the smock races.

***

Charlotte

Drummond came over and whispered to Charlotte. "What spirit she has. I see a lot of you in her."

Charlotte smiled, "No, Tottie, it's the other way around. Her independence has influenced me."

***

Bri

The raucous smock race got underway, and the winners were thrilled with their prizes.

With the official events over, people explored the stalls while the ending dinner of freshly slaughtered, roasted beef rotated on the outdoor spits.

Bri walked up in back of the duchess, who was examining Drea's offerings. "What do you think of the drawers, Grandmother?"

Turning to Bri, Vanessa said, "You should not flaunt these unmentionables in public. It is uncouth, unladylike, and unadvised."

"Here's your purchase, Your Grace."

Bri smothered a grin.

After dinner, people again circled around the cometseekers. Shortly after darkness fell, fireworks began, signaling the end of Summerfest. Sparkling lights in all colors filled the sky.

***

Sunday, August 18, 1811 – The Old Druid Grove, Ravenshire
Charlotte

For those who were interested, the earl hosted a ceremony welcoming the dawn in an oak grove in Ravenshire Forest. Like the ancient Druids, attendees sat on tree stumps felled by time—by nature, not by man.

Trumpets and violins played Handel's "Hallelujah Chorus" from *The Messiah*.

Charlotte's heart leapt at the sound. She reached for Henry's hand. As the dawn broke through the summer leaves, the sun's rays streaming into the grove, she felt as if she were experiencing a true miracle.

Later that day, Charlotte was one of the last guests to depart. As her carriage pulled away, she reflected on how much had changed in her life since the last Summerfest. *I cannot let myself forget that Henry is torn between Taita and me. I must not let myself fall into a false sense of the certainty of his love.*

***

Henry

As he watched her carriage disappear, shrinking to a dot on the horizon moving down the long driveway into Ravenshire, Henry sensed Jean-Louis sidle up next to him.

"Your plan was thwarted. Luckily, Orion was in the right place at the right time, and I know he benefited from your training. But it was

342

an act of Providence that saved me, not our security measures. The grandmother may be emboldened."

The muscles in the Frenchman's jaw twitched in irritation. "Training Orion was not an act of Providence. It was foresight. You had hundreds of people around you for more than two full days. We are lucky no one knows what nearly happened."

"If the grandmother and Blackie are not confirmed dead by next year's Summerfest, we'll need more men and a better plan."

Jean-Louis shook his head. "We can't wait until then. We need both tonight. I've arranged for it with the sheriff."

***

Monday, August 19, 1811 – Ravenshire Pond
Edward

Bri coaxed Edward into an early morning swim at Ravenshire Pond. "You were game to join the swimming event."

"At least I wasn't the last to finish. I can still appear in public, since I wasn't the only one to be beaten by a teen."

They swam out to the island and climbed up into the tree house. Bri pulled a pouch from under her bathing costume.

Edward recoiled. "Here? Now? We're soaking wet!"

"So much the better." Bri removed the sponge, poured a vial of vinegar over it, and handed it to Edward.

They peeled off their wet clothing.

Edward inserted the sponge and pulled Bri to him. "My house is nearly ready. Soon we will have complete privacy."

"I doubt it.. Ravenshire may be the only place we can be alone. Here, or riding, or in the tower."

"Then we shall visit Ravenshire often." He kissed her. "Very often." His arms gently lowered her to the floor, his body covered hers and she moaned in pleasure.

***

After breakfast, Henry rose. "I'd like to see you both in my library. With Jean-Louis."

343

Have we been found out? Edward's palms sweated. He dared not glance at Bri.

Jean-Louis closed the door. "We stopped two intrusions over Summerfest. One by brigands and the other by an assassin."

Bri paled.

"Were it not for Orion, I might be dead now." Henry glanced at Bri. "You or Ian might have been next."

The French former trapper leveled his gaze at Edward. "Treachery is afoot. You cannot disappear on a lark to swim and climb trees. Even at Ravenshire, you will need an escort at all times."

He knows.

CHAPTER THIRTY-SEVEN

Tuesday, August 20, 1811 – Wyndward Trading Offices
Henry

As the day ended, the earl left the trading company offices. Jean-Louis waited outside the back entry with the carriage. A grim expression defined Henry's face.

The Frenchman pushed his black felt hat off his forehead. "What's wrong?"

The earl sighed and ran his hand through his hair. "Sheldon's instincts are correct, but the other directors are chafing under his style. I never noticed before how differently each man running a division approaches his tasks. The competition is getting more aggressive, war is always with us, shipping plans are constantly interrupted, and now, in addition, I have to act as an arbiter among the men in charge of my operations."

Entering the carriage, Henry mused aloud to Jean-Louis, as the Frenchman held open the door. "I never realized how useful Blackie was in herding these directors toward a common goal. Every day at the trading company involves a dispute about something." Henry sat back on the tufted leather bench seat. "Blackie balanced their competing interests in capital allocations and coaxed them into agreement. I didn't realize until Blackie was gone that I have difficulty dealing with such situations."

Jean-Louis shut the door, but the earl continued to talk through the window.

"In fact, the man was far more responsible for the trading company's success than I ever understood." He sighed. "I revel in discoveries, opening new trading links, and negotiating the initial contract. Lately, though, I've come to understand that while I act decisively in a moment of danger, I prefer to avoid confrontation in daily life."

The Frenchman raised an eyebrow and said, in a laconic tone, "You live with someone who revels in confrontation."

Henry nodded. "And I give in every time."

***

Wednesday, August 21, 1811 – Professor Parker's Office
The American

Nathaniel Parker sat in his office at the University of Pennsylvania. He reviewed preparations for his sabbatical at Merton College, Oxford, during which he intended to complete a treatise on the history of philosophy. As a student there nearly thirty years earlier, when he was known as The American, he had sought the soothing silence of the Bodleian Library, where he could read and write for hours.

A knock on the door startled him. He looked up to see the mail clerk. "I didn't think anyone else was around today."

"Mail never stops, Professor. Got one for you from England."

"Thank you." He noted the sender's name and smiled. He broke the seal on the letter and scanned it quickly. *A wedding! The baron is finally getting married. I could write back, but I'd rather surprise them all. Henry alone knows of my upcoming voyage.*

***

Friday, August 23, 1811 – The Blue Bazaar
Vano

Vano had been in a foul mood for days. *No word from Lash or Caló. The Gypsy crone is responsible.*

When Mirela arrived to read fortunes, Vano roughly pulled on her arm to take her aside. "No more men for you."

She shrugged. "One living. Grievously injured, he surviving."

Vano tilted his head and scoffed. "Your wicked cards tell you that?"

"My cards not being wicked. The cards do not lie. I having no more need of your men." She went into the fortune-telling tent and took the first person from the line of eager seekers.

Who survived? I hope it was Lash. If not, I'll kill Caló myself.

***

Saturday, August 24, 1811 – The Catacombs
Alia

Raj delivered an urgent message to Alia in person. "The Pharaoh requests your presence immediately."

It's near midnight. Raj appears on edge.

Knowing better than to ask questions, Alia signaled to Sefu to follow her. When they arrived at The Pharaoh's apartments, her stomach churned. *No one stands at The Pharaoh's door. Why would he send Raj to find me?* She knocked.

"Enter."

The Pharaoh reclined on his couch with a book. He put it down and stood. "Raj, wait outside. Sefu, you stay."

Raj left to take his post and Sefu closed the massive door.

"I've been testing disguises for my voyage. Last night, I followed Raj after I dismissed him for the evening. He darted into an alley and entered a den of hashish. There, he spoke too freely of his service to The Pharaoh. He exaggerated his importance. His poor judgment puts our operations at risk. His usefulness has ceased."

Alia started to speak, but The Pharaoh held up his hand. "Let this be a lesson. When I am gone, you need watchers you can trust. You will be at risk at all times" He turned to the eunuch. "Sefu, make Raj disappear. Before he dies, tell him, "The Pharaoh knows you have been indiscreet. There is no reprieve."

The Pharaoh sat and nodded to Sefu. "Do it now. Alia and I will talk until you return."

After Sefu departed, The Pharaoh gestured for Alia to sit. "A woman cannot be as invisible as a man. Trust is a luxury you cannot afford. Now let us speak of the future."

CHAPTER THIRTY-EIGHT

Monday, September 2, 1811 – The Philadelphia Docks
The American

The American trudged up the gangplank for the limited number of passengers on the Atlantic crossing. His name was on a permanent list for preferred passengers on any Wyndward Trading ship. He also carried a letter from Henry in case someone disputed his claims. Encountering no obstacles, the steward led him through a labyrinthine series of passages that led to his cabin.

Nate couldn't resist mentioning the significance of the name of the ship. Henry's penchant for the goddesses of antiquity had always amused him. "Aboard *Alcyone's Wynd*, perhaps the spirit of Poseidon will guide us."

The steward turned and gave him a blank look.

The American sighed. *I guess they no longer teach the classics in school. There was a time when anyone would have known that. I'm getting older.* "Alcyone was one of The Pleiades and married Poseidon, the god of the sea."

"This way, sir."

Apparently, the provenance of the ship he sails on is of no interest to this steward. Nate had last traveled to London for his sabbatical in 1804-05. Since that year, Henry had lost his father, brother, and brother-in-law. During his years at Merton, Nate had watched Rychard and Aelwyn grow up and fall in love. He'd met Luc de Merbeau and liked him. He'd written letters of condolence to Henry and Gwyneth after each death, but it was Luc's passing that loomed ever present in his mind. *Has Gwyneth found another love?*

In 1776, Nate was at university with Henry when he was caught unawares by the outbreak of the American Revolution. As a result, he had been isolated in England during the long years of war.

Henry persuaded his father to take Nate in as a ward. Nate had spent summers and holidays with Henry's family before coming under his guardianship. When he and Henry were on a tour of Europe one summer, they had encountered Aelwyn as a stowaway on a ship in the Mediterranean. She had also become a ward of the 10th Earl of Ravenshire. Both had been treated as members of the family.

Nate could see romance building between Aelwyn and Rychard, and he could not deny his infatuation with the beautiful and artistic Lady Gwyneth. She could debate him with clever retorts on points of philosophy but also capture life in pencil and paint. From time to time, she would leave a poem around for him to discover. Their first kiss happened one afternoon in the old tower, where she'd found hidden pieces of family history.

Gwyneth was torn between Nate and Jamie Craigfell, whom she'd decided she would marry when she was thirteen. In 1780, when Gwyneth was seventeen and he was twenty, Nate endured the pain of watching Gwyneth marry Craigfell, a boy of sixteen whom Nate knew to be a cad. Since Henry was engaged to Jamie's cousin, Lady Jane, Nate suffered in silence. When he learned that Craigfell died the same day Henry had rescued Gwyneth from Craigfell's brutish treatment, Nate let himself hope she would give him a chance to prove his love.

They spent many hours together as friends, but Gwyneth had become distant. It took a few years until she could be as she had been before her marriage. They talked of a life together, and Nate let himself hope.

When the war was over in 1783, he made a formal proposal of marriage to Gwyneth and asked her to come with him to America. She balked at leaving her family. Perhaps it was because Henry was always away traveling to build his trading company, and she feared never seeing her family again, but she wavered and begged Nate to remain at Merton as a don. He considered that option, but felt she must not really love him if she couldn't leave England. So he returned to America, alone, in 1784.

The intervening years had dealt him many blows. He felt no ties to Philadelphia anymore, and vowed to himself that if Gwyneth was still willing to marry him, he would arrange to teach permanently at Merton after his sabbatical.

"Sir?"

Nate realized he'd let his mind wander as he'd followed the steward.

"Forgive me, I was distracted. What did you ask me?"

"This is your cabin, sir." He unlocked the door and opened it.

A compact room with a built-in bunk and desk awaited him. Bookshelves filled one wall, and a small table and two chairs were to one side. A private bath, a real luxury Henry had installed in each cabin, beckoned.

"Your trunk and valises will be delivered shortly. A welcoming tea will be hosted in the captain's dining room at Five Bells."

"Will we depart on time at four o'clock?"

"Yes, sir. At the end of the Afternoon Watch, Eight Bells. The captain insists on punctuality. Dinner is at Two Bells." The steward moved aside as two crewmen entered carrying Nate's trunk and other luggage.

"Over there," Nate pointed.

After they had left, The American unpacked a few items, and then went up on deck to watch as the sails were set, the ship began to move, and Philadelphia faded from view. Depending on weather, the trip could last from three to six weeks.

A new adventure! And, perhaps, a new life.

***

Monday, September 2, 1811 – Edward's Townhouse
Vaux

In accordance with the schedule Vaux had reviewed with Edward months ago, renovations on the townhouse Edward had purchased were completed in a timely manner. Edward arrived to take possession of the renovated townhouse on the second of September. The final inspection included Vaux, Bri, and Rachel Turtin, the upholsterer and draper.

After the room-by-room check, Edward threw his arm around Vaux. "You've done it!"

"Lady Gabriella and Miss Turtin deserve most of the credit."

"Nonsense," said Bri. "The structure, the design motif, and the execution were in your hands. Miss Turtin's fabric offerings were varied and unusual. My contribution was minor."

By prior arrangement, Vaux suggested that he and Miss Turtin explore the garden while Bri and Edward took another look around the rooms to make any final decisions about function or décor.

The new butler and valet, Shore, brought them tea.

***

Edward

Bri cast a puzzled glance at Edward.

He leaned over and whispered, "I told Vaux to leave us alone for a while."

Bri paled. "I didn't bring the sponge. I had no idea we might be alone."

Edward smiled. "I might have picked one up in the back room at Jane Anne's salon."

"Who told you about the back room?"

"Vaux."

"Well, then, Mr. James. It appears that nothing is preventing us from testing your new bed, now that we know that the roof has been fixed and we are not at risk."

He kissed her neck and pulled her dress over her head.

"Well, in any case, the entire structure has been fortified and rebuilt where necessary. Your bill is forthcoming."

"My bill? Not *our* bill?"

" 'Twouldn't be appropriate for me to pay for anything before we are married."

"Even though you picked out nearly everything?"

She glanced around the room. "True, you are a *very* lucky man."

"I know." He ran his finger across her lips. "Let's make the most of these moments."

"I should hope so. We mustn't dawdle while time is of the essence."

Edward pushed her down on the bed and covered her with kisses.

***

Vaux

Vaux and Rachel sat in the garden.

Rachel tilted her head. "It's serene out here."

Shore arrived with tea and a basket of bread and cheese.

"You and Mr. James planned this private, unchaperoned interlude for them?"

He nodded.

Rachel recoiled. "That is quite forward of Lady Gabriella to take such a risk."

Vaux shrugged. "As a certain Frenchman would say, 'There are ways.' Lady Gabriella plans ahead. I've never known her not to get her own way. She is more clever than any man I've ever met."

"In another life, maybe I would have known her better."

Vaux tilted his head and frowned. "You mean, as a matter of class? That you could never be friends with the daughter of an earl?"

"I think you know exactly what I mean."

Vaux remained silent for a few moments. " 'Tis a lonely life we lead. Have you ever considered marrying?"

"Never."

"Nor have I, although the pressure from my parents, as the only child, is enormous. My cousin, who is next in line to inherit the title, is an absolute prig. I hate him. I should marry to spite him."

"Perhaps you can find a willing partner. Your wealth and title may be enough for many young ladies of the *ton*. Marry and find yourself a willing valet."

"I don't want a servant as a partner."

"You have many more advantages than a woman in such a quandary."

"But a woman isn't as suspect. People pity a woman who has never married. They *label* a man who has never married."

"Then marry you must."

"Marry? Vaux?" Edward's voice carried into the garden as he came down the outer stairs with Bri. He stopped and his mouth fell open. "This garden is delightful!"

"And practical. Nashmir and Vaux worked to create beauty that is ethereal as well as edible."

An odd look came over Edward's face. "Shore?"

"Yes, Mr. James."

"Is there a plan to hire additional staff?"

Vaux stood and put his arm around his friend's shoulders. "I happen to know a very capable woman who could orchestrate that task for you. Perhaps you've heard of her—Lady Gabriella Wyndward?"

A smile brightened Edward's face. "I believe I've heard that name somewhere."

Bri walked up. "My name?"

***

Monday, September 2, 1811 – Aboard *Alcyone's Wynd*
The American

Nate arrived shortly after Two Bells had sounded, meaning it was five o'clock on the First Dog Watch. He smiled. *I'm learning the vernacular of the sailing life. Odd, I've never thought to ask on other sailings.*

The captain and first officer greeted him for the first night's dinner in the captain's quarters. "I am Captain Breslington. This is Lt. Hiller."

Parker was not surprised to see a black man as an officer in Henry's fleet. Tales of Captain Jack Perkins and other runaway slaves finding sanctuary as black mariners were well known. But the image of a Negro captain directing a white officer was not a sight one would witness on an American vessel. *I wonder how he navigates the streets of America? In full uniform, perhaps? With a coterie of aides for protection?* Inwardly, Nate cringed over his country's sin of slavery. As a philosopher, he believed all men were created equal, but even the U.S. Constitution, a document he revered, counted a black man as only three-fifths of a white man. Ideals confronted by prejudice receded in practice.

"Let me introduce all our guests on this crossing."

"Professor Parker, of the University of Pennsylvania, may I introduce M. Étienne, a banker from Geneva?"

"Good afternoon."

"Mrs. Walpole and her niece, Miss Walpole, of Manhattan."

"Good day, Professor. What do you teach?" Miss Walpole flicked her eyelids flirtatiously.

"Philosophy, Miss Walpole."

The young woman's face lit up. "How fascinating! You must explain it to me at dinner."

"In its entirety," added M. Étienne with a roll of his eyes to Nate.

Miss Walpole's face contorted in confusion.

The captain continued, "Mr. John Simmons and Mr. Steffield Helms are U.S. diplomats."

The gentlemen shook hands around the circle until a new guest interrupted the ritual.

A woman in a purple cape, sporting peacock feathers in her upswept hair and waving a fan, entered.

The captain bowed to her. "And finally, may I introduce our famous guest—the actress, Miss Sophie Morel, and her assistant, Mlle. Marie-Chantal Quinault."

Nate tilted his head in admiration. "Your Ophelia in *Hamlet* was haunting, Miss Morel."

"Thank you—"

"Professor Parker, Miss Morel," said the captain.

"A professor. How erudite. I once played a professor in a farce." She sniffed. "Not to suggest your profession is a farce, you understand."

"Of course not. Philosophy is no farce, I assure you."

Simmons and Helms were effusive in their praise of Miss Morel. "We never miss one of your performances when we are in New York," Simmons gushed.

Helms agreed. "We hope we will see you on the stage in London. What role are you performing?"

Miss Morel nodded. "Desdemona."

"And a compelling innocent you shall be, no doubt." M. Étienne smiled. "I thought your portrayal of Dorine in *Tartuffe* was extraordinary. You embodied that audacious and daring character."

"Thank you, M. Étienne."

"And Miss Quinault, it's a pleasure to meet you."

Miss Morel answered for her assistant with a wave of her fan. "She's my costumer and make-up artist. She's rather shy."

Miss Quinault averted her eyes from the group.

Mrs. Walpole turned her attention back to Miss Morel. "I saw you as Desdemona in *Othello* in the New York production *years* ago. It must be challenging to play a woman brought down by rumor and innuendo. And one so much younger than yourself. Tell me, how do you prepare for such a role? And with hundreds or thousands watching you, how do you maintain your focus?"

"Well, Mrs. Walpole," replied the actress in an icy tone, "those are professional secrets. If I told you, you might become a rival."

"Dear God, no! I would never—" She stopped herself in mid-sentence.

Miss Walpole came to her aunt's rescue. "My aunt is shy in public and would be dismayed by such crowds hanging onto her every word."

Nate smiled. *Perhaps Miss Walpole is more astute than M. Étienne believes.*

***

Edward

Bri saw Jean-Louis pull the carriage alongside the garden gate. "Wait here for a moment."

Jean-Louis tipped his hat to Bri with a wink, jumped down from his perch, and opened the carriage door. Bri lifted a basket out and Jean-Louis carried another basket back into the garden.

Confused, Edward stared at Bri. *What is this charade?*

With a broad smile, she handed the basket to him and lifted the edge of the blanket.

"It's empty."

"Not for long. Chérie's pups will be born within the week. As soon as they are weaned, you will have a companion."

Jean-Louis handed a basket to Vaux. "And our lady fair has selected another pup for you, Viscount."

"Smile, Vaux," teased Edward. "You'll no longer sleep alone."

CHAPTER THIRTY-NINE

Saturday, September 7, 1811 – Hanforth's Farewell Party
Edward

A few weeks after the Ravenshire Summerfest, Edward and Bri rode in his carriage to the Pytchley Menagerie before the evening's farewell dinner for Viscount Hanforth, hosted by the Duke and Duchess of Pytchley at their majestic ancestral home, Pytchley Manor. Despite its modest designation, Pytchley Manor rivaled Kensington Palace in size and appointments. Following the farewell dinner, the entire party would be staying for the night as guests of the duke and duchess, followed by a breakfast the following day.

Before dinner, Hanforth would be leading all on a tour of the menagerie originally curated by Bri's grandfather, the 10th Earl of Ravenshire.

Bri squeezed Edward's hand. "We always visit the duchess at Christmas, and I used to spend part of the summer with her. Pytchley Manor is magnificent, surrounded by gardens and an extended area with a greenhouse by a large reflecting pool, and a labyrinth."

"Surely not as majestic as the ruins of Ravenshire Castle." Edward smiled. "A castle being rebuilt to exceed its original glory."

"True. While the Wyndward family's title predates the rise of the Pytchley dukedom, we take care not to mention it."

Edward tilted his head toward his fiancée. "Your father mentioned to me that the duchess may be living at Ravenshire after the duke dies. Lady Abigail wants no advice or interference from a dowager duchess."

Frowning, Bri nodded. "Lady Abigail is a bit full of herself. She and Uncle Oliver invited themselves for this occasion, even though they just met Hanforth at Summerfest."

"Hello and goodbye in nearly the same breath."

"Precisely." Bri turned to Edward. "I've been thinking about the proposal for hotels on the Azores. I think it has excellent potential, but I'm concerned about taking on too much too fast."

"Nothing says we have to implement that venture immediately. We can study its benefits and make a decision after we evaluate the other investments."

"I don't want to miss an opportunity," said Bri.

"Neither do I, but there is a lot of research to do. We must not rush."

Bri put her head on Edward's shoulder and fell asleep.

***

Edward nudged Bri awake as the carriage rolled more smoothly, shifting from uneven roads to the hard-packed ground leading from a gated wall to Pytchley Manor. While footmen unloaded their luggage, Bri and Edward joined the other arrivals as the group walked along the path to the menagerie.

Tables stood end-to-end, set for a picnic meal scheduled for midway through the tour. Bri looked up, and was pleased to see sun breaking through the cloud cover. To ease congestion and avoid upsetting the animals, the group would split in two and explore half the menagerie before lunch and view the remaining half afterward.

***

Bri

A small tent was set up for those who preferred to avoid the sun. The duke had been an outdoorsman in his youth and suffered from recurring bouts of skin cancers on his face, ears and hands, so he took the sun rarely. His surgeon was highly skilled, and though his face was criss-crossed with tiny scars, they appeared to be normal wrinkles that came with aging, so he was not disfigured, except for a missing part of one ear. He liked to say that it was bitten off by a vulture while he awaited rescue in the Alps after he'd fallen off a cliff while hiking, landing on a ledge below the *haute route*. It was a fiction that his listeners permitted without challenge.

The duchess appeared and called all the guests over to her. They stood in a semi-circle as she spoke. "As you know, there will be two groups. I will lead one and our animal-keeper, Mr. Witt, will lead the other. You will each draw a number from the duke's ceremonial beret. The even numbers will come with me and the odd numbers with Mr. Witt."

I wonder how she will control who is in her group? Grandmother does not often leave things to chance.

"After lunch, Mr. Witt and I will switch groups."

Bri smiled. *Grandmother is always a step ahead of me.*

After the tour, Bri convinced Edward to walk toward the reflecting pool and the hedge maze. Entering the labyrinth, Bri began to run.

Edward quickly became disoriented. "Come back, Bri. You know this maze. I don't."

She peeked around the hedge and signaled for Edward to follow her. Once Edward reached her position, she took his hand and pulled him along grassy rows between hedges trimmed to eight-foot heights. Finally, they reached a point where Bri felt isolated enough to wrap her arms around Edward.

Their long, sensuous kiss was interrupted by Henry and Charlotte coming around the adjacent hedge into exactly the same location.

Charlotte took Bri's arm. "You and I shall walk the labyrinth."

Henry threw his arm over Edward's shoulder. "As shall we."

Later, as the afternoon sun shone overhead, the guests headed back to the main house to freshen up for dinner later that evening.

Bri was not surprised to find that she and Edward were directed to opposite wings of her Grandmother's home. *Best not to arouse any suspicion.*

After dressing, the guests were scheduled to meet for a glass of Champagne before dividing into two dining groups.

Bri descended the grand center staircase in a gown of silk jacquard in a hue of green the color of emeralds, one of which hung from her neck on a gold chain. A pearl drop dangled below the diagonally set square-cut emerald. Her eyes fell on Edward.

Her fiancé stood across the room, dressed in shades of gray, charcoal, and black topped by a blue cravat that reflected in his gray eyes. While men's attire varied a bit, mainly an embroidered vest or flashy cravat, there was a comfort in their uniform-like style.

In fashion, Bri noted, women had more freedom. *We have carved out some individuality in a world that demands conformity to the norms of our class.*

Edward walked over to Bri and kissed her on the cheek. "You look dazzling! Your eyes and your jewel," he put one finger under the emerald, "match perfectly."

The duchess entered the room. Vanessa's upswept hair, alternating charcoal and white tresses, almost like stripes, looked stunning with any color. Tonight she appeared in a silvery blue dress with several layers of silver and blue chiffon. She embodied elegance and youth, as *au courant* as any young woman there. Her ice-blue eyes fixed a piercing gaze on Viscount Hanforth.

He bowed his head. "Thank you, Your Grace, for this lovely day. We shall always remember this farewell. The tour of the menagerie was enlightening. I applaud your foresight in designing spaces for animals to roam rather than locking them inside cages."

"How thoughtful of you to notice, Lord Hanforth. I shall look forward to hearing of your efforts to establish the Hanforth Conservancy. Perhaps someday I can visit."

The duchess accepted a glass of Champagne from her butler and raised her glass. "To the Hanforth Conservancy!"

***

Charlotte

As was the custom before dinner, all offered brief toasts to their choice of the duchess, the duke, Viscount Hanforth, the animals, or whatever moved them. Charlotte was the last person to offer a toast. By that time, glasses had been filled again, and she struggled to summon a subject for a toast. Then it came to her. "I toast Viscount Hanforth, on behalf of all the animals he will save from pillagers, poachers, and trophy hunters. May they live free forever."

Henry leaned over and whispered in her ear. "Excellent."

Charlotte smiled, but her heart clenched. *Will Taita be at the next gathering at Pytchley Manor? Am I falling into the faux dream that Henry is still mine? I must guard my feelings.*

Gio cleared his throat. "Your Grace, I have counted the seats and it appears there are seats for only twelve in your main dining room and my name does not appear on a place card. Have you forgotten me?"

Vanessa smiled. "There are fifteen young people, Gio, and you will be the sixteenth, although you're about the farthest embodiment of a chaperone I can imagine. If that role displeases you, then I will join them in your stead."

Bowing in an exaggerated manner, Gio shifted his eyes to the duchess. "Nothing you suggest would ever displease me, Your Grace."

"Ha!" Vanessa scoffed. "I am immune to flattery. Let us go to our respective tables."

Charlotte waited for the others to move toward the table, and her position permitted her to glimpse the duchess wink at Gio. *She is an amazing woman.*

***

Vanessa

The duchess believed in place cards, and amused herself by seating people next to unconventional partners. She and the duke, Bentley, sat opposite each other at the long table, carved from a huge oak tree from the nearby forest. She placed Henry on one side of the duke and Gwyneth on the other. *He will remember them.*

In addition to Henry, Charlotte, Aelwyn and Gwyneth, Vanessa's guests were her son, Oliver, his wife Lady Abigail, Dr. Northcliffe, Count von Dusterberg, and Lady Clementine's parents.

"With Gio banished to the greenhouse, I shall accept the role of court jester." The duchess assumed control with ease. "We will go around the table and each of you will tell me which animal most affected you today and why. The duke and I have our favorites. But no repetitions! My darling, you may begin."

The duke cleared his throat. "Most certainly. The lion is my favorite. A splendid creature. To the lion!"

The group echoed his words, "To the lion!"

The elderly man turned to Henry. "Do you agree with me, my boy?"

"I agree the lion is impressive, Duke, but the lioness even more so. She stalks and kills the prey for the pride to eat. We underestimate the female of the species at our peril, a mistake I have made more than once." He laughed, putting the others at ease. "To the lioness!"

"To the lioness!" toasted the others.

"So the female of the species is to be admired merely because she is a killer?" Gwyneth shook her head.

Henry put his hands up in surrender. "I am simply stating facts. My point is that the female ensures the survival of the pride."

His sister ignored him. "My favorite animal has always been the zebra. Their unique striping, varying hues and stand-up manes fascinate me. I never tire of painting zebra herds." She raised her glass. "To the zebra!"

The others raised their glasses. "To the zebra!"

The duchess nodded to Aelwyn.

"Ian and I were transfixed by the Lady Jane Aviary. The African Grey Parrot was our favorite. Its red under-tail feathers flash color and its ability to mimic is amazing. Ian said, 'I'm Ian,' and the bird kept repeating it! When he said, 'Stop it!' the bird repeated, 'Stop it!'" Aelwyn laughed. "To the parrot!"

"To the parrot!"

Oliver smiled. "I have always been fascinated by the monkey. Agile, clever, mischievous. To the monkey!"

"To the monkey!"

Dr. Northcliffe nodded. "Having lived in Africa, I am more familiar with the meercat than most of you. The meercat calls out warnings when predators prowl too close to the herd. To the meercat!"

"To the meercat!"

Charlotte spoke next. "To me, the grace and beauty of a leaping gazelle around the enclosed meadow was inspiring. To the gazelle!"

Lady Abigail emitted a high, screeching laugh. "Can you guess? I liked the laughing hyena. To the hyena!"

"To the hyena!"

Count von Dusterberg tilted his head. "I was impressed that the Menagerie has a running corridor for the cheetah, the swiftest animal on earth. To the cheetah!"

"To the cheetah!"

The Earl of Hornhill, Lady Clemmie's father, was next. "I know it may sound trite, but the elephant is a majestic animal. To the elephant!"

"To the elephant!"

The Countess of Hornhill smiled at her husband. "The giraffe grazing on the leaves of the acacia trees, extending its purple tongue, is a delightful creature. To the giraffe!"

"To the giraffe!"

Vanessa, the last to speak, smiled. "Interesting selections, all. It may surprise my son-in-law, but my favorite is in the Lady Jane Aviary—the raven. It is the smartest in the bird domain. It can count. It is resourceful. It can learn. It can remember. The lore of the Wyndward family is that a raven led its progenitor, the Roman Ventus, to the shores of Britain. It is the noble symbol of a noble family, now part of my own. To the raven!"

"To the raven!"

***

Gio

Gio walked along the path until he reached the greenhouse. He walked in and bellowed, "Shape up! I am here to insure the conversation does not stray from appropriate topics."

"Ha!" scoffed Bri. "You are the devilish one who will lead us astray."

The dwarf shrugged. "That remains to be seen, my lovely young friend. The duchess instructed me to lead you in the same ritual as their table. We are instructed to toast our favorite animal from today's tour. We have the advantage that we are not limited by the choices they have made because we don't know their preferences, but each person must choose a unique animal. No doubt they have selected lion, elephant and giraffe. Highly predictable. But don't let me dissuade you from your choices."

"Gio, you are incorrigible. You've insulted our choices before we begin." Bri sat at one end of the table and put Gio to her right. She announced to the rest of the guests, "Ignore the comments of Lord Ostwold and speak your minds freely. I always do."

Edward laughed as he took his place at the other end of the table. "You'll get no argument from me on that point."

The younger attendees included Clarissa and Dr. St. Cloud, Banfield, Vaux, Lady Clemmie, Lady Patricia, Lord Lt. Thornton, Lady Marianna, Lady Melanie, Baron Beauchamp, Lady Penelope, and the guest of honor, Viscount Hanforth.

Bri touched Gio on the arm. "You must begin. Dazzle us with your brilliance."

"You mock me, dear Bri. You dare me to dazzle. I pick the ant. I see your surprise. The ants are nearly invisible here, but not in Africa. There they build anthills taller than eight of me. Millions live inside. Tiny, industrious, indestructible."

Viscount Hanforth cleared his throat. "I hesitate to disagree, Lord Ostwold, but what are called anthills in Africa are typically termite mounds. Some are indeed, as you say, thirty feet high."

The dwarf sat silent for but a moment. "I concede I may have been misinformed. Nevertheless, I stand by my choice. The ant is smaller than the termite, and therefore, to me, more interesting. To the ant!"

"To the ant!" echoed the diners.

Lady Clemmie was next. "I find it difficult to choose a favorite, but if I must, I will choose a bird from the Lady Jane Aviary—the yellow-collared lovebird from the Serengeti, near where the Hanforth Conservancy will be sited. It is a type of parrot, beautifully and brilliantly colored in yellow, green and black, with a red beak and white eye-rings. An interesting tidbit is that the external appearance of male and female is identical, an unusual equality of appearance in nature." She raised her glass. "To the yellow-collared lovebird!"

The group responded, "To the yellow-collared lovebird!"

Dr. St. Cloud sighed and shook his head. "How can an animal doctor choose a favorite? But I must say, the caracal—the small cat with the tufted ears—fascinated me. I learned that it can jump over nine feet in the air and was domesticated by the Egyptians as a hunting companion. To the caracal!"

In unison, all called out, "To the caracal!"

All eyes shifted to Lady Marianna. "I'm sorry to disappoint Lord Ostwold, but I loved the elephants. The mother and her babe had their trunks entwined. Were it not for the horrendous odor of the excrement, I would have watched them a bit longer." She lifted her flute. "To the elephant!"

"To the elephant!"

Viscount Vaux swirled his Champagne as he considered his selection. "I am partial to cats, so it is difficult to pick just one. If I must, it would be the leopard, languorously lying lazily on the tree branch. To the leopard!"

Edward could not restrain himself. "How long did it take you to align the alliteration?"

"Ha! Less time than it took you to construct that retort. I have a facility for felicitous flashes of phraseology."

Bri leaned forward. "The end of that phrase is consonance, not alliteration."

Vaux shrugged. "Call me insouciant. It sounds the same. To the leopard!"

"To the leopard!"

Lady Melanie spoke next. "I know it doesn't look beautiful, or graceful, but I felt a connection to the hippopotamus. Bobbing up and down in the water, it looked playful. To the hippopotamus!"

"To the hippopotamus!"

The next choice fell to the baron. "I must disappoint Lord Ostwold as well. The giraffe fascinates me. When it bent down to take a leaf from my hand, its head was nearly half my height. To the giraffe!"

"To the giraffe!"

Edward took a sip of Champagne before speaking. "The chimpanzee's eyes are so human-like. They reminded me of Vaux. To the chimpanzee!"

"To the chimpanzee!"

A retort from Vaux came quickly. "Shall I chortle charmingly?"

Viscount Hanforth smiled. He raised his glass to Lord Ostwold. "Sorry to disappoint you, but I choose the lion, a magnificent animal, a symbol of all that is wild and noble. To the lion!"

"To the lion!"

Lady Penelope raised her glass. "I liked the jungle cats, too. The serval, with its small head, long legs, and interesting line-like splotches, captured my heart. To the serval!"

"To the serval!"

Lord Lt. Thornton raised his glass. "As a military man, the warrior-like rhinoceros charge appealed to me. To the rhinoceros!"

"To the rhinoceros!"

Lady Patricia shivered. "I cannot dismiss the terror I felt as that rhinoceros charged at us, halted by the wall we were looking over to view it. One minute it was foraging, the next it was charging. I was frozen. I choose an unthreatening bird, the ostrich."

"Actually, Lady Patricia, " Dr. St. Cloud interjected, "the ostrich is a most aggressive bird and will chase humans if provoked. But it is an interesting specimen."

"To the ostrich!"

Banfield held up his glass. "I too found the Lady Jane Aviary a fascinating place. African songbirds were competing for attention. The great reed warbler male, a drab-feathered bird, sang complex songs, repeating almost-syllabic notes to attract females. Its melodic interludes inspired me to dash off the beginning of a potential love aria for an opera I'm working on. To the great reed warbler!"

"To the great reed warbler!"

Clarissa's turn came. "I love the zebra. There is something elegant about its black and white stripes. To the zebra!"

Finally, Bri spoke. "I am partial to the gazelle. I named my horse Gazelle because I so admire their jumping, soaring in free flight. "To the gazelle!"

As the last clink of glasses reverberated around the greenhouse, footmen appeared with the soup, a cream of celery with bits of onion. Conversation became centered around immediate seating partners, with competing conversations echoing on the glass enclosure, creating a din that paradoxically created a focus for each conversation, almost a bubble of privacy.

The soup bowls were removed, and dinner platters brought in. Each guest had a pair of quail with wine sauce and capers, roasted potatoes and green beans, raised in the curtained off section of the greenhouse.

Vanessa had reconfigured the greenhouse interior to accommodate a dance area, where a fortepiano sat unattended. Musicians were scheduled to arrive as the dessert was served.

Bri called out to Banfield, "Before the musicians arrive, play us a few notes of your aria inspired by the great reed warbler. The fortepiano is at your disposal."

Encouraged by the others applauding Bri's request, Banfield rose and walked over to the instrument. He opened the lid and fixed it in place, took his seat and began to play a melody that transfixed the listeners. It stopped abruptly. He turned to his audience and shrugged. "That's all so far."

"It's beautiful!" said Clarissa.

Gio tilted his head. "An image came into my head as you played." He moved his hand, as if painting. "I saw swirls of color around trees. What is the subject of your opera?"

"I am working on several. But this tune seems best to incorporate into the opera I'm calling *The Nymphs,* a love triangle set amid a colony of forest nymphs, unspoiled by our civilization, but prisoners of the mores of their own culture, thwarted in their pursuit of forbidden love. They can understand the songs of birds and the whispers of the wind due to the purity of their souls."

Edward's lips curled into a knowing smile as he caught Bri's eye.

She gave him a glance, with a tilt of her head, suggesting, "Why not?"

The dwarf squinted. "Banfield, it seems we may have two operatic collaborations on sets and murals. Years ago, I created some for a ballet company."

"I would be honored, Lord Ostwold, but I am a composer, not an expert in the production of operas. Vaux is interested in constructing the sets and even designing costumes."

Gio raised his hands. "Voila! We have everything at this table to bring your opera or operas—*opere* as the Italians would say—to fruition."

The musicians arrived just as Banfield rose from the bench. Rearranging their chairs, they sat and tuned their instruments

The dinner platters were removed and slices of chocolate cake with white butter cream icing sprinkled with cinnamon appeared in front of the diners. It was in the shape of Africa, matching its topography in colors of the icing, the Sahara desert cutting a wide swath across the continental confection.

"Here's a dessert topic: does anyone know the origin of cake icing or frosting?" Bri forked a small bite of cake and put it in her mouth.

Gio shrugged. "It was probably invented by the French."

"Correct, but whence the terms 'icing' and 'frosting'?'

Lady Patricia offered her view. "I suppose because it is white and resembles snow—that could be the origin of 'frosting'."

"Perhaps, although some version of butter cream have a yellow cast from the yolk of an egg. Still others use egg whites only, so that version, to me, suggests 'frosting' in appearance. So we have one point from Gio and one from Lady Patricia." Bri glanced around the table. "Does anyone have a third?"

Lady Clemmie leaned forward. "I believe the sugar refining process produces granules, which look like ice crystals. Perhaps that is the origin of the term 'icing'."

Hanforth stared at her. "How do you know about the process of sugar refining?"

Shrugging in response, the handsome athletic woman smiled. "My uncle is a chemist and taught me some interesting things."

Gio raised his glass. "To Lady Clemmie for revealing how valuable she will be in Africa! Perhaps she holds many other *interesting* facts at her disposal."

Hanforth raised his glass. "To Lady Clemmie!" The others repeated the toast.

Edward glanced at Bri. "Shall we lead the dancers in the first reel?"

"A slow reel, I hope." Gio scoffed. "All that jumping about might bring up dinner."

Bri glared at the dwarf. "There are no slow reels, and kindly refrain from conjuring images that are unpleasant."

"Unpleasant, unnecessary and uncultured." Vanessa's voice bounced back from the glass panes in the enclosure. "I have come to relieve you of Gio's company. Come with me."

"Your wish is my command, Your Grace."

"No sarcasm. Don't dawdle."

They swept out of the room as the young people formed a line for the reel.

CHAPTER FORTY

Sunday, September 8, 1811 – Lord Ravenshire's Townhouse
Jean-Louis

Just before midnight, Jean-Louis had finished his nightly walk around the neighborhood, looking for anything out of the ordinary and checking on the guards he had placed in the shadows. Chérie had stayed behind over the last week, resting until the imminent birth of her pups. When he got back to the stables, he heard Chérie whimpering.

One of the grooms, who had attended horses giving birth from time to time, knelt next to Chérie, calming her. Hearing Jean-Louis, he turned toward him. "I sent for Dr. St. Cloud."

"I am here." Dr. St. Cloud dismounted and unfastened his medical bag from the saddle straps. "The first litter can be frightening for her. You are right to calm her."

Jean-Louis had faced deadly predators, human and animal, but never had fear gripped his gut as it did in this moment. After he had composed himself, he spoke. "As I recall, you said she might have six to nine pups. We've prepared baskets and blankets for ten, just in case."

Dr. St. Cloud assessed the situation. "Put some more blankets on the floor. Get plenty of towels and water to clean the pups. They'll sleep next to Chérie until they're ready to leave."

"We have a large basket for them over here."

"Excellent. We'll clean them up and move them into a clean set of blankets." He felt her abdomen.

Chérie's brown eyes searched for Jean-Louis.

When Chérie saw her guardian, the Frenchman would swear forevermore that she smiled at him.

She whelped the first pup. The white mound squirmed and whined as it was cleaned and warmed. Other pups followed in rapid succession. Nine in all wiggled out of the womb, but one appeared stillborn. The veterinarian tried to revive the pup, but it was extremely tiny, and no sign of life appeared. He set it aside on the blanket. "It probably died *in utero*. About one in each Dalmatian litter is stillborn." Each dog had a separate placenta, and Dr. St. Cloud counted to be certain all had been expelled.

"A good first litter," mumbled Dr. St. Cloud. "Chérie, I'm just going to push to be certain no more pups or placentas remain." Nothing more was expelled.

Chérie began to eat one of the placentas.

Dr. St. Cloud removed the other afterbirth for disposal. "It's a normal instinct, but eating one is enough."

Jean-Louis had been watching the stillborn pup while Dr. St. Cloud worked on the others. The Frenchman knelt down. "I thought I saw it move." He lifted the dog. "The body is still warm."

The veterinarian glanced at the French former trapper. Once all the dogs were cleaned, he placed a tag on each pup's rear left leg with a number and the gender. "Four males and four females. All appear healthy."

Chérie and the pups were cleaned and settled into the large basket. The pups instinctively sought milk and Dr. St. Cloud helped situate each pup so that all could feed.

Jean-Louis was still massaging the stillborn male puppy's chest.

Dr. St. Cloud put his hand on the Frenchman's shoulder. "You can't will it to live, Jean-Louis."

The pup moved. "*Non?* I think I just did." The Frenchman gently cleaned the runt and placed it next to Chérie, helping it find a teat.

"Watch it closely. Don't get your hopes up."

The Frenchman shrugged. "There are ways."

***

Monday, September 9, 1811 – Aboard *Alcyone's Wynd*
The American

As the first week onboard ship came to a close, Nate made it a point to sit as far away from Miss Morel as possible at meals to avoid her domineering personality. He enjoyed the company of the diplomats, who were educated, well traveled and precise in their use of language. M. Étienne presented a restrained Continental sensibility that contrasted with the brashness of Nate's fellow Americans. His years in London as a young man reinforced Nate's natural reticence. As a philosopher, his discipline required that he be a keen observer of human nature.

The most he could derive from the monosyllabic Miss Quinault in several exchanges was that she was from a far northern province of Canada, fleeing a life defined by harsh weather and bland predictability.

Nate believed in the process of self-examination and the precision of pedagogic explication. To him, an "exchange" signified more than a word or two, but less than a conversation.

Like all Wyndward vessels, the captain's library contained a wide selection of reading material, including some rare first editions and esoteric volumes that the earl or his captains picked up on voyages or that passengers left behind for the edification of others. Nate was absorbed in a treatise on the practices of Brazilian headhunters and other uncivilized tribes contained within a volume on exploring the Amazon when the captain sat down across from him.

"What are the prevailing political winds in America regarding impressments of seamen?"

"It's a serious point of contention, debated constantly in Congress and the newspapers. The rumors of war, no doubt, spurred the diplomats on their journey to London." Nate's face clouded. Putting down his book, he leaned forward. "Has this ship been boarded?"

"Only once. As a former Royal Navy man myself, they'd heard of me and gave me no trouble. But we had two crewmen who'd deserted the Royal Navy and signed on with us. And we feared for Hiller. I was forced to issue him a direct order to hide. When we were boarded and the Royal Navy officers searched our vessel and demanded papers of all crewmen, we complied but hid the emigrants and Lt. Hiller in the cargo area. In coffins, if you can believe it!"

"I wouldn't fancy that."

"Nor did they." The captain leaned back in his chair. "When we left London months ago, rumors of war with America surfaced in conversation. In New York, I heard similar rumblings."

"Of war? I attributed those rumors as fodder to boost newspaper sales. Surely diplomacy will avoid such idiocy."

" 'Surely' or 'perhaps'?"

"I assume you subscribe to the latter."

"I don't subscribe to either. I prefer to be prepared for any eventuality. Lord Ravenshire has made a practice of plotting alternate routing and alternate ports should events require."

"As my old friend always used to say, 'Planning won't prevent the unexpected'—"

"—'but it exercises one's ingenuity.' That's one of ten principles Lord Ravenshire instills in all his ships' officers. We are honored to be in his service."

"As I am to be his friend."

***

Thursday, September 12, 1811 - *La Pâtisserie entre les fleurs*

Gwyneth

Vanessa and Gwyneth had lunch at *La Pâtisserie entre les fleurs*. After their selections were brought, Vanessa requested another pot of hot water. As usual, her tone was commanding.

It was a sunny September day with a chill in the air. The trees in the surrounding parkland sported vibrant hues of yellow, orange, red, and brown.

Gwyneth gestured to the trees outside the window. "I love this time of year."

Vanessa's voice softened. "I'm not sure how many more autumns the duke will be with me. He may breathe, but he will not be himself. We married in the fall, you know. I've always loved the colors. The ebb and flow of life is catching up with me."

I have never heard the duchess speak with such a poignant tone.

Vanessa snapped out of her melancholy. "Have you thought of a gown to match the theme for Bri's Engagement Ball?"

Smiling, Gwyneth sipped her tea. "I'm trying to decide on the color, but I have a concept in mind that will evoke the Great Comet of 1811.

"Wasn't it amazing to see it at Summerfest? Those cometseekers were the hit of the festivities. Did I tell you that Gio dragged a telescope to the Azores and could see nothing? He felt it was a personal rebuke to him by God." Gwyneth took a sip of her tea. "What has the theme inspired you to wear"

The duchess mused, "A mask and head decoration of falling stars, and a blue velvet gown affixed with Austrian crystals. The masks will be judged in best male and best female categories. Gio will paint the two winners' portraits in their costumes."

Gwyneth sat back and tilted her head to conjure an idea. "I see I shall have to devise something stellar."

A smile crept over Vanessa's face. "Clever, Wynnie."

"Have you a preliminary guest list?"

"I am toying with the idea of inviting a diverse crowd, including people that, frankly, I hate. After all, it *will* be the party of the Season."

"Your balls always are."

"I am estimating approximately 200 to 250 people."

"Just a, intimate gathering."

Vanessa frowned. "Sarcasm is unladylike, unnecessary and uncouth."

The comtesse pushed back. "I hardly think it's uncouth."

***

Sunday, September 15, 1811 – The Catacombs
Alia

The Pharaoh looked up from his desk as Alia entered. He was dressed in a westerner's garb. "It is time for me to depart. Remember my instructions."

"I forget nothing, master."

The Pharaoh nodded to Midnight, who jumped into the black leather travel bag. He fastened the flap.

"I'll have Sefu carry your bags."

"No. I must appear as any ordinary traveler from now on. I'll get a carriage to the docks. I'll be sailing on *Bast's Leap*."

"The protection of the cat goddess is a good omen."

"You know I put no stock in omens."

Alia nodded. "Forgive me, master. Many times you have said, 'We make our own Fate.' I will miss your wise counsel."

"You are ready."

The Pharaoh picked up his bags and looked around the Catacombs. "Perhaps I shall return someday."

Alia watched the man who had changed her life walk away, perhaps forever.

***

Tuesday, September 17, 1811 – Riding along Rotten Row

Oliver

Bri and Oliver slowed their horses to a walk after a spirited race.

"Will Gazelle ever beat Scheherazade?"

Oliver smirked. "So it's the horse, not the rider who wins a race?"

Bri shrugged.

"Arabians are bred for speed," Oliver conceded. But they are not jumpers. You always beat me at Ravenshire, over a course and obstacles you know well. That is, some would say, a greater skill."

"Would 'some' include you or is that a balm to assuage my frustration?"

"A little of both."

Gwyneth caught up with them. "Oliver, have you settled on a mask for the Engagement Ball?"

"When one has a mother such as mine, one always has mask ideas in one's head."

Amused at his formal language, Bri commented, "Does *one*?"

Oliver nodded. "If you haven't learned to have a list of masks and costumes in your head by now, you will live a life of repeated mask-selection frustration. It's a malady afflicting the leading lights of the *ton*."

The comtesse added, "And it manifests a heightened severity among relatives of the duchess."

"I have not decided yet. In keeping with the celestial theme, some are coming as their sign of the zodiac. I imagine there will be a surfeit of ice balls and comet tails. Not too imaginative."

Bri's face fell. "I had an image of a dress with a long train in my mind—"

"On *you* it will look beautiful. Ignore my musings." *I hope I have not upset her.*

Changing the subject, Gwyneth said, "Aelwyn tells me you've been visiting once a week on your way back to London from managing estate issues at Pytchley. I hear that you and Ian go off exploring for hours in the old tower and the gardens."

"I love that boy. He reminds me so much of Rychard." His tone turned wistful. "Perhaps I should have encouraged Lady Abigail to have children earlier. She has never become with child and seems to have little interest in children. Frankly, before knowing Ian, I'd put the concept out of my mind."

Bri laughed. "Soon she'll have your puppy around. Maybe that will inspire her."

Oliver scoffed. "Your Aunt Abigail is not partial to dogs. Care of the pup will fall to me. I envision him coming to the park to run alongside us as we ride, like Hector accompanies Henry. I considered the name 'Achilles,' but I thought that might not be fair to my new canine companion. So I've settled on Perseus."

Gwyneth shook her head. "You and Henry are both unnaturally obsessed with the Greek and Roman gods."

Unable to resist the obvious retort, Oliver said, "Hector was a Trojan. Henry and I share a Mertonian obsession for the classics."

***

Tuesday, September 24, 1811 – Aboard *Nekhbet's Wings*
Xie Xie

After the storm, Xie Xie dreamed of Nekhbet often. Before she awoke, she always heard the whisper, "I will protect you on the seas."

The Pharaoh's Chinese apprentice spent most days in the captain's library and spent hours discussing culture, philosophy and history with the Arab professor.

To his credit, the captain enforced civility at his table and the contentious discussions of the early days of the voyage were not repeated.

The Pharaoh had instilled caution in Xie Xie, but also encouraged curiosity and insisted on rigorous analysis of anyone she met. It had been like a game to them. After that training, she instinctively examined their motivations and character. *This voyage is my test. Who am I without the Pharaoh? Can I survive on my own?*

Turmoil in her dreams was calmed by visions of Nekhbet. It was as if the two of them were calmly sitting near a lagoon on a beautiful isle. This imaginary place in her dreams was one she found herself visiting in her mind.

Only days remain until my new life begins.

***

Saturday, September 28, 1811 – Aboard *Alcyone's Wynd*
The American

Nate stood on deck at sunset. The sky's brilliant orange-red was ethereal, illuminating clouds in an other-worldly light.

Lt. Hiller came up beside him.

"Is the ancient saying true?"

"In my experience, yes. 'Red sky at night, sailors' delight; red sky at morning, sailors take warning.' On land they switch 'sailors' to 'shepherds.' At night, the western stream of light means that the east is clear. At morning, it means the west promises storms. This time of year is always uncertain, but most hurricanes stay south of our course."

"May I be so bold as to ask you how you are treated when you are in New York?"

"Well enough. I remain in uniform. But if we stop in South Carolina, I stay on board. No need to tempt Fate."

"And in England?"

"Again, the uniform helps. Still, no one is ever completely safe from harm. I have certain skills."

Nate laughed. "I know a man in England that you would find a kindred spirit. A French former trapper—"

"Jean-Louis."

Surprised, the truth dawned on Nate. "Of course, you've met him through the earl."

"Sailed with him. He's from a family of naval men, you know."

"No, I didn't know that. I thought he served in the French army."

"True, as a form of rebellion against tradition."

"Now *that* I can believe."

"There's no man I'd feel safer with on any continent than Jean-Louis. There was one time where cannibals—"

The dinner bells interrupted their conversation.

The lieutenant tipped his hat to the American. "I must see to my duties."

"But I need to hear more—"

Lt. Hiller had already descended below decks.

Cannibals?

CHAPTER FORTY-ONE

Tuesday, October 1, 1811 – The Blue Bazaar
Lash

Tarps were pulled down to close the market stalls for the night. As shoppers followed the fiddler to the Gypsy camp, Lash showed up.

Vano slapped Lash on the back. "I wasn't sure you'd survived after I heard that Caló had been arrested."

Lash shrugged. "He'll hang by the end of the month."

"How did you get away from the sheriff?"

Lash shrugged. "I was just a poor wandering Gypsy on my way to Summerfest."

"And they bought that?"

"I'm a *very* good liar."

Vano shook his head and roared. "That's the truth!"

"I can stand guard tonight, if you need me."

Vano grunted. "I do. That rabid cur Hedji never showed up this morning. He may be in a drunken stupor, but more likely, he's either lying in a ditch somewhere with his throat slit or lying with a whore."

"If you have any more extra jobs, I'm interested."

"More's the fool you are! Caló nearly killed you." Out of the corner of his eye, Vano glanced at the scarred man with his distinctive bandana. The scar-cover color changed daily, but not the camouflage. " 'Extra jobs' is fraught with meaning, Lash."

"It should be clear by now that I don't flinch from danger."

The huge, muscled stall keeper fastened the last strap and stood up. "I told the old hag that I wouldn't work with her again, but she wants a watcher to be with her at all times."

"Why?"

"She senses someone is watching her."

"So I am to be a watcher for a watcher. I'm interested, and by the way, I got her to pay me in advance, so here is a cut for you." He tossed him a purse with silver coins.

"I told you I didn't want her blood money."

Lash shrugged. "You won't have to listen to Caló whine again. And he doesn't know any details of your involvement. He's trying to blame me, but the sheriff doesn't believe him."

Vano searched Lash's face.

He's looking for a hint of deception.

"She'll be back tomorrow afternoon."

***

Wednesday, October 2, 1811 – Approaching London Harbor
Xie Xie

The child within the Chinese woman could barely contain her excitement as the spires and bridges of London came into view. She'd heard tales of gaslight emanating a pale glow through thick fog of the once-Roman capital of Britannia, but this balmy summer sky held barely a cloud.

More than any of The Pharaoh's acolytes, Xie Xie was privy to his secrets. He roamed these streets for decades, advancing his long scheme to exact revenge on the 10th Earl of Ravenshire and his descendants.

How often she'd imagined these people. She knew facts as told to her by The Pharaoh. The 11th Earl of Ravenshire, the dark-haired Henry Wyndward, was taller than The Pharaoh, but not by much. A brother, mentor and friend, The Pharaoh could not hide his admiration as he spoke of his older brother. And he clearly doted on his red-haired niece, Lady Gabriella, known as Bri, a high-spirited, independent, financially astute woman who'd uncovered The Pharaoh's duplicitous trading partnerships and financial improprieties. He described his sister, the blonde Lady Gwyneth, a widow, as lovely.

The Pharaoh's fabled grandmother also awaited her, presumably now in London to await The Pharaoh's arrival. She came from the mysterious highlands of Scotland where The Pharaoh had grown up. That formidable woman elicited the most curiosity in Xie Xie's mind. According to The Pharaoh, his grandmother nursed a merciless lust to punish what she saw as treachery and betrayal by the 10th Earl of Ravenshire. Xie Xie knew only her part in The Pharaoh's scheme, not his full plan.

A man known as "Arthur" would leave word for her at Durrants, her hotel chosen by The Pharaoh.

The grandmother now lived with a companion, a fortune-telling Gypsy who read Tarot cards to ensnare the gullible. A passing reference to her by The Pharaoh conveyed his disdain. "She is expendable," he'd said. That word sent a chill down Xie Xie's spine. Being "expendable" to The Pharaoh signified an abbreviated lifespan.

Practiced at maintaining an unreadable expression from an early age, Xie Xie tamped down her eagerness to meet these looming figures, yet she ached to make her own assessment of each one.

For years, as a child and prepubescent teen, Xie Xie had dreamed of becoming The Pharaoh's queen. But then she began to understand that the man who had rescued her was incapable of revealing himself to others. Unique among any man she had known or observed, he traveled with a black cat. At night, deep in the catacombs, she'd overheard him talking to the cat, working out his plans, sharing his deepest secrets. After listening to his feline confessions, she realized that her dreams were empty. The Pharaoh would never be hers.

A dream of her own beckoned and began to take hold. Xie Xie would help her rescuer fulfill his declared destiny, a destiny determined by his grandmother. Once her role was completed, she would be free of any obligation. He had promised her she could chart her own life after London. She had beauty, education, intelligence and wit. *I will use all I've learned at The Pharaoh's side.*

***

Wednesday, October 2, 1811 – The London Docks
The American

Leaving the ship, Nate saw Jean-Louis leaning against a Ravenshire-crested carriage. The Frenchman's familiar black garb contrasted with the colorful livery of the Wyndward footmen.

The former trapper tipped his hat to Nate. "Welcome back, Professor."

"The birds flew true."

"The captain knows the drill." Jean-Louis opened the carriage door for the old family friend. After the American climbed in, Jean-Louis opened a small door underneath the bench, revealing a compartment. "Sherry for the ride?"

"Why not?"

Jean-Louis poured the sherry into a small goblet. "Not too full. The roads here are still a bit bumpy. How was your crossing?"

"Thankfully uneventful, unlike my last return to America seven years ago. The seas roiled with fury on that journey. At moments, I believed I faced certain death—an ignominious, watery demise. As I imagined confronting Plato about his *Dialogues* in the afterlife, the seas calmed."

"It was not your time."

"Don't tell me you've become a fatalist, Jean-Louis."

"I am neither a fatalist nor a Platonist, but I believe that some events are foretold. Does this comet the world is watching mean anything at all? Perhaps. It follows a predetermined path, does it not? Does an individual man follow a predetermined path? I think not. There are forks in the roads we tread, diverging paths we select, and options we ignore. One's future changes with each decision. I don't know the time of my death, but I know it is not here and not soon. I have survived wild animal attacks, had my skin pierced by claws, teeth, bullets and daggers, been tossed overboard in storms, been spared by an unexploded cannon ball in war. Why? Unlike you, I do not contemplate the intricacies of philosophical discourse. I live in the moment."

"You've just debated yourself with more philosophical insight than any student I've taught in more than twenty years. Don't deny it, Jean-Louis. You are a philosopher. *Un philosophe extraordinaire.*" Nate raised his glass in a toast and bowed to the Frenchman. "When the Great Comet of 1811 finally vanishes, then we can see what its passing has wrought."

The footmen appeared with Nate's trunk, which he lashed, along with his other large pieces of luggage, to the back of the rig and loaded the remaining valises into the carriage compartment. They nodded to Jean-Louis and took up their positions on the back perches.

Jean-Louis closed the door. "Lady Gwyneth is hosting a welcome dinner for you tonight." He winked at the American before climbing up to the driver's seat.

Nate overheard Jean-Louis coax the team of horses to move slowly into the afternoon's traffic. *I wonder if she is still alone?* The Frenchman's wink said it all. *There are no secrets I can hide from him.* Nate marveled at the city as he passed by the familiar and the new. *I feel more at home here than I do in the land of my birth.*

***

Xie Xie

In the throngs of arrivals milling around the dock, one man stood out. Clad in all black, he embodied the image of someone The Pharaoh had warned her about: A clever adversary, not to be underestimated. She did not reveal herself, shielded behind a large man, who smelled of onions and garlic and worse, an unbathed mass of rancid flesh. It took all her resolve to not distance herself from him. *I would recognize the black-clad man again, but he must not see me.* She heard the man's voice. A trace of a French accent. *It must be him.* He directed another man—tall, light-brown-haired, and lanky—to a carriage with a crest. *The livery colors match the Ravenshire crest that The Pharaoh drew for me. But the other man doesn't match my image of the dark-haired earl. I wonder who that handsome man is. His accent isn't quite British, but he speaks English. American?*

She met with customs and arranged for storage of her trade goods in a locked and patrolled warehouse.

On the bright October day, Xie Xie waited as her luggage was loaded into a carriage, and then she departed for the most expensive hotel in London, Durrants.

***

Lord Ravenshire's Townhouse
The American

Henry bounded down the stairs to greet Nate with a bear hug. "You've arrived at an opportune time. Bri's Engagement Ball is at the end of the month and we have lots of things planned. Gwyneth is hosting a welcome dinner for you tonight. Old friends and new acquaintances."

They went up the stairs. "By the way, your uncle is quite well and Mrs. Wyndward is still as sharp as ever. Barryngton gave me a letter to give to you." Nate pulled a wax-sealed letter from his breast pocket. "Fairfax was in Philadelphia recently and sends his regards as well."

***

In the hours before the welcome dinner, Henry filled Nate in on recent events.

"I can't imagine the turmoil you, Charlotte and Taita must be experiencing."

"Charlotte will join us for dinner tonight. We've been spending time together again. It will never be as it once was, but she knows me better than anyone." He shook his head. "I am undone by events outside my control."

"A philosopher would say that your existence is defined by your reactions to events."

Henry shrugged. "I take life as it comes."

***

Nate rose to toast the other guests.

"Gio, as to your assertion that 'philosophy is the pastime of the indolent—' "

Gio interrupted. "I said '*Despite* the fact that philosophy is the pastime of the indolent, I've missed our debates over issues ancient and current."

"—intellectual discipline is not indolence."

"Sir John and the blond baron from university days bring back so many memories. Lady James and Lady Penelope, I regret to say that I am sworn to secrecy about many events of those days."

"Ah! Were they pranksters or studious? Daring or cautious? Challenging or obsequious? We shall never know." Gio drained his wine glass.

"As as professor, I tell my students that I ignore all interruptions. Charlotte, I look forward to visiting the foundling hospital. I admire your work on behalf of others."

"Bri, your independent spirit has survived our years apart intact, and Edward, you are to be commended for the challenge you've undertaken. Our Bri is a force of nature."

Edward laughed and squeezed Bri's hand.

"Aelwyn, Henry, Gwyneth, and I grew up together. You are more my family than the one I was born into. Ian, your resemblance to Rychard haunts me. How I miss him." He choked up for a moment, but regained his composure.

"I toast you: Friends forever!"

After everyone except Henry and Aelwyn left, Nate embraced each in turn. He lifted Ian up, and the boy said, "I've never met an American before."

Aelwyn took Ian upstairs to bed while Henry went out to the carriage to wait for Nate, leaving him alone with Gwyneth.

"I'm glad you'll be with us for your sabbatical."

"Time has not faded your loveliness, Wynnie. I hope we can spend time together. Perhaps you will visit me at Merton. I'm planning to come back to London every other week."

"I've missed you, Nate." She leaned forward and kissed his cheek.

It took all his self-control to refrain from taking her into his arms. "Goodnight, Wynnie."

"Goodnight."

Their eyes rested on each other for a long moment, and then Nate turned and walked outside to the waiting carriage. *Perhaps it is finally our time.*

***

Wednesday, October 2, 1811 – The Blue Bazaar
Mirela

After the Gypsy bid farewell to her last customer, Lash came through the curtain.

"Vano tells me you need a watcher."

"You? You being paid for a job not done."

"I was paid for the *risk*. Caló nearly killed me."

"Rumors we hearing say Caló will soon hanging for other murders. No mentioning of you."

Lash shrugged. "Caló was never a forward thinker. Sheriffs' deputies are not Roma marks. And I know how to disappear." *J-L warned me that she may try to touch me to steal my thoughts. I must keep my distance or fill my heart with hate to cover my true intentions.* He recalled the rage he felt as his head was being slashed. He felt the ire rise in his blood. *That should work. I can summon it at will.*

"But you were to killing the earl and his daughter. You failed."

"I survived. I know their defenses better now. Vano tells me that I am the only one who has *ever* returned from one of your adventures. The *only* one to get paid. The others died for no coin at all."

Mirela stared at the scarred man. "And?"

"And some might say that you *wanted* them dead after they accomplished their purposes."

"*Some* might. And you?"

Lash smiled. "I thrive on risk. When my time comes, it comes. But until it does, I will take your coin and do your bidding."

"No more killing for now. Watching only. I feeling eyes on me, so I need eyes on the eyes."

"So you want me always in the shadows watching over you?"

"At night, not during days. The eyes at night haunting me."

"Perhaps it is ghosts, the eyes of the dead."

"That is for you to telling me. What is your price?"

Lash gave her a number. "I want to be paid once a week in advance."

Mirela counted out the silver coins and handed them to Lash. "Agreed. You starting tonight."

***

Saturday, October 5, 1811 – Lord Ravenshire's Townhouse
Bri

Invitations to the Engagement Ball bearing seal of the Duke and Duchess of Pytchley arrived by messenger. The most sought-after ball invitation of the year featured calligraphy in scarlet ink. The top of the invitation featured an image of an icy comet streaking across the black sky, each deftly painted individually by Gio.

The honor of your presence is requested by

the Duke and Duchess of Pytchley at

an Engagement Ball

celebrating the engagement

of their granddaughter

Lady Gabriella Jane Craigfell Wyndward

to

Mr. Edward John Ashton James

on the Twenty-Sixth of October 1811

at eight o'clock p.m. at Pytchley Palace.

Preferred attire: a mask, gown or costume

designed to emulate the Great Comet of 1811

Note: No white gowns are permitted.

RSVP by the Twelfth of October

Eighteen Hundred Eleven.

The RSVP offered unmarried guests the option of bringing a companion.

Bri's heart fluttered as she read it. *It's real.*

***

Sunday, October 6, 1811 – Lord Ravenshire's Townhouse
Bri

A fierce thunderstorm roused Bri in the middle of the night. She huddled with Spotty and Monkey until the thunder ebbed and they were able to fall back asleep. Vivid dreams vanished upon awakening.

After breakfast, she and Nate walked down to the garden gazebo.

Nashmir explained the varieties of herbs, vegetables and fruits that he cultivated. In one area, he also nurtured flowering plants and orchids.

"This is serene and beautiful." Nate looked around. "Even more inspiring than I remembered."

Bri agreed. "I love coming here. The energy emanating from living plants gives me hope."

The Tibetan nodded. "The cycle of life is one of renewal. If you will excuse me, I have an engagement at the foundling hospital."

After Nashmir left, Bri said, "I'm glad you will be here for the Engagement Ball. You remember Grandmother's love of costumes and themes."

"Who wouldn't?" Nate laughed. "Jamesey's son seems up to the challenge of marrying a strong-willed woman."

"Not at first. Others saw it, but I didn't. Still, I have occasional bouts of doubt. Father and Charlotte, my grandfather and the nanny, one of Edward's friends...can any man be trusted?"

"We are all subject to temptation. You may look at another man sometime and wonder if he might be a better companion. Most people have 'occasional bouts of doubt.' Temptation is not inherently evil. Hurting another person with intent is evil."

Bri frowned. "One of Edward's friends said that infatuation was normal for any man at any age. But infatuation leads to infidelity, does it not?"

"So is your solution to never marry so that you can never be hurt by infatuation or infidelity?"

"I don't know what to think. Events are proceeding apace. Everyone wants me to set a date. I don't know why I feel this trepidation. Is it fear? Is it premonition?"

"It's normal when on the cusp of a major life change." Nate glanced over at the orchids. "I missed a chance for happiness once. We both hesitated. I moved on, married someone else, had a family, but they were taken from me by pestilence. I have many regrets. Follow your heart, not your fears."

Bri sighed. "I know you're right. No one can predict the future."

At the same time, they both said, "Except Jean-Louis."

Nate's tone became wistful. "I have my teaching, my writing, but I miss the easy comfort of a companion."

Bri brightened. "I can solve that! Come with me." She led him to the stables where Chérie and Hector tended their newborn pups. "We have a couple that are not yet promised. These little white balls will soon have spots. Their eyes haven't opened yet. Which would you prefer, male or female?"

"Female."

"Done." Bri found a piece of chalk and marked "N" on the undesignated female pup. She turned to the groom. "Please tell Jean-Louis that this one is for Professor Parker."

CHAPTER FORTY-TWO

Tuesday, October 8, 1811 – Riding along Rotten Row
Bri

Bri invited Nate to join her riding with Oliver and Gwyneth.

Oliver and Bri talked while Gwyneth and Nate raced.

"Am I rushing into marriage, Uncle Oliver?"

"Nonsense. You two are the envy of the *ton*. 'Beauty and the Banker,' they're calling you." He directed his gaze toward the racers. "Nate and Wynnie were close before she married my cousin Jamie. Though a charmer, underneath his veneer of affability, Jamie was a boor. He bullied me as a child. Vincent protected me from him, put Jamie in his place. But Jamie was fair of face and beguiled Wynnie."

Turning back to Bri, he added, "I believe Nate is still in love with her."

***

Thursday, October 10, 1811 – Bodleian Library, Oxford
The American

Henry put a carriage and driver at Nate's disposal to transport him between Oxford and London. After a week or so adjusting to the city, Nate traveled to Oxford for a couple of days to get settled into a small Merton College office and arrange for the lease of a small house among those that were kept for visiting faculty. When that was accomplished, he headed to the Bodleian Library.

Smiled as he navigated the familiar maze of stacks, he arrived at the rare books section that housed obscure works of philosophy.

Bent over a desk sat Philip Laurence, tutor to Henry, Gwyneth, Nate, Aelwyn, Rychard and Bri. Laurence appeared to be deeply absorbed in a large volume, scratching notes as he read.

Nate sat down, opened his portfolio of papers, and waited for Laurence to notice him.

After about half an hour, Laurence broke his concentration, took off his spectacles and rubbed his eyes. He stared at the man across from him, squinted, and then put his spectacles back on. A broad smile grew as he recognized his former student.

"The American has returned. Welcome!"

Nate rose, walked around the table to embrace Laurence. His tutor's once-firm shoulder bones felt fragile. *I dare not squeeze too brusquely.* He went back to his chair.

The tutor smiled. "I knew you'd be arriving soon. Good timing to arrive for Bri's Engagement Ball. Have you a costume?"

"Henry took me to his hatter, who is fashioning a mask or headdress of some sort. I'm game."

"The duchess told me that she would have a mask waiting for me. A surprise I dare not refuse. She knows I tend to forget dates, so she is sending one of her carriages to collect me."

"She bends Nature to her will. There is a lot of the duchess's personality in Bri. Her fiancé seems a decent sort, more daring than Sir John at his age."

"The younger James is a good match for Bri. The elder James had a domineering father who never let mores, norms or honor impede his will. He was a member of—"

"Of what?"

"To this day, I doubt that Sir John knows, so I must rely on your discretion. Forgive an old man's predilection to reveal his discoveries prematurely. 'Tis not gossip. In my research of the youth of the 10th Earl for my history of the Wyndward family, Henry gave me access to his library at Ravenshire. Behind some of the thousands of volumes there, I found the 10th Earl's hidden diaries. One entry detailed a visit to a notorious Hell-Fire Club with Sir John's father, Sir Balthazar."

Nate interrupted. "I thought the Hell-Fire Club was shut down in the 17th century."

"The original was disbanded. But other secret diabolical cults were begun where rites of paganism, debauchery, devil worship, blasphemy, wenching and worse were practiced, often in former monasteries. The existence of these clubs was kept hidden, guarded jealously by its high-ranking founders. Its membership rosters were burned, so the only remaining evidence is in letters between members and diaries. Sir John knew some of his father's misdeeds, but not all."

"That sounds like something no son would want to know about his father. In truth, Sir Balthazar's manner was forbidding and his gaze withering."

"This incident happened after the nanny had disappeared. After that episode, the 10th Earl began to wonder what else he might not know about Sir Balthazar's methods. He began to doubt a man he had considered a friend. It disturbed him greatly." Laurence removed his spectacles. "But let's speak of other things. This library never changes, does it?" He gestured with a wave toward the massive accumulation of volumes that surrounded them. "I never tire of this repository of knowledge." Tilting his head toward Nate, Laurence paused. "I assume you've seen her."

Nate nodded. "I have hope. I haven't told her, or anyone else, but I am considering negotiating a permanent position at Merton. I should have done it years ago. Then, perhaps—"

Laurence held up his blue-veined liver-spotted hands. "No 'perhaps' this time, Parker. You must seize your destiny. Don't let it slip from your grasp again. Hesitate no longer. 'Tis long past time to act."

The American's face displayed a wry grin. "I know."

"Now, tell me about the book you intend to write during your sabbatical."

***

Saturday, October 12, 1811 – The Streets of London
Aneira

Aneira explored the neighborhood around the restaurant, going into nearby shops and handing out a printed menu with the projected opening date. She had purposely picked a location near a concentration of ladies shops, art galleries and gift emporiums.

She entered an optician's storefront and scanned a selection of tinted spectacles.

The proprietor walked over to her. "These are quite the rage lately. Venetian glass shields the eyes from the sun, or reflections from water or snow. Their use among Society types is not to protect eyes from the sun—not in our foggy city—but these spectacles convey a Continental flair."

"How do you get them from the Continent when there's a blockade?"

"Madame, an inconvenient question. Forbidden items command a premium price. Whether to fulfill a Society woman's desire to appear *au courant* or a dandy's foppish affectation, it's a popular item."

Aneira handed him the menu and explained about her restaurant.

She pointed to a pair of spectacles with dark gray lenses. "I'd like these."

Looking at her look at herself in the mirror, the proprietor frowned. "Perhaps a lighter color lens would be preferable, Madame. This dark shade obscures the lovely unusual color of your eyes."

"My eyes are highly sensitive to light." Aneira lied with a casual ease.

"As you wish. Let me give you a box to store them in at night." He went to the back to retrieve a box and some tissue paper. He placed them in a bag imprinted with the shop name: Joshua Green, Optician. He quoted her the price.

Aneira raised her eyebrows as she opened her purse. "A premium price, indeed." She took a final glance at herself in the shop mirror. *My eyes look gray. Perfect.*

"I hope to see you at my omelet and tea café, Mr. Green."

"I promise to visit you, Mme. d'Aix."

***

Monday, October 14, 1811 – Durrants Hotel
Xie Xie

Xie Xie spent her first weeks in London getting her bearings. Her first request of the hotel concierge was a list of Society dressmakers.

When Xie Xie arrived at Mrs. Watson's, the other patrons stopped speaking when she entered.

Mrs. Watson drew herself up to her full, towering height. "The help goes to the back to pick up their mistresses' packages."

"I am not 'the help.' I came here upon a favorable recommendation that this establishment could provide me with an appropriate wardrobe. My intention is to make purchases here for myself." Xie Xie maintained direct eye contact with the seamstress.

The other patrons looked to Mrs. Watson.

"I don't believe we have anything in our shop that will fit you."

Pausing for a moment for effect, Xie Xie nodded. "I will remember this, Mrs. Watson. You may regret mistreating me."

One patron was taken aback. "Mistreatment? Good Heavens! You are from a mongrel race."

"I believe you mean the Mongol race. We predate your civilization by thousands of years and will exist long after yours is dust." She turned on her heel and left.

Once back in the carriage, Xie Xie admonished herself. *The Pharaoh warned me to use letters of introduction. Rashness imperils my mission. Perhaps the atelier of the notorious Mlle. Bellerobe referenced in the gossip rags I've seen will be more accepting of me. If not, then I will prevail upon someone to accompany me.*

She rapped on the side of the carriage to alert the driver to pull over. She opened the door so the driver could hear her. "Take me to Mlle. Bellerobe's on Portobello Road." She closed the door.

The driver looked back at her, nodded, and coaxed the horses back into the traffic.

The atelier's doorman welcomed her when she arrived at Mlle. Bellerobe's. *This is an improvement.*

After Xie Xie introduced herself, Mlle. Bellerobe welcomed her new client without reservation. "You are more petite than most English women, but we can make adjustments to all of our garments, Miss Li. After all, we are professionals. I always have some samples and some garments clients outgrew before they were delivered, victims of overly-generous portions of sweets."

Xie Xie found several dresses and even a riding outfit that needed little tailoring because it had been ordered for a young girl, tall for her age, but slim. Pleased with her options, she made arrangements for the tailored items to be delivered to her at Durrants. Three other outfits and a cloak were wrapped up for her to take.

"If I might suggest, Mlle. Bellerobe, my family has connections in China, and I have some bolts of silk that you might find interesting. The colors are vibrant and would fit the other offerings of your atelier."

"Ah, Miss Li. You, like me, are a woman of commerce. We understand each other. Bring some samples by next week. Wednesday mornings are reserved for visits with vendors."

"I will call on you the day after tomorrow, then. Good day to you, Mlle. Bellerobe."

"And to you, Miss Li." Mlle. Bellerobe bowed her head slightly in farewell.

The doorman signaled a Hackney for Xie Xie.

After dropping off packages at Durrants, Xie Xie told the cabbie, "Take me to the Asian quarter in the East End."

Xie Xie walked through the area. She was buoyed by the surge of energy of new arrivals. She went back each day for a few hours, to boost her spirits, trying different restaurants, eating food she'd not eaten since her childhood. In truth, the poverty of her early years meant food was rice cakes and vegetables, but she rediscovered the old flavors kindled by the immigrant chefs of the East End.

On her third day, she was startled to hear her own mountain province's dialect spoken. *It's been so long since I've heard it. All my family was killed by the brothel procurers.*

On one walk, an elderly Asian woman pulled on her arm as she approached her destination, *Dreamtime.* "Don't go down that street. Evil is there. The poppy rules. Opium dens of iniquity lie there."

Xie Xie thanked her, walked in another direction, then circled back. She knew that The Pharaoh had acquired an interest in *Dreamtime* before he'd left London as a way to amass funds that he could easily access when he returned. Xie Xie entered *Dreamtime* and gave the manager the code word from The Pharaoh. He gave her a tour of the notorious destination. Part opium den, part brothel, part gaming hell, she saw *Dreamtime* as the perfect lure for the curious denizens of the *ton*, young men with money, no responsibilities and a predilection to dangerous diversions. *Neri's revelation just before I left Alexandria matches a site of temptation within my control.*

***

Thursday, October 17, 1811 – Palace of Westminster
Xie Xie

Some days Xie Xie acted as a typical London tourist, marveling at the city's cathedrals, and Buckingham Palace.

This day she visited the Palace of Westminster where the Houses of Parliament convened. She walked into the courtyard of that deserted edifice and looked up toward its gothic flourishes. She was startled when a voice behind her said, "It was built in 1016, before the Norman Invasion. We've known how to build castles from time immemorial."

The Pharaoh's apprentice turned to see a distinguished man she judged to be around fifty. With graying hair, still full on his patrician head, the well-dressed gentleman exuded confidence. *A politician?*

"May I introduce myself? I am Aristotle Drummond. I work in this building. Parliament is out of session for the balance of the year, but my work never ends."

The one The Pharaoh said the earl calls his "Nemesis?" This is a piece of good fortune. From what I've read in the gossip rags, Drummond is said to be well-connected. "I am Miss Xie Xie Li, recently arrived from Egypt to establish an investment company in London. I am originally from China."

"You speak flawless English, Miss Li. Gigi is a French name, is it not?"

Smiling, Xie Xie shook her head. "It has a similar sound, but my name is Romanized to 'X-i-e' repeated twice. Two words like your British nickname, 'Mary Lou.' " Drummond shrugged. "A natural mistake for a Westerner like me. Tell me, Miss Li, what other languages do you speak besides English and Chinese?"

Again, Xie Xie smiled. "There is no *one* Chinese language, Mr. Drummond. The dominant ones are Mandarin and Cantonese, or Yue, but there are several others in different regions of the country. To answer your earlier question, in addition to English, Mandarin, and Cantonese, I speak French and Arabic."

"You sound like a Renaissance woman."

"One only hears adulation of 'the Renaissance man.' "

"I am not 'one.' "

"Just who are you then, sir?"

"I am a man who helps people get elected to public office. And I am a man who would like to invite you to lunch to welcome you as a visitor to my country." He bowed his head slightly. "We can meet at a public restaurant, so that the other patrons are, in fact, our chaperones. That way, we can avoid any appearance of impropriety."

"You are the expert in protocol, Mr. Drummond, not I. Where do you suggest we meet?"

"Chez Michel is a place you should see. It is very popular among the upper class."

"Very well. At what time?"

"One p.m."

"Agreed. Now, can you tell me more about this magnificent building?"

***

Thursday, October 17, 1811 – *Omelettes de Mme. d'Aix*

Vaux

Vaux and Rachel arrived at the new tea café to meet with the proprietress to review the final design touches. They ducked under scaffolding holding painters working on the outside of the building and lettering the sign. Inside, the framing and flooring were complete. A tea bar had been framed in, and the kitchen cupboards and ovens awaited final installation and testing.

Their delivery men brought in two small bistro tables and chairs for the proprietress, Aneira d'Aix, to approve. In the meantime, they would serve as work areas for small progress meetings.

The only window was in the front of the space but Vaux had obtained city permission to carve porthole-like windows on the wall facing an alley—windows large enough to let light flow in, but not low enough to reveal the ordinary brick and stone walls of the adjacent building.

Vaux laid out the sketches on the tea bar. He and Rachel had collaborated on the color scheme. She had chosen the fabric samples and he had designed or procured the furniture.

Aneira examined the sketches, nodding her approval. "The design is lovely, just as I'd imagined. The kitchen is large with several ovens, as I requested. I once dealt in antiques, so I can appreciate the quality of your furniture selections. For my last years, I prefer to return to my first love, which is baking. Nothing energizes me more than working dough."

Vaux observed her hands. *Strong, callused. No soft Society creature, she.* "It's always gratifying to develop something that reflects your personality and preferences. This space will evoke a sense of warmth in the patrons, a haven of grace and peace." Her tinted spectacles shielded her eyes from him, so it was difficult to read her reaction. "Can you see through those dark lenses? They are *au courant.*" He pulled out his pair of blue-lensed spectacles and put them on. "I fancy myself a British version of a Spanish grandee. I crave stylishness."

Aneira adjusted the fit over the bridge of her nose. "These serve my purposes."

Rachel lifted the samples to catch the light. "Do these meet with your approval?"

Aneira touched them and matched them to their usage, according to the drawings. "You surprise me, Miss Turtin. I have rarely dealt with people who listened to me, anticipated my needs, and then delivered beyond my expectations."

Rachel beamed at the compliment, and Vaux gave Aneira a slight bow of his head in acknowledgment.

The upholsterer pulled out her installation list. "We are on time on all of our deadlines, so we should have all in place one week before your intended opening in September. As far as the extra items of décor, I have a glassblower who could make French blue glass vases for each table, and a florist who can deliver fresh flowers year round from their greenhouses. A spray of yellow and white would match the fabric choices. The rugs should be delivered in time. Is there anything I've forgotten, Lord Vaux?"

"*Lord* Vaux? You never told me—" Aneira stared at him.

Vaux shrugged. "I am a viscount who enjoys design. My family has large landholdings, and, to put it mildly, they're not thrilled that my interests tend toward the commercial aspects of interior design. I am not an artist in the classic sense, much to their chagrin."

"Then they are fools. The world is changing and those who do not change along with it will have a rude awakening. The life of an aristocracy devoted to leisure pursuits cannot last much longer.

Revolutions, wars and science are altering centuries of expectations. You are a visionary, Lord Vaux, in more ways than one. Hard work is not to be belittled."

"I appreciate your observations. To get back to Miss Turtin's question, I thought perhaps some paintings in these colors, scenes from the south of France—fields of lavender, views of St. Victoire, and seascapes of the Mediterranean coast might be appropriate. Many French artists fled here after Napoleon, and might be a good source."

Aneira looked around the room and pointed to her preferred locations. "Perhaps three—there, there and there." She looked at Vaux. "Is there room in the original sum I approved to acquire such artwork?"

"Yes."

"Then do it. Is there anything else?"

"Not today. We should meet again in two weeks to review our status. We are on time for your planned November opening in six weeks."

"I admire efficiency."

"We bid you a good day, Mme. d'Aix."

***

Mirela

As soon as Aneira's guests left, Mirela came downstairs from their flat above. "I have always admiring your confidence. You should being on the stage. You inhabiting your chosen role as if it being real."

Aneira swept her arm around the space. "This *is* real."

"Too real, perhaps."

"What is your meaning? Was something revealed by those devil's cards you turn?"

"For the moment, it being real." Mirela looked at the drawings and samples left by Vaux and Rachel. "If Blackie not living, would you abandoning revenge?"

"Never." A dark mask came over Aneira's face. "How could you think it?"

"Because in making this café, you having joy. You forgetting Blackie. Never having I seeing you in moments of peace as now in this place. Revenge is war."

"I have not abandoned my war against the Wyndwards. Hatred has kept me alive."

"You weakening."

"Never. You *failed* in your last attack against the earl. I listened to you. That was *my* failure. When Duff returns, his destiny will be fulfilled. All Wyndwards must die."

Mirela gazed at her friend. "Duff returning soon. The cards do not lie."

Aneira gathered up the drawings and fabric samples to take upstairs. "Betrayal invites death. Do not fail me again."

CHAPTER FORTY-THREE

Thursday, October 17, 1811 – The Streets of London
Xie Xie

After she bid Mr. Drummond *adieu*, Xie Xie told the cabbie to drive her by the major buildings in London to pass the time before their luncheon appointment.

Her mind whirled. *In my dreams, I never imagined this jarring juxtaposition of filth and the sublime.* The splendor of the architecture of the soaring spaces of worship contrasted with the abject poverty of the average person on the streets. Beggars accosted her. Elderly women sold bird feed for pennies, while young women seeking alms carried near-starving babies. *The wealthy must practice a studied disregard for the welfare of others.* A devotée of Buddhism, the mysteries and contradictions of western religion confused Xie Xie. *The Pharaoh was right – there is no concern for the poor. Money and breeding rule all.*

At the appointed hour, she arrived for lunch at Chez Michel, where Drummond waved her over to his table. An elderly Asian woman sat next to him. He stood to greet her.

"Miss Li, this is Mme. Zhang, who will serve as a chaperone for our luncheon. I mentioned to you, an unmarried woman should not be seen with a man in public without a chaperone."

She bowed her head slightly. "Your culture is unfamiliar to me. My elderly aunt could not accompany me today. Now that I am aware of your customs, I will arrange to have her with me for future meetings. I appreciate your concern for my reputation, although I am in London solely for the purpose of commerce."

Mme. Zhang smiled. "Few women in London are in commerce, Miss Li. Men here are unused to our affinity for dealing."*She speaks with an accent from my province.* A tinge of fear crept up Xie Xie's throat. *The name Zhang is infamous there. She couldn't possibly know my secret.*

Without betraying her thoughts, Xie Xie smiled. "I am simply here for a few months to open up markets for my clients' exports, Mme. Zhang. By the way, Mr. Drummond, I have some Egyptian antiquities I would like to offer to the British Museum as a gift from one of my clients who is a collector. Could you make an introduction?"

Drummond leaned back in his chair and waited for the pre-ordered luncheon platters to be placed in front of them. "I took the liberty of asking Michel to make selections for us. I hope you ladies enjoy his specialties." After they were served, he directed his gaze to Miss Li. "I would be delighted to introduce you to the director of the British Museum. He is a personal friend."

"Our meeting was Fate, perhaps, Mr. Drummond."

"Surely, Miss Li, you know that Fate, *Ming*, is only one of five major influences, although it is the most important. Perhaps you could enlighten Mr. Drummond about the other four factors."

She challenges me. A test suggested, no doubt, by Drummond. Xie Xie smiled. "Luck, *Yun*, is more than a random event, of course. Environment, *Feng Shui*, is respecting the directions of energy patterns and adapting to them. Character, *Dao De*, derives from moral virtue. And Effort, *Du Shu*, is preparation, education and application until the moment presents itself."

"You express the truths of a thousand years," said Drummond.

"Five thousand years." Miss Li bowed her head as she corrected him. "You, Mr. Drummond, are the ideal host for a newcomer to London."

"Miss Li, I would like to introduce you to the *crème de la crème* of the *ton*."

" 'Ton'?"

" 'Tis what we call upper crust Society. There is an Engagement Ball for Lady Gabriella Wyndward and Edward James to which I am invited and may bring a guest. At such an event, chaperones are not needed."

This is the perfect entrée to implement The Pharaoh's plan. "I would be delighted to accept."

"Excellent, as Lady Gabriella's father would say. The date is October 26th. You will need a mask and a gown in keeping with the theme commemorating the Great Comet of 1811. I can give you the names of seamstresses, if you wish."

"The concierge at Durrants has already done so." An expert at reading the reactions of others, Xie Xie's eyes scanned Drummond's face. *I passed the test.*

***

After lunch, Xie Xie hailed another Hackney and directed the jervie to go to the Asian quarter. *I must find an elderly woman who speaks no English to pose as my aunt.* At *Dreamtime*, a worker accepted her offer. "My auntie can be your chaperone."

The aunt spoke only Mandarin, no English. She agreed to act as Xie Xie's chaperone for the next few months. *I must appear legitimate as I pursue commercial connection.* Xie Xie instructed, in Mandarin, "Be as a shadow on the wall.

"Your name will be Li Ling Ling, or as they say here, Ling Ling Li." Xie Xie bought Ling Ling a wardrobe of appropriate Chinese silk clothing and installed her in an adjacent room in her hotel.

Ling Ling thanked her effusively.

The woman followed Xie Xie like a puppy.

In a city where chaperones are expected, her presence will be useful.

***

Friday, October 18, 1811 – The Streets of London
Bri

Bri exited a bookseller's shop and ran into Lady Patricia coming out of an apothecary. They walked in the same direction and nearly bumped into Viscount Vaux leaving a tailor's shop.

"Here we are and it's time for tea," said Vaux. "I know a little place around the corner. *Thés du Monde.* It's a little hole-in-the-wall, but quaintly decorated. Next month a new omelet parlor is opening, *Omelettes de Mme. d'Aix.* Miss Turtin and I worked on that project."

"You are in danger of becoming too commercial, Vaux." Lady Patricia recoiled at the thought.

"No need to be so disdainful, Lady Patricia. It keeps me out of the gaming hells."

Once they were seated in the café, and ordered, Lady Patricia brought the conversation back to a topic of her interest. "Tell me about the gaming hells. Does Mr. Rogers frequent such places?"

"Ah, so the daredevil entices you." Vaux smirked. "He's a confirmed bachelor, he claims."

Bri shrugged. "He is rakishly attractive. Something about the bad boy image calls for the hand of a strong woman."

Vaux shook his head. "No, no, no! Why don't you women understand that you cannot remake men into obedient pets? You must accept men as they present themselves. Believing that you can change a man is a fool's errand. You can nudge him a bit. No more."

"I disagree. Edward has changed." Bri sipped her tea.

"A bit. And so have you." said Vaux. "Incremental change is made by each partner. You keep working at it."

Lady Patricia looked puzzled. "You think love requires *work*?"

Vaux scoffed. "Love isn't something you check off your list and forget about."

Bri wrinkled her brow. "What do you mean? It's quite simple. One meets someone, falls in love, and that's it."

"For life? Hasn't Charlotte's experience taught you anything? Your own father can't decide which woman he loves. What if another woman came between you and Edward?"

Bri's heart clutched.

Lady Patricia shook her head. "Men are fickle. The mere glimpse of an ankle or an inheritance can captivate them."

"An ankle? An ankle could turn a man from his wife?" Bri stared at Vaux.

Vaux shook his head. "It takes a bit more than that—for most men."

Surely Edward would not be fickle. "I'm on my way to the foundling hospital." She waved goodbye to her friends and signaled Jean-Louis.

Holding the door, Jean-Louis read Bri's mood.. "What's wrong?"

"Men."

The Frenchman raised an eyebrow and waited.

"Are men really seduced by the glimpse of an ankle?"

"Not often."

"How could that *ever* be possible? 'Not often.' You are exasperating." Bri climbed into the carriage.

"Most men are driven by baser instincts than most women."

"Most women have no idea what men's lives are like outside the home." Bri sat back in her seat and then leaned forward again. "Do men look at me that way?"

"What way?"

"As if I am a prize pig at a county fair."

"The loveliest pig of all."

"You are not easing my mind. Please take me to Charlotte's."

Jean-Louis gauged the sun's position. "At this hour, she may still be at the foundling hospital. We'll try that first."

Inside, Bri's thoughts flashed in rapid succession. *I thought I could marry and continue to be myself. How much must I change? Can I trust Edward? What if there is a woman from Asia who lurks in Edward's heart as Taita holds sway in Father's? What if I am thrown over as Charlotte was? She is forgiving. I don't think I would ever be so accommodating.* Exiting her carriage at Winters Foundling Hospital. Bri found Charlotte in the reception area.

"I must talk with you. Now."

Charlotte put her hand on Bri's shoulder. "I see you are upset. I was just leaving. Come home with me for dinner and we can talk as long as you like. Is Jean-Louis outside?"

"Yes."

"Good. I took a Hackney this morning because my carriage wheel broke in a rut."

Jean-Louis took them to Charlotte's, where Chérie bounded up the steps, hoping for a bone from Mrs. Holdart.

Morgan was nonplussed, but the cook's voice came from the kitchen. "There's always a bone for you, Chérie."

Bri smiled. "Soon you'll have a pal to play with, Chérie, when the pups are weaned."

The butler said, "Dinner will be served shortly, Baroness."

"Come into the kitchen with Chérie, Jean-Louis. There's plenty for you."

"Let's have a sherry in the parlor while dinner is prepared."

The butler poured their drinks and left the room.

The parlor reflected Charlotte's refined taste. Pale yellow silk wall coverings and drapes framed flowered chintz-covered settees and chairs. Bri glanced around the space. "I love this room. It's like a garden of fabrics. The fresh flowers on the table—are they from the greenhouse Nashmir built in back of your townhouse?"

"Yes. 'Tis a joy to have fresh flowers year-round, especially as fall descends and my roses go dormant." Charlotte reached for Bri's hand. "Tell me what's bothering you."

"Today I ran into Lady Patricia and Vaux. We had tea and they both think men are subject to seduction by the 'glimpse of an ankle.' That can't be true, can it? Can I trust Edward?"

Charlotte nodded. "I understand. Your Engagement Ball is imminent and the prospect of marriage is no longer far off in the future. You are used to being in control, and love turns control upside down. Remember that boy you met at the riding master's? He disappointed you, hurt you by flirting with another girl. You swore off men, breaking the hearts of many country beaux until Gwyneth and Henry persuaded you to attend the Marriage Season."

"Forced is a better description."

"Yet in Edward you found common interests and let yourself care. Witnessing the end of the love your father and I had for so long has affected you. Uncertainty is a challenge. The truth is we tell ourselves we are in control, but all we can really control is our own attitudes and reactions to events."

"What if—"

"There are an infinite number of 'what ifs' in a day. What if Edward hurts you? He will. And you will hurt him. Not intentionally, perhaps, but human emotions are fragile. A deep bond takes time to build. Can Henry and I ever regain what we had if Taita is out of the picture? I don't know. But I have to go forward, one footstep at a time. So must you. You are still in the throes of early romance. Edward is a good man. But you approached the Marriage Season more as a task to complete on a list of things to do than—"

"Than what? Finding a suitable mate? That's what the Marriage Season is all about. Clarissa and Vaux say I've checked finding a mate off a list, just as you are saying. Am I as mechanical as the machines that displace workers? Am I mistaking the convenience of social acceptance with deeper connection? Is it all superficial, shallow, meaningless?"

"You're looking at this as a transaction to analyze in order to avoid your feelings. Pent up feelings. If these feelings are ever piqued by jealousy, you may not recognize yourself."

Bri scoffed. "I am not one of those women who pine over men who have spurned them. I would never tolerate such self-pity."

"You can say that, but in that moment, feelings may overwhelm you."

"Intellect is more powerful than emotion."

"Dearest Bri, you have a lot to learn. Emotions make us human."

***

Saturday, October 19, 1811 – Mlle. Bellerobe's Atelier

Bri

Mlle. Bellerobe greeted her most illustrious client. "Lady Gabriella, your dress is ready for the final fitting."

"Before we do that, I would like to order another classic riding habit, but it should be a costume to make me look as if I were a male. In fact, add a groom's breeches and jacket to that order. And a hat to hide my hair, as if I wanted to disguise myself. It's for a costume party." *Perhaps I shall be like Jean-Louis and track Edward to be certain of his fidelity.*

"I am at your service, Lady Gabriella." The seamstress snapped her fingers. "Anne-Marie, bring Lady Gabriella's engagement gown and mask." Glancing back at Bri, she said, "It's exquisite, if I do say so myself."

CHAPTER FORTY-FOUR

Saturday, October 26, 1811 – Engagement Ball at Pytchley Palace
Vanessa

A steady line of carriages arrived at Pytchley Palace for the ball. After showing invitations and being announced, guests moved through the receiving line. Greeted by the duchess, resplendent in a midnight blue velvet dress sparkling with Austrian crystals and a matching velvet mask featuring falling stars fashioned of white silk on the ends of braided white silk cords, she passed them to the duke.

The duke sported a black mask with a white painted stylized comet, created by Gio. He passed the guests to Gwyneth, who shimmered in a silver silk dress with a comet embroidered in white silk thread. Pearls were interspersed in the design and on her silver mask.

After his sister, the Earl of Ravenshire greeted guests in a mask of white with a small papier maché comet mounted to one side.

Next to Henry was Bri, who looked breathtaking in a white brocade empire-top bodice, with one chiffon puffed sleeve with a self-ruffle, matched by ruffles of chiffon sweeping over the skirt on a diagonal to simulate the path of the comet with Austrian crystals in the tail. Tiny tulle stars embedded at random punctuated the design. Her auburn locks were pulled into a topknot, with one side set free in a long pony tail trailing feathers on one side of her sparkling white mask, evoking an image of a comet's tail falling over one bare shoulder. As was the custom, her long white gloves rose above her elbows.

Edward's mask, jacket and breeches were also white. Next to him, his mother, Lady James, wore a simple pink mask with the same feather flourish that others sported on one side to look like a comet's tail, greeted guests and passed them to Sir John, the last in the receiving line. His attire, all in shades of gray, was topped by a mask with a falling star on one side.

Vanessa drew on her considerable guile to welcome Drummond. "Tottie, I'm glad you could come. All in black...?"

"I represent the vastness of space, the firmament on which the stars sparkle."

"Poetic, Tottie. And who is this lovely guest of yours?"

"May I present Miss Xie Xie Li, originally from China but recently arrived from Egypt."

She is elegant and extremely beautiful. "A stunning dress, Miss Li." *She is one who aims to outshine the guest of honor, but Bri holds her own. This woman may be a dangerous adversary and formidable opponent.*

Xie Xie's black dress with an empire bodice fit close to her body, contrasting with the looser styles of the other ladies. Attached to the black silk were white silk appliquéd stars in a random diagonal pattern that extended down one side. Her mask was painted a glossy red and sported one long red feather on the side, a typical design feature oft-repeated that evening.

***

Xie Xie

Drummond spoke with perfunctory cordiality to Henry, introducing Miss Li.

The earl is a handsome man.

Xie Xie flashed a brilliant smile. "I am honored to be here, Lord Ravenshire."

"You are a lovely surprise to see on Tottie's arm, Miss Li. May I introduce my daughter, Lady Gabriella?"

"Miss Li, it's a pleasure to meet you. This is Edward James, my fiancé."

Another attractive gentleman. Soon he will be under my control.

Once through the receiving line, Drummond leaned over to whisper in Xie Xie's ear. "Attending one of the duchess's balls is the *ne plus ultra* of Society. The Duchess of Pytchley is renowned for her parties and frankly, rivals the Prince Regent in glamour. You may never have an experience such as this again. 'Tis a once-in-a-lifetime ball."

"You have given me insight I could not have imagined." *The Pharaoh would know this life. I have now met his brother, his sister, Mr. James and Lady Gabriella. How long I have imagined these people! The Master's plan is flawless. Lady Gabriella is beautiful but jealousy lies within the heart of every woman. Men are easily manipulated, and Mr. James will be no exception.*

***

Drummond

As the first to introduce the waltz to the *ton*, it was no surprise that the duchess chose a waltz as the first solo dance of the engaged couple. Others were invited to the dance floor, by tradition, after the duke and duchess joined the engaged couple.

Drummond whispered to Miss Li. "It is a difficult step to learn. We can wait it out."

"Do you not know the waltz, Mr. Drummond? I'm adept at its intricacies."

The political manipulator bowed, put his arm around Xie Xie's waist, extended his hand to take hers and swept her onto the dance floor. *Miss Li is more than I expected.*

An accomplished dancer, Drummond guided Miss Li expertly around the wide dance floor.

She matched him step for step. Guests gasped at her long black gloves.

Tottie gave himself silent advice. *En garde, Tottie. 'Tis not often you are astonished.*

The other guests turned their head as the couple in black paced the couple in white.

Drummond was unaccustomed to being the center of attention. Self-relegated to the shadows, he reveled in pulling unseen strings. Tonight, this brief moment of sustained focus on his performance of the quick steps of the waltz with an exotically beautiful woman energized him. *How would I wield a weapon like Miss Li?* He glanced around the room as his feet kept to the beat of the orchestra. *There is much hidden in my guest. Did she know who I was before she met me? Who is her target?*

***

Bri

Bri and Edward moved through the guests between dances, greeting friends and overhearing the stray comment.

Gio wore a red mask with the same stylized white comet that he'd fashioned for the duke. "I am Mars watching the comet pass by on its celestial journey."

***

Lady Patricia

Lady Patricia's dress featured a dark navy empire bodice on her ample bosom, with a skirt fading in ombré shades from dark to light leading to a white tulle comet tail.

Rogers edged by her. "Watch that tail, Lady Patricia. Someone might trip, causing *Scandal & Shame* to accuse you of attempted murder."

She paled. *Does he know my secret?*

"I say, who is the woman in the red mask?"

***

Durwood

"Vaux, the rings of Saturn on that headdress do not flatter you."

"That's because you couldn't pull off such a dashing look, Durwood." Vaux put his arm around Durwood's shoulder. "Glad to see you out and about."

Durwood wore a mask like the cup of the Big Dipper with an upward tilting *papier maché* stick to one side simulating the handle. He needed a cane to hobble around, unable to dance yet.

"I think Saturn trumps the Big Dipper, Durwood." Vaux assumed a faux boxer's stance.

Lady Rose's mask had a similar style, with Polaris on the end of a stick wrapped with dark blue ribbon, simulating the night sky. Like Lady Clarissa, she flaunted the norms of Society by appearing in public while obviously with child. "Dealing with you two prepares me for the future."

Khan and Lady Alice came over.

Vaux nearly choked when he saw them.

Each featured six symbols of the twelve signs of the zodiac painted on their oversized masks.

After they were out of earshot, Vaux said, "I'd make you promise that you will never let me look so ridiculous, but I suppose we should all look in the mirror."

***

Vanessa

Between dinner and dessert, Vanessa announced a musical interlude. "As a surprise for the engaged couple, Mr. Banfield has composed an aria about love for his upcoming opera, *The Nymphs*, and Lady Clarissa will sing it for us tonight."

Banfield wore a yellow mask with *papier maché* spikes simulating the sun with a comet tail to one side. He took his seat on the bench at the fortepiano.

Clarissa, dressed in a blue moiré dress with Austrian crystals placed like stars as well as concentration of crystals on her mask to simulate the comet, sang her first note. The lilting tones of her high soprano voice reverberated in the ballroom and transfixed the crowd.

Vanessa noticed a tear in Bri's eye. *Music touches the soul.*

***

Bri

After dessert, the dances began again, while many went out to the verandah to view the heavens through the cometseekers.

Edward and Bri walked over to greet Oliver, Lady Abigail, Aelwyn, Nate and Charlotte.

Oliver wore a blue-green headdress with a painted comet traversing the planet.

Edward was puzzled. "Who are you summoning, Darlemont?"

"The spirit of Neptune."

Aelwyn wore a pale turquoise gown with a matching mask draped with white feathers.

"The ocean, I presume," said Edward.

Nate's mask was orangey-red with a maroon-hued spot painted over one eye. He pointed to his mask. "To quell your curiosity—Jupiter."

Charlotte's dress of blue and green chiffon ombré was stunning. Her mask used the same colors, with peacock feathers falling to one side as the comet's tail.

"Let me guess," said Edward. "Earth?"

Charlotte curtsied in acknowledgment.

"Tonight you are consort to a princess, James." Oliver took a sip of Champagne. "I know my niece won't let it go to your head." He turned to Bri and kissed her on the cheek. "You look exquisite tonight. I've never seen you lovelier."

Bri blushed. "Thank you, Uncle. This is a delightful evening. I must admit, I wasn't certain I would feel as comfortable as I do."

Lady Abigail was in a dark blue dress with a white tulle ruffle down the back.

As Bri and Edward moved toward the dance floor when Vanessa announced the final dance, Bri overhead someone speaking of Lady Abigail.

"Did anyone not warn her she looks like a skunk?" Muffled laughter accompanied the comment.

They passed by Baron Beauchamp, who wore a light gray mask painted like the man in the moon, and Lady Penelope. The embroidery on her pale gray dress depicted a matching image of the enigmatic lunar face.

The baron's sister, Davinia, wore a dress with a crimson brocade top and a skirt with appliquéd stars, while her son, the Phaeton racer, sported a mask in the shape of a racing rig.

***

Vanessa

After the final dance, Vanessa signaled to the orchestra to cease playing. She walked over to Bri and Edward. Raising her hands to gain the attention of the assembled guests, she waited.

The room fell into silence.

"The last toast of the evening is mine. May the Great Comet of 1811 traversing the heavens above be an omen of peace and love for the life on which Gabriella and Edward are about to embark."

She raised her glass. "To peace and love!"

Edward and Bri kissed.

The crowd echoed, "To peace and love!"

***

Bri

With energies still high, Bri and Edward climbed into Edward's carriage. As François closed the door, Edward said, "All were enchanted by you, my love."

Bri kissed him and then sat back on the tufted red leather bench seat. She pulled off her gloves and glanced at her engagement ring. The huge center pearl was set in gold, surrounded by fourteen round emeralds. "I could not be happier than I am in this moment."

"Nor I."

"This evening was magical. The costumes, the masks, Clarissa's singing of Banfield's composition...it was all perfect." She turned to face him. "I love you, Edward."

"And I you." Edward kissed her. "Are you ready to set a date?"

Bri nodded. "If the central reception hall isn't done, we could hold a reception at an outside tent as we did for Summerfest after marrying at the estate in Scotland now that I have completed the Marriage Settlement research. How about the last weekend in June?"

"I believe my calendar is open." He kissed her deeply, touching her tongue with his.

***

Monday, October 28, 1811 – *Omelettes de Mme. d'Aix*
Aneira

During the final restaurant walk through, Vaux and Miss Turtin completed their checklist.

"Mme. d'Aix," said Vaux, "the only remaining items to deliver will be the food you wish to prepare. Do you agree we have fulfilled all the terms of our contract?"

Aneira took the checklist and noted all the details. "Yes, and may I say, I am impressed by your ingenuity, industriousness, and design solutions. I believe we will be able to open early, a week from today."

Rachel smiled. "We wish you the best of luck and will be among your first customers."

"*Gratis*, of course."

"You are too kind," said Vaux. "I noticed your flyers are ready to be distributed. May I take some for my circle?"

"We left the opening date blank, but I am confident November 4th will be met."

"We will fill that in. I notice you post early hours, opening at seven and closing at four." Rachel tilted her head. "Perhaps you could host occasional private parties in the evening."

"That is possible, but first we must establish a presence and reputation for taste and quality."

Mirela came down the stairs to bid them farewell. "I am pleased with the furniture you designing."

Aneira agreed. "You've created a comfortable retreat for us."

As Rachel and Vaux bid them *adieu*, Mirela took Vaux's hand and pulled him toward her. Tilting her head toward Rachel, the old Gypsy said, "She understands your needs."

***

Wednesday, October 30, 1811 – Lady Gwyneth's Townhouse
Gwyneth

Nambotha brought two wrapped packages to Gwyneth as she worked on a needlepoint design portraying her cats Misty and Mozart playing with a ball of yarn on the fortepiano. "Guy picked something up for you from Kensington Press."

She secured her needle in the canvas and opened the package. Inside each was the same book with a note from Collins, her editor. The first note read: *D.D. – Read this.* The second note read: *P.P. – Read this.*

Guy routinely picked up deliveries for Drusilla Dorset and Persephone Peabody from Collins, who was unaware that Gwyneth wrote the manuscripts of his two most prolific writers, knowing her only as the hidden owner of Kensington Press. He received her completed novellas under both pen names monthly by messenger.

She opened *Sense and Sensibility.* The inside flap read, "Published October 30, 1811 by 'A Lady.' " *Anonymous?* She began to read. After a few pages, she looked toward Misty and Mozart, lying at her feet grooming each other. "This 'Lady' is a formidable competitor. I must up my game."

***

Thursday, October 31, 1811 – Pytchley Palace
Edward

As the earl's carriage pulled into the line of rigs arriving at Pytchley Palace, Edward turned and sighed. "Weren't we just here in costume? I don't know if I can get used to this."

"Grandmother loves costumes and Halloween is her favorite holiday."

"Buck up, Edward," said Henry. "We're both dashing pirates this evening." He adjusted his eye patch.

Bri shook her head. "Brace yourselves. Grandmother's seen those costumes before. She expects ingenuity. I predict she will say that you are 'unimaginative, unconvincing and unsurprising.' " Bri adjusted the petticoats under her Tudor-style gown, and straightened her tiara.

"Being the red-headed queen isn't terribly imaginative either," scoffed Edward.

"Perhaps not, but it's a new costume."

After they exited and entered the palace, Vanessa, dressed as Little Bo Peep, approached them. "Bri, elegant as always." She examined Henry and Edward from head to toe. "Unconvincing, unimaginative, but not unexpected." She moved on to the next guest.

Bri whispered to Edward, "Two out of three."

CHAPTER FORTY-FIVE

Friday, November 1, 1811 – Aboard *Bast's Leap*
Blackburn as di Lucca

T he Pharaoh had transformed into Dragan di Lucca, an
Italian merchant with shoulder length gray hair and a full
moustache, walking the ship's deck with a cane and a faux
limp to be sure he had the disguise perfected. In his cabin, he passed
the time reading his Shakespeare collection. Months aboard ship
provided him time to devour the Bard's works again without
interruption. As a way to keep his mind occupied during the banal
meal conversations in the captain's quarters, he used the insights he
gained from the readings to evaluate the other passengers. *Which
character would he or she be? What motivates him or her?*

It amused him to concoct scenarios of infidelity, theft and murder
among the odd group of travelers. Some nights he read aloud to
Midnight. She seemed interested for a while, but the steady cadence
of his voice and the rocking of the ship calmed her and she rolled
herself into a sleeping ball of fur.

***

Friday, November 1, 1811 – The British Museum
Xie Xie

Through Drummond, Xie Xie set an appointment with the director
of Egyptian Antiquities at the British Museum. Her 'aunt'
accompanied her.

A wiry man with a face mottled by too much time in the sun, greeted her. *I can imagine him in khaki digging in the desert.*

"Mr. Director, I bring priceless artifacts to donate to your museum on behalf of an anonymous Egyptian benefactor." She opened a linen-wrapped package and laid out the treasures on the director's desk. Small carved faience figurines of Egyptian gods, gold rings with lapis stones, elaborate neckpieces, and enameled beads on long necklaces elicited the expected response.

He gasped. "Miss Li, these are exquisite examples of workmanship."

"It is the benefactor's belief that they date to the reign of a woman pharaoh as described by Josephus. Perhaps your scholars can further the identification as you decipher the Rosetta Stone."

"What attribution does your benefactor desire?"

"I have the precise wording here." She handed the director a piece of parchment, which read:

A Gift to the British Museum from an Anonymous Admirer of Civilizations Ancient and Modern.

"May I ask the provenance of these items?"

"Yes, I have the documentation from the Egyptian authorities here, with their seal." She handed a package of documents. Stolen from tombs, the items were authentic, accompanied by an expertly forged provenance from the Egyptian government. *Alia has all the seals to make it appear official.*

The director took off his spectacles, cleaned them, and put them back on. "This looks to be in order. I shall prepare a receipt for this most generous gift."

***

Saturday, November 2, 1811 – Lord Ravenshire's Townhouse
Bri

Bri had invited those who wanted to adopt the pups of Chérie and Hector to afternoon tea. As the tea trays were cleared, nine rambunctious Dalmatian pups burst into the earl's parlor.

Jean-Louis stood in the hallway, amused at the frantic barking.

Bri laughed as the dogs circled around her and the others. "Each dog has a tag marked with the first initial of its new companion's name."

The females went to Edward, Vaux, Ian and Nate. The remaining males went to Oliver, Charlotte, Banfield, and Jane Anne by proxy to Bri, while the runt, who was small but thriving, went to Dr. St. Cloud.

Each had different spot patterns, from brown to black, and blue or brown eyes.

"Father couldn't bear to see them leave, so he went riding with Hector, who loves to run alongside Hermès."

Spotty came downstairs and jumped in her arms.

"When I named Spotty, I had no idea I'd be surrounded by Dalmatians, but I know you'll find a name that fits."

Ian pulled on Dr. St. Cloud's sleeve. "I named my pony after Gio, so you can't use that name for the little dog."

Dr. St. Cloud smiled. "I already have a name for him, and it's not 'Gio.' "

"What is it?"

"Jean-Jean."

The child put his hand over his mouth, widened his eyes, and looked at Jean-Louis.

"He saved him when we thought the pup dead. It's only fitting."

Aelwyn smiled at her son. "What are you going to name your dog?"

" 'Blue.' Like her eyes."

Bri glanced at Edward. "And you?"

"Zori, in remembrance of our happy sailing to the Azores."

Bri smiled. "I like that."

Vaux rubbed his dog's ears. "Diana. A noble name for a noble hunter."

Nate's female put her paws on her shoulders and nuzzled his neck. "Her formal name will be Themistoclea. Clea for short."

Oliver shook his head. "Parker, do you doubt that we'd grasp the reference?"

Before Oliver could answer, Banfield blanched. "*I* don't." He looked around for confirmation.

"Neither would most people, Mr. Banfield," said Bri. "Laurence taught me ancient Greek and philosophy, as he did Father and Nate and Aelwyn."

Aelwyn explained, "Themistoclea was a Delphic priestess who taught Pythagoras the moral doctrines. She is considered a ancient female philosopher."

"Make an opera out of *that*, Banfield!" Vaux laughed.

Banfield shrugged and rubbed his dog's neck. "Well, I'm not as steeped in ancient history as the rest of you." He looked at the Dalmatian, whose tail wagged furiously back and forth. "I'm calling my dog...Wag."

"Come on," teased Vaux. "You can do better than that!"

"I like it Wag, Waggy. It's *my* dog."

"Uncle Oliver, are you still set on Perseus?"

"Absolutely!" The dog sat obediently at his feet.

Bri rubbed Jane Anne's dog's head. "Jane Anne is naming her dog Jak. He'll be her companion and guard at the salon, also called JAK." She turned to Charlotte. "You're the last one...what will your dog's name be?"

"Felix. Look at that smile! He's a happy boy." She petted his head.

Each guardians leashed his or her Dalmatian and headed out the door. Jean-Louis, Thompson and the footmen brought the baskets to serve as beds, filled with blankets, special food, and toys for each dog and loaded them into the waiting carriages.

***

Monday, November 4, 1811 – *Omelettes de Mme. d'Aix*
Aneira

Aneira scanned the café. Pale yellow tablecloths with wisteria blue designs echoed the Provence style she loved. *The viscount and Miss Turtin did an excellent job.*

Scents of lavender infused into oils would complement the fragrances of her teas, imported from the Far East through Duff's connections.

The flyers she distributed in the neighborhood worked. Patrons arrived in waves.

Aneira smiled. *This will work. If the 10th Earl hadn't ruined my life, this café would have been my life's dream.*

***

Tuesday, November 5, 1811 – Riding along Rotten Row
Bri

Oliver and Bri rode without Gwyneth this Tuesday because the comtesse had another appointment. Now that Bri's engagement was official, a chaperone seemed unnecessary when riding with her uncle.

Oliver had just won a spirited race with Perseus at his heels when Drummond rode by with an Asian woman, followed by a small rig carrying an older woman. *Must be her chaperone.*

He called out to Drummond, "Ho, Tottie! Come say hello to my niece."

Drummond headed toward them.

Bri recognized Miss Li. *The woman in the red mask has already made it into Scandal & Shame, touted as a mystery woman.* "How nice to see you again, Miss Li."

"Lady Gabriella, it's kind of you to remember me."

As if anyone could forget such an incredible creature.

Drummond nodded toward Oliver. "This is my card partner, Oliver, Lord Darlemont. His mother is the Duchess of Pytchley. He is Lady Gabriella's uncle."

Miss Li flashed a coy smile at Oliver. "I can't believe you didn't introduce me to this dashing man at the Engagement Ball, Tottie."

Tottie already? Is she his paramour?

Oliver tipped his hat. "Do you keep a horse in London, Miss Li?"

"No, I'm renting from the stables affiliated with my hotel."

"Well, if you decide you prefer your own, I'm a regular at Tattersalls. I'd be happy to guide you through the process."

"Horse auctions," explained Drummond.

"Well, perhaps Auntie and I will take you up on that, Lord Darlemont." She dismissed her aunt with a wave of her hand. "Auntie doesn't understand English."

Drummond and Miss Li rode off, followed by "Auntie's" carriage.

"You certainly made a fool of yourself," chided Bri.

Oliver preened in his saddle. "I don't think I acted in an unusual manner."

Bri scoffed. "You practically drooled on her. Are any men faithful?"

"Bah! 'Twas naught but a harmless flirtation."

"Flirtation leads to infatuation and therein lies the risk."

"Don't be a carper. You're in love, you're engaged. All is new and exciting. Older married men like me are stuck in a routine. Sometimes a little fantasy spices up the day."

"Fantasy? Flirtation? Listen to yourself."

"I noticed 'the woman in the red mask' at your Engagement Ball. She is an exotic presence."

"Do all men dream of exotic paramours?"

***

Oliver

Oliver detected a trace of wistfulness in Bri's voice.

Of course she's upset. Damn that Ravenshire and the island woman.

"I won't lie to you, Bri. All men dream of exotic paramours from time to time. But good sense generally prevails."

" 'Generally' is not comforting."

"Race you to the next post!"

***

Sunday, November 10, 1811 – Riding along Rotten Row
Vaux

Vaux spotted Miss Li riding near them. It was the first time he'd taken Diana to run and had a long leash to keep her in tow. He called out to Rogers, "Look. 'The woman in the red mask' is over there."

Rogers turned to see her, raised his eyebrows and tilted his head toward Miss Li. "Let's be sociable." He rode in that direction.

Vaux followed, noticing that a small carriage with an elderly Asian woman followed Miss Li.

"I believe we were introduced at the Engagement Ball for Lady Gabriella," said Rogers. "I'm Viscount Rogers, and this is Viscount Vaux."

Skirting protocol by suggesting we've been introduced. Daring. And I've never heard Rogers introduce himself as anything but "Rogers." Interesting.

"The evening flew by, and I met so many people. I am Miss Xie Xie Li and this is my aunt, Ling Ling Li."

"Double names are memorable, not that you need any extra boost for people to remember you."

Vaux rolled his eyes.

Some friends rode by, and one called out, "Rogers! When is the next Phaeton Meet?"

"Next summer," shouted Rogers.

Miss Li tilted her head and seemed puzzled. "What's a Phaeton Meet?"

"Last summer I arranged a race among the latest versions of Phaetons. They're racing carriages built for speed. I love speed."

"So do I. I'd like to see a race like that. Next summer is a long time to wait."

"Well, if we have one before then, there will be a lot of publicity and you'll receive an invitation."

Vaux leaned forward. "They called it the 'Trot of the *Ton.*'"

"How clever! Let me know if there is another such race. Good day, milords."

"Enjoy your ride."

As Miss Li and her aunt disappeared around the curve, Vaux scoffed. "That's how you approach women, Rogers? You're transparent as hell."

"It's the notion of speed that gets them every time. Race you to the next marker." He took off.

Vaux spurred his horse to catch up as Diana, transforming into a blur of spots, sped ahead.

***

Wednesday, November 13, 1811 – Mlle. Bellerobe's Atelier

Bri

Bri and Clarissa exited Lord Ravenshire's carriage at the atelier.

Mlle. Bellerobe greeted them. "Lady Clarissa, I have some items for you to choose from."

Clarissa moved slowly, about two months before the expected date of her first child's birth. She sat on a bench. "It's so difficult to find clothes in my condition. I refuse to hide from the world simply because I am with child."

The assistant brought out several dresses for her review.

"We have increased the gatherings on the skirt and the depth of the bodices to accommodate your current size."

Clarissa and Bri looked them over and agreed on a few.

"*Bien.* I have a surprise for you from Lady Gabriella. I will be right back."

Before Clarissa could ask Bri about the surprise, the doorbell rang and they turned to see who had entered.

Bri inhaled involuntarily, but recovered quickly. "Miss Li, how nice to see you again. This is my friend, Lady Clarissa von Dusterberg St. Cloud."

"A pleasure, Lady Clarissa. I read about Mlle. Bellerobe in *Scandal & Shame* when I first arrived in London. Patronage by Lady Gabriella has made her the most popular dressmaker in the *ton.*"

"You have shown up in *Scandal & Shame* as well, Miss Li, as a 'woman of mystery,' and 'the woman in the red mask.' " *Ironic that this siren is famous for attending* my *Engagement Ball.*

Clarissa's eyes darted back and forth between the two sparring women.

Mlle. Bellerobe broke the spell, entering with a small white linen dress.

Clapping her hands together, Clarissa rose to her feet and touched the fabric. "A christening dress!" She embraced Bri. "Our family christening gowns were in a trunk lost during a foreign move long ago. I shall treasure this when our child is born."

Miss Li leaned in. "What is a christening dress?"

"For a child's baptism, of course," answered Mlle. Bellerobe.

"Ah," said Miss Li. "The *Christian* ritual. I follow the precepts of Confucius." She stared at Clarissa's belly. "Oh, you are with child. You western women are so much bigger than we Asians, I wasn't sure if you were simply more plump than Lady Gabriella."

Incensed, Bri stared at her. "Miss Li, it is simply not polite to say such things."

Her eyes widened. "Forgive me, I am still learning your ways." She turned to Mlle. Bellerobe. "I've come to pick up another pair of slippers. They were ruined in the rain yesterday."

"Please have a seat, Miss Li. I will attend to you when I finish my *appointment* with Lady Clarissa."

After their purchases were complete, Bri and Clarissa exited the atelier, grimacing as Jean-Louis held the door to the carriage while they climbed in.

"I assume Miss Li is responsible for your unpleasant glare."

"She called us fat!" hissed Bri.

"Miss Li is no fool. She is baiting you." He closed the door and leaned through the window. "And you bit."

***

Friday, November 15, 1811 – The Docks of Dubrovnik
Blackburn as Di Lucca

Swarms of drivers and guides vied for position as *Bast's Leap* lowered its gangplank and loading deck from the Egyptian vessel. Wagons awaited the few wealthy disembarking passengers. Calls rang out in multiple languages, creating a cacophony of confusion.

Blackburn's hair blew in all directions on the blustery day. *This wig must hold or I am undone.* He appeared on the swaying gangplank from the walkway from the ship to the dock, carrying a small leather bag, followed by a crewman carrying his other bags. Scanning the crowd, Blackburn spotted a would-be driver calling out in Croatian, Greek, English and French, wearing a red hat, about half the height of a fez. Variations of the head topper around him had black sides and a red top, a few had brims, but most were like upside down boxes with rounded edges. The crewman waved him over, spoke to him in French, "*Attendez les bagages.*"

Once the baggage was loaded into the wagon, the driver motioned for Blackburn to sit behind him on the rear bench.

In his disguise as an Italian merchant, Blackburn tossed coins to the crewman and wished him peace in Arabic in leaving.

To Blackburn's surprise, the driver understood and spoke in Arabic.

"Forgive me, great sheik. We have but humble carts here, not up to your expectations. So sorry. To what grand hotel shall I deliver you?"

"The grandest of all."

The driver smiled, revealing several missing teeth, and then guided his horses in silence.

Upon reaching the hotel, a restored 16th century palace, the driver handed the merchant's baggage to a waiting porter at the door. "If you need me for anything else, master, ask for Zagor. All know me."

Blackburn nodded, paid Zagor and then entered the reception area of the once-great palace. The registration clerk greeted him in French, reflecting the governing language of Napoleon's occupation, and offered to book time in the baths after his long voyage.

The porter escorted the merchant to a suite, the best in the hotel, with a verandah with a view looking out over the city and the sea beyond. Under French jurisdiction for several years, the city seemed more vibrant than Blackburn remembered. *War interferes with commerce, but it brings new ways of life, new opportunities.*

Descending to the lowest level, where the baths were located, Blackburn carried a change of clothing and entered the public bathing area. Private dressing rooms off to the side were available for a fee. He paid, disrobed, and stepped into the deep pool of water fed by natural hot springs beneath the hotel.

The weeks on the ship had caused his skin color to fade, so he now appeared more Mediterranean than Arab, but still far from his native British paleness. Blackburn examined the results in the mirror. *By the time I reach London, my skin will help me pass as a man of the Continent.* Now, the worst anyone could say was that he had spent too much time in a sunny clime. Aristocrats valued their paleness as a sign of the indolence bestowed by wealth.

Sinking beneath the surface of the water, Blackburn luxuriated in its warmth, washing the detritus of travel off his body. He ran his fingers over the scars on his shoulder and hand, left by knife and bullet. *They watched me die.*

He laughed out loud as he emerged. The sound bounced off the water and reverberated on the surrounding tiles.

CHAPTER FORTY-SIX

Saturday, November 16, 1811 – Warwick Auctions
Edward

Vaux invited Bri and Edward to attend an art auction to pick up some unusual items to add to their décor, to build their own joint style, even though they both knew Bri would be the deciding vote.

They inspected the items up for auction, and made notes on the program as to which ones they wanted to bid on. Bri noticed some Egyptian antiquities and was drawn to a papyrus scroll with beautiful depictions of Bast, the cat goddess. She waved over the auctioneer. "What is the provenance of this scroll? The papyrus looks modern."

"Oh, no, mad—"

"Lady Gabriella."

"Pardon me, Lady Gabriella, but we have just received this from a seller who gave us an unimpeachable verification of provenance from a prominent Egyptian collector."

"I am not an expert, but I have seen enough of these in my own family's collection to know that this is a copy. A well done copy, to be sure, but a copy nonetheless. It's too thick, not brittle with age, and the colors are too vivid, pure and varied for the time. Paints would have been mixed from the same base colors."

Edward leaned in to speak softly. "My fiancée is generally correct about such matters. I suggest you pull this item from consideration tonight." The auctioneer signaled to someone to do so.

They examined the other items. Bri nudged Edward in front of an architectural drawing of Westminster Abbey that appealed to her.

Vaux pointed out an unusual vase that Bri also liked.

Edward was drawn to a set of colored glass antique inkwells.

They picked out a few more items to consider, subject to what bidding pattern might emerge.

As they moved to sit in their reserved seats in the front row, Vaux stood and scanned the room. "Ah. 'The woman in the red mask' is here."

Bri gave Vaux an icy stare.

Miss Li strode up to the group. "Lord Vaux, how nice to see you again. I enjoyed our conversation riding in the park last Sunday. Lady Gabriella, Mr. James." She slightly bowed her head. "Please excuse me. I must speak to the auctioneer. He seems to have removed an item I wanted sold."

"The papyrus?" Edward's face clouded.

"Yes. It was given to me by a collector to be sold."

"I believe it to be a forgery, Miss Li," said Bri. "I'm sure *you* couldn't have known."

"I shall take your concerns to heart, and speak to the auctioneer."

After she left, Bri turned to Vaux. "You saw her in the park riding and didn't tell me?"

"I didn't think it was important."

Vaux looked to Edward for help.

Edward shrugged. "You don't know her, Bri." Seeing Bri's defiant stance, he added, "And you should know that she has scheduled a meeting with me to inquire as to banking accommodations."

"Surely you are not going to meet with her!"

"She came via a recommendation from a long-standing client. Courtesy demands that I meet with her."

The auctioneer banged the gavel. "One minute. Kindly take your seats."

Edward could feel the heat from Bri's fuming anger. He bid on the drawing, the vase, and the inkwells, winning each.

Remaining silent, Bri bid on a couple of other items she had flagged earlier.

Their paid purchases were bundled for collection. Jean-Louis loaded them into Edward's carriage.

Edward gave Jean-Louis a look that meant, "Ask no questions."

Vaux hailed a Hackney.

Inside Edward's carriage, Bri blurted, *"Must* you engage in commerce with her? She probably knew the artifact was forged and assumed we fools would overbid for it."

"You have no proof of that."

"She's brazen and too independent for her own good."

"Am I hearing this correctly?" Edward couldn't hide a smile. "Is Lady Gabriella jealous?"

"Jealous?" Her voice rose. "Jealous of a woman who peddles a forged papyrus? Why do you think her other commercial opportunities will stand up to scrutiny?"

"Because *I* will scrutinize them."

"Is this what our life together will be like? You and your friends throwing other women in my face? I don't much like this side of you, Edward."

"Nor do I appreciate your lack of trust."

An icy silence permeated the carriage for the balance of the ride to Lord Ravenshire's townhouse.

*** *** ***

Wednesday, November, 20, 1811 – Dubrovnik
Blackburn as Di Lucca

Blackburn sat on the terrace of his hotel, overlooking the Adriatic. Fishing boats as well as large commercial vessels formed multi-hued specks in the cerulean blue sea that extended toward the horizon. *Vengeance has driven me all my life.*

Over twenty years as the earl's protégé at Wyndward Trading, Blackburn had developed secret contacts whose loyalty rested with him, not the earl. He had made them rich, and he could make them poor. He had learned that the two things people feared most were losing wealth and a life-threatening illness. No one could win the insurmountable battle against death. They might delay it, but it would come for them in its inexorable way. But wealth? People would do anything to keep their money, the foundation of their status in society and source of their self-respect. *Year after year, I siphoned off funds without suspicion until Bri figured it out.* Part of him admired her cleverness. She had a flair for numbers that was charming at the age of ten, but vexing at two-and-twenty, when she started to ask too many questions, delving into long-buried accounts.

Over the years, his grandmother had nursed his hatred for his father with every breath she took. Though he'd met his father many times over his tenure with the trading company, he felt no rancor in those meetings, which had always troubled him. *Why didn't I feel the evil she saw in him?*

But his grandmother had been correct about one thing. One death did not destroy a family. One theft would not bankrupt the Wyndwards. Each death brought her one step closer. *How many have there been? I've lost count of the insignificant ones.*

In Egypt, betrayal was met with swift justice from The Pharaoh's sword. His grandmother, in contrast, set assassins upon the innocent as a pre-emptive play.

A son born of Lady Gabriella would be the 12th Earl of Ravenshire and one of the richest men in England. *There is still a chance I could play the role of Bri's husband. I have a deft hand at disguise. Would she believe it? Maybe in a moment of weakness, if her jealousy of Miss Li blooms as I expect, it could still work.*

Since he'd escaped from London months ago, his left shoulder and right hand had fully healed and he had trained himself to use his left hand as adroitly as his right. Now fully ambidextrous, he planned to switch hand-dominance with the disguises he assumed. Hair color, wigs, beards, mustaches, feigned physical impairments—all diverted attention. Spectacles and a cane to accommodate a faux limp completed his physical transformation into an Italian merchant.

The brown eyes would deflect and dispel any inkling of recognition.

Now, like his grandmother's Gypsy agent, he was a ghost, a spectre who could slip in and out of character before his prey could blink. By then, it would be too late. The truth of it was that killing an enemy sparked a thrill up his spine. In that moment, he was as a god, the giver or taker of life, omnipotent. *What a Pharaoh I would have been. My name carved on monuments that still stand after thousands of years. My marker. What will be my eternal marker? Who will know of my prowess? I must work in secret, but secrecy does not beget immortality.*

The next day, Zagor waited outside the hotel, hoping to serve Blackburn. *He may be useful.* " I should like to engage you as my manservant, Zagor."

"At your service, Sig."

They worked out a daily wage.

Blackburn shopped for a wardrobe suitable for a man of Croatian nobility, with the local flourishes. He saw several men sporting red capes and smiled. *I was prescient.*

A knock came at the door.

Zagor, no doubt. Betrayal is always a possibility. One more death, more or less, what difference does it make? Zagor is of use to me now.

Blackburn had learned from the eastern mentality to plan for decades. He developed multiple solutions to problems, multiple sources of funds, and multiple identities as needed. *I am always prepared for a quick escape.*

He opened the door for his new manservant.

***

Thursday, November 21, 1811 – James & Co., Bankers
Edward

Miss Li arrived with Farrukh Aziz, an Uzbek trader with deep connections to Asian markets and a client of James & Co.

After they settled into their chairs, Mr. Aziz said, "A man known as 'The Pharaoh' in Egypt has given Miss Li the highest recommendation. Over the past few weeks, she has impressed me with her knowledge of trade commodities, shipping options, and unique sources. She and I have formed an import-export firm to combine our expertise and we would like to establish letters of credit through James & Co.

Edward picked up the papers in front of him. "Shall we review your proposals?"

***

Saturday, November 23, 1811 – Ravenshire
Henry

A crisp winter breeze from the open window kept the earl alert as he read in his library. An engraving of the original Ravenshire Castle was mounted on the wall above his head. Bookshelves reached the ceiling around the room except in front of the windows and the fireplace, comfortably ablaze. The earl put down the manuscript and removed his spectacles. He'd set aside the tinted ones, preferring clear vision. Rising, he stretched his muscles, and decided to find Philip Laurence.

Young stood in the parlor overseeing the hanging of a recently cleaned portrait of Bri as a child of three. "Yes, milord?"

The earl regarded the painting of his daughter and smiled. "Gio is a master. He captured that glint in her eye, the spark that is Bri."

"Indeed he did, milord."

"Is Laurence about?"

"He's taking a walk around the grounds with Mr. Parker, milord."

"I shall join them." Pulling his cloak off the hook before the butler could reach it, Henry walked outside. He saw them admiring the rebuilt section of the original castle. He waved.

Reaching them, he asked, "Is it vainglorious, Laurence?"

Laurence, a thin, still-straight-backed man of three-and-sixty years shook his head. The scholar of ancient history and former tutor of Wyndward children and wards, had retired after the untimely death of his wife. Now he moved between Ravenshire and Merton College, Oxford, as his research for the history of the Wyndward family required.

The earl's former tutor smiled, revealing his yellowed teeth, long and uneven. "Vainglorious, no. Ambitious, yes. But it's happening, Lord Ravenshire. Your long-held dream is rising before us."

"Laurence, you must cease calling me Lord Ravenshire. Henry is appropriate for old friends."

"I called you 'Young Viscount', as I recall."

"I am no longer 'young' anything."

"Henry, you and I are the same age," argued the American. "Don't drag me down into your melancholy."

The former tutor scanned the scaffolding. "Castles require upkeep."

Henry nodded. "I have set aside an annuity for the ongoing maintenance of Ravenshire, a trust that future Wyndwards cannot plunder. It is merely an attempt to forestall disaster. I have watched other fortunes dissipate. Now that Ian exists, we have an heir. If Bri were to have a son, he would be first in line, but that is an unknown."

"If you and Charlotte were to marry, a child might come of it."

Henry put his hand on Nate's shoulder. "You were not here when Taita appeared. Charlotte is terribly hurt. Taita may return in the spring. She and Charlotte tear equally at my heart."

Nate shook his head. "That cannot stand."

A wrinkled forehead and pinched squint appeared on Laurence's face. "Is it possible that Taita is being held in Madagascar against her will? If the Sultan freed her, why is she still with him? Perhaps you and Jean-Louis could—"

"Free her? Sail to the other side of the world? Demand that an all-powerful monarch do my bidding? Were I to be successful and live to tell the tale, all that I have built would be at risk of being confiscated by the Prince Regent for creating an international incident and depriving him of his spices. I would be a man without a country. That history you are writing would be burned."

Laurence looked off into the distance. "Lucius Ventus started the Wyndward dynasty with nothing. You have many advantages he lacked. Assets in other jurisdictions, for instance. The Earldom of Ravenshire and Ravenshire Forest might be lost. But the trading company would survive. With enough planning, you and your family could continue your lives out of the Prince Regent's reach. You have ships, Henry. *Ships*. Your story would live on. My manuscript will not be burned."

***

Saturday, November 30, 1811 – Lord Ravenshire's London Stables
Jean-Louis

Jean-Louis wore his preferred anonymous black breeches, shirt, vest and coat. Not the clothes of an aristocrat, but not those of a tradesman, either. He might be taken for a merchant, a traveler or someone of indeterminate status. With his long hair pulled back with a ribbon, and his black felt hat pulled low to further obscure his face, he walked into the stables to oversee the saddling of Bri's horse.

He took pride in Bri's riding skill. *I taught her well. That effete riding master taught her prancing tricks, not how to handle a large horse under difficult conditions.*

She walked over to her beloved mount. "Good morning, my Gazelle. Has Jean-Louis taken good care of you this morning?" She patted the horse's nose, rubbed the ash-colored splash between Gazelle's dark eyes, and touched their heads together.

I believe I just saw Gazelle smile.

"I see you've donned your usual costume as a cipher. Ready to swoop to my defense with sword in hand, are you?"

Jean-Louis made an exaggerated bow. "Always at your service, milady. You cannot wander about London alone."

"Very well. But someday, Jean-Louis, women will move about as freely as men." She stepped on a stool and mounted her horse to ride aside.

Jean-Louis made sure she was sitting securely. "Perhaps, but not in my lifetime, Bri. Today, I shall simply be an unidentified rider."

"Ha! As if no one in the *ton* knows who you are." They walked the horses through the streets a few blocks to Gwyneth's house, and rode around the back. Her stableman was adjusting her horse's saddle fastenings as they approached.

Jean-Louis rode silently behind his two charges as they chatted.

When they reached Hyde Park's Rotten Row, Edward was waiting.

Jean-Louis noticed Bri sigh with relief and wave to Edward. She rode ahead to greet him.

Gwyneth stopped riding when she reached Jean-Louis to give Bri and Edward some privacy. "At least we won't have to deal with Bri's envy of Miss Li this morning."

He shrugged. "So far, so good." They followed the well worn trail where the *ton* rode to be seen. "The trees are losing their last leaves."

Yellow, orange, red and brown withered flakes blew across the horse trail as the wind kicked up. Fall's invigorating chill ruled in the late days of November.

Alternating between trots and mock races, Bri took a deep breath of the morning air as Gwyneth and Jean-Louis caught up to them.

"I shall be here in spring when the buds appear, painting en plein air, I expect. I never tire of the endless varieties and features of flowers. They open to the sun with joy and close at night to dream."

"Lady Gwyneth, you are bordering on poetry this morning." Edward smiled as he spoke. "Of what do flowers dream?"

"Of bees, of sunlight, and of soft rain."

Bri tilted her head. "Maybe you should write a book of poetry illustrated with flowers. Call it *When Flowers Dream.*"

"Always full of ideas, Bri. That's not a bad one." Gwyneth looked off in the distance. "I painted that meadow over there, when it was full of poppies and daisies at the height of summer."

Bri followed her gaze, and then felt a tingle on the back of her neck. Out of the corner of her eye she spotted a figure on a horse cantering toward them. She froze.

Edward glanced at Bri. "What's wrong, darling?"

Stiffening in the saddle Bri said, "Your paramour is here. Did you tell her we would be here? Did you ask her to join us?"

Edward seemed perplexed. "What are you talking about?"

Bri waved toward Miss Li, who had slowed her horse to a walk to approach them.

Miss Li called out from a few yards away, "Good morning! Lovely day for a ride, isn't it?" An elderly Chinese woman followed her in a light, uncovered carriage.

Keep calm, Bri. Don't let her goad you. She knows what she's doing.

Bri responded as he'd hoped. "Indeed, it is a lovely day, Miss Li. Do you keep a horse in London?"

"Actually, Lady Gabriella, this remarkable animal," she rubbed her horse's head with familiarity, "belongs to a friend of mine. He lets me borrow her whenever I am in London."

"A beau?"

Jean-Louis closed his eyes in resignation. *Now you've revealed your fear of her hold over Edward.*

Miss Li shook her head. "No, simply an old family friend." Nodding to Edward and Bri, she said, "Delightful to see you again. Enjoy your ride!" Wving toward the elderly woman, Mis Li called, "Come along, Auntie." She trotted off in the other direction, followed by her 'auntie.'

Bri glared at Edward.

Edward erupted in frustration. "She is not my *paramour!* She is a prospective client of the bank. Her contacts and ideas are intriguing."

"You've met with her already?"

"I told you it was scheduled."

"But not that it had taken place."

"You above all others know that the world is changing and the bank must expand its range of commerce. Please cease this constant harangue against Miss Li. It's demeaning for you to behave in such a way."

Bri's cheeks turned scarlet. "Demeaning to whom? You are my fiancé, and everywhere I turn, Miss Li turns up."

Before he could answer, Bri took off at a gallop.

Jean-Louis rode over to Edward. "Give her time. I will speak with her."

Edward put his hand up. "It is between us, Jean-Louis. And don't trouble yourself to look into her background, as I'm sure my fiancée has requested. We have our own bank resources for that task. I'll thank you to mind your own business."

Jean-Louis sat straight in his saddle, his well-muscled shoulders taut. He spoke so softly that Edward had to lean in to hear. "As I have told you before, Mr. James, Lady Gabriella *is* my business. I am charged by the earl with the protection of his family and I do not need your permission or approval to take any steps I deem necessary to provide such protection." He rode off after Bri without a backward look.

Edward, frustrated at both Bri and Jean-Louis, tipped his hat to Gwyneth, pulled tight on his horse's reins, and rode in the opposite direction.

***

Bri

As she rode away, Bri's doubts simmered to the surface. *Can I trust him? What is the attraction of exotic women? Lust? A desire to explore the mysteries of foreign ways of love? Does she remind him of someone he left behind? Will he leave me like Father left Charlotte? Could Miss Li be Edward's Taita?*

CHAPTER FORTY-SEVEN

Sunday, December 1, 1811 – Lord Ravenshire's London Greenhouse
Nashmir

Bri wandered into Nashmir's greenhouse before breakfast and found him tending to his herbs. "I don't suppose you have a love potion you can concoct from these herbs?"

"You need no potions, milady. Mr. James is besotted with you."

"He appears to be under the spell of an Asian temptress. Xie Xie Li." Bri sighed and sat down on a bench. "After the Engagement Ball, I thought our future would fall into place. Instead, it's become more uncertain. I believe Edward is attracted to her."

Nashmir poured some tea, offered it to Bri, and sat down on the bench across from her.

"Attraction of men for women and women for men never ends. You may find *yourself* admiring someone from across a room some evening."

"No, I would *not.*"

"I assure you that you *will.*" He waited for her to raise her eyes to his, and he glimpsed her pain. "Every day, love must be renewed. It must be stronger than temptation, for temptation lurks around every corner."

Bri gazed off into a blur of flowers, her focus diffused by the colors. "As a child, stories warning of the temptations of the devil seemed pointless. I'd *never* follow the devil. I'd *never* be so foolish or stupid. The devil would be an obvious foe, indisputably evil."

The Tibetan softened his tone. "And now?"

"I never considered that the devil would appear as 'the woman in the red mask.'"

***

Monday, December 2, 1811 – The Hanforth Mansion
Jean-Louis

Jean-Louis pulled Bri's carriage up to Clarissa's home.

Bri adjusted the wide swath of her midnight blue hooded cloak trimmed with white rabbit fur. As she stepped out, the cloak swirled, revealing a light blue wool dress underneath. Bri looked up at Jean-Louis and Chérie. "I'll be out in about half an hour."

Jean-Louis tipped his hat, saying nothing.

"Don't look at me like that. I need her advice."

After *The Princess* closed, Clarissa turned one wing of her father's mansion into a music salon, offering private voice lessons for talented children. In the late stages of pregnancy, with the baby due sometime in mid-January, only a few social events remained on her calendar..

While Bri was inside, Jean-Louis considered Edward's situation. *Miss Li appears more often than coincidence would suggest.*

Jean-Louis felt uneasy. *Is some devilish plan afoot? Who would want to entrap Edward and undermine his potential marriage? Drummond escorted her to the Engagement Ball. Is he driving this wedge between Bri and Edward? He's always resented the earl.*

If I hadn't seen Blackburn fall from that ship, and if we hadn't seen his mutilated body, I'd think he was behind this sabotage. The wounds were the same, but the face had been battered by the water slamming him into the rocks. He is clever enough to duplicate the wounds....

He petted his Dalmatian. "Am I becoming suspicious of everything, Chérie? Blackburn is dead." *This new treachery must be the work of the grandmother. Now that the café is open, she is under constant surveillance. I will know if Miss Li is in contact with her. And if Blackburn lives, her will return to the grandmother and I will know.*

***

Bri

Clarissa and Bri appeared at the door. Clarissa waved to Jean-Louis.
The Frenchman tipped his black felt hat. "*Bonjour,* Lady Clarissa."
Inside the carriage, Bri rehearsed her anticipated conversation with Edward.

Clarissa had advised, "Rehearse introducing three subjects with no emotional impact. Use the weather, the food, and other patrons as ways to deflect any anger. Defuse the situation."

Bri took a deep breath. *I have never had cause to doubt Edward. I love him. But why can't he see that his dismissive tone makes me question his love for me? I am not a possession.*

The carriage reached the imposing entrance of James & Co, the bank Edward's ancestors had founded two hundred years earlier. After exiting the carriage, the doorman opened the heavy door.

The chief clerk, Mr. Duncan, stood to welcome the future wife of his employer's son.

She followed the thin, nervous man down a hallway lined with paintings of Edward's predecessors. His grandfather's stern countenance seemed to emanate disapproval, even from a disembodied image. She steeled herself. *I must not lose my temper.*

When Mr. Duncan opened the door to Edward's private office, Bri felt the blood rush from her heart to her head. She felt faint and enraged at the same time. Edward was standing very close to Miss Li, reviewing papers on a table, their heads nearly touching as they looked up to see her.

"Edward?" To her chagrin, her voice cracked. *I must appear in control.* She cleared her throat. "It's a bit chilly out. I should have worn a scarf around my neck."

"December is always chilly." Miss Li's tone was at once cultivated and condescending.

Bri felt disconnected from her body.

∗∗∗

Edward

"Darling!" Edward walked around the table to embrace Bri.
"Good day, Lady Gabriella." Xie Xie bowed slightly to

acknowledge Bri's social status.

"You seem to show up everywhere, Miss Li."

"Bri, Miss Li and I were just reviewing the bank documents for her new venture. Perhaps you would be interested in—"

Miss Li smiled and raised her eyebrows. "Really? I was under the impression that western ladies did not dabble in commercial transactions. We shouldn't want to bore you, Lady Gabriella."

Bri's pale pink English complexion deepened into a purplish hue. "Bored? Indeed, I just don't have a head for numbers, do I, Edward?"

"On the contrary, Miss Li, my fiancée is quite adept at mathematics and languages."

"Do you speak Mandarin, Lady Gabriella?"

"Not yet, but I've engaged a tutor. I intend to be as fluent in Mandarin as you appear to be in English, Miss Li."

Edward hid his surprise at Bri's assertion that she was learning Mandarin by taking her arm. "I thought we'd all have lunch together and discuss the import business Miss Li is proposing."

"How delightful." Bri smiled but her eyes flashed a warning.

I must be on guard.

Donning their cloaks, the trio left the bank.

Miss Li told her "Auntie," who had been waiting in the carriage Miss Li had leased for several months, that she would see her back at their hotel. "I don't need a chaperone with Lady Gabriella present."

They climbed into Lady Gabriella's carriage.

Edward saw Bri glance briefly at Jean-Louis, whose eyes bored into Edward's.

This is going to be a delicate balance. They're allied against me.

***

Monday, December 2, 1811 – *Chez Michel*
Gio

Michel escorted Gio to his usual table. It had the best view of the large dining area.

"Michel, I would like my usual omelet—you know how I like it."

"*Oui.* Soft in the middle, full of fungi and spinach, sauce on the side. In the meantime, a lovely Chardonnay?"

"Excellent! Ah, here is Charles." Gio waved his grandson over to the table.

Michel nodded to the young man, and said, "You like your omelet dry, as I recall."

"With soft cheese inside, like Camembert, with diced tomatoes."

"Very fine, very fine. And some greens dressed with buttermilk as usual?"

Gio nodded. "*Magnifique*, Michel." He took a sip of the Chardonnay. "Perfect."

Charles nudged his grandfather. "I believe Lady Gabriella has just entered with Mr. James and an Asian woman I don't recognize."

Gio waved to Bri.

She brought the group over to greet her friends. "Gio and Charles, how delightful to see you."

Both men stood to acknowledge Bri and Edward. "Miss Li, did you meet Lord Ostwold at our Engagement Ball?"

Gio raised his eyebrows. "You are 'the woman in the red mask.' I also wore a red mask, but all the talk was of you. Contrary to my plan, I was not the center of attention."

Miss Li bowed. "Forgive me, Lord Ostwold, but I don't remember seeing you."

"As I recall, you were too busy being swept around the dance floor by Tottie Drummond to notice me." He gestured to Charles. "This is my grandson, Charles da Garfagnini."

Miss Li squatted to Gio's level. "I've never seen a dwarf before. How interesting you are, Lord Ostwold."

Gio tilted his head. "I am not an oddity in London, Miss Li. Within China are there no dwarfs?"

She rose to her full height, looked down at him and replied, without guile, "No. They are killed at birth, as are all defective children."

Bri's face reflected her shock. "Miss Li, Gio—Lord Ostwold—has been a valued friend and confidant of my family for over forty years. Please apologize to him for your rudeness."

Edward tried to salvage the situation. "Gio, please forgive Miss Li. She is not schooled in our social norms."

"I knew there was a reason I disdained travel beyond Greece. Ah, Miss Li. Despair not! My dwarfism is not contagious. You will not shrink for having seen me."

Miss Li downcast her eyes. "I humbly beg your pardon, Lord Ostwold. I am ashamed to have acted in an inappropriate manner."

Gio shrugged. "No dwarf experience is a decent excuse. No harm done, Miss Li. I've heard worse. And kindly close your mouth, my dear. My grandson is no dwarf."

Clearly flustered, Miss Li bowed to Charles, holding her hands up to her chin in a steeple-like position. "Forgive me, sirs. I have acted as a foolish child."

Edward bowed slightly. "Our table is ready. Enjoy your meal."

"We always do," said Gio. "The wine covers a multitude of cooking mishaps. Not all, but a multitude."

After they left, Charles said, "You have an equanimity about you, Grandfather, that I admire."

"I know what I am, Charles. It's hardly a secret. I think that Miss Li has never been caught in such vulnerability before. She strikes me as an unusually self-assured young woman. Perhaps a challenge to Bri."

"Surely not!"

Gio rubbed his hand on his chin. "The whole *ton* knows that her father had a love from the South Seas, a woman of copper skin, once a slave. Who knows what mischief might be afoot? The *ton* may no longer be simply...pink. "

"Grandfather, you are incorrigible."

The luncheon platters arrived.

Gio stuck his fork into his omelet and liquid oozed out. "*C'est parfait*, Michel."

Charles cringed. He stuck his fork in and no liquid flowed. Relieved, he echoed, "*C'est parfait*, Michel."

Beaming, Michel clasped his hands together in satisfaction.

***

Xie Xie

"What do you recommend, Mr. James?"

"Perhaps we should let Michel make suggestions."

The chef and owner appeared almost immediately. "Lady Gabriella and Mr. James, how delightful to see you. I believe I've seen your companion here, but I apologize for not recalling your name."

Edward introduced Miss Li.

"I last dined here with—"

"Tottie Drummond and Mme. Zhang. Of course."

Miss Li flashed a wide smile at the susceptible Michel.

He appeared flustered. "Today's special is *Moules à la crème Normande*—mussels cooked with white wine, Normandy cider, garlic and cream. And fresh greens from our greenhouse with buttermilk dressing."

"I look forward to that, Michel," said Miss Li.

Edward agreed.

Bri smiled at Michel, but said nothing.

"Don't worry, Lady Gabriella, I know your preferences. *Poulet à la bretonne* for you."

Miss Li leaned forward, her tone one of faux concern. "Do you have a sensitive stomach, Lady Gabriella?"

"No. I do not like fish or most shellfish."

"But you live on an island surrounded by seas full of fish."

"Which means there is more for others to enjoy." Bri sipped her wine.

"Exactly what is the *Poulet à la bretonne?*"

Bri said, "I thought you spoke French." She paused. "It's chicken simmered in apple cider, a specialty of Brittany. Not dissimilar to the recipe for your meal."

"Perhaps you'll share a taste with me."

"If you wish."

This iciness in Lady Gabriella is precisely what I hoped to elicit.

When Xie Xie returned to Durrants, she found Ling Ling nearly unconscious, smelling of whiskey. She mumbled in a slurred manner, "The bitch treats me like a slave."

In the woman's hand was a piece of Xie Xie's jewelry.

Xie Xie ripped it from the woman's hand and shook her to get her attention. "You've stolen from me. You speak English."

"Of course I do, you arrogant whore. I've had enough of you."

"And I of you. Get out."

"My clothes—"

"They are *my* clothes, purchased for you to wear at my request. You leave with better clothes on your back than when I found you. You've grown fat on my money, eating like a glutton. Begone!"

***

Tuesday, December 3, 1811 – Riding along Rotten Row
Oliver

Bri was oddly silent during their ride.

Oliver pulled up on the reins of his Arabian. He patted her. "Scheherazade is a marvel. But you are distracted. What is troubling you?"

"I think Edward is enamored of Miss Li."

Oliver listened as it spilled out. "You were concerned about her when we ran into her here a month ago. Is it so unusual that you should run into her three or four more times?"

"I no longer think it was a coincidence. She is after Edward."

"As your uncle, as a man, as a friend, I warn you that expressing your jealousy can destroy love faster than the actions of another woman. Don't drive him into her arms. You must let him continue to choose you. Temptation is ever present. Miss Li is playing you both into where she controls your actions."

"Maybe I should flirt with one of Edward's friends to make him jealous."

"*No.* That will rebound to you. Trust James. If you don't *really* trust him, *act* as if you do until the truth is evident."

"But—"

"Lack of trust will destroy your love faster than anything Miss Li might do. Fostering jealousy may be her stock-in-trade. So far, it's worked. Only you can stop her in her tracks. Don't engage."

Bri looked away. "I'll think about it."

***

Wednesday, December 4, 1811 – *Dreamtime*
Xie Xie

Arriving at *Dreamtime* late in the evening, the barkeep waved her over. "I got your note. The worker has been let go. But there's something you've got to see."

She followed him into the opium den.

Ling Ling lying prone on the floor, her eyes open in a glassy stare. "Dispose of her useless body in the usual manner."

"Understood." The barkeep signaled to a burly man.

Xie Xie left them to their tasks.

CHAPTER FORTY-EIGHT

Friday, December 6, 1811 – Edward's Gentlemen's Club
Edward

Edward had dinner most Fridays with friends from his university days while Bri spent time with Charlotte, Gwyneth, Aelwyn and Ian. Tonight he was reeling from the rage Bri had leveled at him a few days earlier after their lunch with Miss Li at Chez Michel. He was the first to arrive at their regular table.

Vaux sat down, wearing his colored-lens spectacles. "Why so glum? Is some client behind on payments?"

"Do you remember the Asian woman Drummond escorted to the Engagement Ball?"

"Who could forget 'the woman in the red mask?' "

Edward grimaced. "Bri believes I am attracted to her."

Vaux sipped a glass of wine and shrugged. "Well, you're engaged, not dead."

Banfield and Rogers sat down, also wearing their spectacles.

"Who's dead?" said Rogers as he waved over the server. "None of *us*, it seems."

"Lady Gabriella thinks Edward is going to run off with 'the woman in the red mask.' "

"Ha! Not if I can beat you to it. Although I prefer a more voluptuous look."

Banfield smirked. "Like Lady Patricia?"

Rogers sat back and drained his glass. Signaling the server for more, he frowned. "Pressure to marry is ever present. Lady Patricia *is* quite lovely, and the daughter of a earl."

Vaux wrinkled his brow. "No one's seen him for years."

The server brought their regular dinner orders.

"They say he's ill." Rogers ate a piece of roasted chicken. "His younger brother is chomping at the bit to seize the earldom."

The server refilled their wine glasses as they discussed the latest gossip in the *ton*. Their plates were served shortly thereafter.

"See here, James, you can't mean Lady Gabriella is jealous of the Asian woman?" Banfield's face conveyed the dawning of a realization. "Oh."

" 'Oh,' what?" Edward's delivery was clipped as he picked at the lamb chops.

Banfield finished chewing his beef roast. "Perhaps the earl's desire for the island woman is causing Lady Gabriella to think you are attracted to another exotic woman."

"Miss Li is a bank client and nothing more."

Vaux disagreed. " 'The woman in the red mask' is definitely *more*." He smiled with satisfaction at the taste of his veal Marsala.

"Then why don't *you* run off with her and release me from my fiancée's wrath?"

Vaux shrugged. "Maybe I *will*."

Banfield scoffed. "Your parents would disown you."

"Maybe then I would be truly free."

As they rose to leave, Edward said, "Unless you run away before Gio's exhibition on January 1st, I'll see you all then. Family holidays will consume my next three Fridays."

The viscount put his arm on Edward's shoulder. "This will blow over James," said Vaux. "She'll come around." He reached into Edward's waistcoat pocket and pulled out his spectacles. "Join us for a drink at the bar and look *au courant*."

"The Engagement Ball was such a perfect evening. She agreed to set a date for the wedding. Now, only weeks later, I wonder if there will ever be one." He donned the spectacles and headed toward the bar.

"That's the spirit!" Vaux nudged Edward with his elbow.

***

Saturday, December 7, 1811 – Durrants Hotel
Xie Xie

Xie Xie sat at a small writing desk at her hotel, reviewing her calendar. The Pharaoh would be arriving at any time. By then she must have Edward James under her spell. Lady Gabriella was clearly jealous of her, and Edward was unsettled by the situation. Their engagement might be in jeopardy, just as the Pharaoh predicted. If so, it had been easier than she had expected to drive a wedge between the two lovers.

Her major task loomed ahead. She must exploit Edward's weakness to further The Pharaoh's scheme.

She looked into the mirror and reviewed her future. *I have been an attentive student, O Pharaoh. One day, you may no longer need me. I have seen what happens to those whose usefulness has expired.*

I am close to our goal.

***

Wednesday, December 11, 1811 – The First Night of Chanukah
Annabelle

Annabelle and Eli Sterling checked the final preparations before their guests arrived to celebrate the first night of Chanukah.

With Edward and Bri's engagement, the family circle expanded. Coming tonight, in addition to Annabelle and Edward's parents, Sir John and Lady James, and Edward and Bri, were Henry, Nate, Gwyneth, Aelwyn and Ian. Charlotte had been invited, but demurred given her uncertain future with Henry.

The doorbell sounded and guests began to arrive. The three Sterling children, Hannah, Sarah and Aaron, captured Ian when he arrived, showed him the menorah and explained that during the Festival of Lights, they lit candles.

Hannah, the oldest said, "We light one candle each night and open one present."

"*Every* night?" Ian's eyes opened wide. "You get a present *every* night? I only get a few gifts on Christmas Day. You get," he counted out on his fingers, "eight presents?"

He looked at Aelwyn, confused. "We're here to learn different traditions, Ian."

Sarah took Ian's hand and they went to the nursery to play.

Annabelle smiled at Aelwyn. "I felt the same way when I first met Eli. He'll get over the initial envy."

Bri came over to Annabelle. "Where would you like Jean-Louis to place the gifts?"

"I have a table set up over here."

While Annabelle and Bri arranged the gifts, the butler, Shapiro, passed a tray filled with glasses of sherry.

At sunset, the children were called and the group stood around the *chanukiah*. Eli gestured toward the table candelabra. "Some call this a menorah, which is inaccurate because it holds 7 candles. A true *chanukiah* holds eight candles and the Shamash." It was the first experience for all the Christian attendees and they watched in awe.

Ian reached for Aelwyn's hand, entranced by the spectacle.

Eli explained. "First we light the Shamash, the 'attendant.' This is the first candle we light each night and the only one we use to light the other candles." He placed one candle in the *chanukiah* in the holder on the far right. "Tomorrow night we will replace this candle and add another, and so on for each night of Chanukah. We light from left to right, but we place the candles from right to left." He reached into the tinder box and pulled out a tinder pistol to strike the spark to light the Shamash. "Two blessings are recited each night, and a third on the first night. We say 'Amen' after each." Eli sang the blessings, along with Annabelle and the children. After each blessing, all in the group said, "Amen." After the third blessing, Eli lit the candle on the far right. The family held hands and sang a Chanukah song. The others held hands too but did not know the words.

"What a lovely ceremony," said Bri. "I never experienced this before."

Ian walked over to Eli. "But what does it mean?"

"Let's sit down and I'll tell you." He lifted Ian onto his lap. "Once upon a time, a Greek king ruled in Judea and said that Jews could no longer practice their religion. He took our Temple in Jerusalem and put statues of Greek gods and goddesses inside."

"That's not fair."

"No, it wasn't. And so the people revolted and went to war, and when they finally won back the Temple and purified it, they needed pure olive oil to light the menorah. But there was only one jug of olive oil that was pure, which meant that it had been properly prepared and blessed. That jug would last only one night. Their challenge was that they needed to keep the flames lit for seven nights and it would take seven nights to purify more oil."

Worry crossed Ian's face. "What happened?"

"A miracle. That one jug burned the flames for seven nights until new oil could be purified. And that is the celebration of Chanukah."

Annabelle led another song, and then said, "It's time to eat."

Aaron clapped his hands. "Latkes!"

Ian turned to Annabelle. "What's a latke?"

"It's a potato pancake fried in olive oil."

Ian brightened. "Like the miracle oil!"

***

Friday, December 13th, 1811 – Lady Gwyneth's Townhouse
Aelwyn

Charlotte arrived for dinner. It had become a standing date for the women of the family to meet on Friday nights at Gwyneth's, save any other obligation. Bri sat on the floor playing with a dreidel with Ian.

"Look Baroness! I got a dreidel from Uncle Eli."

Charlotte hugged Ian. "Your excitement is contagious." She laughed.

"What does that mean?"

"It means you make *me* excited too."

Aelwyn reached for Charlotte's hand. "I wish you had been there. It was lovely. I had no idea what happened on Chanukah."

"Neither did I," said Bri. "It was a life-affirming event. Our Christmas seems more about parties and presents, less about the bonds between us. We need to come up with new traditions that bring us together at a deeper level."

Aelwyn glanced at Charlotte. "We're going again on the last night of Chanukah. Please come with us."

"Yes, please come, Aunt Charlotte. I'll let you play with my dreidel if you promise to come."

Charlotte pulled Ian onto her lap. "Then how could I say no?"

Bri mused aloud. "We have Christmas Eve with the duke and duchess, Christmas morning in London, and then go to Ravenshire for Boxing Day on the 26th, hosting the reception for our servants. What if we designated Christmas afternoon to spend at the foundling hospital so the women awaiting childbirth, new mothers, and children in the orphanage can have a full Christmas?"

Gwyneth shrugged. "We wouldn't arrive at Ravenshire until nearly midnight on the twenty-fifth."

Charlotte sat back. "On the afternoon of Christmas Eve, we have traditionally provided a small gift for each person living in our shelter, and for the staff, who work in shifts so that there is always someone of responsibility on premises at all times. It's been a small affair, with someone playing the fortepiano donated by Gwyneth and singing Christmas carols. But it is a lonely time for most."

Gwyneth stood and paced. "Then the afternoon of Christmas Eve makes more sense than the afternoon of Christmas Day. What can we do that's different, inclusive and joyful?"

***

Sunday, December 15, 1811 – Pytchley Palace
Vanessa

For two Sundays before Christmas, Bri and Gwyneth joined Vanessa in a family tradition of making puddings, fruitcakes and confectionary items that could be stored for use during extended Christmas festivities. The pudding aged in the ice box, and fruit cakes were preserved with brandy.

Bri asked her grandmother, "Now that I am engaged, do you think I should learn to cook?"

"Heavens, no! One hires cooks. Why slave over a hearth? Here we are simply mixing things measured by my cook. She cooks the cakes. The pudding is simply mixed and chilled. Biscuits are cut, then we decorate with icing she has prepared."

Bri smiled. "So we organize the preparation."

"Precisely."

"That's perfect."

***

Sunday, December 15, 1811 – Flat above *Omelettes de Mme. d'Aix*
Aneira

Aneira tallied the week's receipts, put down her pen and pushed her spectacles farther up on her nose. The little omelet café became a favorite of the ladies of the social set almost from the day it opened.

An ideal location, an innovative menu, and the flair of a French proprietress on the run from Napoleon, a fiction Aneira fostered, appealed to Londoners. Her furniture and antiques shop in Inverness had been a success, but baking was her first love.

She swept her eyes over the little restaurant with a back garden and tables on the front street, weather permitting. Sometimes the yellow-striped awning provided adequate cover, but the fog's chill made most of the year impossible to serve outside.

This week she'd fielded the third request for a catered luncheon in a client's home. The lure of expansion beckoned, but so did her long-planned revenge. She could taste the sweetness of victory. *Catering would provide an entrée into society and serve as camouflage for overhearing secrets. The rich ignore us at their peril.*

She smiled. *My boy, our vengeance is near. I poisoned your wicked father, and others had to die. Soon, the last brother, his vile daughter, and the newfound heir much vaunted in the Times will meet their fate. And we will be free.*

***

Monday, December 16, 1811 – *Omelettes de Mme. d'Aix*
Gio

Vaux, Banfield, Rogers and Gio finished breakfast after discussing ideas for *The Nymphs* and *Macbeth*. Gio and the others sported the Venetian glass spectacles that were spreading through the *ton* as the mark of devotés of fashion. Their wide-ranging discussion energized them and they agreed to meet once a month to continue refining their creative vision.

As they stood to leave, the proprietress came over to their table. Vaux introduced Mme. d'Aix to his dining partners.

Rogers smiled and said, "I see you are wearing the latest fashion in eyewear, Madame."

"As are you gentlemen."

From his unique lower vantage point, Gio glimpsed her eye color. *I've seen that color before.* A cold fear clutched his heart and he lost his balance. He reached for a chair and pulled it to the floor with him as he fell. Banfield and Rogers were closest and went to his aid.

"A bit too much wine, Lord Ostwold, at breakfast?" teased Rogers.

"It's never too early for wine. A momentary faintness came over me, but it has passed."

"Good day, Mme. d'Aix. Few get my omelet preferences correct the first time. I congratulate you." Gio welcomed the fresh air once they were outside.

Vaux wanted to call a Hackney for Gio.

"I'm fine. I'll just walk a bit to get my bearings. Vision of opera sets must have dazzled me. Gentlemen, I look forward to our collaboration." He watched as their carriage pulled away, and noticed a familiar black hat across the street dip back in the shadow, talking to another dimly lit figure.

Gio caught the eye of the man in the black felt hat.

Jean-Louis tilted his head toward the next block. Gio moved in that direction and waited for the Frenchman to join him.

"You're here because you know about the eye color. Is she the grandmother who killed the 10th Earl of Ravenshire?"

The former trapper nodded. "Since our dinner in Ireland, only the earl knows that we have her under watch. I must ask you to maintain that confidence."

"Do you sense imminent danger for Bri and Ian?"

"It is always possible, but—." Jean-Louis looked around to see if they were being watched or overheard."

"—our watch is to see if Blackburn seeks her out."

Gio paled. "You think he lives?"

"His fall was a clever ruse. I've employed a similar maneuver myself. Nearly ended up dead in *that* stunt." He hailed a Hackney for Gio. "You are another pair of eyes for me. If you would like a watcher for your protection, let me know."

The dwarf waved him off. "I'm of no consequence to either Blackburn or the grandmother. If I see anything, I will inform you immediately."

Jean-Louis helped Gio climb in to the cab and shut the door. His last words before signaling the jervie to go were, "Beware of Gypsies."

***

Tuesday, December 17, 1811 – Aboard the *Muse of Porto*
Blackburn as Di Lucca

After two nights in the ancient city of Dubrovnik, Blackburn and Zagor left on a Croatian ship and arrived in Porto more than three weeks later.

After spending a night in a hotel and transforming himself from di Lucca to Count Vlarić, a dandyish rake with an *au courant* hairstyle and short-trimmed beard, Blackburn and Zagor boarded the *Muse of Porto* for the last week of their journey to London.

In his cabin, Blackburn petted his black cat. "Midnight, only you know *all* my secrets. We have much to do before we are free."

***

Wednesday, December 18, 1811 – The Last Night of Chanukah
Charlotte

At the Sterlings' home, transfixed by the ceremony of the Festival of Lights as the seven candles were lit from left to right by the Shamash, holding Henry's hand on one side and Bri's on the other, Charlotte was gripped by a deep sadness. *This was once my family. Who am I now? Where do I belong?*

CHAPTER FORTY-NINE

Friday, December 20, 1811 – Durrants Hotel
Xie Xie

When Xie Xie went to the hotel dining room for dinner, she was surprised to see James, Vaux, Banfield and Rogers sitting at a table in the corner.

Rogers saw her and waved her over. "Please join us. We usually eat at our club on Friday nights, but this time of year people rent out the club for parties and it wasn't our crowd."

"Septuagenarians," said Banfield.

Edward seemed withdrawn. "Good evening, Miss Li."

Lady Gabriella will not like that Mr. James is here with me. Tonight may plant the final seed of temptation.

"You are not with Lady Gabriella tonight, Mr. James?"

"Most Friday nights are spent with the ladies in her family. Her Aunt Aelwyn was missing for three years and presumed dead, so there is lost time to recover."

"Presumed dead? That sounds mysterious."

"After Bri's Uncle Rychard was found dead, there was fear for her safety. She fled under the protection of Jean-Louis, the earl's driver."

"Jean-Louis has quite a reputation," said Miss Li. "I've heard he killed a polar bear in Canada with his bare hands."

"Not true," said Vaux. "He used a knife."

"But the animal weighed over a thousand pounds," said Edward.

Xie Xie laughed. "And you believe that?"

453

Edward nodded. "I have learned not to underestimate the Frenchman."

After dinner, Miss Li asked if any of her dinner partners had visited the Asian quarter and was surprised to learn that none had. "My clients have made an investment there in an establishment for drinking, gambling and companionship. Would you care to see it?"

Rogers was game. "Drinking and gambling and companionship? What could be better than that?"

Vaux and Banfield begged off.

Rogers, Edward and Miss Li climbed into a carriage.

"Where is your aunt?"

"Sadly, she breathed her last a few days ago. Don't worry, Mr. James. It's late and no one will remark on my lack of a chaperone."

"That's what I like," guffawed an already-inebriated Rogers. "A woman who dares to challenge the petty conventions of Society."

When the carriage stopped, the passengers exited at *Dreamtime*.

***

Edward

After three games of cards, Edward feigned exhaustion. "It's time for me to go." *Bri must never know of this night.*

"Wait. There's one more room I want to show you." Miss Li led them to the back of the establishment, pulled back a curtain and Edward stared at the contraption in front of him.

***

Xie Xie

Rogers stared at it. "Hell's Teeth! Is that what I think it is?"

"A simple puff is nothing to worry about. A harmless distraction."

She drafted a breath of the opium into her mouth and expelled it into Rogers's face.

He blinked rapidly.

She took another drag and blew it toward Edward.

He turned to avoid inhaling, but she detected smoke wafting up his nose. She focused on his eyes. The faraway stare told her all she needed to know.

"I must go." Edward departed immediately without a look back.

***

Sunday, December 22, 1811 – The London Docks
Blackburn as Count Vlarić

Descending the gangplank, dressed as Count Vladimir Vlarić in a red cape, Blackburn waved over a Hackney, and waited for Zagor to load the luggage. The servant climbed in and took a seat opposite him.

Rapping on the side of the carriage, Blackburn said, "Take us to Durrants."

"How can he hear you, master?"

"He can hear me. Here is a lesson for you, Zagor. Drivers, called 'jervies' in this city, can hear conversations inside a carriage. Watch your tongue."

Zagor said nothing more until they arrived at the hotel.

After they checked in, Blackburn left the red cape on the bed and donned a non-descript cloak. "I'll be back later. Tell the front desk if you want a meal and they can bring it up. Put it on our bill."

The servant nodded.

Blackburn hailed a Hackney. "Take me to the Blue Bazaar."

He walked among the stalls, picking up items that might be of use, workmen's breeches and jackets, boots, and a brimmed hat. He passed by a table with colored-lens spectacles. Signaling to the stall keeper, he asked, "What are these for? I see people wearing them."

" 'Tis the latest rage, sir. From Venice by way of Portugal. The expensive ones are over at Wyndward Emporium, but these are just as good at half the price." Blackburn smiled. *Lady G. at work, no doubt. She is clever to spot a trend.* I'll take two pairs, one green and one gray."

"This blue is a favorite."

"I don't like blue." *No need to stir a memory.*

As he turned, he noticed a colorful tent. *Gypsies?* And then he saw her, the old crone, hobbling with a cane, exiting a fortune-telling tent. *'The cards do not lie.' Fools will pay for her gibberish. Now I know grandmother is in London.* Keeping a discreet distance in a Hackney, Blackburn followed Mirela to the back entrance of an omelet shop. *So, Grandmother, you finally get your dream, courtesy of my townhouse proceeds.*

***

Monday, December 23, 1811 – Atelier Maximilian
Gio

A familiar boot step echoed on the marble floor.

Dog ran up to greet the visitor.

"Bri." Gio didn't change position. "I wasn't expecting you."

"I have a favor to ask."

The dwarf turned around, put down his brush, used a rag to wipe his hands, and gestured to her to have a seat on an adjacent stool. He leaned against his worktable.

"Name it."

"You don't know what it is yet."

Dog jumped into her lap.

Gio shrugged. "Tell me."

"I know you have plans for Christmas Eve night with your family, but I was hoping you might help us entertain the children and mothers-to-be at the foundling hospital earlier in the afternoon."

"Entertain? My voice is hardly of operatic quality and my feet are not those of a dancer."

"I was thinking you might sketch the children and women so they have something personal to remember this Christmas. I have generic Christmas boxes, but I thought something personal might be appreciated. I acquired some crates of unclaimed cargo for Wyndward Emporium that contained an assortment of toys, and a cache of magical-looking carved rocking horses, rabbits, zebras, lions and other animals from Germany, including one unicorn, that have been held in customs since before Napoleon came to power. They're in excellent shape. And I've had clothing brought from Drea's in Ravenshire village to fit the children's measurements, so they will each have something of their own, not a hand-me-down from charity."

"You hide it well, you know."

"Hide what?"

"Your thoughtfulness and concern for others. You are always

thinking of how to help people but your matter-of-fact veneer disguises it from the shallow crowd." He looked off into the distance. "If you give me the unicorn, I will do it. I'll sketch them all."

Bri bit her lip in hesitation.

"What else?"

"I am my grandmother's granddaughter."

"No. Please tell me you don't mean—"

"I am coming as Cinderella. Not in a costume really, but my engagement gown. I might as well wear it one more time. Mlle. Bellerobe fashioned a tiara for me. Edward is coming as my Prince. I found a glassblower to fashion a miniature pair of glass slippers. Charlotte is dressing as Little Red Riding Hood, Gwyneth as a herald angel, Father as a shepherd, Nate as the Ogre who is tricked by Puss in Boots. Aelwyn as a Cinderella's faerie godmother, and Ian wants to dress as a Christmas pixie like his imaginary friend, Nym. I'd like you to wear the costume of Puss in Boots."

"I would have drawn the line at the pixie. That is too predictable. Or one of your mice, Cinderella. That is too obvious. But that clever cat? I can don that costume. Who created them?"

"Miss Drea, on short notice. When I told her why I needed them, her seamstresses all wanted to do it for the foundlings." Bri hesitated.

"And?"

"And I promised them you'd sketch all of us in costumes to display in their shop."

Gio shrugged. "I was as a foundling once. Disposed of, disinherited, alone. And it *is* Christmas."

"Jean-Louis will bring in your costume when I leave. Now, show me what you are working on."

***

Monday, December 23, 1811 - *Dreamtime*
Blackburn as Count Vlarić

Blackburn walked in and admired the progress that had been made since he'd left London. He didn't identify himself. *Not yet.*

He left *Dreamtime* and retrieved his horse from the all-night stables. His senses told him he was not being followed. Mounting the gelding he'd bought after his arrival the day before, he rode through the pre-dawn streets to Durrants. *I'm riding from the most scurrilous to the most fashionable section of London.*

Over deserted streets, it did not take long. After leaving his horse at the hotel stables to be patted down and rested, he entered the hotel.

Zagor sat in front of Blackburn's room.

"You can retire now."

"Yes, master."

The Croatian walked to one of the servants' room at the end of the hall.

Inside his room, Blackburn removed his false beard as Vlarić and resumed his normal clean shaven visage. He detested the longer curly style that was *au courant* in the *ton,* but it framed now-brown eyes. With his medium brown hair darkened to black with the apothecary's potions, streaks of white around the temples, flourishes he improvised, his persona conveyed an aura of maturity. Spectacles with green tinted lenses completed the look. *I don't look like the Blackburn from a year ago.* He squinted at his image in the mercury glass mirror. He knew not how long his visit to England would last, but Blackburn and all his alter egos were men who prepared for all contingencies.

Placing his faux spectacles on a table next to the bed, he reclined. As was his habit before sleep, he mentally listed any problems he had encountered that day and the plans he had for the next day. He had learned from an Egyptian mystic that this exercise trained the mind to send guidance in dreams. Not the fantastical visions of *Dreamtime* patrons, but lucid dreams, messages he could interpret and use to his advantage to survive. Survival at all costs was paramount to exact revenge. Once he fell asleep, dreams came.

***

He turned into a raven, flying over the rolling fields of Ravenshire, his ancestral home. The only portrait of his mother, Brigid, was in a locket that his grandmother had given him as a small child. His mother did not have the same unusual blue eyes tinged with turquoise that he and his grandmother did. Hers were hazel, her hair a light brown unlike his dark locks with hints of auburn, like his father's.

Wavering images passed before him. Finally, he could discern his father standing next to Henry. Their hands reached out to him. *Why? To pull me into hell? Harbingers of death?*

His mind went blank.

***

Xie Xie next came into focus. She was walking away from him. *Is she betraying me? No. I told her she could leave after she delivered James to the poppy. She is simply following my instructions.*

He fell back into a deep sleep.

***

His grandmother's image flickered before him. Above the café, she sat as the Gypsy witch turned the cards of the Tarot.

He was wary of Mirela's powers. The death card, the skeleton knight, lay face up.

Whose death?

Mirela took Aneira's hand.

What does the crown know?

***

Blackburn awoke with a start as the early morning light streamed into his suite. *Acceptance? Betrayal? Death?* His mind spiraled into alternate explanations while his heartbeat accelerated. Sitting on the edge of the bed, he analyzed the messages in his dream, speaking aloud to his cat, as was his habit.

"Acceptance or death. I am never sure what my family offers me. My path has diverged too far for any reconciliation. Aneira filled me with hatred, but I always would have been the bastard, the outsider, the unwanted remembrance of my father's dalliance."

Midnight meowed.

"Grandmother is not young, although she looks twenty years younger, she is near eighty. I must prepare myself for her loss."

Another insistent meow came from his companion.

"But Xie Xie...might she betray me? Or is the dream telling me that her goal is accomplished? That all the chess pieces are in place for checkmate?" He paused. "A seed of doubt is not a bad thing. It will prevent me from becoming complacent. Nothing in this life is certain. I must remain ever vigilant."

His cat jumped into his lap and rubbed her face against his cheek.

***

Tuesday, December 24, 1811 – Durrants Hotel
Zagor

Outside the door, Zagor overheard his master talking to himself and withheld his knock. Usually his master spoke only a few words, not a long rambling monologue. The master always rose at dawn. He was later than usual today, a departure from his regimented schedule. *Is it possible? Could this Xie Xie betray him?* Zagor waited until he heard water splashing in the wash bowl and knocked in the requisite code.

"Enter, Zagor."

The servant entered.

"Run my bath and lay out the dark blue ensemble."

Silently, the servant complied.

***

Blackburn as Count Vlarić

'Tis time to let Grandmother know I have returned.

Throughout his childhood, Blackie and his grandmother had never celebrated the Christmas holiday, other than stocking historical seasonal ornaments and artifacts for sale in the Inverness antique store during the days of the Advent.

Along with the other merchants on the boulevard, they decorated their shop "to attract the susceptible and sentimental who will buy on impulse," according to his grandmother.

Every year, at least one of the antique Christmas ornaments was stolen. "Too easy to slip in a pocket," complained his grandmother. One year it was a pull-string toy soldier. Other years saw the theft of a small white bunny stuffed with muslin, a miniature painted horse, a spinning top painted in Christmas colors, a small clay pipe for blowing soap bubbles, and the last year they carried any such merchandise, a blue bandalore—a disk on a string that, when rolled tightly, was carried back up by momentum—went missing. When only a few items remained from their inventory, Blackie made a proposition to his grandmother. "Let me sell them at school."

"An enterprising boy you are. But you'll have to pay me for them, just as I buy them from vendors. This will be a good lesson for you." She named a price.

Blackie, adept at maintaining a mask in public, suppressed a smile. *I have squirreled away much more money than you know.* He bargained with her, eventually paying half of what she had originally requested.

He sold what he didn't care for and kept the rest. He came out ahead. *I always do.* She never found the missing toys. Just as Neri had given Alia a hollowed-out book, Blackie had one that he carried with him to this day in his black travel bag. Inside was the cache of missing miniature toys.

I never told her that I love this season. She would have thought me weak. The scent of fresh pine garlands they hung around the shop made him smile. The harmonies of carolers streamed through the inched-open window. His grandmother had ignored the sound, but as Blackie had worked in candlelight adding up accounts, the joyful voices stirred his heart.

One night, Blackie went out to fetch firewood, but sneaked away to listen to a choir rehearsing in a nearby church. The majestic chords of the massive organ touched his soul. Ever since that night, he'd loved sacred music, a secret passion.

Tonight, he walked the streets of London amid fiery torches, flickering candles in windows, touches of light snow on the gaslights that melted in moments. *People are happy.*

He heard church bells in the next block and filed in behind other parishioners. Listening to the children's choir and congregation sing hymns of joy, his mind was in turmoil. *Will I ever feel joy?* He left before the sermon, slipping out unnoticed.

Strangers embraced him, saying, "Happy Christmas!"

He laughed, replying, "And a Happy New Year!" *Is this what life might be like after my last task is accomplished? Will I ever know a happy day?*

Every year, he'd been invited to the Ravenshire Christmas event for key trading directors, villagers, and old friends. For nearly fifteen years until his grandmother had poisoned his father, he'd shaken the hand of the 10th Earl of Ravenshire, a momentary greeting or words of general goodwill. He never sensed the man was evil. *What might my life have been like if he had known I existed? Nothing can excuse his behavior with my mother, but a man is more than one act. I am more than a murderer, though murderer I be.*

CHAPTER FIFTY

Tuesday, December 24, 1811 – Winters Foundling Hospital
Bri

Bri, Henry, Nate and Edward arrived at noon. The foundling hospital was decorated with garlands, wreaths, and bowls of sugared fruit. The large reception area was set up with long tables. A fortepiano stood on a wall near the fireplace.

Felix, Charlotte's dog, patiently let the children pet him.

Charlotte, Gwyneth, Gio, Aelwyn and Ian paced around the piano, talking and pointing.

Nate laughed. "I think they're planning how we should introduce ourselves."

Bri watched her father gaze at Charlotte, her ebony hair peeking out from under her red hood. *Will they ever regain the love they once shared?*

Gwyneth waved them over and explained how they were going to be presented to the guests.

"It's time to open the doors," announced Charlotte.

Children and women in various stages of pregnancy entered. Some were no longer with child, but stayed in the dormitories until they were trained by the Seminary for Women's Work. Dozens of children of various ages and half as many young women walked in to find their seats, all marked by calligraphed place cards.

Edward, dressed as a prince in an Elizabethan type puffed sleeve doublet and short puffy pants over stockings, leaned over to Bri.

"You were able to persuade Drea to make clothing for all these children in the appropriate sizes?"

"And for the women, too. They worked without much sleep this last week. It's amazing what they accomplished. The Ravenshire cobbler enlisted his sons, daughters and apprentices to make the shoes."

Henry overheard. "And *our* costumes?" He wore the robes of a shepherd. "I look more like a monk than a shepherd."

Bri rolled her eyes. "Mlle. Bellerobe, of course."

Gio had been listening, and turned toward them. "Why are you amazed at what Lady Gabriella can accomplish? Her vision is extraordinary and her persuasion is legendary." He turned to his muse. "Cinderella, I am your dwarf forever."

Bri curtsied to Gio.

Nate's Ogre mask was green and orange, but not frightening to children. "Come, Puss in Boots," he said. "Let us take our places."

Gwyneth, garbed as an angel heralding the birth of the Christ child, sat on the fortepiano bench. Henry, as a shepherd, stood next to her.

Bri as Cinderella with Edward as her Prince, and Aelwyn as her faerie godmother stepped into place next to Nate as the Ogre and Gio as Puss in Boots. Ian, as the Christmas pixie, stood next to Gio.

Charlotte, in her red riding cape, signaled to Gwyneth, who played a few notes on the piano to quiet the din. "Welcome to our Christmas Eve festivities. Father Christmas has sent a pixie to greet us."

Taking his cue from Charlotte, Ian stepped forward.

Edward leaned over and whispered to Bri. "He takes after you. He commands the room."

Ian bowed at the waist and began to recite, in a singsong voice.

A clever Christmas Eve pixie am I,

Dancing on toes under a moonlit sky.

He began to twirl and do a little jig, to the laughter of the guests.

Cinderella's Prince a glass slipper wields,

Edward held up a miniature glass slipper.

While the Angel sings to Shepherds o'er fields.

Gwyneth played a few heavenly sounding cords.

The Ogre tries, but the cat will not scare.

Nate feigned big paws over Gio, who dismissed the large predator with the wave of his hand.

While Red Riding Hood says, "Of wolves, beware.

Charlotte waved a warning finger.

Let the faerie godmother wave her wand,

Aelwyn waved her wand in an arc over the crowd.

And I welcome you with a great big kiss.

Ian blew a kiss toward the rapt listeners.

The room erupted in applause and the costumed performers spread out to take their seats among the children.

After the meal, a huge layered cake in the form of Christmas boxes was brought in to murmurs of admiration.

After the cake was finished, the group gathered around the fortepiano to sing carols.

While they were so occupied, Jean-Louis, Guy, Gilles and François matched the Christmas boxes to the names on the empty chairs. Two boxes were left at each place with a personal tag. A toy for each child and a set of personal grooming items, such as a comb, mirror, and hair bobs for the adults. Each child and adult received a new item of clothing, shoes, and a nightshirt.

When the still-costumed crew arrived at Pytchley Palace for the duchess's Christmas fest, they entered to another round of applause.

***

Tuesday, December 24, 1811 – Exterior of *Omelettes de Mme. d'Aix*
Voutain

Colvert took a bit of snuff, sniffed and rubbed his finger under his nose.

"He's right, you know. About the snuff." Voutain kept his eyes on the door.

Colvert scoffed. "It's a cold night in December. I have little else to warm me."

"Hold! Who is that man in the red cape?"

***

Tuesday, December 24, 1811 – *Omelettes de Mme. d'Aix*
Blackburn as Count Vlarić

In late afternoon as winter's light waned, Blackburn spotted an urchin lurking in the doorway to the upper level of the omelet café.

This will be a test. Will the goatee, hair and brown eyes fool them? How long will it take? Blackburn gave the boy some coins. "Knock and announce me."

The boy threw the coins on the ground.

"I know better than to go against the Gypsy. She'd be having a spell put on me, she would."

"You are a feisty one." Blackburn smiled. "I could smite you to the ground with one hand."

"But she would curse my eternal soul."

Blackburn laughed at the boy's audacity and shook his head.

"Pick up the coins. I assure you no curses will plague you. Knock on the door."

The urchin did as he was told.

The Gypsy's voice could be heard through the closed door. "Do not disturb us, boy."

"Tell them a Christmas beggar has arrived."

"A Christmas beggar has arrived," loudly called the urchin.

"From Scotland."

"From Scotland," the boy repeated.

The sound of someone trudging down the stairs elicited a smile from Blackburn. Turning to the boy, he said, "Watch."

Aneira threw open the door, "Ar—

"Not Arthur, Mme. d'Aix."

She stared at him for a moment.

He watched her eyes scan his face from head to chin and then stop at his brown eyes.

"How did you—?"

"Would you invite a stranger in for Christmas dinner? I smell the goose roasting."

She put her hand on his shoulder. That was the limit of her warmth. "Come upstairs."

"Let the boy bask in the heat from your fire."

She shrugged. "If it pleases you. There is food enough for a waif like him."

Blackburn signaled to the boy to pick up the coins he'd tossed.

When they got upstairs, Mirela nodded. "I telling you he lived."

"Curb your tongue while the boy is here. And threaten him no more with your empty curses."

The old Gypsy shrugged. "Not empty, but if you wishing, then no more."

Blackburn looked around their rooms. He found a storeroom. "Let the boy stay here. Get a mattress and let him be sheltered from the cold. He will not speak your secrets, will you boy?"

The boy shook his head.

As The Pharaoh, Blackburn had learned that gratitude was a far greater motivator than fear.

All eyes were on Aneira. She nodded. "You can stay, boy. We have extra blankets until we get a mattress." She walked back to the main room. "Mirela, set two more places."

Aneira placed platters on the table, with goose, potatoes and a special bread his grandmother always made for Christmas.

"I haven't tasted a Christmas goose for a long time." Blackburn looked at the urchin, who was awkwardly wielding a knife and fork. He carefully modeled how to cut the goose.

The boy watched and improved.

Blackburn lifted his glass of wine.

Even the boy had a touch of wine in his glass. He followed Blackburn's gesture.

"Happy Christmas!" *This may be my last Christmas with Grandmother. The next steps I take will change everything between the Wyndwards and us.*

***

Colvert

"It's not him, " The snuff sniffer said. "It can't be."
"Fool." Voutain spat on the ground. "Of course it is."

***

Wednesday, December 25, 1811 – Ravenshire
Bri

The afternoon of Christmas Day, Bri and the family went to Ravenshire to prepare for Boxing Day on the 26th. Christmas boxes for the servants had been ready for weeks, hidden away in an unused bedroom in the family wing.

Bri and Edward left on the morning of the 27th with François, but Henry, Gwyneth, Aelwyn, and Ian planned to stay a couple of more days. Henry wanted to go over details on the castle constructions, while Gwyneth and Aelwyn wanted to rest after all of the holiday festivities. Jean-Louis and Guy stayed with them.

***

Friday, December 27, 1811 – Lord Ravenshire's Townhouse
Bri

Arriving in early afternoon from Ravenshire, François dropped Bri at Lord Ravenshire's townhouse.

Edward kissed her goodbye. "I'm going to stop at the bank for a few hours and the crew is coming for dinner at my house while you have dinner with Charlotte."

Bri adjusted the cravat and gold tie pin she gave him for Christmas. "Do you really like this?"

"Absolutely."

"Good, because I love my pearl-and-emerald earrings." She kissed him on the cheek and climbed out of the carriage.

***

Edward's Townhouse
Edward

At seven, Banfield and Vaux arrived with several bottles of wine. "From the Vaux cellars. My parents are in Scotland. They'll never miss them."

"Isn't Rogers with you?"

"He's always late," said Banfield. "I must say, Vaux, you and Lady Gabriella did a marvelous job here."

"What about me?"

"James, you don't have a designing bone in your body."

"Hold on, I chose the colors for my office."

"Let me guess...gray?" Banfield smirked.

Edward grimaced. "Am I so predictable?"

Vaux and Banfield answered in unison, "Yes!"

The doorbell rang.

Edward's butler announced, "Mr. Rogers and Miss Li."

The blood drained from Edward's face.

"Hope you don't mind, James, Miss Li's a stranger here, alone at Christmas. I'm out to spread goodwill and joy," he rolled his hands in a spiral, "and however the rest of it goes."

"Miss Li, welcome to my home." *Surely Bri will realize I had no choice.*

Dressed in a peacock blue silk dress in a combination of empire and Chinese styles, and, as usual, more fitted than the dresses that were currently in fashion among the ladies of the *ton*, Miss Li flashed a brilliant smile. It was not the same dress she'd worn earlier in Edward's office. Her hair fell to below her shoulders, unencumbered by the normal bamboo sticks that held her straight, raven tresses in a bun. *She is breathtaking.*

"You are incorrigible, Rogers," said Vaux.

"I hope so. I shouldn't want to be boring."

Vaux gestured to the wine. "I brought a sampling from the family wine cellar. Some smuggled in from France, of course, courtesy of a certain Frenchman we all know."

Just hearing a reference to Jean-Louis sparked ire in Edward. *I must calm myself.*

Miss Li accepted a glass of wine from the butler, and eyed Vaux. "Why do you all call each other by your last names?"

They shrugged. "It's always been that way."

Banfield added, "The *ton* can be a bit stodgy, eh?"

Rogers grinned. "Do you want to be one of the boys? Shall we call you 'Li'?"

Miss Li gave an impenetrable glance toward him, and then shrugged. "Why not? For tonight only."

After dinner, they played Whist. The men donned their Venetian spectacles.

Vaux had an extra pair and handed them to Xie Xie. "Happy Christmas, Li."

Disappointed in his play after two games, Edward threw his cards on the table. "I'm out for the next game. It's a good thing we're not gambling or Li would have fleeced us."

"You're almost as good as Lady Gabriella, Li." Vaux dealt a hand for Edward, despite his capitulation.

"Beaten by two women, James. We should stage a Whist Meet like the Phaeton Meet, featuring Li and Lady Gabriella." Banfield leaned forward. "Betting would be fast and furious."

Vaux scoffed. "You only bet on sure things, Banfield. Where would you put your money?"

Li tilted her head and eyed Banfield. "Yes, Banfield, who *would* you put your money on?"

Banfield slowly curled his lips. "All betting is private, Li. I reveal nothing."

Rogers howled with laughter. "Banfield, you gossip like a source for *Scandal & Shame*. You'd never be able to keep that secret."

After that game, Xie Xie announced it was time for her to depart. Edward walked her to the foyer while Shore retrieved her cloak. Edward took it from the butler and placed it around her shoulders. They waited on the doorstep while the butler waved down a Hackney.

Rogers took his Phaeton, while Banfield and Vaux climbed into Vaux's carriage.

"I think they're off to the gaming hells," said Edward.

"Come to *Dreamtime* with me. Take another look when it is at full capacity. It's a *very* lucrative enterprise. You don't need to stay long, but you really should see it when it's busy, if only to make an appropriate evaluation. If you still advise me to sell it, then I shall give your arguments their due."

Perhaps I should see it in full operation.

***

Bri

As Bri returned from Charlotte's, she decided to have a Hackney take her by Edward's townhouse. *Without Jean-Louis watching over me, perhaps Edward and I can steal a few moments alone. Father is still at Ravenshire. No one at the townhouse will know what time I left Charlotte's as long as I don't stay too long. Edward and I had a lovely Christmas together.*

She closed her eyes and imagined them in Edward's bed. *Miss Li cannot come between us.*

Approaching Edward's townhouse, the warmth she felt for him froze in a flash.

There on the steps to his townhouse, Edward embraced Miss Li, wrapping her in a cloak. *Her hair is down. What does that mean? Have they been intimate?*

She rapped on the side of the carriage. "Stop. Wait until they are in the carriage, and then follow them."

The jervie held back after the carriage he was following stopped.

Bri rapped on the side of the carriage. "What is this *Dreamtime?*"

"No place for you, milady. 'Tis a bawdy place, a gaming hell, a brothel and an opium den."

Bri sat back in her seat, her mouth open. *It can't be.*

After an hour, she could no longer keep her eyes open. She rapped on the side of the carriage again. "Take me home." *I'll follow him again tomorrow night. I have the perfect disguise from Mlle. Bellerobe.*

CHAPTER FIFTY-ONE

Friday, December 27, 1811 – *Dreamtime*
Xie Xie

Edward stayed for about an hour. "I can't deny the place is hopping. But it is not an appropriate investment to build on. You would have to keep it secret or other partners for your trading proposals would withdraw."

"Come see the traffic on the pipes."

He demurred, but when she pulled his arm, he didn't resist. On the way to the back room with the opium pipes, he bumped into a man with long gray hair and a goatee. In Italian, the man said, " "*Scusami*."

"Pardon me, sir," said Edward.

The denizens in the opium room included dandies of the *ton* as well as one or two well known wealthy older gentlemen with ladies of the night. Only one pipe was free.

Miss Li walked over to it, took a puff and blew it in Edward's face.

This time he didn't turn his head.

"It's just a puff, Edward." He caught another glimpse of the Italian man standing in the doorway.

A huge man hustled the interloper out of the room, as he said, "This is for invited guests only."

Edward resisted. "It's time for me to go."

Leaving, Edward made his way through the crowd to the street where he took deep breaths of invigorating winter air.

Watching him from inside, Xie Xie turned away, feeling satisfied that she had begun to nudge James into his descent into dependence on her and the opium pipes. When she reached the office, Xie Xie pulled out a key hanging on a chain around her neck, turned it in the lock, and opened the office door.

There, sitting in a chair was the interloper. The man took off his spectacles, revealing deep brown eyes. Something about him tugged at her memory, despite his unfamiliar appearance. Xie Xie's first inclination was to scream, which would bring the security man to her aid. But then the man spoke.

"Buonasera."

***

Blackburn as di Lucca

Xie Xie stared at the stranger. "Master?"

"You have done it, Xie Xie. He is delivered to us. Your task is almost finished. Once he fully succumbs, I can implement the next phase of my plan."

***

Saturday, December 28, 1811 – The Blue Bazaar
Bri

Bri, Jane Anne and Dana walked through the Blue Bazaar. Bri stopped and scanned the area. "Let's split up and we'll each take one row of stalls, and then meet at the end. Examine the wares and see if there is any purveyor who offers anything like our proposed hair styling products."

Nothing was observed in the first three rows, nor the second group, nor the third. After the fourth row, they were back at the front and decided to sit at the café to review their options.

Jane Anne bit into a pastry and tilted her head toward the rows of stalls. "No stall is selling such products."

Dana nodded. "There is more room toward the back. It's not a very easy area to access."

"Maybe the cost is less. If they will only lease to immigrants, then Jane Anne can be the lessee, funded by Wyndward Investments, of course. I was thinking some of the items at Wyndward Emporium could be sold here too. And we could add hair products there. The shoppers are different, but the need for products is universal."

"I think we should start with the smallest size stall," said Jane Anne. "And I would have to hire attendants."

"Jean-Louis can provide men for their protection," added Bri. "Let's go to the owner's stall and inquire."

They rose and walked over to the leasing stall at the entry of the Blue Bazaar. Within an hour, they had selected a space, purchased a tent from the owner, and arranged for set up to begin the next day, with sales beginning after the first of the year.

Standing in front of their stall space, Bri said, "Jean-Louis knows some of the stall keepers. Perhaps he can recommend those who have relatives who are familiar and could serve as attendants. She turned and the Gypsy stall caught her eye. A hand-lettered sign read: Tarot Reader & Fortune Teller. "I'd like to shop for a while. Why don't we start walking to the front when the church bells strike one?"

Jane Anne and Dana walked off to shop.

Bri walked over to the large Gypsy who appeared to be in charge. "How much for the Tarot Reader?"

"No more after the one who's in there now. Come back another day."

Disappointed, Bri picked up a crystal ball and other trinkets. As she was paying, the client exited the fortune reading tent. A few minutes later, the Tarot Reader herself appeared.

Stepping forward, Bri said, "I had hoped to see you today."

"A matter of love?"

Bri nodded. Perhaps she can enlighten me as to Miss Li's true intentions.

The Gypsy reached out to grasp Bri's hand, turned over her palm, and gazed into Bri's eyes. "You will lead a long life, and an extraordinary one. Much adventure awaits you."

Bri smiled and said, "Good day to you. I hope to see you again soon."

***

Mirela

As Bri walked away, Mirela asked Vano, "Do you know who that woman is?"

"Everyone knows who that is. The likeness of Lady Gabriella Wyndward has been splashed over the gossip rags for the last year."

Mirela displayed no surprise, but as she walked away, her mind was in turmoil. *A long life? I cannot tell Aneira, but this woman has a good heart. She is not destined to die soon. Perhaps all Wyndwards will not die.*

***

Lash

Lash watched Lady Gabriella walk away from the Gypsy stall. *J-L won't like this. The old Gypsy touched Lady Gabriella.*

***

Bri

Late that night, after all in the household had retired for the night, Bri donned the black riding outfit Mlle. Bellerobe fashioned for her, grabbed a cloak, slipped out of a basement casement window, and trod along the back alley until she spied a Hackney coming along the street. She hailed it and first directed the jervie to go to Edward's townhouse. The lights were on.

Perhaps he will not go back tonight. The carriage is in the stables, not out front. She saw a figure come around the side of the house. *Edward.*

He hailed a Hackney and she rapped on the side of her carriage. "Stay back, but follow him."

The jervie pulled out.

Dreamtime again? She waited. After about an hour, Edward came out, staggering a bit, with Miss Li watching as a security man helped him walk.

Drunk?

Edward practically fell into the Hackney.

Bri rapped on the door rim. "I've seen enough. Take me home."

***

Sunday, December 29, 1811 – Lord Ravenshire's Townhouse
Henry

Nashmir knocked on the earl's bedroom door. "Your bath is prepared, milord."

"The ride from Ravenshire was delayed by the muddy roads. Most of the way is paved by cobblestone, but there are some treacherous stretches. Remind me to speak to someone in the interior ministry about it."

"As you wish, milord."

The valet stood behind the earl and removed his robe, shielding Henry as he stepped into the copper tub, and then silently left the room.

Henry lay back in the hot water, rested his head and closed his eyes. All throughout the ride, he had tried to understand his deep feelings for both Charlotte and Taita. To see his long lost love, a mere ghost of a memory for so many years, only to be separated from her again, tore at his heart. But Charlotte had shared his life for fifteen years and was as close to a mother as Bri had ever known. He opened his eyes. *It is not my nature to be indecisive. Is Taita's love for me a dream from the past that will fade in the present? I can't stop thinking about her. Would he, could he, risk all for Taita? I must know her true feelings. Should I go to Madagascar?*

Confused as ever, Henry sank beneath the water and emerged no wiser than before.

***

Sunday, December 29, 1811 – Lord Ravenshire's London Stables
Jean-Louis

Jean-Louis stood in the door of the stables, scanning the alley behind the earl's townhouse. A man of action and discipline, he never retired for the night until his instincts permitted. Under the blue-tinged crescent moon, he listened to the sounds of the night. He had turned to return to his room adjacent to the stables when he heard a window open. He stepped back, hidden in the darkness.

A black-clad figure twisted as it flattened and maneuvered its way out of a cellar casement. The lithe, shadowy shape emerged, lit by the midnight glow of the moon. An arm reached back to pull a heavy woolen cape through the narrow aperture.

Bri? Has she learned nothing from Blackie's kidnapping of her last year? He had vowed not to let her headstrong nature put her at risk again. The Frenchman followed her, an invisible spectre, as always.

After walking a short way through winding side streets, Bri hailed a Hackney.

Jean-Louis signaled another and discreetly pursued his prey. The streets of London were alive at all hours of the day and night, but traffic slowed after midnight. As they entered a nefarious part of the Asian quarter, a haven for whorehouses, opium dens and gambling hells, his curiosity turned to alarm. *What is she doing here?*

Her driver pulled over to the dark side of the street, giving Bri a vantage point to the gaslit but unmarked doorway of a private entry club, *Dreamtime*. A man in control of his desires, Jean-Louis had known others who had fallen victim to the lure of the poppy. *It's not possible. Not Bri.* The door to Bri's cab opened. He quickly told his driver to wait and sprinted silently until he was close enough to grab her arm before she reached the middle of the street. He pulled her back into the darkness.

"How dare you?" Bri's green eyes appeared luminescent in the cloud-filtered moonlight. "Let me go!"

"Not until you tell me why you are visiting this disreputable sewer."

Bri tried to wrench her arm from his grip, but he held firm. "It's none of your concern."

"Everything you do, by definition, Lady Gabriella, is my concern. Your father put your safety in my hands. After last spring's escapade, how can you be so foolish as to risk your life among the degenerates who frequent these despicable dens of iniquity?"

The young woman looked at him with defiance, yet he saw pain behind her mask.

Softening his tone, he said, "Tell me, Bri. What is it?"

Bri blinked tears away. "It's Edward. I followed him here the last two nights when you and Father were at Ravenshire. I think he's here again tonight."

"*Foutre!* Must I set spies on you at all times? What would James be doing in such a place?"

"What do you think?"

"James is neither gambler nor womanizer."

"But he must be. I'm going in there."

"*Jamais!* Never will you enter such a place. I will go in and find him." Jean-Louis paid her cabbie and walked her back to his cab. He knew most of the jervies in the city, and this one was no exception. "Archie, don't let her out."

"Anything you say, J-L." He tipped his hat to Bri. "Sorry, Lady, but he's the boss. You'll have to stay put."

Bri nodded.

Her sadness propelled the Frenchman forward. He pulled silver coins from his pocket, hoping to persuade with bribes rather than his knife. It worked on the door guard. Inside, the majordomo, an imposing man with a single long braid woven from still-extant wisps of hair on the back of his mostly bald pate, towered over Jean-Louis. When offered the silver, the Asian cupped it in his hand and immediately turned away, allowing Jean-Louis to survey the layout of *Dreamtime.*

Canopied private enclosures circled a central bar area where liqueurs in bottles of varying sizes and colors sparkled in front of a mirrored backdrop. A drape in the back right corner opened, revealing long opium pipes spoking out from a central glass well. A white liquid bubbled as it transformed into smoke that flowed through the hollow bamboo pipes to the mouths of wide-eyed patrons seeking release. Scantily clad Asian women offered themselves to the addled clientele, counting out their own wages from their patrons' pockets.

The former fur trapper approached the scene as if stalking a kill. Adrenaline flowing, his muscles taut, he methodically pulled open the private curtained lairs around the room, peered in and moved on. After moving more than halfway around the establishment, he found his target.

"When does the cargo—" Edward looked up from his position reclining on a floor cushion. "Jean-Louis, what are you doing here?"

Miss Li lay next to Edward. *I should have paid more attention to Bri's unease about James and the mysterious enigma known as Miss Li. Perhaps Bri's jealousy is not irrational.*

"Looking for you. It's time to leave."

The woman rose to her feet. *She moves in the lithe and limber manner of a jungle cat.* "This is a private meeting to discuss the import and export of Asian silk and artifacts. I do not recall inviting you."

Edward rose. "This is Jean-Louis Chevalier. He works for the private bank client I mentioned who might be interested in your clients' wares. Jean-Louis, I'd like to introduce Miss Xie Xie Li. She represents an Asian-Egyptian trading company seeking new markets. This is one of their establishments."

Jean-Louis leveled his gaze at Edward. He did not look at the woman. "Must I repeat myself? It's time to leave."

Edward shook his head. "You don't understand, Jean-Louis. Miss Li—"

"Don't make me say it again." The Frenchman's tone was unmistakable.

"Miss Li, please forgive me. I will resolve this misunderstanding with M. Chevalier. We can continue our conversation tomorrow at my office."

She nodded. "You will excuse me then, gentlemen," and left the veiled enclosure.

Jean-Louis took Edward's arm, pulled him to his feet and steered him out of *Dreamtime.* "When we get in the cab, you'd better have the explanation of a lifetime."

"Explanations be damned, Jean-Louis! I am not used to being manhandled. 'Tis not your place to monitor my whereabouts."

When they reached the cab, Edward opened the door and stared into the face of his fiancée.

CHAPTER FIFTY-TWO

Early Monday, December 30, 1811 – Exterior of *Dreamtime*
Blackburn as di Lucca

Engrossed in their confrontation, his prey hadn't noticed when the Italian merchant exited *Dreamtime*, peered across the street when Edward opened the carriage door. Blackburn smiled at his luck and retreated back into *Dreamtime*.

***

Early Monday, December 30, 1811 – Exterior of *Dreamtime*
Edward

The fury sparking from Bri's piecing green eyes singed Edward's soul. "Bri! Why did you follow me here?" *She must never learn the truth.*

"You are the one skulking around in the darkness of the night. I have followed you for the last three nights. I know you are not a gambler; therefore you must be enjoying the company of that Asian woman, Miss Li, who suspiciously shows up at our private events."

Edward shook his head in disbelief. "Why are you still harping on that? As I keep telling you, Miss Li is a bank client, looking to arrange trade contracts for dealers from Egypt and the Far East." He pointed to the non-descript building he had just exited. "This establishment is one of the operations she represents."

"Women do not negotiate international contracts for such operations."

Edward scoffed. "As a woman in this country does not secretly act as the 'man of affairs' for her father's vast trading empire? Are you so thoroughly familiar with all the customs of all the countries and cultures of this world?"

Jean-Louis scanned the area before speaking. "Do not discuss private business in the street. Ears may be hiding in the shadows. Get into the cab."

With a shrug of resignation, Edward climbed in.

Jean-Louis jumped up to sit next to the driver and the horses moved into the street.

Inside the carriage, the two occupants sat across from each other in silence for several minutes. The wheels bumped roughly over cobblestones that paved this section of the city; several times, a jolt nearly knocked them off the benches during the first part of the journey.

"I thought your arrogance had abated. It appears I was mistaken." Bri wrenched her fingers together, holding them tightly in her lap.

Edward sat back and folded his arms across his chest. "You do not need to know every detail of my banking business. You must trust me."

"Oh, must I? Trust you to sneak out three nights in sequence to meet that Miss Li? She has seduced you into an unsavory area of the city frequented by gamblers, whores and drug addicts." She leaned forward. "I do not want to find out too late that you are a scoundrel."

"And I do not want to be tracked like a wild animal—"

"Then don't behave like one."

"—by a woman harboring bizarre fantasies of my intentions. This behavior is beneath you, Bri. As your husband, I would not tolerate a repetition of this evening."

"Perhaps you won't have to."

Edward uncrossed his arms and placed his palms on his knees. "What's that supposed to mean?"

"I mean that without an immediate and satisfactory explanation of your recent actions, I am not sure I still want to marry you."

Color began to rise in Edward's cheeks. "Bri, I pride myself on control of my emotions, but you are testing me to my limits. You are spying on me as if I were an enemy, misinterpreting my actions, attributing the basest of motives to my client, threatening me with withdrawal of your love and support. Where is the trust that we built over the last year? We are to be wed in a few months' time. You must trust me."

Bri shook her head in disagreement. "Not without an explanation."

"I've told you already. Miss Li is a client, not a lover." He reached over to take her hand. "I made clear to Miss Li in our conversation tonight that the type of establishment she bought is not conducive to establishing the lucrative contracts she seeks. I've advised her to sell *Dreamtime* immediately and reinvest the proceeds into a restaurant in the part of the city frequented by the type of clientele with whom she would like to transact business, and, furthermore, to act only as a silent owner. Men are uncomfortable dealing with women in commerce."

"Perhaps you have forgotten that *I* am a woman in commerce." She bristled with defiance.

"In secret, Bri. In secret. Your father is the face of the trading operation and my bank is the face of the financial operation. You work in the shadows. I am merely stating that Miss Li must also retreat to the shadows to manipulate events without attracting undue notice."

"So women must retreat to the shadows to behave properly in your world. Thank you for making it clear."

Exasperated, Edward threw up his hands in surrender. "What do you want me to do, Bri?"

"Do whatever you please, Edward. You always do." She turned away and stared out the window.

"Bri, it's late and you're upset. Let's talk about this tomorrow."

"It already *is* tomorrow."

"Fine. Please have lunch with me at the bank today. I'll show you her business papers—after all, Wyndward Trading is the main partner we intend to recommend to her."

"And what if I do not approve of her and her clients?"

"Then I will respect your wishes, of course."

The carriage pulled up to the earl's townhouse and stopped.

Bri's reluctance softened. "Very well. Lunch today. What time?"

"One p.m."

Edward tried to kiss her goodnight on the lips, but she turned her cheek to him so the kiss was but a glancing one.

The door opened and Jean-Louis extended his hand to help Bri. She took his hand and briefly turned back to look at Edward. "Good night, Edward."

"Until later, my love."

She turned and walked up the step with Jean-Louis at her heels.

Edward told the cabbie to take him home. *My new home, where we are to live after we are married. She followed me. She embarrassed me. She makes demands on me. I love her independence, but will it ever be tamed? If she learns my secret, will I lose her forever?*

***

Jean-Louis

Lash was waiting in the stables. "I saw Lady Gabriella at the Gypsy stall yesterday. She wanted to see the fortune teller, but the old crone was done for the day."

"Did the Gypsy touch Lady Gabriella?"

"Yes. She appeared to briefly read her palm."

"I'll take care of it."

***

Monday, December 30, 1811 – A London Newsstand

Bri

Despite being out late, Bri slept for only a few hours. She ate breakfast quickly and called for her carriage.

On her way to Gwyneth's, she asked Jean-Louis to stop at a newsstand. She stepped out of the carriage to buy a copy of *La Belle Assemblée,* a ladies fashion magazine that also featured poetry and articles. As she reached into her reticule to pay for it, Vaux came walking by.

"Looking at the fashion plates?"

"I can't deny I find them fascinating. Where are you off to?"

"I'm just out for a stroll. It's a brisk clear day."

"And you?"

"I just wanted the magazine and fresh air, the same as you. May I walk with you a bit? Jean-Louis will follow us so it wouldn't be improper." She signaled to Jean-Louis that she would walk for a while with Vaux.

"Nothing you do would be improper, Lady Gabriella."

She shrugged. "I'm worried, Vaux. Edward is enamored of Miss Li."

"Impossible."

"Quite the contrary. She shows up everywhere! It's as if she is playing some infernal game with me. Durwood, Father, Edward...do all men act this way? Am I naïve, believing in faerie tales of love? Too much of Lord Byron?"

"Edward would never dally with another woman."

Bri hesitated.

"What troubles you?"

"I followed him the last three nights. He was with Miss Li at a brothel, gambling hell and opium den."

"*Dreamtime?*"

Bri recoiled. "How did you know?"

"Rogers, Banfield, James and I went there the other night with Miss Li after we ran into her when we had dinner together at Durrants."

"You had dinner with her?" Bri's voice became more shrill with each word. "And went to *that place?*"

"It was nothing," he protested as she signaled Jean-Louis to stop the carriage.

Vaux paled. "Good God! You didn't go in?"

"No. Jean-Louis went in and pulled Edward out."

"James loves you," Vaux protested.

"So I must accept his dalliances? Is no one on my side?"

She climbed in the carriage, leaving Vaux speechless on the street.

***

Monday, December 30, 1811 – Lady Gwyneth's Townhouse
Gwyneth

In the library, Misty and Mozart, Gwyneth's cats, slept curled next to her on the divan, purring softly as their human companion read a book. The late afternoon light streaked through the two-story paned windows, making the lacquer finish on the two grand fortepianos sparkle. A knock on the door startled her.

The deep voice of Nambotha, her butler, announced the arrival of her niece. "Lady Gabriella is here, Comtesse."

Bri walked into the room and hugged her aunt, then burst into sobs.

"Nambotha, bring tea and scones for Lady Gabriella."

The butler nodded and left.

"What is it, Bri?"

Bri couldn't catch her breath, so the comtesse guided her over to the divan. Misty and Mozart meowed at their displacement, but quickly found places on the carpet where the light shone and stretched out in the warmth.

Gwyneth pulled out a handkerchief from her pocket and dabbed at her niece's tears. "Bri, please tell me what's wrong."

"It's Edward. He is acting strangely, prowling around the city in the middle of the night with a seductive Asian woman he says is a business client."

"How do you know this?"

"I followed him."

"Bri, you very nearly were killed by Blackie last spring. Danger lurks in the night. Have you learned nothing about controlling your headstrong nature?"

"But Aunt Gwyneth, I don't know if I can trust him with that woman."

"What possessed you to follow him in the middle of the night?"

"For the last three nights, he has gone to the dregs of the Asian quarter."

"Three nights? You've followed him for three nights? Good heavens, Bri. Why not talk to him first?"

"Because I wanted to know what he was doing. He was so arrogant when we first met, and lately he's been hiding something, I'm sure. I wanted to know what he was up to. And I didn't know it when I went out, but Jean-Louis followed me, so I was safe."

"Safe only by the grace of God and Jean-Louis."

"Jean-Louis went inside and brought him out."

"Shaming Edward in public? Bri, this is an affront to Edward's pride."

"His pride? What is he doing in such an offensive place? He said the Asian woman owns it. Who knows what kind of decadent activities are conducted there? How can I ever trust him again?"

Gwyneth shook her head. "And how can he trust you?"

"I am not frequenting a gambling hell that houses ladies of the evening."

"No, but you are spying on him. That itself is a breach of trust."

"We are supposed to meet for lunch today at the bank. He plans to show me proposals for trading clients of the Asian woman."

"Then he appears to be committed to allaying your worst suspicions."

Bri hung her head, dabbing at her eyes. She took a deep breath. "Perhaps I am simply nervous about the wedding. I have been unusually emotional lately."

Nambotha returned with the tea.

Bri waited for him to pour it and leave.

She took a sip.

Misty jumped up into Bri's lap and rubbed her furry cheek against Bri's face.

Bri smiled. "Misty, you are a darling. I have been very foolish. My stomach is jumping around, but this tea should help settle it."

The cat jumped down and Bri sighed with a slight smile..

The comtesse smiled. "You're smiling. You must be feeling better."

"I knew you would cheer me up, Aunt Gwyneth. Thank you."

Gwyneth put both hands on her niece's shoulders. "Repair the rift with Edward. He is a fine man and he loves you."

Bri nodded. "I know you're right. Uncle Oliver warned me not to let jealousy prevail. It's unlike me to be so emotional. Now that we've set a wedding date, the reality of it is affecting me more than I realized. And I slept intermittently last night."

"Be kind to Edward and be kind to yourself. Curb your judgmental nature."

"In my mind, I know you're correct. But when I am with Miss Li, in the moment, I feel completely out of control. I must fight to reign in my anger."

Bri hugged her aunt and together they walked to the door.

***

James & Co., Bankers
Edward

The shame of being dragged out of *Dreamtime* the night before ate at Edward's gut. He could not find the courage to tell his father or the earl the truth. But the Frenchman knew, so it was only a matter of time. He would have to face it at some point, but he wasn't ready yet. *Worse, Bri is due here for lunch this afternoon.*

He heard the earl's voice and looked up from his desk to see the earl and his father walking by. They stopped in his office. "We're talking about Gio's Gala Exhibition," said Sir John.

"Gio says it will be the event of the year...until the next day," laughed the earl. "He is uncharacteristically modest in the description."

"Will you be bringing the baroness?"

Henry lowered his eyes.

Edward immediately regretted his question. *I've embarrassed him. The baroness must not be attending.*

"The baroness will attend, but not on my arm. She feels it is too public an event for us to appear as a couple while facing an uncertain future together. We had a lovely Christmas, and I was hopeful we could regain our past closeness. But alas, my indecision has hurt her. I may never see Taita again. I may very well have lost them both."

"Maybe at the gala—" Sir John was interrupted by Duncan's arrival with a bank client.

"What gala?" asked Miss Li.

Sir John bowed his head slightly. "Good day, Miss Li. A gala for the artist Gio, Lord Ostwold, at the Musée de Merbeau on the first of January."

"Ah, of course," said Miss Li. "I met him when I had lunch with Mr. James and Lady Gabriella at Chez Michel." She glanced at Henry. "You were depicted on the wall as Louis XIV, I believe, sir."

"This is Lord Ravenshire, Miss Li," said Sir John.

"We met at Lady Gabriella's Engagement Ball in the receiving line, Lord Ravenshire."

The earl bowed his head slightly. "One is unlikely to forget 'the woman in the red mask.'"

She lowered head and placed her hands together under her chin, as if in prayer.

Sir John glanced at his son. "Could we arrange an invitation for Miss Li to Gio's Gala?"

Edward paled, but quickly recovered. "I'm sure we could prevail upon Lady Gwyneth—"

Henry shook his head. "No need to prevail on anyone, Miss Li. I will be pleased to escort you as a member of my party. I will send a carriage to pick you up at seven p.m. on the first of January."

"I should be delighted to accept, Lord Ravenshire. I am staying at Durrants."

"The best. I would expect no less."

Edward's recent scenes with Bri flashed before him. *When Bri finds out—*

Miss Li interrupted his thoughts. "I look forward to seeing your lovely daughter Lady Gabriella again. She is *delightful*. How are her Mandarin lessons progressing?"

Edward saw the confusion on the earl's face. Before Henry could voice his surprise, Edward cut in. "Very well. As a matter of fact, I may join her. Your language contains the wisdom of the ages."

"We revere what our ancestors have taught us," said Miss Li, with a bow.

Bri's voice broke in, translating, "*Wǒmen chóngjìng wǒmen de zǔxiān jiào gěi wǒmen de dōngxi.*"

Edward's mouth fell open. *Bri has been taking Mandarin lessons?*

Bri directed her gaze toward the Asian woman. "Tell me, Miss Li, do you find it as fascinating as I do that the word for "we" in Mandarin is *women* in Romanized letters?"

"No. I never thought of it before."

"*Really?* As a student of languages, I *assumed* you would take note of such coincidences. I've been studying some Mandarin proverbs about women. They are not particularly flattering. Patriarchal cultures, ancient and modern, seek to diminish women."

"I cannot disagree. 'Tis a shame we were not alive to see the Amazons wielding swords of victory."

"Perhaps we can explore that history another day, Miss Li." Bri looked toward her father. "Our agenda for today is full."

Taking his cue, Henry kissed Bri goodbye, followed by Sir John. "We'll leave you to your meeting."

Edward sighed inwardly with relief that the earl hadn't mentioned the gala in front of Bri. *How can I keep Miss Li from blurting it out in a verbal fencing match with Bri?*

Miss Li held out an envelope. "I wanted to deliver the documents you requested, Mr. James. I didn't intend to interrupt your day."

Edward accepted the envelope. "Thank you and good day, Miss Li."

Duncan escorted Miss Li out of the bank.

Once the bank client was out of view, Edward took Bri's arm and led her into his office. "I'm sorry, but an urgent problem arose this morning, and I will have to cancel our lunch together, but I've prepared a summary of Miss Li's proposals for your review."

Bri accepted the papers. "I shall review these with great interest. As for lunch, it's just as well. I have much to attend to myself." She rose to her feet.

"Miss Li may appear from time to time. I cannot control her movements."

"That is clear, but as long as our interaction is over for today, I am grateful for small favors."

Bri kissed Edward on the cheek and left.

How can I tell her about the gala? Maybe tomorrow night at Vaux's New Year's gathering.

CHAPTER FIFTY-THREE

Tuesday, December 31, 1811 – Interior of Edward's Carriage
Bri

Bri took a deep breath. "Before we see Vaux, I think you should know that I told Vaux the other day that I thought you were enamored of Miss Li."

Edward's face briefly showed purplish blotches but he exerted control. "Is there anyone to whom you haven't expressed your distrust of me? I am not enamored of Miss Li."

"Was there an Asian woman in your past? You spent a lot of time in the Far East. Perhaps you are like Father, nursing a long lost love that haunts your dreams. I won't wait, like Charlotte. I won't be your loyal pet."

"I'm not asking you to be subservient. You are the only woman in my heart."

Bri pressed. "You didn't answer me directly. Was there a woman in Asia?"

"I am a man who traveled the Far East for six years. I was not unfamiliar with the charms of women during that time. Have I grilled you over former beaux?"

"No."

"Then kindly give me the same courtesy. The past is the past."

***

Tuesday, December 31, 1811 – Lord Vaux's Townhouse
Vaux

Among his set, Vaux's small, exclusive New Year's Eve dinners spawned conversations for months afterward. This year it preceded Gio's gala, so the usual all-night revelry would be cut short.

Once the Champagne was poured, Gio held up his flute and announced, "We are all like Cinderella this year, leaving on the stroke of midnight. If anyone is late to my gala, woe be unto him or her. The wrath of Gio is harsh and long."

Vaux always invited his auntie to these soirées. His parents spent holidays in Scotland. "Not for me," said his Auntie. "Think of hell as if it were an eternity of damp, bitter cold." She paused for a moment. "Add a drafty castle with frozen privies. That's Scotland."

Gio laughed. "Acerbic wit becomes you, my dear."

"I know," said the septuagenarian. "When I was young, my eccentricity was scandalous. Now people pretend it's charming."

"Auntie is a devotée of astrology, so she is going to analyze us all tonight according to our birth signs."

Lady Marianna was taken aback. "Is astrology not an offense to our Lord?"

"Nonsense. 'Tis but a trifling game. The stars have fascinated humankind since time began," said Vaux.

"*Was* there time before time?" Bri asked.

"That can be next year's topic."

The doorbell rang as they toasted.

Rogers entered with Miss Li.

Vaux saw a stricken look flash on Bri's face and then disappear. *She is in control, but for how long? Edward looks like he might vomit.*

The butler appeared. "Dinner is served."

Over dinner, Vaux's aunt gave uncanny insight into each person based on astrological signs.

Lady Patricia's interest piqued. "I saw an old book on astrology at the Gypsy stall at the Blue Bazaar. I think I'll go back and get it after this evening." She glanced at Bri. "No matter what your Frenchman says."

Confusion overtook Bri's face. "What do you mean?"

"He warned me away from the Gypsy fortune teller and told me never to go again."

The clock struck midnight.

"And the spell is broken," said Gio.

"We had the Great Comet of 1811," said Bri. "What will define 1812?"

"My gala," said Gio. "Until tonight, all!" Gio stood to leave and the rest followed.

"Obedience?" Rogers scoffed. "Not often seen in this crowd." He shepherded Miss Li out to the waiting carriages.

Vaux watched them leave. *Watch yourself, Rogers.*

He signaled to Diana and they went upstairs to bed. *She is the best female companion I could ever hope for.*

***

Edward

In the carriage on the way home, Bri sat back on the leather bench, shivering in the bitter, icy night. Her cloak was lined with fur, but a chill wind blew outside, under the door, and their breath fogged up the windows. She leaned her head back and closed her eyes. "If we are to believe Vaux's aunt, you are the stubborn Taurean bull and I am the industrious Capricornian mountain goat."

"I never put much stock in astrology, but her brief descriptions matched the people in uncanny ways."

Bri opened her eyes and glanced at her fiancé. "You are in a bull ring and I on a mountain top. If we live at differing altitudes, will we ever meet on common ground?"

Edward reached for her hand. "I hope so. I love you, Bri. Miss Li means nothing to me."

"I saw you embrace her on Friday when I rode by in the carriage on the first night I followed you."

The muscles in Edward's face tensed. "It meant nothing."

As the carriage approached Lord Ravenshire's townhouse, Edward leaned forward. "It appears we may see Miss Li from time to time whether we expect to or not." He paused. "I meant what I said. If you want me to decline her as a bank customer, I'll do it."

Bri scanned his eyes. "You will?"

Edward nodded.

"I appreciate your offer. I'll think about it."

The footman opened the door and extended his hand to help Bri exit.

Edward hesitated. "Bri—"

She put up her hands. "No more tonight. Let's sleep on it and enjoy Gio's gala tomorrow. A new year begins."

"But—"

"Good night, Edward." She kissed him on the cheek and exited.

Surely the earl will mention that he invited Miss Li to accompany us.

***

Wednesday, January 1, 1812 – Musée de Merbeau

Gio

Gio announced his arrival, startling Gwyneth.

"Why are you here so early?"

"I wanted to see the final décor. I will leave to pick up Charlotte and return to make a grand entrance. By the way, you look lovely in that shade of blue—azure I'd call it—like the sky over the southern coast of France." His brow wrinkled. "Why are your workers setting up an additional table?"

Gwyneth sighed and shook her head. "Sir Reggie just sent word that the Sultan and several of his wives and Taita will be attending at the personal request of the Prince Regent."

"What? They're back in London? Does Henry know?"

"How could he? I've sent Guy over to tell Jean-Louis. He'll know how to break it to Henry. You'll have to tell Charlotte."

"I'll do it in the carriage where no vases are available for her to crack over my head."

"If there was any doubt that tonight would be a dramatic evening, it has vanished."

"I shan't be upstaged at my own gala!"

"As if that could ever happen. Behave." She paused. "Nate is coming tonight."

"Mr. Parker is still a dashing man, were I the sort to notice such things."

Gwyneth hit him with her fan. "That was all a long time ago."

"But he is here. Now. Love is still in his eyes when he looks at you. Don't destroy the poor man a third time."

***

Lord Ravenshire's Townhouse
Henry

As Nashmir buttoned the last button on the earl's dinner jacket, the valet asked, "Will there be anything else, milord?"

Henry walked over to the mirror to judge his appearance. "No. Ask Thompson to bring me a sherry in the parlor. Is Bri ready?"

"Almost, milord."

"Excellent. We should be early, as Gwyneth requested."

Descending the stairs, followed by Hector, Henry walked into the parlor, where Thompson handed him a glass of sherry. As he lifted the glass to sip, his cravat pin fell on the floor.

Before he could stoop down, Jean-Louis materialized, picked it up, and affixed it to the cravat. The pin featured the Ravenshire crest engraved on a gold oval topped by a ruby. "The Sultan has returned with Taita and will be at the reception tonight."

Henry froze.

Bri's voice startled him out of his shock. "Why so glum?"

Henry kissed Bri on the cheek. "I just found out that the Sultan and Taita will be at Gio's reception tonight. Sherry?"

Bri's mouth dropped open but she recovered quickly. "I think not. Some tea only."

"You look marvelous tonight. Emerald velvet matches your eyes." Bri's auburn hair was pulled high on top, with wisps on the sides while the back was formed into dangling ringlets. Under the empire-waisted velvet bodice with off-the-shoulder puffed sleeves, the skirt a black watch taffeta with a ruffle at the hem reached the top of her ankles. "Edward will not be able to resist you. Have a bit of sherry with me."

"Not tonight. I must keep my wits about me in the event that the devious Miss Li were to appear. She seems to show up *everywhere*."

Henry grimaced.

"What does that expression mean, Father?"

"Miss Li will be joining our table tonight."

Bri blanched. "What?"

"Before you arrived at the bank yesterday, I invited her to join us."

"So I must be humiliated in public?"

"There is no reason for you to be humiliated."

Bri looked away. "I think...." Bri turned back to look at her father. "I think Edward is enamored of her."

"Nonsense!"

Bri shook her head. "I suspect his meetings with Miss Li touch on more than mere commerce."

"That is female jealousy getting the better of you. I thought you were more rational that that."

"She appeared to dazzle Edward on the arm of your Nemesis at our Engagement Ball. I accepted her coincidental morning ride on Rotten Row in November. But after I saw her at the art auction in December, I became suspicious. She was in Edward's office one day when I arrived to join him for lunch and he invited her to accompany us to Chez Michel. I accepted her commercial expertise as it was explained to me. But Edward's fascination with her became a constant topic. So while you were at Ravenshire last week, I followed Edward a few nights in a row to a brothel and gambling hell disguised as a restaurant in the old Asian sector."

"What? Are you mad? That area is not safe for any young woman!"

"I used a disguise. And, unbeknownst to me, Jean-Louis never let me out of his sight on the third night."

The earl glared at the Frenchman. "And you didn't tell me?"

"I had the situation under control."

"Apparently not." The earl's face reddened. "The first two nights could have proven disastrous."

Bri continued. "Jean-Louis made me wait outside while he brought Edward out of what appeared to be a brothel, though he protested it was a restaurant. Painted women paraded along the street outside the entrance. I could tell he was lying." Her jaw tightened. "I despise her."

Henry gestured to Bri to sit down. "I have never heard you use that word. Jealousy is not becoming to you, nor to anyone, in fact. But since I also am held in its clutches, I can sympathize." Henry was silent for a moment. "I don't know many Chinese merchants who would put a woman in such a sensitive position. She impressed me in our brief meetings as an extraordinarily poised and intelligent young woman. I thought you might like her."

Bri stood up, appearing exasperated. "You, too? Must everyone I *know* prefer her to me?"

Henry reached for her hand and pulled her back to the divan. "I didn't say that, Bri. But as a woman who secretly handles my business affairs, I would think you would admire her and perhaps learn from her."

"She is interested in Edward. He is keeping secrets from me."

"Perhaps. But I suspect that she is merely interested in the bank's support of her business interests. You must trust Edward, my dear. Over the course of a lifetime, there will be many temptations. If he is that sort of man, and I don't believe he is, then best to know now, before you marry."

"Charlotte trusted *you* and *her* heart is broken." Tears welled up in the corners of Bri's eyes. "I am undone by these feelings. Overwhelmed, helpless—"

Henry dabbed at her eyes with his fingers. "You? Helpless? Never. No woman, nor man for that matter, can match your determination when you set a goal. That was true when you were three, and it's true today. Don't let your emotions rule your head."

"That is precisely the advice I would have given another before this incident. Now, I don't know how to react. Edward will arrive shortly to accompany us to the gala and that vixen will be here. It will take all my resolve to restrain myself from screaming at him."

Henry took Bri's hands in his. "Nashmir taught me a practice from Tibet. I imagine Edward and Miss Li also have learned how to disassociate from the immediate. It is a method of breathing, a willing of the mind to float above the fray, not engaging in thought. It is accomplished by taking slow and deliberate breaths. Adopt the persona of an enigmatic queen. Assume a regal demeanor and do not fall into the trap of uncontrolled emotion. Act as if you are watching a play, and wonder what the next scene is going to be without getting pulled into another person's drama. Analyze behavior as you would numbers."

Bri sat up straighter and breathed slowly. "Very well, that is soothing." She closed her eyes and spent two minutes breathing in silence. She opened her eyes and looked at her father. "It worked. I will be tested immediately at tonight's gala. I must attempt it with my eyes open."

"Indeed you must."

The noise of hooves outside alerted them. "Edward!" Bri put her hand to her throat.

"Stop that!" Henry rose and took her hands to help her to her feet. "You are my daughter. You swoon for no man."

Steely resolve overtook her. "I don't want to become one of those women who only see themselves as an appendage to a man. If Edward does not want my love, I shall direct my energies elsewhere."

Henry's tone softened. "Don't give up yet, Bri. Something tells me that there will be many acts to this play. Tonight is but one of them."

Thompson opened the door and said, "Milord, Mr. James and Miss Li have arrived."

Bri turned to see Edward standing next to Miss Li, her long black hair piled up high on her head, held in place by enameled Chinese sticks. A long, intricately carved necklace of rubies on her swan-like neck was accentuated by a red silk dress in the Chinese style, fitted close to the body in contrast to the empire style favored by women of the *ton*. The cut of the garment showed every curve of her nubile, lithe body. A slit up the side exposed part of her lower leg, which was considered quite scandalous. Matching silk slippers completed her outfit.

Bri breathed deeply and extended her hand to her Chinese guest. "Welcome, Miss Li. I'm delighted you could join us tonight on such short notice." Bri kissed Edward hello and stood next to him.

Henry reached out and took Miss Li's hand and kissed it in the Continental manner. "How lovely you look in red, Miss Li. A lucky color for the Chinese, if memory serves."

Miss Li nodded. "You are correct, Lord Ravenshire."

Pulling out his pocket watch, Henry said, "I was hoping we'd have time for an *apéritif*, but I know Gwyneth will expect us to arrive in advance of the other guests. Shall we?" He extended his hand toward the door, where Thompson held the greatcoats for the gentlemen, Miss Li's silver-tipped fox cloak, and Bri's black velvet opera cape.

Lined with white rabbit fur, the cape's hood, trimmed in white fox, framed Bri's face. A spray of auburn curls peeked out from underneath the fur. She fingered the earrings Edward had given her for Christmas to match the emerald and pearl pendant that hung on her neck.

As the ladies were helped down the steps to the carriage, Henry glanced at Jean-Louis, who was leaning against the carriage. *The look in his eye is urgent.* Jean-Louis cocked his head and pulled on his right ear, a signal perfected years earlier that meant information needed to be conveyed at the earliest possible moment.

Before he got in the carriage, Henry walked over to the Frenchman.

Jean-Louis whispered in the earl's ear. "A red-caped Croatian count is creeping around the *ton.* He has visited the grandmother."

Henry paled. "The same one Bri saw riding with Miss Li and bidding at the art auction. Could it be—?" He inhaled deeply, and waited until the color had returned to his face.

Jean-Louis shrugged. "His eyes are brown, he favors his left hand, and a beard hides the contours of his face. I cannot be certain, but the height is the same. Not much to go on. But we are following him."

"Say nothing to anyone else. Especially not to Bri."

The Frenchman nodded.

***

Bri

In the carriage on the way to the gala, Bri sat next to Edward, and across from her father and Miss Li. Vowing to act blasé, Bri smiled at her unexpected companion. "Did you attend many galas in China?"

"No, Lady Gabriella. I was orphaned as a child and taken by caravan to Egypt by a family friend who raised me in her nephew's household in Heliopolis, in the shadow of the pyramids. Her family had extensive trading contacts throughout the Far East, and she engaged tutors in English, French and other languages she thought might be useful in trade. It was there, through my benefactor's contacts in the international world, that I attended many embassy balls and receptions in Alexandria and Cairo."

Struck by how this exotic woman fascinated men, Bri suddenly felt provincial. Her stomach fluttered. *What if Edward is attracted by her foreign sophistication? He spent a great deal of time in the Far East.* "Cairo and the Nile enthralled me. The pyramids are unforgettable. Father took me when I was quite young—we saw them on camelback, as I recall."

Henry nodded. "Magnificent. I still cannot fathom how many slaves were used to erect those monuments. I wonder if we will ever know their secrets."

Edward joined in. "Weren't they tombs for the pharaohs?"

Henry tilted his head. "That's the official version. I met a desert-wizened camel driver, who claimed the pyramids were older than recorded history. He whispered to me that they were built by off-worlders and the stones carried by sound vibrations to their final location."

"Off-worlders! You mean life from beyond Earth?" Edward leaned forward.

"That's what the camel driver believed. Someday, mankind may know its origins." Henry shrugged his shoulders. "As the bard said, 'There are more things in heaven and earth...'"

Miss Li smiled. "There are many stories spun about the origin of the pyramids. A Gypsy fortune teller once told me that in ancient times the pyramids functioned as beacons to the stars."

"Beacons for what?" Edward was flummoxed.

Miss Li looked up at the moon and gestured toward the sky. "To the off-worlders."

"Balderdash!" Edward retorted.

Bri's mouth dropped open. "Miss Li, I didn't take you for someone who would seek out a Gypsy fortune teller." *No one knows that I almost visited one.*

Henry shrugged. "Why not? I've been to one."

"What? Father, I'm shocked."

Henry shrugged. "It was at university, a lark. Your father went too, Edward. And Nate, the baron and AJ. It was of no consequence. But back to Egypt. The meandering Nile, the towering pyramids, the fascinating hieroglyphics—altogether, that ancient land inspires awe in all who visit. The magnificence of that civilization! Mysteries, hidden tunnels, and secrets buried in the desert, hidden in scattered tombs swept from memory by the sand storms of antiquity. Incredible discoveries await us."

Bri smiled at Miss Li. "Father is a student of ancient civilizations. He would like nothing better than to wake up some foggy morning

and find himself in ancient Greece or Rome or Egypt."
Edward laughed. "At least it would be sunny weather!"
Miss Li giggled. "Oh, Mr. James, you are so amusing!"
Bri froze, willing her blood to drain the flush from her cheeks. *I will not let envy capture me.* But momentary silence unnerved her. *What topic can I bring up now?* She looked out the window and saw that the museum was in view. "We are almost at the museum my Aunt Gwyneth founded. She took art lessons as a child from Gio, the artist being honored tonight, whom you met at Chez Michel."

Miss Li blushed, and said, "Please forgive my inept comportment on that day. I had never seen such a little man before. He deflected my *faux pas* elegantly. I look forward to seeing his work."

Henry leaned toward her and said, "You will be impressed, my dear. *Very* impressed."

CHAPTER FIFTY-FOUR

Wednesday, January 1, 1812 – Gio's Gala at Musée de Merbeau
Henry

Henry led the group up the quarried gray-shaded granite steps to the Musée de Merbeau entrance, past uniformed guards on each side of the massive, arched iron double doors, salvaged from the entrance of the ruins of a 15th century French castle. Invitations in hand, the earl guided Bri, Miss Li and Edward through the foyer, framed by giant urns of fresh flowers three feet high on each side, toward the director of the museum. M. du Bois greeted them and gestured toward the end of the foyer where Lady Gwyneth stood at the head of a receiving line for the guests, with Gio standing next to her.

***

Charlotte

Nate, Aelwyn and Charlotte had arrived before Henry's party and stood nearby sipping Champagne.

Ian stood transfixed by the trio of violinists.

Nate nodded toward the boy. "Unusual to see a child at a gala such as this."

"It was Gio's idea," said Aelwyn. "He said he wanted another person as short as he was. Ian is thrilled."

Wearing a miniature version of the earl's breeches, shirt and waistcoat, Ian sported his first cravat, a personal gift from the earl.

"The 12th Earl-in-training," observed Charlotte. *If Henry and I had married and had a son...*

***

Gio

As the earl's party moved through the receiving line, servers brought trays filled with flutes of Champagne from the de Merbeau vineyards, smuggled through Napoleon's blockade through the efforts of Jean-Louis. When Henry reached his sister, he kissed her on the cheek. "The museum looks magnificent, Gwyneth."

"I do hope so, Henry."

Gio added, "Hope is superfluous. As usual, Lady Gwyneth has seen to every detail. And," he pulled the earl's arm down so their heads were closer together, "she has even kept me almost sober so far."

Henry shook his head. "Always the rake, Gio. Decades have not tamed your impudence."

"Impudence is my trademark. Life would be ever so dull following rules."

"Bri told me that you've met Miss Li."

"An unforgettable encounter." Gio clicked his heels together in a mock Prussian posture.

Miss Li bowed her head in greeting. "Forgive me, Lord Ostwold. I spoke out of ignorance. I look forward to your exhibition."

"Some of the paintings are for sale. Feel free to double the asking price of any of them." He shrugged. "If it eases your conscience, that is." He smiled. "I detect a faint blush, Miss Li. Perhaps my sense of humor is not common in your part of the world."

"It is not common in any part of the world, thank God," added Henry.

"How lovely you look tonight, Miss Li."

Xie Xie bowed to Gwyneth and Gio. "I look forward to seeing your work, Lord Ostwold."

"Perhaps you'd like to commission a portrait of *yourself*, Miss Li. In your red mask. Beat the *ton* at its own game of gossip."

"Perhaps, Lord Ostwold. Perhaps."

"Miss Li, may I introduce my son, Maximilian?"

Henry tilted his head toward Miss Li. "When I first met Maximilian, he, like Gwyneth, was taking art lessons from Gio and Mme. Victoire. At that time, he was introduced as the orphaned son of a noble family."

Miss Li looked confused.

Gio tilted his head to one side. "Yes, Miss Li. Until my family accepted Maximilian, I felt it best to hide his ancestry. Eventually, their shame of not drowning me at birth in the nearest lake subsided, as I became somewhat well known in Society. And Maximilian, not being as 'unusual' a creature as I, pleased them. So now, all is known."

Smiling a mysterious smile, Miss Li said, "I have learned, Lord Ostwold, that 'all' is never known."

"Indeed, Miss Li? Tell me what *you* are hiding." Gio took a sip of wine.

Betraying no sign of awkwardness, she answered, "We all have secrets, do we not?"

Gio took her measure. *There is something nefarious beneath this beautiful exotic exterior. Surely the earl, a man of the world, is no fool and knows this. I shall endeavor to learn her secrets.* He shrugged and turned to kiss Bri's hand. "Ah, my darling Lady Gabriella, a vision in the darkest green of the farthest nebulae in my astronomical paintings. If you tire of James, I am always available as a suitor."

Bri leaned over and whispered in his ear. "It is not I who may have cold feet. I need your advice, later." Gio played his role, reacting in mock horror. "Lady Gabriella, you make me blush!"

From his expression, Gio could see that Edward found no humor in his antics. "James, watch your step or I shall dance her out of your arms and into my heart."

Edward shook his head in exasperation. "Gio, were you not such a monumental talent, someone would have challenged you to a duel long ago."

"But many have, young James." He gestured with his hand as if skipping stones onto a lake's surface. "And each has been disposed of, one by one by one. I happen to be an excellent marksman but even more lethal with a knife, as you no doubt saw at Summerfest. You see, Edward, I should have been in the circus, billed as 'Knife-thrower extraordinaire'!"

***

Bri

Bri searched for Clarissa and Dr. St. Cloud. She found them admiring one of Gio's newest paintings, created for this exhibition: *Birth of a Nebula.* "Ethereal. Fantastic. It pulls you into its spell," said Dr. St. Cloud. Absorbed in examining the artwork, he didn't see Bri approach.

Clarissa flouted convention by being seen in public when she was great with child. She greeted Bri with a kiss on the cheek and then nudged the doctor.

He turned and kissed her other cheek. "Where's James?"

"Bringing more Champagne. And Miss Li is here tonight, escorted by my father."

Dr. St. Cloud and Clarissa looked at each other, not knowing what to say.

Trying to affect an air of nonchalance, Bri said, "Both Edward and Father consider her an important liaison for the bank and the trading company. Apparently, we are going to be enjoying her company at *every* major social occasion for as long as she stays in London."

Edward appeared with the Champagne, and Bri took one and turned away from him to look at the painting. She took a deep breath, and regained her composure. "Edward, darling, isn't this painting magnificent?"

"A bit fanciful for my taste. Farfetched imagination in that Gio."

"Again, Edward, your tendency to dismiss what you don't understand is annoying." Bri turned to him and said, "Gio went to France to see through the largest telescope in Europe—by changing lenses and refractors, he saw the colors—colors are all a trick of light anyway."

" 'Again'? This will be a long night, my darling, if your tone does not lighten."

"Would you dictate my behavior tonight and forever?" Bri's eyes bored into Edward's.

Clarissa said, "We should find our table. We'll see you later."

After they left, Bri continued. "Now you are embarrassing me in front of our friends."

"I? It is *you* who called me 'annoying.'"

"Why did you not tell me Miss Li would be accompanying us tonight?"

"It was a last minute request by your father. He had planned to go alone because the baroness felt it was too public an event to be seen as his escort."

"And that was *before* she knew Taita would be in attendance."

"What?" Edward glanced back toward the large gathering. "I had no idea. Ah, there she is with the Sultan."

"You know I do not like her."

"Taita?"

"No. Miss Li."

"I know she makes you uncomfortable, but there is nothing between Miss Li and me. Nothing."

Bri resolved to be calm. "Very well. Let us enjoy the evening. It's about Gio, not us."

"Precisely."

Always alert to proper decorum, Edward offered Bri his arm and guided her to their table.

The last of the pre-dinner toasts had been offered and the guests wandered about the exhibition, with the violins lending a lilting cadence in the background, until the formal call to dinner would be made.

Bids were being taken by museum representatives for a silent auction. The artworks would hang on display for the month-long exhibition, and then be delivered to buyers at its conclusion. Gwyneth had already purchased some paintings for the permanent collection of the museum, and some had been loaned out for the gala, but the hope was that collectors tonight would make donations to fund the museum's endowment. The Wyndward family could fund the museum in perpetuity, but Gwyneth hoped to broaden appeal and generate a long-lasting legacy in the de Merbeau name.

Bri saw Gio standing by himself near the portrait of her mother in her wedding dress. She walked over to him. Most people were in the main gallery looking at the astronomical paintings. He looked up at her and suggested they sit on a carved oak bench placed in front of the wall facing the paintings. "We are alone," he whispered. "Tell me what is troubling you."

"Every time I see Edward now, Miss Li is there. First at our Engagement Ball, then riding in the park, at an art auction, at his office, at luncheon, at Vaux's New Year's Party, and tonight. I think she is hiding something. And worse, Gio, although I am ashamed to admit it, I followed him to the Asian sector a few nights ago."

Gio leaned back in dismay. "Bri, that is dangerous! What were you thinking? You could have been—"

Bri held up her hand. "Jean-Louis followed me. At first I was angry, but then realized I was lucky. Jean-Louis has always looked out for me. He went into an establishment of ill repute, found Edward with Miss Li and brought him out. Edward said he was advising her against investing in such dens of iniquity. Gambling, ladies of the night, frequented no doubt by murderers and worse—"

"What could be worse than murderers?"

Frustrated, she shook her head. "I don't know. I only know that his behavior has changed and I wonder if our marriage is a bad idea. Maybe my interest in him was just a reaction against Blackie's treachery. Edward rescued me and I imagined it was love. Maybe it was just gratitude. We are very different."

"My dear, you and James are very well matched. I have a sense about people. It's a benefit of my stature. I can't look in people's eyes, but I can read their minds."

Bri laughed.

"On one point, you are as prescient as I."

Bri gave Gio a quizzical look. "Which point?"

"I think Miss Li is hiding more than the usual cache of secrets. Under that Far Eastern mask of control lurks more than an exotic mind. Her mysterious aura obscures a truth that suggests danger to me. Perhaps Jean-Louis should undertake a surreptitious investigation of her background."

Looking to the shadows, Bri signaled for the ubiquitous Jean-Louis to come over.

Gio twisted to see the bodyguard and raised an eyebrow. "*Bon soir, mon ami.*"

Jean-Louis smiled. "I bow to the master of brush, canvas, color and composition."

"Jean-Louis, Gio suggested that I could put my misgivings about Miss Li to rest if you investigated her. Without letting Edward know.

Or Father, for that matter."

"Lord Ravenshire may not approve." Gio looked at Jean-Louis for confirmation.

"The earl has charged me with defense of his family and has never questioned any device of mine. It will be done."

Edward called from the entry of the portrait room. "Here you are, Bri darling. I've been looking for you. If we want to bid on any paintings, time is running out. Gio, your fortunes shall no doubt increase tonight."

Jean-Louis disappeared into the shadows of the back hallway.

***

Charlotte

The baroness admired Gio's featured painting of the Great Comet and its arc across the spray of stars.

A voice startled her. "My *chef d'oeuvre*, don't you agree?"

"Yes. It *is* a masterpiece."

"Let me paint you. I've begged for years. I won't be around forever..." Gio took a sip of Champagne.

"Why not? I don't know why I've resisted for so long."

Miss Li approached them. "Is this the Great Comet everyone is talking about?"

"Yes, Miss Li. Let me introduce the Baroness Glasspool."

Charlotte nodded in greeting. "Hello, Miss Li."

"Baroness, I've read about you in *Scandal & Shame*."

Charlotte dismissed the reference with a wave of her hand. "It's all true. The earl is still a friend, but we are not as close as we once were. The island woman is seated over there." Charlotte pointed in the direction of the Sultan's table. "Maybe you'd like to speak to *her*."

Turning on her heel, Charlotte walked away.

Gio scowled at Miss Li. "You have been the subject of speculation in *Scandal & Shame* as well as the baroness. 'The woman in the red mask' is notorious in the *ton*." Without waiting for Miss Li to respond, Gio hurried to catch up with Charlotte, calling, "Wait!"

The baroness turned to say something to Gio, unexpectedly bumping into someone.

"Henry!"

"I'm stumbling into a lot of people tonight. I nearly knocked over a Croatian count moments ago."

Charlotte nodded as Gio caught up to them. "I saw him earlier when he came in. He swirls that red cape around him like a bullfighter."

"I didn't *intend* to charge him." Henry shrugged.

"*I* would have." Gio raised his glass and disappeared into the crowd.

***

Henry

It was no accident that I bumped into the man in the red cape. I wanted a closer look at him. Could it be Blackburn? He craned his neck to see the man, but the red cape was nowhere to be seen. *Vanished like a wavering spectre in a dream.*

CHAPTER FIFTY-FIVE

Wednesday, January 1, 1812 – Gio's Gala at Musée de Merbeau
Charles

Charles leaned against a pillar on the periphery of the ballroom, observing the most important arbiters of London society from a distance. For a moment, he imagined one of those medieval tableaux where the knights bowed before the king at a coronation.

Gio walked over to join him.

Laughing softly, Charles said, "You beat them at their own game, Grandfather. They come to fête you, the reigning dwarf of British aristocracy."

"The *only* dwarf of British aristocracy, so far as I know," said a voice Charles didn't recognize. Turning his head, his eyes absorbed her while his mind translated her image into a poet's vision. *An untamed curly head of pumpkin-colored hair tumbling over irises of raw umber offset by skin as pure as cow's cream.* He was lost for a moment, and then recovered. "The gallery's art restorer, I believe—Miss Rybicki?"

"Yes, Mr. da Garfagnini."

"Please call me Charles."

"As you wish, but only for this evening. And you may call me Bettina."

"Only for this evening." He moved over to her. "May I escort you to your table, Bettina?"

She nodded toward the back of the room. "We are practically

seated in the Colonies, Charles. We may be surrounded by noble savages. But yes, you may escort me there."

Gio patted Charles on the back, smiled at his art restorer, and continued to circulate.

Charles offered Miss Rybicki his arm, and they maneuvered around the chattering nobility, overhearing the odd comment about Gio's art.

"Stunning."

"An amazing body of work."

"He must have used a ladder."

"What an imagination! It's fantastical!"

It was not lost on Charles that Bettina turned a few heads in her gown, the color of fuchsia in high bloom, cut high in front, but very, very low in back, nearly to her waist. The contrast of her hair and dress would deter most women from the pairing, he knew. *This is a woman unafraid to stand out in a crowd. No wonder my grandfather recommended her for this position. Most art restorations were done by men, but Grandfather, and the comtesse, for that matter, are iconoclasts.*

Arriving at her table, he said, "I see no noble savages at your table. Rousseau would be disappointed."

"Would he?"

"Perhaps we can discuss his ideas later, after the festivities."

Smiling, she sat down and looked up at him. "Perhaps."

He bowed slightly, and walked to the front of the room to his table.

***

Henry

The earl signaled Jean-Louis.

When the Frenchman came over, the earl whispered to him, "I bumped into the Croatian count accidentally."

Jean-Louis raised an eyebrow.

The earl shrugged. "On purpose. He did not resemble Blackburn, but there was something about him that felt familiar."

"I'll study him from the shadows."

***

510

Gio

Gio watched as Charles's gaze fell on Bettina a bit too long after she was seated at her table. *Will he make the same choice as I? Elevating love over an aristocratic bloodline? Maximilian grew to normal height, without any of my deformities, as did Charles. Perhaps I am the only anomaly, the only freak in the family, a divine punishment for some ancestor's transgression.*

Lady Gwyneth nudged his arm. "Are you prepared to be fêted, Gio?"

The guest of honor bowed to his benefactor and said, "I am always prepared to receive adulation, my Lady Gwyneth, but tonight you have *commanded* it of these guests."

Gwyneth touched him lightly on the shoulder. "Nonsense. Your life's work surrounds us. The crowd stands in awe, as do I."

Shrugging, Gio offered her his arm to escort her to the head table, but first they stopped at the Sultan's table to pay their respects. After all the introductions, the Sultan pointed to a painting of the Great Comet. "I must have that one. Name the price."

Gio glanced at his *pièce de resistance* and quoted an outrageous figure.

The Sultan's ample belly shook as he laughed. "A man who knows his worth! My Fy admired it, so I will meet your price for my sweet wife."

Gio didn't flinch. "Perhaps you should buy one for each of your wives."

"A droll dwarf you are, Lord Ostwold."

"I am not a troll."

"*Droll.* Perhaps my accent made my intention unclear. I meant your wit."

Gio bowed as he guided Gwyneth to their table. He overheard another wife say, "*I* like that one. Why does Fy get a painting?"

The Sultan took her chin in his hands. "Rana, you are my newest wife. It is my nature to be generous. Do not demand things of me."

Gio whispered to Gwyneth, "His touch is gentle but his tone leaves no doubt that she misspoke."

After they were seated, Gio whispered to Gwyneth, "If I had a shilling for every time I was called a 'droll' dwarf, I'd be richer than Ravenshire. Were I to object to strongly, the Sultan could smite me and the Duke could ostracize me. I have to bow to their taunts and appear amused." He took a sip of wine. "Gwyneth, you are a goddess, captivating me since you first walked into Mme. Victoire's gallery. I may never say this again, so listen closely—thank you."

Gwyneth shook her head. "You don't fool me, you old devil. Under that gruff exterior, there *is* a beating heart."

Tilting his head, he smiled. "For tonight, perhaps. Then back to stone-cold marble tomorrow."

"So will that be your memorial stone? A hunk of marble carved to look like a heart?"

"Broken or with a chunk out of it, for as you can see, I am not a whole man."

Gwyneth's anger seethed to the surface, her cheeks blushed to a magenta hue, and she hissed, "Enough! You are a magnificent artist, a dear friend, and the kindest soul I know. Cease these protests! I won't have it tonight. Tonight you are as a star in one of your astronomical paintings, the one who lights the room."

Softening to her entreaties, Gio reached for her hand. "Forgive me, Lady Gwyneth. I have mastered the art of the quick-tongued response and fell into that habit without thinking of its impact on you. "

Focusing directly into his eyes, Gwyneth smiled. "I know you deflect pain with humor. Tonight, however, you are among friends. We accept you. Accept yourself."

Gio's eyes misted a bit, and he reached for the wine to regain his composure.

Henry raised a glass. "I'd like to make the first toast of the night, if you two would stop conspiring in whispers and join in conversation with us all. When I was young, shortly before I left for university, I was annoyed that Gwyneth got so much attention for her artwork. I decided to try to sketch the main house at Ravenshire. When no one else was about, I presented Gio with my drawings. He paged through the sketches, looked at me, and said, 'Art is about skilled drawing, deft brushwork, color mixing, and compelling composition, all of which one can learn, but it also requires a gift for translating the visions of the soul to paper or canvas and an overriding desire for self-expression. I believe your gifts lie elsewhere, Young Viscount.'

"I stomped away in anger. But he was correct—art was not my destiny. Tonight, Gio, I toast your counsel, and the visions of your soul depicted in the marvelous work that surrounds us. Raise your glasses for Gio!"

"Hear, hear!' the table cheered.

Gio smiled and raised his glass in thanks. "Lord Ravenshire, Lady Gwyneth, and the late Mme. Victoire were my second family after Maximilian's mother died. I spoiled Bri since before she could speak, but even at that age, she could glower." He glanced around the table. "To all of you, Henry, Bri, Gwyneth, Maximilian, Ginette, Charles, James, Nate, Aelwyn, Charlotte and Ian—you are my family. And, Miss Li, I hope to learn more of your fascinating life this evening." He held up his glass. "To family!"

"To family!"

The table of honor had fourteen chairs but only thirteen people. The artist leaned forward to speak to his grandson loudly enough for all to hear. "Charles, there is an empty chair for a guest you neglected to invite. Perhaps you would care to escort Miss Rybicki from her table to join us?"

Charles blanched.

Maximilian looked at his son. "By now, you know your grandfather's unerring ability to embarrass. He doesn't want an empty seat."

Charles looked at Lady Gwyneth. "I would not want to presume, Lady Gwyneth—"

"No need to hesitate, Charles. Bring the young lady here at once."

Gio echoed, "At once!"

Charles pushed his chair back and gathered his nerve. "I shall return shortly."

"I always return shortly." Gio sipped his Champagne.

Making his way to the back of the room, Charles spotted Bettina.

Gio twisted in his chair to watch the exchange. "This could lead to a duel, I suppose, if she has an escort already."

Gwyneth grimaced. "Gio, it is unseemly to speak of duels when it may be your grandson's life at stake."

"I jest. *I* placed the people at that table, and I can assure you, my dearest Lady Gwyneth, Miss Rybicki has no escort." He watched as Bettina stood and waved adieu to her table companions. "I see our Charles has been successful." Turning back to face the others, he added, "Miss Rybicki is a talented art restorer. She has an eye for color and brushwork that are unique. I think she may become a well known artist in her own right."

Gwyneth looked at Gio. "You planned this from the start, you old devil!"

"As if he could ever be stopped from trying to manage the lives of everyone he knows." Maximilian leaned back in his chair.

Ginette laughed. "And you love it, my darling. He is almost always correct."

Bri agreed. "He painted my portrait as a child, and we talked for hours as I held the pose. Gio told me I was willful, brilliant, difficult, insightful and impatient."

"Really, Lady Gabriella?" Gio raised an eyebrow. "I thought all you heard was brilliant and insightful."

Edward laughed. "No, Gio, she has an excellent memory. Complete conversations are repeated to me verbatim should I misremember a salient point."

Bri glared at Edward.

Henry laughed. "You're not the *only* one to experience that."

"In my culture, a woman *never* criticizes a man in public." Miss Li twirled her Champagne flute in her fingers.

Gio could feel the heat of Bri's anger in the air. "Well, Miss Li, in *our* culture, we don't drown defective children."

The servers broke the chill as they brought the dinner selections to the table.

Between courses, Gio circulated around the room and the exhibition gallery.

Vaux and Banfield approached him.

The viscount shrugged. "According to the bids, it will take our joint inheritances to purchase one of your masterpieces."

"That is how it should be." Gio smirked.

Banfield elbowed Vaux. "Just before the final announcement of bids, Vaux will take another look. I'm out of the bidding process."

"Once your opera is produced, I'll give you the original of the advertising poster. *Gratis.* I've always wanted to work on an opera."

Banfield extended his hand. "That's an offer I can afford to accept."

Gio shook Banfield's hand. Over the composer's shoulder, Gio noticed that Henry was talking to Taita. "Please excuse me, gentlemen." He approached and heard a bit of their exchange.

Henry's sentence ended, "—Sultan's permission."

Taita's response was measured. "I don't need the Sultan's permission to do anything. You know I am free. It is my choice to stay with the palace entourage. The Sultan will be in residence in London for a few months—"

Gio interrupted. "Mme. Taita, I am honored that you are attending my exhibition."

***

Charlotte

Watching Henry and Taita talking tore at Charlotte's heart. She turned away and was startled to see Drummond. "Tottie, I didn't know you were here."

"It's the event everyone has been talking about for months. How could I *not* be here?"

"I should know better by now than to underestimate you."

"You look beautiful in that shade of blue." He tilted his head toward the Sultan's table. "Do you see the Chinese woman talking with the Sultan?"

Charlotte nodded.

"I met her by chance shortly after her arrival in London."

"She is a business associate of Edward James."

Drummond raised an eyebrow. "She works fast. And how does Lady Gabriella like her involvement with James? Miss Li's body in that red dress leaves little to the imagination. And I have *quite* an imagination."

"I'm sure their association is limited to arranging trading company contracts. She appears to have connections in Egypt and throughout the Far East."

"Connections. Of that I am certain." Drummond narrowed his eyes.

"What is it?"

"Our Chinese friend seems to have sparked jealousy in one of the Sultan's wives. She's arguing with him, pulling on his arm and pointing to Miss Li."

Charlotte glanced in that direction and gasped. "He's raised his hand as if to strike her!"

"The wife is feisty. She's not cowering. The Sultan's face is purple

515

with rage, but look at the muscles flexing in his jaw. He's recalibrating his reaction."

Exhaling, Charlotte said, "He's lowered his hand."

"An ugly incident averted. But a man with many wives must practice self control in public."

"And in private?" Charlotte tilted her head toward the fixer.

"I prefer not to think about that."

***

Taita

After dinner, guests revisited the paintings. The number of bids on the silent auction forms grew.

Vanessa approached Taita as she admired one of Gio's paintings. "Madame Taita, I am—"

Taita turned to address her. "I know who you are, Duchess."

"I do not blame you for the winds of Fate that brought Henry to your island. But that tempest has now reached my world. Turmoil is not conducive to happiness. Not for you, not for Henry, not for Charlotte, not for Bri. All admire you, but their world is in disarray with your presence. You hold the key to their future happiness. Turn it wisely." She turned and left before Taita could answer.

A formidable woman. If she knew, she'd understand.

***

Early Thursday, January 2, 1812
Henry

After dessert and the final fêting of Gio, Gwyneth thanked everyone for coming and bid adieu to all.

Henry shepherded Bri, Edward and Miss Li toward his carriage. He caught the eye of Jean-Louis, who pulled the carriage out of the queue and toward the steps to the museum. Since they were among the last to leave, the crowd had dispersed, so their waiting time was negligible. *Jean-Louis can't get here soon enough. The chill between Bri and Edward is palpable.*

Edward tried to keep the conversation light. "The night was

516

successful for Gio. Many of the paintings have multiple bids already."

As they climbed into the carriage, Henry told Jean-Louis to stop first at Miss Li's hotel, Durrants, which was near the museum. All were aware of the tension, and Henry tried to shift the mood. "Miss Li, I noticed you spoke briefly to the Sultan and there seemed to be some kind of misunderstanding."

"Yes. One of his wives thought the Sultan was being too friendly with me."

"How awkward for you," said Bri.

Henry intervened. *I must change the subject.* "What did you think of the exhibition?"

"It was imaginative and fascinating, I—"

Before Miss Li could finish her response, Bri spoke. "Ah, Miss Li, we have reached your hotel. Thank you so much for joining us tonight."

Miss Li bowed her head. "I thank you all for your generous invitation. The gallery exhibition was marvelous, and as I told Lady Gwyneth, I might have buyers for some of Lord Ostwold's paintings."

After Miss Li had exited and the carriage was underway again, Bri gazed directly at her fiancé. "*Must* Miss Li be with us at all times? What's next? Shall I expect her at my breakfast table?"

Edward turned toward her. "She has the potential to be an important banking client. It's mere courtesy, Bri. The bank must attract new clients and bankers with international expertise if we mean to grow as the world changes and be ready to re-enter Europe when Napoleon falls. That means dealing with different cultures, languages and extensive travel abroad."

"Extensive travel abroad?" Bri twisted in her seat to face him. "You never told me that! How can we both be abroad when I need to be here to handle Father's commercial interests and Wyndward Investments? You'll be traveling alone and I'll never see you."

Edward sighed in exasperation. "Sometimes I wonder if that matters. You're always finding fault with me."

"What are you saying, Edward?"

Henry put up his hands to stop their verbal sparring before it got out of control. "Bri, don't say something you'll regret tomorrow."

"Every time someone says that to me, it already *is* tomorrow."

"Your father is right. Let's talk more of this after we've slept on it."

"The facts will not change with sleep." Bri glared at Edward.
Edward looked at Henry.
Henry shook his head in resignation.
Jean-Louis pulled the carriage to the steps of Henry's townhouse.
Bri exited first. "Goodnight, Edward." She did not look back.

***

Edward

The earl and Edward shook hands before parting.

Edward signaled to François, who had been waiting patiently with Zori since he had driven Edward and Miss Li to the earl's townhouse earlier that evening.

Zori jumped down and into the carriage with Edward.

As his carriage pulled away into the moonless night, lit only by flickering gas lamps, Edward's stomach churned as he petted Zori. *I used to feel energized by the verbal sparring between Bri and me. Now I find it exhausting. Miss Li confines her conversation to commerce. She is beautiful. I must take care not to be alone with her at any time.*

CHAPTER FIFTY-SIX

Early Thursday, January 2, 1812 – Interior of The Sultan's Carriage
Anja

The Sultan's chief wife calmed him as their carriage traveled back to the palace after a late night at the gala for Gio's exhibition. "You nearly struck Rana in front of two hundred people, my love. There are consequences to that, even here. From censure and ostracism to possible legal jeopardy. We are not in our country where you control all."

"I am not an unfeeling brute, but she wounded me." The Sultan's eyes hardened. "She defied my command in public."

"Only those at our table heard her. You must release the episode from your mind. I will speak to her and take her off the rotation for the week. That should be punishment enough."

The Sultan smiled and squeezed Anja's hand. "You always help me, my darling. I shall spend an extra night with Fy."

That will further upset Rana, but so be it.

***

Thursday, January 2, 1812 – Gio's Studio
Henry

The earl's carriage arrived at Gio's gallery. Although the gallery had closed for the holiday week, Henry guessed that Gio had slept unitl at

519

least noon after the gala the night before and would be working in the late afternoon.

Before knocking on the door, Henry's past flashed before him. He remembered Gwyneth taking watercolor lessons here as a young girl with Gio and Mme. Victoire. Gio had bought adjacent buildings and expanded to encompass an entire city block.

The earl rang the bell, and Charles came to the door. "Lord Ravenshire, we weren't expecting you. Please come in."

"Thank you, Charles. Is Gio about?"

"Yes, he's putting the varnish on the wedding portrait of Lady Clarissa. The painting has been drying for more than nine months. The unusually rainy winter delayed his schedule. The varnish itself will take a few months to dry. I'll take you back to him."

Henry followed Charles through the teaching room into the back where diffused north light shone through leaded glass windows into Gio's studio. "Grandfather, Lord Ravenshire is here to see you."

Gio stood on a ladder, working on a canvas that exceeded his height. He did not turn around. The air chilled him because the windows were flung open to dissipate the foul, pungent odor of the varnish. "Just a little more here to finish before I stop; can't have it drying with a streak, now can I?" Completing his task, Gio climbed down the ladder.

"What brings you here, Henry?" In private, all pretensions of formal address were dropped between old friends.

"I need a favor, but don't say 'Yes' immediately. There will be subterfuge involved."

"I thrive on subterfuge! How do you think an artist survives among the nobility? I know secrets…you can't imagine."

Charles cleared his throat. "May I get you some tea before I leave you two alone?"

"Yes, and Charles, please join us. Perhaps you can help. I know I can trust you as I trust your grandfather."

Charles left to prepare the tea.

Henry looked at the portrait of Clarissa. "You've captured her, Gio. I remember when you painted my mother with only your memory and a tiny portrait to define her features…" The earl stared out the window.

Charles returned with the tea.

Gio gestured to the student room. "There's more room in there.

Let's sit down." He led the way.

Once seated, Charles poured and they waited for the earl to speak. Henry watched Charles and Gio exchange a glance. Gio shrugged his shoulders, and waited.

"I am about to ask you to do something that you may not like. You can refuse. I think the Sultan is holding Taita against her will. She denies it, but there's something more she's not telling me. I want to know what it is."

"You want to know her secret."

"Yes."

Gio mused. "Why not? I like knowing secrets."

Henry smiled. "I hoped you'd agree. I would like to find someone who has access to the Sultan's household to act as an intermediary with Taita, to let me know what her life is really behind those pink walls."

"I've seen the Pink Palace in passing, but I've never been inside. I've heard it was built from a specially quarried stone imported from Turkey."

"True. I imported it in the early days of the trading company." Henry ran his fingers through his hair. "I need to know if Taita remains with the Sultan truly out of her own free will or if she is a prisoner with velvet chains. It occurred to me that you have a patron in the Sultan. Since he bought one of your paintings at the gala, he might want a portrait of himself. If you could persuade him that he *wants* such a portrait, you would gain entry to the palace and be in a position to observe the situation and bring me the vital information I crave."

Gio frowned. "The Sultan likes my work. Who better to paint his portrait than the artist who painted his newest acquisition? With an emerging artist as an assistant—perhaps to paint the wives." Turning toward Charles, he asked, "Are you thinking of the same candidate I am?"

Charles smiled. "Miss Rybicki has a following of merchants for her portraits. Doing portraits of the Sultan or his wives would vault her to a new level of client."

Henry smiled. "You have a conspiratorial turn of mind, Gio."

Gio preened and raised an eyebrow.

"Of course, I will compensate her fully for her assistance, in addition to whatever the Sultan pays."

Gio nodded. "Charles, ask Miss Rybicki to join us for dinner tonight."

"And I will inform Gwyneth." Henry grimaced. "She won't like it. Miss Rybicki is valuable to her, but it won't be for long."

"Lady Gwyneth's wrath is indeed severe, Lord Ravenshire. Better that it be directed toward you than me." Gio motioned to Charles to leave him alone with the earl.

"Is there any word on Blackburn?"

"Perhaps, but his eyes are brown. Jean-Louis is watching her. I need you to keep an eye out when you are with Bri. We can't be too careful."

"I am, by profession, an observer *par excellence*."

***

Thursday, January 2, 1812 – Bettina's Garret
Bettina

Bettina sat at a small table in her attic room in a boarding house that catered to single women. The diffused northern light of the late afternoon from a dormer illuminated her work. She had assembled a still life: White-painted twigs arranged in a blue-and-white Chinese-style painted porcelain vase in front of the window, which was open for ventilation of the oil painting solvents.

A gray tabby stray, a frequent visitor, perched outside on the window sill, watching Bettina. The cat tilted her head, unaware that she was a subject of the composition.

"Hello, my petite friend." Over the past months, Bettina had sketched the tabby in multiple positions, so that she could place the cat into any painting with the stance she preferred. She mixed the colors in her palette, kept fresh with a small linen patch soaked in clove oil, a trick that Gio had taught her. The canvas was small by Gio's standards because Bettina could not afford a large one. "All my money goes to painting supplies, little one. Luckily for you, mice are plentiful in this old turreted building. I wonder what your life is like, exploring the towers and roofs of London, finding shelter and companionship wherever and whenever possible. If only you could talk, perhaps I would not be so lonely, but it is lovely having you here."

Bettina heard footsteps on the stairs and a knock at her door. She opened it to see the landlady's errand boy, out of breath from running up five flights of stairs.

"A note has come for you, miss. The messenger is waiting for a reply."

Bettina took the note, smiled, and read the note while the boy waited.

The note was from Gio:

Please join Charles and me for dinner tonight at eight o'clock at our home. I will explain all then. If you agree, a carriage will be waiting for you at half-past seven.

"Tell him I will be there."

Tipping his hat to her, the boy left.

Bettina twirled around and clasped her hands together. "Darling! Something unusual awaits me tonight! You don't know Gio—he has an air of mystery about him. And Charles...he is a most attractive young man." Her face fell. "But I am not on the same rung of Society. Do cats have a hierarchy of class importance? I must be on guard not to fall in love with Charles. He would never marry me." She smiled again. "But tonight will be an adventure!"

She looked at her few outfits. "What can I wear?" She could sew, but there was no time to create something like the dress she wore to the gallery event. She settled on a dark blue dress and a silk scarf with orange flowers that she hoped would drape well and give it a look more suitable for evening. She had hand-painted the scarf using a wax resist technique. She'd never worn it, so it would be something neither Gio nor Charles had seen before. *It will give me confidence.*

Until the light was gone, she painted with her stray friend.

That evening, she dressed and turned to her friend. "Wish me luck!"

The cat tilted its head and stared at her.

Bettina descended the multiple levels until she reached the ground floor. She saw Gio's carriage pull up, and the landlady's husband, who functioned as an occasional doorman, opened the door for her to exit.

"Have a lovely evening, miss, and be home before midnight."

Bettina smiled. She knew that the young ladies living there were expected to comport themselves to be above suspicion. "I will, Mr. Jackson. Good evening."

She descended the boarding house steps and entered the carriage.

***

Friday, January 3, 1812 – Mlle. Sabine's Brothel
Jean-Louis

Mlle. Sabine's brothel operated in a townhouse in a luxe neighborhood. The ground floor housed a men's tailor, an excellent diversion to a steady stream of well-dressed men going through its doors. The Italian tailors, in fact, had become nearly as wealthy as the madam and her female associates.

Jean-Louis passed through the main shop, nodding to the tailors, through the fitting rooms and up the back stairs to Sabine's office. He smiled at the name, which meant "catlike." The hennaed Mlle. Sabine painted the edges of her gray-green eyes with kohl to mimic cat eyes.

In the elegant reception area, Mlle. Sabine met with her clientele at a discreetly placed desk behind a screen, where the clients handled the financial part of the transaction. When that was completed, she rang a velvet roped bell for the appropriate companion for each gentleman.

She looked up to see Jean-Louis and greeted him. "*Bon jour, mon cher.*"

"*Et toi.*"

Jean-Louis followed her away from the reception area into her office. "What can I provide you today?"

"I need to employ another one of your associates for a project that may last a week, a month, or longer, I am not certain. She would have to play a role in the household of a Sultan, only while he is visiting here in London, and be my eyes and ears to the one known as Taita."

"We have heard of the earl's tragic love."

"Gossip undergirds the structure of Society."

"Indeed. What type of role?"

"A Lady's maid or tea server. I don't believe her unique pleasuring skills will be required, but I cannot disavow that potential."

"Some raised in his culture have the reputation of being brutal. I will not have my girl harmed in any way. The Sultan may be well bred, but his entourage may be less educated."

"I also have a man in the household who will be charged with her safety. Satisfactory?"

"Trained by you? As good as you?"

Jean-Louis smiled. "Sabine, you must know no one is as good as I am. But I have trained the man and vouch for him."

"Very well. I think that Giselle would be our best option. Do you agree?"

"She is my first choice."

Sabine rang the bell for Giselle's room. "She doesn't have an appointment until an hour from now."

They waited longer than normal until Giselle appeared, a bit flushed.

"Giselle? I rang for you nearly ten minutes ago."

"*Oui, Mademoiselle*, but I was in the bath and had to dress. *Excusez-moi*, forgive me." She looked at Jean-Louis for help.

"Do not trouble yourself with apologies, Giselle. I have another lucrative opportunity for you. I want you to seek employment with the Sultan of Madagascar in his palace. As I explained to Mlle. Sabine, its duration is uncertain. Your task will be to inform me as to what is taking place in the household, specifically related to the woman known as Taita."

Giselle's eyes widened. "*Mais, oui. Certainment, Jean-Louis.*"

Jean Louis continued. "You will seek employment through the kitchen entrance. Ask to speak to Wally Connors. He will see to it."

"Will it be the same payment arrangement as the last time?" Giselle waited for confirmation.

"Yes, the money will be deposited in your name in the same bank." Jean-Louis looked at Sabine. "When can she start?"

"Tuesday would be best to start, I think. Will that work for you, Giselle?"

"Yes."

"I will have some appropriate clothing and instructions delivered to you here."

Giselle nodded.

"That will be all, then, Giselle." Sabine checked the time. "Your next client is due soon."

"Yes, Mademoiselle. And thank you, Jean-Louis. I won't let you down."

The girl left and Mlle. Sabine twirled her quill pen in her hand. "I should be angry with you, Jean-Louis. Giselle is one of my best girls, and your little jobs will make it easier for her to return to France with enough to buy a little flower shop, her dream."

"As usual, Sabine, you will be handsomely compensated."

"And by such a ruggedly handsome man. Someday, Jean-Louis, you will tell me who she is."

Jean-Louis pretended to be confused. "Who?"

"The woman who broke your heart, of course. Whoever and wherever she is, she must be extraordinary."

Jean-Louis tipped his hat and exited out the back entrance.

CHAPTER FIFTY-SEVEN

Friday, January 3, 1812 – *Dreamtime*
Xie Xie

Xie Xie met The Pharaoh in the back office of *Dreamtime* late Friday evening, as previously agreed.

If he hadn't been seated behind her desk when she came in, she wouldn't have recognized her master. Dressed as a dandy, with ruffles and flourishes to his attire, his moustache and blond wig with curly front-swept short hair and spectacles, his disguise made him look completely different than his prior appearance as an Italian merchant or the Croatian count.

"What happened with the Sultan? I saw the dispute you caused with one of the wives at the gala."

"You were there?"

"I even bumped into Henry and apologized. He never guessed."

"Changing your eye color is a masterful touch."

"Has James renewed his attachment to the poppy?"

"Last week he took more small puffs. It is an excellent start because he stopped. Now he believes he can stop at will. I made a comment in passing to his racing friend, Rogers, suggesting that games of chance were loose here, and that a distant relative of mine owned this establishment. I drew him into my confidence and asked him not to tell too many people, as we wished to keep its attractions to only a chosen few."

"Perfect. You fed his vanity."

"I told him it didn't get busy until midnight. I even gave him a secret code word, 'moonglow.' The staff is on alert."

"Ha! James will fall into the pit of his own weakness."

A knock came at the door. "Enter."

The spare barkeep said, "Miss Li, a group of young 'swells' has arrived, using the word, 'moonglow.' "

"I'll be out in a moment. Make them comfortable in the card room. Don't push them to the pipes. Let them get comfortable here. Maybe on the next visit. Let them win so they'll be eager to return."

The Pharaoh agreed. "Make the pipes only for special clients. The more secretive and forbidden that room appears, the more their interest will be piqued."

Before the barkeep left, he added, "One of the 'quality' is that man the Frenchman dragged out of here last week."

A slow smile came over The Pharaoh's face. "He is ours."

***

Edward

"So Rogers, this is the 'new place' that you insisted had better betting odds than the usual gaming hells? I didn't expect to end up *here* again." Edward had chafed under the opprobrium of Bri's temper lately, and had looked forward to an all-male evening.

"You left so quickly last time I thought I'd surprise you, James."

Now, standing again in *Dreamtime*, the scene of his recent humiliation, his stomach turned over. *I know what is behind these curtains. And the last one in the far back is where the pipes flow. The pipes of dreams I dare not dream.*

***

Early Saturday, January 4, 1812 – *Dreamtime*
Blackburn as the Dandy

Rising to his feet, Blackburn glanced at Xie Xie. "You should stay out of sight. In fact, leave through the back exit. I'll handle our Mr. James and his weakness."

"As you wish. Good night, master."

***

Xie Xie

I have done what was requested of me. It is time to start planning my exit. Will The Pharaoh let me go?

***

Blackburn as the Dandy

Hovering just out of sight in the card room, Blackburn watched until the last game was over. He sidled over to a guard and said, by pre-arrangement, loud enough to be heard, "Show me the pipes of pleasure."

"Yes, let's go try the 'pipes of pleasure,'" said Rogers.

"The dreams of ecstasy, the elixir of the angels, the secrets of the poppy." As the dandy, Blackburn took his fingers to his lips, kissed them, and threw them in the air as if sending the kiss to the ceiling.

Rogers looked around his companions. "I'm game. Are you?"

The burly guard shook his head. "That room is only for special guests."

"We are all special guests, are we not?" Blackburn pulled silver out of his pocket. "I'm sure you can arrange something for me and my companions?" *Why wait when a perfect opportunity has presented itself? James may refrain tonight, but his desires will be whetted.*

The guard pocketed the money and turned away.

Edward and the other two players followed Rogers and Blackburn into the opium den.

***

Saturday, January 4, 1812 – Riding along Rotten Row
Bri

As Bri and Edward rode in the early morning, Edward's energy waned. He pulled up on his horse's reins to catch his breath.

"What's wrong? Did you not sleep well?"

529

"I played cards with Rogers and some others at the club until quite late. Too late." He averted his eyes from hers.

This is odd. He told me he was glad to be away from the club and mindless drinking and gambling, but now it seems he's participating fully.

A woman's voice called out from behind. "Hello! Mr. James and Lady Gabriella, our paths seem to cross so often. Isn't that an odd coincidence?"

Summoning what she hoped was a believable smile, Bri answered, "Indeed it is, Miss Li."

"May I present my associate, Count Vlarić from Croatia."

"Good morning, Count."

He nodded and in heavily accented English, said something that sounded like, "*Gud Murnig.*"

"I just met the count at the stables this morning. He is new to London and I invited him to ride with me. Are you game for a race?"

"Not today. Edward is not feeling up to it, and neither am I. Perhaps another time."

"Good day, Miss Li." Edward smiled, "Count Vlarić."

As they rode away, Bri said, "She has an uncanny ability to show up wherever we are." She glanced in the direction where Miss Li and the count had ridden. "I could have beaten her."

"Probably." The banker glanced at his fiancée, and tried to lighten the mood. "Shall I ride around town with a red cape flying behind me like the count? Rather dashing, don't you think?"

Bri curled one edge of her lips. "Rather *arriviste*, I'd say, Mr. James."

"Mr. James again, eh?"

Gwyneth rode up behind them. "Was that Miss Li? Who was that man in the red cape? I think I saw him at the gala."

Edward smirked as he turned around to answer her. "An *arriviste*."

***

Sunday, January 5, 1812 – The Pink Palace
Gio

In response to his thank you note to the Sultan for buying his painting of the Great Comet of 1811, Gio had received an invitation for an audience with the Sultan at the Pink Palace.

Xerxes, who had introduced himself to Gio as the Sultan's vizier, maintained a thoroughly chilling presence as he strode through the pink granite hallways.

Gio struggled to keep pace with him.

Bare-chested, pate-shaven guards stood at attention every fifteen feet along the walls, one hand on their sword hilts, the other fist held taut against their chests. At the end of the hallway, double doors loomed.

Two guards there moved aside to let Xerxes rap his two-knock-pause-three-knock signal.

Another bare-chested slave opened the door, but this one wore peacock blue silk harem pants with a white silk sash. A peacock blue silk turban topped his head. No weapons were visible, but Gio silently vowed to tread carefully.

The Sultan turned and clapped his hands. "Lord Ostwold! You are a genius. I hate to wait a month for my comet painting. It is vibrant, sparkling—a cosmic omen of peace and goodwill."

Gio bowed. "I am gratified that you appreciate my work, Your Royal Highness." He leaned in, peering closely at the Sultan's face.

"Why do you stare at me so?"

"Forgive me, Your Royal Highness. I can't help but notice the shape of your jaw, the noble angle of your brow. It reminds me of a bust I once saw of Alexander the Great or...was it Julius Caesar? Could you have had a mutual ancestor in antiquity?"

The Sultan strutted around the room in his purple turban and gaudily trimmed gold pantaloons and purple tunic. He waved his hand with a flourish. "Some have suggested it."

"If only—"

"If only what?"

"I do not wish to be impertinent, Your Royal Highness."

"I have just had an amusing thought. If you were Sultan, you would be known as 'Your Royal Lowness'!"

Gio feigned laughter. "Few have your gift for humor, Your Royal Highness."

"So? Your impertinent thought?"

"I would like to paint your portrait. And perhaps my female assistant could paint one or more of your wives." Gio grinned. "For an outrageous sum, of course."

The Sultan laughed so hard that his girth undulated like the movements of a jellyfish. "You are not the first to suggest it."

Good. The courtesan plowed his vanity and planted the seed. Adopting a stance of faux outrage, Gio said, "No other artist could do you justice, Your Royal Highness."

"Of course not. Come back tomorrow morning at ten. Bring your paints and your assistant. We will discuss my posing."

Done! "As you wish." Following Xerxes's instructions, "Never turn your back. It would mean instant death," Gio backed out of the room while still facing the Sultan.

*****

Sunday, January 5, 1812 – Interior of Lord Ravenshire's Carriage
Bri

Her internal turmoil had not dissipated after the encounter with Miss Li on Rotten Row the day before, but Bri and Edward had invited their circle to celebrate Twelfth Night at Edward's townhouse. As Bri rode there, she sighed. *I must put on a show, but at least I control the guest list, and Miss Li will not be attending tonight.*

Edward's staff had worked with Bri to prepare the evening's menu. Her favorite Vichyssoise, along with Edward's favorite pureed potatoes, would accompany quail in red wine sauce with peas and onions from the earl's greenhouse. A selection of de Merbeau Merlot and Chardonnay would be on hand. *I had enough Champagne at Gio's gala to last me for a long time. I prefer a non-sparkling variety of grapes.*

Earlier in the day, the same local confectioner who had created the cake for the foundling hospital's Christmas Eve celebration had delivered a similar the multi-layered cake arranged in a series of diagonally placed smaller and smaller layers, each decorated as a Christmas box, in keeping with Twelfth Night tradition as the night of the gifts of the Magi. Chocolate, vanilla and cherry fillings alternated between layers of chocolate and vanilla cake with varying colors of cinnamon-flavored butter cream icing and fanciful bows of spun sugar.

Jean-Louis pulled the carriage to a stop in front of Edward's home.

This is intended to be our home. Will I ever live here?

He leapt down to open the carriage door. "Don't look so glum. Tonight's party requires a smiling hostess."

After rolling her shoulders to dissipate the tension, Bri shook her head. "You know I am no actress."

"You can do whatever you set your mind to."

He held her hand as she exited the carriage.

***

Twelfth Night at Edward's Townhouse

Bri

Shore, the butler, whom Edward had liked during their Azores trip and selected over more experienced applicants, waited at the door. "Lady Gabriella, welcome. You're a bit early. Mr. James is out walking Zori." Jean-Louis followed her in, carrying a box of party favors. Setting them down, he left to take the carriage and Chérie around to the stables in the back.

Bri looked around the dining room. The table comfortably sat twelve. *Baron Beauchamp is game to socialize with us for the sake of Lady Penelope. He is a thoughtful man.* She heard Edward's steps on the back stairs.

Edward's voice called out, "Bri! Come look at Zori and Chérie!"

Bri walked back through the kitchen and looked out over the garden to the stables. Zori was nuzzling Chérie.

Edward put his arm around her and kissed her on the cheek. "No Miss Li to disrupt our evening. Truce?"

Bri nodded, but averted her eyes to the dogs. *Can I trust him?*

Jean-Louis and François threw sticks for the playful mother and daughter to chase. Their competitive natures drove them toward their target and they each pulled on the end of a stick.

Brightening, Bri laughed. "Like us—close one minute, fighting the next."

"The cake is a tower of gift boxes, just like at the foundling hospital."

Bri nodded. "It was such a success, I decided to repeat it with a few changes. The confectioner exceeded my expectations."

Tilting his head, Edward smiled. "That's a high bar to vault. I keep falling back on my haunches."

Before Bri could mount a retort, the doorbell rang. "Our guests have arrived."

***

Edward

After the candlelit dinner, Shore brought out the cake to a round of applause.

"I say," exclaimed Vaux, "I couldn't have designed anything better than that!"

Bri smiled. "You've inspired me to new heights of imagination."

As the butler and footman cut the slices, Lady Penelope said, "The phrase 'heights of imagination' gives me an idea. The Comtesse de Merbeau wrote a series of faerie stories about the elves and faeries, pixies and devas. She told one story about Christmas traditions where one elf started a story and they went around a circle, each adding a detail after repeating the words that had come before. Let's do that tonight!"

"I'm game," said Edward. He raised his glass. "To elf and faerie stories!"

"To elf and faerie stories!"

Bri tilted her head and glanced at Lady Penelope. "It was *your* idea, so you must begin."

Baron Beauchamp leaned back and put his arm around his violet-eyed, raven-tressed voluptuous fiancée.

The future baroness thought for a moment. "Crimson, a holly faerie, missed the last flying caravan to the Faerie Mountain in the Mists for winter hibernation because..."

Rogers blanched but gamely went next. "*Because* her leaves were still green and her red berries fresh despite the falling snow..."

Lady Melanie tilted her head. "*Snow* that was early in the season and made it difficult to fly..."

Banfield picked up the narrative. "*Fly* through the spiraling swirls of snowflakes...."

"Alliteration is *my* specialty." Vaux scoffed.

"You're out of turn," said Edward.

Lady Marianna poked Vaux with her elbow. *"Snowflakes.* Crimson spied candles in the window of a farmhouse dimly visible in the blinding white storm..."

Vaux nodded. *"Storm* that showed no sign of abating. The holly faerie flew against the wind..."

Lady Patricia wrinkled her brow. *"Wind.* Icicles dripped from her wings and tears froze on her eyelids..."

Dr. St. Cloud took a deep breath. *"Eyelids,* but still Crimson flew toward the flickering flames..."

"More alliteration," mumbled Vaux.

Clarissa *"Flames* that glowed through the window, diffusing into a beam of light to guide Crimson's way until..."

Edward glared at Clarissa. *"Until* she alighted on the window sill. Limbs shivering, teeth chattering, and fingers numbing, she pressed her frozen nose against the glass..."

Bri glanced up at the ceiling to gather her thoughts. *"Glass,* attracting the attention of a little girl inside, who stood and ran to open the window..."

The blond baron scanned the expectant eyes of his dinner companions, as it fell to him to complete the story. *"Window* a crack to let the faerie in. No one else but the little girl could see Crimson as she settled under a sprig of holly leaves and berries interspersed between the candles, warmed by the light and love of the season in the company of friends."

Spontaneous applause from the group surprised the baron. "Bravo!"

"Why a 'Bravo' for him? What about me?" Vaux pouted.

"Bravo to all!" toasted Edward. "To faeries and friendship!"

A scream pierced the air.

"Clarissa!" Bri leaned forward, concern on her face.

"I think the baby is coming. Now."

CHAPTER FIFTY-EIGHT

January 5, 1812 - Twelfth Night on the Streets of London
Blackburn as Count Vlarić

As a child, one of Blackburn's favorite memories was his grandmother baking for Twelfth Night. She taught him how to pound dough, roll out shapes, and decorate cookies and pastries with icing colored with berry juice.

Tonight, for a few brief hours, he relived that childhood tradition, forgetting their shared pledge of vengeance. He pretended that life could be a series of pleasant rituals shared with people he loved. *But does she love me? Did she love my mother? Or is it merely her oath of vengeance she loves? Or the old Gypsy? Would she sacrifice both of us in pursuit of her prey?*

As he rode back to his hotel, he realized that the end of the Christmas season tonight saddened him. *It feels like the Gypsy's death card in the Tarot Deck. A change is in the air. Perhaps I shall not escape the grip of death this time.*

***

January 5, 1812 - Twelfth Night at Edward's Townhouse
Dr. St. Cloud

Clarissa closed her eyes and grimaced, but could not suppress another scream.

Rogers raised an eyebrow. "Dr. St. Cloud, you may have to deliver your own child."

Bri took charge. "Gentlemen, carry Lady Clarissa to the guest bedroom at the top of the stairs." She rose. "I'll send Jean-Louis to get the midwife."

Dr. St. Cloud and Edward carried Clarissa up the stairs.

Lady Penelope slipped into the guest bedroom and pulled back the bedcovers so they could put Clarissa on the bed.

Lady Marianna went into the bathroom, wetted a towel, and returned to blot Clarissa's forehead.

Lady Melanie smoothed the covers on the bed.

They looked to Dr. St. Cloud for direction. "First babies usually take a long time. I'm sure the midwife will be here soon. James, you should leave now." After he left, the doctor said, "We need to get Clarissa out of her dress so that she is unrestricted. Are you ladies squeamish?"

"I helped my mother deliver my little brother when no one else was around," said Lady Marianna.

"Good, we'll need your expertise."

"I wouldn't call it expertise—"

"You're the only one in this room who's seen a human birth."

***

Bri

Bri came back inside. "The midwife should be here in about half an hour."

Edward and the other men moved to the parlor with Lady Patricia.

Lady Patricia started to shake. "I think I might vomit."

Bri guided her to a chair and whispered in her ear. "You should come upstairs. We all should know what awaits us."

The stricken face that stared back at her convinced Bri to ask the butler to bring water. "I'll be upstairs if you need anything."

Edward stood. "What can I do to help?"

Bri shrugged. "None of us can do anything but wait."

Another scream from upstairs reverberated through the house. Bri looked at the men. "Please feel free to leave if you wish. Clarissa wouldn't expect you to stay all night."

"A Twelfth Night baby is a good omen," said Vaux. "We'll wait."

Bri went upstairs to be with Clarissa.

"I'll get some cards." Edward opened a drawer and took out two decks of cards.

Vaux, Banfield, Rogers and the baron waited until the dining room table was cleared.

"You need a card room, James."

"I guess my interior designer failed to anticipate my needs."

"Indeed. I shall admonish myself later."

Another scream came.

Lady Patricia jumped.

Edward leaned over. "Would you like me to have François take you home?"

She nodded wordlessly.

"Lady Patricia is not feeling well. My driver will see that she gets home safely. I'll return shortly."

"Goodnight," said Lady Patricia. "I hope all goes—"

The next scream caused her to lose her balance, but Edward caught her.

"—well for Lady Clarissa."

Once outside, the cold January air helped calm her as she climbed into Edward's carriage.

Jean-Louis arrived before Edward's carriage carrying Lady Patricia was out of sight.

The footman jumped down and opened the door.

The midwife directed her gaze at Edward as she exited the carriage with a small satchel. "I am Mrs. Carter. Have your men bring the birthing stool." She gestured to the stool tied on the back of the carriage. "Take me to Lady Clarissa."

***

Early January 6, 1812 – Edward's Townhouse
Mrs. Carter

The midwife, a middle-aged woman with a stout frame, trudged up the stairs to the bedroom where Clarissa screamed in pain. The footman and Jean-Louis followed, carrying the birthing stool.

Moments later, Count von Dusterberg's voice called out from the first landing. "Clarissa! I'm here!" The count bounded up the stairs and gripped Clarissa's hand. She screamed again.

Mrs. Carter assessed the situation. "Must we have a crowd in this room?" She felt Clarissa's forehead, and felt her belly. "The men should leave."

"I'm a veterinarian. I could help."

"Your wife is not a dog, Doctor. Please leave. If I require your help, I shall call you."

Dr. St. Cloud kissed Clarissa on the forehead. "It will be over soon."

"No it will not and kindly do not fill your wife's head with falsehoods. First babies take a long time."

Clarissa screamed again.

The count and Dr. St. Cloud went downstairs.

"Have any of you young ladies ever seen a birth?"

Lady Marianna nodded. "My brother's."

"Lady Clarissa, is there anyone you'd like to stay?"

"Bri."

"Which one of you is Bri?"

Stepping forward, Bri answered. "I am."

"You other ladies can leave. I'm sure Lady Clarissa—"

A scream interrupted Mrs. Carter, but she did not flinch.

"—appreciates your concern."

Lady Melanie, Lady Marianna and Lady Penelope descended the stairs to join the others in the parlor.

Mrs. Carter lifted the sheet and examined progress on the baby's position. "Hmmm. Help me get her off the bed and to the birthing stool."

They maneuvered Clarissa into place.

"Bring more sheets and towels. Boil some water in a tea kettle and bring it up here." The midwife glanced at Bri. "The baby is coming faster than I expected."

Clarissa moaned and screeched.

Zori whimpered.

"Get the dog out of this room," ordered the midwife.

***

Bri

Bri dashed out to ask the cook to boil water.

By the time Bri and the cook came back upstairs, holding the pot with a towel, Clarissa's screams were nearly constant.

"The baby is crowning."

"What does that mean?" Bri froze.

The cook stood with the pot in her hand.

"It means birth is imminent. Put the pot in the bathroom. The water will still be pure, but it will cool before we need it."

Clarissa's scream pierced the air and set Bri's nerves on edge.

Zori's continued whimpering and scratching on the door heightened Bri's anxiety. She went to the door. "Edward! Please take Zori downstairs."

The whining stopped but the screams of her friend continued.

How do women survive this? And then she remembered her own mother's death and her heart clutched, as if pressed in a vice. *What if Clarissa dies?*

***

Edward

The men waited downstairs, unable to concentrate on cards.

Banfield glanced at the others. "What was that chair they took upstairs?"

The count answered. "A birthing stool. Gravity aids in the birth process."

Edward looked upstairs toward the screams. The reality of family responsibilities overwhelmed him. *Am I ready for this? They've been married less than a year...she became with child immediately.* Edward blanched. *What if the sponges don't work? I never considered the possible outcomes, assuming Bri knew what to do. I have approached life analytically—now I am acting without thinking. What is happening to me? And the poppy? Just a bit here and there lightens the pressure. I can stop anytime.*

***

"The head is out." The midwife continued to massage Clarissa's belly.

All Bri could see was matted hair covered with blood. Then a shoulder appeared.

Another scream came.

And the other shoulder came into view. The midwife pulled gently, and the rest of the baby slid out. "She's here, Lady Clarissa." The midwife pulled on the umbilical cord and rubbed the baby's chest. "A breath. Now I like to wait a few minutes to cut the cord. It gives a babe a chance to get used to breathing."

Bri came over and stared at the blood-covered infant. "Should I wet a towel and clean her off?"

"In a moment. Push down Lady Clarissa."

A bloody, blob of tissue was expelled from Clarissa's body. Clarissa groaned.

Bri gasped and her eyes opened wide. "What's that?"

"The afterbirth."

Bri suppressed a gag reflex.

"You can rest now, Lady Clarissa." Turning to Bri, she said, "Take the twine from my satchel."

"Tie off the cord. Here and here." Looking at Clarissa, the midwife said, "Your baby will be in your arms in moments."

Following instructions, Bri tied off the cord.

The midwife took scissors from her satchel and snipped it.

"Now wet a couple of towels and bring them to me along with one to wrap the baby in."

Bri returned with the towels. Mrs. Carter started at the head and meticulously cleaned the babe.

"Clarissa, you have been so brave. An inspiration, really. I've been transfixed." Bri looked at the baby girl. "Her fingers are so tiny! She is perfect."

Mrs. Carter wrapped the baby in a towel, lifted the girl, and laid her on Clarissa's chest. Then she cleaned the birth area and packed it with clean linens she had brought with her. "I don't see excess bleeding. You should be fine in a few days."

Bri moved toward the door. "I'll get Dr. St. Cloud and your father."

***

Monday, January 6, 1812 – Interior of Gio's Carriage
Gio

Gio and Bettina rode in the dwarf's carriage, carrying leather portfolios containing sketchbooks. When they arrived at the Sultan's palace, Bettina's mouth dropped open. "The Sultan *lives* in the Pink Palace?"

"When in London," Gio answered. "Apparently his palaces in Madagascar make this look like a country cottage. He comes for the Season with his favorite wives and the healer, Taita. Are we clear on how to proceed?"

Bettina nodded.

They drove through the arched entrance and the carriage pulled up to the palace doors. "I'm glad there are no steps here. My knees are feeling their age."

The butler was there to meet them. "Welcome, Miss Rybicki. As I told Lord Ostwold on his last visit, I am Xerxes Arsama, vizier and butler to His Royal Highness, Sultan Sarduba. You may call me Xerxes. Please follow me."

They walked through a wide foyer with multiple hallways leading from it, turned down one and then another. At several points, they encountered large bare-chested men with criss-crossed leather straps across their chests, curved swords on their belts, and odd puffy pantaloons. Gio's heart skipped a beat and he felt Bettina jump when the guards first came into view.

They reached the Sultan's large drawing room, ringed with paintings of ancestors, palaces, and landscapes. *God help me, they're appalling.*

The Sultan swept into the room in his desert robes. The vizier announced, "His Royal Highness, Sultan Sarduba of Madagascar." A man of fifty-five, the Sultan was short and rotund, but his gaze left no doubt that he was a man accustomed to total control.

"Gio, my friend. This lovely child is also a painter? How quaint."

The doors opened and a regal woman Gio recognized at the Sultan's chief wife entered the room. She wore the latest London fashion, as she had at Gio's gala.

With dark upswept hair interspersed with white streaks at random intervals, the elegant woman towered over the Sultan by six inches.

"This is my chief wife, Anja, Sultana of Madagascar."

Gio tilted his head. "Your Highness, are you of Persian ancestry?"

His wife opened her mouth to answer, but the Sultan held up his hand to silence her while he narrowed his eyes and stared at Gio. "Why do you ask this?"

Gio walked over to the painting hanging on the wall in back of the Sultan's throne. "This is Persian," pointing to the depiction of a peacock throne. "The cheekbones of the figures match those of Her Highness, the length of the head, the shape of the jaw. It is my *métier*, Your Royal Highness, to observe. Would you not agree?"

The Sultan clapped. "Precisely! This is why I chose you! Where shall we pose? What clothes should we wear?"

"The clothes are up to you, traditional garb or London fashion. The pose depends on light, shadow, time of day, and so on." Gio looked around. "Is this the room you prefer?"

"Yes."

"Let us arrange some furniture and we will sketch." Gio stopped and put his hand on his forehead. "Forgive me, Your Royal Highness, this is Miss Bettina Rybicki, who will be painting portraits of the other wives."

"The lesser wives," the Sultan corrected.

"The light from this large window is diffused by the clear leaded glass, which is perfect." Gio looked over to the vizier. "Can you help me? I can't move heavy furniture by myself."

The Sultan nodded to the vizier.

Xerxes bowed. "Of course." He snapped his fingers and two bare-chested brutes appeared to do his bidding.

"Move this table to the side. Take this chair over here, and Your Royal Highness, please sit. Your Highness, please stand here. Place your hand on his shoulder. Look forward. Miss Rybicki and I will sketch."

The Vizier escorted the others out, left, and closed the door behind him.

The artists sat and sketched with vine charcoal to set the direction of light, and the figures. By prearrangement, Gio focused on the Sultan and Bettina on the chief wife in the first sketches. They would shift depictions in the second version and compare images to create the final composition.

After a few minutes, Gio said, "Excellent. Now let's have the chief wife sit and Your Royal Highness stand in back of her, with your hand on her shoulder." The artists sketched again.

Gio took both versions over to the subjects.

The Sultan looked at the sketches, and said, "I am astonished! How could you capture us in such a short period of time? I want both poses."

Taken aback, Gio asked, "Why?"

"Don't you see, Gio? One can be in traditional garb, as you call it, and one in London fashion. I will sit in the portrait of us in traditional garb and Anja will sit in the portrait of us in London fashion." He clapped again, pleased with himself.

"Miss Rib—"

"Rybicki," said Gio.

"Miss Rybicki, your work is quite good. You may paint the lesser wives and Taita, our healer, in whatever attire Anja approves."

"I think London fashion. We are shopping for new gowns tomorrow, darling." She smiled at her husband in a seductive way. *She knows how to get him to do what she wants.*

Anja spoke. "Miss Rybicki, can you come Wednesday at one p.m. to sketch the lesser wives and Taita as you have sketched us?"

"Of course, Your Highness."

The chief wife said, "Miss Rybicki, you will come daily. Lord Ostwold, Monday, Wednesday and Friday. Will that be satisfactory?"

Gio agreed.

The Sultan looked out the window, which faced east. "This light is good, Gio, but I prefer the light of dawn. Please come Wednesday at dawn to capture the light in this room from this window. That is the light I want in the painting."

"Dawn? Your Royal Highness, I rarely rise before noon."

"Xerxes will meet you at the gates the day after tomorrow about half an hour before dawn."

Gio shrugged. "As you wish, Your Royal Highness. Half an hour before dawn the day after tomorrow."

Anja glanced at Miss Rybicki. "Again, for you, Miss Rybicki, Wednesday at 1 p.m. is best. We have plans for tomorrow all day."

Bettina nodded.

"Come, my dear." The Sultan strode out of the room with his chief wife following several paces behind.

Gathering up their sketches, Bettina and Gio followed Xerxes back to their carriage. As they passed the guards on the way out, Gio turned to look at their scimitars again. *Terrifying. I must keep my head about me or else it will surely roll down this hallway.*

***

Monday, January 6, 1812 – Edward's Townhouse
Clarissa

After the other guests departed, the housekeeper had instructed that a room be made up for Mrs. Carter, who would remain until she was certain Clarissa had mastered the intricacies of nursing and had been instructed on baby care.

A baby nurse had been arranged in advance through Charlotte's foundling hospital training program with the Seminary for Women's Work. She was scheduled to arrive later that day, intending to prepare for the baby, but the child had arrived earlier than expected.

The count, Dr. St. Cloud, Bri and Edward stood around the bed where Clarissa held the baby. Jean-Louis, by invitation, stood by the door. Jean-Jean, the male runt from Chérie and Hector's litter, lay next to the bed.

The mother beamed. "We have a name chosen. My grandmother's name was Luise. We were always close, but after my mother's death, she acted as both mother and grandmother. This is Luise Clarissa Gabriella St. Cloud," she kissed her on the forehead, "and we will call her Lulu. We are honoring my grandmother as well as Bri and Jean-Louis. If not for you," she glanced at the Frenchman and at Bri, "We might never have met and Lulu would never have been born."

***

Monday, January 6, 1812 – The Pink Palace
Jean-Louis

After visiting Lulu, Jean-Louis took Bri back to the earl's townhouse and got about three hours of sleep.

Jean-Louis rode his horse, followed by Chérie, to the servant's entrance of the Pink Palace. Once Jean-Louis confirmed through Vaux that the palace had been fully renovated and was seeking staff, he'd placed a footman named Connors there before the Sultan's return.

Wally Connors saw the Frenchman ride up and waved him over to the far edge of the stables.

Jean-Louis whispered in his ear.

Wally nodded and said he would return in a few minutes.

While Jean-Louis waited, he looked up at the massive structure and squinted when he saw a woman standing on a small terrace looking out over the city on this rare winter's day where fog did not obscure the view. She climbed onto the wall surrounding the terrace. Just as she began to move her other leg over the edge, a bare-chested man grabbed her from behind and pulled her back in. *What horrors go on inside this pink prison?*

When Connors returned, he spoke softly. "It is arranged. Send her to meet with Xerxes at eight a.m. tomorrow morning. She will begin at once." Connors petted Chérie and started back toward the house when Jean-Louis asked him another question.

The Frenchman pointed up to the terrace and asked, "Whose room is that?"

Counting over and frowning as he recalled the order of the rooms, he said, "That is the room of Sultana Nomena."

Jean-Louis tipped his hat and rode off. Securing work for Giselle at the Sultan's temporary palatial London house had been arranged with minimal effort.

Knowing Xerxes's weakness, Jean-Louis had placed Connors in the Sultan's household, the only logical choice.

For his part, the young man was only too happy to have a high-placed protector.

Jean-Louis shrugged. *What people do behind closed doors is of no import to me, but knowing their proclivities can be helpful.*

Information was always available to those who knew whom to ask. Jean-Louis made it a point to know as many Society drivers and Hackney jervies in London as he could. People talked freely as they rode in cabs because few knew that their drivers could hear them. The well off patrons paid little attention to those who served them. Drivers knew which men frequented brothels and the names of the women, or girls, and occasionally, boys, they preferred. Jervies knew who was a gambler, who had affairs, who was cruel, who was kind, who was a thief, who was a drunk, who was a braggart, and who was humble. As a result of relationships cultivated over decades, Jean-Louis tapped into the pulse of the city.

Installing Giselle as a tea server and occasional Lady's maid allowed her access to the women's section of the palace. She would be in a position to observe Taita, as male servants were not permitted in the women's quarters. *Giselle will be my eyes and ears.*

CHAPTER FIFTY-NINE

Tuesday, January 7, 1812 – The Pink Palace
Giselle

Giselle sat in a high-backed chair, waiting for the butler to speak to her. She took a deep breath. *Remember the advice Jean-Louis gave me. I know how to flatter. Watch and learn.*

Xerxes, who called himself a vizier instead of a butler, walked in. A Persian, born in Tehran and educated in Britain, he was tall and regal looking. *He looks like a Sultan or a king.*

Giselle stood to greet him.

He picked up a piece of paper with some notes on it. "I see your name is Giselle Lumière. My name is Xerxes Arsama. You may call me Xerxes. In this household, English, Arabic, French and Farsi are spoken. In which languages can you converse?"

"English and French, Mr. Arsama."

He nodded. "You come highly recommended. You will train with Frau Schumer, the housemistress. She will direct your efforts. Watch in silence from the edge of the room as others perform their tasks. You speak only if spoken to. You will be assigned a room on the top floor of the women's section. A uniform will be provided." He rang a bell.

A stiff-postured woman appeared. Her graying hair was pulled back in a severe bun. Spectacles sat on her nose. Cold gray eyes stared at Giselle.

Xerxes introduced Frau Schumer. "She will see that you have a uniform and begin your training. That will be all."

Giselle stood and followed Frau Schumer out the door. The palace had many long, wide hallways and Giselle was completely lost by the time she entered a room with many mirrors and closets.

Frau Schumer opened the double doors of one of the closets. It was stocked with uniforms of different colors. When Frau Schumer spoke for the first time, Giselle noted her Prussian accent. A "w" became a "v" and vice versa. An "s" or a "th" became a "z". "You will wear a different color every day, depending on the day of the week. These colors were selected by the Sultan based on astrological signs. Today is light blue. I think you are this size." She pulled out a uniform and held it out to Giselle.

"Is there a place to change?"

"No. Try it on here. Now."

Giselle, who removed her clothes several times a day in her normal course of work, had never felt more uncomfortable and exposed. Something about Frau Schumer unnerved her. She needed help taking off her dress. Frau Schumer's hands were cold; her fingers pricked like little sticks on Giselle's back. Once the dress was off, she donned the blue uniform, a long-skirted stiffly starched dress with a high white collar. She was given white gloves.

"Pack up your clothes, and I will show you to your room, and then you will start your training."

Giselle tried to do as instructed, but her valise did not have room for her dress, having already been fully packed, so she carried the dress over her arm and followed Frau Schumer up several flights of stairs.

The room was small, with two beds. A muslin nightshirt was on one bed. Frau Schumer pointed to it and said, "You will wear this shift to the uniform room every morning and a freshly laundered one will be waiting for you at the end of the day to wear back to your room. The water closet is down the hall. Zana will be in the other bed."

Giselle put her valise and dress on her bed, turned and followed Frau Schumer back down the stairs to the kitchen. After being introduced, the cook showed her how the Sultan and each wife and the healer, whom Giselle knew was Taita, liked to be served. Some preferred to put in their own sugar while others expected it to be done for them. "Don't worry, dearie," said the cook, Mrs. Collins.

"You'll figure it out soon enough."

Will I?

A bell rang and they all looked toward the wall with the markings of the origin of the request. Frau Schumer took Giselle by the arm. "The bell is for Sultana Anja. She is the chief wife. Come with me and we will begin your training."

Giselle again became disoriented by all the hallways and passages. It seemed as if the palace were a giant maze, a labyrinth of pink-veined marble. Two uniformed men in exotic silk embroidered pants such as she had never seen before, with bare chests crossed by leather bands and scimitars affixed to their belts, stood at attention before double doors. One knocked, and opened the door for Frau Schumer and Giselle. "Your Highness, this is the new server."

Seated in the room were five other women. Giselle felt her stomach churn. *How will I remember their names?*

The Sultana pointed to Giselle. "You, my dear. Approach."

Giselle looked at Frau Schumer, who nodded at her to do as she was told. She approached the Sultana and bowed her head. "And who might you be?"

"Giselle Lumière. I am a new tea server."

"In French, your name means 'light,' *noor*, as we say. Giselle, I am sure that Frau Schumer will instruct you as to our preferences, but it must be difficult to remember it all on your first day." She pointed to each woman in order. "These are the other Sultanas in residence on this trip. Of course there are many more in Madagascar. I am the chief Sultana, the Sultan's first wife. These wives are Nomena, Mialy, Fy, and Rana. And of course, the Healer, Taita, is a special adviser to our Sultan. No men enter these rooms. I think you should know, Frau Schumer, that we will be requiring more service in the next weeks, as Lady Winifred, the duchess of Warwick, has convinced the Sultan that his portrait as well as those of his wives should be painted. While the Sultan and I will have our joint portrait and my individual one done by the dwarf artist Gio, the Sultan has forbidden it for the other wives. A female artist will complete the portraits of the lesser wives and Taita."

Giselle noticed pinched expressions at the term "lesser wives" from two of the women.

"We shall need additional Ladies' maids to properly dress us for the painted images. The Sultan wants us to look like European royalty, but—"

Giselle, an expert in reading subtle signs from clients, detected a flash of jealousy.

"—our Healer will pose in her traditional island garb, such as can be reproduced in London. Today we will be visiting the dress salon of Mlle. Bellerobe, who has arranged to assemble a selection from which we will choose our attire. Frau Schumer, we will take Giselle to assist us."

Frau Schumer was speechless for a moment. "She is but a tea server, Your Highness."

"She knows London, and I would appreciate her insights."

"Shall I notify the carriages, Your Highness?"

"Yes. We will need two carriages to transport us and two for our purchases. Giselle can ride in one of those. We will leave in half an hour. Giselle may remain with us. You are dismissed."

Frau Schumer left the room, clearly annoyed, but unable to dispute the Sultana.

The Sultana rose and walked over to Giselle and hugged her.

Caught completely off guard, Giselle's mouth fell open in shock.

The Sultana laughed. "That old frau is efficient, but as icy as the North Sea in February. In our country, my dear, the waters are always warm. Now, a test. Can you remember our names?"

Giselle took a breath. "You are the Chief Sultana, Anja, first wife." Pointing to the next woman, Giselle said, Sultana Nemona."

Nomena corrected her, "Nomena"

Giselle repeated, "Sultana Nomena."

To the next, Giselle continued, "Sultana Mialy, Sultana Fy and Sultana Rina."

Rana shook her head. "My name is Rana."

"Sultana Rana."

"Dear Giselle, you do not address as Sultana this or Sultana that. Your Highness Anja, etc., etc. The sultan is addressed as Your Royal Highness, although I doubt you will ever meet him or need to know that."

"Yes, Your Highness. Forgive me."

"There is nothing to forgive. I wanted to shock the old Frau by taking you with us to the dressmaker. We have so little fun here." The other women laughed. "She did not anticipate this, and it is only your first day. We don't behead servants for mistakes on their first day."

Giselle blanched.

The women laughed again.

Taita spoke. "We are not so formal in private, Giselle. But don't tell Frau Schumer."

Nomena spoke. "She would not approve."

Rana laughed. "It's bad enough that the Sultan has five wives here for the old frau. Back in Madagascar, there are twenty more in his harem."

Mialy nodded. "And the Sultan is young, barely over fifty. He will take many more wives."

Giselle started to speak, but stopped herself.

"What is it, Giselle?" asked Anja.

"Pardon me, Your Highness. I was told not to speak unless spoken to. It is not my place to ask questions."

"I give you permission to ask questions. What would you like to know?"

I would like to know how these exotic women please the Sultan in bed, but I cannot ask that. "How many children does the Sultan have?"

"Sixty-three."

Giselle said, "Oh, my! I can't imagine!"

Anja smiled. " 'Tis a large number! When you are with us alone, you can ask us anything. When Frau Schumer is about, stay silent."

"Yes, Your Highness."

"Have you heard of Mlle. Bellerobe?"

"Yes, Your Highness. She is rumored to have 'known' Napoleon, but it may be just a Society rumor. I have heard that her salon is a marvelous place, with silks and velvets hanging all around in huge rooms with seamstresses working all hours to clothe the wealthy. I am thrilled that I will get to see it."

Anja smiled. "We've seen snippets in the gossip rags about how notorious she is, but the *ton* has made her busier than ever. We're anxious to see her atelier. Giselle, sometimes we like to pretend we are British, Queen Anya, Princess Nomena, Lady Taita...whatever we please. It's a bit of a game. Do you like to play games, Giselle?"

Giselle didn't know what to say. "I suppose." *You cannot imagine the types of games I play.*

"I think we should buy Giselle a dress today. What do you think?"

"Yes, yes," they echoed.

"But...but Frau Schumer would not approve."

"Frau Schumer has no right to approve or disapprove anything, Giselle. You will have a dress. What is your favorite color? Your coloring is part French, of course, dark flowing hair when released, milky skin. Your cheeks have a tinge of pink. I think a deep pink, near-purple, color would look dramatic on you."

Giselle started a bit. "I love that color." *This woman is intelligent and astute, yet she lives in a sort of prison.*

Taita spoke again. "Does something trouble you, Giselle? Another question?"

"How...how can you live with no freedom within these walls?"

"Who is really free?" asked Nomena.

Anja shot a disapproving glance at Nomena. "All freedom is relative, Giselle. We are free in our minds and our wealth conveys advantages unknown to you. You must work to live. One person's prison may be another's sanctuary. Few women in this world have true freedom."

Giselle nodded. "Forgive me, Your Highness. I did not mean it as a criticism. I am just too curious."

The chief wife waved her hand in dismissal. "Nonsense. We live in a world you have just entered and do not understand yet."

A knock at the door signaled the carriages were ready. The women stood and walked toward the carriage entrance at the back of the palace.

Giselle looked back at the huge bare-chested men. "Why are those men allowed near you?"

The sultanas who heard the question giggled. "They are eunuchs," said Rana.

Confused, Giselle said, "I thought eunuchs were more like women, not such muscled men as those."

Anja smiled. "That is true of men who are castrated as boys. These men, who are of the Royal Guard, were castrated when fully grown."

Giselle gasped.

"Don't worry," said Fy. "They volunteered."

Giselle's eyes widened. *Volunteers for castration? Beheadings? Harems? How can I wait until my day off to talk to Jean-Louis?*

***

Tuesday, January 7, 1812 – Edward's Townhouse
Bri

Bri stopped by to bring an assortment of baby clothing and gifts to Clarissa.

Upstairs, she held Lulu. "Clarissa, I wonder if I will ever have a child."

"Of course you will. This business with Miss Li will fade with time."

"I hope so."

"The midwife says I can go home on Thursday. The baby nurse is lovely and helpful. I want Edward's home to be private so that the two of you have a place to be alone on your birthday on Friday."

Bri scoffed. "With Grandmother in charge? I doubt we will have more than a fleeting moment alone."

Clarissa stood and took Lulu from Bri's arms.

Releasing the babe reluctantly, Bri cooed at her and kissed Lulu on the forehead.

***

Tuesday, January 7, 1812 – Interior of the Sultan's Carriage
Giselle

The Sultan's carriages pulled up to the salon of Mlle. Bellerobe. Giselle's quick step conveyed her excitement. She had heard of this salon, and talk of the Society balls, but never expected to be able to see it in person. *Did Her Highness Anja mean it when she said I would also get a gown? Could it be possible?*

She followed the sultanas and the healer into the salon, where Mlle. Bellerobe was waiting to greet them. "Welcome to my salon, Your Highnesses and Honorable Taita. Please follow me."

The sultanas and Giselle walked through the velvet curtains into a room with mirrors and gowns tied with ribbons onto displays. Rana walked over to one of the gowns to feel the fabric.

Anja cleared her throat and Rana quickly moved back into the group, head down in shame.

Mlle. Bellerobe smiled at Anja. "Your Highness, shall we start with you in this room? We can move the other sultanas to adjacent rooms."

After Anja nodded, Mlle. Bellerobe gestured to her associates, who escorted the women into the adjacent rooms. Taita stayed.

"Giselle, remain here with me for a moment. Look through those gowns and see what style you think I might like."

Anja motioned to Taita to speak.

Taita reached into her pocket and pulled out a folded piece of paper. She opened it and handed it to Mlle. Bellerobe. 'I sketched something unusual. Can you make this for me?"

Mlle. Bellerobe stood up a bit taller. "We can make anything, Madame." Her tone conveyed irritation. She studied the sketch and snapped her fingers.

An assistant appeared. "Bring me the fuchsia silks and the turquoise chiffon."

She gestured to Taita to have a seat. "Would you like some tea?"

"Not now, thank you."

While Taita waited, Anja and Mlle. Bellerobe reviewed the selections on one wall while Giselle looked at an armoire full of folded gowns.

Something regal for Sultana Anja, I think.

She could hear Anja saying, "No, too fussy."

No frills.

"Too high a neckline."

I didn't think she would want to reveal her bosom. Interesting.

"Green is not a good color on me."

Giselle stopped in the middle of the armoire and lifted out the garments above the color that caught her eye. "I think this might meet your approval, Your Highness." Giselle pulled it out, unfolded the garment, and shook the gown. "It's elegant. The quilted teal brocade bodice and the peacock blue skirt remind me of the painting of the Peacock Throne in your drawing room."

Anja walked over, and said, "Maybe a stand-up collar of lace to match the throne would complete this." She looked at Mlle. Bellerobe for concurrence.

"*Absolument.* Absolutely. Let us try on this sample size to see if adjustments need to be made."

Giselle helped Anja undress. She fastened the bodice over the skirt. "It's a bit loose, I think."

Mlle. Bellerobe disagreed. "One needs to move, my dear."

Feeling foolish, Giselle stepped back.

"I think more fullness in the skirt is needed. We have more petticoats in the back." Mlle. Bellerobe snapped her fingers and sent an assistant to retrieve them.

After the assistant left, Anja said, "Mlle. Bellerobe, I want Giselle to have a gown as a gift from me."

"Well, my dear, do you see anything you would like?"

Giselle's eyes widened. She turned around and selected a dress she had passed over for Sultana Anja. The dress was constructed with a pink the color of fuchsias in a *peau de soie* bodice with puffed sleeves and a midnight blue silk skirt embroidered with fuchsia *fleurs de lys*.

Mlle. Bellerobe nodded. "That will complement your hair and dark blue eyes."

Giselle took off her uniform and tried on the dress. It fit perfectly.

Anja smiled. "You look lovely my dear."

"Thank you so much, Your Highness. I can't believe this could be mine!"

Mlle. Bellerobe looked at Anja. "We have matching shoes."

The Sultana nodded.

The assistant returned with the petticoats. After Anja used two, there was still one left for Giselle.

Both sat down while the assistant measured their feet for shoes.

"Giselle, please dress and go see what the others are up to. None of them should have the same color I do."

"Of course, Your Highness." Giselle quickly disrobed and folded her new gown, placing it on a chair. She quickly put on her uniform.

As Giselle was leaving, an assistant returned with the fabrics Mlle. Bellerobe had requested for Taita.

Giselle could not resist speaking before being granted permission. "The colors are so beautiful, Lady Taita."

Taita smiled at her. "I agree."

Moving to the adjacent room, Giselle found two of the other sultanas. Nomena was in apple green, Mialy in lavender. They seemed delighted. Nomena was tall, and the dress had to be lengthened. She was standing on a stool while the seamstress took out the hem. The bodice fit. Mialy's dress was a little too long, so she was also on a stool, having the dress shortened.

Finding the next room, she could see there was a problem. Fy and

Rana were arguing over a burgundy dress.

Fy stamped her foot. "I saw it first!"

"No, I want it!" Rana's face was red with anger.

Giselle put up her hands. "Your Highnesses, please stop! Do you want the chief wife to hear you?

Both Fy and Rana were quite young. Giselle guessed that neither was over seventeen.

Rana let go of the dress. "I want to see the hanging sails of color I've heard about." She ran back through another set of curtains.

Horrified, Giselle went after her. "Your Highness, please stop! The chief wife will be embarrassed."

"Let her be embarrassed. The Sultan likes me best. He's tired of her old body."

Giselle guessed that Anja was not yet forty.

Rana looked at the flowing fabrics hanging from the ceiling. Velvets, chiffons, silks, brocades. She wandered around as if in a trance, touching the fabrics, swirling them around her, walking farther and farther back into the waves of color until she stopped.

A man's voice boomed. "Who is accompanying you?"

Fear froze Giselle in place. Men were not permitted to be alone with any of the sultanas. She reached Rana and pulled on her arm. "She got lost, monsieur. We need to get back to the main salon."

He parted a curtain of fabric, and a path appeared. Giselle held fast to Rana's arm and guided her back, whispering. "Say nothing of this."

Rana pouted.

Returning to the room where Fy was being fitted, Giselle said, "Let's find you something special, Rana." Lowering her voice to a whisper, she asked, "What is the Sultan's favorite color?"

Brightening, Rana said, "Yellow. 'The promise of dawn on the horizon,' he calls it."

Giselle found a white dress with a bodice of quilted velvet and a silk skirt. "This could be dyed." She helped Rana take off her dress and put on the selection.

Giselle called over the assistant. "Can this be dyed a pale yellow?"

"Perhaps. Let me ask Mlle. Bellerobe." The assistant left to get the couturière.

Mlle. Bellerobe swept in, and rubbed the silk between her fingers. "Pale yellow, oui? Boiling burdock burrs in water is my preferred method."

Rana beamed.

Giselle smiled in relief. She heard Anja's voice approving of Nomena and Mialy's choices. She appeared in their room and frowned. "White, Rana?"

Breathlessly, Rana answered. "It will be dyed, Anja. Pale yellow."

Anja smiled, "As His Royal Highness likes to say, that color is 'The promise of dawn on the horizon.' "

Rana's face fell.

In that moment, Giselle understood. Rana thought she was special to the Sultan, but Anja knew how to assert her status as chief wife. *She knows her Sultan.*

Mlle. Bellerobe snapped her fingers and her assistants wrapped the dresses in tissue paper. "The yellow dress will be delivered tomorrow with the shoes. I trust that will be satisfactory." She presented the bill to Anja, who signed on behalf of the Sultan.

"It will." Anja led the sultanas out to the waiting carriages, followed by the assistants, who placed three dresses in the first carriage, and Anja's and Giselle's with Giselle in the second carriage.

Riding in the carriage with her lovely new gown, Giselle wondered where she would ever wear it? At twenty-three, she had spent seven years with Mlle. Sabine, who provided tutors for her girls in manners, and proper English. She had saved as much of her earnings as possible, hoping to go to America within two years. The money she would get for this special work for Jean-Louis might make that dream come true sooner. She could start over in a new country with no past to haunt her. No former clients to see her on the street. Maybe the chance for a love and marriage of her own. She could invent a dead husband, perhaps a soldier killed in Napoleon's wars.

The carriages made a turn she didn't recognize. *Are we not going to the Sultan's palace?* They pulled up to a tea room, *Omelettes de Mme. d'Aix.* Giselle looked at her uniform. *What now?*

The chief wife's footman walked over to Giselle's carriage. "Her Highness requests that you remain in the carriage. She will have nourishment brought to you."

Giselle nodded and waited. *He must be a eunuch and the drivers too. What an odd world these sultanas inhabit.*

A voice came from the other side of the carriage. "Learn anything?"

Recognizing the accent, Giselle whispered. "Not yet. I have just met everyone. They are inside having tea. The chief wife bought me a gown from Mlle. Bellerobe! Taita holds a position of honor, but I have not been alone with her."

Jean-Louis nodded. "The chief wife must like you. Excellent work. I'll find you another day." He disappeared.

All I have to do is listen and report, for more money in a week than I make in a month. And I'm the most in demand of Mlle. Sabine's girls. I could get used to this.

The footman brought her a basket. She opened the napkin to find a selection of fresh-backed breads, with rolled slices of ham and cheese. *I didn't realize how hungry I am.* Giselle made a sandwich and bit into it. She noticed the footman still standing next to her carriage.

"Did you get any food?"

"No, miss."

"Would you like some?"

The footman shook his head. "The chief wife would not like it."

"May I ask you a question?"

"Yes."

"Are you a eunuch?"

He grimaced at the concept. "No, miss. The chief driver is and we are not permitted to speak to the sultanas. I thought you being a tea server, it might be acceptable, but he is glaring at me. I must go." He walked back to the lead carriage.

She watched him walk away. *A handsome young man. Too bad he could never afford me.*

CHAPTER SIXTY

Wednesday, January 8, 1812 – The Pink Palace
Gio

In silence, Gio followed the butler down the long hallway toward the bare-chested eunuchs guarding the Sultan's drawing room. *Curb your tongue and keep your head.*

The doors opened and Gio tilted his head. "I see you've set up a special curtain to contain the area for painting, but it impedes the light. I must have the proper light!"

Xerxes held up his hand. "One moment, please." He walked over to the curtain, which had been attached to a rod suspended from the high ceiling, and pulled it aside. "We can open it while you paint and enclose the area at other times."

Gio squinted toward the ceiling and walked around the enclosure. "Ingenious. Hmmph. Clever." He nodded to Xerxes. "Well done."

"We will have some tea brought to you."

"I prefer wine."

Xerxes raised an eyebrow. "The Sultan permits wine only during official functions. He, of course, does not imbibe."

"So you have it, but won't provide it to me?" Gio shrugged. "So be it. Tea will do very well." Gio dropped his bag between the two easels then stood back to assess his progress. Each stretched canvas was seven feet high and five feet wide. He had sketched in the poses in graphite pencil and had tested skin colors on a canvas on a smaller easel. "At the end of the week, I would like to schedule another

posing session with the Sultan and Sultana. Can that be arranged?"
"I will endeavor to arrange that and let you know before you leave today." A pile of wood planks had been placed in the painting area. "The Sultan's carpenters will build scaffolding to your specifications." The doors opened and three men came in, each carrying a bag of tools.

Gio gave them instructions, and worked on two small studies of his composition while they constructed the painter's scaffolding.

***

Wednesday, January 8, 1812 – Bettina's Garret
Bettina

After a fitful night, Bettina, who usually awoke at dawn, rose to paint before her appointed time to arrive at the Sultan's palace. She laughed, thinking of Gio trudging to his carriage before the first rays of the day glowed through the clouds. *But don't laugh too much. You have the portraits of five women to paint.*

She sponged herself clean and dressed.

Around 11 a.m., she began gathering up her sketch books, easel and canvasses, for the trek to the Sultan's palace, and realized it was too much to carry. An unexpected knock at her door frightened her. *Who can that be?*

The messenger boy twisted his cap in his hands. "Miss Rybicki, there's a man downstairs who told me to tell you his name is Charles and he brought you a carriage to help you transport some materials." Looking at the pile of equipment, he added, "I'll help you. He already paid me, don't worry about it."

Bettina smiled. "Then you are a welcome visitor, Forsyth, but we may need even more hands to carry all this."

The sound of boots on the stairs caused both of them to turn.

"So I thought." Charles stood at the door.

Forsyth had a look of terror on his face. "Mrs. Jackson won't like this, sir. She won't like it at all."

"I am here with her blessing, Forsyth, but if we stand here babbling, she'll get suspicious. Don't worry about your easel, Bettina. I've already had five delivered to the palace, along with canvases and drop cloths. I'll take the paints and turpentine. Forsyth, you take the brushes, the charcoal, the palette. And you," he added, looking at Bettina, "should be able to manage the rest."

Once in the carriage, Bettina sighed. "You're right, of course. I was only thinking of sketchbooks and charcoal for today, but this morning I was overwhelmed with all the equipment I would need, and would have to leave there. The Sultan might not want others to see his wives without his permission, even in paintings."

"The 'lesser wives,' you mean."

Bettina nodded. "I hope I can remember all that is said. Perhaps I need a scribe."

"The Sultan would not permit me to be there, but Forsyth is a boy. What do you think?"

"Perhaps. I'll know more after today."

Adjusting his weight on the bench seat, Charles pulled out his pocket watch. "It's mid-morning now. I'll have the carriage waiting to pick you up at dusk. If it takes a bit longer, don't worry. I'm patient."

Smiling, Bettina added, "And resourceful. And somewhat annoying."

Taken aback, Charles stared at her.

"I would have managed on my own, you know." Bettina leaned back in the seat and looked away from Charles, out the window.

"I'm sure you would have. I was just trying to make it easier for you."

Bettina sat in silence until the carriage reached the palace. She turned to Charles and spoke in a soft, measured tone. "I appreciate your thoughtfulness, but next time, ask me what I need. Don't assume you know." She took a deep breath, and to her own surprise, she leaned over and kissed him on the lips.

***

Wednesday, January 8, 1812 – Outside the Pink Palace
Charles

Momentarily dazed by Bettina's kiss, Charles embraced her.

She smiled. "We have to unload all these materials."

Charles exited the carriage and helped Bettina climb down, and then directed the footman to unload the easels strapped onto the back of the carriage. A line of the Sultan's servants took the easels, while others took canvases from the inside of the carriage, along with Bettina's equipment bag.

Holding her sketchbooks, Bettina turned to Charles. "I'll see you at dusk."

He grinned and made a mock bow. "As you wish, Your Highness." He watched as she walked through the palace doors. His heart fluttered. *She's amazing!*

***

Wednesday, January 8, 1812 – The Pink Palace
Bettina

Bettina was greeted by Xerxes, who led her toward the drawing room in the sultanas' quarters. When she entered she found Anja, the chief wife, waiting for her.

"Your Highness, I wasn't certain of what protocol I should follow, so I am grateful to see you this afternoon."

The elegant woman smiled. "Miss Rybicki, I thought you might need some help understanding our culture. The 'lesser wives' are sometimes jealous of each other. I thought it best if I determined the order of portrait sitting to avoid any squabbling. Then you would not be in an awkward position. How would you like to proceed?"

"I would first like to sketch everyone in a pose or two. In that way, I can study their features to achieve the best likeness of each on these large canvases. I expect to vary the poses—some sitting, some standing. Of course you and the Sultan will make the final choice."

Bettina bowed her head slightly in deference to Anja. "Another point is that this room has many functions, so it may not be the best choice for this process. We will need to leave the drop cloths, canvases and easels in place for several months. Is there another room that you feel would be better suited to this endeavor? For some people, the odor of the paint solvents can be a problem. So before your men in the hallway enter this room to set up the room for painting, it would be prudent to be certain of the room's continued availability for a singular purpose. That way, my presence won't interfere overmuch with your daily lives."

"I have also considered that issue, Miss Rybicki. We have an adjacent room that would work quite well. The windows can be opened to air out any objectionable odor from the paint solvents. Please follow me." Anja walked into the next room which was even larger than the drawing room, with high leaded windows that could be opened.

Bettina looked around. "This is perfect! If I were the most famous artist in London, I would never have a north-facing studio this grand!"

Anja smiled. "The most famous artist in London recommended you, Miss Rybicki. The Sultan and I posed for your mentor this morning. We set up a dedicated painting room for Gio, but in truth," she tilted her head closer to Bettina, "it is not *this* grand."

"Your Highness, you mentioned you would help me understand your culture. Is there a hierarchy among the 'lesser wives' that I should observe in my interactions?"

The chief wife nodded. "It is a bit of the delicate matter, as the Sultan's preference shifts over time. In order of marriage, it's Nomena, Mialy, Fy and Rana. As the youngest and most recent wife, Rana is currently the favorite. However, Taita is valued by the Sultan above all others. He reveres her as one would a goddess of ancient mythology. In truth, she means more to the Sultan than I do."

Bettina wondered how the chief wife felt about Taita's history with the Earl of Ravenshire, but she knew it was wisest for her to remain silent. She wondered if she would ever truly be alone with Taita to fulfill the earl's request of her. "Your Highness, once I have completed the sketches and we have all agreed on the best pose for each woman, it would work better for me if I were alone with each subject so that I could concentrate on one portrait per painting session. Since there are five subjects, rotating each for one day a week would be best. Would that be possible?"

The chief wife tilted her head and looked directly at Bettina. "As long as you understand that I may enter at any time. Taita will be Wednesday, Mialy Thursday, Fy on Friday, Rana on Monday and Nomena on Tuesday. Of course you may have privacy within this room. It is now *your* studio as a guest in our home. A lavatory is attached."

Frau Schumer appeared at the door. "Your Highness, do you need anything of me?"

"Yes. Alert the other sultanas and Lady Taita that we will begin in about an hour."

"The lesser wives and Lady Taita are dressing now."

"Very well. Please ask Giselle to bring tea for Miss Rybicki and me."

After Frau Schumer left, Anja leaned toward Bettina and whispered, "As far as interfering with our lives, I assure you that the paintings that Gio and you will create are the talk of the palace. It is quite exciting. You won't be interfering with our lives, but we most definitely will interfere with yours! Making five women happy is a challenge for the Sultan, let alone a young woman charged with making each one beautiful on canvas."

Two massive eunuchs brought in the easels and canvases, setting them up as instructed by Bettina, along with a work table and another table for mixing her paints. As she directed them, Bettina smiled as she remembered the shocked look on the face of Paulo, the Italian easel and canvas maker who supplied materials for Gio and her.

Initially dumbfounded at the size of the order Bettina placed, after she had received the initial payment from the Sultan's agent for her five commissions, Paulo jabbered in Italian for nearly two minutes. But he delivered exactly what she had described in a wagon the day before.

"Is that a rug?" Anja watched as two men carried an obviously heavy cylindrical item.

"No," Bettina answered. "It's woven linen to place over the floors and rugs to avoid damage." They unbound the linen, and covered the floor. Bettina instructed them to put extra linen around the mixing table, where kettles of linseed oil and solvents had been placed.

She set her bag and sketch pad on the work table and pulled out the vine charcoal.

Turning back toward Anja, she waved her hand around the room. "What do you think?"

Anja shook her head and laughed. "Miss Rybicki, five paintings is quite a task! Do you feel the light is adequate?"

"It's ideal." She walked over to the window. "It's diffused through these panes." She motioned to Anja to join her. "See the rays of light? The trick will be to get the subject's best side toward the light."

"Best side? I don't understand."

"Nor did I, before I studied art. I learned that everyone's body is asymmetrical—one side is larger than the other. One foot is larger than the other; one leg is longer than the other and so on."

Anja looked at her feet and turned them from side to side. "It's difficult to tell."

"To most of us, it's not noticeable, but in the face, it becomes more pronounced. One eye is usually larger, one ear is higher on the head, the left and right sides of the lips are uneven. The jaw line can be noticeably different. Gio set us on an exercise where we went to several museums in London and counted how many poses featured the left side of the face as compared to the right side. There are more with the left side featured, so I use that as a guide. Extremely asymmetrical faces look better in three-quarter views than in straight-on, and that is generally a flattering pose for almost everyone."

Giselle arrived with tea. She stopped in mid-step as she confronted the changes to the room. The eunuchs had moved six chairs and two small tables to one side of the room, away from the easels.

Anja gestured to Bettina to have a seat while Giselle poured the tea.

"Your Highness, the other sultanas and Lady Taita will be here shortly. I brought them tea as they were dressing."

Anja nodded in acknowledgment.

Giselle left.

Sipping her tea, Bettina's face clouded.

"What is it, my dear?"

"I just realized that I cannot lift these canvases or easels without help."

"The eunuchs outside the doors are at your service." Anja rang a bell and the doors opened.

Both bare-chested eunuchs came in as summoned.

"You will help Miss Rybicki lift and move canvases and easels at her direction."

They both bowed and waited for instructions.

"That will be all."

Taita entered.

Anja turned to look at the healer, inhaling a gentle gasp of air. "You look exquisite, Taita."

Bettina agreed. "A marvelous costume. I've never seen anything like it."

Smiling, Taita explained her choice. "The pink-shaded feathers on the gold headpiece are the closest I could find in Madagascar that approximate the ones from my lost island. The carved turquoise talisman on the headpiece is similar to a stone from my native land. Mlle. Bellerobe worked with me to fashion a *lamba* from this vibrant deep pink silk." The *lamba*, one long piece of fabric, draped off one shoulder, leaving the other bare. Gathered at one side under her breasts, it fell to the floor in gentle gathers down the front. A sheer shoulder cover in turquoise chiffon was attached with a small ruby brooch set in gold over the uncovered shoulder and at the top of the shoulder on the other side, so it streamed down the back of the dress like a train. Her still-black hair cascaded over the chiffon in the back to her waist. At her neck turquoise and pink shells formed a necklace, on hand-woven leather strips. Earrings of small shells hung from her ears, and a large turquoise ring surrounded by rubies dominated her right hand.

The next to arrive was Nomena, her apple green dress accented by a large jade jewel embedded in a thick gold collar, with matching earrings and ring surrounded by diamonds.

Fy entered in her burgundy dress. A necklace of graduated-sized rubies covered her chest, ruby-and-diamond earrings dangled from her ears, and a large ruby circled by diamonds was on her finger.

Mialy's single amethyst the size of a fist dangled from a thick gold chain, setting off her lavender ensemble. Amethysts set in gold hoops were on her ears. She wore a ring with one large amethyst circled with lighter amethysts.

Anja smiled in approval with their choices, but her face clouded. "Where is Rana?" She rang for Frau Schumer.

Almost immediately, Frau Schumer appeared.

"We are waiting for Her Highness Rana. Please see to her progress."

"As you wish, Your Royal Highness." Frau Schumer left.

"We will not let Rana's lateness delay us. Sit down ladies. Today Miss Rybicki will sketch and then each of you will be assigned a day for posing. It will be the same day each week. Wednesday, today, will be Taita. Thursday—Mialy, Friday—Fy, Monday—Rana, and Tuesday—Nomena. Please give them instructions, Miss Rybicki."

"Miss Taita, please stand in front of this window." Adjusting the healer's stance, Bettina stood back and arranged the folds in the dress to capture the light and shadows, spreading the train out the back. She took out her sketch paper and set it on the easel and quickly sketched Taita in the standing position from a three-quarter pose. She then moved a chair over and had her sit, looking in the other direction, and sketched that pose. A side profile and full face front sketch completed her work. "Thank you, Miss Taita." She showed the sketches to Taita and Anja.

They nodded approval of her sketches, in awe that Bettina could sketch a likeness so quickly.

Heads turned as Rana arrived. "Forgive me, Your Royal Highness. The Sultan wanted to see me in this dress." Her flushed look suggested that it was more than a quick glance.

Bettina felt invisible daggers flying toward Rana. *Jealousy among this group must be rampant.*

Nomena, Mialy and Fy completed their poses and giggled in delight at Bettina's depictions of them.

Finally, it was Rana's turn. Bettina thought Rana felt the tension. She said to Anja. "The other wives can leave if they wish."

Anja tilted her head toward the other wives. "You may leave now. Taita, you may stay if you so wish."

Demurring, Taita said, "This headdress is a bit heavy. I shall leave you as well."

The lesser wives and Taita left the room. Anja, Rana and Bettina remained.

Rana wore an oval yellow diamond that sparkled in the late afternoon sun. She assumed the poses requested by Bettina, uncharacteristically silent. Between poses, however, she could not contain herself. "Let me see! Let me see!" When all the poses were completed, she asked Bettina, "Am I the most beautiful, Miss Rybicki? The Sultan thinks so."

Bettina struggled to be diplomatic in front of Anja, whose tight lips signaled her displeasure with the Sultan's youngest, and favorite, wife. "All of you are uniquely beautiful, Your Highness. You have a particularly symmetrical face, which is very pleasing to the eye."

"So it's perfect? Symmetrical is best, is it not?"

Stopping Bettina from answering an impossible question, Anja said, "That will be all, Rana. Your session is completed."

Rana nodded and left the room.

Bettina gathered her sketches to take home. "I have made notations as to colors to mix for their dresses. The vibrant jewel colors of the gowns are stunning."

"Miss Rybicki, each wife wants to be the favorite, but the Sultan's desires change with time. I chose the days for their posing after their scheduled night with the Sultan, so they should be in a good mood. There is a rotation. Ring for Frau Schumer if you need anything while you are working here."

"To maintain the light, I think afternoons are best, for about three to four hours at a time. I hope that will not interfere too much with your household. And a full day for Miss Taita."

"Not at all. I will see you tomorrow for Mialy's session."

Anja escorted Bettina to the hallway where the butler was waiting to shepherd her through the warren of hallways. "Tomorrow, then."

Bettina bowed slightly. "Tomorrow, Your Highness."

The butler carried her sketches to the carriage, where Charles waited. *He is so handsome.*

As the carriage pulled away, Bettina sighed. "A cut from a eunuch's scimitar may bleed, but the hatred of a jealous sultana cuts just as deep."

"Then stay away from the Sultan. He might want to make you his umpteenth wife!" Charles laughed.

"Never. He demands compliance from a wife. I am an independent woman."

"You and Lady Gabriella have an indomitable spirit." Charles remained amused.

Bettina frowned. "The Pink Palace is a nest of vipers."

.

CHAPTER SIXTY-ONE

Thursday, January 9, 1812 – Edward's Townhouse
Jean-Louis

Clarissa, Dr. St. Cloud, the baby nurse carrying Lulu, and Count von Dusterberg gathered all their belongings to return to the Hanforth mansion.

Edward and Bri bid them farewell after accepting their profuse thanks.

Zori nuzzled against Clarissa's skirt.

Jean-Louis put his finger on Lulu's nose and she seemed to smile. "I am smitten," he said.

***

Friday, January 10, 1812 – Pytchley Palace
Bri

Vanessa always hosted Bri's birthday dinner. After the meal, the family gathered in the parlor to watch as Bri opened presents.

Gio sat next to Bri. " 'Tis always a challenge to find an appropriate gift for the woman who has everything. I have painted her portraits for years, so that is not an option." She opened the box to find a note describing his gift. To the group, he added, "But this year, I shall paint the Ravenshire pets as if they were playing Whist—Chérie, Hector, Spotty and Monkey."

Bri clapped her hands together and beamed. "That makes me smile just thinking about it."

Nate smiled as he handed her a book wrapped in bright paper. "We have discussed psychology and psychiatry, and I came upon an English translation of Reil's book, *Rhapsodies about applying the psychological method of treatment to mental breakdowns.*

"You've expressed an interest in such things, Bri? I am astonished." Vanessa stared at her granddaughter.

"Nate can explain it better than I."

"Reil postulates that madness is a reaction to social conditions, in some cases. He believes it signifies a harmonic disturbance in the workings of the mind."

"That sounds like a thinly veiled attack on the social order," countered Edward. He turned to Bri. "Why would you want to read such things?"

"So that I can increase my knowledge of human behavior."

Laurence interjected, "I must admit, my gift is in a similar vein."

Bri opened her former tutor's gaily wrapped box.

"A first edition of John Locke's *An Essay Concerning Human Understanding.* Thank you, Professor. I shall treasure it."

Eli and Annabelle's gift was also a book. Two leather covers contained large sheets of papers with drawings and writing. Bri opened it and read the title and inscription aloud:

Horses on the Mountain
A story by Hannah, Sarah and Aaron Sterling,
for Lady Gabriella Wyndward
January 10, 1812

She leafed through the pages. "I shall treasure this. Thank you!"

The Sterling children ran up and embraced her.

Bri kissed each one on the forehead in turn. "We'll read it together after all the other gifts are opened."

The box from Sir John and Lady James contained a piece of blown glass in the shape of a tulip. "It's exquisite!" Bri carefully wrapped it in the tissue paper to protect the delicate sculpture.

Next, Bri opened a velvet-covered box and gasped.

The duchess explained. "My grandmother's sapphire pendant."

Bri lifted the large stone surrounded by moonstones from the box.

"Thank you Grandmother and Grandfather." She rose to her feet and walked over to kiss them.

Oliver and Lady Abigail's gift was in a huge box, too heavy to lift. Bri opened it and shrieked. "A new saddle and harness! The leather is so fine and supple."

"I wrote to an old university friend in Italy and described what I wanted. It was smuggled through the blockade under the auspices of a certain Frenchman," said Oliver.

Gwyneth's gift was a watercolor of Spotty and Monkey.

Likewise, Ian painted a picture of pony Gio.

Gio nodded his approval. "My student may exceed me one day." Ian beamed.

Aelwyn gave Bri a crystal ball from the Gypsy stall at the Blue Bazaar. "To gaze upon and dream," was written on the card. *She must know I am uncertain of the future.*

Bri opened Charlotte's box next to find a red fox boa. She pulled it out and wrapped it around her neck.

"It looks like your hair, cousin Bri," said Ian.

"That's the idea," said Charlotte.

Henry's box contained an envelope. Bri opened it and her mouth dropped open. "I am not a Greek goddess."

"You are to me," said her father.

The other guests looked confused.

The earl smiled. "My next ship will be named *Gabriella's Wynd.*" He pulled another gift from behind him and handed her another box. She opened it, to find an antique gold torc with ancient Celtic symbols carved on it.

"Like Bodicca," said Sir John.

"As I said, my goddess," Henry said.

One gift remained on the pile. A small box from Edward. She opened it. A deep intake of breath came as a tear formed in her eye. "Edward, it's dramatic and beautiful!" She pulled out a gold bracelet to match the torc.

The duchess's butler brought in another gift. "This was just delivered." He brought it to Bri.

She read the card and her cheeks slowly turned a deep shade of pink. "It's from Miss Li." She opened it to discover an Egyptian carving of the cat goddess, Bast, in blue-green faience. *How did she know it was my birthday and where I would be?*

Ian broke the spell of silence. "Can we read the horsey book now?"

"Yes, let's," said Bri.

***

Henry

In the carriage on the way home, Bri asked aloud the question she thought when she opened the gift. "How did she know it was my birthday and where I would be?"

Henry shook his head. "I did not tell her."

"Nor I," said Edward. "Someone might have mentioned it at Gio's gala."

"Your father?" Bri's brow wrinkled.

"I doubt it."

"Rogers?"

"Unlikely that he would remember the date, although I bowed out of our normal Friday night dinner due to your birthday." Edward shrugged. "It's possible. He's infatuated with her."

Bri scoffed. "The faience is probably a fake. I'll have it examined at the museum."

Henry said nothing, but his mind raced. *He knows the date, he knows the place, for it never changes: Blackburn.*

***

Lord Ravenshire's Townhouse
Jean-Louis

When Bri and Henry arrived home, the earl went inside. Trailed by Jean-Louis, Bri stopped to say goodnight to Nashmir, who was still working by candlelight in the greenhouse.

"I was hoping you would stop by. I have a birthday gift for you." He took her back to the canvas flaps segregating the orchids, where steam from a line of coals from an ingenious drip system he'd constructed maintained the proper levels of humidity. A silk cloth obscured a lone stem. He lifted it off to reveal an orchid unlike any Bri had ever seen. "It has been accepted as a new species by the

Horticultural Society of London: The Lady Gabriella Mokara Orchidaceae. The deep orange petals have the fire of your hair, and the parallel purplish veining is subtle. As you can see, the flowers show five star-like petals with a truncated yellowish column in the center. Each stem will produce an average of ten blooms."

Bri, stunned into silence, embraced Nashmir. A tear ran down her cheek. "You have bestowed a great honor upon me. I am without words to express my gratitude."

"Let it be a symbol to remind you of the harmony in the universe. Mokara is a Sanskrit name that developed from a branch of Hindu philosophy teaching that each individual is comprised of three states of consciousness, with Mokara representing the state of form, or the physical body, which joins with the causal body and the astral body to create harmony, which is the natural state of the human spirit." Nashmir bowed to Bri. "Happy Birthday, my friend."

"My gift is not so grand, nor of the earth." From his pocket, Jean-Louis pulled a gold Admiral's whistle. "This is a whistle of honor, a boatswain's pipe. If you need me, blow on it. I'll hear it and come when you call. 'Tis an antique I received long ago as a gift from my grandfather, an Admiral, which I now offer to you."

Nashmir nodded. "To give a precious gift one has harbored to another is a great gesture of friendship."

Bri turned it in her hands, and saw that it was engraved. "Bri. 10 January 1812."

***

Edward

François dropped Edward at the front and took the carriage around to the back stables in the alley.

Edward couldn't sleep. After tossing and turning, he slipped out the door, hailed a Hackney and exited at *Dreamtime*. Bri's family traditions for her birthday coupled with the birth of Clarissa's baby in his home brought to the forefront the seriousness of marriage. *Am I ready? I just need a little toke to help me sleep.*

***

François

At this hour, Edward's driver watched as a passenger in a waiting Hackney. He suspected Edward would steal away. *Mr. James is on a dangerous path.*

Edward exited *Dreamtime* after about an hour.

At a discreet distance, François followed his employer home. *Jean-Louis will not be happy.*

***

Monday, January 13, 1812 – Exterior the Sultan's Pink Palace

Giselle

Leaving through the servants' entrance, Giselle walked out into the rain. She tried to hail a cab, but demand was too heavy. She pulled her coat tighter, and walked toward to the meeting place designated by Jean-Louis.

A voice from a Hackney perch startled her. "Miss Giselle, J-L sent me to collect you. He had to travel to Ravenshire. The Prussian will meet with you."

She looked up and nodded, grateful for the shelter. Opening the door, she climbed in. Jean-Louis had told her that either he or the Prussian would be her contacts, and she knew that many Hackney jervies in London were loyal to Jean-Louis.

When the driver stopped at the designated spot, a dress shop, the Prussian opened the door and got into the carriage. "Change of plans, Miss Giselle. Jean-Louis asked me to get your report. Are you being well treated?"

"Oh, yes! It's a fascinating place—another world, really. I have seen Taita. She seems to have special status in the household and has the freedom to roam the palace. I have not yet been alone with her, but she knows my name and I am unobtrusive in my service to the sultanas. I'm sorry I have nothing of substance to report."

The Prussian waved a hand, as if to dismiss her apology. "This is to be expected. They would not speak freely so soon. I have seen the green sign in your window. In the event of danger, we have a man stationed outside at all times. Do not put yourself at risk. Simply observe and report. In my experience, those of noble birth ignore the presence of servants. The earl is an exception. Again, take no chances. If a red sign appears in your window, we will come immediately. Otherwise, either Jean-Louis or I will meet with you in a week's time in this same location."

***

Tuesday, January 14, 1812 – Riding on Rotten Row
Oliver

Bri smiled. "My new saddle provides a cushioned, luxurious ride."

"Excellent! I intend to order one for myself and perhaps for Lady Aelwyn and Ian as well. "

"Ian adores you."

"He boosts my spirits. His pixie friend is a fond fiction."

"Nym. Somewhere in the back of my mind, I might have dreamed of a little pixie with a yellow hat. When Ian mentioned his name, an image flashed into my mind. Odd."

"Perhaps not so odd. You have willed yourself to discount fantasy."

"Fantasy is not practical, Uncle Oliver."

"Perhaps not, but sometimes, 'tis a welcome diversion."

***

Wednesday, January 15, 1812 – The Pink Palace
Bettina

Bettina had spent one afternoon a week with each sultana, and a full day on Wednesday with Taita because the Sultan had requested two portraits of her—one in native dress and one in a London gown.

Today would be the second posing with Taita. Bettina's canvases were smaller than Gio's, four feet high and two-and-a half feet wide. Some of the sultanas posed seated, others standing. Their likenesses were depicted life-size, in half-body poses. Today she would begin painting over the charcoal outline of Taita's portrait, and hoped they would be alone so that she could establish a rapport, both for the painting as well as gaining trust. Eventually, Bettina would tell Taita of the earl's proposal. First, though, she would complete the paintings. *If my conversation with Taita does not go well, I can ill afford for the portrait commissions to be withdrawn. The earnings from these commissions are intended to be my nest egg. I need to secure my future.*

Absorbed in her paint mixing, Bettina did not hear the door open, and her brush slipped when she heard a voice.

"Good morning."

"Good morning, Miss Taita. You look marvelous in your native costume." She guided Taita to the desired position. Bettina stood back to check the light, angles and pose. She frowned.

Noticing the frown, Taita asked, "What troubles you?"

"Forgive me, Miss Taita. Your hairpiece of feathers is magnificent, but your hair is styled in the English way, not as I sketched you originally. How would your hair be styled in the land of your birth?"

"It would be free flowing."

"May I take out your hair pins and arrange your hair?"

"Very well."

Bettina carefully let down Taita's hair so that it fell over her shoulders. Its silken blackness set off the turquoise and pink colors of her clothing and the feathers in her crowning headpiece. As she was standing back to evaluate the results of her efforts, the doors opened and Anja entered the room.

"Your Highness, welcome." Bettina bowed slightly.

Anja smiled. "Good morning."

Anja waved for the servant to leave. She had an unopened letter in her hand, held it up. "Where shall I put this?"

"On the side table over there. Who is it from?"

"Vaitea."

Taita smiled.

Who is Vaitea? I cannot ask this soon.

Anja stood behind Bettina as she applied paint to canvas. Because Bettina restored old paintings, she was used to people watching her. She explained to Anja and Taita how she approached a portrait. "First I put a light underpainting where I want the figure to be, and block in the colors of the clothing."

"I was wondering where you would start. This is very interesting. When do you do the details of the face?" Anja seemed truly interested in the process.

"After I have it blocked in. I work until I feel that the real person is looking back at me, and continue to adjust the features in minor ways to achieve the best likeness. Sometimes it comes together quickly, other times…not so quickly." She shrugged and smiled.

Anja watched for a while, and then left.

Bettina worked a bit longer and then stepped back to assess her progress. "This might be a good time to stop on this costume. How long will it take you to change into your gown?"

"Perhaps an hour. I will have the kitchen bring you some food. May I see the painting?"

"Of course!"

Taita moved out of her pose, and stood next to Bettina. "I see now. You have reproduced the colors perfectly!"

"The range of hues is dazzling. Would you mind leaving the headpiece here so I can study the details while you change?"

"Certainly." Taita lifted the headpiece off her hair and placed it on the table next to Bettina. "I'll eat and change into the gown, returning in an hour."

Bettina nodded. "That sounds ideal."

***

Gio

The late afternoon sun illuminated the reception area of the Pink Palace. Gio studied the marble mosaic patterns on the foyer floor while waiting for Bettina. Intricately set, like tiny puzzle pieces, the swirling spiral design fascinated him. Built a century earlier, he marveled at the level of workmanship involved, an ancient skill.

The tapping of Bettina's heeled shoes diverted him from his reverie on mankind. He made a faux bow to her, extending his hand in sweeping motion.

Bettina laughed. "Are you my courtier now?"

"Always, my princess."

The disapproving eyes of Xerxes bore into them.

"Don't let yourself sink into frivolity, Xerxes. I am clearly an example that it never ends well."

A curl of a sneer crept over Xerxes's mouth.

Gio missed nothing. Looking toward Xerxes, he held his thumb up, squinted as if adjusting his artistic perspective, and nodded. "That is the visage I should paint. Intense, brooding, disdainful. You and I have a lot in common, Xerxes. Don't argue with me. You know it's true."

Xerxes drew himself to his full height. "Do you need assistance to your carriage, Miss Rybicki?"

"No, thank you. I can manage." Bettina balanced her portfolio, sketchbooks, and accoutrements as she walked toward the main entrance with Gio at her side.

"I left my materials there so I don't have to bring them daily," Gio said in a near-whisper.

"Perhaps I will do that tomorrow. Tonight, however, I have some details I want to review and refine."

Striding in long steps that led him to the entrance before the departing artists, Xerxes opened the door for them and stood at rigid attention.

As Gio and Bettina climbed into their waiting carriage, the dwarf turned and winked at Xerxes.

***

Thursday, January 16, 1812 – The Pink Palace
Bettina

Mialy, petite and shy, maintained her pose without complaint as Bettina worked on the details of her face. Although all the lesser wives had brown eyes, Mialy's had sparks of gold in them that Bettina painstakingly captured. *This girl is sweet, at the mercy of wives like Rana.*

"Tell me about yourself, Mialy."

"I am not very interesting, Miss Bettina. I grew up in a small village that overlooked the sea. I used to love to sit on the cliffs and dream of sailing away, although my country is very beautiful and flowers bloom all year. Forgive me, but I do not care so much for London. It is cold, foggy and makes me sad."

With such demanding other wives, I can see why her sweetness appeals to the Sultan.

CHAPTER SIXTY-TWO

Friday, January 17, 1812 – The Pink Palace
Bettina

F y fidgeted in her burgundy gown, altering her pose.
"Please, Your Highness, I am trying to capture your eyes and you keep moving your head."

"I'm sorry. I just can't get comfortable in these western clothes and I am upset."

Bettina put down her brush and pulled a stool over closer to Fy. "What is bothering you?"

"I love the Sultan but Rana is undermining me, and even the chief wife is cold to me. I'm afraid of Rana. I know a secret that she does not. When she finds out, she will be enraged because she will be displaced in the Sultan's heart. By me."

"Please do not tell me secrets I should not know."

"I feel better now. I'll sit still."

"Very well. I'll only keep you a short while longer."

***

Saturday, January 18, 1812 – Riding on Rotten Row
Bri

Riding with Edward, paced a few horse-lengths back by Jean-Louis and Gwyneth, Bri saw Vaux, Rogers and Lady Patricia approaching with Sir Reggie as the chaperone.

From the other direction, Bri spotted Miss Li.

Rogers waved and rode over to speak with her.

Edward shook his head. "Rogers is besotted with 'the woman in the red mask.' "

Bri nodded. "It seems Miss Li is the most memorable attendee of our Engagement Ball."

Bri rode off, forcing James and Vaux into a race to catch up.

Gwyneth glanced at Jean-Louis. "Will she ever listen?"

"Apparently not. But why should we expect her behavior to change, given that she has been the same since the age of three?"

***

Monday, January 20, 1812 – The Pink Palace
Bettina

Xerxes opened the double doors to the designated painting room for Bettina. Glancing around the empty room, she began to set up to continue Rana's portrait.

"Her Highness Rana will be with you shortly." The imperious butler shrugged, which struck Bettina as out of character. "Punctuality is not a habit she values."

"Very well. I can work on the palette for her dress while I wait for her." Bettina worked the pigments on her palette and tested color mixes until she felt confident she had a range of hues to blend to create the lights and shadows of the pale yellow fabric and diamonds.

The doors opened by the eunuchs, and Rana swept into the room, followed by a maidservant Bettina had never seen.

Without greeting Bettina, Rana grabbed her servant by the arm and pulled her toward the row of paintings-in-progress. "Do I not look more beautiful than the others?" She held her head high, expecting only one answer.

The maid looked at her mistress. "Yes, Your Highness. You are the most beautiful." Her Cockney-accented voice wavered in fear.

Rana slapped the maid across the face. "Liar! You have not looked at the other paintings! I want the truth." She pushed the frightened girl to look at the other paintings one at a time, arranged in an arc around the room, then returned to hers. "Now, who is the most beautiful?"

"You are the youngest and the loveliest of all of the sultanas."

Rana slapped her again. "I must be the only one the Sultan desires when he looks at these paintings."

The maid took a deep breath as she appeared to regain her composure. "You are the most beautiful, of course, Your Highness. Your eyes sparkle. Your bosom is high and firm. No one else compares. The color of your gown is most becoming."

The youngest sultana pouted. "Why didn't you say so immediately?" Her eyes narrowed into slits. "Do you know something? Does the Sultan whisper to the others about me?"

Shaking her head, the maid's eyes widened with fear. "No, Your Highness! I know nothing of the other sultanas. I have never even seen the Sultan, except at a great distance."

Dismissing the maid with a gesture toward the door, Rana ignored the servant as she left the room.

Rana walked around the partially finished portraits again, and examined them closely. "Taita's headdress of feathers distracts from her face, and the distinctly foreign slant of her eyes is unattractive." She looked at Bettina and grinned. "Besides, the Sultan never sleeps with her, so it matters not."

Standing in front of Nomena's likeness, she tilted her head. "She is so tall. Her face is long like a horse." She laughed. Edging toward Mialy, she frowned and shrugged. "Mialy is so tiny, almost like your dwarf friend, Mr. Gio. She has a face that looks squashed."

Bettina tried not to betray her reactions. *This one's jealous nature is poisonous.*

Looking at Fy's portrait in the burgundy dress they had feuded over, Rana remained silent. Turning her head toward Bettina, she said, "Fy is my only true rival. We are nearly the same age. Neither of us has been with child yet."

Rana walked toward her chair to assume her pose. "Once a sultana is carrying a child, the Sultan does not sleep with her for one year. That is the most frightening time. He may find another, younger woman to rank higher in his affections. A baby is a joy to the Sultan, but sometimes the sultana dies or the baby dies. If the baby dies, the sultana is banished to a separate palace because everyone knows it means she is weak."

Not knowing what to say, Bettina began to apply the pale yellow paint on the canvas over her outline of Rana's gown.

***

Monday, January 20, 1812 – Exterior of The Pink Palace
Giselle

This week, Jean-Louis was waiting for Giselle outside the palace.

Giselle apologized. "There is nothing new to report. Jealousy simmers under the surface. The Sultan visits each sultana in a set rotation."

Jean-Louis squinted and pointed up to the far part of the palace. "The day I dropped you off, I saw the one called Nomena try to throw herself off the balcony."

Giselle gasped. "To kill herself?" Her hand flew to her heart. "How terrible! Her Highness Rana mercilessly teases Nomena, saying she has a face like a horse and makes horse sounds when Nomena approaches. The Sultan doesn't know it and the others are afraid to tell him. It's every sultana for herself.

"Taita, however, is set apart in honor and respect. I haven't had a moment alone with her yet. The chief Sultana is always present."

"Don't force it. Steiner or I will see you here next week."

***

Tuesday, January 21, 1812 – The Hanforth Mansion
Bri

Bri stopped in to see Clarissa and Lulu.

Jean-Jean jumped up on her as soon as she walked in.

As she held the baby, Bri seemed far away. *Will Edward and I marry? Will I ever have a child of my own?*

"What is wrong? Not that Miss Li again."

"I can't help but think about it. I worry about Edward and her."

"This is all you talk about lately, Bri. You must stop. You're making it worse by reliving every moment in your head, endlessly analyzing their actions and intentions."

"I know you're right, but I can't shut off my emotions."

"Maybe that's progress."

"What do you mean?"

"You never admitted to having emotions before you met Edward."

***

Wednesday, January 22, 1812 – The Pink Palace
Bettina

Anja brought in another letter for Taita and laid it on the side table.

When their session was done for the day, Bettina waved Taita over. "What do you see that I should change?"

Taita's mouth dropped open. "The depiction amazes me. You have made the eyes seem alive. I am most impressed, Miss Rybicki. Your talent will be recognized widely, I predict."

She walked to the door, but before she could turn the handle, Bettina called out, "Miss Taita!"

"You forgot your letter."

Taita shook her head, walked back, and smiled. "It's unlike me to forget. Lately a lot has been on my mind."

Perhaps she will tell me in time. "Is is from Vaitea again?"

Taita nodded.

"It is such a lovely name. What does Vaitea mean in your language?"

"It means 'clear water.' " Taita picked up the letter. "Vaitea is the name of my son."

***

Wednesday, January 22, 1812 – Interior of Gio's Carriage
Gio

Once in the carriage, Charles reached over to take Bettina's hand. "How did the second full week go?"

Bettina took a breath. "Taita has a son in Madagascar. It must be the Sultan's, even though the other wives say she is not a sultana. From what the earl said to you, I don't believe he knows."

Gio rubbed his chin. "No. He would not broach the subject of marriage if he knew the Sultan had fathered her child. Odd. Why did she not tell him when they met again? Why let Henry believe the Sultan might approve their renewed courtship? It makes no sense."

Charles frowned. "I think you're missing the obvious alternative. Could it not be the earl's child from their liaison on the island?"

Tilting his head, Gio shrugged. "Perhaps. Life can be strange. Her Royal Highness Anja would know. Let me deal with her, Bettina. You shouldn't be seen as asking too many questions. I can get away with more outrageous behavior. A perk of my stature."

"How go the portraits? Are you pleased with your progress?" Charles directed his question to Bettina, but Gio answered.

'Why wouldn't I be? The Sultan is the most infuriating subject I've ever painted. An impatient man. He moves around, he pouts, he changes his stance repeatedly. I shall have to paint details from my initial sketch."

***

Friday, January 24, 1812 – The Pink Palace
Gio

Anja sat in her pose for Gio, but the Sultan had not yet appeared. "Your Highness, when do you expect the Sultan? I may lose the light to capture his face properly."

"My husband is often distracted by the demands of his subjects. I am certain he will be here soon."

Gio stood back from the large canvas, tilted his head and squinted to determine perspective. "Your Highness, may I adjust the folds of your skirt to catch the light?"

Anja nodded.

After adjusting the fabric to match his initial sketch, Gio reached over to move a stray lock of hair back into place.

The doors opened, the Sultan swept in, and stopped in shock.

"Never touch my sultana!"

Gio immediately pulled his hand back. "Your Royal Highness, I meant no disrespect. I was simply fixing a wisp of hair."

"My darling, he asked my permission."

The Sultan strode toward Gio, his direct gaze paralyzing the artist.

The dwarf held his breath. *The scimitars. Will the eunuchs come for me now?* Although he was a short, stocky man, the Sultan towered over

Gio. *If we were in Madagascar, I would no doubt be dead.*

Stopping within inches of Gio, the Sultan glared. Muscles in the Sultan's face pulsed as mottled shades of magenta and crimson intensified.

Summoning all of his bravado, Gio rose to his full height and stared back.

The Sultan guffawed. "Did I scare you, little man? Ha! You asked permission and it was granted. No consort of mine would ever want another man."

Gio relaxed and breathed. *If it were not a matter of life or death, I would point out my prowess, but silence is prudent.* "Why would she? You are a leader, a ruler, a man of unique accomplishments."

The Sultan rolled his hand in a forward circular motion. "Continue, continue. I like to hear how wonderful I am." His laughter caused his oversized paunch to quiver. He walked over to look at the progress on the canvas. "You will, of course, make me look virile."

"That, Your Royal Highness, is undeniable. I can capture the spark in your eye."

"No, I want you to show my readiness."

Gio's head wobbled at this request. He pointed to the canvas where the Sultan's ceremonial pantaloons met his legs. "Do I understand you to mean that you want a bulge here?"

Patting the dwarf on the head, the Sultan smiled. "Precisely."

"May I request that you stay a moment so I can depict the light falling on your face?"

The Sultan nodded. "Quickly. Important matters await my attention."

Gio sketched out with graphite the highlights revealed by the dawn's light. When done, he stepped back and glanced once more at the Sultan. "Your Royal Highness, I have what I need."

Leaning over to kiss Anja lightly on the cheek, the Sultan left.

As soon as the door was closed, Gio bowed to Anja. "Your Highness, thank you for coming to my defense."

Anja smiled. "I know my husband. But don't touch Rana or Fy. They are his current favorites. His attentions are fleeting, easily turned by a pretty ankle, a delicate cheekbone. He values my wit and insight. The others have shallow skills beyond their youthful looks. They come and go. I have endured."

"I always say, wit carries you farther than long legs." Gio leaned over his worktable and mixed paints for the tones of peacock blue he needed for her portrait.

Picking up his brush, he became absorbed in creating a lifelike representation of the sultana who sat before him. The wet paint on the canvas shimmering in the light and he lost track of time.

CHAPTER SIXTY-THREE

Monday, January 27, 1812 – Exterior of The Pink Palace
Giselle

Giselle met with Steiner in front of the pre-arranged location. Steiner handed her a sandwich from Nellie. "Anything to report?"

"Yes. I brought tea to Taita, and she was reading a letter. I apologized for disturbing her. She smiled and said a letter comes once a week, after months in transit." Giselle leaned forward. "*Then* she said, 'I miss my son.'"

Steiner recoiled. "The Sultan's son?"

Giselle shrugged. "I don't know. I said, 'It's thoughtful of him to write to you so often.'

"She said, 'Like all young men, he believes himself to be in love and wants to shout it from the rooftops, but cannot.'

"I asked, 'Why not?'

"Taita's answer showed fear. 'Never mind. I have said too much,' and she looked toward the door in fear."

Steiner mused aloud. "If she had borne the Sultan a son, he never would have freed her. Could there be another man in Madagascar?"

"She has never mentioned one."

"Don't call attention to yourself by asking too many questions. I'll talk to J-L and we'll think about the best way for you to proceed." Steiner opened the door. "Now, tell me where you'd like to go on your day off."

***

Monday, January 27, 1812 – The Pink Palace
Bettina

Rana was late, as usual. She came in and plopped herself in the posing chair, petulant and pouting.

"Are you unwell?"

"Last night was my turn with the Sultan, but my bleeding came earlier in the day. The Sultan hates the sight of blood. I tried to please him without letting him know it was my time, but he found out, and left my room as if I were dirty. Why do men act so?"

Bettina walked over and whispered to Rana. "Perhaps you should not speak openly of these things. The guards may hear."

Rana whispered back. "They are not *all* eunuchs. Some remain virile."

Bettina's eyes widened. "Say no more of this!"

The sultana waved her hand dismissively. "Eunuchs can't give you a child, but they can give you pleasure."

"Please stop!"

"You are so old. Have you never been with a man?"

"I do not discuss such things."

"So you are probably afraid of men."

This sultana's ignorance and arrogance will be her undoing. Rana chattered for the next few hours, telling Bettina about her tribe and how she caught the Sultan's eye.

As the afternoon sun dimmed, Bettina put down her brush. "I think I have all I need of your time for today."

"Let me see." Rana walked over and examined her likeness from several perspectives. "My breasts are more turned up. The Sultan always calls them 'alert.' You'll have to fix that." Rana swept out of the room.

***

Tuesday – January 28, 1812 – Lord Ravenshire's Townhouse
Edward

Edward arrived late, after breakfast, for their regular meeting to discuss Wyndward Investments.

"Forgive me for being late."

"Did Miss Li detain you?"

"As a matter of fact, she did. She had some suggestions for Wyndward Investments—"

Bri bristled and left Edward no doubt about her resolve as her icy tone chilled the room. "Kindly refrain from discussing *my* family's investments with Miss Li."

"I understand, but—"

Her stare terminated his efforts at persuasion.

"Bri, you are the client and all decisions ultimately rest with you. I shall respect your wishes."

"Good. I have prepared an agenda." She handed him a page of topics.

***

Wednesday, January 29, 1812 – The Pink Palace
Bettina

Although she wanted to learn more about Taita's son, Bettina felt it would be too direct to bring it up early in the posing session.

"I know so little of your customs, Taita. Where are you from?"

"A small island in the South Seas. Idyllic. Pearl-filled oysters swept onto the beaches bordering sheltered lagoons. Shipwrecks washed lost sailors ashore. The gossip rags have detailed the story, which I'm sure you know by now. The Earl of Ravenshire was once such a lost sailor, though he was but a viscount then. A fierce hurricane caused the water to surge into a huge wave. The power of that mountain of water cleaved the island in half. I trekked to find my father, the chief, but I was swept out to sea as parts of the island sank beneath the turbulent waters. I didn't know the viscount had survived until I saw him at a ball last year. You see, I only knew him as Henry. He told me he was viscount of nothing, as he felt he had lost that life forever, marooned and isolated." Taita sighed. "Life has such twists. My heart is now split in two as was my island: Henry or my son. I cannot have both."

"Forgive me, but why must you make a choice?"

"Though he dotes on Vaitea, the Sultan might punish my son

were I to stay in London. He would consider my abandonment of his largesse an unforgivable betrayal. And he would never let me see Vaitea again. I have lived without Henry for five-and-twenty years. I cannot live without my son."

Bettina set down her brush. "Please come review your likeness. What do you think?"

Taita walked over to view the progress and gasped. "You've done so much in the last week! You've captured the headdress perfectly. I must confess, I was annoyed at the amount of time I would have to spend sitting for a portrait. But now I am excited to see the final results!"

The doors opened and Xerxes appeared. "Gio is finished for the day, Miss Rybicki. He awaits you in the foyer."

***

Friday, January 31, 1812 – The Pink Palace
Bettina

Fy entered with a broad smile on her face.

Bettina smiled. "You seem very happy this afternoon, Your Highness."

'I am."

"Your skin looks lovely and your long neck is so elegant, and the rubies set off your coloring perfectly."

Bettina spent most of the session perfecting the skin color and highlights.

After a couple of hours, Fy put her hand on her forehead.

"Are you unwell?"

"Perhaps I ate something untoward. Where is the lavatory?"

Pointing, Bettina said, "Should I call Frau Schumer?"

"I don't think so."

Bettina could hear Fy vomiting. She knocked on the door. "Can I get you anything?"

Fy opened the door. Her pale face looked drawn. "I think I need to rest a bit. I'll see you next week."

Bettina nodded, and watched her leave. *I hope Rana is not poisoning her. Could her jealousy be that extreme?*

***

Monday, February 3, 1812 – The Pink Palace
Bettina

Dancing into the painting room, Rana took her seat.

"Are you celebrating something?"

"I am. I think I have displaced Fy in the Sultan's heart."

I have entered dangerous terrain. "Perhaps we should not speak of this."

"Fy is getting fat. The Sultan is fat, but he likes his women to be lithe." She stood up and twirled in her dress. "Like me."

"Forgive me for being so bold, Your Highness, but with so many wives, how can you remain the one he prefers?"

The sultana smirked. "I have a special potion that prevents me from becoming with child. I won't be tossed aside."

Bettina stopped, shocked. "What if the potion doesn't work?"

Rana did not break her pose. "It always has. And I have another that will bring on the bleeding if necessary."

"How long can this continue? Won't the Sultan expect to make a child with you?"

"Another few years and I will have replaced Anja in his heart. Then I can present him with a son." Rana jumped at the sound of voices outside the door. "Who is there?" Her face flushed.

Bettina put down her brush and palette and went to open the door. "Is something amiss?"

Frau Schumer stood there. "It is nothing, Miss Rybicki. I caught Fy listening at the door and was reprimanding the eunuchs for not turning her away immediately. I'll send Giselle up with some tea and small bites to eat." She closed the double doors in Bettina's face.

Open-mouthed at the doors closing so abruptly, Bettina walked back toward Rana, whose flush had faded into the paleness of fright. "The doors are very thick. Our voices were low. She probably could not hear you. We only heard their voices because they were raised in anger."

Rana breathed in deep heaves. "The Sultan can never know. You must lie for me if Fy says anything."

Caught unawares, Bettina agreed. "All our conversations are private. You have my word, Your Highness."

Rana resumed her pose, her breathing still labored.

Bettina picked up her brushes and continued. *This palace façade hides a strange world. I must tread its hallways with care.*

Giselle brought tea and admired the paintings, looking at each one.

"I am the most beautiful, am I not, Giselle?"

"You are indeed, Your Highness."

"More beautiful than any of the others." She stamped her foot. "You must repeat my words."

"More beautiful than any of the others, Your Highness."

Giselle shot a questioning glance at Bettina and quickly left.

***

Late Monday, February 3, 1812 – The Pink Palace

Rana

Rana peeked around the corner as the Sultan headed toward Nomena's room. She was in a robe and pirouetted for her master, giggling and motioning with her finger to be silent and teased him to follow her. *He cannot resist me. I am his favorite.*

The Sultan stopped for a moment, then smiled, shrugged and waddled after her, his belly jiggling like a gelatinous mass. He chased her into her room and closed the door. The eunuchs who accompanied him everywhere stood guard outside. He shook his finger at her in mock scolding. "This is Nomena's night. You are violating palace protocol."

In a purring voice, Rana cajoled the Sultan. "You determine protocol. You are our master. Your will is paramount. I am yours." She dropped her robe and stood naked in the candlelight.

The Sultan tilted his head. "What is that on your arm? Your time should have ended by now. You know I would never touch you under such conditions!"

Rana looked and saw blood on her elbow. "Oh, no," she stammered. "It is not my monthly flow. It must be paint from that portrait. I perhaps touched the painting without knowing it."

The Sultan grabbed her arm and looked closely. "This is blood." He wiped it off with his hand and stared at her. "There is no wound. Whose blood is this? Have you beaten a servant again?"

Struggling to escape his grip, she protested. "No, it was nothing. Just an accident."

"What kind of accident?" He raised his hand to her. "I ask once more: whose blood is this?"

Rana had never seen such fury in his eyes Icy arrows of fear pierced her heart. *He must understand how much I love him.* "Fy's. She threatened me. She was not worthy of you, my Sultan."

He tightened his hold on her. "Was? What have you done?"

Straightening to her full height, Rana was defiant. "I slit her throat."

The Sultan struck her across the face, knocking her to the floor. He straddled her, preventing any movement. Steely-eyed, his voice took on an unnaturally soft tone. "You killed my Fy?" He slapped her again, harder. "Why?"

"Because she would tell you lies about me." Rana's mind raced. "She was using a potion to prevent becoming with child and when I found out, she threatened to kill me if I told you. She was dangerous, my love, dangerous to us."

Loosening his grip, the Sultan's eyes bored into hers. "When did she start using this potion?"

It's working. He believes me. She relaxed slightly, although his massive weight suppressed her lungs. "For many months, maybe a year. She is so vain, my love, she does not want to deform her body to carry your child."

She didn't see the blow that split her forehead, not the next one that knocked out several teeth. She sputtered blood. "M-my love…"

"I am not your love anymore, you daughter of snakes." He struck her again. Leaning in close to her ear, he whispered. "She took no such potion. She was carrying my child. My son. You have killed my Fy and my son. Now you shall die and be forgotten forever."

He struck her again and again until she could no longer hear his condemnations.

***

Early Tuesday, February 4, 1812 – The Pink Palace
Xerxes

Xerxes edged into Rana's room, having come when the eunuch

informed him that the Sultan required his presence.

The Sultan sat on the bed, staring at him. He spoke in a flat tone. "Rana killed Fy and now she is dead too." He tilted his head to the other side of the bed.

The butler walked to the other side of the bed. His voice betrayed no emotion. "We shall remove her body and clean the room. You should prepare to leave London on your ship immediately. Tonight. Where is Fy?"

"I have not had the courage to look. I cannot bear to see her. Go to her room and report back."

Xerxes exited.

***

When the vizier returned, he confirmed the Sultan's fear. "She is dead and her lute was smashed to pieces. There is only one option. The eunuchs outside will dispose of Rana. We will say she ran off. Tomorrow, the staff will find Fy. I will alert the police. The killing will be put off on some itinerant footpad. There will be nothing more to occupy the British authorities. A domestic dispute. You will be off premises and the episode will fade."

"But the paintings…"

"They will be finished or destroyed, as you wish."

"All but Rana's should be finished. Destroy Rana's or give it to the artist. I care not which."

"You can tarry no longer, Your Royal Highness. You must depart now. Sail to the south of England, and the sultanas will meet you on the coast. I shall meet up with you in Porto. Leave this issue to me."

Rising to his feet, the Sultan touched the arm of his vizier. "Your loyalty has always given me strength." He departed without looking back.

Xerxes walked to the door to address the eunuchs. "Wrap Rana's body in a sheet and clean this room. Speak to no one."

Watching as they efficiently worked, Xerxes frowned. *Loyalty. These eunuchs have been loyal to the Sultan and to me. Now they must die.*

***

Early Tuesday, February 4, 1812 – *Dreamtime*
Edward

Just a quick inhale is all I need.
Half an hour later, Edward came out and hailed a Hackney. He didn't see François watching across the street.
I have conquered my desire. I can partake and stop at will.

***

Tuesday, February 4, 1812 – The Pink Palace
Giselle

Giselle knocked on Fy's door. There was no reply. *Perhaps she is sleeping late this morning.* Looking at the tray of hot food, Giselle hesitated. Her instructions were to bring breakfast trays to all wives in a specific order. Given Fy and Rana's dislike for each other, if she skipped Fy and gave the tray to Rana, that would incite another loud disagreement. She knocked again.

Frau Schumer entered the hallway. "Is there a problem?"
That woman makes everything sound like it's my fault.
"Her highness Fy is not responding, Frau Schumer."
Shrugging with a frown of disgust, Frau Schumer came to Fy's door and knocked loudly. "It is time to awaken, Your Highness. If you are unwell, please tell me." Still no answer.

Frau Schumer reached into her pocket and took out a ring of large keys, put one in the lock and opened the door. The bed stood undisturbed. Walking inside, she walked to the far side of the bed and screamed.

Giselle put down the tray on a table near the door and ran to Frau Schumer's side. She grabbed the housekeeper's arm in horror.

Blood stained Fy's white satin sleeping gown and pooled around her head. Vacant eyes stared at nothingness. Her head had been half-severed from her neck.

CHAPTER SIXTY-FOUR

Tuesday, February 4, 1812 – The Pink Palace
Bettina

U neasy at the previous day's events, Bettina was setting up the position of the chair for her portrait of Nomena. Studying her preliminary strokes, she couldn't forget the cruel assessment by Rana of Nomena's long face, likening her to a horse. There was something regal about Nomena, like pictures of Egyptian busts and statues of ancient queens. *Pride, confidence and elegance must be evident in the eyes, the way her head is held. The challenge is to find what attracted the Sultan to each woman and reveal it in the portraits.*

The sound of the doors opening caused Bettina to turn her head.

Nomena entered in her apple green gown. As she took her place, she fidgeted with her sleeves and kept shifting her position.

"Please be comfortable, Your Highness. To achieve the best likeness, I need you to remain still."

Wounded eyes turned up at Bettina. A whisper escaped Nomena's lips. "He did not visit me last night. It was my turn, and I waited and waited." Tears burst forth from her eyes.

Bettina searched for clean rags to blot the flow of tears, and dabbed at her subject's cheeks. "Perhaps matters of state interfered."

Nomena shook her head in disagreement, still not able to speak.

Both were startled when the doors to the room flew open and Frau Schumer appeared carrying clothing.

"I am sorry, Miss Rybicki. Your Highness, the Sultan has

commanded that all the sultanas meet his ship on the coastline. He has already departed."

Nomena protested. "But my portrait! It will not be finished."

"It will be finished before we return again. I'm sure Miss Rybicki can finish it at her leisure. We have had a tragedy. Her Highness Fy has been found murdered."

Bettina and Nomena gasped. They looked at each other, then back to Frau Schumer.

"And Her Highness Rana is missing. The constable has been notified, over my objections. This matter should have been kept private. You must leave immediately. Remove your gown, don this dress, and go downstairs to the waiting coach."

Nomena meekly stood, glancing at her unfinished portrait for the last time.

Frau Schumer helped her undo the ties of her gown and placed it on a chair. Turning to Bettina, she said, "We will provide a similar maid to pose in the dress so that the portrait may be completed."

Bettina remained silent. *Did Rana kill Fy?*

Dressing quickly, Nomena tossed a grateful look at Bettina as she was rushed out the doors to Xerxes, who waited outside to usher her to safety.

After Nomena left, Frau Schumer closed the doors and sighed. "The constable may want to question you. It would be best if you waited here. Lord Ostwold is also being detained. You could," she waved her hand in a dismissive gesture, "mix your paints until the constable arrives. Tomorrow you should be able to return. I will have suitable maids to sit in the gowns for the portraits. The Sultan does not want Rana's portrait—he left instructions for you to destroy it or keep it. Simply see that it is removed from the palace. I will have Rana's dress delivered to you tomorrow to take with you. We'll burn Fy in hers as soon as we get her body released. Perhaps you can substitute another face on your painting, for another commission. Of course, you will be paid in full for all portraits, as agreed."

Even after gathering her composure, Bettina found it difficult to speak. "Her Highness Fy was a lovely person. So tragic." She paused, "Her Highness Rana thought Her Highness Fy was listening at the door yesterday. Do you think—"

Steely eyes glared back at her. "It is best *not* to think, Miss Rybicki."

"Of course. I know nothing of the workings of the palace." *Must I lie to the constable?*

Xerxes knocked on the doors before opening them. "The sultanas are in transit. The balance of the household is to assemble in the foyer to await the arrival of the constable and coroner."

Bettina bent to gather up her materials, but Xerxes stopped her. "We must go now. Leave these items until tomorrow."

Obeying, Bettina followed Frau Schumer and Xerxes out of the room.

***

Tuesday, February 4, 1812 – Lord Ravenshire's Townhouse
Edward

After riding with her Uncle Oliver, Bri met with Edward to conduct their usual weekly meeting to discuss Wyndward Investments. As Edward rose to leave, he noticed Bri had something more on her mind.

"Is there something more?"

"Are we taking on too much? These investments are small operations compared to your large clients. And I must keep the trading company foremost among my tasks. When Father starts traveling again, we may be pulled in many directions."

"I agree. The board can help. Perhaps we need to expand it."

"Let's both think about it and discuss it next week."

"Your wish is my command." His kiss brushed her lips. "Too many eyes here."

Bri nodded, but pulled him closer for a deeper kiss.

She doesn't see a difference in me. The poppy has no impact. I have harnessed its power by controlling my cravings.

***

Tuesday, February 4, 1812 – The Pink Palace
Gio

Gio sat on a bench in the huge reception hall. When he saw Bettina appear, he waved her over. "I never got to see the Sultan or Her Highness Anja this morning. I was instructed to sit and wait. It's been over three hours. At least they brought me some tea. I took a nap for a while. It is no secret that arriving at dawn is not my preference, so I welcomed the respite." He took a sip of tea and waved over the servant. "Miss Rybicki would like some tea."

Bettina leaned toward her mentor, whispering, "Don't you know what happened?"

"No. I assume it was some whim of the Sultan." He examined her face and squinted. "*You* know."

The young artist nodded, and continued in a soft tone, so as not to be overheard, "Her Highness Fy was murdered, and Her Highness Rana is missing. The Sultan and the sultanas are en route to their ship as we speak."

Gio raised an eyebrow. "At least we got a partial payment."

"Lord Ostwold! For shame. One woman is dead and another most likely murdered as well."

Shrugging, the artist defended himself. "We must be practical. The Sultan lacks not for food, but we must always keep an eye to our coffers."

Bettina shook her head. "Do not worry. Frau Schumer and Xerxes said we would be paid in full as contracted. I am to finish the portraits with maids posing in the gowns except for Rana's. That is what the servants brought. The brown bag contains her posing dress."

The dwarf leaned back against the wall and stared at the ceiling. "There will be no one to give final approval of the portraits until the Sultan returns to London. Of course, that day may never come." He slumped. "Taita must have departed with the others. The earl will be unhappy that she has left London."

"But her son would always pull her back to Madagascar. The earl can never win."

Smiling, Gio squeezed her hand. "Ah, my dear, you are so young. 'Never' is a long time. But our problem is immediate; not only do I have to tell the earl that his love may never return. I have to tell him that she has a son. Whether that son be the Sultan's or another man's, even the earl's, we do not know. Of course, we could sail to Madagascar and see for ourselves. One look at the boy should tell us if the earl is his father."

"Are you mad?"

"Some think so."

Their conversation was interrupted by the arrival of the constable and the coroner.

Accompanying the constable was Boyd of the Bow Street Runners. When the detective saw Gio, he approached him. "Lord Ostwold, may I request your assistance? We need sketches of the scene."

"Hardly my métier, Mr. Boyd, but I shall welcome the distraction. Miss Rybicki can assist me."

"Fine. Please follow the coroner." Boyd pointed to the staircase. "He's over there."

Gio pulled Bettina by the hand, giving her some of his materials to carry.

As they walked, she murmured in low tones. "You appear excited to see such a gruesome sight."

"Have you seen it?"

Bettina shook her head. "No."

"Then how do you know it's gruesome?"

Bettina sighed with a note of exasperation. "She's dead."

When they reached the coroner, he led them to the upper levels of the palace.

Whispering as they struggled to keep up with the long-legged coroner, Gio continued, almost giddy in tone, "I've never seen a murdered body."

"It's not an adventure to be wished. You are a scurrilous interloper."

"I think of myself as a dashing vagabond who fears nothing. And, may I point out, I was invited by the Bow Street Runner."

Bettina had no retort before they reached Fy's room.

A bare-chested scimitar-wielding eunuch stood at attention near the body.

The coroner stared at him. "Has anyone touched the body?"

The man shook his head from side to side.

"Do you speak?"

The guard repeated his action.

Gio came over to the coroner. "Some of them lose their tongues as well as their...well, you know. The other parts."

The coroner focused a withering gaze on the dwarf. "Sketch the scene."

Gio reached into the leather portfolio that Bettina carried, and retrieving paper and charcoal, quickly depicted the position of the body. He bent over closer to the neck, to gauge the depth of the slice, careful to avoid stepping in the blood pooled on the floor. "The killer was left-handed. And probably a woman."

"And just how do *you* determine that?" The tall coroner did not try to hide the disdain in his voice.

"The cut is right to left, and it's shallow, though deep enough to kill. One of these gentlemen," he waved a hand toward the eunuch, "would have sliced off her head with a single swift stroke."

"You're correct. Jealous woman, probably."

"A lot of those around here."

Another voice came from the door. "Why do you say that?" Boyd walked in.

Finishing his sketch while he talked, Gio asked, "Have you been to the Pink Palace before?"

"No."

"He has many wives. He brought his chief wife, four favorites and his healer for this visit. This was one of the youngest wives."

The detective frowned. "Foreigners. The Persian says the Sultan had to leave the country on urgent business. Where are the other wives?"

Bettina cleared her throat. "They all left this morning to meet the Sultan. They will rendezvous with his ship on the southern coast. Maybe you could catch them—"

"Not our jurisdiction. By the time we got to the coast, they would be far away and I can't commandeer the Royal Navy for one woman's murder."

"Maybe two. There is another sultana who is missing, but—" Bettina hesitated.

"But what?" The detective walked over to her. "You must tell me all you know about this murder."

"I don't know anything about the murder. But yesterday, Her Highness Fy, who is lying there," she pointed to the prone figure, "was listening outside the door as Her Highness Rana, who is missing, told me something she should not have revealed. Then, this morning, Her Highness Nomena sobbed as she told me the Sultan did not come to her last night, when it was her turn. She feared he had tired of her."

The coroner cocked his head toward the dead woman. "The dead woman was with child. Maybe he tired of *her*."

"Are you daft? We just agreed a woman killed this Fy, not a man." Indignant, Gio's face flushed in anger. "It's quite obvious."

"Is it now? Why don't you enlighten me?"

"You have no gift for sarcasm, detective. Fy listened and learned something that Rana wanted kept secret." He turned toward Bettina. "Was Rana left-handed?"

Bettina nodded.

"*Voilà!* Rana slit Fy's throat to protect her secret. A simpleton could see that."

"So where is Rana?"

"That is your mystery to unravel, detective. I solved your murder. A missing woman? Child's play. Perhaps she hid rolled up in a carpet the Sultan took to his ship, perhaps she lured him to her room away from Nomena and bewitched him. Maybe the Sultan killed her. Maybe Nomena killed her. Maybe one of the other wives did it. That's your job."

Gio took his charcoal drawing and handed it to the detective. "Here is your sketch. May we leave?"

"Yes, just give me a way to contact both of you."

They dictated their places of residence and the gallery, and left.

Settling into a Hackney cab, Gio sighed. "How can I tell the earl his love has left for Madagascar and that she has a son?"

"Who is the father?"

Gio shrugged. "We may never know. The son could be the Sultan's, but I think not. The other wives all liked Taita. There was no underlying jealousy. Perhaps another man in Madagascar, perhaps even the earl. Before the typhoon separated them, they were lovers. As I said earlier, there may only be one way for us to find out."

"We're *not* going to Madagascar." Bettina sighed in frustration. "You *are* mad." She sat back on the leather bench seat until a rut in the cobblestones lurched her forward. "This carriage ride is turbulent enough. A sea voyage holds no appeal for me."

"The meek shall *not* inherit the earth. They never go *anywhere*."

Bettina glared at the dwarf.

***

Giselle

The staff assembled in the large main foyer to be questioned in sequence by the constable and the detective. Xerxes, Frau Schumer and Giselle were taken to a separate room and instructed to wait for Boyd.

Will Mr. Boyd reveal that he knows who I am? Giselle tried to sit stock-still, but her mind was racing.

"Stop fidgeting." Frau Schumer's ever-present frown and air of disdain for Giselle were accentuated by her snapped command.

The tension was broken when Boyd entered. Turning toward Xerxes, he looked at his notes. "You are the butler, Mr. Arsama?"

"The vizier. It is similar to a butler, but with more authority."

Boyd took a chair and moved it to a position opposite the three subjects of his interrogation. "Tell me how you learned of Sultana Fy's death."

Xerxes cleared his throat. *"Her Highness* Fy," he paused to emphasize the correct form of address for the dead sultana, then continued, "was found by the maid, Giselle. The eunuchs guarding the hall of sultanas summoned me. When I arrived, I found Frau Schumer and Giselle in the room looking at Her Highness Fy's body lying in a pool of blood. Her throat had been slit."

Looking up from his notes, the detective asked, "What did you do then?"

"I instructed no one to touch the body."

"Where was the Sultan?"

"The Sultan had grown bored with London and decided to return to Madagascar in the middle of the night. He was gone by the time I was called to Her Highness Fy's room the next morning. The sultanas left in another ship after the body was found."

"In Britain, sir, people living in a household where a murder has taken place do not leave the country until an inquest has been completed. You may have aided the escape of a killer. While I cannot pursue them out of this jurisdiction, I can detain *you.*"

"When the Sultan decides to leave, it is customary that the sultanas follow. He did not know of the murder of Her Highness Fy. It is true that the other sultanas were aware of Her Highness Fy's death when they left that morning, but frankly, sir, this is a dangerous city, and we were afraid for their safety."

An icy stare met Xerxes as the detective tapped his pencil on his pad. "Men with scimitars guard these halls. It is unlikely that a footpad gained entrance to this fortress. However, it is highly likely that someone in your household committed this act. To my mind, suspects abound—the Sultan, another lover, or one of the other sultanas. Jealousy is a familiar motive, in any culture. Death by knife almost always defines a personal vendetta.

"We have a phrase in this country: 'obstruction of justice.' You, sir, may be adjudged guilty of it. I am instructing you not to leave this country. Is that clear? We shall station men around this compound to prevent anyone else from departing in the middle of the night."

"I am not subject to your laws."

"You are in this country and, therefore, you most certainly *are* subject to our laws. Make no mistake about it, sir: you are in legal jeopardy and will be held here under house arrest." He walked to the door and signaled to one of his men to enter the room. "Escort Mr. Arsama to his room. He is not to leave it. Arrange for meals to be delivered to him."

Xerxes spluttered in frustration. "I run this household! Chaos will reign if I do not remain in charge."

The detective shrugged. "Chaos has already reigned—a woman's throat has been slit and the key members of the household have fled. How much worse can it get?" Boyd glanced at one of his subordinates. "Take him away."

Turning to Frau Schumer, Detective Boyd asked the same question, correcting his reference to Fy, "Tell me how you learned of *Her Highness* Fy's death."

"Giselle could not gain access to Her Highness Fy's room, so I unlocked it and we found the body. I told the eunuchs guarding the hall of the sultanas to summon Xerxes, which was a violation of protocol."

"How so?"

"No man is to enter the hall of the sultanas. However, since there had been a murder, I believed his presence was required. He dispatched a runner to inform the constable of the situation."

"Do you know of anyone who would wish ill toward Her Highness Fy?"

"No."

"Did you know she was with child?"

Frau Schumer looked genuinely surprised. "No! Oh, *mein Gott!*"

Giselle gasped and her eyes widened in horror. *Poor Fy! And a baby too.*

"Frau Schumer, do not leave London."

"I have nowhere else to go. This is my home now."

"You may leave." He walked to the door and opened it for her.

Before she left, Frau Schumer turned to Giselle. "The sultanas are gone. You are no longer needed. Remove yourself and any possessions from these premises immediately after the detective is finished with you. The footman will summon me when you are leaving, and I will give you your final wages at that time." The German housekeeper spun on her heel and departed with her customary disdain for lesser humans.

Boyd closed the door and walked back to his chair. "What brought you to this place, Giselle? And why are you masquerading as a serving maid?"

***

Tuesday, February 4, 1812 – Lord Ravenshire's Townhouse
Henry

Arriving home from the trading offices, the earl was met by Thompson

"A note from Gio, milord.".

> One of the Sultan's wives is dead. Fleeing London, the Sultan has taken Taita with him back to Madagascar.

A cryptic postscript ended the note:

> More to be discussed in private. Gio

After reading it, the earl walked back to his study and placed the note on his desk. He paled and gazed out the window into the foggy late afternoon. *All that matters is that she is gone.*

***

Tuesday, February 4, 1812 – The Pink Palace
Giselle

"Thank you for not acknowledging my normal profession."

Boyd smiled. "Wouldn't add to my credibility, either."

"Jean-Louis asked me to help find out if Taita, the healer, was happy at the palace or if she would like to be with Lord Ravenshire."

"I've heard the rumors of their liaison."

Giselle bristled. "The gossip rags are a scourge."

"Perhaps. In any case, the romantic pursuits of Lord Ravenshire are not my concern. What do you know of this murder that you could not say in front of Frau Schumer?"

"Her Highness Rana is missing. She was not with the other sultanas when they left because I had to prepare baskets of food and took them to the carriages. When I asked why Her Highness Rana was not among the other wives, Xerxes said it was none of my concern."

"And?"

"Rana was the youngest and newest of the favored wives. Impulsive, scheming, and jealous, she fought with Fy at the dressmaker's because she felt Fy picked the gown that the Sultan would like best."

"Could she have killed Sultana Fy?"

"*Her Highness* Fy. They are very particular how we refer to them. As to whether Her Highness Rana could have killed Her Highness Fy, I have no inkling. I have been here only a few weeks. The palace is very secretive. People fear the Sultan's temper."

Boyd raised an eyebrow. "Could the Sultan have killed *Her Highness* Fy?

Giselle looked off in the distance. "I never met him. He is said to be charming but possesses a fearsome temple. The whispers are that the murder was done by a woman."

"Why?"

"They say men cut off heads, woman slit throats."

Boyd closed his notebook. "We're done. Time for you to gather up your belongings, I guess."

"Thank you again for not publicly recognizing me."

"Don't need to compromise myself, do I?" The detective smiled.

Giselle laughed. "I will be very grateful the next time I see you, Detective."

Boyd stood and escorted her to the door.

***

Tuesday, February 4, 1812 – Lord Ravenshire's Townhouse
Bri

Thompson responded to the knock at the front door.

"Who is it at this hour?"

Gio had overheard her comment as he entered. "*Moi.*"

Henry rose. "Bri will excuse us." He and Gio walked toward his study.

"I will not!"

Henry stopped in his tracks, looked at Gio.

The dwarf shrugged. "What I have to say affects her too." In the earl's study, Gio climbed into a wingback chair. His legs dangled over the cushion edge.

Henry closed the door. "Well? What have you learned?"

"Let me begin at the end, for Bri. One of the Sultan's wives was murdered in the Pink Palace."

"How awful!" Bri leaned in, glanced at her father, and then back at Gio.

"A young sultana had her throat slit, and another sultana is missing. The Sultan, his remaining wives and Taita were spirited off to his ship and are now en route to Madagascar."

"I know all that, and now Bri does too."

Gio bit his lower lip, and stuttered, "Th-there's more."

Perplexed, Henry frowned. "Out with it!"

"Taita will never leave the Sultan…well, maybe 'never' is the wrong word. Let us say it is unlikely."

Crestfallen, Henry shook his head, denying he'd heard Gio's words. "When last I saw her, I knew our bond had remained strong. I believed that her love for me had not dissipated."

"Perhaps her love is as it ever was. But there is someone she loves more."

"Not that fat Sultan! It cannot be!"

"No, not him."

"Damnation, Gio! Stop speaking in riddles. Another man? Tell me. Now."

"Taita has a son."

Henry's chest was seized by a spasm, his face flushed, and he clutched his hand to his breast.

"Henry, are you unwell? Let me call Nashmir—"

Bri jumped to her feet and ran to her father.

Henry put up his hand to stop her. Breathing in deep gasps, he finally spoke. "I'm ashamed to reveal such weakness. Speak naught of this episode."

"Nonsense," said Bri. "Don't expect me to remain silent. Nashmir must attend to you." She put her arms around her shoulders. "Father, has such a thing happened before?"

"No."

"I'm older than you, Henry. Do not ignore such warning signs."

Dismissing the dwarf's concerns with a wave, Henry leaned back in his chair and stared at the ceiling.

Gio jumped out of the chair and put his hands on the desk. "Forgive my impertinence, Henry, but the boy was born in 1787. Was not that shortly after the period you were thought lost to us, when you met Taita?"

"What are you saying?" Henry sat up and leaned forward.

"You know very well what I am saying. You may be the father of Taita's son."

Bri's mouth dropped open.

Henry stared at the diminutive artist he had known since the age of twelve, gripped his chest again and collapsed on the floor, unconscious.

"Nashmir!" screamed Bri. She knelt by her father's side.

Pain flared in her eyes as she glanced at Gio. "He's still breathing."

CHAPTER SIXTY-FIVE

Tuesday, February 4, 1812 – Lord Ravenshire's Townhouse
Nashmir

The Tibetan came downstairs to report to the waiting guests.

"The earl is resting now. Jean-Louis has sent a bird to Ravenshire to alert Dr. Northcliffe and will return with the comtesse."

Despite knowing her father was out of danger, Bri could not stop the tears. "But he is not elderly. Is his heart damaged?"

"More by love than by Fate."

"I am undone, finding out I have a brother. I know my father. He will seek out my brother."

"Half-brother," said Gio.

***

Wednesday, February 5, 1812 – Lord Ravenshire's Townhouse
Jean-Louis

Dr. Northcliffe and Gwyneth had arrived a few hours past midnight. They went upstairs to join Bri and Gio, who had fallen asleep in chairs surrounding Henry's bed.

Gwyneth sank into an empty chair.

The doctor took the earl's pulse, palpated his chest, and leaned in to speak into his ear.

Henry opened his eyes and blinked rapidly. "What happened?"
At the sound of his voice, Bri and Gio awoke.
"You scared us half to death, that's what happened. You passed out after hearing the news—" Gio jumped off the chair and walked over to the bed.
Henry closed his eyes. "—of Taita's son."
"Can you sit up?" The doctor held up his hands to prevent others from helping him. "I must assess his strength."
Raising himself to a seated position, Henry rubbed his eyes and threw his legs over the side of the bed. He stood but lost his balance and fell back onto the bed.
The doctor felt his chest. "The heartbeat is normal. Try to sleep. I will assess your condition in the morning." Turning to the others, he said, "I'll stay with him. The rest of you should go to bed for a few hours, at least."
Bri and Gwyneth kissed Henry goodnight, and Gio saluted.
Jean-Louis stretched out on a chair and closed his eyes.

***

Bri

Gwyneth sighed. "I am nearly as stunned by the news as Henry. I thought it might be his heart, but possibly shock overcame him."
Bri nodded. "We'll know more soon, but now we must sleep. Your usual rooms have been prepared."
Climbing the stairs to her own room, Bri's mind fought the jumbled thoughts that assailed her. *A brother? How will Charlotte feel? And Father? I thought he might die. He's always been there, strong and comforting. I thought I could overcome anything. How naïve I have been. Life is so much more uncertain than I knew.*

***

Thursday, February 6, 1812 – Aboard *Zainab's Dream*
Taita

Taita was ushered into the Sultan's private suite on his ship.
"Taita, I need your wise counsel."

611

I could be in danger if he confesses to me. Taita breathed deeply to calm herself. "Join me in deep breathing, my Sultan. Close your—"

"I have no time for that!" Tears welled up in his coal-black eyes. "My Fy! And the babe. A son, perhaps. Could you tell?"

As the palace healer, Taita had attended Fy during bouts of morning distress. Only she and the Sultan knew that Fy was with child. "It was too early to tell if she carried a son. With a first child, it is often difficult to predict."

The Sultan hung his head, then stood and paced in anger. "Such betrayal!"

"My Sultan, I have not seen Rana among us."

"Nor will you see her deceitful face again. Never speak her name!"

"She is banished?"

"She rests at the bottom of the sea, to be devoured by the swimming beasts of the deep."

Did he kill her or order her death?

"Is this why you seek my counsel?"

The Sultan waved his hand dismissively. "No. I want you to plan Fy's memorial and burial. Xerxes will see that she is burned on a pyre at the London palace. Her bones will be gathered and returned to us. I cannot think of it, it is too painful. You must think for me. There will be two caskets, one for Fy and one for our son. Xerxes has been instructed to open her body and remove the baby so that they will be burned separately. All will know the horror of her death."

The thought of ripping the corpse of a baby from a dead woman's body caused Taita's face to blanch.

"I shall not make you guess, healer. The evil one had Fy's blood on her person. The accursed witch confessed her wicked act to me. I avenged my Fy," he cupped his palms, "with my own hands."

The die is cast. I know too much. "Justice is your right, my Sultan. I shall attend to the burial matters. Do you wish a large gathering?"

The Sultan shook his head in disagreement. "I shall declare a month of mourning, but the burials will be private. We will announce an accident, a fall, something." He gestured in the air. "I leave it to you. Write words for me to speak to my people."

"As you wish, my Sultan."

Taita left and walked slowly down the hallway. *If I leave the Sultan, I endanger my son. If my son does not want to escape, my Fate is sealed.*

***

Thursday, February 6, 1812 – Lord Ravenshire's Townhouse
Henry

Henry awoke at noon.

Dr. Northcliffe rose to his feet. He felt Henry's forehead. "No fever. Let me check your heart." He listened. "Can you stand?"

Henry stretched. "My legs feel weak, but I haven't eaten for more than a day, I hear."

"Splash some water on your face and let's see how you feel after you eat."

***

Friday, February 7, 1812 – Musée de Merbeau
Gwyneth

Gwyneth sat in her office at the back of the museum. A portrait of her as a child, drawing in the garden at Ravenshire, painted by Gio, hung on the wall behind her desk. A small table held place settings for two, while a large table for meetings at the other end of the room was covered with artwork for a book she was preparing for publication. While art books were the mainstay of Musée de Merbeau Press, the occasional work of poetry captured her interest.

The museum was closed today, but the doorman stood on duty for security and knew that Lady Gabriella was due for luncheon. Gwyneth's cook, Dominique, had brought ingredients from home, and was in the museum kitchen preparing a meal of cold chicken and walnuts mixed with mayonnaise and mustard, with fresh cuttings of an assortment of lettuces and tomatoes from the comtesse's greenhouse, defying seasonal limitations.

She heard footsteps along the marble hallway and Bri walked in, followed by Jean-Louis.

"Darling!" Aunt Gwyneth held out her arms to embrace her niece. "Jean-Louis, Dominique is preparing luncheon in the kitchen. There is plenty for you."

"Thank you, Lady Gwyneth. I shall walk the perimeter first to confirm the exits are secure."

Gwyneth shook her head and smiled. "Ah, Jean-Louis, I know your procedures.

"Never take anything for granted, Lady Gwyneth."

"Thank you. I'm sure you will find that all is in order."

Jean-Louis shrugged. "*Peut-être*. Perhaps." He exited soundlessly. Dominique brought their plates and left.

Bri sighed. "Father seemed back to normal this morning."

"Dr. Northcliffe believes it to be—I hesitate to say this—a manifestation of severe melancholy brought on by a shock to the nervous system. Naturally, Father resists any label suggesting infirmity. But to me, 'tis better than a weak heart. He's always had a prodigious work ethic."

Gwyneth nodded. "Now that you are dealing with more aspects of commerce, you can appreciate the importance of time and the impact of pressing deadlines. Henry has been able to juggle multiple demands for years. He thrives on it. But the emotional toll of loving both Charlotte and Taita, then learning he might have a son...might kill a lesser man.

" 'Tis a time to review the demands all of us face. The fact is, with my work at the museum, writing, and publishing, I am very busy now and cannot do everything myself. I shall have to consider hiring an assistant or two."

Bri nodded. "Time restraints are affecting me as well. I've recognized that I have to expand beyond myself as a resource, create a staff of advisors and directors." She frowned. "Wait—I thought you had written the books and simply needed to print them. Are you engaged in more writing?"

Gwyneth directed her gaze at her niece. After a moment of silence, she answered, "Yes. In addition to publishing through Musée de Merbeau Press, I work through another publishing company." Gwyneth sat back, put down her fork. "I own Kensington Books, secretly. The publisher has never met me. Under pen names, I write novellas, submitting one or two every month."

"Novellas? Not the scandalous romances that the *ton* talks about incessantly?"

"Yes." Gwyneth poured some tea and stirred in some cream. "Have you ever heard of Persephone Peabody or Drusilla Dorset?"

"Drusilla Dorset? She's the author of the scandalous Demeter Price novellas. Clarissa gave me one. It was shockingly descriptive—and informative. Inventive, to be sure. Wait—you're not saying *you* are Drusilla Dorset?"

"One and the same."

Bri leaned forward. "How did you conjure the idea of a brothel madam solving cases of murder and blackmail? Her love affair with the constable allows her to feed him details about the corruption of moneyed gentlemen from whispers in the brothel. I could not put it down, surprising myself. That material is outrageously addictive." Before Gwyneth could answer, Bri had another question. "But who is Persephone Peabody?"

Gwyneth shrugged. "Demand increases during the Marriage Season. Persephone Peabody is a new pen name for a series centering on Gavina Lachlan, a heroine whose name means 'hawk woman.' She has a psychic connection to hawks and other birds, who tell her about wrongs that need to be righted. She works with a sheriff in the highlands of Scotland. The presses can barely keep up with demand."

"I know. Bookstores stock them wrapped in brown paper. Every month, buyers place orders for the next volume. I should think that sales of the novellas would pay for the painstaking copying process for your art books."

"With the addition of Persephone, sales have more than doubled."

"Persephone and Drusilla *are* prolific. A new book from each author comes out every other month—how do you find the time?"

"The premises are simple, with a twist here and there."

Bri leaned forward. "Do these stories burst into being entirely from your imagination?"

"For the most part, although I recognize occasional reflections of well-publicized crimes or characters I've met."

"Astonishing.

"You said you read one of these books. Don't you remember at the back of the book was an offer to send in ideas for other plots? For a small fee?"

"The last couple of pages were torn out." Bri dropped her fork. "Is Clarissa one of the authors?"

"I cannot say, as that is confidential unless you become a partner in the enterprise. But stories and ideas come from many people. I weave together elements from disparate sources."

Bri sat back in her chair, speechless for a moment. "How clever! The readers become part of the process, enlarging your audience with each newly published novella. They tell their friends, never breathing a word of their participation, and sales expand."

"And the contributors earn money on their own, a secret cache."

"And you, Aunt Gwyneth. Such secrets you keep!"

"More than you will ever know."

"I realize more and more that I know far less than I thought I did."

"That is the one of the secrets of growing up."

***

Saturday, February 8, 1812 – Mlle. Sabine's Brothel
Jean-Louis

Giselle, Sabine and Jean-Louis met in her office.

"I'm glad it's over," said Giselle. " 'Twas terrifying to contemplate the nature of their lives. Trapped in a gilded palace forever."

"We are free." Sabine stood. "We are not prisoners."

"Thank you, Giselle." The Frenchman tilted his head, pinching his lips. "I had no intention for you to be placed in danger."

"I was never in danger, but I *was* frightened on the last day."

Jean-Louis handed her a purse. "Here is your payment, plus extra for the problems."

"I'm sorry to have disappointed the earl. Taita will never leave her son."

***

Monday, February 10, 1812 – A Newsstand on the Streets of London
Drummond

After paying for the latest issue of *Scandal & Shame*, Drummond scanned the featured items. He shook his head. *One wife is enough to confound any man. But a harem? How does the Sultan maintain his sanity? A murder, intrigue and betrayal in the Pink Palace. How will the Sultan ever be able to return?*

His mind went to Miss Li. *Exotic currents roil our stodgy* ton. Miss Li exuded an undeniable allure. *But my position would never permit me to marry a woman of her race. Too bad. Her intelligence would be of value. Perhaps*

I can use her in other ways, from time to time, to seduce my prey-of-the-moment.

CHAPTER SIXTY-SIX

Wednesday, February 12, 1812 – *Omelettes de Mme. d'Aix*
Gio

Gio arrived early at the busy restaurant favored by the ton. Gwyneth had requested this meeting place. *Can I feign insouciance when I see the Grandmother? Gwyneth chose this place—will she notice my discomfort or make the connection about the eye color?*

Quiches, omelets, salads and fresh-baked breads attracted a busy crowd wanting lighter fare than Chez Michel. The limited menu met popular demand after its opening in November.

A different host from the one who attended him when he visited the café in December recognized Gio. "Lord Ostwold, the famous artist! We are delighted you will be joining us today."

Gio bowed in acknowledgement of the praise. "I am meeting the Comtesse de Merbeau here at one p.m. May we have a table by that wall with the painting of the lavender fields of Provence? I'd like to look at it more closely."

Nodding, the host led Gio to a table. He did not take a seat at first, examining the painting of the lavender fields leading to the slopes of Mont Sainte-Victoire. Vineyards, thatched farmhouses and barn silhouettes dotted the background. "Who is the artist?"

The foppish host shrugged. "I do not know, sir. I shall ask the proprietress. Please excuse me for a moment."

While studying the painting, Gio became so absorbed in his examination that he did not hear anyone approaching from behind.

"Lord Ostwold, how lovely to see you again. I understand you have inquired about the artist who painted the mural. She was recommended to me by your friend, Viscount Vaux, who designed my interiors. Although she has never visited Aix-en-Provence, she went to the British Museum for inspiration, and then I described scenes from my memory, as I spent time there with my mother, who was from Aix, although I was born in Wales."

The dwarf nodded. "I thought I detected a Gaelic accent. I visited Aix for most of a year long ago. I was inspired by the colors, the vibrancy of the people. It was a magical year, with my young bride. Who is the artist, may I ask? She has real talent, a distinctive style."

"An unusual last name. Forgive me, but I will have to look it up. Her first name was Betty, no, wait," she looked off before continuing, "Bettina, I think."

"Bettina Rybicki?" Gio was incredulous.

"Yes! Now I remember. Have you heard of her?"

Gio nodded his head. "She works for me in art restorations. I never knew about this aspect of her talent. Astonishing!"

Looking up at the proprietress, he squinted. "Madame, your spectacles are *au courant*. I have some in my pocket that you have inspired me to don." He pulled a blue-lensed pair out of his pocket and put them on.

Aneira laughed. "You flatter an old woman's heart, Lord Ostwold."

Gwyneth joined them and admired the painting.

"Guess who painted it?"

Gwyneth looked at the canvas and then back at him. "Not you?"

"No. Bettina."

"The lovely young woman Charles is interested in? The art restorer. How extraordinary! That lavender pulls you into the scene, as if you could jump into the pastoral splendor and live in her imagination."

"Poetic this afternoon, aren't we?"

"You've been here before. What is their specialty?"

"I think the poached eggs over brioche sounds divine. Nothing comes close to the brioches I had as a child at Ravenshire, as I told you during Summerfest. There was a bakery in the village where we bought them as treats, but once the under-baker left, the taste was never the same. And you?"

"My dear, I am, as you know, a creature of habit. The *Omelette Florentine avec champignons* is my choice. After all, what artist could resist anything Florentine?"

"I hope they make it runny inside so I don't have to listen to you complain incessantly."

Gio shrugged. "Last time it was perfect. If my meal again meets my standards, I'll be delighted."

They ordered, and the server brought a selection of tea leaves.

"How exotic!" Gwyneth picked an orange pekoe blend with cinnamon.

Gio held each glass vial up to inspect the contents.

"Really? You can predict the taste from the leaves?"

"Of course. Can't you?"

Gwyneth scoffed in exasperation.

Grinning, Gio picked a white tea. "Baby tea leaves. *Petit*, like *moi*."

Individual pots were brought, and the leaves brewed in front of them in little silver holders, steeping.

"I think I am going to like this place." Gio removed the holder and poured a cup, adding a sugar lump and waiting until part of it had dissolved. He took a sip. "Mild but a bit of vanilla, I think. Delectable."

Gwyneth tried hers. "The orange and cinnamon are perfect. They've passed the first test."

The meals arrived. Gio poked his omelet, and the center ran out. "Perfect!"

Gwyneth cut into the brioche, slathered with poached egg, and tasted. She looked puzzled, and took another small bite. "The brioche tastes just like the ones I remember as a child."

"The baker must have a secret recipe." He waved his hand as if to dismiss her memory. "It's too long ago to remember a specific taste."

"But *you* can remember the shade of one iris in a field of purples or a stray blade of grass in a sea of greens?"

"Without dispute." Gio mumbled with his mouth full. "We should make it a regular practice to eat here."

"I wonder how the desserts are?" Gwyneth winked.

He held up one hand. "We can share, that's it. I'm too big for my britches as it is."

"That is an understatement."

"I knew that was a mistake as soon as I said it. Respect your elders, don't ridicule them."

"Then don't say anything ridiculous."

"Why did I agree to have lunch with a woman who is a champion archer with words?"

"To talk about my art books. We need to find a way to do engraving plates of my animals, and even revive the faerie books. I did them one at a time for Bri, but they could be published just as well as the alphabet book. Bri wants me to do one of flowers too."

"We could sponsor a contest of engravers. We'll need more than one. Let's see what we can develop. If they're good enough, maybe a book of my portraits is possible. Until now, it seemed impossible. Lithographers in Germany are developing new processes all the time. Very time consuming and expensive, but promising."

"Musée de Merbeau could sponsor a contest. An excellent idea from my old teacher."

"I prefer immortal. It's my new response to being called 'aged' or 'elderly.' "

"Or decrepit, shriveled, waning…"

Gio put down his fork. "Now you're getting a bit too close to home, Comtesse."

"I meant it to be funny. To me, you *are* immortal. A master of technique, color and light. Always and forever."

"That's better. Keep the praise coming."

"I think you've had enough for one day."

"I can never have enough praise. I'm a man."

Gwyneth waved to the server. "What do you recommend for a sweet end to our meal?"

The proprietress never returned to their table.

Gwyneth didn't notice the eye color.

***

Gio's carriage took him home. He climbed the steep steps to the front door, where the man who served as his valet and butler waited. "Maybe I am getting old, Hawkins. These steps seem to get steeper every day."

Hawkins took his coat.

Gio walked back to the kitchen, Dog at this heels. He talked over his shoulder as he walked. "I'd like to go to the attic—can you pull the dumb waiter chain?" He slid the door open, took a seat on the stool, and muttered to himself, "Maybe I need one of these outside before I need to be carried up the steps."

The butler restrained Dog from jumping onto the platform and pulled on the chain, twisting it on the wheel that Arches had fashioned long ago when he'd fixed the broken contraption.

The earl's clever, inventive former stable boy never ceased to amaze Gio. One of the things Gio admired about Henry was that he valued and rewarded talent no matter a person's birth station, gender, racial heritage or stature. It was a rare man, Gio knew, whose riches enabled him to defy the conventions of Society.

When he reached the attic, Gio rang the bell twice, so the butler knew to secure the chain.

Gio pushed the sliding door aside, and slid out into the attic. Here were discarded canvases—commissioned portraits declined, unfinished, discarded. Mumbling to himself, Gio searched the rows of canvases stacked against the wall in sections. "I know it's here somewhere. One painting was quite large, but the other was small." He moved enough aside to move toward the back of the stacks, to the largest. More than a year earlier, he had begun a portrait to hang in the offices of Wyndward Trading. "It must be here." He tried to move several large canvases at once, lost his balance and stumbled backwards. "Damn!" He righted himself and kept moving back toward the largest canvases. He recognized the top and painstakingly moved each obstruction out of the way until it was revealed. The unfinished portrait of an unrepentant murderer, an arrogant turncoat, perhaps un-dead. Staring back at him were the ultramarine and turquoise eyes of Duff Blackburn. *Just like Mme. d'Aix.*

If that evil woman can be stopped, the Frenchman is the one to do it.

***

Wednesday, February 12, 1812 – Aboard *Zainab's Dream*
Taita

Taita sat at an ornately carved desk in her elegant, gold silk-draped cabin. The Sultan's words had been reverberating in her mind for days. *He killed Rana with his own hands. He ordered her body to be tossed into the sea.* Until two days ago, Rana had been the Sultan's favorite, but her act of double murder was unforgiveable. *I may never see London again...unless I flee Madagascar. How could I escape the Sultan's vengeance for leaving him? And my son, what choice would he make? He has known no other life but that of the Sultan's court.*

Dipping her quill into the small bottle of India ink, Taita tried various phrases on a blank piece of paper to honor Fy's life. Like many in the Sultan's harem, Fy had been offered by her father to incur favor with the Sultan. Barely thirteen at the time, Fy had accepted her fate without question. The lure of the palace fueled the dreams of a girl from a mountain village. Ignorance of the ways of men was common among young initiates to the harem. The chief wife and Taita taught the girls palace protocol, manners, how to dress, and languages. In addition, she helped each one develop a specific skill to please the Sultan and set them apart from the other wives. Like Taita, Fy had a high, clear singing voice. Taita helped her train her voice and taught her to play the lute for accompaniment. She had felt especially close to Fy, almost as if she were a daughter.

The healer felt a sharp pain of loss as she thought of Fy. Dead before the age of eighteen, the late sultana's first three years in the palace had been a happy time. But with Rana's arrival two years earlier, that happiness frayed. Jealousy of the newest wife was common in the harem. Setting Rana's impact aside, Taita smiled as she recalled Fy's excitement over her first visit to London and joy when she learned just weeks ago that she was carrying the Sultan's child.

Crossing out her first attempt at the Sultan's words to his people, she tried again.

Fate is written for each of us.
Who are we to argue ?
All are subject to the directives of Destiny.
Fate brought Her Highness Fy to me
And Fate took her and our unborn child away.
Now her joyful voice will serenade the angels.
She and our child will live on in heavenly glory
Until I join them in Paradise.
Today I return these bones to the earth to nourish the soil
And infuse it with Fy's spirit of goodness.

Go in peace, my people.

Taita put down the quill, picked up the paper and read it aloud. *The Sultan likes short speeches. This should satisfy his demand.*

Rana's disappearance would not be acknowledged. Her name would never be spoken again. *I fear for her family. How vengeful will the Sultan be?*

A knock came.

"Enter."

The captain opened the door. "The Sultan wants you to accelerate his introduction to the Princess of Ethiopia immediately upon our return, and arrange a trek around the country to pick another sultana from his subjects."

Taita nodded. *The Sultan is not one for extended mourning.*

***

Wednesday, February 12, 1812 – Gio's Townhouse
Gio

I might need proof. Gio's mind swirled. It was more than the eyes. The cheekbone, the chin structure matched Mme. d'Aix. *Where is it?* He turned toward the other side of the attic. "*Merde!*"

He moved more canvases, pushed things aside, but careful to make a pathway this time. Henry and Gwyneth's mother, Lady Rebecca, a blonde, had blue eyes, but this girl, the children's nanny, Brigid, had light brown locks pulled back from her fresh-milk face, and combination of green and gray flecks in her eyes. She had disappeared after the first sitting, but he'd been able to finish the larger portrait from this study as well as from earlier portraits of Lady Rebecca and another servant posed in the dress. That first day, he'd done a quick watercolor study of Brigid's face to set his focus and establish his color values. *It's here somewhere.* Under some books, he found a worn tan leather portfolio full of watercolor studies.

He flipped though the paintings, smiling at his quick watercolor impressions of Lady Gwyneth as a child. Looking at a few during his search, he smiled. "An excellent likeness. These papers have survived nearly forty years of musty storage." The paper was still firm, the colors vibrant. He kept looking until he found the value study of

Brigid in the cache.

Here it is! The painting showed a three-quarter view of his model for Lady Rebecca's wedding portrait, done shortly after her death. "Yes!" He closed the portfolio and carried it back to the other side of the attic, and held it up next to the painting of Blackburn.

His eyes darted back and forth between the two depictions, Blackburn's unfinished oil portrait and the watercolor study of Brigid. The jaw was like Henry's, the ears and lips like Brigid's. *There is no doubt. The Frenchman knows it. Henry knows it. I know it.*

Gio took a deep breath. *May the Frenchman be as good as his legend.*

CHAPTER SIXTY-SEVEN

Thursday, February 13, 1812 – Lord Ravenshire's Townhouse
Henry

Gio's tone was uncharacteristically somber. "After the deaths at the Pink Palace, I can't subdue my fears about the safety of you, Bri and Ian."

The earl leaned forward. "Gio, do you remember the man you joked about at your gala, the one you described as swirling his cape like a bullfighter?"

"I always remember a man with a flourish."

Henry pursed his lips. "Jean-Louis told me you recognized the grandmother's eyes. We think the man in the red cape may be Blackburn, masquerading as a Croatian count, but he has brown eyes."

"By God! The man tempts Fate!" Gio squinted at Henry.

The Frenchman glanced up at the ceiling. "I heard rumors among crewmen on some of our voyages, of potions with strange properties peddled in bazaars, trade caravans, and black markets. I have never seen it, but all signs suggest the man is Blackburn." Jean-Louis paused. "I have a related theory."

"Don't hold back," the earl ordered.

"That Miss Li is an agent of Blackburn."

Henry sat back. "My brother *is* a clever devil. Why didn't we see it before? What's next?"

"Unknown. But we have a slight advantage."

Gio nodded. "We're onto him but he doesn't know it."

***

Tuesday, February 18, 1812 – Riding along Rotten Row
Oliver

A flash of red diverted Oliver's attention from the marker as he raced Bri. When Scheherazade beat Gazelle by a nose, he tilted his head toward the approaching rider. "A bit obvious, isn't it?"

Bri shook her head. "What?"

The Croatian count approached, removed his hat as he rode by, and called out, "*Gud Murnig.*"

Perseus barked at the red cape.

Once he was out of earshot, Oliver gazed after him. "Few gentlemen call attention to themselves in such an obvious way."

"Perhaps he wants to be talked about. Remembered."

"Where is 'the woman in the red mask' today?"

"I don't know and I don't care." Bri leaned over to pat Gazelle.

***

Thursday, February 27, 1812 – Bodleian Library, Oxford
Laurence

Philip Laurence was a scholar, but he vowed not to become an old bent-over shell of a man like colleagues who buried themselves in books, secreting themselves in libraries, never interacting with the world nor observing it outside of the confines of a university.

Today he was meeting with Arches in the rare royal documents section of the Bodleian Library, where a diligent clerk had found the original Ravenshire Castle plans.

An elegantly dressed man, unwigged, with hair pulled back in a pony tail, entered, carrying a large flat leather case.

"Arches! My word! You look like the lord of the manor today." Laurence stood to greet him.

The architect laughed and extended his hand to Laurence.

Laurence put his arm around the clerk. "Arches, Mr. Booker is the clerk who discovered the plans we will examine today."

Extending his hand to the young man, the architect introduced himself. "Peter Groom."

The clerk's face wrinkled. "Arches?"

Laurence smiled. "Mr. Groom exhibited mathematical skills as a youth, building new types of windmills, piping and so on. We likened him to Archimedes—hence the sobriquet."

Booker looked sheepish. "Sobriquet?"

"Nickname."

Booker nodded and took his leave.

Arches sat next to Laurence. They put on the cotton gloves and gingerly lifted the drawings, spreading five large pieces of parchment across the table. "We have the front and back elevations, the cellar, the first floor, the second floor, the third floor. There are more for the stables and a plan for tenant houses."

They began with the façade. Pointing to the towers and battlements, Arches said, "I can see how the towers were connected. We were correct in our design before these documents became available."

Laurence studied the diagrams and pointed to the west end of the façade. "The main fortress and battlements stretch farther west than we thought. The excavations should reveal more of the foundation at the west end. It's almost as if it was deliberately covered – could that hill have been man-made, like a mound?"

"Mounds were ancient, far before this time. Why would it be there now, and not in the original plans?"

"Burials after centuries of war destroyed that section of the castle? It may be rather gruesome if we dug it up to extend the castle footprint another 50 feet to match the original."

"Didn't the earl say that we should be as accurate as possible?" Arches waited for the professor to speak.

The don nodded. "That was his paramount objective."

"Remember when, as a child, Lady Gwyneth found the parchment, rubies and pearls hidden behind a loosened stone in the tower?"

"Yes. We came here, to this very library, in this very room, to decipher the message."

"As I recall, a young girl in the 14th century jumped from the west end, near the keep? Could the mound have been created to commemorate her death?"

"No. 'Tis of unlikely size for a single grave." Laurence shook his head in disagreement. "I believe it must have been after a battle, maybe one where the western end of the fortress was destroyed. There are more diaries at Ravenshire to read. Perhaps the answer is there. Not all the earls were dedicated to maintaining history of their home. Occasionally I've found the lady of the castle kept the details in the earls' diaries, or in those of a son or daughter."

"The mysteries of Ravenshire continue to reveal themselves." Arches smiled. "I hope we live long enough to unravel them."

Laurence scoffed. "If not, other generations will follow us, delving into secrets we have not yet imagined."

***

Monday, March 2, 1812 – *Omelettes de Mme. d'Aix*
Voutain

Colvert slipped into the shadows behind Voutain. "Have you seen the man with the red cape?"

"Not in the back. He went in the front once, about a month ago." Voutain leaned back on the brick wall of the building.

"That Gypsy boy's back at Ravenshire, eh?"

"Right. Didn't have the stomach for this business."

Colvert scoffed. "Lucky him. He likes the country. The life out there would bore me to death. What the hell would you do at night? Howl at the moon?"

"Probably. Or kiss a goat."

"Ha! No goat would have you, Colvert."

"Can't argue with that, Voutain. I haven't *your* animal magnetism." Voutain scoffed. "Few do."

"This endless watch is boring. How long do we have to do this?"

"Until J-L says to stop."

"I say cut the old crone's throat and be done with it." Colvert took a bit of snuff.

"Which one? The grandmother or the Gypsy?"

"Both."

Voutain slapped him on the back. "Watch yourself, Colvert. That bloodthirsty side of your nature may do you in."

" 'Twould be better than this. Watching's like practicing being dead."

***

Tuesday, March 10, 1812 – Lord Ravenshire's Townhouse
Henry

Nate had stayed over in London for the week. He and Henry sat in the study, sipping wine.

"I haven't traveled abroad in over a year. 'Tis unusual. Am I losing my sense of adventure?"

"It sounds like you're mulling a trip."

"After Bri's wedding in June, perhaps."

"Where?"

"Madagascar."

***

Saturday, March 14, 1812 – Riding along Rotten Row
Bri

Bri and Edward rode in the light rain, Zori at their side.

As the downpour turned heavier, they turned their horses to return home. Out of the corner of her eye, Bri caught a glimpse of red.

"Was that the man with the red cape?" Edward craned his neck, squinting to discern the figures.

"No doubt. The long black hair in the pony tail of the woman riding next to him can only be one person. Perhaps we should choose a different day for our ride. Miss Li has an uncanny ability to track us."

CHAPTER SIXTY-EIGHT

Friday, March 20, 1812 – Mme. Mottier's Atelier
Bri

About a month before Lady Penelope's wedding, the bridesmaids met at Mme. Mottier's for the final fitting of their dresses.

Lady Prudence was her sister's maid of honor. The baron's five sisters, all quite a bit older than he, provided a stark contrast to Bri and the young women absorbed in courting rituals.

Bri knew the baron's five sisters from his father's first wife. Lady Portchallont was the youngest, only slightly older than Henry and the baron. The others were in their sixties. Some were unsteady on their feet. *What is the baron thinking?* Mme. Mottier dealt with them first. *She is amazing. The design looks good on all sizes and ages. Penelope was right to come to Mme. Mottier instead of Mlle. Bellerobe for this group.*

Standing in front of a large mirror on a pedestal, Penelope had been accommodated beautifully by a clever design created by Mme. Mottier to accentuate the bride's curves.

Bri's eyes sparkled. "You look absolutely beautiful, Penelope."

The other bridesmaids chattered in agreement while Penelope beamed.

Will I ever see my own wedding day? Guilt pushed aside Bri's selfishness. *Forgive me, Penelope.*

In varying shades of lavender, in gradations, the gowns flattered all the women. *What color will I choose for my bridesmaids? What if Edward suggests Miss Li as a bridesmaid?*

Clarissa nudged Bri out of her thoughts, whispering, "What's wrong?"

Bri shook her head and said very softly, "Not now. I'll tell you after this fitting is over."

Clarissa nodded.

The dresses were constructed with satin bodices, in an off the shoulder style from which puffed chiffon sleeves extended to below the elbow. In empire style, the chiffon under the bodice bow was gathered over a satin underdress. Mme. Mottier's seamstresses made adjustments to the lengths of the gowns, taking into account the height of the matching dyed-silk small-heeled slippers the bridesmaids would be wearing on the day of the wedding.

When all the pinning was completed, Mme. Mottier thanked them. "I will have these delivered to you individually with the slippers the week preceding the wedding." She curtseyed to the bride.

Penelope nodded her appreciation.

The bridesmaids went out the back to carriages lined up in the alley behind the salon, giggling and laughing in excitement.

***

Friday, March 20, 1812 – *Omelettes de Mme. d'Aix*
Clarissa

Clarissa and Bri left the atelier after the fitting to have a late lunch at the omelet café everyone was talking about. This marked the first outing for Clarissa since the birth of Lulu.

Their carriages arrived at *Omelettes de Mme. d'Aix* at the time, and they entered the small, already crowded café. A host met them at the door, and suggested they have a seat at a small parlor-style waiting area arranged with settees until a table was open. "It shouldn't be more than a few minutes. I shall have a server bring a selection of teas for you while you wait."

They picked a secluded spot near the wall. The server brought a selection of vials with different teas. Clarissa picked Songs of India, a cinnamon-flavored variety, while Bri picked a lavender ginger mint.

The tea was poured and they sipped in silence.

"My stomach is churning." Bri grimaced. "Perhaps the ginger will calm it."

Clarissa leaned toward Bri and took her hand. "What's the matter? You were distracted at the fitting."

Bri took a deep breath, and said, "I am wondering if I should break off my engagement to Edward. I haven't told anyone else. He's changed and so have my feelings for him. I cannot imagine marrying a man I no longer love."

Tilting her head, Clarissa asked, "Does the exotic Miss Li have something to do with this?"

Bri shrugged her shoulders and raised her hands in exasperation. "Partially. It's no secret that Miss Li vexes me. Father would like Miss Li to act as an intermediary with her associates in Egypt to secure a meeting with someone Blackie called The Pharaoh who could protect our cargo in transit. He is despondent now that Taita and the Sultan have left London after the murder in the Pink Palace." She leaned forward. "The gossip is shocking."

"And that surprises you?"

Shaking her head, Bri's shoulders slumped. "No. It is simply an unwelcome reminder of how limited is our free will."

"Philosophy doesn't explain why you want to break your engagement. Do you intend to find another fiancé? This year's Marriage Season has already begun. Penelope's wedding is but weeks away. Yours is set for the end of June."

"Those thoughts are what spiral through my mind at all hours of the day and night. Maybe I shall never marry. I never really expected to fall in love. Edward swept me off my feet, but now that thrill has faded. Now I fear I have fallen out of love. I don't know what to think."

"Because you should *feel*, not think."

The host came to tell them their table was prepared, and showed them to a table for two by the café window and left hand-printed *menu du jour*.

"This is a charming place. The poached chicken and asparagus omelet sounds perfect." Clarissa put down her menu. "And you?"

"The *omelette de Lorraine* with fresh greens appeals to me."

The server came to take their order and left a basket of brioches.

Bri took a bite of brioche with fresh butter and a dab of raspberry jam. She gazed at Clarissa with a quizzical look and took another bite. "There's something about this brioche…"

Clarissa tried one. "It's delicious, actually. Is there a dash of cinnamon and vanilla?"

Bri nodded. "And something else I can't pinpoint...."

I've never seen Bri get so lost in her own thoughts. "What are you thinking?"

"I was just remembering life at Ravenshire. Father used to say that the brioches were never the same after Brigid left."

"Who was Brigid?"

"The nanny for Father, Aunt Gwyneth and Uncle Rychard. She left without a goodbye about a year after their mother, Lady Rebecca, died. I attributed that comment about brioches never being the same as a metaphor for his sense of loss. Somehow his pain now stabs at my heart—losing his mother, then a caring nanny. And my mother's death on the day of my birth."

Clarissa put her hand over her friend's. *Bri's never talked about this before.* "I think Lady Penelope's upcoming wedding is weighing on you. You're afraid of marriage. That's why you are toying with a break up with Edward. You pushed off any closeness until Edward. I think your fear of losing him is pushing you to end the engagement."

"Watching the birth of your child reminded me of how much I've buried. Longing for a mother I never knew, willing the loneliness to vanish. All sorts of emotions have been running through me. Nothing makes sense. If I'm afraid of losing him, why am I the one who wants to break it off?"

The server brought their meals and fresh hot water pots.

Once they were alone again, Clarissa spoke. "You are afraid you will lose him as you lost others close to you, and so you want to end the engagement so that you can avoid pain later."

Nearly hissing in a whisper, Bri countered, "That is completely wrong! I want to end it because I mistook gratitude for love. I do not love him anymore."

"Yes, you do."

"No, I do not."

"It is all you speak of. You still love him." *I best be careful or she will turn her wrath on me.*

"I speak of it because ending an engagement is a serious step, which affects my family." She put down her fork and nearly choked on her words. "Dear God, why must I be a brood mare to save Ravenshire?"

Clarissa blanched and whispered, "You're not with child, are you?"

"Good heavens, no! We have hardly spent any time alone together these last few months.'

"Perhaps you and Edward *need* intimacy. It might bring you back together after all the intrigue with Miss Li."

"I'm far too angry with him to consider 'intimacy.' "

The server returned to take their plates. Clarissa said, "That was delicious. Could we share a *crème brulée?*"

"*Mais, oui, madame.* But of course."

"How can you think of more food? I just picked at my lunch."

"I noticed. I have to keep up my strength." She leaned over and whispered, "I'm breastfeeding Lulu. The idea of a wet nurse repelled me."

Bri was silent. "I had a wet nurse because my mother died. I would have liked to have had that experience...even if I couldn't remember it. I think the bond would be embedded deeply. You are doing the right thing."

The *crème brulée* was served, and the proprietress came over to thank them for their patronage. Bri looked up at her to thank her, but froze.

Clarissa expressed her delight at the meal, and Bri nodded without making a sound.

After the woman left, Clarissa noticed Bri's demeanor. "What is it?"

Bri spoke in a whisper. "When that woman came to our table, a chill reached my core. Her eyes, Clarissa...despite the spectacles shielding her gaze, the color of her eyes...was the same."

"The same as what? She has blue eyes. Many people have blue eyes."

"But in her eyes, there is a hint of turquoise. Just like Blackie's."

Clarissa recoiled at the thought. "You must be mistaken. In any case, it is not him. And he is dead."

"Yes, but those eyes brought him back to life in the instant she looked at me. I cannot stay here another minute. We must leave now."

"Calm yourself. I am not abandoning the *crème brulée.*"

Bri took a spoonful, but a look of brooding took over her face, and she put down the spoon. "I can't taste it."

"It's delicious."

Bri waved the server over and paid the bill. "I have no more appetite." She stood, impatient to leave.

Clarissa insisted on finishing her dessert, so Bri sat down again. At their carriages, Clarissa asked, "Do you want me to come home with you? Do you need to talk more?"

"No. I want to be alone for a while."

Jean-Louis held the door for her. After closing it, he glared at Clarissa as if to suggest she were responsible for upsetting Bri.

Clarissa shook her head and signaled him she had something to say.

Jean-Louis jumped down and walked her to Clarissa's carriage. "What is it?"

She pulled him close to her and whispered in his ear. "The proprietress of the café has turquoise blue eyes. Bri insists they are the same as Blackburn's and she will not be dissuaded."

***

Jean-Louis

The Frenchman nodded, walked back to the Wyndward carriage, and opened the door a crack. "We have been following her for months. We believe she is his grandmother. I didn't want to worry you."

Bri's face drained of color. "Is Blackie alive?"

"I don't know. But we are prepared for anything."

"You always say, 'There are ways.' This time, make sure he's dead."

CHAPTER SIXTY-NINE

Friday, March 20, 1812 – Lord Ravenshire's Garden
Bri

After her lunch with Clarissa, Bri sought the shelter of the garden.
Dana brought her some tea, but retreated when it became clear that Bri wanted to be alone. Spotty lay at her feet.

Daffodils, hyacinths, irises and tulips bloomed on the lovely spring afternoon. She tried to focus on the colors, the petals, the butterflies and bees that brought life to the garden.

It didn't work. *The color of her eyes...of his eyes.* All she could think of was the horror of Blackie kidnapping her, trying to rape her, threatening to kill her. When she closed her eyes, she could see his unusual blue and turquoise eyes laughing at her. The same as that old woman's. Cold fear gripped her soul, as if her ordeal were happening again.

Edward had saved her then. *Can he save me now? Can he save me from my doubt?*

Bri wanted to get out and walk, but a cloudburst drove a pelting rain in a swirling wind. *Trapped.* She quickly ran up the backstairs to the townhouse. *Where can I go? Who can I talk to? It's Friday.*

She summoned Jean-Louis and climbed into the carriage. Rapping on the side of the door frame, Bri said, "Take me to the foundling hospital." *Charlotte will understand.*

***

Friday, March 20, 1812 – Winters Foundling Hospital
Charlotte

Bri burst into Charlotte's office, startling her. "Blackie is alive."

"No! It cannot be." She rose to embrace Bri.

Felix rubbed his head against both of them, signaling he wanted to be part of the hug.

Petting Felix with one hand, Bri continued, "Father and Jean-Louis know and have kept it from us. They think the owner of the omelet café is his grandmother. The eyes. I knew the moment I glimpsed her eyes. I felt a chill, as if he were standing in front of me."

Charlotte held Bri. "This time Henry's silence could have been deadly. Instead of providing protection as it did for Aelwyn and Ian, it exposed you and Ian to danger. Henry should have warned us all."

***

Friday, March 20, 1812 – Edward's Gentlemen's Club
Edward

Rogers threw his cards on the table. "Why can't we play at your house, James? Li can't play here."

Vaux shrugged. "True, Rogers. No women here. 'Tis, after all, a *gentlemen's* club."

Edward averted his eyes.

When the game was over, Edward hailed François and went home. Pretending to retire, he slipped out about an hour later.

Arriving at *Dreamtime*, Edward told himself he wouldn't stay long.

When he exited, his pinpoint pupils made it difficult to focus.

Miss Li bade him good evening with a kiss on the cheek.

***

François
Edward didn't see François sitting in a Hackney across the street.

***

Saturday, March 21, 1812 – Lord Ravenshire's Townhouse
Bri

Bri sat down to breakfast and glared at her father and Jean-Louis.

Nate had arrived late the night before from Oxford. The American glanced around the table. "What's going on?"

"Father and Jean-Louis have known for a while that Blackie is alive and didn't see fit to tell me." Bri took a bite of toast.

Recoiling, Nate turned to the earl. "Have you seen him?"

Henry nodded.

Bri's mouth fell open. "Where?"

"He has taken to wearing a red cape."

"The Croatian count who rides with Miss Li?" Bri scoffed. "He didn't resemble Blackie."

Henry glowered at Jean-Louis. "Where were *you* when this happened?"

"I was nearby and suspicious at that point but, as Bri observed, he doesn't resemble Blackie. He has brown eyes."

"Wait—" Nate's brow wrinkled. "—Ravenshire, didn't a man in a red cape bump into you at Gio's Gala?"

The earl shrugged. "*I* bumped into him because I suspected he might be Blackie. At that moment, my senses told me it was Blackie, but my mind resisted."

Nate's eyes moved between Henry and Jean-Louis. "How could Blackburn change his eye color?"

The Frenchman shrugged. "I've hear rumors from sailors, but I've never seen it before."

Bri pushed back from the table. "I don't know how he changed his eye color, and I don't care. I'll tell you both what I told Jean-Louis yesterday: This time, make sure he's dead."

She got up from the table. "And you'd better tell Aunt Gwyneth, Aunt Aelwyn, Edward, and Gio. I've told Charlotte. "This time, Father, your secret could have been deadly."

"Gio saw the grandmother's eyes," said Jean-Louis."He knows."

Shaking her head in frustration, Bri fumed. "When will you stop hiding the truth from me?" She stomped out of the dining room.

***

Monday, March 30, 1812 - Wyndward Trading Offices
Bri

Harriet Fong, Hiram's sister, arrived and met with Bri in a small conference room. A linguist in a private school for the children of Chinese diplomats, Miss Fong had been coaching Bri in Mandarin for a few months.

The earl stuck his head in. "*Huānyíng. Zhè shì guānyú wǒ de pǔtōnghuà de chéngdù.*" Henry laughed. "Welcome. That's about the extent of my Mandarin."

Bri glanced through the small window overlooking the harbor, and her mind wandered. *Edward has become more distant and unpredictable. It must be Miss Li. He is changing because of her.*

***

Saturday, April 4, 1812 – Baron Beauchamp's Gentlemen's Club
Edward

A pre-wedding dinner for the groomsmen was set for eight o'clock at the baron's gentlemen's club. More than thirty years older than his fiancée, the baron mixed well with her younger friends and appeared to truly love the charming, effervescent Lady Penelope. And, after all, he needed an heir.

Henry, Nate, Sir John and Edward arrived in the earl's carriage.

Edward was the last to exit. As the others stepped out, he sighed. *I love Bri, but she has been so combative of late. Is marriage the right step now? Her irrational jealousy of Miss Li has torn us apart. And now Blackie's return has threatened all of us. We must be a united front.*

Henry put his arm around Edward's shoulder. He leaned in to whisper. "She'll come around. Be patient."

Edward grimaced. "I am not so certain."

Nate tilted his head toward the baron, standing at the canopied entrance. "The baron, the earl and I had a don at Merton, Willoughby—"

"He was still there when I attended. Ancient history from an ancient don." Edward shook his head.

"The baron always said he liked the idea of the Spartans' celebration of a prospective husband's last night as a single man." Nate laughed. "I got the impression that his ne'er-do-well cousin, Teddy, may have arranged something bawdy for after dinner. I'll take my leave of you then."

"As will I," said Henry.

Sir John nodded. "This is a young man's evening. I plan to leave as soon as politely possible."

Edward grimaced. "I may not be far behind."

Henry laughed. "The baron has always been a bit of a joker, a bon vivant who was hit by the proverbial *coup de foudre* when he met Lady Penelope. The age difference is encouraging to unmarried men such as Nate and I."

Edward recoiled and stared at the earl. " 'Encouraging?' Do you intend to marry someone of Bri's age?"

The earl shook his head. "Not remotely possible. I prefer the mature conversation of a woman who understands the vicissitudes of life. But, as you know, I've enveloped myself in a quandary. Two divergent pathways. Both may be lost to me as the chasm widens between my path and theirs."

Nate, as always, took the philosopher's approach. "The plight of men! Despite our projected bravado, each of us is subject to the whims of a woman's heart."

Henry raised his eyebrows and elbowed Nate. "What were you saying about ancient dons, Edward? We seem to be in the company of another ancient professor tonight, spouting proverbs."

They walked into the club, were led to a private room, and greeted their friends. Edward shook hands with the baron. "Congratulations, Baron! Lady Penelope is a lucky woman."

"No, James, I am the lucky one. Her heart is pure. I never thought I would find anyone like her. Just like you and Lady Gabriella, eh?"

Edward murmured an unintelligible response, but the baron didn't notice as others pulled him away.

Dr. St. Cloud waved Edward over to a seat next to him.

*I wonder if Bri and Clarissa have talked about our potential split. Maybe the doctor knows something about how to approach Bri—*Edward caught himself in mid-thought. *Am I a besotted schoolboy?* He twisted his shoulders from side to side, attempting to physically shrug off his unsocial mood before he sat down.

"Is that a dance move, James?" Vaux teased.

Edward nodded to Banfield and Vaux, but was surprised to see Rogers, who sat on his other side.

Rogers leaned over and whispered, "I can see you didn't expect me, James. The baron and his nephew, Davey Portchallont, have taken a heightened interest in carriage racing since the Trot of the *Ton*. They ask my advice on Phaetons." Taking a look around, he added, "The nuptials may require an impresario. The wedding party itself may exceed all the other attendees in number."

"Doubtful," said Vaux. "The guest list exceeds six hundred."

Teddy Fitz-Hough, the baron's cousin and best man, began the *de rigueur* rite of passage of toasting the groom. A few toasts, by the baron's contemporaries, voiced traditional wishes, while the younger men tended toward ribald, risqué, and downright improper comments.

After dinner, Teddy called for more toasts. Interrupting a particularly bawdy one, Teddy made an announcement. "Gentlemen, tonight we are going to tread in dangerous waters before allowing my cousin, Beau, to be tamed by marriage. Do I have your attention?"

The crowd settled down.

Edward's stomach churned. *What now?*

Taking a swig of whiskey, Teddy looked around, smirking. "Tonight will be an experience you will never forget. I have several carriages waiting. You will be blindfolded. Come let us be merry!"

At the carriages, Teddy handed out blindfolds, and most of the younger groomsmen complied, while most of the contemporaries of the baron begged off.

Dr. St. Cloud's eyes widened. "I've never been to anything like this." He glanced at the others for confirmation.

One of the men he had just met, Roderick "Roddie" Chambers, said, "Teddy was known for his shenanigans at university, but that was years ago. We got to know the baron at Merton reunions. We are ten years younger, but met at a pub there fifteen years ago and have been friends ever since. Still, I've never known Teddy to use blindfolds. I think I'm too old for this."

"Oh, Roddie, don't be so nervous." Cousin Pequie, a beefy, ruddy-complexioned and balding individual, dripped with sweat. Standing next to Edward, his bulk pressed against the banker as he jockeyed for position. "Teddy will probably just take us around the block."

Edward made light of it. "At least we'll have a doctor in *our* carriage."

Nick demurred. "A veterinarian, James."

"Sounds about right." The bald man guffawed."We're a bunch of mad dogs, aren't we?"

Teddy shepherded the baron, Roddie, Vaux and Rogers into the first carriage, he corralled Edward, Dr. St. Cloud, Banfield, Davey and Cousin Pequie into the second.

Reluctantly, Teddy dismissed the other carriages after paying the drivers for their time. "Spoilsports and old men would dull the fun anyway." He climbed into the first carriage and yelled, "Blindfolds on. Now!"

The guests complied.

The carriages bounced over the cobblestones. After nearly fifteen minutes of off-color stories from Cousin Pequie and Davey, Edward was ready to jump out.

Dr. St. Cloud had made the mistake of saying, "Don't call me Nickie," and that was it.

"Why not, *Nickie*? Don't you *like* to be called Nickie?"

If they call me Eddie, I may knock out their teeth.

The carriage rolled to a stop. After a few moments, Teddy announced he was opening the carriage door and lowering the steps, since he was the only one who could see.

Edward's patience had been pushed to its limit. *I cannot bear being herded about like an animal.*

After Teddy had emptied the carriages, he lined up the groomsmen shoulder to shoulder and instructed them to remove their blindfolds.

Annoyance turned to fear. A gut-punch of anxiety swept through Edward as the sign of their destination confronted him: *Dreamtime.*

***

Early Sunday, April 5, 1812 – *Dreamtime*
Edward

The baron put his arm over Edward's shoulder. "Guess we won't tell

643

our future wives about this clandestine visit, will we?"

"Perhaps we should terminate this soirée now."

"Indeed not, James! This is an adventure! Saddle up, my boy. Saddle up! 'Tis as if we were on a hunt."

"If we're not careful, we will be the prey."

"Nonsense. Simply an evening among friends." Teddy nudged them toward the door.

Edward felt the back of his neck tingle. He felt as if he were being watched. Turning to look, he saw nothing but shadows. Then a slight movement in the darkness spiked his adrenaline. *Someone is out there. Did Bri set Jean-Louis to spy on me again?* Incensed, he entered *Dreamtime*.

***

Xie Xie Li

Xie Xie sat in the back office of *Dreamtime*, planning her next moves. Her part in The Pharaoh's scheme of revenge had been completed. James had fallen under the spell of the poppy again. She needed to think of her own future, to implement her escape plan. Opening the safe, she removed a cache of British and foreign currency, and stuffed it into a flap of her leather portfolio. She had just tied the closure ribbon when the back door opened. She jumped, gripped by fear at the sight of an unknown man in black. Mustachioed, the assailant pulled off a cap to reveal light brown hair tinged with blond. His sleek physique signaled danger to her. She willed her nerves to be still.

"Who are you and what are you doing in my establishment?"

The man broke into a smile. "So my disguise is that good?"

She released her taut muscles and bowed her head. "Master, that is an amazing transformation."

He took a chair. "Indeed." He now assumed a Cockney accent. "An Italian merchant, a Croatian count, a Cockney cut-purse—my options are unlimited. How is our plan coming along?"

"Very well. James is now outside with groomsmen celebrating an upcoming Society wedding. I had planned to have one of the other girls handle it. It would not be good for the wedding party gentlemen to see me here."

"It *must* be you."

"Master, it is a very delicate situation."

"Yes, a situation of my design. You will take him to the room where I can watch through the curtain. Persuade him. You are a mistress of persuasion. Do it now."

"It might throw off your entire plan."

"You must make sure it does *not.*"

She knew that tone. There was no turning back now. She led him from the office through a hallway to a peephole where he could watch, and then she entered the main serving area.

Edward did not see her at first, but the other men did. "Come here, darling," shouted Teddy. She walked over. Edward gaped at her.

"Good evening, Mr. James."

"I thought you were going to divest of this operation."

"Not yet. It is quite lucrative, you know."

The baron looked confused.

"Won't you introduce me to your guests?" Miss Li's tone had a flirtatious lilt that Edward had not heard before.

Edward put down his drink. "Absolutely not. We are leaving immediately."

The baron put his hand on Edward's shoulder. "Slow down, James. This place looks interesting."

Rogers took Xie Xie's arm. She snapped her fingers and women appeared. Each took the arm of a groomsman and guided him to a private, curtained area. Edward and Rogers were guided to the room at the back with the opium pipes.

This is dangerous. I must keep my wits about me.

The pipes puffed with smoke. Xie Xie feigned taking a puff and gave the pipe to Rogers.

He inhaled deeply and passed the pipe to Edward. "Just a taste, James. It will calm you, nothing more."

He declined. "I must take my leave of you now." *Something is not right.*

Xie Xie blew smoke into Edward's face.

He could not react quickly enough. It filled his lungs. The infrequent puffs he had taken over the past weeks had rekindled his desire. He remembered the euphoria, the sensation of peace from his days in the Far East. Maybe this was just what he needed to forget the pain. The pain of Bri's coldness, of sending spies to watch him.

It's only a puff. I won't go too far. Not again. Just another puff. Just one more. I can stop at anytime. Anytime.

***

Blackburn as the Cockney Cut-Purse

Peering through a slit in the curtain, Blackburn watched Edward take puff after puff of the opium pipe. *All is unfolding as I envisioned. James is weak.*

CHAPTER SEVENTY

Early Sunday, April 5, 1812 – *Dreamtime*
Vaux

Vaux stationed himself at the bar where he had a view of the layout. Dr. St. Cloud quickly released himself from the grip of his escort and joined Vaux at the bar.

"I planned to leave, but I feel compelled to wait until the others leave."

"I'll stay to make sure all get home safely." Vaux waved toward the door. "Go home."

After taking a final sip of his whiskey, Dr. St. Cloud nodded to Vaux and left.

Eventually, the groomsmen stumbled out of their rooms, inebriated and confused. There was no set closing time, but the party had come to an end. Teddy lay prone on the floor.

Vaux watched as two groomsmen carried Teddy to the waiting carriages.

The baron approached Vaux, his brow wrinkled. "Where are James and Rogers?"

Just then, Rogers stumbled into view.

Vaux answered, "I'll look for James. You can leave." Vaux circled the inside perimeter of *Dreamtime*. "James?" He methodically opened curtains. Finally, at the last enclosure, Vaux spotted Edward, nearly unconscious. Glancing at the pipe apparatus, he gasped. "Opium!"

Lifting Edward, who stirred to a semi-conscious state, Vaux

whispered. "Come on, James. We have to leave."

The other private rooms offered the charms of women, gambling, fine wines and other alcohols, but no opium. *Dreamtime* was a uniquely exotic locale. Vaux had slowly sipped a whiskey and paid a woman to sit next to him until the others were ready to go. *No one suspects the truth.*

I never dreamed that James would fall prey to the pipes. Vaux supported Edward as they all stumbled outside, but no Hackney was to be found. Vaux looked to one side, and his burden lightened. He turned to face Jean-Louis, who supported Edward on the other side. "I have a carriage in the alley. Let's go."

"Damnation!" Vaux stopped to catch his breath as they loaded James into the carriage. "James is as heavy as a bag of salt."

***

Xie Xie

After the groomsmen departed, Xie Xie walked back to her office to find The Pharaoh sitting in her chair. Her portfolio appeared untouched. *Does he know I took the money? Does he suspect I am ready to vanish?*

"I trust you saw James take the bait."

The Pharaoh shrugged. "It was almost too easy. It seems our Mr. James welcomed release into the ecstasy of the poppy. I thought I might have to hit him and force it into his lungs." He stood. "No matter how it happened. It happened. That is enough."

"What now?"

"I shall be in touch soon. Tonight, I will leave first. We should not be seen together. When I need you again, I will get a message to you."

***

Lash

Once James had been safely escorted out and in the carriage with Jean-Louis, Lash continued to hide under the eaves of a stable, invisible in the early morning fog descending over the dirt alley.

Jean-Louis had instructed Lash to follow his instincts.

A man in black left *Dreamtime* by the back door that led to an alley, bypassing a waiting carriage.

He marked the strange man's height and gait. He detected a slight limp. And something else that he couldn't describe. *A sense of danger. Should I follow him?*

At that moment, Miss Li, the Chinese woman Jean-Louis had described to him, exited to enter the waiting carriage. Without making a sound, Lash stepped onto the back of the carriage and crouched down, securing his position.

***

Early Sunday, April 5, 1812 – On the back of a Hackney

Lash

The carriage made no stops before turning toward the entrance to Durrants. *Someone gave Miss Li the name of the best hotel in London.* Lash silently slipped off the back of the carriage and waited across the street to be sure she entered the hotel.

He walked back to the earl's townhouse, mulling over the night's events. He had enlisted a runner in the slums surrounding *Dreamtime*, whom he knew from the demi-monde, to go into *Dreamtime* from time to time and report back to him. He could not risk entering himself. Hat or no, his scar would make him all too easy to identify. *Why would such an elegant lady own such a scurrilous establishment? And what could Edward James be seeking there? Surely not—.*

And then he understood.

***

Jean-Louis

Vaux got in with Edward. "He was in the opium den. I fear he is lost to it."

"Speak of this to no one."

Viscount Vaux nodded. "What are you going to do?"

Jean-Louis directed his gaze at the viscount. "What I always do. Protect this family. It seems I must protect James from himself."

"But how?"

"There are ways." Jean-Louis shut the door, leapt up to the driver's perch where Chérie waited, and headed to Edward's townhouse.

The Frenchman analyzed the situation. *I was wrong. I thought James was drunk. But opium? I need to speak with Nashmir. He has seen more of this obsession than I. He is the only one who can help.*

***

Edward's Townhouse
Vaux

François heard the carriage and came out of the stables, despite the pre-dawn hour.

Jean-Louis looked at Vaux. "Would you stay with James to keep him from leaving? François is here to help."

Vaux nodded.

They carried Edward to his bedroom, placed him on the bed, and removed his boots.

Zori whined, nuzzling Edward in an attempt to wake him.

"The butler is off tonight," said François. "The household will not know."

"I'm sure it's just a momentary lapse." Vaux ran his hand through his hair. "James and Lady Gabriella have battled over Miss Li."

"Let's keep tonight's events between us and watch his behavior. Time will tell." Jean-Louis frowned. "I'll be back with Nashmir soon."

Within an hour of leaving Vaux at Edward's townhouse, Jean-Louis returned with a potion from Nashmir and forced it down Edward's throat.

Turning to Vaux, the Frenchman said, "François will watch James. Select another bedroom to be close. You may be needed to calm James when he awakens."

***

Monday, April 6, 1812 – Winters Foundling Hospital
Bri

650

The quarterly meeting of Wyndward Investments had been rescheduled until this morning. Eli, Charlotte, and Bri waited, but Edward did not appear.

"He must have had an unexpected matter to attend to," said Eli.

Bri nodded. "Of course. Let's review today's agenda. The first item is my proposal that we add a permanent fifth trustee in order to ensure an odd number of votes to avoid being deadlocked. As a temporary trustee, I nominate Professor Parker as a neutral third party. He possesses common sense, an analytical mind, and a keen sense of human nature. His sabbatical will end in August, but that gives us time to consider a permanent trustee."

As the discussion ensued, her mind was in turmoil. *Where is Edward?*

***

Edward's Townhouse
Vaux

Edward slept all day Sunday. Awakening Monday afternoon, Edward's vision was dimmed and his memory groggy. His eyes focused on François. "What is going on?"

Vaux came in.

"The staff is back. Keep your voice down. You passed out at *Dreamtime* and we brought you home."

"We?"

"Jean-Louis and I."

Edward closed his eyes and sighed, "*Damnation!* I sensed him in the shadows when we arrived at *Dreamtime*. What day is it?"

"Monday."

Trying to sit up, Edward fell back. "But the groomsmen's evening was Saturday. I have been—"

"Out for more than a day."

"What time is it?"

"Two p.m."

"I have to get to a meeting."

"You're going nowhere. I'll send word you're ill. To whom?"

"To Bri at the foundling hospital. But it's too late. The meeting started at ten."

Edward stumbled to the bathroom and retched.

François ran his bath. He glanced at Vaux. "I don't want Shore to see him like this."

"I told the staff at breakfast that he ate something that didn't agree with him at the groomsmen's party."

Jean-Louis appeared, startling them. "Nashmir says clear broth and toast."

***

Tuesday, April 7, 1812 – Riding along Rotten Row
Oliver

When Bri and Oliver stopped, Gwyneth rode up to join them.

"Perseus seems to be keeping up with you."

"He's born to run."

Oliver leaned toward Bri. "You are distant."

Gwyneth nodded. "You seem distracted."

"Edward did not join me for a long-scheduled meeting of the Wyndward Investments trustees yesterday. Late in the afternoon he sent a note that he had eaten something that made him quite ill."

Shrugging, Oliver said, "It happens."

Bri remained silent for a moment. "There are too many coincidences lately that separate us."

Oliver started to respond, but thought better of it. "Let's see how the flowers are popping up in the meadow Gwyneth likes to paint every year."

***

Tuesday, April 7, 1812- Comtesse de Merbeau's Townhouse
Gwyneth

Later that day, Bri and Gwyneth sat in the comtesse's Music Room.

"I am considering breaking off my engagement to Edward."

Gwyneth sat back, her brow furrowed. "Because an illness prevented him from attending a meeting? That seems arbitrary. Edward is a fine young man who is clearly in love with you."

"It's not just his incessant attention to Miss Li. It's more the assumption that I will 'fall in line' and accede to *his* expectations for our life together. It is as if he expects me to cease being who I am."

"I think you are mistaken. Edward accepts your independence. Not many men would. Do not fool yourself, Bri. Most men, even those of your generation, still cling to myths of male superiority."

"I am not interested in 'most men,' and I do not have to marry. It was never my intention to marry; meeting Edward was what changed that. I can change back."

Gwyneth reached over to touch Bri's hand. "Are you so certain? I have experienced a terrible marriage, a wonderful marriage and a lonely widowhood. Being alone takes a lot of inner strength, which you have, but it might not be a formula for lasting happiness." Gwyneth withdrew her hand and sat back in her chair.

"Remember, all that we have discussed today, all that I have accomplished, has been done in secret. No recognition, no outside support. You are not a monk spending hours in silent meditation. You are a young woman with desires and ambition. You might need a man to help you transform those ideas, those sparks, into reality."

"Father will help me."

"My brother is an unusual man. But as he is mortal, and will not be around forever. With Ian, he now has an heir to groom, and he travels for long periods of time. Granted, the trading company is large and successful, but clients may demand a man in charge, not you. The world will not reform itself to meet your demands on your terms for decades, perhaps not in centuries. 'Modern' is defined by those who dominate. Right now, that means men, as it has been for nearly 5000 years."

"So I should just give up and marry Edward no matter how I feel?" Bri's eyes flashed anger.

"No, but I think you should give yourself more time to decide on an unalterable course for your future. Everyone who marries makes concessions. Edward is not perfect, but neither are you. You need to talk through these issues, not demand his capitulation to your conditions."

"But he's hurt me." A tear formed at the corner of her eye.

"And you have no doubt hurt him and both of you will hurt each other in the future. It is the way of human beings. If you can't be hurt, you don't care. Forgive and try again to reclaim the love you felt. All of us need to learn to forgive. Let the past go or it will choke your future."

"But—"

"Promise me, Bri. Promise me that you will talk to me again before you make your final decision. Please do not, in a moment of anger, discard a lifetime of happiness."

***

Tuesday, April 7, 1812 – Wyndward Trading Offices
Henry

After a frustrating day of confronting differing opinions among his key directors, Henry went back to his office to review their opposing proposals.

When the earl left the trading company, he found Jean-Louis in the driver's perch seated next to Chérie.

Sir John, Lady James and Edward were due for dinner. *How will Bri behave? Will she spar with Edward? Are all the Wyndwards star-crossed?*

He remained lost in thought on the ride home to his townhouse.

When his guests arrived for dinner, Henry embraced the man he had known all his life, a man whose health had nearly returned to normal through the ministrations of Nashmir. "Sir John."

Reaching for Edward's hand, Henry pulled him closer and leaned in to whisper, "Edward, could I speak to you privately for a few moments?"

"Thompson, please fill sherry goblets for our guests. I'll be back in a moment."

Edward fidgeted as he followed the earl into his study.

His eyes seem darker than normal. "What's wrong, Edward? Bri told me you forgot the meeting of Wyndward Investments."

Edward averted his eyes from the earl. "Nothing's wrong. I had an unavoidable conflict. Why are you interrogating me?"

"No interrogation. Simply a question and an observation. You seem unlike yourself, nervous."

"Why would I be nervous?" His eyes blinked repeatedly.

"Have you and Bri fought again?"

"Not today. Does she have a *new* complaint about me?" Edward waved his hand to dismiss such notions.

Henry frowned. "Perhaps this is not a good time to talk."

"Correct. Your guests are waiting."

When they returned to the parlor, Bri had joined Sir John and

Lady James. She moved to embrace him.

Edward's movements seem awkward and forced.

Sir John looked troubled. "Edward? Are you still unwell?"

"Nothing is wrong, Father. I am late for another meeting that, unfortunately, must take precedence over this dinner. I wanted to tell you in person. Forgive me, Bri. Goodnight, Mother." He nodded to the earl. "I must depart." He left without looking behind him.

Henry and Sir John glanced at each other, puzzled.

"It's not like Edward to behave in such an ill-bred manner. I apologize, Ravenshire."

Henry saw a tear form in Bri's eye. "Bri, what is going on between you two?"

She shook her head and rapidly ascended the stairs, leaving Henry and his guests open-mouthed.

Thompson broke the spell. "Dinner is served."

***

Jean-Louis

After Edward left, Jean-Louis exited and hailed a Hackney. When he reached Edward's townhouse, he sought out François.

James was not there.

The two Frenchmen headed to *Dreamtime.*

After they arrived, François remained watch outside.

Jean-Louis signaled with a wave. "Pull around to the back."

Jean-Louis entered and took a seat at a small table near the door, where he had an unobstructed view. He gambled that the staff would not recognize him from his late-night ruckus with Edward from a few weeks earlier.

After half an hour, he knew his assumption had been correct. No one paid attention to him. It was early evening, and sparse patrons were about. He waved over an Asian woman. Show me the dreamtime you advertise."

She led him to the back of the bar, to the last curtained area. "This is our best room." She pulled the curtain aside and gasped.

A man was using the opium bubbler, alone.

"I must get the manager, sir. This is highly irregular." She left.

The man's eyes were dilated, glazed over, as if in a trance. "So you

655

found me again, did you? Damn you! Damn the Wyndward arrogance! Leave me alone!"

"James, come with me. Now."

"Who are you to give me orders? You are no one. A servant, nothing more. Begone!"

"This compulsion for the poppy is stronger than most men can resist, James. Come with me now, before it is too late and you have lost everything."

"I've already lost her. I know it. She hates me." He took a deep puff.

"No, James. She loves you. In fact, she loves you so much that it frightens her. She would not tolerate this behavior. You must put it behind you. Nashmir can help you."

Edward laughed in a bizarre, shrill way. "You don't understand. I've been under the poppy's spell before. The ecstasy! Some call it nirvana, others paradise. It is an escape from those responsibilities you want to thrust down my throat, chaining me to tradition, to what is expected of me. No! I refuse!" He inhaled deeply from the pipe.

The manager appeared at the door. He assessed the situation, looked at Jean-Louis and said, "Take him. Now."

Jean-Louis headed toward Edward, who was taking another long draft of smoke.

Edward passed out.

Jean-Louis lifted Edward and threw him over his shoulder and carried him out the back entrance to avoid scrutiny. Signaling François, they loaded Edward in the carriage and left *Dreamtime* in the dust-filled fog of evening.

CHAPTER SEVENTY-ONE

Tuesday, April 7, 1812 – Lord Ravenshire's London Stables
Jean-Louis

Jean-Louis pulled into the alley next to the Ravenshire stables. He and François lifted Edward and carried him to the greenhouse, placing him on the floor. *If I put him on the bench, he might roll off.*

He went to find Nashmir and they went back to the greenhouse.

Looking at Edward's unconscious body, Nashmir felt his neck pulse. "He's not dead. That's a point in his favor. What happened?"

"He has succumbed to the lure of the poppy. Can you wean him from its hold?"

Nashmir leaned over Edward, using his fingers to open his eyelids. "I just gave you a potion for him a few days ago. How long has this been going on?"

"I don't know. The night of the groomsmen's party and tonight for certain. According to François, probably since Christmas. Tonight he told me that he was drawn into its power during his extended sojourn in the Far East."

The valet looked off into the distance. "The need is always there for a victim of the poppy. If he conquered it once, there is hope, but there is a dark side to the compulsion. I do not know if this is true of every user, but of those I have seen, if one stops for a long period of time, it is even more dangerous to start again."

"But why? Wouldn't it be as if it were new and easier to end the impulse?"

Shaking his head, Nashmir motioned to both Frenchmen to sit on a bench across from him. "My personal theory is that, in the depths of our life force, called '*qi*' by the Chinese, there is latent memory. The '*qi*' remembers the euphoria of the opiate state and seeks it again. A whiff of the smoke can return the victim to a heightened state of desire for the poppy.

"A former user must be ever wary of its enticement. If Edward has been locked in its clutches in the past, the danger I alluded to is that the addiction will be deeper and come on more quickly than the first time. The acceleration is dramatic. Too soon it takes over the victim's life and it is far more difficult to eradicate the desire."

"Are you saying that one or two nights, like this one, could cause James to descend into that hell?"

"It is possible, although probably the point of no return would be more infusions, which François has suggested Mr. James has experienced."

"Do you have an antidote?"

"I must augment the one I gave you a few days ago. Clearly, it did not reduce his desire. In any case, James cannot remain here."

"I know a place I can take him."

"Good. I will prepare a sleeping potion until I isolate the proper combination of herbs to counteract the effects of the poppy."

Waiting for Nashmir to prepare the sleeping potion, Jean-Louis paced about the large greenhouse that held pots of Nashmir's herbs as well as orchids, vegetables, fruit trees. "You have a veritable Garden of Eden, Nashmir. Is there a solution for James that grows here?"

"Not an antidote *per se*, but I can mitigate some of the symptoms. I have learned through bitter experience that if he does not want to stop, there is not much anyone else can do."

Nashmir looked at Jean-Louis, and sighed. "My brother fell under the spell of opium. Three times I brought him back, but the fourth time, I could not. He took the pipe again and again until his life was forfeit to visions of ecstasy that led to oblivion." He stood up, and looked toward the house. "Does Lady Gabriella know?"

"No. Nor have I told the earl. Perhaps I am too hopeful. I believe that James is fundamentally a good man. I have known drunks that functioned fairly well throughout their lives. What about the poppy is different?"

"There are similarities, but whiskey and wine are readily available and socially acceptable, even expected in some circles. Opium is also legal, but more hidden, so there is the thrill of the chase. It sends the user into a euphoric state. Nothing in the universe matters but the lift, the sensation of freedom that one experiences, so I am told. Watching my brother battle the demon poppy, throwing his life away left me with no desire to find out what he experienced. I prefer to keep my wits. And my life. James must be watched over."

"He is expected at work. How can he disappear?"

"Could he not travel to see clients? We would need at least a week, probably longer." Jean-Louis looked off into the distance. "The place I have in mind might offend your sensibilities, but he would be watched over in complete privacy."

"If you feel it is safe, I shall not question you. However, the earl must be informed. I will not lie to him and I cannot disappear several times a day without his approval."

"I agree. Let me handle it."

Nashmir began to mix a concoction of herbs to bring on sleep.

Jean-Louis went into the house. He found the earl in his study at the late hour, walked in and closed the door.

Henry was startled, but knew that this must be important. "What is it?"

"Edward James lies unconscious in the greenhouse."

"What?" Henry wrinkled his forehead. "I thought he seemed ill earlier today. He left in a most unusual manner. Bri was left in tears and his parents dumbfounded."

"Not ill, milord. It is the reaction men have when they have developed a need for opium. Their nerves shatter without another dose. I have followed him to *Dreamtime*, an opium den in the Asian quarter, more than once. This place is owned by Miss Li and her associates, no doubt Blackburn.

"Tonight, James was sucking on a rubber hose of opium, lost in delusion. He told me that he had once had this compulsion while in the Far East, but he had beaten it. Miss Li, apparently, introduced him to it again. Probably by design. She should be eliminated with Blackburn, at the appropriate time, of course."

Henry appeared stunned. "When I was grievously injured, and Nashmir brought me back to life, he used a tincture of opium to dull my pain, but I was drifting in and out of consciousness. I recovered and never felt drawn to it. But I've known sailors who fell victim to the poppy and never recovered."

"Before James succumbed to opium dreams, he thought he had convinced Miss Li to divest *Dreamtime* from her holdings. That was the first night I found him there. François followed him on a few more late nights. I know for a fact he was there with the younger groomsmen from the baron's wedding, and again tonight. His desire for the poppy has accelerated. It must end or it will be the death of him."

Henry stood up and looked out the window toward the greenhouse. "What do you suggest?"

"The first thing is to get James out of the greenhouse and to a safe place I have selected, where he can be looked after for at least a week. Nashmir will have to visit frequently. It would be best if you could invent a reason for James to leave town that would explain his absence. I don't know if he will be well enough to attend the baron's wedding. The date is nigh, less than two weeks' time."

"Very well. I'll tell Bri and Sir John that something urgent and unexpected developed in Scotland." Henry put his hand on the former trapper's shoulder. "Thank you. More than once you have prevented disaster for my family."

"I didn't prevent *this* disaster and I may not be able to change its outcome. But I vow to do my best."

"Your best effort exceeds other men's guarantees."

Jean-Louis slipped through the garden to the stables and readied the carriage. He went back to the greenhouse, and said, "The earl has agreed. We will take James now."

"Very well. I have prepared some medicine but he is still unconscious. Will there be someone there who can administer my tinctures and potions?"

"Yes."

Together, they lifted James and carried him to the coach. The dead weight of his body made it difficult to maneuver, but they managed to pour him onto the bench seat.

Nashmir climbed in. Before the door closed, he reached out to touch the trapper's shoulder.

Jean-Louis looked back at him.

"And one more thing, although I hesitate to say it. James may need to be restrained."

The trapper smiled. "The place I have in mind can accommodate all your requirements."

He climbed up to the driver's perch, petted Chérie and gave the horses their instructions.

***

Late Tuesday, April 7, 1812 – Mlle. Sabine's Brothel

Sabine

The bell outside the back alley door to the brothel rang in Sabine's office. Frowning, she signaled to Pierre, her majordomo and bodyguard who kept order when the occasional brothel patron over-imbibed spirits or threatened one of her girls.

Pierre went to see who was ringing at this hour, instead of following the normal process of entering through the front of the tailor shop. Even at night, there was a sign on the front door instructing patrons to ring for service. Painted on the windows was "*Service at all hours to our valued clientele.*"

Hearing grunts and boots trudging up the back stairway, she went to see what was being delivered. The majordomo and Jean-Louis were carrying a body up the stairs, followed by a slight Asian man with black hair pulled into a bun on the top of his head.

"Is he dead?" Her voice had more than a hint of a scold.

Jean-Louis answered. "No, but close."

Pierre stopped at the top of the stairs, and turned his head toward Sabine. "Is there a room you'd like us to put him in?"

She indicated with a toss of her head to take the unconscious man to the private area on the upper floor. *I may regret this, but Jean-Louis has never let me down.*

Sighing at the task of carrying the dead weight up another flight of stairs, the majordomo walked backwards toward the next flight, while Jean-Louis followed. Once on the upper floor, the majordomo maneuvered the body into the closest room.

Sabine dismissed Pierre and closed the door.

"What do you keep this room for? It's rather spare, not up to your usual decorating standards." Jean-Louis raised an eyebrow with a hint of a smile.

The proprietress ignored his silent jab. "Who is this and why is he here?"

"His name is Edward James, and he needs to be watched closely to recover from the scourge of the poppy."

"Edward James, the banker who is engaged to Lady Gabriella? Are you mad?"

"Not yet." Jean-Louis glanced at James. "He is officially on a trip to Scotland. We hope to have him back to functionality," he shrugged at the word, "in time to attend a Society wedding in two weeks' time."

"And exactly how do you propose to do that? I have seen people writhe in agony emerging from the spell of opium. Most die. I cannot have a screaming maniac frightening away my clients, no matter who he is or how much you pay me."

Nashmir cleared his throat. "Mlle. Sabine, if I may speak."

She glared at him, and then nodded her permission.

"I have herbs that will keep him sedated. Nourishment will counter the effects of the cravings until they subside. Is there someone here I can instruct on how to administer these potions?"

Sabine paced the small room, fuming. She didn't speak for a few moments. She turned to take the measure of Nashmir. "People talk, even my girls. It would be too delicious a scandal to conceal. I am the only one who can do it. What is required?"

Nashmir opened a well worn woven satchel, retrieving small vials of liquid, a folded paper, a container of salts of hartshorn, and a jug of broth. He opened the container of salts. "He will sleep most of the time. When it is time to give him the contents of a vial, use the salts to revive him.

"Your majordomo should assist you in the event James is disoriented and strikes out. In fact, he should probably be restrained for the first three to five days. Every six hours, give him a glass of water and an equal amount of this broth. I will bring more each day. After he has taken nourishment, he should drink the contents of one vial of this liquid. If he resists, it should be poured down his throat." Nashmir brought out a funnel. "Use this."

"So am I to be a jailer *and* a nurse?"

Jean-Louis raised James up in the bed so that he would be able to swallow, positioning him in a near-sitting position, with pillows to prop him up. Pulling rope from Nashmir's satchel, he restrained Edward's arms and legs to the metal bed frame. "We'll do the first ministrations now, and you can decide. If I must come here every six hours, I'll do so. Do you agree?"

Sabine nodded. She walked over to the cabinet next to the door, lifted a pitcher, and poured a glass of water. Back at the bedside table, she took a salt crystal and waved it under Edward's nose.

James stirred, coughing and looking around. "Where am I?" His eyes appeared unfocused, then settled on Jean-Louis. "You! Blackguard!" Trying to move, he realized he was confined. "Release me at once!"

Jean-Louis lowered his voice to barely more than a whisper. "Listen to me and listen well, James. I have asked Nashmir and Mlle. Sabine to help save your life. The earl is telling Bri and your father that he dispatched you to settle urgent business for him in Scotland. You are expected to be gone for a few days, perhaps as long as a week. During that time, we will attempt to wean you from the draw of the poppy. You will cooperate with Mlle. Sabine or I will administer your 'medicine', and in a less-kind manner. At the end of four days, we will review your condition. Nashmir?"

Nashmir stepped forward. "Mr. James, you are on a dangerous precipice. You have recently fallen into the grip of this affliction, as I understand it, for the second time. If you do not overcome this desire now, intense though it may be, there may not be another chance. You could descend into the spirals of hell, never to return. Do you understand?"

James was defiant. "I am not 'in the grip' of anything except your illegal abduction of me! I tell you again, release me!"

"No." Jean-Louis leaned over the bed, his face very close to Edward. "Were you to leave here still under an opium trance, you would threaten Bri's happiness. The love of the poppy might kill you eventually, but I assure you that I would not wait for that to happen. Is the meaning of my words clear?"

James squirmed against his shackles and eyes shot arrows of malice toward the trapper. "Submit or die? Is that your offer?"

Jean-Louis stood back. "Precisely."

"You'll regret this, Jean-Louis, I promise you that."

"Perhaps." Jean-Louis shrugged. "Perhaps not."

James nodded his assent.

"Mlle. Sabine will give you a glass of water, which you will drink. Then, you will drink another glass, filled with broth from Nashmir, containing a mixture of herbs to counter the effects of the poppy. Then you will swallow the contents of this vial to sleep until you are awakened for the next dose. Understood?"

Again, James nodded.

He drank the water and the broth.

Sabine dabbed excess liquid that had dribbled down his chin. She opened the vial and he complied.

He blinked a couple of times until his eyes closed.

"It works almost immediately." Nashmir placed the contents of his satchel on the cabinet.

Jean-Louis indicated they should leave the room. Outside, he said to Sabine, "I will be here in six hours, and wait outside in case there is any problem. He handed her a small drawstring pouch of velvet. In the dim light, it reflected the color of plums.

Sabine untied the drawstrings and looked inside and looked back at Jean-Louis, revealing nothing. "Fair."

Jean-Louis tipped his hat. He and Nashmir descended the stairs. Nashmir climbed back into the carriage, Jean-Louis leapt to his driver's perch where Chérie waited. They disappeared into the night.

Zori sat between Jean-Louis and François on the driver's perch, whimpering.

Jean-Louis petted her, whispered calming words, and took the reins. "François will take care of you, Zori. Maybe when James is better, you can watch over him."

***

Early Wednesday, April 8, 1811 – Lord Ravenshire's Townhouse
Jean-Louis

It was past midnight when Jean-Louis and Nashmir knocked on the open door of the earl's study. Standing, looking out the window, he turned toward them. Without deflecting his eyes, he asked, "How did it go?"

They followed his eyes and saw that he was watching Bri in the garden.

She walked along the circular cobblestone path, her head down.

"Clearly troubled, she can't sleep either, and I cannot tell her the truth about Edward. I hate to see her in pain." Henry turned to them.

"Will *Edward* comply?"

Jean-Louis shrugged. "He did not have much of a choice, but he consented. I may have to stop by occasionally."

"Of course. Do whatever is required." Looking at Nashmir, the earl asked, "Will your potions work?"

"For now, milord. However, if he succumbs again, I may not be able to bring him back."

Shaking his head, Henry's sadness emphasized the lines in his face, making him look ten years older. "Then we must have faith that our efforts will be successful. The alternative would be tragic. Nashmir, in your experience, how likely is it that if weaned, he will be able to resist the poppy?"

Nashmir hesitated. "Milord, each man is different. I cannot predict the future. I lost my brother to the enticement of opium's phantasms. I thought he had the strength to refuse its flights of rapture, but I was wrong. Others, whom I thought weaker, surprised me by thwarting its power over them by sheer force of will. Only time will tell."

The earl sighed. "Patience is a trial like no other."

***

Wednesday, April 8, 1812 – Mlle. Sabine's Brothel

Sabine

Sabine had a habit of writing down what needed to be done to help her mind focus on tasks at hand and clarify their most efficient order of completion. Due to the high caliber of her clientele, the proprietress had the funds to incorporate private water closets next to each private room, a major advantage over her competition. Still, having Mr. James restrained meant that his necessary functions might be a problem.

While Sabine had a laundry operation behind the tailoring shop, including large boiling pots for linens, and special lifts for inside drying racks, that had proven too small as her brothel business had grown, so she had recently purchased a building directly across the back alley and turned it into a commercial laundry for small rooming houses and hotels as well as her brothel.

Sabine rang for Pierre. "It is time for the next dose for our special patron, and I want to avoid any unsanitary problems, therefore it may be necessary for you to help him into the water closet to do his business. However, I do not want you to do something you feel is too distasteful. Of course there will be extra compensation for your participation and silence in this matter."

The majordomo, an imposing former military man, always stood at attention when speaking with his employer. "Mademoiselle, on the battlefield, I aided many men in dire circumstances. I have seen, heard, smelled and carried things you cannot and never should imagine. This is a limited need and I am here to serve you."

"I am pleased I can rely on you, Pierre. Let's see how our charge is doing. I left Praetorian to watch him. Jean-Louis should be arriving soon."

They walked up the stairs until they reached the upper floor where James was hidden. They walked in to find him asleep, as promised by Nashmir. "I don't notice any unusual odor, so perhaps we don't have to disinfect the bed sheets at this moment. However, I would like to do it every day if there is a problem, and every other day if not. We can put them down the dumb waiter, and then disinfect the linens with vinegar and lye soap."

Praetorian, a large German Shepherd, lay next to the bed. He was gentle unless given specific protection commands in Latin, a protection Sabine felt would avoid any miscommunication by others to her dog.

Sabine had a dumb waiter at the end of each hallway for sheets to be delivered to the laundry. Sheets were changed after each client, as a sanitary precaution. London was a notorious breeding ground for disease, and Mlle. Sabine had vowed to mitigate any such risk at her establishment.

"I see your charge is still breathing." Jean-Louis stood at the door.

"We didn't hear your footsteps on the stairs," said the majordomo.

"Of course not." Jean-Louis curled the right edge of his upper lip.

"We were just about to wake him, and Pierre will help him to the water closet before we give him his medicine."

Jean-Louis nodded.

Sabine held a salt crystal under James' nose.

Crinkling his face at the odor, James blinked his eyes multiple times. Trying to move, he felt the ties and said, "What now?"

"Now, we are taking you to the water closet, then we will feed you, and then you will sleep some more."

"I have no strength to resist."

Sabine untied the ropes, and helped James sit up.

Weak, he tried to stand and fell back toward the bed. Pierre lifted Edward and supported him as he stumbled toward the water closet. When Edward had voided his bladder, he lurched toward the bed and sank down into it. Pierre propped him up again with pillows, and Sabine brought a glass of water. When he finished that, he drank the broth.

"I have had fantastical dreams. Please restrain me again. I dreamed I could fly and I might have jumped out the window if I had not been tied up." He looked toward Jean-Louis. "Your methods are an affront, Jean-Louis, but I needed this retreat from temptation."

Edward was restrained, and then he started to shake uncontrollably. He screamed. "Monsters! Horrible deformed twisted forms coming at me from all sides! Stop them! Stop them!"

Jean-Louis moved forward to stabilize Edward. "The funnel! I need the funnel!"

Sabine brought the funnel. While the majordomo forced open James' mouth, Jean-Louis poured the sleeping potion with anti-opiate herbs down the thrashing man's throat.

After twitching violently a few more times, Edward dropped into a deep sleep.

"For the duration of his time here, I will be needed. I shall return in six hours' time. I will speak with Nashmir to see if we need to increase the dosage." Jean-Louis left as silently as he had arrived.

Sabine signaled Praetorian, who came to her side. She bent down to pet him and whisper in his ear. She opened the door to the cabinet where she had placed his food, and filled a water dish for him. After she had checked on James earlier, she had taken the dog for a walk to the park.

Pierre and Sabine stood for a while watching their charge.

"Have you ever seen anything like this?"

The majordomo nodded. "More often than not, we ran out of drugs to knock out wounded soldiers. Delirium, visions, violent bursts of energy. But this man's wounds were self-inflicted."

Sabine had seen girls and clients bedeviled by alcohol, but this was her first observation of someone trying to break the hold of the poppy. "But the pain is just as real."

Before leaving, she gave the *stay* command to Praetorian, "*Mane.*"

***

Wednesday, April 8, 1812 – Lord Ravenshire's Townhouse
Henry

At dinner with Bri, Henry aimed to sound matter-of-fact. "I've sent Edward to Scotland to deal with some banking issues there. He'll be back in a few day's time."

"But the parties preceding Lady Penelope's wedding start soon. Surely he will return by then!"

"I expect so."

"He's been so odd lately. Missing the meeting of the trustees for Wyndward Investments, acting so strangely at dinner last night. And then that Miss Li—"

"Stop imagining things. Miss Li means nothing but business to Edward."

Bri sighed and ate her roast lamb.

***

Early Thursday, April 9, 1812 – Lord Ravenshire's Townhouse
Bri

The candle next to Bri's bed had burned to a waxy blob in the well of the candleholder. The fire's embers cast an ethereal glow over her bedroom. Bri sat up in the near-darkness, pulling extra pillows behind her back, wide awake and unable to sleep.

Does Edward truly love me?

He fell under the spell of that Asian temptress. Jean-Louis thinks Miss Li is a disciple of Blackie that he used to split Edward from me. If I break with Edward, then Blackie wins. I can't let his plan work.

But I feel such conflict. I don't know why I feel this way. Am I still jealous? Am I going mad?

Bri threw off the covers and went to her curved writing desk. She thought of her Aunt Gwyneth's comment, "Bri is analytical to a fault."

Perhaps it is a fault, but it is the only way I can move forward. Before she saw Edward again, she wanted to have a plan in place. She took out a sheet of her monogrammed writing paper, dipped the feather pen in the inkwell, and began to write. At the top she wrote the question:

Should I marry Edward?

Yes

I love him because I admire his mind and his bravery for trying to save me from Blackie. He is witty, a long time family friend with similar views on life and commerce. He is an honorable man. He is attractive.

No

I have begun to doubt his love for me because Miss Li has captivated him. The sparring wit we shared has turned biting lately. He can be domineering, controlling, and arrogant. He is mysterious about his past. Does an unknown Miss Li exist only to reappear in his life as Taita did in Father's?

If he loved me, he would have done what he promised and turned down Miss Li as a bank client. If he keeps things from me, it means he doesn't trust me. If we have lost trust in each other what is left?

Kissing and dancing are fleeting over a lifetime. Most of life is conversation built on trust.

What if we differ in raising children? I've never thought of it—what if he and I fight over children the way we fight over investments? Will he travel the world like Father, leaving me alone for long periods?

How could he disappear tonight without notice? Father Seemed as surprised as I.

She reviewed the list and pushed it off while she stared into the fire. Her dog and cat had awakened when she did. Spotty lay at her feet while Monkey stretched across her lap. She petted the cat and spoke to both of them as she often did when searching for a solution to a problem. It helped her focus. "The joy, the passion I felt when I got to know Edward as an adult is pierced with anger and jealousy. I fear these emotions will consume me. I thought my nature was rational. Who knows when Miss Li will appear again? Her spectre haunts me.

"I always vowed to be an independent woman. I didn't expect to fall in love with Edward. She looked toward the ceiling in exasperation. "Intervening events have thrown me into a whirlwind of doubt. Does any love survive, truly?

"Ian's existence means that I no longer must produce an heir. How demeaning that concept is. Was it the spectacle of it all that convinced me I was in love? The gowns, the balls, the attention, his rescue of me from Blackie? Was I seduced by such trivialities? Has the poetry of Lord Byron implanted a romantic ideal in my mind? Is my heart ruling my head? Am I a fool?"

Looking into her dog's eyes, she sighed. "Will I always wonder about the next woman Edward might meet?"

Bri rubbed her cat behind his ears. "Breaking off the engagement is a big step. Perhaps we could postpone the wedding date indefinitely. We could remain engaged but never actually marry. Father and Charlotte had fifteen years of companionship."

She pulled out another piece of stationery and wrote to Edward.

Dear Edward:

I am and will always be grateful that you rescued me from Blackie's clutches. In retrospect, the feeling I imagined was love is wavering. I no longer believe that we should marry in June. We need more time. If you wish, I hereby release your from your proposal of marriage.

Sincerely,
Bri

Postscript: I see no reason why a delay in marriage or breaking of our engagement should impact your continuing to act as banker to my family.

She held the letter up to read it again, then tore it up and threw it in the fire, watching as it burned and smoldered into ashes. "I'll keep thinking about it, but somehow I feel better having written down my thoughts." Looking at her cat, she added, "'Maybe the answer will come to me in my sleep." She rolled the emerald engagement ring around her finger but didn't take it off.

Yawning, she stretched and gave in to exhaustion. She walked to the bed, waited for the dog and cat to jump up to snuggle into the covers. Then she lay down and fell into a deep sleep.

CHAPTER SEVENTY-TWO

Thursday, April 9, 1812 – *La Pâtisserie entre des fleurs*
Vanessa

When their plates were delivered, Vanessa gazed directly at her granddaughter. "You are upset, Bri."

"Father sent Edward to Scotland for a week or longer. He may miss all the parties for Lady Penelope's wedding."

"My intuition tells me there's more." Vanessa took a deep breath. "I dismissed your mother's bouts of melancholy. I don't want to make the same mistake again."

"I think Edward is in love with another woman."

" 'The woman in the red mask'?"

"Does *everyone* in the *ton* know about Miss Li?"

"I am not *everyone*. She came to your Engagement Ball on the arm of Tottie Drummond. I doubt that they met by accident as he suggested." The duchess tilted her head. "I am right. I see it in your eyes."

"Father and Jean-Louis think she is an agent of Blackburn and that he is here in London in disguise."

Vanessa sat back, taking in the implications. "You and Ian are at risk."

"Jean-Louis is arranging for additional protection."

***

Interior of Bri's Carriage
Bri
I need advice from someone with more experience with men than I have, but more objective than Grandmother. As she stepped into her carriage, the perfect person popped into her mind. Bri smiled and rapped on the side of the door. "Please take me to Mlle. Sabine's."

***

Thursday, April 9, 1812 – *Dreamtime*
Xie Xie

When Xie Xie walked into *Dreamtime* in the late afternoon, the manager motioned to her to come into the private office. "We had a little problem again yesterday with your banker and that French thug."

All of Xie Xie's senses heightened in fear, but she was skilled in not showing it. The Pharaoh would not like it if he found out that she did not know of this problem immediately and report to him. "Why did you not inform me at once?"

"I did not know until the daytime barkeep told me. He came in the late afternoon, not at night. The banker apparently slid into the opium room without anyone seeing him—"

Xie Xie interrupted him. "How could that have happened?"

He shrugged. "It did. The watcher will not make that mistake again. Ever."

She nodded her approval. "That should keep the *new* watcher on his toes." She paused a moment. "Toby?"

The manager nodded. "Especially since he helped me dump the body of the terminated watcher off the docks. He knows what is expected of him."

All who worked for The Pharaoh knew what was expected of them. No one knew that better than Xie Xie. Sometimes she had seen a glimmer of a lost boy in her master's eyes, but it was masked in the next instant by a ruthless instinct for survival.

"How much did the banker use?"

"More than is wise."

"Speak of this to no one. Who found him?"

"Gina."

"Can she and the barkeep be trusted?"

"Yes, they have been tested. They know what is expected of them too."

"Make sure of it."

She walked out to the alley and hailed a Hackney. She instructed the cabbie to take her to the stables behind the earl's townhouse. Once there, she sat inside the cab, not wanting to exit until she saw Jean-Louis.

A stable boy was sweeping and she called him over. "Is Jean-Louis here?"

From the other side of the carriage, a voice said, "I am." He opened the door.

Xie Xie jumped, nearly falling off the jump seat. *That never happens! I must control my nerves.*

She stepped out of the cab and reached into a pocket hidden inside her jacket to pay, but Jean-Louis tossed the driver some coins.

"Thanks, Joe."

"No problem, J-L."

"Shall we talk in the garden?" Jean-Louis led the way. He gestured to her to take a seat on a garden bench and joined her. "He is safe. Your seduction plan is thwarted."

Xie Xie knew she was cornered. *Jean-Louis is a man not unlike The Pharaoh. He can see through people. I will have to shade the truth enough to be convincing without revealing all.* "I just found out he came to *Dreamtime* and took the opium pipe without the appropriate supervision. I am so relieved to know he is well."

"I said he is *safe*. I did not say he is *well*. How did you know?"

"I just told you, I came directly to you from *Dreamtime*."

"No. I mean how did you know he would succumb to the bait?"

"Bait? I had no idea-"

"Do not attempt to lie. Your charms are useless on me. You knew he could not be seduced by you as a woman, but the poppy...you knew of its power over him. How?"

Xie Xie shook her head in protest. "No! I showed him *Dreamtime* as an investment property of my associates. He counseled me to dispose of it. I have advised my clients that they should do so, but of course, communication to and from Egypt takes weeks under the best of circumstances. It will be done. How was I to know he would seek opium dreams? He seemed to be a solid, disciplined man."

"You're lying. I will find out the truth. It is best if you tell me now."

A brief shudder of fear shot through her.

Jean-Louis saw her dread. "You're afraid to tell me. I know how deadly he is. I can protect you, get you to Canada or America. You could start a new life. Walk away now and you will have two deadly enemies instead of the one you are most afraid of." He waited for the words to sink in. "It's your choice."

She gathered her wits. "If I appear afraid, it's due to your unveiled threats." Her professed defiance gave her confidence to continue. "I came here to tell you that Mr. James might be in danger, due to his own, ill-advised actions, out of respect for Lord Ravenshire and Lady Gabriella. I demand an apology from you!"

Jean-Louis nodded. "Perhaps I spoke in haste. Forgive me, Miss Li. Let me get one of our carriages to take you to your hotel."

Xie Xie nodded. As the carriage pulled away, she could feel Jean-Louis watching her. *I must be constantly on guard, against The Pharaoh and Jean-Louis. All must be prepared. When I disappear, no one will know where I have gone.*

***

Thursday, April 9, 1812 – Interior of Bri's Carriage

Bri

After Bri's lunch with Vanessa, Jean-Louis drove the carriage to Mlle. Sabine's brothel and told Bri to remain inside the carriage. "I will bring her to you."

"But I'd like to see—"

"You will *never* set foot inside this establishment, is that clear?"

"But—"

"No."

The French trapper returned in about ten minutes and opened the door. Sabine climbed in. "Hello, Lady Gabriella. This is fortuitous timing. I would like another crate of sponges." She handed Bri a handwritten order.

Bri took a deep breath. "I actually came here for a different purpose—to ask for advice."

Sabine tilted her head and raised her eyebrows. "I'm happy to listen."

"I could not sleep last night and made lists of whether I should marry my fiancé or not. I am still unsure. He has disappointed me and I fear he is attracted to an exotic Asian woman."

Sabine nodded. "Exotic women spur men's fantasies, but the thrill fades as differences in culture are often too great to overcome. Time usually tempers such attractions." She leaned forward. "It may surprise you, but many men are afraid of women, especially strong women like you. Sometimes, just listening and remembering they were once little boys dreaming of dazzling their paramours with feats of daring is all you need to do. They crave approval."

Bri looked away. "I'm afraid I haven't been very approving lately. Ever since that woman started showing up everywhere—"

"You've never felt jealousy before?"

Bri shook her head. "I feel so out of control."

"Love is about relinquishing control and accepting the other person. On your list, do you have common interests?"

"Some. He's learned to swim and to roll with the waves on a sailing ship."

"And what have you learned of his world?"

Bri thought for a moment. "I've learned to respect his opinion more than I did in the beginning, to value the insights he's gained from experience. But—"

Sabine waited for Bri to gather her thoughts.

"But I can't dismiss the feeling that Edward is hiding something from me. That is perhaps why I assume it is Miss Li. Perhaps it was another woman during his six years in Asia."

"Like the earl's long lost love?"

Bri sighed. "The gossip rags tell all. Have we no privacy?"

"Not much, given your father's position in the *ton*." Sabine sat back and looked directly into Bri's eyes. "My advice is this. Forget the Asian woman, spectres of long lost loves, and focus on the moment you are in and savor it. 'Tis a cliché, but time heals. When you are next with your fiancé, listen. Say things like, 'I hear you saying such-and-such, but that makes me feel uncomfortable because...and explain it instead of becoming angry or issuing ultimatums. Nothing lasts forever, but don't deny yourself the chance for happiness when it is offered."

"I am used to adding up numbers and not having stray variables enter into an equation."

"But Lady Gabriella, love is not an equation. Life is dealing with stray variables."

Bri looked out the window. "I've lived a life where I could control most things. I know I'm very lucky to have an indulgent father and access to funds for whatever I want to do. But people are not numbers, they are far more complex. This engagement experience is showing me that I need to analyze myself the way I analyze accounting ledgers."

Sabine shook her head and smiled. "Lady Gabriella, you are not listening. Love is not an intellectual exercise. Emotions are powerful and do not fall into columns on an accounting ledger. Emotions frighten you. You fear losing yourself. But in true love, you find yourself."

Bri sighed. "I have a lot to learn. Just when I thought I had life figured out, love toppled my assumptions."

"It happens to us all. I must go now."

Bri reached out and squeezed Sabine's hand. "Thank you. I'll practice listening more."

***

Sabine

Back in her establishment, Sabine checked on Edward. She peeked into his room. His form remained unconscious. *I hope this young man proves worthy of Lady Gabriella. She is a unique woman.*

Sabine resumed her planning. She had recently bought the adjacent townhouse to expand, and was considering purchasing a third to house her girls. Currently they lived in their client rooms, but Sabine's vision was of offering more like a hotel experience, a pristine room where fantasies could play out, maybe decorated with themes and costumes available. She could charge more for a unique experience. Imagining a room for Ancient Rome with couches and togas, a room canopied by a camel-caravan desert tent, a captain's cabin on a ship of discovery, she let her mind wander until it was interrupted by an urgent knock.

"Mademoiselle! Mademoiselle!"

She recognized the voice of Lizzie. "Come in. What is it?"

The girl was in the grip of sheer panic. "I don't know what happened, Mademoiselle. Please believe me! You must come now!"

Sabine followed the terrified girl to her room on the second floor. "Stay calm. Do not attract attention," she instructed. Opening the door to Lizzie's room, Sabine pulled Lizzie inside and closed the door. There, a naked man's body lay draped across the bed, his head hanging off the mattress, eyes wide open in death.

***

Friday, April 10, 1812 – Tattersalls
Henry

Henry and Jean-Louis visited Tattersall's on Hyde Park Corner to look over former race horses deemed unsuitable for stud fees, not having won any races. They were being offered at auction the next week, and today marked a preview period.

With an eye for horses, Jean-Louis advised the earl on purchases. He had found more than one winner in the past. Not that Henry put them on the racing course, but they had sired winners, and performed admirably in the annual Ravenshire Fox Hunt, held each November, as well as frequent recreational riding and jumping.

For this event, Jean-Louis had summoned Orion from Ravenshire. This was Orion's first exposure to Tattersall's and he was enthralled.

After deciding on their targets and bid ranges, Jean-Louis left Orion with the earl to handle the transaction, and headed to Sabine's to look in on Edward.

After their mostly winning bids, Henry and Orion tagged their preferred selections.

Orion had some astute observations.

The earl put his hand on Orion's shoulder. "I can see why Jean-Louis values your opinion. Good job, Orion. I'll want you here next week for the auction."

The Gypsy boy beamed.

The earl flagged a Hackney for Orion, and decided to eat lunch at his club.

As he sat alone at a table, reading the morning newspaper, a familiar voice called out, "Ravenshire! Mind if I join you?" The man took a chair before Henry could respond.

Henry looked up to see Asgard Fitz-Hatton, Marquess of Norbury, an old schoolmate from Merton. They had been nodding acquaintances, but not close. Fitz-Hatton's father's estates had been ravaged by flooding rivers, crops had been destroyed and livestock killed on more than one occasion in the past. Out of deference to their old acquaintance, Henry had provided interim loans when the bank had refused.

As many in England in the early years of the nineteenth century, Fitz-Hatton was land rich and cash poor. The upkeep of such vast acreage and the stately castle became more burdensome each year. Even today, Ravenshire received twenty-five percent of the profits from all Norbury estate income in return for past and possible future financial support. Blackie had not liked the marquess, believing that he was cheating Henry. *Odd, despite Blackie's nefarious actions, I believe he was sincere in his assessment of the marquess, although I dismissed his suspicions. I should ask Bri to look over the loan and Norbury income documents. I never thought much about theft from the Ravenshire estates.*

"Asgard, you still look like a Norse god."

Asgard's white-streaked blond hair, tied back in the pony tail style of the day, and steel-blue eyes were still vibrant, even at the age of fifty-two. "As you know, Ravenshire, 'Asgard' is an entire realm in Norse Mythology, not a god. But my mother misremembered the childhood stories she was told." He shrugged. "What have you been up to?"

Henry signaled the server to come over.

Asgard ordered his usual open sandwich of turkey and spinach, with goat cheese garnish, and a glass of white wine. "Your best, of course. The earl is paying."

"Irrepressible and insolent as ever, Asgard." Henry laughed. "I have been at Tattersalls, looking over the horse stock prior to next week's auction."

"Anything remarkable?"

"A couple."

"I'm out of the horseflesh business, as you know. Sheep are a better investment; they can be shorn year after year."

"I agree. These horses would just be for our riding stables, most likely."

"Ah, 'most likely', eh? I know what that means, old friend. You have a ringer in there, a winner that no one else has identified. Jean-Louis picked him, no doubt."

"A mare."

"Now I'm intrigued. I look forward to the next installment of the story."

Both lunches were served at the same time. Henry's sandwich was rare sliced roast beef, slathered with mustard mayonnaise.

"How are the wedding plans coming for your daughter and Sir John's son?"

Henry had to keep up public appearances about the wedding until Bri made a final decision and Edward recovered from his affliction. "Down to the colors of flowers and bridesmaids' dresses, hair styling and so on. Quite a production."

Asgard had once been in love with Lady Jane, but she had eyes only for Henry. After recognizing she would never love him, Asgard married an older woman, a wealthy widow whose two older children eventually squandered most of her late husband's wealth. Still, she and Asgard remained together, and had three daughters and a son. "Yes, I am all too familiar with the theatrics of it all, with three daughters, one married, two to go. My son is still looking for the perfect combination of Freya and Helen of Troy. Too bad Lady Gabriella chose young James—she could have been a marchioness!" He laughed. "Don't worry, Henry; having known Lady Gabriella all her life, I doubt she would tolerate a dreamer such as my son." He frowned. "He would rather read history than manage animal husbandry and cultivate crops."

Henry recognized that Asgard's son, Valgard, would never manage the Norbury estates properly, and hoped that Valgard's son, should he ever have one, would be up to the challenge. Valgard had the same Nordic looks as Asgard, but was an introvert.

"He is heir to a title and many women have tried to entrap him. This year's Marriage Season may be the one where he finally secures a match."

"Perhaps. There's always a new face, is there not?" They finished their sandwiches and sipped wine. Long ago, Henry had set up an account for Asgard, which he replenished when it was below a certain level. Each year, it was repaid, when possible, from that year's profits from the Norbury estates. That arrangement meant that each meeting between them did not require an awkward discussion regarding money.

"Interesting evening at the gallery recently." Asgard nodded with a tilt of the head, "That dwarf is a master. He painted my wife as a young bride, and when he painted us together on the occasion of our twenty-fifth wedding anniversary, she paid him extra to eliminate any signs of aging. He bowed to her wishes, not without a brash retort, but he did it all the same. Very accommodating man, I must say."

They rose to leave. "See you at the blond baron's wedding."

"Beau is besotted with the lovely Lady Penelope."

On his way home, Henry mulled over their interaction. *I don't think Blackie was right, but I will still ask Bri to look over the reports on the Norbury estates.*

***

Friday, April 10, 1812 – Interior of Lord Asgard's Carriage

Asgard

In his carriage, Asgard reviewed his meeting with Henry. *He doesn't suspect anything. If the Norbury income is down, he will attribute it to my poor management skills, not improper reporting or hidden accounts in the Colonies.*

Asgard's fingers twisted his left hand into a fist so tight that the blood drained from his fingers.

CHAPTER SEVENTY-THREE

Saturday, April 11, 1812 – County Kerry, Ireland
Hinton

U nder dark, scowling clouds, cold rain thrashed the umbrellas of mourners at a cemetery next to a small country church in County Kerry. The widower, a smattering of friends, and the parish priest released Lee Anna Hinton from her earthly bonds.

"We shall be together as one in spirit, now and forevermore." The priest blessed the grave, closed his eyes in silent prayer, and walked back to the church. The group broke up, and Hinton walked back to the waiting carriages with Lee Anna's friends.

"Are you sure you must go to London first? Your daughters are waiting for you in America." Lee Anna's oldest friend, Morag, reached for Stephen Hinton's hands and held them in hers.

Hinton nodded. "There is an unfinished piece of business there. I shall join our girls once that is completed. And I hope you will visit us in Boston someday." He looked around. "I will miss this verdant isle and the warmth of its inhabitants."

Morag began to sob, and her friend Mary put her arm around her shoulder. "Not here, Morag. Not now. Lee Anna is at peace."

"God sent the rain to mourn dear Lee Anna. I mirror His tears with my own."

"I shall miss your poetic turn of phrase, Morag. All you Irish are walking poets. We British are so dull in comparison."

Morag tried to smile. "I won't argue with that."

Hinton helped them into their carriage, then got into his and went home to close up the house.

He'd made arrangements for a caretaker, and the priest had requested that the parish use the house for ruined women and their illegitimate children. "Lee Anna would have liked that, Father, to give poor suffering girls and their unfortunate children a new beginning. Someday our daughters may want to return here. I want them to have this house forever, but it should be put to some good use until that day." Knowing the house would not be empty made it easier to leave.

Before traveling to America with their husbands and children, knowing their mother was deathly ill, the house had been thoroughly cleaned. Lee Anna had insisted that the children and grandchildren bid her goodbye while she was still able to talk. She did not want them to see her ravaged by cancer as her mother had been. Hinton and her daughters had accommodated their mother's last wish.

Now it was his turn to set someone's mind at ease, if it were still possible. He packed his necessary traveling items in a small leather bag, and closed the door on his life in Ireland.

I must keep my last promise to Lee Anna.

***

Sunday, April 12, 1812 – *Omelettes de Mme. d'Aix*
Aneira

Aneira looked over the books for the café. Since its opening in November, it had become more successful than Aneira ever imagined. Her plan to have a small unobtrusive place to observe the implementation of her final revenge against the Wyndward family was threatened by that success. The café and its patroness were now talked about, bringing unwanted visibility. She hadn't anticipated the word-of-mouth among Society women, or the twitter about the "grandmotherly proprietress." Her intention to infiltrate Society's inner circle by subterfuge and gossip had been turned upside down—she had become the center of attention.

A knock at the door startled her. She rose to see who it was. Her suspicious nature made it impossible to have any permanent personal staff. A servant might learn too much and killing them might bring unwanted investigation. Only the urchin knew secrets. No one would miss him if he had to be eliminated.

Self-reliance had kept her alive. She opened the door.

"Hello, Grandmother."

"This is imprudent. Your proficiency at disguise is masterly, but I advised you not to return and to communicate only by coded message. There are things that spark a memory you might not expect, such as a tilt of the head, a turn of phrase, a scent. Your love of danger threatens our plan. I won't permit it."

She scanned the surrounding area. "Don't stand in the light. Come inside now."

***

Sunday, April 12, 1812 – Lord Ravenshire's Townhouse
Henry

Henry rubbed his brow. If Taita could never be his, and Bri followed through on her intention to break the engagement with Edward, then he had to face reality.

Ian was young, but no one had a guaranteed lifespan. In order to protect what he had built, he might be forced to marry to protect his family's future. As a man of three-and-fifty, the prospect of marrying a young woman of childbearing age seemed a chore. *How could she understand me the way Charlotte does?*

He and Lady Jane had known little about life or each other when they'd married shortly after Henry returned from his first sea voyage. When he began to assemble the elements of his trading company, their life was ruled by the necessity of travel for the trading company as well as their social calendar and expectations of others in their class. If he were honest, the pace of life at Ravenshire was too slow for him.

After losing Lady Jane, Henry spent long periods at sea, alone, brooding, courting death with daring escapades. *Maybe Laurence should write a swashbuckler about me instead of a dull history of our family. But he is an historian, not a novelist.*

The swashbuckling days were long over. When he'd arrived home with Jean-Louis one day in 1792, Bri greeted him with crossed arms and demanded that he never travel without her again. He'd given in ever since. *I can't force her to marry against her will. Can I force myself to do so to save Ravenshire?*

***

Sunday, April 12, 1812 – Mlle. Sabine's Brothel
Edward

Drifting in and out of consciousness for several days, Edward's pupils could not focus. *Is that a wolf? Am I in a wild forest?* A low growl rumbled in the background.

He found himself in the deep woods. A spectre in the distance glowed, illuminating the dark horizon. The growl came again. Terror drove shards of ice into his gut. The wispy figure's hand reached out. "Come! Come to me." The apparition came closer. "We can fly together. Soar around the earth, touch the stars. The universe awaits us. Leave this bondage behind. Be free, with me! Come! Come!" The voice receded. He tried to reach out, but found his hand restrained.

Where am I? Why am I bound? He struggled against his bonds and fought to regain lucidity.

Breathe deeply. Center yourself. He opened his eyes, willing them to sharpen their focus. He turned to the side and two deep brown eyes stared back. *Not a wolf—a dog. But where am I? This small room is totally unfamiliar. Why am I being held against my will?*

He vaguely remembered *Dreamtime*. Miss Li jumped into his mind. *Is this a blackmail ploy? Was this a plot to seduce me with the poppy?* His head fell back onto the pillow. *I fell under its spell again.*

Rage and shame simultaneously flowed through his body. Unable to control his emotions, the banker who valued self-control was undone by tears. *I have lost Bri. I have lost myself.*

***

Monday, April 13, 1812 – Exterior of Sir John's Townhouse
Hinton

The former cavalry soldier had been watching Sir John's house since the banker had returned home. As a boy, this man had seen Hinton at least once as he was leaving the alley behind this very same house. Attuned to senses developed over years of dangerous, surreptitious work, Hinton believed he'd been observed more than once. Hinton had assumed at the time that it was the son watching.

Tonight, forty years later, the time had come. Hinton hid in the shadows in the alley across the street, where he hid his horse and watched the house where the younger James still lived.

The banker's carriage pulled around to the front of the house.

Hinton moved further back into the darkness as the front door opened, and the banker and his wife walked to their carriage.

He mounted his horse to follow.

Based on the instructions given to him by his employer, Sir Balthazar James, so many years ago, Hinton did not believe that the 10th Earl of Ravenshire knew of the death decree the elder James had issued for Brigid. *If the earl were complicit, and his son knows about his father's duplicity, this night could be my last.*

***

Monday, April 13, 1812 – Lord Ravenshire's Townhouse
Bri

Dana helped Bri step into a midnight blue dress and lace up the quilted empire bodice for dinner with Sir John and Lady Anne. *I hope I never have to tell Edward's parents of our broken engagement.* Her maid fastened the clasp on the chain that held her new sapphire pendant.

Bri sat at a vanity cabinet in front of a mercury glass mirror while Dana stood behind her, trying different effects with her hair. "How about pulling your hair up on the sides and leaving it in long curls in the back? The curling tongs are heating in the fire."

"I like that idea. Let's try it." Bri sat back patiently as Dana wound sections of Bri's hair around the movable tong, and then pressed it to the grooved tong to set the curl. It took about thirty minutes. Spotty lay at her feet, while Monkey jumped up on the vanity to watch.

"You must be excited to see Mr. James tonight."

Bri shook her head slightly, so as not to burn her head or Dana's fingers. "Father told me that Mr. James left for Scotland to deal with an urgent matter."

"Isn't Lady Penelope's wedding in little more than a week?"

"He must return in time. He and I are both in the wedding party." Changing the subject, she asked, "How do you like spending your day off working at Jane Anne's salon?"

"It's exciting and exhausting. I'm doing what you told me to do—observing and listening." She whispered, "The sponges in the back room are very popular."

"Only a few know about it." Bri peered at her face in the looking glass. "I love the way you made my hair look! You and your sister both have a talent for hairstyling."

"The shop is busy. Even men are bringing in wigs! Do you know that some of them take their wigs to bakers to bake in their ovens to kill lice? Jane Anne refuses to accept them."

Recoiling in disgust, Bri's hand went to her throat. "Do you mean to say that wigs are placed on baking racks next to bread?"

Dana nodded with a slight shrug. "Wigs seem to be falling out of favor except for the lord judges and special court occasions." She shivered involuntarily. "It's disgusting."

"Dear Heavens, yes! I am appalled at the very idea of such a practice. It's unhygienic and revolting. I cannot think of it while I eat or I might vomit." Bri took a deep breath, smiled at her cat, petted a few strokes on Monkey's head, and snapped her fingers for Spotty to follow her downstairs.

"I'll lay out your bedclothes and come back when you are ready to go to bed."

Bri and Spotty descended the two stories to the parlor.

She found Henry at his desk in the study, absorbed in the designs for rebuilding the old Ravenshire Castle. He looked up when she came in and removed his spectacles. "Sir John and Lady James should be here shortly." He stood and went to the window, looking out toward the greenhouse. I hope Nashmir can keep Sir John in good health. Your wedding is not far off."

Bri felt her face flushing in irritation. "Father, you know very well that there may never be a wedding. If you are asking me to pretend that I will marry Edward because Sir John is near death, I shall try, but as you know better than most, I am not much of an actress."

"It is a skill that helps one navigate the seas of Society. If people can easily read what is on your mind, they have the advantage, not you. You must learn to control your temper. There is no need to blurt out the truth at every turn. We British could learn something from impenetrability of Asian facial expressions."

"Miss Li again? Am I *never* to be free of her?"

"Stop it. You demean yourself with these outbursts of petty

jealousy. Miss Li is of no interest to Edward other than as a potential client and intermediary with associates of The Pharaoh."

Bri started to answer, but was interrupted by Thompson's knock. "Sir John and Lady James have arrived, milord."

Henry and Bri followed the butler to greet their guests.

***

Monday, April 13, 1812 – Lord Ravenshire's Townhouse
Jean-Louis

After delivering Edward's medicines, Jean-Louis left his horse in the stables. He decided to walk the perimeter of the immediate neighborhood to get the cramps out of his legs from the day's riding. "Never used to be this stiff," he mumbled to himself.

Strolling back toward the earl's townhouse, his heightened senses told him he was not alone. Although the man was hidden in the shadows, Jean-Louis spotted him. The stranger appeared to be watching the earl's home. *Who is this?*

Jean-Louis walked along the other side of the street from where the man was obscured by shrubbery.

From the observer's position, he had full view of the front parlor windows.

Circling back around, Jean-Louis crossed the street and walked toward the shrouded spot.

A low voice said, "I mean you no harm."

"Then why are you hiding in the shadows?" Jean-Louis conveyed danger in his tone.

"I want to speak to the earl and Mr. John James."

"Sir John?"

Hinton raised his eyebrow. "Knighted, eh? Yes."

"Why?"

"I have kept a secret for forty years. I want to unburden myself. This secret affects both the earl and Sir John."

"And you expect to simply march up to the earl's door and reveal this secret?"

"I prefer the straightforward approach."

"Give me your weapons."

Earlier in the day, Hinton had learned of the near-mythic

reputation of the French former trapper who worked for the Earl of Ravenshire. He tendered the knife in his belt, hilt first.

"And the one in your boot."

Hinton smiled. "Can't be too careful, eh?" He handed it over.

Jean-Louis took him by the arm and escorted him through the garden and up the back stairs to the kitchen entrance. He guided him to the hallway. "Wait."

Jean-Louis stood at the edge of the dining room and caught the earl's eye.

The earl waved him over.

Bending over, Jean-Louis whispered something in Henry's ear.

The earl whispered back.

The guests ignored the interruption, finishing their desserts.

Jean-Louis left and stood silently outside the dining room in the hallway.

Henry said, "Jamesey, I need to speak with you in my study. Bri, perhaps you and Lady James could sit in the parlor and have a bit of sherry until we are done."

Jean-Louis swallowed a smile as he watched Bri control her annoyance at being dismissed.

When Henry stood, Jean-Louis guided Hinton to the study. Henry put his arm around Sir John, and they followed Jean-Louis down the hallway.

Once inside the office, Henry and John sat by the fire.

Jean-Louis stood by the door, motioning Hinton to start. "Sir John, I worked for your father for several years. I disappeared forty years ago."

Sir John peered at Hinton. "You were my father's driver. I remember once seeing a man of your same height in the alley being rebuked by my father. I was home over a school holiday."

"On one occasion, you stood close to me in the street. On other occasions, you watched from your window while I met with your father."

"I could not say if it was you. Much time has passed."

"Your father did not tolerate people who displeased him. I was the instrument he wielded to rid himself of such people."

"By what means?"

"I think you know what kind of a man your father was beneath his well-bred veneer."

Sir John nodded. "He could be cruel. In truth, I hated him."

Henry stared at Sir John and then looked at Hinton. "So you have come here forty years later to tell Sir John his father told you to kill people for him? After all this time, what is the point?"

"The point is, Lord Ravenshire, that Sir John's father sent me to track down and kill your nanny, Brigid, and her unborn child. He told me your father knew nothing of it. In fact, your father had provided the nanny with a generous settlement to leave London. She died shortly after childbirth in Scotland. Neighbors said the child died, but I believe they were wrong. The story of the child's death was a lie, concocted by Brigid's mother, a wicked woman. That child lived. If he lives still, he is your half-brother."

CHAPTER SEVENTY-FOUR

Monday, April 13, 1812 – Lord Ravenshire's Townhouse
Bri

B ri couldn't stop looking toward her father's office.
   Lady James sighed. "We are left out of men's lives from
time to time. You'll get used to it."
"No, I won't. I refuse to be shunted aside. I'm going in there." Bri
stood and walked toward the earl's study.

Lady James followed.

Bri opened the door to hear a strange man speaking.

"I took the assignment intending to protect the nanny and her
child. I knew I would have to disappear afterwards—"

Henry frowned at the uninvited visitors. "Come in and listen. This
is Hinton, who was employed by Sir John's father." Turning back to
Hinton, Henry directed, "Continue."

"—I would have to disappear afterwards, as Sir Balthazar would
never tolerate me as a threat. His only protection would be to have
me killed. When I told him the nanny and child were dead, as the
local people would corroborate, he had no more use for me. He
engaged two potential successors to compete in my assassination, but
both proved unsuccessful. I vanished that same night."

Henry stood and paced the room in frustration. "You could have
told my father at the time!"

Sir John spoke up. "Would he have believed it? My father had
many gifts, of which persuasion was one. The probability is that

Hinton is correct. He would have been eliminated as a threat."
Turning to Hinton, he said, "You were right to disappear."

"Agents of your father attacked and stabbed me. I managed to kill both and escaped. I boarded a ship to Ireland the next morning."

"But still," Henry looked exasperated, "years ago, after Sir John's father's death, you could have told my father. The fact is, on his deathbed, my father told me the truth of Brigid and the possibility that his son lived. Not only did I meet my brother, unbeknownst to me due to his invented persona, I entrusted my company to him when I was overseas for long periods. He embezzled from me, masquerading as a valued associate for nearly twenty years. His grandmother killed my father, and he killed my brother, my sister's husband and probably more we will never know. We saw him die." He paused. "Or at least, we thought we did."

"How?"

"In an attempt to evade pursuers, he fell to his death from a ship's deck after trying to rape and kill my daughter," he pointed to Bri."

"Did you see the body?"

Henry glanced at Jean-Louis."We share your doubt."

"The child's 'death' was faked shortly after his birth, so it is not too far a notion to suppose that the man's 'death' was designed as a similar feint. The grandmother would be elderly now, perhaps late seventies. When revenge takes over a man's soul, it propels him forward. His prey is never released until dead. But he may feel safe now. If we know he is alive, we have an advantage."

"We suspect we have seen him, but his eye color has changed."

"Some sorcery may be afoot."

"No doubt." said Jean-Louis. Turning toward Henry, he continued, "When I came to London with you, your father asked me to search for information on Brigid and the child. I found what Hinton did in the old church records in the small village. An old woman there remembered a Gypsy who visited the grandmother. Gypsies were unusual in that part of the coast. I suspected the boy lived.

"I learned that the Gypsies set up camp outside Inverness once a year. I followed the caravan and saw a Gypsy meet with a woman, whom I suspected was the grandmother. I saw the boy. When I went back a few months later, they had disappeared and I could find no trace of them. What I didn't know, until we discovered Blackburn's journal last year, was that the boy grew up to be a fraud and a killer."

Hinton's voice conveyed his anguish. "Should I have killed a baby? Or an old woman? How many lives would have been saved if I had committed such a depraved act?"

Henry shook his head. "At some point, Blackburn made his own decision to pursue his grandmother's vengeance. Twenty years I knew the man! 'Twas only in the last year that I saw negative aspects of his behavior toward others. Arrogance, disdain and self-aggrandizement were becoming more apparent. None of us knows how a child will turn out. He is responsible for the deaths by his hand, not you. You gave him a chance to live; he is the one who twisted his life's purpose into one driven by hate."

Jean-Louis glanced at Henry and then back at Hinton. "We believe Blackburn is in London, but he does not suspect are onto his subterfuge. We could use your help. Will you work with us?"

Maintaining direct eye contact with the earl, Hinton nodded. "Yes. I want to clear my conscience. After this discussion, I fear Blackburn may try to finish what he started."

Jean-Louis nodded. "He is masquerading as a Croatian count, one we call 'the man in the red cape' and he may have other disguises. We know where the grandmother lives."

Unable to restrain herself any longer, Lady James pointed a finger at Hinton. Her hand shook. "You come here to unburden yourself, but you have *added* to our burdens! You accuse, you frighten, you conjecture. What are we to do now? How do we know, if Blackburn is still alive, that you are not his agent, sent here to create discord among us?"

Bri stood up. "I think we should bring Detective Boyd into this situation. He is the one who told us Blackburn was dead. He has access to sources we do not." She walked toward the fireplace and stared into the fire.

***

Monday, April 13, 1812 – Interior of a Hackney
Blackburn as Count Vlarić

Disguised as Count Vlarić, Blackburn asked the jervie to take him around the Mayfair area, one of London's finest neighborhoods.

Practiced in his exaggerated Croatian accent, he said, "I may want to buy property here. I've heard these streets are particularly lovely. Just drive up and down the neighborhood until I rap on the window to alert you to return me to the hotel."

The driver shrugged. "Whatever you say, sir."

When the carriage approached the earl's house, Blackburn tensed. The pace of the carriage slowed, as the driver avoided another rig, giving Blackburn more time to observe the people leaving. He recognized Sir John and Lady James. *Where is Young James?* Henry and Bri stood at the top of the stairs as their guests stepped into their carriage. *My brother and niece.* For the briefest of moments, a thought of what might have been flashed through his mind.

Around the side of the house, Blackburn saw two men come out of the side alley. They were talking as they watched the dinner guests leave. One he didn't recognize, but the other one was Jean-Louis. *That French dog. He'd slit my throat in a second or pierce my heart with a knife-toss tossed with a mere flick of this wrist.*

Hell's teeth! Blackburn closed his eyes. *I've been careless. The trapper knows all the Hackney drivers in London.*

***

Monday, April 13, 1812 – Mlle. Sabine's Brothel
Edward

Sabine entered Edward's room in the middle of the night to find him awake. "Are you ready for the broth?"

"I want more than broth! I haven't eaten real food for days."

Praetorian sat up, rigid and growled.

"According to Nashmir, your body cannot yet tolerate it. The opiate residue must be fully cleansed from your blood. Nashmir will be here for the first dosage tomorrow and you can discuss it with him. I can give you extra broth."

"Are you a nurse? Your clothing seems too fancy for that. Where am I? Is this a hotel or some private hospital?"

"Full of questions, are we?" She prepared the broth.

"Does Jean-Louis know every beautiful Frenchwoman in London?"

"I am immune to flattery." She held the cup to his mouth.

He drank it eagerly.

"I thought you didn't like it."

"I said I was hungry. It's not dreadful." His gaze was direct. "Untie my hands."

"No." Taking the cup, she walked over to the cabinet. Measuring a slightly larger dose of the herbal sleeping potion than the last one because he should not have awakened early, Sabine mixed it with more broth, went back to the bed and held the cup to his lips.

"Wait." He turned his head to the side. "Talk to me first."

"No."

A booming male voice came from the hallway. "Drink it."

Edward sighed. "Your enforcer? Are you afraid I'll attack you? With that wolf watching my every move?"

"Drink."

Cornered, Edward did as instructed and almost immediately fell back into a deep sleep.

Praetorian lay down, resuming his watch.

***

Early Tuesday, April 14, 1812 – The Streets of London
Boyd

"A jervie?" Detective Reggie Boyd looked down at the open-eyed stare of a corpse.

The cab master nodded. "He'd just finished for the night. He usually picks up from small hotels where foreigners stay."

Boyd smirked. "So he can charge more, driving them in circles."

The cab master shrugged.

"He didn't get very far." Boyd looked around the alley adjacent to the stables. He bent down to go through the man's pockets and pulled out a full week's wages. "Why wouldn't his assailant take the money?" The detective frowned. "Anything like this happen before?"

"Never. All my jervies are spooked now. Find who did this."

"Give me the names of the hotels where the cabbie usually waited for passengers. Does he have a family we should notify?"

"No. He was a quiet guy. Kept to himself."

"Then I guess he'll like it where he's going."

"How's that?"

"Coffins tend to be quiet."

***

Early Tuesday, April 14, 1812 – Lord Ravenshire's Townhouse
Henry

The door knocker alerted the butler, despite the fact that it was past midnight. He opened the door to see Detective Boyd. "Ah, Mr. Boyd. The earl is expecting you."

Thompson showed Boyd to the earl's study, where he found Jean-Louis and another man waiting with the earl. The men stood while the earl shook Boyd's hand. "Sorry to be late, but we found a jervie murdered earlier tonight."

Henry introduced the detective to Hinton.

"I got your urgent message, Lord Ravenshire. What's afoot?"

The earl leveled his gaze at the detective. "Blackburn may not be dead after all."

Boyd took a seat and leaned forward. "On what evidence?"

"Nothing concrete."

Hinton brought the detective up to date on their suppositions.

"That's it? A man in a red cape with brown eyes? An elderly woman with turquoise eyes and a Gypsy consort? An assumption that because the man's death as a baby was faked by his grandmother, he faked it again last year to fool us? We chased him that night. We saw the body fall. The wounds were the same. The clothes were his."

Henry nodded. "But the identification was not definite. We cannot be certain."

Boyd stood to leave. "Forgive me, gentlemen, but I have a murder to investigate: A real case, not an imaginary one."

Jean-Louis asked, "What happened to the jervie?"

"He was stabbed after he left work. Money left in his pocket. No family. No reason we can figure. Just unlucky."

"What's his name?"

"Donald Grimes."

"Gopher Grimes? I knew him. He liked to pick up foreign passengers from the small hotels—"

"Because they didn't know he was taking them in circles," Boyd interrupted.

Jean-Louis looked out the window.

Boyd noticed. "What is it, Jean-Louis?"

Jean-Louis turned back and looked at the detective. "I saw him last night, driving down this street." He gestured toward the front of the house. "Sir John and Lady James were leaving. The earl and Lady Gabriella were on the steps. Hinton and I were in the side alley."

"I know you have legendary skills, Jean-Louis, and that you can stalk and trap any prey. But late at night, how could you recognize a passing Hackney driver?"

"His hat. It had a musket hole in it that the gaslight shone through. He used it once for target practice in the army. Seeing his handiwork, he decided that the hat had a rakish quality to it and he kept it. Said it was his lucky hat."

"Not anymore." Boyd sat down again. "So you think that Blackburn drove by this house last night and when Jean-Louis recognized the driver, Blackburn decided to kill him?"

"He probably saw me," Jean-Louis said. "Blackburn is aware that I know most of the drivers in London."

Detective Boyd grimaced. "I'll check the hotels."

Jean-Louis said, "Try Durrants and the Holton Arms. A footpad followed the man in the red cape to both."

"A red cape is hardly a way for a dead man to remain incognito."

"A Croatian count gallivanting about the *ton*." Jean-Louis shrugged. "A testament to confidence in his disguises."

Hinton cleared his throat. "Respectfully, Detective Boyd, I think that inquiries might best be made by me. Blackburn doesn't know me. He would recognize Jean-Louis and if you were known to be asking questions, he might vanish. I can report back and we can devise a strategy to stop him."

"*Foutre!* I hate to admit it but Hinton's correct. Blackburn knows all of us. I'll see what other spies I might place in the hotel after we determine where he is."

"It would be clever to change his appearance," mused the Bow Street Runner. "It would be too brazen to come back to London without a disguise. But brown eyes? He was wounded in the left shoulder. Sometimes that affects the whole side of a body if the damage hit a nerve. He may limp now. Wigs, glasses, accents and affectations can be very effective. His right hand would be scarred. The man kills without a second thought. We must be on guard at all times. Lady Gabriella should never be alone, nor you, Lord Ravenshire, nor the Comtesse de Merbeau, Lady Wyndward or the boy."

Henry disagreed. "If he sees that we are never alone, he will know something is wrong."

"Then you must curtail your movements."

"No. Our lives must appear normal. Jean-Louis, you will stay with Bri. Hinton will report back to us as our eyes and ears."

Jean-Louis stood. "My men can blend into the shadows. Gilles can stay at Ravenshire, but I will summon Steiner here. Nambotha and Guy can protect Lady Gwyneth."

"And at Ravenshire. He might try something while we are in London. What about Edward?" Henry looked at Jean-Louis.

"I will evaluate his condition. He may be ready to go back to his house. François is up to the task, but I will add more guards."

"What's going on with Edward?" As an old schoolmate of Edward's, Boyd face registered a perplexed look. "What 'condition' needs to be evaluated?"

The earl spoke. "I would prefer that this information not leave this room. Lady Gabriella does not know. Edward is recovering from a desire to lose himself in opium."

Boyd's brow pinched with concern. "I never knew James to overindulge in anything."

Henry shrugged. "It was a shock to us all, but apparently, he had fallen under its spell years ago during his travels in the Far East."

"I will get word to Steiner and set the others to their tasks." Jean-Louis stood. "Then it will be time for me to check on James."

"I'll come with you." Boyd rose and nodded adieu to the earl.

Chérie rose to accompany them, but Jean-Louis signaled to her to stay.

She whimpered.

"Not tonight. Go to sleep."

She rejoined Hector in front of the fireplace.

***

Early Tuesday, April 14, 1812 – Mlle. Sabine's
Edward

Jean-Louis and Boyd took an indirect route to Mlle. Sabine's, taking care to be certain they was not followed. He hoped that Blackburn was overly confident. But a fresh kill signaled the man was dangerous to any and all who came into contact with him.

Silently ascending the steps to Sabine's office, Jean-Louis and Boyd reached the landing where Sabine was waiting for him. "I didn't expect to see you, Detective."

"I'm an old friend of James, Mademoiselle."

Sabine turned to Jean-Louis. "He's waking up earlier and earlier. I gave him some of the extra potion the Nashmir made up, but I was hoping you would be early just in case. He seems better."

"The situation has changed. For your safety and his, I am moving him today. Is your man about?"

"Yes." Pierre emerged from the office.

Jean-Louis led the way up to Edward's attic room.

Edward was awake. "A full contingent." His eyes focused on the Bow Street Runner. "Boyd?"

"I'll help however I can, James, but danger is afoot."

Jean-Louis took charge. "James, unforeseen events suggest we are all in danger. I am taking you elsewhere to hide you until you are well." He untied the bonds. "Can you stand?"

Edward tried, but was unsteady.

"It may take awhile, but your strength will return. Drink the broth now. We must make haste."

Edward did as he was told.

Jean-Louis and Pierre lifted Edward and helped him down the stairs.

As they reached the lowest level, Edward was out of breath. Before they were out the door, he turned to Sabine, and said, "I am indebted to you, Mademoiselle. Thank you."

"*De rien*, Mr. James. Take care."

Jean-Louis loaded Edward inside the carriage with Boyd and closed the door. He leapt up to the driver's perch.

Edward stared at Boyd. "What is going on?"

"In all probability, Blackburn is not dead. We believe he is in London to finish the murder spree he began last year. No one is safe."

CHAPTER SEVENTY-FIVE

Early Tuesday, April 14, 1812 – Interior of a Hackney
Edward

Despite bouts of vertigo as the carriage wheels rolled over uneven cobblestone streets under foggy moonlight, Edward's mind focused on Blackburn. *Bri is in danger.* He shuddered to think about what might happen this time.

"The depraved blackguard might kill her. We must turn his drive for revenge against him. He believes his intellect is superior to ours."

Boyd nodded. "Arrogance is a flaw that has undone many men."

Before he could comment, Edward passed out.

***

Early Tuesday, April 14, 1812 – Lord Ravenshire's London Stables
Jean-Louis

The acrid odor of smelling salts revived Edward. Jean-Louis and Nashmir helped the incapacitated banker stumble toward the stables.

"Where are you taking me?"

"To safety." Jean-Louis led them to a small stable room that was used for storage. Behind miscellaneous equipment, a screen hid a bed. They placed him on the mattress.

Nashmir felt Edward's forehead and cheeks. "The fever remains elevated, but it is slight. You appear to be on the mend, Mr. James."

James reached up to grab Nashmir's arm. "I want to help."

Jean-Louis shook his head. "In your current state, you would impede us. Sleep, take the medicine, and we will evaluate your condition tomorrow. Lady Penelope's wedding is in a little more than a week. We want to keep you in hiding until then. In the meantime, we will track Blackburn and try to discern his plan. The element of surprise is on our side, but the man is the devil's spawn. We must be prepared for anything. No one is safe."

"You said that before." Edward tried to rise up on one elbow, but fell backward.

"And I'll say it a hundred times more until Blackburn is dead. Drink."

Edward drank as instructed. He quickly fell into a deep sleep.

Jean-Louis turned to Nashmir. "I will stay with him until morning. Tell Steiner to knock on the door when the clock strikes seven tomorrow morning."

"That's only a few hours from now."

"It is enough." Closing the door, Jean-Louis set make-shift bolts in place, sat down on the floor next to the bed, and willed himself to sleep.

***

Wednesday, April 15, 1812 – Lord Ravenshire's Townhouse
Bri

Bri came down for breakfast and confronted a house full of strange men, guards hired by Jean-Louis and security staff selected by Boyd to protect their family. An equal crew had been dispatched to Ravenshire to protect Aelwyn and Ian.

Despite the disruptions, Bri insisted on leaving after breakfast. "Father, I need to talk to Aunt Gwyneth."

The voice of Jean-Louis settled the question. "Lady Gwyneth is also well guarded. I will take you." Turning to the earl, he said, "Steiner will be your driver today."

Henry agreed. "I am reluctant, but we must not give Blackburn any reason to believe we have altered our normal patterns. But as Jean-Louis has warned, 'No one is safe'. Therefore, from now on, none of us should be alone."

***

Wednesday, April 15, 1812 – *Omelettes de Mme. d'Aix* Blackburn as di Lucca

Miss Li and a gray-haired gentleman, whose locks touched his shoulders, walked into *Omelettes de Mme. d'Aix* for breakfast, and were shown to a prominent table in the intimate café that had rapidly become a favored meeting place of the women who controlled Society. The man's closer-cropped beard obscured his jaw line.

Looking down at the table, Xie Xie whispered, "I think this is highly risky."

Blackburn ignored her concern. "Nonsense. Everyone thinks I am dead. I bear no resemblance to my former self."

The server, wearing the traditional costume of Provence, greeted them and placed the *menu du jour* on the table. "We have a selection of teas listed on the reverse side."

Xie Xie and Blackburn chose their preferences and looked over the menu after the server left to brew the tea. "I've developed a taste for the spicier food of the Orient. This bland continental fare no longer suits my palate."

"Aneira generally comes around to meet patrons near the end of the meal. Is she expecting you?"

"Not in this guise. Let's see whether she recognizes me. If not, no one will." His eyes bored into hers. "You question my judgment." His voice had lowered so that it was barely audible.

"Forgive me, master. I know how important your goals are. I am not as experienced in this culture as are you. Perhaps I overestimate your enemies."

Blackburn's lip twisted into a pernicious curl. "I thought *my* goals and *my* enemies were *our* goals and *our* enemies." *Could my most valuable creation be moving away from me? The slave rebelling against the master? Her usefulness may be waning.* For a moment, a shadow of doubt came over Blackburn. *My planning is meticulous. Have I forgotten something?*

The server brought the tea and the confrontational moment passed. They ordered their omelets. *For the moment, Xie Xie, you are safe. But once a doubt is sown, it rarely stagnates. It sprouts.*

After the server left, she answered. "Of course I mean *our*. I have infiltrated their web to unravel it, as you requested."

"As I *instructed*. It was never a request." *Things have changed since Alexandria. Is she wavering?* "I saw my dear brother and niece Monday night."

Xie Xie's shoulders tensed involuntarily. "Did they see you?"

"You flinched. Again, you underestimate me."

"Forgive me, master. Your safety is my paramount concern. It is but my love for you that weakens me."

"Your weakness may be our downfall. Either control your impulses or return to Egypt." *Will she betray me?*

Xie Xie sat in silence, with bowed head.

Blackburn ignored her and ate his meal. Taking a brioche from the basket, he bit into it. "Ah, these brioches are Grandmother's finest concoction. A mere bite elicits fond memories of her baking them for me as a child. Part of me rather hates that she has shared this treat with others. It should be reserved for me alone."

Indicating with an inclination of her head that Aneira had entered the café, Xie Xie continued to eat in silence.

Aneira came to their table. "Miss Li, who is your distinguished friend?"

"Mme. d'Aix, this is Sig. di Lucca, newly arrived in London. He is an investor in my family's companies."

Di Lucca stood, clicked his heels together, and took the hand of the proprietress and kissed it with a flourish. Everyone in the room turned to look at the display of continental flair.

Aneira played her part, appearing flattered. Her face flushed and she bowed her head to him in thanks. "Please sit, Sig. di Lucca. I hope that you enjoyed your meal."

"Wonderful! The peppers in the omelet were particularly piquant. And the brioches reminded me of those I ate as a child. I never thought to taste such delights again."

The proprietress smiled. "The brioches are my specialty. I'm so glad you enjoyed them." She moved on to the next table.

"She didn't appear to recognize you."

"You need to hone your observation skills. Her hand remained in mine too long for a stranger." After finishing their meal, Xie Xie and Blackburn left the café and waved down a Hackney.

Blackburn looked up at the weathered face of the driver and gave him their destination. "Musée de Merbeau."

Inside the carriage, Xie Xie asked, "Not to Durrants? Why the museum?"

Blackburn whispered in her ear so that the jervie could not hear. "Why not see the collection and gallery of the Comtesse de Merbeau, my sister? I sailed with her and her husband in the early years. Lady Gwyneth is a lovely woman, past childbearing age now and no longer a threat to me. And Gio has a permanent exhibition there. Did you know he began my portrait? It remains unfinished, due to my untimely death." His laugh echoed in the silence.

Adopting his *sotto voce*, Xie Xie spoke. "Master, my spies have not been able to discover the whereabouts of James. However, his absence may accomplish our goal of dividing him and Lady Gabriella without further action on our parts."

Blackburn mused as he looked out the window. "Perhaps I should revert to my original plan."

"Master?"

Another whisper followed. "Marry Lady Gabriella and secure my revenge through our children."

Softly, she questioned him. "The risk of discovery," she modified herself as she spoke, "is mitigated by your changed appearance, but she is a strong-willed young woman, highly intelligent, and independent-minded. She may not want to marry."

In a more normal tone of voice, Blackburn mused, "Society will dictate what she does. Even her father wishes her to marry. He told me that years ago. He prefers that it be her choice, but in the end, the needs of the family must prevail."

"What if he—the earl—were to marry again? Wouldn't any children of that union—"

Blackburn dismissed her concern with a wave of his hand. He leaned in to speak into her ear. "As soon as I have an heir with Lady Gabriella, Henry will gladly cede precedence and chase after his island woman or marry Charlotte. I can't see him with a debutante."

"And what of the boy? The one that was recently revealed?"

"My son will be the designated heir." He shrugged. "As for the other...many children die before reaching their majority."

"You sound as if this marriage is more than a passing thought, master."

"We'll see. I have many paths to victory."

They arrived at the museum. Blackburn exited the carriage, tossed payment to the driver, and said, "Take Miss Li to Durrants." He turned on his heel and walked toward the museum.

***

Hinton

As the driver waited to pull into traffic, Xie Xie rapped on the door of the carriage. "Take me back to the café."

Hinton smiled. Jean-Louis had been right. Masquerading as a jervie, he overhead the entire conversation, despite their attempts to speak softly. *Di Lucca, this phony merchant, is Blackburn. It all fits. Now we can set the trap.*

***

Wednesday, April 15, 1812 – *Omelettes de Mme. d'Aix*
Aneira

Aneira was surprised when her messenger boy appeared in the café. He whispered in her ear, "Miss Li is waiting for you upstairs."

She finished her conversation with the host and went upstairs to her rooms above the café. Xie Xie was pacing in front of the window. "What's wrong?"

"I am here to ask for guidance. All my training from The Pharaoh has emphasized strategy, subterfuge and secrecy, all planned with consideration given to the most minute detail. Something is wrong. He has always said, 'No one is invincible; all have weaknesses for us to exploit.' Now I fear he is taking ill-advised risks."

The older woman nodded. "Like his visit here today?"

Xie Xie nodded.

Aneira gestured for her to take a seat before continuing.

"And to the Musée de Merbeau after we left here. And now," Xie Xie breathed deeply, "he is seriously considering reverting to his earlier scheme to marry Lady Gabriella to father an heir to Ravenshire."

"That was last year's plan." Aneira sat forward in her chair. "Breaking up James and Lady Gabriella is working. Commercial dealings to damage the trading company are underway. He is disrupting his own design for destruction of the Wyndwards."

Clasping and unclasping her hands, Xie Xie continued, "Ever since I have known him, The Pharaoh has always been careful, precise, patient and single-minded in pursuit of his goals. He planned revenge against the Wyndwards for years before it failed last year.

"Instead of adhering to his principal caution—that unforeseen circumstances can destroy any well-plotted scheme—he seems now to believe that his disguises give him immunity to identification. He perfected the use of his left hand to deflect any connection to his former self, takes potions to darken his irises, and exaggerates the limp to imply infirmity. He believes he can move freely among those who knew him as Blackburn for twenty years.

"He appears to be playing a game rather than executing his meticulously crafted war plan. He always told me that one must master the details to achieve one's goals.

"But now, glee has supplanted focus. But, Madame, this game is a deadly one. Today, I began to fear that he has been seduced by his own rhetoric. Victory was supposed to be measured by financial ruin for the Wyndward family, destruction of James by opium, shame and spinsterhood for Lady Gabriella.

"She is no shy flower. A piercing intellect and keen intuition define her. The financial fall of Ravenshire was the linchpin of The Pharaoh's strategy after last year's failed effort. Now it has faded behind the renewed fantasy of courting Lady Gabriella."

Silent as she considered Xie Xie's news, Aneira finally spoke. "How much of your doubt have you revealed?"

"I suggested some of this might be risky and he accused me of disloyalty for questioning his choices when his success is my most fervent desire."

"He must never know you came to me. It could mean your death. I set my grandson on this path, but men, as you know, can be easily deluded by their sense of self-importance. I cannot rein him in as I could in earlier years. I got my revenge against the 10th Earl—he died by my hand. The destruction of their wealth was my next goal. Duff siphoned off a portion of their fortune and has built it up to be substantial in its own right. I inspired his revenge, but I can no longer shape it. "

"Madame, I fear he underestimates the Wyndwards. If they knew he lived, the power they could wield is prodigious. The Pharaoh killed members of their family. Their desire for revenge is no less than his."

"The time is nigh for you to disappear. Do not come here again."

After Xie Xie left, Aneira became lost in thought. *Could he betray me? It's folly to imagine he can fool the Wyndwards for long. He was furious with me about the failed Summerfest assassination. Has he turned against me?*

***

Wednesday, April 15, 1812 – The Holton Arms Holton
Blackburn as a Cockney Cut-Purse

After donning his disguise as the Cockney cut purse, Blackburn left his hotel and walked the neighborhood, depending on his highly attuned senses to alert him to danger. His mind wandered to Lady Gabriella. *Xie Xie is jealous.*

His slightly upturned lips gradually turned downward into a frown. *She questioned my judgment. 'Tis not a good sign when the student doubts the teacher.*

A beggar boy bumped into the cut-purse's bad leg, catching him off guard.

Before speaking, he regained his composure, shouting in a Cockney accent. Watch out, boy!"

The miscreant scampered out of sight.

As The Pharaoh, no one would have dared approach me.

His mind returned to his grandmother. *She likes the restaurant too much. She has become too visible. Her carelessness threatens my goals.*

And Xie Xie doubts me. She could thwart my plans. The Wyndwards must fall under my spell. I can wait no longer. The time to act is now.

***

Wednesday, April 15, 1812 – The Holton Arms Hotel
Hinton

The stable boy had played his part well, distracting the Cockney-accented man. Hinton had been waiting across the street from one of the two hotels they suspected Blackburn of using. Knowing that Blackburn specialized in the art of disguise, Hinton's senses were alerted when a shabbily dressed man left the hotel. His clothing seemed out of place in this part of London without a pushcart or a tradesman's wagon.

Hinton sent the boy on his errand.

Observing the man's reactions, Hinton smiled.

The targeted man stood up straight, revealing his true height. His feigned mannerisms fell away, as expected. The limp was there, but not as pronounced in the immediate aftermath of being thrown off by the boy's action until he deliberately bent down and exaggerated his difficulty walking. Because the man blended into the crowds, only a tracker as experienced as Hinton could follow him. *I haven't lost my skills.*

After about a mile, Blackburn stopped at a pub that catered to the working class.

Following his instincts, Hinton walked around to the alley behind the pub. After a few minutes, he saw the man exit. He smiled. *Keep trying.* He followed the man over a circuitous route that finally ended at another hotel.

Hinton walked into the hotel just as his prey turned the corner on the first landing of the stairs and enter a room.

The former soldier went back downstairs and found the carriage door. He flagged a Hackney.

"Do you know the Frenchman?"

"Of course."

"Tell him to meet the old banker's soldier here." He pushed some coins into the man's hand.

Jean-Louis will send two men to watch this hotel and a third to follow Blackburn.

***

Wednesday, April 15, 1812 – Interior of a Hackney
Xie Xie

As she rode away from the café, Xie Xie wondered if she had hastened her death at the hand of The Pharaoh. *Can I trust Aneira? Is she really on my side? She has killed too. Am I a fool?*

It's time. I cannot wait another day.

She didn't notice a tracker following her on horseback.

***

Wednesday, April 15, 1812 – Lady Gwyneth's Townhouse
Gwyneth

Arriving at her aunt's home, Bri saw more footmen than usual.

Nambotha opened the door.

"New footmen?" Bri's concern was evident on her face.

"For the protection of your aunt, Miss Bri. She awaits you in the Music Room."

Before Nambotha closed the doors to the Music Room, he said, "Tea will be served momentarily, milady."

Bri sat down on the settee. "We are like prisoners."

Gwyneth nodded. "But we must behave as usual, and believe that these guards will keep us safe. Have you shot a pistol lately?"

"Yes, the last time I was at Ravenshire, Gilles took me out with Orion to demonstrate his skill. But we must be frank. No one can be prepared for an attack at all times. The pistol would have to be loaded, close at hand, and I would have to have time to reach it. In the manner that Blackburn seized me last year, it would have made no difference.

"Edward is knowledgeable in the Asian fighting arts, and he and Nashmir taught me a few defensive movements. I think that would be more effective for me." She raised her hand to her forehead and ran her fingers through her hair. "I just don't know what to think or do anymore. Edward is in Scotland, Lady Penelope's wedding is coming up, and I don't know if I love Edward, or hate him, or just don't want to be married."

"The dark reality is that Ian might be Blackburn's target now. He is without remorse. A child's life is naught to him."

A knock on the door signaled that the tea had arrived. They sat in silence while Nambotha poured.

Until the servant left, Gwyneth looked out at the window. The rose bush on the window sill showed buds ready to bloom. "I want to visit Ravenshire this week. Would you like to come with me? Blackburn can't be both in London *and* at Ravenshire."

"As long as I'm back for Lady Penelope's pre-wedding parties, which sounds like a welcome respite from the tension in London," said Bri, "I'd like to walk around the village and feel normal again."

"And I will bring my books to finalize the text and design the order of the etchings." She rang the butler's bell.

Nambotha appeared.

"We are going to Ravenshire. Ask my maid to pack enough for a few days. Send a runner to the earl's to get some clothes for Lady Gabriella, and please ask Jean-Louis to come in. We want to speak to him."

The butler left and shortly afterward, Jean-Louis appeared.

"We want to go to Ravenshire for a few days. Guy and Nambotha will accompany us. The earl will remain behind with Steiner and Hinton."

Jean-Louis agreed. "You'll both be safer at Ravenshire. Nashmir should come as well. I'll have him follow us in another carriage with a few other men."

Gwyneth waved her hand. "Whatever you suggest. Ask Nambotha to send in Felicity."

Jean-Louis nodded. "Be ready to leave in about an hour."

When Felicity appeared, Gwyneth said, "Pack a basket of meat, bread, cheese and wine. We will eat on the way to Ravenshire.

"And pack up my rose bush in a box. I like having it with me." She heard a rustle in the leaves and smiled. *Petal will like seeing Ravenshire in the springtime.*

***

Jean-Louis

Jean-Louis sent a stableman to ride to the earl's townhouse with one note for Nashmir and another for the earl.

He pulled Nambotha aside. "After we load the carriages, I will ride to Ravenshire to ready the property. I can get there faster on a horse. You and Guy will drive." *This will give me a chance to alert the sheriff, reinforce the Ravenshire guard contingent, and shore up defenses.*

After selecting the men to accompany the carriages to Ravenshire, Jean-Louis instructed the remaining guards as to their duties in his absence. *Steiner and Hinton can surveil the London base. I must protect Bri and Lady Gwyneth.*

***

Wednesday, April 15, 1812 – Interior of a Hackney
Blackburn as the Cockney Cut-Purse

Before returning to The Holton Arms, Blackburn took a Hackney to Berkeley Crescent where Lady Gwyneth lived. He recognized Jean-Louis loading bags into the comtesse's carriage. *They must be going to Ravenshire.*

He smiled. *This will be an interesting opportunity to test the strength of my disguise.*

CHAPTER SEVENTY-SIX

Wednesday, April 15, 1812 – The Streets of London
Hinton

Threshe earl had given Hinton authority to search out Blackburn. Drawing on his past army training, Hinton set up primary and back up teams, while Steiner guarded the earl.

When Hinton had been introduced to Steiner, the Prussian minced no words. "I am by nature a distrustful man, Hinton. Prove yourself."

While Steiner knew many of the cabbie contacts Jean-Louis used, he did not know all of them, but added a few of his own to the network of watchers. One team was set on Miss Li while others were stationed near each of the two hotels they had confirmed that Blackburn was using. A third team was available to track a disguised Blackburn if he left either of the hotels. Knowing that his affinity for evasive maneuvers could lead them astray, multiple trackers were employed. Cabbies were alerted and ready to report any passengers they suspected might be Blackburn. Because Miss Li had been seen entering the café run by Mme. d'Aix, they stationed a team there and intended to place a server or cook in the employ of Mme. d'Aix.

Lash followed Mirela whenever she left Aneira's flat. Still another team staked out *Dreamtime*. Steiner stayed with the earl at all times, while Hinton rode between teams for constant surveillance updates.

The plan entailed teams working around the clock. Steiner would sleep from midnight to four. Hinton from four in the morning until eight.

Hinton at on a perch on a Hackney as he drove Blackburn, in a new disguise, to Lady Gwyneth's street and then back to the rear entrance of The Holton Arms. Blackburn exited the carriage and entered the hotel.

Once Hinton was certain that Blackburn was inside, he signaled to one of his men. "Tell Steiner I think they are headed to Ravenshire. I'll trail the Asian woman and be back shortly."

***

Wednesday, April 15, 1812 – The Holton Arms Hotel
Blackburn as di Lucca

Once back in his suite of rooms, Blackburn shed his identity as the Cockney cut-purse became di Lucca again. He outfitted Zagor in black clothing and tested a mask. He handed him pistols, secured on a belt. Wearing a greatcoat, the pistols could not be seen.

Zagor fidgeted, visibly nervous.

"Don't worry; you'll not be hurt. It's all part of my plan."

The persona of the count in the red cape is too flamboyant. This disguise will fool them.

***

Lord Ravenshire's London Stables
Steiner

The Prussian walked into the stables to find Jeffries, a stableman from Ravenshire who ferried horses back and forth between London and Ravenshire as needed. The former cavalryman was a trusted hand.

"Jeffries," Hans lowered his voice, "I have a special assignment for you. Lady Gabriella and Lady Gwyneth are going to Ravenshire. Head out there yourself, with a groom or two, just in case you need to provide extra protection. The roads to Ravenshire are not yet rid of highwaymen. Once at Ravenshire, let Jean-Louis instruct you whether to stay or return here."

Jeffries nodded. "I'll get the men saddled up and we'll be off within the half hour. The cavalry will ride to the rescue, as usual."

Steiner turned to leave, but thought better of it. "Jeffries, you and your men should arm yourselves well."

The stableman gestured in a half-salute. "We always do, *Oberleutnant* Steiner. The enemy is *überall.*"

"This is no time for mocking. The enemy *is* everywhere. No one is safe. Not you, not me. Be mindful."

"Forgive me, Herr Steiner. Black humor is my way. I'll fulfill my duty."

"I expect no less."

***

Exterior of Lady Gwyneth's Townhouse
Jean-Louis

Bri and Gwyneth were in the de Merbeau carriage. Guy sat in the driver's perch. Two footmen rode on the back of the carriage and one of the Merbeau stablemen accompanying them on horseback.

Dana and Isabella, Lady Gwyneth's maid, climbed into the second carriage with Nashmir, with Nambotha driving. Jean-Louis had drafted another de Merbeau stableman as well as one of his Ravenshire men to ride along the second carriage. The back of this carriage was loaded with footmen rather than luggage.

A Hackney waited across the street.

Before leaving to ride ahead, Jean-Louis walked over to the second carriage and opened the door. "Ladies, there will be another guest. Under no circumstances are you to reveal the identity of this person to Lady Gabriella or Lady Gwyneth. Is that clear?"

The tone of his voice was unmistakable.

They nodded in silence.

Jean-Louis turned to Nashmir. "After I depart, Guy will leave. When he is out of sight, the driver," he indicated the jervie with an inclination of his head, "will help you transfer the passenger from the Hackney to this carriage." He shoved a leather bag onto the floor. "I trust you ladies know how to shoot?"

Dana and Isabella gasped. They shook their heads, speechless.

He opened the bag and took out one of the pistols. "It's easy enough. They're already loaded, so be careful. If you're attacked,

714

you'll learn fast. Just point and pull the trigger."

He fastened the flap on the bag, closed the door, and then opened it again.

"And don't miss."

***

On the Road to Ravenshire

Zagor

Zagor rode alongside his master, the late afternoon sun in his eyes, afraid to speak but unable to stop himself. "How can you be sure they're on this road?"

"I'm not. But it's more likely than not that they are going to Ravenshire."

"Master, what and where is this Ravenshire you speak of?" The servant was from Croatia, and while he spoke English quite well, he was unfamiliar with Britain.

"Ah, Ravenshire. What is Ravenshire? My birthright, Zagor."

"Birthright, master?"

Blackburn answered in a clipped tone. "We'll be there in four or five hours."

"Why—"

"Ask no more questions or you will suffer my wrath."

Sweat trickled down Zagor's face.

They resumed their pace as a soft rain began to fall. The rutted road was dangerous for the horses, so they rode along the side where the wheels from carriages and wagons had not carved uneven pathways.

"Odd." Blackburn, disguised as di Lucca, looked behind them. "The roads are lightly traveled today. So much the better. Recite your instructions. Now."

The Croatian began, "When we see a carriage, I will ride by to confirm the passengers, then wait up ahead. If it is not the right carriage, we will continue to ride until we find it. When I can identify the carriage, I will wait for you. When you reach me, we will ride ahead through the woods until we see a good place for an ambush. I will shoot one pistol into the air to stop the carriage, hold the other to rob the passengers, and then you will come to stop me, retrieve their purses and save the ladies."

"Correct. Now this is important. Your pistols and mine are loaded only with false balls that will make a loud noise, but not kill. We are expecting the passengers to comply without your needing to shoot."

"Expecting? What if *they* shoot?"

"Duck."

He laughed at the look of terror on Zagor's face. "Don't worry. Most men can't shoot very well. Pistols are notoriously unreliable."

They rode on in silence until they spotted a carriage ahead.

Zagor rode faster, passed the carriage, and rode into the trees.

When Blackburn reached him, he waited for Zagor's report.

"A single elderly gentleman."

"Let's move ahead. We have the advantage of speed."

They passed two more carriages without the passengers they sought.

They came upon another and Zagor performed his task and retreated to the woods.

"There were two women as well as an Asian man and someone else, a figure I could not make out. The carriage was driven by a huge man, black as iron."

"Nambotha, an African. The earl's carriage must be ahead. We'll ride through the trees until we are ahead of them by half a mile."

They passed the carriage driven by Nambotha, and rode for quite awhile until they saw the earl's carriage ahead. They spurred their horses to increase the pace. When they were comfortably ahead, Zagor stopped.

When the first carriage came into view, the merchant nodded at Zagor to attack. Riding toward the carriage, Zagor shot one pistol into the air while he held the other pointed at the carriage driver. "Stop."

Guy reined in the horses, calmed Chérie, and shouted to the other men, "Do as he says. Make no move."

Climbing down from the driver's perch, he asked, "What do you want?"

"Money, of course. Empty their pockets." He waved toward the passengers.

The driver opened the door slightly, saying loudly enough for the brigand to hear, "Hurry, give me your purses."

The passengers complied.

As the driver walked over to the highwayman and handed him the purses, the second carriage approached, a black man driving.

Zagor hesitated, and then heard a voice shouting from behind, in a Continental accent. "Stop, thief! Drop your pistol!" The rider fired a shot that barely missed the robber.

Zagor, the faux-highwayman, froze in fear for a moment, and then turned and fled.

The Italian-accented shooter followed in hot pursuit.

Mounted escorts that had been trailing the second carriage closed in on the shooter.

Zagor looked back at his pursuers and saw that the driver had drawn a pistol. The footmen were moving toward the door to protect the occupants.

A bullet knocked Zagor off his horse.

***

Blackburn as di Lucca

Di Lucca reined in his horse a few paces ahead, jumped off, and then ran toward the man he had wounded just as the mounted escort arrived.

The highwayman was bleeding. His eyes were out of focus but then he looked at the man who had shot him and started to talk, "Mas—"

A shot to the head silenced him. The gunman reached down and retrieved the purses from the dead man's pocket. He handed them to the mounted escort, a triumphant look on his face.

Guy, the lead driver reached the scene and leveled his gaze at the man before him. "Are you familiar with English highwaymen, sir?"

"No, I am out for an afternoon's ride to see the countryside. I left Dubrovnik when the French arrived. My family comes from the Principality of Lucca in Italy. I am still learning English ways."

"First lesson: highwaymen work in pairs, at a minimum. More likely, a gang. Second lesson: passengers carry false purses for just such purposes. Experienced highwaymen know that. The reason we didn't resist is because the brigand was clearly a novice thief. Third lesson: never kill unless you must, and then only after you know with whom you are dealing."

The man appeared offended. "See here! I thought I was saving you from harm!"

"Yes, you *thought* so. But you were wrong."

A voice from the carriage contradicted the driver. "Guy, this man tried to save us! You are being quite rude." Turning to the man, who was still holding the pistol that had killed the highwayman, Bri asked, "Who are you, sir?"

The man removed his wide-brimmed hat with a flourish. "I am Sig. Dragan di Lucca. My father was Italian, my mother Croatian. I am a dealer in fine olive oil, at your service."

"Very pleased to make your acquaintance, sir. I am Lady Gabriella Wyndward. Please accept my invitation to dine with us tonight at Ravenshire. You can follow alongside our carriage. The old Ravenshire Castle is visible from the road after you pass through the village. It's another two hours from here."

"You honor me, Lady Gabriella." He trilled the "r's" in her name as he spoke. "I would be delighted." The merchant bowed, and remounted his horse. *This disguise is better than I imagined.* He glanced at Guy, a man he knew to be trained by Jean-Louis. The driver's face was unreadable. *I know you're watching me.*

***

Bri

Closing the window inside the carriage, Bri was unprepared for the approbation of her aunt.

"How could you invite a stranger to stay at Ravenshire when we are all in danger? Are you mad?" Gwyneth leaned forward to press her point.

"Aunt Gwyneth, Sig. di Lucca bravely fought the highwayman. Guy lectured him as if he were an ignorant schoolboy. It was the height of rudeness."

"I have learned, through bitter experience, neither to jump to conclusions, nor to take first impressions as fact. Last year, Blackburn nearly raped and killed you. He wounded Edward and almost killed Jean-Louis. You must learn to heed advice. Strangers must earn trust, not be accorded unlimited deference. You are far too headstrong for your own good." Gwyneth sat back in frustration.

The second coach pulled up alongside.

Looking out the window, Gwyneth continued. "Nambotha has arrived. Our 'incident' allowed him time to catch up. At least we have safety in numbers."

Bri closed her eyes for a moment to restrain herself from mounting a defense. "I'm sorry, Aunt Gwyneth. I feel safe with Guy and Nambotha. Perhaps I acted impulsively."

"Perhaps? Do you not comprehend the danger we face? Until Blackburn is dead, we are all at risk. Any stranger is to be distrusted. You may have invited the wolf into a pen of lambs."

"Or the fox into the henhouse. I understand."

"No, clearly, you do *not*. All of these men are risking their lives for us. You have now made their task more difficult. I am too old to have children; you and Ian are our only hopes for the future."

Bri's anger exploded in a staccato barrage. "No! I *refuse* to be categorized as a brood mare!" She turned her head away from her aunt and stared out the window.

Neither woman spoke for the next two hours until they arrived at Ravenshire.

***

Guy

Jean-Louis had driven home to Guy the necessity of maintaining a perpetual state of alertness. His senses were attuned to anomalies. Anomalies such as a lone, inexperienced highwayman, a "savior" arriving at the precise moment of danger, the convenient elimination of the highwayman who might have recognized his executioner in the moment preceding his death. *If I were going to arrange a false rescue, I would concoct something similar. No loose ends. Too convenient.*

The driver's peripheral vision kept the Italian merchant in sight.

The stranger sat a horse well. Although he had shot the highwayman with his left hand, he seemed to guide the horse with his right, unconsciously. Blackburn was right-handed. *An easy disguise would be to switch hands.* His shot had been at very close range, easier to control than at a long distance. The Italian had brown eyes, but Blackburn's were blue, an unusual aqua color. *I've never heard that anyone could change his eye color. I've only seen Blackburn at a distance. Jean-*

Louis will sense his identity.

***

Wednesday, April 15, 1812 – The Streets of London
Hinton

Everyone was on edge. With Lady Gabriella and Lady Gwyneth on the way to Ravenshire, the only person to protect was the earl, which freed up teams to focus on their prey rather than protection.

Hinton had arrived to reconnoiter with the team watching Miss Li's hotel when a veiled woman, approximately the same build as Miss Li, exited and hailed a Hackney cab driven by one of their informants. Shortly afterward, Miss Li herself came out of the hotel with a small satchel and walked by the shops lining the street, stopping periodically to look in the windows. She went into an apothecary shop and stayed for a while. Two watchers followed. Hinton on horseback and a woman on foot. The woman tracker followed Miss Li inside and overheard her purchasing some medicine to induce sleep.

Leaving the apothecary, Miss Li went in to a children's clothing store and emerged with a package wrapped with twine for ease of carrying. She flagged down a Hackney, driven by another one of their informants. The woman tracker continued to walk while the mounted watcher followed the Hackney. It stopped at a bank, and Miss Li instructed the driver to wait, handing him partial payment to induce him to stay.

The watcher dismounted, and walked into the bank. Inside, he saw Miss Li sitting with a clerk, handing him a piece of paper. The watcher got close enough to overhear the conversation.

"Yes, a letter of credit will suffice, along with the currency noted on my request."

The clerk stood to fulfill her request. When he returned, he held documents in his hand along with a bulky envelope. He handed her a piece of paper to read. When the watcher tried to get closer, another clerk approached him, "May I help you, sir?"

Hinton, the watcher, shook his head in indignation. "Do you know how long I have been standing here? The service in this establishment is abominable!" He turned and walked outside. He mounted his horse and, after giving a silent signal to the Hackney driver, continued along the street until he reached an alley where he could watch and wait.

When Miss Li exited the bank, she directed the Hackney driver to go to the docks.

The watcher raised an eyebrow. Women rarely frequented that area alone. She stopped at the ticket bureau and again asked the cabbie to wait. Once she was inside, the watcher said, "Extra money for you to find out where she's going. Any friends inside?"

The cabbie nodded and tipped his cap. "I'll get it for you guv'nor, don't you worry none. J-L always does right by me. I'll circle back later and find you at the lady's hotel."

The watcher nodded and rode farther down the block, turned and watched from a distance.

***

Wednesday, April 15, 1812 – The Streets of London
Xie Xie

Xie Xie Li left a wigmaker's shop in a run-down part of London that catered to the demi-monde. Gripping her package, she shoved her way through the fast-moving stream of people in the busy shopping sector. She hailed a Hackney, and donned her disguise inside the cab as the driver navigated the narrow streets of the city until they reached the docks. When she exited, she appeared to be an elderly, slightly bent woman. She signaled to the jervie to take her bags down and wait for her return.

She entered the departure ticket office, where a bell hooked over the hinges signaled her entry. A chalkboard listed the departure times and destinations of ships. While she would have preferred Paris, Napoleon's wars blocked that future. Besides, she knew she must travel farther than France to escape The Pharaoh's reach. *Someday I'll see Paris again.*

XieXie's innate self-control prevented her eyes or actions from betray her wistful thoughts. She tightly held the ticket to Boston in her hand. She checked to see that her ship was leaving on time, and then went out to the docks to await boarding.

When she'd bought her ticket on an earlier visit to the area, the clerk had laughed at her initial inquiry. "Depends on what you mean by 'first class', missy. A mail ship with a few cabins ain't no palace. Can't count on white glove service."

"The best available, then. It's for my grandmother. My uncle awaits her arrival in Boston."

***

Wednesday, April 15, 1812 – The London Docks
The Jervie

The jervie watched the Asian woman and shook his head in admiration. *She has adopted a disguise, doing as Jean-Louis predicted.*

His gut clenched. *She is walking toward me. Was I wrong? Is she not boarding?*

Looking up toward him in his perch, Xie Xie handed him a letter. "Give this to Jean-Louis."

Stunned, the jervie said nothing.

***

Wednesday, April 15, 1812 – *Omelettes de Mme. d'Aix*
Aneira

Is Duff unbalanced? Ever since her grandson had recklessly returned to London from Alexandria, convinced that his mastery of disguise could fool anyone who had known him as Blackburn, Aneira had been preoccupied with his true purpose. *He is obsessed with the illusion that he can marry Lady Gabriella and seize his birthright through their to-be-born child. His judgment is clouded.* He was no longer the meticulous planner she had raised. The deliberative, strategic thinker was gone. *Duff has become lost in the web of his own threads of conspiracy and revenge.*

Vengeance had taken hold of her soul long ago. *Will Duff's arrogance destroy my best chance to inflict the final blow to the Wyndwards?*

Mirela interrupted her friend's thoughts. "All Wyndwards may not die. I seeing Lady Gabriella and touched her. I feeling long life."

"Then maybe Duff's plan will work. Surely she could not escape the fate I have decreed for her."

An uneasy feeling came over Aneira. *My grandson, my disciple, my life's work, rebels at my efforts to control him. He plots his own course. Is the inconceivable possible?* A chill ran through her. *The distance of the last year has stretched the bond between us beyond repair. The end has come.*

"Mirela!" The café was empty and Mirela was upstairs in their flat. The Gypsy appeared at the top of the stairs.

"Send more of your Roma to Ravenshire. Duff is there. All Wyndwards must die."

"But Duff is a Wyndward."

"*All* Wyndwards must die."

Mirela did not argue. She trudged down the stairs, went out to the street, and hailed a Hackney to find Vano and Lash.

***

Wednesday, April 15, 1812 – The London Docks

Xie Xie

An elderly Asian woman with a cane hobbled over the unevenly paved dockside, holding a ticket in her hand. When she reached the gangplank, the First Officer reviewed her ticket, and welcomed her. "Mrs. Li, welcome to the Royal Mail *H.M.S. Queen Anne.* The porter will take your luggage."

The uniformed porter placed her trunk and valises on a portable hand truck and extended his hand, indicating she should precede him up the ramp. She stepped slowly, deliberately and stopped a few times to catch her breath. Reaching the deck, she moved to the side until the porter had ascended, then she followed him to her room.

The room was compact, but satisfactory. The porter placed her trunk and valises in the corner and explained where the "conveniences" were located. She tipped him a few coins, and asked in a faux French-accented English, "How many passengers are there on this voyage?"

"Six or seven," said the porter. Meals are served in the captain's dining room at six bells in the morning and evening and two bells for lunch. Tea is at two bells in the late afternoon." Seeing her confusion, he added, "Don't worry. I will knock on your door if you do not appear. We sail in less than two hours, at ten o'clock."

When the door was closed, Xie Xie rose to her normal height and rubbed her back. *This disguise may be difficult to maintain in public. I may be permanently bent over by the time we reach Boston.*

Keeping her surname, Li, was logical. It was the most common surname in China. She'd given Alia several aliases under which to prepare passports. She had picked a traditional French name, Anne-Marie, for this voyage, ironically on a ship named *Queen Anne*. Once in America, another French passport held the name of Monique Li for her new life.

Xie Xie had been on the Mediterranean, but never the Atlantic. She had heard rough seas were more likely in the late summer, but in April, there could still be icebergs in the northern Atlantic. She refused to let herself dwell on it. Monique would be Anne-Marie's niece. Anne-Marie would conveniently die in a few months, and she would emerge into the light as Monique. Xie Xie had learned at the feet of The Pharaoh. She'd feigned indifference, but, in fact, nothing had escaped her observation of his techniques. Cotton balls stuck in the cheeks to age a face, an altered gait, a stooped stance, wigs, spectacles—all were effective.

Eating with the cotton balls would be a challenge, though she doubted she'd die from ingesting them. She'd practiced moving them to one side and chewing on the other. *I'll either master it quickly or choke to death.* She laughed at her own precipitous choices. *I am almost away. I am almost safe. In less than a month, I'll be in Boston.*

Exhausted from executing her escape, she sat in the room's only chair and fell fast asleep. She awoke when the ship began to move. Rising, she made her way to the deck. Grabbing the rail with one hand, she held her breath for a moment, and then exhaled in victory. *Free. I am free.*

Strangers next to her lined the rail, watching the lights that defined the city of London recede into the distance. *Once I was thrilled to approach it. Now I am relieved to leave it. Alive.* She walked to the other side of the ship, slowly in keeping with her new persona, and looked toward the endless new horizon that beckoned her.

Stars shone overhead in the unusually clear night. She smiled as the dancing moonlight sparkling on the rolling waters. *I could dance too, but it wouldn't be appropriate at my "age."*

She closed her eyes, willing herself to be safe. *The Pharaoh will not know I have disappeared until I am already on the open sea.* Once she completed five years of residence, she could become a citizen of the new United States. *A new life in a new country. Again. But this time it will be on my terms.*

CHAPTER SEVENTY-SEVEN

Wednesday, April 15, 1812 – Lord Ravenshire's Townhouse
Steiner

Thompson, followed by Steiner and Hinton, knocked on the door of the earl's study.

The earl looked up from his desk, took off his spectacles and nodded.

"What is your report, Steiner?"

The Prussian frowned. "Miss Li appears to be planning to leave London for America. Hinton drove Blackburn in a Hackney to Lady Gwyneth's street and he saw the carriages being loaded. He and the servant headed toward Ravenshire on horseback."

Henry stood. "Good God! So Blackburn may be lying in wait to strike at Ravenshire. Our plans to protect Lady Gabriella, Lady Gwyneth and Mr. James are a folly. We must not let him gain the advantage. He thinks we remained behind."

Steiner nodded. "But your movements are hardly invisible, my lord. Pomp and circumstance accompany you everywhere. We have devised a ruse, if you are game."

Henry sat down and motioned for them to do the same. "Explain."

"Our men will remain here in London, and one of them, who resembles you in height and physique, will occasionally leave and attend your usual haunts. We can track if anyone follows. We propose," Hinton looked at Steiner for corroboration, "that Thompson go to Ravenshire in disguise as a flower carter. The wagon will be covered with a tarp, with men and guns underneath. When we are close to Ravenshire, we can disengage the horses and reconnoiter before arriving at the manor house."

"Should we inform Detective Boyd or the Sheriff of Ravenshire?" Henry looked out the window. "Ravenshire is outside Boyd's jurisdiction, but perhaps we should alert the sheriff of our plans."

Steiner cleared his voice. "We have discussed our concerns with Boyd, and he is willing to accompany us and consult with the sheriff."

"How will we maintain the element of surprise with so many people involved?" The earl twirled his spectacles in his hand.

"Blackburn is a dangerous man with considerable resourcefulness. It takes but a few seconds to kill, Lord Ravenshire." Steiner leaned forward in his chair. "He has ingenuity, but we control Ravenshire. It is a better place to set a trap than London, which has myriad ways to escape."

"No one knows Ravenshire as well as Jean-Louis. Blackburn's first move will be to eliminate him." Hinton rubbed his chin. "Perhaps we should do it for him."

"Another ruse, I assume?" Henry directed his gaze at Hinton. "Continue."

"If Blackburn thinks Jean-Louis is out of the picture, he may relax his guard enough to give us the advantage."

Henry nodded. "Send a bird to Ravenshire and get a message to Boyd. If we ride now we should arrive around midnight. Thompson should leave in short order. We'll leave later this morning, to arrive around dinnertime. They will not be expecting us."

Steiner cleared his voice. "Lord Ravenshire, Jean-Louis told me that he believes Blackburn to be a specialist in poison. All must be alert. Nashmir has a larger greenhouse at Ravenshire. I hope he has an antidote for any poison."

"We seem to be assembling a veritable army." The earl grimaced.

Hinton tilted his head to one side. "Lord Ravenshire, splitting our defenses in two locations hinders our actions. By concentrating our resources, we improve our odds of success."

"Still," Henry mused, "this all remains mere speculation."

"With all due respect, Lord Ravenshire, I think not." Steiner shook his head. "Neither would Jean-Louis."

"Then it's off to Ravenshire we go." Henry stood. "Make ready the preparations."

***

Wednesday, April 15, 1812 – Ravenshire
Gilles

A carter pulled into Ravenshire after the dinner hour.

"Flowers?" Gilles innate skepticism kicked in. "I don't recall ordering flowers. I shall see to the carter."

The footman nodded and left.

Gilles went outside to the courtyard.

The carter's brown felt-brimmed hat was pulled low over his eyes and a long grey scarf was wrapped around his face, obscuring his features. Gilles tensed, his hand moving to one of the daggers concealed on his person. "We ordered no flowers."

Pushing his hat up, Thompson smiled. "I'm sure you'd be interested in these flowers, sir. Perhaps I could show you more in the stables."

Gilles nodded, and followed the cart to the stables across from the back of the house. He extended his hand to aid the butler in climbing down from the wagon's seat and led him into a private area of the stables. "What's afoot?"

"The earl, Hinton, Steiner and Detective Boyd and some of their men are assembling in the forest near the clearing you use for target practice to rendezvous with Jean-Louis. They believe Blackburn is heading to Ravenshire. They will reconnoiter and request that you meet them at midnight by the broken oak."

"Blackburn is not *heading* to Ravenshire. He is here as we speak."

Thompson's brow wrinkled. "I don't understand."

Gilles glanced around to be sure they were not overheard. "He is disguised as an Italian merchant, but Guy and I believe it is Blackburn. He concocted a theatrical highway robbery with a lackey, rode to the rescue and killed the unfortunate pawn before he could speak. In her naïveté, Lady Gabriella invited him to stay for the night. I could spare no man to alert the earl, so I am grateful for your arrival. I've not slept for two days. Help will be welcome."

"How can Blackburn hope to kill anyone and get away from here?"

"My mind is awash with horrible imaginings. However, I have become convinced over the last two days that he's overly confident of his ability to disguise himself. I believe he intends to seduce Lady Gabriella."

"No! Is he that good a dissembler?"

Gilles tilted his head and shrugged. "His disguise and accented English are convincing. He is left-handed. I am told Blackburn was right-handed. Occasionally I notice a reflexive action with the right hand. I believe it is a studied subterfuge. One can change one's girth, voice, hair, tint of skin, gait..." Gilles hesitated. "But I've never seen a man change his eye color. I've been told he had piercing aqua eyes. How can they now be as brown as mahogany bark?"

Thompson squinted. "Nashmir might know."

They found Nashmir in the back rooms of the stables.

"Thompson?"

The butler nodded. "I've brought more men and guns."

Directing his gaze at Nashmir, Gilles asked, "Can a man change his eye color?"

Nashmir glanced upward, as if trying to remember something. "I once heard a tale I attributed to exaggeration for the purposes of self-aggrandizement, but perhaps it was not as fanciful as I believed." He moved closer to Gilles and Thompson and lowered his voice. "The story was that an Arab alchemist had discovered such a formula by mistake and that it had no effect on those with dark eyes, but would turn light eyes dark. It was passed down generation to generation, a closely guarded secret, because of course it would give non-Arabs an advantage. Some, as we know, would sell out their own mother for financial advantage. The last known practitioner was based in Alexandria."

Thompson raised an eyebrow. "Blackburn used to travel to Egypt for the trading company and spent months there at different times over a span of decades. He set up the trading offices in Alexandria. In addition to chartering illegitimate companies and forging ledgers, it's not much of a stretch to imagine him learning the finer points of poisons and potions."

Gilles's mind flashed to the Gypsy woman.

Nashmir nodded. "On the earl's instructions, I have been working on an assortment of antidotes for various poisons. Come back to my greenhouse."

The Ravenshire greenhouse was three times the size of the one in back of the earl's townhouse. The Tibetan opened the door and shook his head. "Immediate dosing is needed for some poisons. Not all can be detected. I have one antidote that is effective against most venoms, and because it is eastern in origin, it may work if his primary source is Egyptian. Still, we must be ever vigilant."

Gilles sighed. "If I am to meet the earl at midnight, I must have my wits about me. I shall speak to Lady Gwyneth, then return here to get a few hours' sleep. I'll send one of my men to help Thompson unload the guns from the cart and distribute them to the guards. Set aside some extra guns for me to take to the earl. Thompson, you should stay out of sight."

Gilles headed over toward the house while Nashmir followed his instructions.

Finding Aelwyn and Lady Gwyneth in the library, Gilles spoke softly. "Take care. We believe the stranger is Blackburn."

***

Guy

After talking to Gilles, Guy offered to guide di Lucca on a walk around Ravenshire Castle in the twilight while supper was being prepared. Fluent in several European languages, Guy questioned the merchant in Italian, "*Qual é la campagna, come a Lucca?*" *I want to hear his Italian, to see if he can answer my question,* "What is the countryside like in Lucca?"

The merchant smiled and chattered in Italian. "Groves and groves of olive trees outside the walled city! That is my passion—*olio d'oliva Lucchese.* I am looking for new markets for my father's family's olive oil from our own orchards that overlook the Ligurian Sea. The Ligurians, you know, preceded the Etruscans and Romans. Olive groves have been cultivated in Lucca since the beginning of history. The Lombards minted coins in Lucca, it remains a center for the oriental silk trade, and holds a major place in history. Oh, yes, my friend, the First Triumvirate of Julius Caesar, Pompey and Crassus sealed their agreement in 56 B.C. in Lucca."

"A walled city, you say? How high are the walls?" Having seen it as a child, Guy wanted to further test the merchant's knowledge.

"The walls are thirty-nine feet tall, or twelve meters high and there are trees planted there, for walking between the bastions. And green fields lay without. It is truly a place of beauty. Lucca is now ruled by Napoleon's sister, Elisa, our *principessa*."

He knows Lucca. Overconfidence is dangerous.

"Enough of politics." Napoleon had no friend in Guy. "Have you samples of your olive oil with you?"

"Alas, my supplies have all been given out as enticements for future orders."

"How unfortunate." *And convenient.* To an Englishman, the merchant's Italian would have sounded like a native-speaker's. But to a Frenchman, the nuances of Italian were unmistakably missing. *He's a fraud. He may or may not be Blackburn, but he's assuredly not Italian.* "Tell me, Sig. di Lucca, how do you evade Napoleon's blockades?"

The merchant shrugged. "Smugglers find it a game to evade the incompetent French navy."

***

Gilles

In the kitchen, Sallie scurried to prepare a light supper, which was still an intricately planned meal.

Gilles slipped by the kitchen staff, climbed up the servants' stairs to the door that led to the family's quarters, and edged through, taking care to be sure no one was in the hallway. He softly padded to a room on the left, entered and went into a closet, where he moved some storage items camouflaging another door, which gave him access to back passages known only to a few. Jean-Louis had shown him when he had first arrived from Ireland. He crept along silently until he reached the wall of di Lucca's room. Gilles looked through a small section of black screen disguised as the pupils in a painting of a Wyndward ancestor.

Di Lucca had declined a valet to help him dress, but he had not expected to dress for dinner. The butler had provided a clean shirt, vest and jacket from the earl's closet for him to use, since they were of similar height, although the earl was slightly taller. Di Lucca removed his jacket, vest and shirt, and splashed water on his face and chest. He combed his hair and then straightened it.

A wig. Not unusual, but a hint of deception. Di Lucca peered closely at the mirror, tugging on the lower corner of an eye.

"Damnation!"

Gilles could tell that di Lucca didn't like what he saw. *What is it?*

When di Lucca turned to get something out of his traveling bag, Gilles noticed the scars. A scar about four inches long showed on his left shoulder. *That's where Jean-Louis said the count's knife stabbed Blackburn.* A round unevenly edged scar marred his right hand. *He was wearing gloves earlier. That's where Mr. James shot him.* His pants hid his legs, but his stance was even. *The limp is feigned.*

Di Lucca took a vial from his traveling bag, opened it, and poured the contents into his mouth. *What can it be?*

Once dressed, di Lucca preened in the mirror. He murmured. "Now I wear your clothes, brother." He walked to the window and looked out over Ravenshire's rolling hills. He whispered, audibly. "The desert is open and intoxicating, but these verdant fields are ordered and calming. I was ripped from my birthright, my ancestral home."

Grim-faced, Gilles held his breath. *Brother? Ancestral home? Traces of a highland brogue. 'Tis Blackburn.*

Taking out his pocket watch, di Lucca began to limp as he made his way toward the door.

Gilles replaced the screen shield and waited enough time for di Lucca to pass through the hallway to the main stairs before slipping away.

CHAPTER SEVENTY-EIGHT

Wednesday, April 15, 1812 – Ravenshire
Bri

Bri rested her head on the back of the armchair turned toward the window so she could look at the progress on the old Ravenshire Castle reconstruction. *I thought the Marriage Season was a labyrinth I had to walk through, not become entrapped in its endless barriers.*

Dana knocked on the door. "Are you ready, milady?"

Bri stood and answered. "Come in. I have not dressed yet."

The maid moved toward the armoire. Throwing open its doors, she pulled out an ivory dress embroidered with tiny pink blossoms. "You always look lovely in this, milady. Let's get you out of the dusty travel dress."

Bri turned so that Dana could pull the empire ties in the back and pull the dress over her head.

Her languorous bath had been a relief after the long carriage ride. "That attack by the highwayman unnerved me."

"I thought nothing could unnerve you, Lady Gabriella. You are always strong."

"It's less the shock of the attack, which our guest helped stop. It was more Aunt Gwyneth's anger that I invited the guest to stay with us. I don't know why she thinks a man who helped us would be a problem. I supposed I wanted the distraction of polite conversation to forget the potential danger we face."

"We've all been warned to be alert, milady." Dana finished fitting Bri's fastenings on the dinner dress. "You must not worry. Jean-Louis is nearby. Gilles and Guy are protecting us. She leaned in to whisper, "Lady Gwyneth told Isabella to watch the stranger. Isabella told me the comtesse thinks that the merchant is the blackguard in disguise."

Bri's face lost all its color.

"Oh, milady, I shouldn't have mentioned it! I thought you knew. Please don't tell Lady Gwyneth that you know."

Regaining her composure, Bri shook her head. "Don't worry, Dana. It will be our secret." She smiled at the maid. "Perhaps Aunt Gwyneth is overwrought and mistaken."

Dana finished dressing Bri and fetched her shoes. "Will there be anything else, milady?"

"No. I'll be down in a minute."

Dana closed the door as she left.

Bri looked at herself in a full-length mirror as her mind raced. *Blackie! How did I not sense it? Could Aunt Gwyneth be right? Blackie is a master of detecting miniscule clues. I have been told many times that I cannot hide my feelings.*

She settled on a plan, took a deep breath and exited her room.

***

Blackburn as di Lucca

Di Lucca used his cane to descend the stairway. He'd perfected the ruse. *Everything is going as planned. I rescued her. Women fawn over their saviors. James was once her hero.*

A trim footman dressed in Ravenshire livery stood at the bottom of the stairs. "Sig. di Lucca," he moved his arm in a wide gesture toward the drawing room, "Lady Gwyneth and Lady Wyndward await you."

Di Lucca sensed the man at his heels. When he entered the drawing room, Lady Gwyneth and Lady Wyndward were seated. He walked over, bowed and reached for their hands one at a time, kissing their gloves in the continental manner. "You are so kind to invite me to stay as your guest, Lady Gwyneth. And I thank you as well, Lady Wyndward."

Lady Gwyneth smiled. "You were so brave, Mr. di Lucca. And you saved us from harm. It is the least I could do." Looking at the butler, she nodded. "Sherry, Young."

Young poured dry sherry from the leaded glass decanter into three small goblets and brought them to the guests.

Di Lucca sat across from Lady Gwyneth and raised his glass to her. "To two lovely, gracious ladies."

Lady Gwyneth smiled and raised her glass toward him. "And to a daring rescuer."

As they took a sip, Bri appeared at the door, Ian at her side.

Young brought her a glass of sherry.

Ian ran in and pulled on Di Lucca's sleeve. "Are you the brave hero who killed the highwayman?"

"I did what any man would do when a brigand approaches. I am no hero." *The child resembles his father. 'Tis uncanny.*

"Yes, you are!" The boy clambered into Di Lucca's lap.

Pulling down his glass of sherry on the table, Di Lucca shrugged. "I acted out of instinct." *If you only knew the truth.* Di Lucca hugged the boy.

Bri stared at di Lucca hugging Ian and dropped her glass on the carpet.

The thick Persian rug protected the glass from breaking, but the butler quickly signaled the footman to mop it up.

Recovering quickly, Bri said, "How clumsy of me. I guess today's events have rattled my nerves."

The butler poured another glass of sherry for her.

Taking the goblet, Bri raised it to the others. "To a delightful conversation this evening."

"Delightful conversation," they echoed, raising their glasses in return.

"Ian," said Lady Wyndward, "it's time for you to go to the nursery."

"Yes, Mother. I'm tired after riding Gio all afternoon."

"Gio? Is there an Italian countryman of my father's here?"

"No, sir," said Ian and he squirmed out of di Lucca's arms and ran to kiss his mother goodnight. "Gio is my pony. I named him after my friend Gio, the artist."

"I have heard of this Gio. Even in Europe, they speak of his talent."

Once Ian had left with Lilyanne, Bri took the armchair next to di Lucca, across from Gwyneth, and glanced toward him. "I must confess, Sig. di Lucca, your valiant actions today calmed me. We have fled London, you see, in fear. My father believes us to be in danger."

Gwyneth's face turned a reddish-pink. "Please do not bother our guest with wild speculation, my dear."

Bri took another swig of sherry. "Speculation! We were nearly murdered today, save for Mr. di Lucca's actions." She leaned over the arm of her chair, moving her head closer to di Lucca. "My *bastard* uncle wants to kill us. I believe he hired that highwayman who attacked us today."

Di Lucca was caught off-guard by her candor. He assessed her demeanor. *Has the sherry loosened her tongue?* He feigned concern. *"Che Dio ti protegga!* God protect you!" He limped to the windows, pretending to peer through, scanning for attackers. "Can the French driver assemble a guard force?"

"Oh, yes." Bri waved to Young to refill her sherry glass. "We have many French drivers. Jean-Louis, Guy or Gilles—any one of them—could slit that bastard's throat like a flash of lightning."

Gwyneth stood. "That will be enough vile and vulgar talk, Gabriella. We should not alarm our guest. Please forgive my impetuous niece, Sig. Di Lucca. Perhaps the sherry has altered her judgment. No more sherry for Lady Gabriella, Young."

Whirling to face her aunt, Bri raised her voice. "How dare you! If I want more sherry, I shall have more sherry! Young, I want more."

The guest noticed that Aelwyn stared at Bri with a look that expressed concern.

"Dinner is served." Young waved them toward the dining room.

"Very well, Young. If you won't pour me more, I'll get it myself. This *is* my home." Bri walked over and poured herself more sherry. She walked into the dining room ahead of everyone else and sat before her aunt or Aelwyn.

Di Lucca knew this to be a breach of protocol. *I've never seen this petulant side of Bri. It is a weakness I can exploit. She was always so proper in our previous encounters.* He extended his elbow to Lady Gwyneth. "May I escort you, Comtesse?"

Seeing a puzzled look overtake her face, di Lucca smiled. "The footman told me that you are the Comtesse de Merbeau."

"Of course, Sig. Di Lucca."

"May I tell you a secret?"

"If you wish, sir."

"I am a conte, but after Napoleon installed his rulers in my native country, I do not disclose that fact to many. My lands may be confiscated at any time in Croatia or Lucca should I fall out of favor."

"How awful for you, Conte di Lucca."

"Not at all. Fate is out of my control. Please maintain my secret. *Sig.* di Lucca is best for now."

Lady Gwyneth nodded.

When all had taken their seats, Lady Gwyneth motioned to Young to serve and glared at her niece.

***

Gwyneth

Young and the footman served the soup.

Di Lucca took a spoonful. "*Fungi!* Mushrooms are such a delicacy."

The comtesse nodded. "St. George's mushrooms are at their peak for the next month. And we also have a greenhouse where we grow vegetables year round."

Bri directed her gaze at di Lucca. "Sir, you were so gallant today. Did you kill anyone in Croatia? Is that why you fled your homeland?"

Gwyneth stared at Bri. *What is wrong with her?* A staccato laugh from di Lucca caused Gwyneth to turn her head toward him. *What an odd sound.*

"Ah, Lady Gabriella, you have the wild, romantic imaginings of a young girl. Would you make me so daring, a dashing cavalier, perhaps?"

"But you are, Sig. di Lucca. I am so glad you are here to protect us. Jean-Louis is getting old. He may not be up to the challenge of killing my evil uncle. That, you see, is why I asked you to stay. We may need a man unafraid to kill for our protection."

"Bri, stop this rude banter at once! I will not have it."

"Aunt Gwyneth, Blackburn is depraved, conniving and scheming his way through life. He betrayed our trust for nearly twenty years, learning all of our secrets and using them against us. But he doesn't know what we know." She tilted her head back in near-manic laughter. "Wait until he finds out what we have in store for him!"

"Bri, be silent!"

The servers took the soup and brought platters of roast chicken, potatoes and asparagus.

After the plates were filled, Gwyneth changed the subject. "How long will you be in England, Sig. di Lucca?"

The Italian merchant moved his hand in a gesture signaling that he was uncertain. "It depends on my success in finding markets for the products of my family's olive groves and vineyards. With Europe in a state of near-perpetual war, transportation of goods is fraught with danger. Of course, the French don't want Italian wines, so I am exploring other markets. Evading the French navy or pirates means some shipments are lost. I cannot afford to lose too many more. I came through Portugal." He took a sip of wine. "This is a delightful dry white wine. Where is it from?"

"My late uncle Luc, Comte de Merbeau, owned vineyards in western France that are still held by his family. He was murdered by Blackburn too."

Di Lucca leaned toward Gwyneth. "Lady Gwyneth, I am so sorry for your loss."

Aelwyn had remained silent until that point. In a soft voice, she added, "He killed my husband, Rychard, too."

"Ian's father," explained Bri. "I hate Blackburn. Yes, hate. Sig. di Lucca, it may shock you to learn the murderer was my best friend as a child. I called him 'Blackie.'" Bri took a gulp of wine. "Now I want to *kill* him. *Myself.* Torture him perhaps. Cut him into little pieces as I'm cutting my chicken and feed him to the pigs."

"Bri! Cease this rude and unforgiveable talk or leave the table." Gwyneth felt her face flushing with embarrassment.

"No! Sig. di Lucca understands. He killed the highwayman. He knows how it feels to kill. I want to know. I want to kill Blackburn. I care about nothing else."

Gwyneth threw her arms up in the air. "Sig. di Lucca, I apologize for my niece's abominable behavior. The wine is clearly too much for her."

"Nonsense. I haven't imbri...imbibed too much mine. Too much wine." Bri giggled in an unnatural high-pitched way. "Sig. di Lucca and I should be a team to track and kill Blackburn. Put a pistol in his face as you did with the highwayman. Well done, sir. Well done. Would you let me try the pistol? Would you let me kill Blackburn when we find him?"

At the breaking point, Gwyneth signaled to Young and said, "Escort Lady Gabriella to her room. She is finished."

Weaving her head, Bri said, "No, I'm not," even as Young and the footman lifted her from her chair and forced her from the room. "Stop!" she stumbled as they led her to the stairs.

The footman closed the doors to the dining room so her rebuttals could not be heard.

"A spirited young woman," said di Lucca. *I can use Bri's lapse in judgment to my advantage.*

***

Jean-Louis

Jean-Louis had circled back to Ravenshire to check on the situation. The earl was due at the clearing at midnight. Without announcing his arrival, he caught a catnap in the stables while the others ate dinner. Jean-Louis was awakened by a commotion outside his door. He rose, checked his knives and pistol, and opened the door.

A scullery maid and stableman were laughing, but stopped when they saw Jean-Louis.

"What is so amusing?"

The kitchen worker shifted foot to foot, nervous in the bodyguard's presence.

The stableman spoke up. "It's Lady Gabriella, J-L. She's drunk and misbehaving. Lady Gwyneth made her leave the table because she was rude to the guest."

"It's true, J-L. I heard it through the door—we all did."

"Speak no more of it. Go back to work."

Jean-Louis followed the kitchen maid toward the house. *I've never known Bri to act in such a way. Something is wrong.* Entering through the kitchen, he went up the back stairs and down the hallway to Bri's room. He knocked.

"Go away, Aunt Gwyneth. I don't want to speak to you."

"*C'est moi.*"

The door opened and Bri pulled him into the room. "Thank God you're here! Our guest Sig. di Lucca is Blackburn."

***

Henry

Henry rode under a pale spring moon rising over Ravenshire Forest along the route to Ravenshire. As they neared their destination, green fields filled with grazing wildlife gave way to a wooded glen. *Maybe I should ask Gio to paint a series of pastorals around Ravenshire.*

The horses expertly avoided the ruts from wagon tracks and the incessant impact of rain on the unpaved road. Arriving at their appointed meeting place, Henry pulled on the reins, and dismounted. Hinton and Steiner followed. Steiner calmed the horses with handfuls of oats and tied them to a nearby tree.

"We're far enough away. It's safe to build a small fire." Henry pulled out his pocket watch. "Jean-Louis should be here in about an hour."

Hinton set about building a fire, warming them on the cold clear spring night.

Lash appeared. "The Gypsy sent me with two assassins. They won't be troubling us."

***

Jean-Louis

"I was told you were in a drunken stupor."

"Good! I was afraid my rage and suspicion would give me away to Blackburn, so I decided to act in a way that would shock people and divert their attention. Everyone knows I'm no actress, but I channeled my anger into a memorable dinner performance."

"Did he appear convinced?"

"Confused, I think. He'd never seen me behave in such a way, nor had Aunt Gwyneth, nor Aelwyn for that matter. Only you..."

"As puppeteer for the marionette theatre I built for you. You played all the parts with remarkable diversity and inflection." A wry smile crept over his lips. "I remember." The smile turned to a thin line. "But Blackburn is a killer. Take no chances, Bri. Exactly what did you say?"

The French former trapper shook his head in amusement as Bri recounted the dinner conversation. "You've left him with the impression that we have something planned. This is an advantage for us. He may overreact. A normal man would bolt in the dead of night. But this one thinks he is smarter than all of us."

"He's wrong, of course." Bri searched the Frenchman's eyes for a sign of agreement.

Jean-Louis betrayed no emotion in his reply. "Deep wounds of abandonment by the Wyndward family, and the death of his mother have festered into a putrid fount of hatred-fueled vengeance. We thought him dead a year ago. We must not be complacent. He is a wily foe."

"But *you* can stop him. *We* can stop him."

"I don't want to put you at risk. Not again."

Bri hardened her gaze. "I want to stop him! What do you want me to do?"

"I think he may still operate under the delusion that he might marry you. The servants told me they overheard him tell Lady Gwyneth that he is an Italian count, a complete fiction that he begged her to keep secret, but a revelation meant to imply that he is a worthy suitor. Clearly expert in assuming new identities, he believes himself to be impervious to detection."

"And?"

"Can you maintain your control of the puppet strings to manipulate him into believing that you are angry with your family and have tossed Edward aside? Could you convince him that to spite them you might accept his courtship?"

Bri's face grimaced in distaste. "I don't know if I could maintain *that* ruse."

"I have to leave to meet the earl in the forest. Stay in your room, speak to no one." He turned to go. "Did you sense di Lucca was Blackburn?"

Bri grimaced. "I'd only seen him at a distance. Isabella told Dana and she told me. She thought I knew."

Jean-Louis nodded, peered out the door to be certain the hallway was empty, and slipped out.

CHAPTER SEVENTY-NINE

Early Thursday, April 16, 1812 – Ravenshire Forest
Henry

Henry's ear turned toward the pounding clops of horses' hooves over the glen's floor of hard earth. Fog had obscured the formerly clear night. The moon's eerie glow cast a gray light through the cloud cover over the canopy of branches budding with leaves where Henry, Hinton, Lash and Steiner waited.

Jean-Louis came into view, dismounted, and greeted the men with a curt, "Blackburn is here."

The earl and his two companions sat in rapt attention as the French trapper outlined the snare he proposed to immobilize their prey.

***

Young

The butler bolted awake a few hours after midnight. Windows in his room overlooked the stables and estate servicing complex. He saw the earl dismount.

Young rapidly dressed, descended the servants' stairs to the kitchen entrance, and walked toward the stables. His mouth dropped open when he saw his father, still serving as butler to the earl in London, standing next to the earl.

"Milord, we were not expecting you."

Henry turned and walked toward Young, and spoke in low tones. "My plans changed. I didn't intend to disturb you, Young. Trouble is afoot. Your father is here at my request."

Jean-Louis stepped forward. "Here is the plan."

Young listened, nodded, and returned to the main house.

***

Blackburn as Di Lucca

Always a light sleeper, Blackburn heard footsteps in the hallway. *Is the Frenchman spying on me?* He effortlessly slipped from under the covers, tiptoed to the door and eased it open a sliver. *Henry!* He quashed the hint of a smile. *If I can fool my dear elder brother, then victory is within my grasp.*

Closing the door, Blackburn paced the room for nearly an hour, planning all possible ways to escape whatever traps Henry and Jean-Louis had no doubt set. Finally, confident in his ability to adapt to alternative scenarios, he went back to bed, willing himself to wake at first light.

Rising with a plan for an early morning horseback ride around Ravenshire before breakfast, Blackburn took extra care with his wig and disguise, strutting in front of the mirror. Entering the hallway, he almost bumped into Henry. "Lord Ravenshire, I presume?"

***

Henry

Henry stopped in mid-step. "You have me at a disadvantage, sir. I don't believe we have been introduced."

"Dragan di Lucca. My father's family is from Lucca, my mother's from Dubrovnik. Honored to meet you, Lord Ravenshire. I had the honor of overpowering a highwayman attacking the carriage of Lady Gwyneth and Lady Gabriella. Your lovely daughter invited me to stay overnight. I intended a short ride this morning before I go on my way. Will you join me?"

Shrugging with a smile, Henry answered, "Why not? The fog has lifted. I can show you around some of the estate. Then we can breakfast together."

"Ravenshire is vast."

"Indeed it is. One of the largest in England, as a matter of fact."

"But you are only an earl?"

Henry smiled. *Trying to rile me, brother?* He waved his hand dismissively. "Antiquated, these titles. The time may come when, as in America, dukes and earls are simply men."

As they went down the stairs, Henry noted di Lucca's limp, studied the wig, and discerned the favoring of his left hand. *Believable.* But then di Lucca turned and the light from the main window illuminated the corner of his eye behind his tinted spectacles. There was a gleam, a tiny speck of aquamarine on one eye. The color vanished when Blackburn turned, blending with the near-mahogany tint of the surrounding eye. *There is no doubt. My brother has fallen into our trap.*

***

Jean-Louis

While grooming his horse, Jean-Louis first heard the earl's voice, then di Lucca's. *Part of the plan is in play early.* He was hidden behind a stall divider, but peered through the wood slats.

While Orion saddled their horses, Henry described where they would be riding. "The eastern edge of Ravenshire Forest is an invigorating ride, across streams and fences. Does your horse jump?"

He knows either that I'm listening, or that the Gyspy will tell me.

Di Lucca shook his head. "I doubt he is jumper. I should not care to test him and break my neck."

Jean-Louis grinned. *A good plan for us, but you are no fool, Blackburn.*

"There is another route we can take, where the horses have naught but a shallow stream to traverse. I love to ride through the silence of the wooded glens, past the sheep at pasture, under the birds in flight. This hour of the morning is contemplative."

"An earl *and* a poet. You are an interesting man, Lord Ravenshire."

"Merely a steward of nature and of my birthright." *That should sting. A bastard has no inheritance rights.*

After Henry and di Lucca rode off, Jean-Louis gathered Hinton and Steiner, who had also overheard the conversation. Lash emerged from the shadows.

Hinton smiled. "Perfectly in line with our favored scenario."

"What can I do?" Orion looked pale.

Jean-Louis put his hand on the Gypsy boy's shoulder. "We have it in hand. Stay behind with Steiner. We must be vigilant here. Bri, Lady Wyndward and Ian are depending on us."

The Frenchman, Hinton and Lash rode off in pursuit, while Steiner remained behind to patrol the grounds with his men.

***

Gwyneth

Isabella arrived to dress the comtesse. After she had laid out the clothes for the day, the maid hung her head. "Milady, I must confess that I told Dana about your suspicions about Mr. Blackburn, and she told Lady Gabriella. Please forgive me. I thought she knew."

"When I told you to speak to no one—"

"I thought you meant not to speak to other staff, not Lady Gabriella."

"When I say 'no one,' I mean 'no one'."

"Forgive me, milady."

"Do not overlook the possibility that Blackburn may have a spy here. Be discreet. Revealing even insignificant facts could be fatal. That man killed my brother and my husband. He wrote of it in a diary in his own hand. His lust for treachery and revenge is ever on my mind. No one is safe while he lives. Observe only."

Once dressed, Gwyneth went downstairs, through the kitchen, to the stables to find Jean-Louis. She was surprised to see Nashmir. "Where is Jean-Louis?"

"Good morning, Lady Gwyneth." Nashmir tilted his head to induce her to follow him to a more private area. He lowered his voice. "Jean-Louis and Hinton followed the earl and the 'other' on horseback."

"Where are they riding?"

"To the eastern part of the estates."

Gwyneth's heart jumped. "Where Rychard was killed?"

Nashmir nodded.

A groan came from a nearby room.

Gwyneth glanced at Nashmir, and walked toward that room.

Nashmir stepped around her in an attempt to stop her from reaching the room.

She glared at him.

Moving aside, he whispered, "The earl prefers that this be kept secret from Lady Gabriella."

Perplexed, Gwyneth turned the handle to open the door. She gasped. A pale man lay on the cot. Unkempt and haggard, the near-skeleton managed a wan smile. "I'm much better today."

"Mr. James!"

***

Blackburn as di Lucca

Henry and Blackburn rode across the fields. A light spring rain began to fall. Henry pulled up on his horse's reins by a stream. It was the place of his brother Rychard's death.

Henry turned to his riding companion. "You Italians aren't used to English weather, sir. Shall we return?"

"No need on my account, Lord Ravenshire. I must acclimate." A subtle movement caught his eye. "What's that?"

"Perhaps a deer. They drink from this stream on occasion."

A bird call alerted Henry to the arrival of Jean-Louis. He stared into Blackburn's eyes. "I know who you are and what you are up to."

Still in character, di Lucca threw his hands up in submission. "Guilty, Lord Ravenshire. I have taken a liking to your daughter, Lady Gabriella. Naturally you are protective, but—"

"We saw your body hit the rocks."

Blackburn sat back in the saddle. Calm at his unmasking, he dropped his faux-accented English and smiled. "You saw *a* body hit the rocks. An itinerant seaman no one missed. You look well, brother. What do you propose to do?"

Henry's voice was icy. "This is the spot where you killed our brother. And this is where I will kill you."

"Indeed? Where is that Ravenshire sense of justice? The law and all that drivel? Is my self-righteous elder brother going to commit murder on his own property?"

"You forget, Blackburn. You're already dead."

"But your sense of honor won't permit it, brother. You have never killed anyone."

"How little you know, brother." Henry pulled a pistol from his boot and fired at Blackburn just as his younger half-brother pulled the reins on his horse.

The shot merely grazed Blackburn's temple as he spurred his horse to a gallop. At the same moment, a knife flew into Blackburn's right thigh from across the stream.

"Damned Frenchman!"

"*Non. Je suis en arrière de vous.*"

Blackburn turned around to see the Frenchman, knife in hand.

Another shot from Henry rang out.

"Missed again, brother." The horse bolted at the gunshot, and Blackburn was off but not before Jean-Louis threw a knife, hitting Blackburn in the right shoulder. Wounded, he spurred his horse along the edge of the stream with three men in pursuit.

***

Henry

Hinton, who had been lying in wait across the stream, rode on the other side of the water, to cut off Blackburn from that direction.

Henry and Jean-Louis were closing in on Blackburn when their prey turned and fired.

Jean-Louis was hit by a musket ball in his left side, and fell off his horse. Henry stopped but Jean-Louis protested, "It's nothing. Stop him!"

***

Jean-Louis

Once Henry was out of sight, a man emerged from the woods and stanched the flow of blood from Jean-Louis's side.

"It's not 'nothing'."

"Thanks for shadowing me. I wanted to have a hidden weapon."

"Brothers stick together. Always."

Jacques du Bois looked toward the sound of hooves. "I must disappear. I'll be close by if needed."

The Jackal vanished as quickly as he had materialized.

***

Henry

Henry regained speed, but Blackburn's lead had increased. *I can't lose him now. Lash took a short cut and should be up ahead. We still have that advantage.*

Hinton was ahead of Henry, keeping up with Blackburn, but riding on the other side of the stream, which began to widen at this point. Crossing it slowed down his horse as he fought the current. By the time Hinton had forded the stream, he had fallen behind the earl.

Blackburn's lead was about fifty yards.

Hinton caught up with Henry and they raced to subdue their wily enemy. A former cavalry man, Hinton was accustomed to shooting while riding. He pulled out a pistol and fired.

Blackburn fell limply to one side, but kept riding.

"I think I hit him." Hinton shouted over the noise of the horses hooves hitting the ground.

"Looks like it. We can't let him escape." Henry prodded his horse and began to close the distance between him and Blackburn.

Hinton grunted, distracting Henry. Clutching his chest, Hinton's face drained of color and he slumped on his horse, and then fell to one side, being dragged by one stirrup.

Henry turned back and grabbed the reins of Hinton's horse, slowing him to a stop. He dismounted and released Hinton's foot from the stirrup. Cradling the man's head in his arms, he called his name. "Hinton! Were you hit?"

Ashen-faced, the former soldier shook his head and whispered. "Chest exploding. Leave me to die. Stop that blackguard!"

Henry shook his head. "I must get you back to the house. I owe you that loyalty."

Hinton shook his head. "This is my time. I matter not."

"Were I to leave you here, I would be no better than Blackburn.

His time will come another day." *Lash is our only hope.*

Hinton gasped for breath, his eyes searched Henry's as he tried to speak, but a guttural groan escaped his lips and he was gone.

Henry closed the dead man's eyes, and lifted him over the saddle of his horse, securing the body as best he could, and then turned around to ride back to Jean-Louis.

***

Lash

Hearing a shot, Lash spurred his horse to circle back to the sound of hooves.

From the wooded area that surrounded them, Lash saw a lone rider slumped over his horse moving toward the London road. *He's wounded. Where is the earl? Jean-Louis? Hinton? I must stop Blackburn.* He pulled out his pistol and rode forward.

***

Jean-Louis

Jean-Louis could feel the sticky ooze coming from under his left arm. He placed a hand over the wound, to try to stanch the bleeding. *I dare not close my eyes. I must fight to stay conscious.*

He saw Henry riding toward him, with a body over a horse. "You got him!"

Henry dismounted and knelt by Jean-Louis. "No, it's Hinton. His heart gave out. Blackburn was wounded by Hinton's knife and yours. My bullet merely grazed him, but Hinton got off a shot that clearly hit the mark.

"Blackburn rode off, injured, perhaps grievously. We may find his body in a few days, but we'll need more people. My urgent task now is to get you back to the house." Henry examined the wound. "You are a lucky man, once again. The bullet appears to have passed through you, but we must stop the bleeding."

***

Lash

Blackburn's pace had slowed.

Lash judged that the wounded man was barely conscious, as Blackburn wielded his pistol with little control.

After shooting wildly, the gun fell from Blackburn's hand.

Lash ducked but maintained his pace. *He can't reload but he may be feigning injury and have another weapon.*

His Gypsy bandana flicking in the wind, Lash advanced.

Blackburn slumped over, but clung to his horse's neck.

I've almost got him. Lash missed the glint of an errant ray of sun through the intermittent clouds as it struck the blade flying toward him until the last minute. He fell to one side as the knife embedded itself in his gut.

Damn! He didn't slump, he reached into his boot to flick the knife. Lash shot at the fleeing man, but knew he could no longer catch him.

***

Henry

A single shot rang out, followed by the clomping of hooves.

Henry called to the rider. "Lash! Jean-Louis is wounded. We need a makeshift litter." He stopped and stared. "A knife is sticking out of your side."

"I think it missed my liver." The Gypsy lost his balance, but Henry caught him.

Lash's voice wavered. "Blackburn is severely wounded, perhaps unconscious on his horse. I don't know how far he'll get, but I could ride no farther." He looked at the body on the horse. "Hinton?"

Henry nodded. "His heart gave out in the chase, but I'm glad to hear we've wounded Blackburn badly. I chose to stay with Hinton as he took his last breaths rather than maintain pursuit."

Jean-Louis tried to sit up. "I can ride," but fell back.

Searching Lash's eyes, Henry hesitated. "If I remove the knife, it might accelerate your bleeding."

The Frenchman shook his head. "You must. We can't have him bouncing over uneven terrain with a knife in his abdomen. You need to remove it while applying pressure at the same time." Henry pulled off his cravat and pressed it into the wound while removing the knife. Lash groaned.

The pounding sound of an approaching horse alerted them.

Henry maintained the pressure with his left hand and reached for his pistol with his right, hiding it behind Lash's body.

A lone Gypsy rider approached. Looking at Lash, he said, "I never trusted y—"

A thin blade emerged through his neck, spilling blood as his eyes widened in horror. He fell to the ground.

Orion appeared. "I saw this one," he gestured to the dead man, "skulking around the woods in back of the stables and followed him."

"Not a moment too soon, Orion." Henry tilted his head toward Jean-Louis. "I need your help. Jean-Louis and Lash have serious wounds. I can't risk the time to go back and get a carriage—that's more than an hour each way. We can use the saddle blanket from Hinton's horse, and this Gypsy's, creating makeshift litters laced with the horses' reins. Cut some branches and we can get this done quickly." He glanced at Lash, who had closed his eyes but was still breathing, and then back at Orion. "And things at Ravenshire?"

"Steiner, Guy, Nambotha and Gilles are with the ladies and Ian."

Jean-Louis pulled himself to the slumped Gypsy in the bandana. "My bleeding has stopped. I'll see to Lash while you two build the litters."

Henry and Orion constructed a sort of hammock between Lash's and the Frenchman's horses to shelter Jean-Louis and Lash from the ground.

Orion and Henry mounted their horses, guiding the others, tying the one carrying Hinton to Orion's. They couldn't move quickly. Jarring the injured men would be dangerous. In a little less than two hours, they managed to cover the distance back to the main house, keeping both men talking to maintain their consciousness.

When they arrived, Orion jumped off his horse, ran to the stables and called out to Nashmir, who came at once, followed by Steiner.

They carried Jean-Louis inside to his bed and Lash to another room.

Nashmir pulled off the improvised bandages and examined the wound. "Lucky again, old friend. If the bullet had hit on the right side, it would have destroyed your liver and taken your life."

"No. I will not die in this country."

The Tibetan raised an eyebrow. "I shall return with medicine." He left the room to look at Lash.

Jean-Louis groaned in pain. "I wanted that bastard dead."

Orion looked at the earl and back at his mentor. "What can I do, Lord Ravenshire?"

"Watch over my friends." Henry put one hand on the Frenchman's shoulder. "I leave you in Nashmir's hands. Blackburn has been hit. We're going to search for him, or his body. If he survives, he is severely weakened, but hatred drives him. Blackburn's final reckoning lies ahead."

***

Blackburn, unmasked

I must not close my eyes. I must keep going. Henry will attend to the wounded men. I have but a brief time to escape. He gripped the reins and grasped his horse's neck with both arms to regain stability and remain in the saddle. *I wounded the man in the Gypsy bandana, probably sent by that old crone, Mirela.*

Once he had known these woods, but many years had passed, and he wasn't sure the direction to ride to reach the road back to London. Riding aimlessly, he began to lose consciousness until the clap of other hooves on hard-traveled ground revived him. *I am close to the road.*

He slowed the horse and approached the perimeter of the road, took a sip of water from a pouch, and checked to see that the bleeding from his wounds had stopped. *Lucky today.* His throat was raw from hard breathing, and he took another swig of water. His head cleared, and he pulled off his wig and stowed it in his saddle bags, carefully so as not to reopen his wounds. He rode toward London as fast as his wounds could tolerate.

***

Thursday, April 16, 1812 – Ravenshire

Bri

The word spread rapidly to the main house. "Jean-Louis is wounded!"

Bri heard and ran toward the stables. Fear, an unfamiliar emotion, gripped her heart. Henry and a party of men were riding out. Steiner was directing others to patrol the perimeter of the main house.

She followed Nashmir's voice to the room where Jean-Louis lay, Orion at his side. She knelt by the bed and grabbed the trapper's hand. "Thank Providence you are safe!"

"It takes a lot to kill me. Many have tried. None have succeeded." He grimaced.

"Nashmir, give him something for the pain!"

Nashmir turned to Bri and spoke with a patient, but reproachful tone. "It's working its way through his body, Lady Gabriella. Healing is a process. It is not magical."

Jean-Louis scoffed. "You *are* a magician, Nashmir. Don't deny it!"

The Tibetan shook his head. "I simply know more than most westerners—secrets of the lamaseries, herbs from the sacred mountains, and tinctures created by years of experimentation."

"Maybe the head of a Tibetan mountain goat will sprout from my wounded side. I'll call him Nashmir."

Bri laughed. "Jesting in the face of death, as expected."

"Jousting, I say, not jesting. I'll spear death's head and stake it on the turrets."

Nashmir shrugged. "*Now*, Lady Gabriella, you can see that the herbs are working."

***

Edward

Edward leaned against the wallboards to listen. *I must stay still. Bri must never see me like this.* He pulled the covers over his head in case the door opened. *I must not be discovered.*

CHAPTER EIGHTY

Thursday, April 16, 1812 – *Omelettes de Mme. d'Aix*
Blackburn

Darkness concealed Blackburn as he rode into the alley behind his grandmother's omelet parlor. Strength waning, he spied a gas lamp in the apartment above the café, dismounted in a near fall, and stumbled to the door. He pounded several times.

The urchin appeared.

"Take me to Aneira."

The boy unlocked the door.

"My horse needs to be wiped down and sheltered." He tossed the boy a coin.

Catching it in mid-flight, the boy grabbed the reins and led the horse to the neighboring stable.

Blackburn tried to climb the stairs, but fell, groaning.

Aneira appeared, came down to help raise Blackburn to his feet.

Blackburn crawled up the stairs. They put him in the storeroom where the urchin had been staying.

Aneira pulled off his clothes to examine his wounds. "I'll boil water."

Blackburn tried to speak, but lost consciousness.

***

Thursday, April 16, 1812 —*Omelettes de Mme. d'Aix*
Colvert

Voutain had taken his turn following the Gypsy crone, leaving Colvert in charge outside the café's back entrance.

In the wee hours of the night, Colvert had slipped into a nearby pub for a quick brew. *Voutain will never know.* After relieving himself in an adjacent alley, Colvert ambled back and saw the urchin scan the area before going up into the grandmother's lair. *How much longer must we be sentinels for two old women?* He took a pinch of snuff.

Voutain's voice came from behind him.

"Some wicked Gypsy ceremony lasted half the night. All the old crones casting spells, I'm sure. An evil coven."

A carriage pulled up and Mirela climbed out, unlocked the door, and disappeared upstairs.

"Do you think they drink blood and—"

"Don't say it. It's disgusting to think about."

Colvert shrugged.

***

Sunday, April 19, 1812 – The Comtesse de Merbeau's Carriage
Gwyneth

Temporarily safe from Blackburn, Gwyneth, Bri, Jean-Louis and Henry rode in his carriage back to London, each absorbed in thought.

Guy followed with the maids, Nashmir and, unbeknownst to Bri, Edward.

Bri broke the silence. "Blackburn is alive, somewhere. Will we never have peace?"

Henry leaned forward. "He is wounded, perhaps gravely. He will go to ground, heal until he is fit enough to leave London for his own safety. He cannot return to his hotels—we have both under surveillance. He may break into an unoccupied home, or go to some obscure hotel or rooming house. He may seek out the grandmother, where we have stationed watchers. He always carried money, passports, or had them hidden where he could access them quickly. We are vigilant now, but he will wait until we slacken. In a month, two months, or a year, he will try again."

"I refuse to live in fear." Gwyneth's jaw hardened with resolve. "Lady Penelope's wedding is at the end of the week. Perhaps a happy occasion can lift our spirits. I must say, I am amazed such a young woman is marrying my old schoolmate. The 'blond baron' always got attention from the ladies. Were it not for Ian, perhaps I should have been forced to marry again, Bri. To one of your young friends."

A look of horror crossed Bri's face. "Father, what an appalling thought!"

"You don't want to be a 'brood mare'." Gwyneth shrugged. "Either Henry or I might be called on to save Ravenshire."

"*You?* At nine years past forty?" Bri could not hide her disbelief.

"I seem to recall Lady Brookmont giving birth at two past fifty when we were children." Henry looked toward Gwyneth for confirmation.

Gwyneth nodded. "She had a youthful appearance. It was whispered that she hennaed her hair."

"Have you two lost your senses entirely?"

"It appears you have left us no choice. Ian is but a child. You have agreed only to continue the engagement to Edward for the wedding of Lady Penelope. Then, depending on your decision, we may have to make a carefully worded announcement to avoid ruining your reputation."

Bri blanched. "How bad would it be?"

Henry shrugged. "You are still an heiress. That can overcome a lot for an ambitious suitor."

"I don't want an ambitious suitor. I want to fall in love!"

Gwyneth threw up her hands in frustration. "Forget the pretentious poetry of Lord Byron! Most people of our class marry for purpose. You are an heiress. Do not delude yourself with dreams of passion. That bond is rare."

"But you had it with Uncle Luc."

"Yes, but what I thought was love in my first marriage was naught but fantasy. I grew into love with Luc. My wariness nearly drove him away, but he was patient with me."

"So you doubt Edward will be patient with me?"

Henry flushed with visible anger, but kept his voice low. "You are the one who talks of breaking it off with Edward. Over a suspected liaison with Miss Li, which was a mere figment of your overactive imagination. Jealousy is pernicious. It destroys more than intended."

Frustrated into silence once again, Bri looked out the window.

Gwyneth winked at Henry. *Maybe she'll grow up a little.*

***

Sunday, April 19, 1812 – Mlle. Sabine's Brothel
Nashmir

After dropping off Dana and Isabella, the carriage stopped at Mlle. Sabine's brothel.

Nashmir reached for a small satchel. "It's not safe for you to return home for a bit longer, Mr. James. Just a night or two."

The Tibetan healer handed Edward the satchel. "I have prepared a set of vials to complete your treatment. You will need to take one every day with breakfast for the next seven days. By the end of this regimen, you should feel like your old self. You don't have to stay here that long, but you need to be able to walk and appear fit when you leave."

"I am in your debt forever, Nashmir."

"Your energy is limited, Mr. James. Do not overly tax yourself during the wedding festivities."

Edward directed his gaze toward the Tibetan. "Do I have a chance to win her back?"

Nashmir considered Edward's question. "She's headstrong and proud, like an unbroken horse. She will come to you, James, but it must be of her own volition. Never, ever, give Lady Gabriella Wyndward an ultimatum. It didn't work when she was a child, and it won't work now. Give her freedom, as you would lift the reins on a horse to let it run free. Then she will return, but it may not be soon. Kindness and patience, even in the face of abuse, are your only options.

"She is more fragile that she knows. Her unbridled jealousy at Miss Li's presence in your life surprised even her. Never before had she cared much for a beau, let alone fallen in love with one. You have pierced her heart. Let that heart heal and she will be yours."

Edward smiled with an air of frustration. "Too bad you didn't tell me that when I first met her."

"You weren't ready to hear it then."

Edward's face clouded as he looked at their destination. "Why have we stopped at a tailor's shop?"

"I have arranged for you to stay above the tailor's shop for a few days. Stay out of sight. They sheltered you before we went to Ravenshire. I will check on you daily."

Nashmir led Edward through the tailor's shop and up several flights of stairs, supporting him as he stopped frequently to catch his breath.

"I guess I'm weaker than I thought."

As they reached the final landing, the fierce eyes of a wolf-like dog greeted him.

"You? I thought you were a phantasm."

***

Tuesday, April 21, 1812 – Edward's Townhouse
Edward

Have improved over the prior two days, Edward exited the earl's carriage. He saluted Jean-Louis, and greeted François at the door, and went into his study. He leafed through his mail while Shore drew his bath.

He dashed off a note of thanks to Mlle. Sabine, offering private banking services should she require them.

The invitations on his desk were for three receptions preceding Lady Penelope's wedding. *I'll have to ask Bri which ones we should attend together.* He closed his eyes and sat back in the wingback chair. *This is going to be difficult. When I tell her the truth, will she leave me?*

***

Tuesday, April 21, 1812 – Lord Ravenshire's Townhouse
Bri

Still a bit shaken from recent events, Bri tried to distract herself. This afternoon, she sat in the parlor, reading one of Persephone Peabody's novellas. She turned the pages mindlessly. *Once again we don't know if Blackie is alive or dead. He might strike at any time. I cannot let myself be fearful.*

Bri's internal debate raged. She had lost confidence. Fear was a new emotion. She tried to bury it, but she felt its grip at inopportune moments, like a cold hand of ice squeezing her heart.

Thompson cleared his throat, startling her and causing her to loosen her fingers, letting her book slip to the floor with a thud. She reached down to retrieve it.

"Lady Gabriella, pardon the interruption." He handed her several letters, sealed with various colors of melted wax. "These were received while you were at Ravenshire."

Invitations for various pre-wedding receptions were among them, but one from Edward was the first she opened. It was dated earlier that day.

> *Dearest Bri:*
> *I should like to meet you for a private lunch tomorrow*
> *at one o'clock at the museum.*
> *Lady Gwyneth has agreed to chaperone.*
> *Lovingly requested, E.*

Bri's initial excitement turned to anger at her aunt for arranging this meeting without her knowledge, rage at Edward for assuming she'd comply with his request, and annoyance at herself for wanting to see him.

Just before dinner, Bri joined her father and Aunt Gwyneth in the study.

Thompson brought her a glass of sherry.

Holding the letter from Edward in her hand, she waved it at her aunt. "Did you not think to tell me that you arranged a luncheon for me with Edward?"

"He requested my intervention this morning and after the disturbances with Blackburn, I thought it prudent. I hope you intend to accept."

Bri sighed. "I will. We should not appear angry with each other at Lady Penelope's wedding. Perhaps we can mitigate any awkwardness. I don't want us to stumble around in a fog of silence."

The butler cleared his throat. "Dinner is served."

They took their places at the long table.

Gwyneth took a spoonful of her tomato bisque. "If Blackburn

survived, what will he do next?"

Henry took a bite of a baguette, chewed for a moment, and moved his gaze between the two women. "He may come back to London, but Boyd has cleared out his belongings from both hotels, although he may have a third location we don't know about. Jean-Louis has people watching the grandmother.

"Blackburn is nothing if not a careful planner, anticipating all potential roadblocks. He may have sailed away, as did the Sultan and his entourage, perhaps to points east. One thing we know for certain. If he lives, his thirst for revenge will never be quenched. He could come at us at any time, especially if we think we are free of him."

"No!" Bri leaned forward. "I simply won't succumb to fear. Blackie is a wounded animal. Dangerous, but the element of surprise has evaporated."

The earl nodded. "Despite his prodigious capabilities, he is wounded, perhaps grievously, which will delay his treachery. He trusts no one, kills those who aid him, and must always look over his shoulder. Further, our intrepid Jean-Louis, the canniest tracker on any continent, escaped, although he is ailing."

"Ailing? Recovering from being shot is more than ailing." Gwyneth glared at Henry. "He is not up to his usual feats of valor."

Henry sipped his wine and laughed. "He repeated his belief that he will not die in England. Valor? Are we back in the days of knights on white horses riding to the rescue of a damsel in distress?"

Bri's defiance increased. "His surname *is* Chevalier. He's always been my protector. A wounded Jean-Louis is better than Blackie with five accomplices."

Gwyneth sighed. "You are lost in a delusion, no doubt caused by a lack of sleep."

Bri sat back in her chair in exasperation.

Henry directed his gaze at his sister. "We both know that Jean-Louis is nothing short of amazing. He's beaten death no less than a dozen times. Don't court defeat. We've had a setback. Blackburn may disappear for a time and tend to his wounds, if he survives. But he will no doubt leave London with all due haste."

Taking a spoonful of soup, Bri considered the situation. "Risks await us daily. Falling down stairs, carriage accidents, attacks by highwaymen, illness or injury from innumerable sources. We go forward in spite of these risks and we can go forward despite

Blackie's escape."

Henry rang the bell for the server to remove the soup tureens. "The next time, I will not miss. Make no mistake: Blackburn will die by my hand."

CHAPTER EIGHTY-ONE

Wednesday, April 22, 1812 – Lord Ravenshire's Townhouse
Bri

In a state of semi-consciousness, Bri felt pressure on her chest. A tongue licked her nose. Stirring, she opened her eyes. Monkey, splayed across her chest, fixed his azure eyes on her and meowed.

Rubbing his ears, she cooed. "Good morning, my little Monkey, my prince charming. Why can't a man be more like you? Loyal, devoted, a wonderful listener." As she raised herself to a sitting position, the cat slid off. He landed in the folds of the down comforter, rolled into a ball, closed his eyes and purred.

Spotty woke up and came over to lick her too.

Bri laughed.

A knock at the door signaled Dana's arrival. She placed a tray with a pot of hot water, tea leaves steeping, on a small table next to a reading chair. A cinnamon scent wafted through the air.

"Good morning, Lady Gabriella. I shall run your bath." Dana's Irish brogue brightened Bri's morning.

"I'm meeting Aunt Gwyneth at the museum at mid-day. Please lay out my pale green dress. It looks like a lovely spring morning."

"There's still a bit of chill in the air, milady, but the buds are on the branches, so it won't be long now before the blooms of spring appear."

Pulling on her robe, Bri walked into the bath and splashed water on her face while the tub was filling.

Dana poured lavender-colored liquid into the water, which began to bubble and create a foamy surface.

"How lovely! It's like stepping into a cloud." Bri stepped into the claw-footed tub, and sank down into the warm, welcoming water.

The maid left to lay out her mistress's clothes for the day, then returned to the bath and moved a stool to a position where she could sit behind Bri's head. "A quick duck, milady."

Bri submerged herself so that her hair was sopping wet.

Dana doused Bri's long auburn locks with her sister's special liquid shampoo, blended in the Wyndward kitchens with ingredients imported from India. "This has the essence of hibiscus, milady. I like the way your hair settles afterwards."

One of the Wyndward trading partners in Bombay had brought shampoo to Henry's attention and provided him with recipes. At Bri's suggestion, Jane Anne had spent months testing the ingredients and formulae and made specific refinements. Her salon was busy and her products were popular.

After Bri's hair was thoroughly soaked with the hibiscus shampoo and shaped into a topknot with a foamy consistency not unlike that of the bathing waters, Dana asked, "Are you ready?"

Bri closed her eyes. "Yes."

Picking up a bucket of water, filled before the tub was full, Dana tilted it to rinse Bri's hair with the cooled water until all the frothiness dissipated. She reached for a towel and wrapped her lady's head in a turban-like style.

After Bri leaned back to relax, Dana placed a small towel soaked in lavender essence over Bri's face to soothe away any eye puffiness.

"You're a marvel, Dana."

Bri stood to leave the tub, enveloping herself in the thick-looped cotton robe that Dana held for her.

After Dana fixed her hair, Bri dressed.

Monkey and Spotty followed her downstairs to the kitchen for their breakfast.

Henry was seated and reading the *Times*. He looked at her over his reading spectacles. "Good morning, Bri. You look like a breath of spring this morning. Perhaps your garb will hurry it along. 'Tis a clear day. Not a cloud to be seen."

After kissing her father on the forehead, Bri took her place, and the servers brought a plate of eggs and bacon with a basket of croissants. "I'm meeting Edward at the museum today for the mid-day meal. And I'm considering breaking off our engagement."

Henry stopped in mid-bite. "You say that in a matter-of-fact way, Bri. This is a serious step, don't you agree?"

Without looking at her father, Bri continued to eat, speaking between bites. "I have given it constant thought over these last weeks. I am not yet certain. His behavior with Miss Li was intolerable. He fell into Blackie's treacherous plan like a chess pawn. I've been wondering if I've mistaken gratitude for love. Edward saved me from Blackie last year, but is that enough of a basis for marriage? I am not certain he loves me nor that I love him."

Her father set down his fork. "Love is an invention of modern life, Bri. Arranged marriages are still the norm. Mine was a combination of attraction and family compatibility. Although it ended in tragedy, it was not a loveless match. But you and Edward have a strong intellectual as well as physical attraction. I had hoped he could make you happy, though God knows, that would be quite a task."

Bri stiffened. "Whatever do you mean, Father? I am not the scold Edward makes me out to be."

"No?"

"No! And his constant preening in front of that ever-present Miss Xie Xie Li pushed me to my limit."

"Did it?"

"Why are you throwing questions back at me? Do you think I don't know my own mind?" Sparks flew from her emerald-hued eyes toward her father.

"I think your mind is not what is ending this engagement. I think it is an immature and jealous heart that is overcoming your rational side. Edward is a fine man, despite the lapse in judgment that allowed Miss Li to distract him from his responsibilities."

"So I am one of his 'responsibilities'?"

"And whatever possessed you to follow him to *Dreamtime* in the wee hours of the night months ago marks an equal lapse in judgment on your part. Save for the quick action of Jean-Louis, you might have found yourself in serious danger, as you did when Blackie kidnapped you."

"It was impudent of Jean-Louis to follow me."

"Jean-Louis has been charged by me with your protection since you were three. I trust him with my life, as you should. He deserves your gratitude, not criticism. You are quite a handful for any man, Gabriella Jane Craigfell Wyndward. And it was *you* who invited Blackburn to stay at Ravenshire."

"I will not be 'handled' by any man, Father. Ever. Perhaps I shall never marry. And as for Blackburn, better to have him in plain sight than vanished as he is now."

"I do not require you to marry, my dear, and Ravenshire no longer needs you to produce an heir because Ian can become earl. I might marry again and produce an heir, but my age does not favor reproduction and it is probable that neither Charlotte nor Taita will have me. In your case, Miss Li is gone."

Bri paused for a moment. "How do you know?"

"She sent a note to Jean-Louis revealing her role."

Initially taken aback, Bri resumed her musings. "The absence of Miss Li doesn't change my feelings. I'll always wonder about him now. If I had known Miss Li was a pawn in Blackie's game, it might have made it a difference at the time."

"I think it already has. 'Tis your wounded pride. Blackie's planting of Miss Li into Edward's life irked you to the point of poor judgment. If you break off your engagement to Edward, you are letting Blackie win."

"I have not made a final decision. Perhaps we could just delay the wedding."

"Only to relive this indecision each time Edward does something you don't like? Commitment means working through good and bad. I believe you are not giving Edward a fair hearing. I ask you to wait a month. Do not break off the engagement before Lady Penelope's wedding. She is a friend and you don't want your break-up to cast a pall over her special day, as both you and Edward are in the wedding party."

Bri sighed in resignation. "Very well, Father. I would not want to hurt Penelope or let gossip about Edward and me overshadow her wedding. I have written him letters ending our engagement, but always end up burning them. Perhaps Edward can prove his love for me by the wedding."

Henry shook his head. "Bri, if you give Edward an ultimatum to 'prove his love' for you, in a set time frame, you will push him away. He doesn't have to prove anything. You must weigh this decision very carefully. I believe Edward loves you. He accepts your role as my 'man of affairs'. He enjoys your intellectual sparring matches. He is a good-looking man, as near as I can tell. Many women will set their caps for him if you reject him. Bri, listen carefully to what I say: A man never forgets rejection. You may lose him forever because you are temporarily angry with him. Do not let a fit of pique destroy your chance for a happy marriage."

Bri nodded. "Why must I be the one to understand him? What about Miss Li? When will the next 'Miss Li' come along? But I will wait until after Penelope's marriage." She finished her now-cold breakfast in silence.

Mlle. Sabine said to listen. I do not want to be angry when I see Edward.

***

Edward

Edward arrived at the museum looking thinner than when he had last seen Bri, nearly two weeks earlier. She'd noticed that he'd been losing weight since Christmas, but he'd brushed off her concern. Recent events had accelerated the loss. His clothes hung on him, ill-fitting.

The museum manager escorted him to Gwyneth's office. She and Bri were seated, waiting for him.

Bri stood and a look of alarm crossed her face. "Edward! Have you been unwell?"

"Yes. But I have recovered. I feared for your safety with Blackburn bent on revenge."

Gwyneth intervened. "Jean-Louis warned Edward that he was also in danger from Blackburn."

The server brought two plates and removed the silver covers to reveal portions of poached chicken and vegetables.

"I will leave you two to eat in private." Bri's aunt left the room.

They embraced. Awkward at first, they clung to each other for longer than Bri had expected.

"Tell me of your illness, Edward. I've not heard of any outbreak of influenza."

Edward pushed away his plate.

Concerned, Bri reached for Edward's hand. "You must eat. You must regain your strength. I insist that you eat half before we speak of anything."

Relenting, Edward took a bite and managed to eat a little less than half of his meal as his fiancée instructed.

Breaking the silence, Bri smiled. "Excellent. Now…what did you eat in Scotland that made you ill? Bad fish?"

"It was not an illness. It was a weakness."

Bri's face clouded. "I don't understand. What weakness would affect your health if not an illness?"

Edward breathed deeply, steeling his nerves. "A weakness for the poppy."

The fork in Bri's hand dropped and clanged on the plate. "You are an opium-eater?"

"I am mightily ashamed to admit it. During a trek in the Himalayas, I tripped over a rock and fell partially down the peak, saved only by a slab extending over the crevasse below. A companion lowered a rope to me, but I was too weak to grasp it. He ran for help and the indigenous natives scaled the rocky terrain to bundle me in a sort of hammock to lift me to safety and then carry me back to their village. They treated the pain during my recovery with a miracle plant that I only later learned was the opium poppy. Not only did the infusion of poppy remove any trace of pain, it imbued my entire being with an indescribable euphoria. Once my injuries were healed, I was unable to function without it. With the help of the local healer, it took over a year to separate myself from its power over me."

Bri frowned. "But why now?"

"Recently, I experimented with an opium pipe at *Dreamtime*—"

"With Miss Li? Are you blaming her?"

"No, the fault is entirely my own. In retrospect, it must have been Blackburn's plan for Miss Li to lure me back to the pipes of ecstasy. I will probably never know how he learned of my weakness. I thought I could take a puff occasionally, as someone sips wine. I experimented with deeper infusions once in anger, and again at the baron's party for his groomsmen. After the second session, my efforts at resistance proved futile. The temptation overwhelmed me. The lure of the poppy eclipses all other desires. Only the help of Jean-Louis, Nashmir, your aunt and father helped me recover."

Bri's face flushed. "So everyone, literally *everyone*, knew of this affliction except me! All of you conspired to maintain this veil of secrecy to deceive me?"

"No. It was to protect you from my shame."

Rising from the table as her voice increased in volume, Bri stared at him. "How many times do I need to tell you that I don't need to be protected?" Her face flushed to a deep purple color.

Raising his voice to match hers, Edward countered, "How many times have you told *me* that Jean-Louis is your protector?" He slammed his hand on the table. "As your future husband, *I* should be your protector!"

***

Bri

"Men! Always the same useless competitive madness!" Bri waved a hand dismissing the notion. *I have lost control of myself. Remember Nashmir's breathing instructions. She regained her composure.* "But we have been diverted from the topic at hand. How do I *know*—how do *you* know—that the poppy will not capture your will again?"

Edward looked directly into her green eyes. "I don't. No one can know what the future holds. But I know that to choose that path would be certain ruin. And that I would lose you forever. I love you, Bri. I do not want to lose you."

Bri looked down at her untouched food.

"Now it is you who must eat." Edward leaned closer. "Please."

His fiancée pushed her plate away. "Perhaps we are doomed. I'm not a believer in Fate, but neither can I trust in such an uncertain future."

"Uncertain? So you doubt my resolve."

"I doubt myself as well as you. We rushed into this engagement. I have no interest in other men, particularly, but perhaps we owe ourselves some time, a delay in our marriage plans, to know that our futures are truly with each other."

Edward sighed in resignation. "How much time?"

"I don't know, a month or two? To test our love, ourselves."

"Months can turn into a year with neglect."

"I am not saying that we should neglect each other. After Lady Penelope's wedding, we'll simply tell people we've pushed off the wedding date until the fall. No one will take any notice."

Edward's voice was soft. "Fall is farther away than a month or two. I understand your hesitation, but I'll not beg, Bri. I love you."

"Edward, be sensible. A few months to absorb the horrors of Blackburn's treachery is not so very long."

Her fiancé gazed at the face of the woman he loved. "So I am your fiancé without a wedding date. The date was set on the evening of our Engagement Ball for the end of June. It's embarrassing for both of us to delay it."

"Embarrassing?"

"Yes. Breaking our engagement would be a major embarrassment for both of us and a blow to your reputation. Think carefully before you act."

"Are you suggesting I am rash? An overly emotional woman, perhaps? Hysterical? A word men always use to describe women?"

"I have not said that. I have to regain my strength. Let's also try to regain the happiness we had in the Azores and at the Engagement Ball."

Bri's resolve softened as she gazed at him. "I was so happy with you then." Their eyes locked and she felt a surge of energy. "I want to try, Edward. I still love you."

"I know I have disappointed you. I'm asking for another chance."

"You could not fight the poppy as I could not surmount the jealousy that consumed me. I am at fault for not trusting you. We must give each other another chance."

Edward rose.

She stood, walked toward him, and let him envelop her in his arms. "If we break up, Blackie wins."

Edward whispered in her ear. "Blackburn will never win."

Their embrace continued until Gwyneth entered the room. She smiled. "I am happy to see you together."

Edward released his hold on Bri. "There are several events preceding Lady Penelope's wedding. Shall we attend them all?"

"Yes," answered Bri, "but you must put on weight or *you* will be the center of attention, not the bride. I shall have Nellie send over cakes and pastries every day."

"The first invitation is for tonight. According to Jean-Louis, Miss Li has left London. Forever. What shall we tell Rogers and the others about her departure?"

Bri's forehead wrinkled as she considered his question. "We can't say that Blackburn sent her to break us up. To all, he is dead and 'tis best that he remain so."

Gwyneth pursed her lips. "Just say that her family requested her urgent return to Egypt and leave it at that. 'The woman in the red mask' will not be soon forgotten by any in the *ton,* but with time, her memory will fade."

Bri nodded. "Why don't you come for a sherry first. You, Father, Nate and I can go together."

"Fine. I'll see you at five." Edward kissed her lightly on the lips.

After her fiancé left, Gwyneth embraced Bri.

"Why didn't you tell me you'd seen him?"

"It was to protect you. I only stumbled on Edward, hidden in the stables at Ravenshire. Nashmir was tending him."

"Do you jest? He was right under my nose when I went in to see Jean-Louis?"

"Edward was in danger from Blackburn as much as any of us. In his weakened, depleted state, we dared not leave him unattended. His condition was quite horrifying. I was not certain that he would survive."

Bri backed away from her aunt. "Now you tell me he might have died and I wouldn't have been able to say goodbye? Why does everyone but me know these things?"

"I followed Nashmir and found Edward. Henry and Jean-Louis arranged a way to allow Edward to fight the poppy's hold over him as well as keep him safe from Blackburn."

Bri walked over to the window and stared off into the distance. "I never thought to marry before Edward."

"He's the only man who's ever been an intellectual match for you."

"We've disappointed each other."

"Edward is human. You expect ideal behavior, which does not exist in this world. In your mind, imperfection is an unforgiveable weakness."

Bri fell back into her chair and absorbed the sadness in her aunt's eyes. "Am I such a terrible person that he would sink into the poppy to escape me?"

"That is not the way it was, I am sure. You both made mistakes. Learn from them."

CHAPTER EIGHTY-TWO

Wednesday, April 22, 1812 – Ravenshire Stables
Jean-Louis

Nashmir changed the dressings on Jean-Louis's wounds after preparing a tincture of salt and herbs.

The Frenchman flinched. "It stings."

"That means it's working."

Jean-Louis grimaced. "When will I be able to resume my duties?"

"Tomorrow, if you are prudent. I will give you something to sleep and heal. But no fights or riding. Sit, listen, advise. No more."

Looking askance at first, Jean-Louis finally nodded.

Nashmir stretched to his full, though short, stature. "Make no mistake, Jean-Louis. You will be of no use to anyone if you try to do too much too fast."

Sitting back, Jean-Louis shrugged. "Much as I hate to admit it, I know you are correct, Nashmir. I shall obey your instructions—just this once. Don't expect it to become a habit."

"Then don't get yourself shot again. You bear more scars than most men I've seen."

"What? Have you seen another with more scars than I?" He tried to rise.

Nashmir restrained him. "You challenge my patience, Jean-Louis. Lie down. I must admit that others who sustained wounds such as yours breath no more. That claw mark on your side—"

Smiling, Jean-Louis pointed to the claw carvings into his flesh. "A cougar in the wilds of Canada left me this souvenir."

"And that puncture near your lung?"

"A buffalo tossed me into the air like a feather."

"The gouge in your leg?"

"A wolf attack."

"Who is a more fearsome adversary—Blackburn or a wild animal?"

His face set in grim resolve, Jean-Louis answered. "Blackburn is by far more dangerous. He has the cunning of a predator, the cleverness of a courtesan, and the patience of a viper. Still, he is but a man, and mortal. The earl's shot grazed his temple. I wounded him grievously by knife and Hinton by knife and pistol. He may never regain his former agility, so that is a fact in our favor."

"So you expect to meet him again?"

"That is in the hands of Fate. In the next encounter, he will not survive. I will not die by Blackburn's hand. Even if I am wrong...should Blackburn and I die in conflict with each other, it would be a victory for me. Bri would then be safe."

***

Wednesday, April 22, 1812 – Tattersalls Reception Hall
Gio

Looking over the décor for the first pre-wedding evening reception for her brother and Lady Penelope, Davinia nodded in satisfaction. The private club at Tattersalls, where she and the baron habitually spent prodigious sums on racehorses, would be the scene for a myriad assortment of old friends of the bride and groom. Walls featured oil paintings of famous thoroughbreds.

Startling Gio from behind, Davinia asked, "Any painted by you?"

"Only one." He pointed to one of the earl with a champion Arabian racer and stud. "I specialize in humans, more's the pity. A horse wouldn't complain that I made her look too fat, or too old, or too," he waved his hand in a gesture of dismissal, "whatever."

"Perhaps you should paint *me*, Gio."

"An elegant subject you would be. Anytime you would like to pay my exorbitant fee, I would be happy to comply." He bowed and clicked his heels in the Prussian manner.

"I am tempted."

"That's a dangerous statement to overhear," said Henry.

He and Nate came closer to view the paintings.

"We are found out, Lady Portchallont," said Gio. "*Scandal & Shame* will have us engaged in a raging love affair in the next issue."

Nate shook his head. "Gio, you have not changed in all the years I've known you. A provocateur of the first order."

"And what, pray tell, is a provocateur of the second order?" Gio took another flute of Champagne from a passing waiter.

Davinia tilted her head toward Edward. "Mr. James looks unwell."

"A bout of food poisoning in Scotland. Spoiled fish, I'm told." Henry hoped the lie would quiet anyone impolite enough to inquire."

"We've heard Lady Gabriella's wedding will follow Beau's shortly, but I've not received an invitation. Have I not been invited?"

"No slight intended, Davinia. There has been discussion that the date should be postponed until his doctor says Mr. James is fully cured. No date has been set."

Gio walked over to Vaux and Rogers. "This is quite an event."

Vaux nodded. "We are taking note of the preparations."

"We might ourselves as *Rogers and Vaux, Impresarios of Intimate Gatherings*," whispered Rogers as guests began to flood the room.

"I was thinking we should call ourselves Vaux & Rogers, Virtuosos of Receptions."

Gio scoffed. "You are far too fond of alliteration."

"It's memorable. That is the secret of successful advertising." Vaux pulled on Rogers's arm. "Hold! James is looking even worse than rumors suggested."

"He looks how I felt after reading in *Scandal & Shame* that 'the woman in the red mask" had departed for destinations unknown. She lives in my dreams."

"Let her go. She could never have been anything but a courtesan for you, anyway."

"True, but what I would have given for just one night..."

Bri and Edward walked over. "You two look like you're conspiring to rob a bank."

"Just as long as it's not yours, eh, James? Being an impresario is more expensive than I anticipated." Rogers drained his wine glass.

***

Bri

Edward became unsteady on his feet after a stroll around the room, so he and Bri sat at one of the tables set up randomly around the large reception area. The lavender tablecloth and napkins echoed the colors Penelope had chosen for her wedding.

Edward lowered his voice. "Did you tell Penelope about the unmentionable device?"

"You mustn't overtax yourself with thoughts of engaging in sponge games. You're not ready." She winked at him. "Or *are* you?"

"Not yet."

Bri reached over and squeezed his hand. "To answer your question, the bridesmaids under the age of fifty met at the salon to try different hairstyles, and we introduced them to the secret stash in the back room. We've had to double our imports."

"Always thinking. That's my Bri." He noticed her attention was directed at Sir Reggie speaking to Rogers. "An odd pair, those too."

"Sir Reggie strikes me as someone who never makes a stray remark. A diplomat, to be sure, but perhaps more."

"More?"

"I may have read too many novels, but I can't help but wonder if he isn't one of those men behind the scenes who pulls strings, deeply involved in international intrigue of the sort we cannot imagine."

"You are weaving your uncovering of Blackburn's treachery into fantasies of subterfuge being conducted by the most unlikely characters."

"Perhaps. I am affected by the truth of Miss Li 's motivation. It never occurred to me that Blackburn would have set her to the tasks of tempting you with the poppy and instilling jealousy in me at the same time. They almost succeeded in breaking us apart. I'm ashamed to say I was played by someone who recognized a weakness in me that I didn't know I had. Tonight, every time I look at someone I *think* I know, I wonder what weaknesses *they* are hiding or harboring without acknowledgment."

"You sound as though you're concocting a plot for one of those scandalous novels with outrageous plots that circulate in the *ton*."

Bri winked at her fiancé. "Perhaps you don't know *everything* about me, Mr. James."

"And I probably never will. You keep me guessing, Bri."

***

Thursday, April 23, 1812 – Ravenshire Stables
Jean-Louis

After leaving his room at the Ravenshire stables despite Nashmir's warning that he needed more rest, Jean-Louis rode directly to Mlle. Sabine's. The Frenchman climbed the back stairs, stopping twice to catch his breath. "*Foutre!*" *I shall rest when I get back to the stables.*

Reaching Sabine's private office, he paused again.

"Are you unwell, Jean-Louis?" Her face registering alarm, she rose and moved toward him.

Shrugging off her offer of help, the Frenchman lowered himself into a chair.

"Sherry?"

"*Oui.*" He accepted the glass and took a sip, closed his eyes, and gathered himself to his purpose.

"I came to thank you for sheltering young James."

Giselle entered.

Jean-Louis started to rise, but Giselle put her hand on his shoulder. "No need. Detective Boyd told us of your heroics."

"Not *très* heroic." He grimaced as he shifted his position. "I got shot and my prey escaped."

A voice came from behind. "Perhaps he is mortally wounded."

Jean-Louis turned to see Boyd. "We can hope, but I want him dead. Preferably by my hand."

"Not what a detective wants to hear from an ordinary citizen."

Jean-Louis raised an eyebrow.

"But of course, you are not *ordinary.*" Boyd smiled in resignation. "Just be sure it's self-defense."

"Always is." Jean-Louis laughed. "I dance with death, but the spectre has not yet vanquished me."

"Nevertheless, you and the earl were foolhardy to take on Blackburn alone," scolded Boyd. "We searched the rooms in the hotels here in London where he stayed, finding assorted disguises, but no clues as to where he came from or planned to go. He led us to a *cul-de-sac* of deception."

Jean-Louis nodded. "He knows how to disappear, but we believe him to be grievously wounded. He may be hiding out nearby with an as-yet-unknown accomplice." *Unknown to you. I know where to go. I have Blackburn's grandmother under surveillance.*

Boyd bid them farewell. "Remember my warning."

Jean-Louis nodded.

After Boyd left, Sabine inclined her head at a questioning angle. "Something crossed your mind just before the detective left."

Waving his hand in a gesture of dismissal, Jean-Louis demurred. "Just a momentary ache. Nothing more."

"I've learned to read your facial expressions. There *is* more." Sabine shook her finger at the French trapper. "Don't take any more chances until you have recovered. Your pallor concerns me."

The former trapper rose to leave, took Sabine's hand and kissed it. "I will not—"

"I know, I know. You will not die in England." She moved in closer for a lingering kiss goodbye.

***

Thursday, April 23, 1812 – Boston

Barryngton Wyndward

Barryngton walked Fairfax to the door after a quiet dinner.

Looking around to be sure he would not be overheard, even in Barryngton's home, Fairfax whispered, "I fear war may come again, old friend."

Frowning, Barryngton listened.

"Mumblings are growing louder. The Revolution was not the last battle. A blockade may come. Set aside provisions for a siege." Fairfax took no pains to hid his concern. His furrowed brow and grim visage were not lost on Barryngton. "War is terror. The Revolution was exhilarating, but I was younger then, idealistic. I often marvel that I came to America as a British loyalist and found myself pulled to the cause of independence. But this will be no war for freedom and ideals."

"I shall take your warning to heart, Fairfax. You take care as well."

"At my age, death awaits by a loose cobblestone or uneven step, an errant horse, or a rabid dog." He laughed. "I'm beyond the ire of a jealous lover with a pistol, thank God. But in my youth, your brother, Neyl, was my second in a duel. A misfire is the only reason I stand before you today. But I digress. War is in the offing."

Barryngton watched Fairfax ride off toward his nearby Boston residence, purchased years ago to house him on extended trips from his home in South Carolina. *War? I must write to Henry before all communication is cut off.*

***

Thursday, April 23, 1812 – The Hanforth Mansion
Bri

The second pre-wedding reception for wedding attendants at the Hanforth Mansion, hosted by Clarissa and Dr. St. Cloud, was atwitter with gossip about Edward's emaciated appearance. "A bad meal in Scotland" was overheard several times.

Bri, at his side, resplendent in a burnt orange dress the color of her hair, did her best to allay all concerns.

Lady Patricia pulled Bri away for a private moment. "I hear Miss Li has left London. Do you think that means I might capture Rogers's interest? He seemed besotted with that exotic Asian vixen."

Will I ever escape talk of the exotic Miss Li? "He struck me as interested in you before Miss Li descended on us."

"That was at your Engagement Ball, of all things. By calling her 'the woman in the red mask,' they elevated her to a figure of mystery."

"I am grateful that Edward and I are engaged and that I need not worry about this medieval ritual of courtship."

"Well, you are still in the game whether you recognize it or not."

"Edward and I are engaged. Life is not a game."

"Then you don't understand life, Bri. Courtship is the oldest game of all."

"But if you win the game, win a beau, do you lose yourself?"

"Oh, for Heaven's sake, Bri, this is no time for philosophy! Look at Penelope. She is clearly in love. And with a much older man."

Bri nodded. "I asked Penelope if conversation was difficult and she laughed and said the baron was a delightful conversationalist. He told me that he adores her openness and exuberance."

"No doubt as a contrast to that scheming half-sister of his, Davinia. Not exactly divine, that one."

"Why do you speak of her thus? She seems quite lovely."

"If you think the baron is old, her now-dead husband was a walking skeleton. The joke's on her, really. He didn't die right away. Lived nearly as long as Methuselah. They married when she was but nineteen and he over fifty." Lady Patricia lowered her voice. "She had a child less than nine months later. Now Davinia is fifty-four and her husband died a mere two years ago. By then," scoffed Lady Patricia, "she was way past her prime for attracting any man. If her husband hadn't died when he did, she probably would have poisoned him."

"Heavens!" Bri glanced around to make sure no one had heard that comment. "You must curb your tongue in public."

"Oh, it's just us, my dear. Just us. His stepdaughter from his late wife used to live with them, you know. Rumored to be an invalid. Succumbed to a mysterious illness shortly after he married Lady Davinia. Their son is here as a groomsman, tonight." She scanned the room and pointed with her fan. "There he is."

Bri glanced in that direction. "Davey and the baron share a striking family resemblance."

"He looks as if he could be the baron's son!" Lady Patricia raised an eyebrow and took another sip of punch.

Bri noticed and shook her head. "Surely I do not take your meaning—"

"Mere gossip, my dear. And the baron is clearly besotted with Lady Penelope, raven-tressed and plump, but still lovely. Quite a contrast to the icy blonde goddess of a half-sister. As for the nephew, well…"

Narrowing her gaze, Bri leaned closer. "There's more?"

In a whisper, Lady Patricia added, "The nephew is a bit dim. Overfond of wine and they say he frequents the gambling hells. Quite a rake. Has taken to racing Phaetons, you know. Two breach-of-promise suits have been quashed with money. Davinia dotes on him. Spoiled beyond redemption, I'm sure."

"You really must be more judicious in curbing your penchant for gossip."

Lady Patricia waved her hand in dismissal of Bri's admonition. "Lady Clarissa is a delightful hostess. We love her, of course, and

Lulu is adorable, but many look down on her, you know, for marrying a doctor, and not even a doctor for people," she scoffed, "but for house pets. Still, she has regained her figure after the recent birth of her daughter."

Exasperated, Bri shook her head. "Are you not being somewhat arbitrary?"

"Somewhat? Indeed not. I am being precisely arbitrary. Every Society has its hierarchy, Bri. From tribal chieftains to royal monarchs, there is a pecking order. Deny it at your peril. 'Tis easy for you, as you're centuries ahead of other titles. Though not as high as *some*, it *is* ancient. You are still an heiress, even though the title will go to Ian unless you have a son. In fact, you are the richest of all the unmarried women in the *ton*, more than any of the king's daughters, they say. Make no mistake, Bri, you are a catch for any man, even a prince."

"Let us no longer speak of me. I have been 'caught,' to use your description, by my fiancé, Mr. James. 'Tis Penelope's evening."

Lady Patricia took another sip of wine. "Have you heard her plans for the honeymoon?"

Bri nodded. "To avoid Napoleon's navy on the high seas, they are sailing to Scotland, and from there to Iceland and Norway."

"A Viking pilgrimage. That awful Napoleon has kept me from Europe for too long." She sighed. "How I miss Paris!" Lady Patricia shook her head in frustration, as if Napoleon existed simply to annoy her. "How did such a coarse man become elevated?"

Bri frowned at Lady Patricia's single-minded fixation on everyone's position in Society. "The other officers either lost their heads to the guillotine or fled France. He was a man ready to seize opportunity at the moment it presented itself. There were no rivals. He rode the winds of Fate to his destiny."

Lady Patricia laughed. "Bri, you have the mind of a novelist. Maybe you should write under a pseudonym, like Persephone Peabody or Drusilla Dorset."

I know them both.

CHAPTER EIGHTY-THREE

Friday, April 24, 1812 – St. George's Church
Bri

Mid-morning, the wedding party practiced the procession and order of the wedding service. The sheer number of bridesmaids and groomsmen required more than one run-through as people forgot where they were supposed to stand, ignored the cues from the priest, or stumbled along the aisle.

Bri found herself stealing glances at Edward. *He looks stronger than a few days ago. Will he be able to withstand the pull of the poppy? Can we regain the happy days of the Azores?*

***

Friday, April 24, 1812 – Lord Ravenshire's Gentlemen's Club
Henry

Ensconced in a small private room at Henry's club, old schoolmates, the baron, Sir John James, Henry, Nate and Asgard joined to toast the baron's marriage the next day.

Sir John lamented, "A shame AJ could not be here. Haven't seen him since he left school."

Henry nodded. "AJ fulfilled his dream of becoming an architect, teaching at the University of Padua in Italy until his health failed these last few years. He designed the blueprints for the rebuilding of Ravenshire Castle fifteen years ago. It's been constant construction since then, with masons and historians from Oxford contributing to the project. Maybe it will be done in another fifteen years, or a hundred."

"Sad to hear AJ can no longer walk." The baron sighed. "His wife and children are arriving today with the family doctor, so we will see them at the wedding. They are revitalizing the ancestral Smithton family home, quite a large undertaking. They intend to move back after AJ's death, which may not be far off, I've heard."

"As have I," agreed Nate. "AJ insisted that they come for your wedding. Selfless, really. Can't believe one of our old crew might pass the torch sooner than expected."

"Not so long ago, I thought I would be the first." Sir John's voice sounded wistful.

"Hold on, old boy! You sound disappointed!" Asgard slapped Sir John on the back.

"Not at all. I was just thinking how lucky that I met Ravenshire at university, and that Ravenshire met Nashmir in the Himalayas, and that Nashmir's exotic knowledge of herbs and potions cured me of pain."

Henry put his arm around Sir John, acknowledging his comment.

The American turned his sherry glass slowly in his hands. "I'm worried, old friends, that another war may be brewing between our countries over trade embargoes and the impressment of American sailors on the high seas."

Sir John shook his head. "Wasn't one Revolution enough? And don't we have our hands full with Napoleon? Why fight on two continents? Napoleon is a true threat. I don't believe we will fight America again. No, it will not happen."

Henry was non-committal. "I hope not, but we must prepare for anything. But, see here! Talk of war dulls the joy of the baron's impending nuptials."

"Indeed," agreed Sir John.

The baron took a sip of sherry. "Jamesey, a few nights ago, Edward looked like the bout of food poisoning had hit him quite hard."

Sir John cleared his throat. "It did, but he is stronger every day. It's possible it triggered a recurrence of an illness he suffered in the

Far East."

The baron leaned forward. "We all hope that he recovers completely." He glanced at the earl. "And what of you and the baroness? Is there any hope of reconciliation?"

Henry frowned. "Not soon. Charlotte and I faltered when Taita appeared in London again. Moreover, the scandal of the Sultan's rapid departure after the death of one of his wives has tainted the Prince Regent's opinion of anyone in the Sultan's company. Taita may be lost to me forever. Love seems a distant possibility for me, regardless of the breathless fictions dished by Lord Byron or *Scandal & Shame.*"

"Balderdash, Ravenshire!" The American slammed his hand on the table. "You cannot mean you are star-crossed as that Gypsy witch predicted so long ago. There are no such things as magic spells."

"True, I've never believed in such things. But now…sometimes I wonder."

"No," the baron disagreed. "Each of us charts his own course. Those predictions that fortune teller made so long ago are whispers on the wind. Ravenshire, you have led an exciting life, traveled the world, tempted Fate, beaten Fate, and met fascinating people. And, may I point out: you're not dead yet."

Asgard held up his glass. "Here! Here! Drink to Ravenshire. He's not dead yet!"

***

Saturday, April 25, 1812 – St. George's Church
Bri

As was the custom, Penelope's wedding was scheduled for the morning. The fog was so heavy that it became a candlelight affair.

The day began at dawn in a whirlwind of activity. Bri, Clarissa, Lady Patricia, and the other bridesmaids dressed in gowns of lavender to violet, the colors of an elusive spring. As the bridesmaids and groomsmen took their places flanking each side of the church altar, they turned at the sound of trumpets from the choir loft and Lady Penelope and her father, the Earl of Somervale, walked down the aisle.

Bri choked back tears. *Will Edward and I ever share such a moment?*

She willed herself to focus on the bride.

Penelope beamed, Her lovely gown accentuated her curves and minimized her bulges. In a daring off-the-shoulder chiffon and embroidered brocade in the empire style, her head was topped by a trailing veil set with pearls. *She is a vision.* Her dark hair was pulled up into a top knot with stray tendrils framing her face. Her skin glowed a pale pink. Ribbons of lavender and violet were woven into her bouquet of white roses interspersed with violets the color of her eyes.

A tear fell from Bri's eye. *Is it the ceremony? The music? The promise of love?* Always analyzing her reactions, her self-absorption confused her.

The baron's seven nephews from his five sisters were among his groomsmen. *Lady Patricia's observance is correct. Only Rupie resembles the blond baron.*

When the baron kissed his bride and the trumpets sounded again, Bri was startled into following the choreography of the wedding party. They exited in order, and then boarded carriages for the wedding breakfast at the Library of the British Museum, where both the baron and Lady Penelope's father were benefactors.

***

Saturday, April 25, 1812 – The Library of the British Museum
Gio

The wedding party was seated in the front at long tables with huge topiaries of flowers. Gio, Gwyneth, Henry, Davinia, Lady Anne, Sir John, Nate, AJ's wife, Alexandra, and her family friend, Dr. Capehart, sat together with the baron's widowed sister, Petunia.

Gio leaned toward Gwyneth. "During the vows, did I discern a tear in your eye? Getting soft in your old age?"

"Who are you calling old, you wrinkled-up gnome?"

Gio laughed heartily. "Since a child of nine, you have been remarkably rude."

"I most certainly am not rude. *You* think you can get away with outrageous statements at all times—"

Gio held up a hand. "That's a given. You are in fighting form again." He shrugged. "But I did see a tear."

Gwyneth tilted her head. "Perhaps." She looked off into the distance. "The shimmering light and reflections on the stained glass windows transported me, as if by magic, to another time and place. A simpler time."

***

Henry

Across the table, Henry leaned toward Nate. "We miss you while you are at Merton."

"My book is coming along. I hear I missed a wild time when Blackburn returned, although I'm not sure I would have been much help." Nate shifted in his seat. " 'Tis the turmoil of politics that concerns me. Despite the others' doubt, word in America is that cannon balls may fly by summer."

Henry nodded his head. "No one wants to believe it. Impressment is foolish baiting by the Royal Navy. Napoleon is a much greater threat to us. The HMS Leopard against the USS Chesapeake altercation was over five years ago. Still, I share your concern. Months ago, a contact at the Foreign Office warned me, and I have taken steps to reposition my trade routes and recall vessels from the American coast. But with Napoleon patrolling the Mediterranean and the North Atlantic, it's a challenge. Pirates prowl all coastlines for plunder. South America, Africa and India beckon. But, truth be told, there is no easy way to redeploy a fleet."

"I warn you, Ravenshire—be quick about it. The rhetoric is accelerating in belligerence."

"Your cautionary advice is appreciated, Parker. I shall not be caught unawares."

"They jest about my sober assessment at the university. The other faculty have taken to calling me the 'Cassandra of Oxford.' "

***

Henry

At the wedding breakfast, Sir John smiled at Alexandra Smithton. "My, my, Mrs. Smithton," he muttered. "And you are a professor of architecture as well as AJ?"

"Yes. The University of Padua granted a degree to a woman in 1678, so it is not unusual there as it would be here in England. That is why AJ and I remained in Italy. His fondest hope is to see his ancestral home once again before he dies. I fear that day may come soon, but I refuse to let the thought stay with me long."

Sir John's face clouded with sadness. He peered at Alexandra. "There is something so familiar about you, my dear. I just can't put my finger on it."

Alexandra toyed with her dangling earring. "I am an English girl born in Northern Italy, where my parents settled after a life as diplomats. The children thought it adventurous to evade Napoleon's ships to get here, but I must confess I was terrified the whole way. My ancestors came from Sweden, they say, maybe with the Vikings, but I have not that sailing spirit that the earl does."

"Vikings?" Henry chimed in. "The baron is going to the Viking homelands on his honeymoon, I hear. He wants to see the geothermal springs next to volcanoes in Iceland, a country of contrasts." Turning toward the Smithton family doctor, Henry asked. "Have you visited Iceland, Doctor?"

"No, although I've heard it's very beautiful. We spend a lot of time in the Alps." He leaned over toward Henry. "Can you give us a ride back to our hotel in your carriage so that we may speak privately?"

The earl nodded.

***

Bri

After the wedding breakfast, a sudden exhaustion overcame Bri. She glanced around for Edward, who had been seated at the far end of the table. She rose and walked over to him, leaned in and whispered in his ear, "I realize how terrible it would have been to have lost you to your illness. I love you."

Edward rose and kissed her on the cheek.

Henry came up to her. "We are taking Alexandra and the doctor to their hotel." Seeing Bri's reaction, he admonished, "Do not pout. It is not becoming. Alexandra is an old friend."

Pinched eyebrows conveyed Bri's disapproval. "She is the *wife* of an old friend. You're just being polite."

"You think you have all the answers, don't you?"

Taking Edward's arm, Bri walked with him outside and waited with her father for their carriage to pull up. Edward helped her inside and kissed her goodbye.

Henry followed.

When Alexandra Smithton and the doctor arrived, the earl put his arm around Bri. "Lady Gabriella, unbeknownst to the world, is my 'man of affairs.' She is fully aware of all my business matters and maintains confidences as do I."

Confused, Bri deferred to her father. *What is going on?*

Nate came up to join them in the carriage.

Once inside, Alexandra said, "It's been so long, Henry! Thirty-five years since I've been in London. It's changed but still the same. I can't explain it."

Dr. Capehart leaned forward. "The children are out in the country at the ancestral home. Word will arrive of AJ's death in the next week. The inheritance papers have been resting with solicitors here for years. All is in order. Alexandra will inherit all from AJ's estate to hold in trust for Alan, her son. That should proscribe any legal action by AJ's uncle or his sons. We are assured that her claim is inviolate."

Bri struggled to reveal nothing externally, but internally she was roiling. *How can they calmly talk about a death that is planned for a date certain? Is Father complicit? Is the doctor Alexandra's lover while AJ lies dying? Is the father I thought I knew a conspirator? A killer?*

***

Saturday, April 25, 1812 – Interior of Lord Ravenshire's Carriage
Bri

Nate glanced at Henry. "Bri is horrified. You must explain before she calls the constable."

Alexandra reached over and took Bri's hand. "I was born a twin. My brother, AJ, died at birth. I have the same initials. To protect the family's wealth from falling into the hands of my uncle, my parents disguised me as a boy. I didn't tell Henry until just before I left England. Dr. Capehart tended to my father on his deathbed. He accompanied me to Italy and there we have lived ever since."

Nate spoke up. "Ravenshire only told me the truth earlier today. No one else knows."

"It would ruin everything. My son is the rightful heir, as my uncle only has daughters, but my uncle is a wicked, greedy man. He would have looted the estate before my son reached his majority."

Bri sat back and absorbed the facts. *Is there anyone without secrets?*

***

Sunday, April 26, 1812 – Riding along Rotten Row
The American

Gwyneth and Nate rode horses on a cloudy spring morning. Intermittently, the sun would illuminate a grove of trees, only to pass into the shadows moments later

Nate began, "Did you ever think—"

"Yes, but—" Gwyneth looked at him. "I wasn't ready then. Hurting you was not my intention. I was afraid to leave my home and all I knew. It was selfish of me to expect you to make such a sacrifice for me."

"I find myself thinking of you frequently over the months I've been back."

"Shall we...spend more time together?"

Nate searched her eyes. "My sabbatical will end in August. And the ocean will separate us again if I return to Philadelphia. Perhaps I should stay at Merton. Nothing awaits me in America anymore."

"Perhaps this is our time, now." Gwyneth glanced ahead. "Race you to the marker?"

"You're on." Nate spurred his horse as the sun caught both of them in its rays breaking through the ever present clouds.

***

Thursday, May 7, 1812 – *Omelettes de Mme. d'Aix*
Aneira

Aneira nursed her grandson, silently cursing him for his foolhardy scheme and at the same time fuming that Mirela's assassins had failed.

As Duff lay delirious from pain, fever and infection, she feared for his life. At times, she wondered if she should take it. But with the help of her Gypsy friend's potions, they fought to bring him back to health. After a week, his fever broke and he began to improve to the point where, by the end of the third week, he was coherent, alert, and strong enough to walk to the table.

"I feared the worst, but you have survived two bullets and two knife wounds."

Still taking Mirela's potions, Blackburn's voice was weak, but he no longer blinked in and out of consciousness. "That damned Frenchman."

Aneira stared at her grandson. "Duff, I planted the seeds of revenge in you, but we are not finished. I failed to kill the earl and his niece during Summerfest—"

***

Blackburn as himself

Blackburn's face flushed. Bile rose to the back of his tongue. "You didn't wait until I returned, as instructed?"

Wielding her words as daggers, his grandmother hissed, "*You* don't instruct me. *I* instruct you."

Unhidden, unadulterated hatred flashed in his eyes. "Do not presume to tell me what to do, nor where to go. It is *my* birthright. *My* decision."

Aneira's eyes bored into her grandson's. "All Wyndwards must die. I shall never abandon my revenge." She paced. "My attempt at Summerfest was thwarted. You do not have to be at risk next time. Others can do my bidding. Ravenshire shall crumble."

The Gypsy stood silently at the door.

"And don't think I don't know you're there, Gypsy. Begone."

Midnight, who had been delivered to Aneira for safekeeping before Blackburn left for Ravenshire, rubbed against her master's leg.

He stood. "I need rest." *The time is nigh.*

CHAPTER EIGHTY-FOUR

Saturday, May 9, 1812 – Pytchley Palace
Edward

After his birthday celebration, Bri and Edward stole a few moments alone in the duke's massive two-story library.

Bri smiled. "By now, you know that your birthday is no longer your own. Grandmother appropriates all special occasions."

"Dinner for fifty was not what I expected."

"That's a small intimate dinner to Grandmother. At least costumes were not required."

Edward laughed. "A small mercy. The cake with a depiction of Glaslough Pond pleased Ian. The layers of the tree house were inspired. He made me climb up there with him one day when you were not around. I'll never forget the view of green fields stretching in all directions."

"Today is more than your thirtieth birthday. It is the anniversary of your learning to swim. I hoped you'd find the image in the icing amusing. Sailors must know how to swim. Wyndwards sail into the wind on the oceans of the world. And you will be a Wyndward as much as I am."

"So we shall sail into the wind together. After our wedding in the fall. No one seemed to mind the postponement." Edward kissed Bri. When they parted, he scanned the thousands of volumes of books that surrounded them. "Everyone in your family has a magnificent library that puts my meager collection to shame."

"We have a lifetime to build our own."

As he took her in his arms again, Vanessa appeared.

"Unchaperoned? 'Tis unacceptable and unwise. But you shall remain *undiscovered* for a bit longer." She closed the door.

"Fleeting moments are all we can expect." Bri kissed Edward until she had to break for breath.

***

Sunday, May 10, 1812 – Baroness Glasspool's Mansion
Charlotte

Over dessert after an intimate Sunday dinner with Henry at her home, Charlotte asked, "Has there been any sighting of Blackburn since the events at Ravenshire?"

Henry's jaw set. "Not yet."

"He might have killed you!"

"Actually, I shot him, grazed his temple."

"He didn't shoot first or shoot back?"

"No, he took off. Hinton and Jean-Louis loosed knives that hit their mark. Blackburn shot Jean-Louis and Hinton got off a bullet that hit Blackburn before Hinton's heart gave out."

Charlotte frowned. "If he hadn't hesitated, you would be dead."

"Probably, but I'm still here." Henry took a deep breath.

"Taking a deep breath means you have something difficult to say."

Henry nodded. "After Taita left again with the Sultan, I learned that the reason she returned with him is that she has a son."

Charlotte paled. "With the Sultan?"

"I am not sure." His face contorted as he gazed at her.

"Dear God! Not yours?"

Henry shrugged and shook his head. "I don't know. Perhaps. An illegitimate son could never inherit the title, but I feel driven to find him. To see him for myself."

"So you are sailing to Madagascar?"

He nodded. "After Bri's wedding in the fall."

Charlotte remained silent for a moment, but her eyes betrayed her pain. *I may have lost you forever.* "Do what you must."

Henry rose and kissed her goodbye, a long and lingering kiss. *Will this be our last embrace?*

When the door closed behind him, she walked back into the parlor, as if in a trance.

Felix put his head in her lap.

She picked up a carved crystal globe, a memento from a trip she, Henry and Bri had taken to Bohemia years earlier. She turned the heavy object over and over in her hands.

The words he had spoken on that day echoed in her ears now: "You are my world. I have never been happier than I am with you in this moment."

Slippery with her tears, the globe escaped her grip, bounced once on the rug and then hit the marble floor. A chunk broke off and rolled until it hit the bookcase. *It did not shatter completely. Perhaps there is hope.*

Felix licked the tears from her face. She held him close to her as she sobbed.

***

Monday, May 11, 1812 – Drummond's Gentlemen's Club
Drummond

Drummond entered his gentlemen's club a little after six o'clock. By seven p.m., after stopping to speak to several of his clients at the club, he had met up with Oliver, and they had just toasted each other's health when a commotion ensued.

"Assassination! The Prime Minister's been assassinated!"

Oliver and Drummond ran outside to hear news hawkers calling out the grim event, "Prime Minister Dead! Assassinated! Shot by a bankrupt!"

Drummond hadn't seen this coming. "I didn't anticipate this treachery. But now...who will rise to replace him?" *Will he be one of mine?*

Oliver's tone scolded. "Cold and pragmatic as ever, Drummond. A man is dead."

"A politician, Darlemont. The opportunity is now. The world goes on. Someday I'll die, you'll die. We all die. Power is for the living."

"Do you not believe that in death we meet the real power, our Lord above?"

Drummond scoffed. "Where is power? In this life or the afterlife?"

Oliver recoiled. "You don't believe?"

"I believe what I need to believe to accomplish my goals. And I tell people what they need to hear to get them to do my bidding."

"You are a craven, stone-hearted manipulator of weak men."

"Thank you, Darlemont. You have summed me up with precision."

***

Tuesday, May 12, 1812 – Aboard *Zainab's Dream*
Xerxes

Xerxes stood on deck as the ship sailed close to the North African shore. He had paid the requisite bribes to buy protection from the Barbary pirates.

The Sultan styled himself as a bit of a rogue, adopting the swagger of pirates whose ships attacked from hidden coves on the coastline. Most paid him tribute, but the peace was an uneasy one.

Upon reflection, Xerxes realized that he liked London. Fewer factions conspired for the Sultan's attention. *That damned scribe, Ariapses, will have the Sultan's ear again. But now? Do I know too much? Am I a loose thread to be tied off like Rana?*

Power bases in Madagascar have been built in my absence. I must be on guard, ready to leave on a moment's notice.

***

Wednesday, May 13, 1812 – Boston
Xie Xie

The bent-backed elderly Asian woman slowly descended the gangplank, daring to breathe freely. *I am safe.* The voyage had been uneventful, but for Xie Xie, it had been her first foray into the world without calling on the power of The Pharaoh to exploit others' fear.

A Chinaman with a wagon offered to take her to an Asian hotel, and she accepted. He loaded her baggage into the cart, and helped her climb up into what appeared to be the driver's perch.

Xie Xie looked around, confused. "Where is the horse?"

"Ha, ha, Lady! I your horse."

He took straps from the wagon's front end, looped them over his shoulders, attached them to a leather harness, and expertly pulled the wagon out into the street and over the cobblestone streets of Boston.

Xie Xie was impressed. *For a small, wiry man, he can pull a heavy load. Perhaps he might be useful to me.*

Her mind wandered as they meandered over wide boulevards until they reached the narrow streets of Chinatown. *The Pharaoh's tentacles have a long reach. I must take care not to reveal myself. The master taught me well. Disguises work on the undiscerning masses.*

Reaching a small hotel that catered to older women, mostly widows, the wagon man stopped and spoke to the proprietor on her behalf. It was a different dialect than her native one, but she understood most of what was said.

She paid for the ride, and the proprietor snapped his fingers for his idle workers to take her luggage to her room.

To her surprise, it was spacious and clean. *I expected a hovel.* She tipped the bearers, and walked to the window. Two floors below, the street was teeming with activity. Carts selling fruits, vegetables, candles, and assorted trinkets engrossed her.

She unpacked a few items, and put them in a leather satchel, and then descended the stairs, as an elderly woman would, stopping from time to time while pretending to catch her breath.

Once downstairs, she asked the proprietor for a map, told him she might visit her niece for a few hours, and went out to explore Boston.

After stopping at a restaurant, listening to conversations around her, she immersed herself in her native language, identifying the speakers' origins by their pronunciation of an odd word here and there. She smiled. *The Pharaoh taught me to listen.*

Walking through the colorful streets, she hailed a carriage-for-hire and asked to be taken to the finest hotel in the city. Walking inside, she took a seat in the lobby and watched the traffic flow, clientele, and staff to evaluate the venue. She left, walked across the street to another hotel, and asked to use the washroom. It was quite luxurious, with several private stalls with wash basins.

Inside the one farthest from the door, she changed clothes and became Monique Li, a woman in her twenties instead of late fifties.

Releasing her hair from the gray-streaked wig, she pinned her sleek black locks into a topknot and stood back from the mirror to appraise her appearance. Satisfied, she put her former costume in the satchel, and exited the hotel.

Back at the first hotel, she registered for a long stay, saying her trunk from the ship would be delivered the next day.

The elegant suite overlooked the toniest area of the city. She spotted a storefront and leaned closer to the window, squinting. *Can it be?* The sign read: *Barryngton Wyndward, Fine Antiques and Collectibles.*

***

Friday, May 15, 1812 – James & Co., Bankers
Edward

Edward hung his head. *This is going to be difficult.* "Father, do you feel it is absolutely necessary for me to be there?"

"Yes."

"But it means being out of the country for at least three months. The wedding is planned for October."

"That's plenty of time to set things in motion and return. Bri will understand, given her involvement in the earl's operations. She's far more used to the concept of foreign travel than most women. Eli can work with the trading company in your absence.

"A new branch of our bank being established in another country requires a high level emissary to encourage clients to deposit their funds with us."

Sir John leaned forward and placed his hands in front of him on the desk that had been in his family for generations. "Once Napoleon is defeated, all of Europe awaits as well."

"Understood. When do you think I should leave?"

"I'd like you to be in New York by the middle of June. Two to three months should give you enough time to find the appropriate directors and get things set up properly according to our standards. You can leave at the beginning of September, and be back in time for the wedding.."

"But that means I must leave—"

"Within the week."

Edward stared at his father. *If I don't go now, I'd have to go if Father dies. Banking is based on personal and governmental relationships. We must begin on the right foot. Bri will understand.*

***

Lord Ravenshire's Townhouse
Edward

Thompson announced, "Mr. James has arrived, Lady Gabriella."

Bri looked up from her reading in the parlor. "Aren't you playing cards tonight with your friends? I am due at Charlotte's tonight. Shall I cancel?"

"Perhaps." Edward took a seat on the divan across from her. "Father wants me to establish a branch of James & Co. in New York. Our agent there has set things in motion, but Father feels very strongly that I must meet with governmental officials and potential clients to establish the bank's presence."

"That makes sense logically, but—"

Edward nodded. "I know. We've been through a series of trials and we both expected a normal summer."

"I suppose in the world of commerce, there is no 'normal.' Wars, uprisings by Luddites, and assassinations are being shouted about by news hawkers daily. The world is in turmoil. I would go with you, but Wyndward Investments needs supervision, just as the New York branch does. We both need to develop people we can trust to act in our stead when we are away." She grimaced. "Ironic, isn't it? The lives of leisure of our peers are less demanding. We laughed at their indolence, but we are being separated by our respective obligations." She took a deep breath. "How long will you be gone?"

"Probably around three months in New York, returning in September for our wedding in October. It means I won't be here to help you plan it."

"As if we had any choice regarding those plans!" Bri raised her hands in submission. "Grandmother has taken charge of the wedding. We have few decisions that will be truly our own." She leaned forward. "When must you leave?"

"In two weeks .A Wyndward leaves for Boston on the 29th."

Bri blanched and rang for Thompson.

When he arrived, she said, "Send word to the baroness, Lady

Wyndward and Aunt Gwyneth that I cannot join them tonight."

Edward cleared his throat. "Might I impose on you, Thompson, to tell François, who is waiting outside, to let Rogers, Banfield and Vaux know that likewise, I cannot join them tonight?"

"I shall." The butler left to fulfill his instructions.

Bri stood. "Let's go into Father's study and discuss the plans we need to complete. Father has a ship going to New York on Wednesday. I know that because I arranged a shipment to Granduncle Barryngton."

Once inside the study, Bri closed the door and embraced Edward. She held him close to her. When she pulled away, she gestured to him to sit down. "We are strong enough to do this. You are nearly back to your former weight. You look well. This unexpected development may define our future life together. We may literally be pulled in different directions by our commercial responsibilities. This impending trip gives us the impetus we needed to face the implications of our decisions. We can give each other the freedom to be independent people who love each other."

"Few that we know could accept these conditions."

"We are of a mind, Edward. Our love has been tested and survived. Miss Li could not part us, the poppy could not part us, and distance is merely a temporary parting. Our souls are connected."

"We have a lot of decisions to make." He smiled as she sat down at the earl's desk. "You know I like to see you with a quill."

"So it's a dominatrix you seek?" Bri playfully twirled the quill.

"Best not to do that after you've dipped it in the inkwell. You would splatter your father's office with indelible ink."

Bri pulled out a blank sheet of paper, readied her quill, dipped it, and glanced at Edward. "The first item of business is to set the formal wedding date."

***

Sunday, May 17, 1812 – Sir John's Townhouse
Sir John

Lady James and Sir John sat in their parlor after dinner.

Sir John cleared his throat. "Now that Nashmir's potions have restored my health, I think it is time for Edward to establish a branch of the bank in New York."

"But what of the rumors of war?"

"Bah! Spats over impressments of sailors do not signal war."

"A small tax sparked a revolution, dear."

Shrugging, Sir John grimaced. "Perhaps. But the Treasury could not support it, as we have Napoleon on our eastern shores, hungry for territory. War is merciless and expensive. A fool's errand."

"But all men are fools."

Sir John raised an eyebrow. "All?"

"What about Lady Gabriella?"

"She is used to Henry traveling. Edward can return in the fall for the wedding. She is a good match for his temperament. They may divide their time between London and New York."

"Edward has barely recovered from the food poisoning he suffered in Scotland."

Sir John had not told Lady James of Edward's weakness for the poppy, and vowed it would remain unspoken. "Edward can rest on the voyage. Once in New York, he will be totally engrossed in the building of our bank's presence in America. Let him become a separate entity from me. That will appeal to Lady Gabriella's independent streak."

Lady James's voice cracked. "I am not prepared to lose you both." Tears misted her eyes.

Squeezing her hand, Sir John spoke gently. "I am no longer unwell. And Edward must make his own way in the world. It is the course of human history."

Sitting back in her seat. "I don't care about the course of human history. I care about my family."

"Edward needs to become his own man."

***

Friday, May 29, 1812 – Aboard *Aphrodite's Wynd*
Bri

"One more kiss, darling." Edward pulled Bri close to him. He whispered, "Until September."

Zori jumped up to be petted by both of them.

"I'll miss you Zori. Take good care of Edward, promise?"

The Dalmatian barked.

"She's almost as smart as you are." Edward gave Bri another quick kiss. "You must get off the ship now or you'll have to swim back to shore."

"Are you going to climb the rigging?"

Edward shrugged. "A long voyage can get boring."

"Our fleet has excellent libraries. And you have bank documents to review. Don't forget to see Granduncle Barryngton when you get to Boston—"

"And Alastair Fairfax if I get to South Carolina. You've told me more than once."

Zori scratched at the door.

"Come, it's time to go."

Bri followed Edward up to the deck, kissed him one more time, then went down the gangplank to where Jean-Louis was waiting and waved.

"I wish you would have let me send François with him."

"Edward doesn't need a minder."

Jean-Louis raised his eyebrows.

"Stop it. He'll be fine." Bri climbed into the carriage.

***

Jean-Louis

A crewman on deck waited until Bri was out of sight, and then flicked his fingers toward the Frenchman, pulling his sailor's cap lower on his forehead.

His tribe doubts him and Boyd cannot make him a Bow Street Runner. Lash will have a better future in America. And Edward has never met him, so the Gypsy can keep watch over him without the banker's knowledge.

Lash will be my eyes and ears. He knows of the birds. James will not be alone.

CHAPTER EIGHTY-FIVE

Thursday, June 4, 1812 – The Sultan's Palace in Madagascar
Taita

On her first day back in Madagascar, Taita walked with Vaitea among the Sultan's flower gardens, now in full bloom. Gentle scents wafted through the air. The tropical sun kissed her face as she maneuvered along the winding paths.

"Rija is responding to a herb mixture. Aripases and you together carefully followed my notes while I was gone. Your diligence saved Rija's life."

"I've been visiting him in his quarters, remembering what you said about people seeming to be unconscious but being able to hear, so I've been speaking words of love and encouragement."

Taita's heart brimmed with pride at the man her son had become. She squeezed his hand, slipping a note into Vaitea's sash in a fluid, practiced move while she brushed her lips against his cheek. In their native tongue, which she had taught her son in secret, she whispered in his ear, "Eyes and ears are everywhere. You know what to do."

She had long ago taught him to unobtrusively slip notes under his waist sash into a special pocket she had added to every brightly colored sash in his wardrobe.

In English, Taita spoke to Vaitea about her time in London. Palace guards generally did not understand English, but given the Sultan's penchant for spying and the omnipresence of servants under the tutelage of Xerxes, she never spoke anything aloud that could not be repeated verbatim to the Sultan.

Rumors surrounding the death of Fy had spread like a black mist through the palace grounds. Rana, whose name was never again to be spoken, would suffer the worst their culture could impose—she would be erased from memory. The Sultan issued a decree that any girl or woman in the Sultanate with the same name must immediately be renamed in a ceremony before their tribal elders.

"We will stand next to the Sultan at the ceremony of honor for Her Highness Fy at sunset. You will release the doves, my son. The timing is precise."

"Of course, Mother. I have practiced releasing the cord on the net with the Royal Birdmaster—it will be executed flawlessly. I have been wondering," he lowered his voice but continued in English, "Will I still be permitted to study medicine in France?"

Taita took her son's hand again. "It was the Sultan's wish that you learn Western medicine as well as Eastern practices, but I cannot predict his reaction at this moment. Paris is still possible despite Napoleon's wars, as the Sultan has remained neutral. I shall seek out the French ambassador."

The Malagasy language had been influenced by French traders for centuries. Vaitea spoke fluent French as well as English and Malagasy, which itself had traces of Polynesian languages similar to Taita's native tongue.

"*C'est bien, maman.* You know that my fencing master conducts our sessions in both French and English to ensure my proficiency."

Frowning, Taita shook her head. "For medical terminology, you will need specialized instruction. That is the basis on which I will speak to the French ambassador." With another kiss on her son's cheek, she spoke too softly to be overheard, "I want you safe and far away."

Vaitea nodded as they walked in an ambling arc around the gardens in silence.

Vaitea must be safe. Henry can protect him in France. Jean-Louis has contacts throughout Europe.

***

Vaitea

Vaitea had never seen his mother so rattled. No one else could tell, but their psyches were attuned and her hand had been damp with fear.

When he returned to his rooms, Vaitea asked a slave to stoke the fire and fetch some wine. Once the servant had left, Vaitea bent over the fire and surreptitiously pulled out the note from the hidden compartment in his sash. Secret holes in the painted murals might disguise watchful eyes on him at any time. By now, it was second nature to Vaitea to subvert surveillance at will. He read the words written in his native tongue in a single glance and tossed the missive into the flames, disguised by stirring its embers with the fireplace poker. He watched as the paper flared into ash before he turned around.

Born with the same gift of sensing as his mother, Vaitea sensed a watcher's eyes. He sat by the fire with a book of verse in French, and read it aloud to practice the language, knowing that any spy most likely could not understand what he was reading. Still, his mind raced, unable to concentrate. The note told him that the Sultan had killed Rana by his own hand after she had ripped open Fy's throat with a ceremonial dagger, a gift from the Sultan. The savageness of Rana's death made his mother fear that the Sultan's wrath might be turned on any who, like Taita and Xerxes, knew the truth, or others who might suspect his role in Rana's death. The reigning monarch had become a raging madman in a moment of passion. It was no longer safe for Taita or Vaitea to stay in the Sultanate.

Taita wanted Vaitea to be safe in Paris, but his mother's fate was his primary concern. *How can I leave her to an uncertain future at the hands of the Sultan, a man who had been as a father to me? What if she cannot escape?* Vaitea shut the book and closed his eyes to meditate on his dilemma. He knew in his heart he and his mother would no longer be safe in the palace. *Will mother's escape plan work?*

Sadness washed over Vaitea. He caught himself dreaming of a place with no palace subterfuge, and then laughed silently. *As if any place where humans congregate will be free of subterfuge or subjugation.* He would miss the wild exotic beauty of the only land he had ever known. It was a world of dazzling colors. Scents of spices floated on the trade winds. Music rose from many corners of the palace. *But I must leave.*

During his mother's most recent time in London, he had matured. The scribe, Ariapses, had warned him to beware Szilard's ambition before the Sultan's oldest son had returned from England months in advance of the recent arrival of the Sultan's entourage. Jealousy had defined their relationship from birth, as the Sultan treated Vaitea as his own.

Vaitea was ready for change. The ways of the palace were regimented, secretive and sometimes nefarious. Now he was pulled by the promise of ocean ships holding out the open sea of the future before him. How he had begged the Sultan to take him on an ocean voyage! But always the Sultan had resisted. Now Vaitea understood why.

His mother would never abandon him and the Sultan would never relinquish his power. Keeping one of them with him at all times ensured his control. *I must leave first, so Mother can escape without fear for my fate.* Vaitea's adrenaline surged. *Freedom lies within reach, but it is fraught with danger.*

And what of Zainab? As beautiful as the delicate bougainvillea flowers daily woven into her hair by a slave, Zainab stirred his heart as no other. Favorite daughter of the Sultan, whose name meant "a father's precious jewel," Zainab was a beauty and his secret love. *How can I leave her behind to marry some lout of an old man who offers political gain to the Sultan for some strategic tribal alliance? Or worse, Szilard, her wicked half-brother? Would she...could she...defy the Sultan? If I ask her to run away to Paris with me, will she come willingly or betray me?*

***

Sunday, June 7, 1812 – *Omelettes de Mme. d'Aix*
Blackburn

My wounds have healed. Blackburn pursued his usual calisthenics in secret, by candlelight, while his grandmother and the gypsy slept. As always, he operated in secrecy to maintain his advantage, doubting the loyalty of everyone, including his own grandmother. *She is anxious to complete her plan of revenge. Planning is essential, not rash impulse.*

***

Monday, June 8, 1812 – Lady Gwyneth's Townhouse
Gio

The ebony-skinned Nambotha ushered Gio into Lady Gwyneth's parlor.

"Your blonde tresses sparkle in the light."

"Sherry?"

"Have you ever known me to refuse?"

Nambotha poured.

Gwyneth glanced at Gio. "Will you ever marry again?"

Waving dismissively, Gio shook his head. "I have no taste for the chase. I simply cherish my friends." He narrowed his eyes. "Why ask?"

"Just wondering."

"You're thinking of Parker. Yes, *you* should marry again. That is your real question, is it not?"

Smiling, she raised her glass. "To old friends. Student and teacher."

"Patroness and artist."

Gwyneth sat back in her chair and stared at the sherry in her glass. "I told Bri about my novellas."

"Was she shocked?"

"At first. But not for long."

"Not much throws her off her game. Except 'the woman in the red mask.' "

Gwyneth looked off. "I can't get Blackburn out of my mind. He is wounded, but probably alive, nursing his hatred for all of us into a frenzy of treachery and revenge." She shook her head. "All those years, I thought I knew him."

"Last time, he disappeared for over half a year. We have time to plan for his return. But what of Bri? The wedding is merely delayed, isn't it, until Edward returns from New York?"

"She's enamored with independence. Who knows what trials lie ahead?" Gwyneth sighed. "Perhaps I shall have to save Ravenshire."

"And how, pray tell, will you do that?"

"I could still conceive a child."

"At nine-and-forty?"

"It's not unheard of."

"I've 'unheard' it."

"Well, hear it now."

Gio smiled. "Parker has always loved you." He leaned forward. "Now we have an interesting subject for dinner conversation. I assume the child will be named Gio or Gia."

"Not Natalia or—"

"Absolutely not. Gio or Gia."

***

Monday, June 8, 1811 – Exterior of *Omelettes de Mme. d'Aix*
Voutain

The watcher whispered under his breath. "Hold!"

A candle shone through the window, though it was past midnight. Under his breath, he continued to himself, "A shadow is moving." *Foutre! How did he get by us? Jean-Louis will slit my throat.* "Damn that Colvert!"

***

Tuesday, June 9, 1812 – Flat above *Omelettes de Mme. d'Aix*
Blackburn

Back to full strength after nearly two months, Blackburn reached for his hidden cache of potions. *It's a good thing I didn't kill that old apothecary in Alexandria. I may need her again.*

During his recovery, his grandmother hadn't known to continue the potion to keep his eyes brown. *My mind is clearer. Could the potion have affected my judgment? Perhaps that potion has served its purpose.* He checked his reflection in a mirror. The small aqua dot in the corner of his eye had not grown.

He retrieved the red vial from the hidden compartment in his travel bag.. Merely one drop would constitute a lethal dose for a strong man. *Two drops each will no doubt kill two old women.*

Peering off into the distance, he considered his situation. *Grandmother molded me into her instrument of death. Hatred consumes her.*

The success of the omelet parlor among smart Society had not softened his grandmother's lust for treachery. Worse, that Gypsy, a mistress of darkness, had contempt for him. "You not being the *only* dagger of destruction in your grandmother's quest for revenge."

Mirela's influence over Aneira had grown while he had been gone. *Time to act.*

She knows most of my secrets, but not all. There is still time. To his grandmother, the chant endured: All Wyndwards must die.

It was time that Aneira and that damnable Gypsy faced the final phase of his plan. *It is time for me to become The Pharaoh again.*

***

Aneira

Sitting alone in the drawing room, Aneira clasped her hands together as she considered her situation. *He has changed. He looks at me with hatred in unguarded moments. I have lost control of him. He will come when I least expect it. He no longer trusts me.*

Mirela entered the room, nodded in greeting, and sat on the divan, next to her oldest—and only—friend. Aneira had asked her to look through a peephole to watch Duff.

The nod signaled Mirela had seen Duff preparing something deadly. *A pistol? A knife? A bludgeon? Poison?*

Mirela whispered. "What we'd hoped." She reached for a pouch that hung around her neck and emptied a powder into her palm. Taking Aneira's palm into hers, she placed most of it on her friend's fingers. "Suck your fingers—swirl them around the inside of your teeth and your tongue. Do not swallow it. It must stop the poison in your mouth. The antidote is powerful."

Aneira looked at the small amount left in Mirela's hand, and whispered back, "But you don't have enough."

"I have taken this before. My system can withstand more of the poison." They waited.

Blackburn entered the room holding his black travel bag. He wore the garb of a gentleman and sported a blond pony-tailed wig and spectacles. "I must take my leave of you, Grandmother." He put down his travel bag.

"Must you?" She stood and stared at his hands. "Those odd gloves look like the skin of a snake."

"I am myself again. I will get word to you of my new plan. Be patient."

He kissed her on the cheek, then pulled her head back and released two drops from the red vial into her mouth. She sputtered, foaming at the mouth, struggling to escape his grip.

***

Blackburn as himself

Blackburn released his hold on Aneira. She fell to the floor with a thud as Mirela grabbed him from behind. He wrestled the Gypsy to the floor, forced open her mouth, and delivered two drops to her tongue. "Die, Gypsy witch." She struggled for a moment. Resistance ceased.

Pushing her away like an old blanket, he muttered, "Good riddance."He replaced the top of the vial and secreted it in the special compartment in his travel bag. He removed the snakeskin gloves and checked them with care. *No splatters.* He placed them in a separate compartment in his bag and donned another pair of gloves.

He glanced at his cat. "Ready?"

Midnight jumped into the travel bag.

Exiting through the alley, Blackburn pulled a hat low on his brow and headed into the near-deserted streets of the predawn London morning, shrouded in fog.

***

Voutain

Voutain saw Blackburn leave.

"Colvert, stay here."

Deep in the shadows, Voutain tracked his prey.

***

Wednesday, June 10, 1812 – Lord Ravenshire's Gentlemen's Club
Henry

Malcolm, the operative from the Foreign Office, twirled the wine glass in his hand and looked around Henry's club. Walls lined with books and a smoky ambiance punctuated with low pitched conversation defined the upper class enclave. He waited for Lord Ravenshire to speak.

"Based on your advice, Malcolm, I've made arrangements to reposition my ships to South America. I have one more shipment to Boston for my brother through Portugal. After that, I will pull back. If the Royal Navy stops any of our ships, the flag ruse may be found out. As we discussed, if you need some of my ships for the crown, we can agree to reasonable terms."

The older man's lips curled into a wry smile. "The crown could seize them in wartime."

"True, but a lease is so much more acceptable among gentlemen. Besides, the Royal Navy has the largest fleet in the world."

The Foreign Officer pulled out a pencil and wrote a number on a piece of paper and shoved it toward Henry. "Per ship for the duration."

Henry scoffed. "A paltry sum. Suitable as an offer per month."

"Per month! What if the war lasts for years?"

"Precisely my point. Under that scenario, you will need more ships."

"Which we can commandeer as needed." He took a swig of wine. "For the good of the Empire."

"The Empire needs its reputation for good credit and goodwill to wage war. Materials are in short supply."

Malcolm waved his hand dismissively. "We can acquire what we need. There are many other sources, Lord Ravenshire."

"There are not and you know it. Ten ships now and another fifteen when they return from the Americas and the Mediterranean. We've been successful in avoiding Napoleon's navy, but his officers are becoming more difficult to bribe. I will accept that number per month per ship, and full restitution if a ship is lost in battle."

"Yes to the first, but we'll pay the insurance to Lloyd's for the ship. Let it be their risk."

"Done."

Henry raised his glass and said. "To peace. To the day when man forgoes war!"

"That day will not come until human beings no longer rule this planet. War is in our blood, Lord Ravenshire."

Raising his eyebrows, Henry sipped his wine while directing his gaze at Malcolm. "A pessimist?"

"Try working at the Foreign Office for as long as I have. No, Lord Ravenshire, I am not a pessimist. I am a realist. From the Roman legions to the Vikings, we have been shaped by war. We wear only the veneer of civilization."

***

Wednesday, June 10, 1812 – Lord Ravenshire's Stables
Jean-Louis

The trapper listened as Colvert finished his report. "And he has not returned."

"If Voutain has not appeared, there is only one conclusion to be drawn." Jean-Louis set his jaw. "You can go back to the estate in Scotland."

Colvert departed without objection.

Jean-Louis mounted his horse. *Boyd must know.*

***

Saturday, June 20, 1812 –Aboard *The Azure Star*
Blackburn as The Pharaoh

A dark-haired man dressed as a gentleman stood on the deck of the ship, rolling with the vessel as it moved over the waves. He could see the shores of Oran in the distance. The captain had changed the ship's flag to that of the Barbary States to thwart attacks by pirates. Further, a crewman held by a rope-lowered basket had painted over the name of the ship, previously *The Asian Star.*

Once in Oran, The Pharaoh planned to secure passage to Alexandria where he would evaluate his options. He smiled into the cool ocean mist. Intrigue always piqued his curiosity, for it offered insight into the players' weaknesses.

Weaknesses could always be exploited. *I have survived death many times. Now, at last, I shall begin to live on my own terms.*

***

Sunday, June 21, 1812 – Aboard *Aphrodite's Wynd*
Edward

On the deck near the bridge, Edward breathed the salty air. His breath blew white. Days ago, they had passed by the frozen mountains and molten volcanoes of Iceland. The northeastern coast of Nova Scotia lay a day or more away. A low sound directed his gaze in another direction. A flash of orange. He gasped aloud, "Cannon fire!"

The ship's bell rang, the crew rushed to their appointed stations. No warship, *Aphrodite's Wynd*, as others of the Wyndward fleet's cargo ships, had minimal crew. At same time the warships cannons roared, storm clouds appeared out of nowhere, obscuring their view of the approaching battle.

The captain shouted to his crew. "We're caught between warships! We'll head for land. May Providence be with us!"

Edward looked to the captain. "What can I do to help defend the ship?"

"Nothing, James. Go to your cabin. Get off the deck. Many of the crew sailed for His Majesty in the American War of Independence and know what to do. We carry no cannon, but there is a stash of rifles on all of Lord Ravenshire's ships. This is not the first skirmish we've encountered. Your safety is my priority. Go to your cabin. Now."

With reluctance, Edward climbed down the ladder to his cabin.

The sounds of battle were unnerving to Zori. She whined and paced.

Not knowing what was happening made each lurch of the ship, each pistol shot, each scream of a wounded crewman more threatening.

Edward leashed Zori and held her close to him.

A sudden jolt told Edward the ship had been hit, perhaps rammed. Another violent roll of the vessel toppled him. He hit his head on the side of the bunk and passed out as water began pouring in from the gash in the side of the hull.

CHAPTER EIGHTY-SIX

Tuesday, August 11, 1812 – Lord Ravenshire's Townhouse
Henry

Bri joined Henry for breakfast after her ride with Oliver. "By the way, Bri, I've been meaning to ask you to look into Asgard and the Norbury accounts. Blackie always suspected him of dishonesty, but I set those notions aside. A recent conversation with Asgard brought Blackie's suspicions to the fore."

"We've always accepted the Norbury harvest totals without question. Perhaps we should send our agricultural steward out to evaluate the true yields." Bri took a forkful of fluffy egg whites with dill.

Thompson placed the morning newspaper on the table.

Henry picked it up. "Good God! Thompson! Have I had any urgent messages delivered this morning?"

"No, milord."

Henry's outburst alarmed Bri. "What is it?"

"Official confirmation of war. The birds brought the news days ago. The British Minister Plenipotentiary to America fled to Halifax. Word has just been received that war was declared on the 18th of June."

"Your foreign contact gave us an advantage in repositioning ships in advance. Britain has the largest navy in the world, but how can we fight wars simultaneously in the east and the west and patrol all the seas?"

Henry paused until his silence caused Bri to look up.

"There is something you're not telling me. Her mouth dropped open as she realized the possibilities. "But surely Edward is already in America. He left over two months ago."

The earl handed the paper to her.

Bri read the brief article aloud:

"A merchant ship sailing under the flag of Portugal, A*phrodite's Wynd*—"

She glanced at her father before continuing,

"—was caught in a skirmish between British and American warships on June 21st. It sank beneath the waves in minutes,"

Bri's voice cracked as she read:

"engulfed in flames. It is unknown if there were any survivors."

Paling, Bri stared at her father.

"He's missing." Henry reached over to cover Bri's hand with his. "I was once missing and thought dead."

Bri could not speak for several moments. When she did, the anguish in her cry pierced her father's heart.

"Edward!"

ABOUT THE AUTHOR

Noëlle de Beaufort weaves insights from her background in finance, her studies of French language, culture and literature, and her love of history, travel and art into novels exploring generations of the Wyndward family. The *Secrets of Ravenshire* series, an epic historical family saga with elements of romantic suspense, spans centuries. Occasionally, the author writes short stories about secondary characters in the series.

Under her birth name, the author holds a B.A. in French from Denison University, and an M.B.A. in Finance and International Business from NYU Stern. She currently lives in Nevada with two very demanding felines. One is an organic shredding machine, attacking any stray piece of paper that flies off the desk (or that she captures in a furtive move), while the other (when he isn't sleeping) drapes himself above her keyboard and bats her fingers with his paw as she writes.

www.noelledebeaufort.com

Made in the USA
Columbia, SC
25 April 2021